A Gallery of Mothers

Brathius Legacy Book 2

JS Latshaw

fernweh books

FERNWEH BOOKS

Published in the United States by Fernweh Books.

ISBN-13: 979-8614343491 (Fernweh Books)

Cover artwork by Daria Brennan

1

THEN

Pound, pound, pound.

Sean Brathius ignored the knocks at his door. He knew who it was and couldn't face her.

He'd avoided her all day. He'd silenced her calls, deleted her text messages without reading them and finally tossed his phone into a pot of boiling water and watched the bubbles swirl until the screen flickered and died. He wanted no connection to the outside world.

Now she was here in person.

"Father! Please," her words spilled out, feeble and pathetic, "I need you. *They* need you."

The knocks continued, but weaker this time. Her will was waning.

The sound of Laura Lee suffocating into silence prickled the hair on the back of his neck. She was losing heart, and that woke him from his stunned paralysis. He couldn't lose them *all* today. There was fresh desperation in her voice. She was on the edge of being lost, too.

He opened the door and stared at her, bereft of words, filled with a desire to turn his face away from her searching eyes.

"They need you, Father."

He shook his head. She was talking to an empty shell, flushed of vitality long ago. "There's nothing that can be done," he answered. "Nothing more, that is. I've fought this for so long and I've lost."

He was seized by a sharp loneliness. "Come in — sit with me and wait for the worst to come. Let's be broken together."

Anger flashed across her face. She grabbed him by the shoulders and shook. "I have come from there. They are frightened children. What is wrong with you? Just because you're broken doesn't mean you have to be useless. You owe this to them. At least be with them when they pass. Look them in the eyes — don't just let this happen while you're sitting in the dark, trying to baptize yourself in your sadness. Let them feel the love you have for them. If you won't do anything to save them, at least let them die in your embrace."

"It's too late," Sean whispered. "Shai has…" He trailed off.

"Go back with me," Laura Lee urged. "They deserve to know you love them."

"Laura Lee," he started, hoping to explain, but everything he'd been thinking made no sense to him now. Why wasn't he there? Why had he let Shai handle this without him?

"Don't let them die abandoned, Father. Don't."

Sean's sense of unease grew as he neared the facility

He knew what had happened before he saw any evidence. He tried to ignore the rippling current of desolation crackling through the air. This was why he'd kept himself locked away in his apartment, far away from here. He'd felt traces of this shadowy aura of violence all along, but while hidden away, he'd been able to pretend he hadn't. Now, it was unavoidable.

A glimmer of light shot through his thoughts.

At least they're not dead.

It was a foolish thought. Whatever Amperous and Omathis were now was worse than dead. They'd turned. He couldn't blame them completely; they'd only become what he'd designed them to be. Or, rather, they'd grown into one aspect of what they were. He'd created them to be many things, regardless of whatever his official governmental goal was. Tragically, his creations had chosen to define themselves by their most lethal qualities.

Sean pushed through the steel door.

It should have been sealed, but it wasn't. Emergency lights flashed dimly. The electricity was down and it appeared that the backup generators had been damaged too. He'd made his creations smart, so he wasn't surprised. They were problem-solvers. Sean struggled against conflicting feelings of pride and shame. They'd been trained to infiltrate and destroy fortresses.: breach, disable, surround, slaughter.

Their training had been successful.

The reinforced plexiglass wall that had held them captive was broken into pieces.

Breach. "No living creature is strong enough to crack this, I can assure you," he'd been promised by the engineer who'd designed and installed it. "Heck, it could withstand being struck by an asteroid." Again Sean wrestled with a dark, overwhelming sense of admiration for the elite horrors he'd birthed. Omathis and Amperous weren't supposed to possess enough strength to break this wall. Yet they had.

They were greater than he'd even imagined.

He heard a steady dripping and turned his head to examine a darkened corner of the room. He staggered backwards in disgust.

Shai, carved out, hung from the wall like an offering made to a bloodthirsty god. His instinct was to run to her, hold her, wash her face with his tears. But he stood frozen in horror by the gratuitous savagery.

They were good. They were gentle and kind. He had trained them to love. How could they do this?

On some level, he realized, he'd always known it would come down to either them or Shai. He loved them dearly, but Shai couldn't accept what he'd done in creating them. He thought he had chosen Shai wholeheartedly, but now it was clear. Choosing her was never a realistic outcome. They were too powerful.

By choosing her, he'd lost control of them. He'd lost them all.

He could feel Omathis and Amperous, distant, wandering in the outside world, calling to him, confused by the evil they'd committed.

He thought frantically about how they could be captured before they did any more damage. Were they truly indestructible? No, not yet. As a mass, a Croathus army would be unstoppable. But only two of them? It would be difficult, but they could be contained.

He put aside his thoughts of Omathis and Amperous. Shai deserved his attention now.

He pushed through his disgust and walked toward Shai's empty carcass. He held her lifeless hand in his. "I'm sorry," he whispered. "I thought we'd have a family, have children, and..."

He froze. *My god. There are only two that escaped. But what if...*

Sean Brathius suddenly knew where they were headed.

He needed to stop them before they got there.

Amperous and Omathis dove headfirst into the outside world, though it bewildered them as much as it attracted them. A dizzying cocktail of scents flooded their nostrils. Of sweet-blooded humans that they could tear to pieces, of enticing baked and frozen treats (how were there *so many* desserts in this world, when they'd only tasted a few?), of an enchanted variety of multi-colored flowers, of rich brown soil, of all the barking, flying, chirping beasts in this world, of the briny saltwater, of the tall gracefully arching trees, and of the angry screeching wheeled vehicles the humans used to travel.

This world was a chaotically beautiful canvas, alien and unpredictable, with countless paths, noises, and sights. They'd read stacks of books, seen television shows and movies, and studied illustrations and photographs. They thought they'd known what it would feel like. But compared to the sterile cell where they'd spent their lives, the brothers had found a terrifying and exhilarating freedom that overwhelmed them.

They knew by instinct that they should keep to the shadows. Though they were mighty, they were only two. Two could be destroyed. They must become many — and then indestructible.

Amperous leapt from the darkened alley where they were resting and in a flash returned with the lifeless body of a woman. Omathis was surprised. He'd barely noticed Amperous was gone and hadn't even heard a scream. Amperous had improved his hunting just from being outside the cell for a few hours.

"She looks like Shai," Amperous observed. He was right. This woman was wearing all black, like the men who dressed as dark as night. Amperous sensed hesitancy in Omathis at the slaughtering of this woman, and he offered him the first drink of her still-warm blood to make him feel better.

"I don't know," Omathis faltered, "She isn't Shai. What has she done to deserve this?"

"But still you feel hatred for her. Mister Sean gave it to us. Do not deny his gift." Amperous urged.

Omathis drank. Whatever bothered him washed away in the searing thirst the taste of human blood awoke in him.

Their instinct needed to be satisfied, so they slaughtered another handful of humans as they cut through the city. Yet they maintained their discipline, limited themselves to only a sampling, and hid the torn-apart bodies, They didn't hang them high and display their trophies to all to stoke fear and bring glory, as they wanted to. All in time.

After all, there were so many humans. Multitudes of the weak could overwhelm a pair of the strong. Amperous and Omathis needed to make their number uncountable.

They were in agreement that they should head north, north, and always north until they found the Other Batches that itched the place where their eyes and brains touched. However, Amperous couldn't resist the first bakery they stumbled across. Omathis didn't deny him. They were still so hungry from their years in that sterile, empty cell. So hungry that they'd probably never be sated, no matter how much they ate.

"I knew about cookies, brother, but here are cakes and pies and éclairs and lady fingers and donuts and…" Amperous rattled off the names of the sugary concoctions, reading the labels with rapt enthusiasm while tasting each. Humans, while vile, did have a knack for gathering materials from the world's vast landscape and mixing them together until they formed delicious treats.

After all, that's how Omathis and Amperous had been created, too. No wonder they liked these pastries and baked creations. "We are kin to this sweetness, in a sense," Amperous declared to Omathis, between chomps of tiramisu and napoleons.

"What are you rambling about, you gluttonous fool?" Omathis teased, though he knew exactly what his brother meant. Oh, the magnificent wonders humans could create! Like an exquisite croissant filled with chocolate and cream—or two tall muscled brothers who were more and better than human, who were strong and smart and driven.

Though not (and probably never!) satiated by their rampage through the bakery, it was time to move north again. They could do nothing else —not even reunite with Mister Sean before finding the Other Batches and making themselves more. They stowed the bloody remains of the baker and a couple of his customers in a cramped back storage room and slipped into an alley, then quietly ducked into a tunnel below the surface where they could travel undetected.

NOW

The baby named Merond held her plump, sticky fingers toward Istoch. She exhaled with bubbly gurgles as he inched his face toward her and broke into breathless laughter when he ran into her outstretched hand.

"You got me again! How do you keep catching me?" he marveled, for indeed it was miraculous considering Merond could only lie on her back and flail her arms and legs.

Istoch took a deep breath of her sweet baby scent, of renewal and innocence, and closed his eyes.

Cracks were forming in the glacier that had hardened strong and mean around his heart. Even his sadness—stronger than stone—could not resist the New Ones, and it seemed to be giving way under their constant flow of tears, giggles, coos, and hiccups. There'd never been a scene like this in Mountaintop before, twenty-two babies born within a month of one another, the next generation of humanity gathered together in one cozy Round. He let it wash over him, grateful for new beginnings.

Another child started to cry, jealous from Istoch's playtime with Merond.

"Oh now, how about you chew on this?" He held out a wooden stick, polished and smooth, to Dransinth, ornery and stuffed full of morning grumpiness, to ease the pain of teething. "And that's for you. And you. And you, too," he whispered, soothing and warm, to Erlth, Crian, and Akbula, who'd waited as patiently as one could expect, considering they were infants.

Istoch arranged the four children so he could feed them their morning milk at the same time, despite only having two arms. "Won't be too long before you can hold these bottles on your own," he encouraged, himself as much as them.

When he fed them, he imagined their lives far into the future. First steps, first words, first kisses—becoming adults who contributed to the Kith, who fed a wee child of their own. He saw only good things ahead for them.

Istoch was grateful to Adorane for assigning this duty to him. He'd never thought he would want to be in charge of the New Batch. But every moment he got to spend with the squiggling, squeaking bunch—dewy pure in their untouched newness and soft rolls of infant flab—restored him in unexpected ways.

"Isn't that a task better suited to a Veritas woman?" Istoch had asked, worried he may be teased.

"People have said that," Adorane had mused, "But this idea that one thing is for Veritas and another for Cognate, that one thing is for women and another for men—we've tried those answers many times before, and they haven't served us well. It's time for new answers, just to see how it goes." This had been Adorane's most recent mandate: Try new answers, because the old ones had failed.

Istoch liked the idea of trying new answers because he didn't fit into any of the old ones anyway. He had been born a Veritas but then adopted into a Cognate family, so he was at the same time both and neither. And at this point, if anyone thought it was strange that a teenaged boy would relish this role, they'd quit worrying about it a long time ago. Nobody expected Istoch to be normal—not after what he'd been through. He'd walked outside the edges of what was acceptable as long as he could remember.

With his satisfied quartet of babies finishing their breakfast and gently descending into a milky haze, he turned to the last unfed child. He was his favorite—Talia—the little boy who had smiled first out of all of them, and at Istoch more than any other.

"Now why haven't you wakened yet, my little Tay-Tay?" Istoch sang the words, making up the melody as he went along. "Are your dreams so rich this morning that you don't want to leave them just yet?"

Istoch gently lifted Talia and an ugly shock passed through his gut. Everything was wrong. Babies were hot little pockets of sticky sweat in the morning, portable furnaces working overtime to keep themselves toasty. But Talia was a frozen stone. The baby's normally soft skin was cold and tough.

Istoch felt a familiar panic swell inside. He'd hoped he'd left this behind in a past life—but horrors had followed him.

Talia's cheek and neck were messy with the dried remnants of drool that had run out of his mouth.

"No. No. No." Istoch dipped a rag into a basin of water and washed Talia's face and neck clean. He scrubbed gently, determined to clean the little boy up. If he couldn't be alive, Istoch thought numbly, he'd at least be bathed. He owed this to his precious boy.

The water soaked into the skin. As Istoch watched, a small pattern of blotches appeared behind the baby's left ear: three reddish-purple dots, in the rough shape of a triangle. The mark felt menacing, like an infection, like the threat of death. Only the death had already happened; the mark was death gloating.

Istoch stifled a moan, pulled Talia close to his chest, and took a deep breath.

This is who I am at my core. I can never escape.

He was overcome by sadness and anger. He screamed until his throat hurt.

Can anyone truly ever divorce himself from who he is?

Istoch was a boy stalked by death. And death had visited him again.

In the following weeks, Istoch begged and prayed to make this stop. He pled with each child. *Hold on, keep breathing. You are alright, We can get through this.* With terror, he grew to recognize the sound of muscles choking in the back of each of their throats. Of their own tiny bodies strangling themselves for no good reason.

The three blotches of death were present behind every one of their left ears.

The babies didn't even have enough air to cry, as infants in distress should. Under an eerie blanket of silence they passed away, one after another, over the space of the next few months. Neither Istoch nor anyone else in Mountaintop had been able to stop the advance of the dreaded three dots. In time, every single child under his care, the entire future of Mountaintop and humanity, quietly expired.

When each passed, he held their soft hands, kissed their springy cheeks and smelled the intoxicating tops of their heads. In an unfair twist of irony, for him their scent still evoked the essence of life.

ICELYN

I climb, my arms and legs pleading with me to stop, please, just for a moment. I push through their shaking.

"Twenty-nine, thirty, thirty-one..." Omathis bellows the count, unrelenting and constant.

"I don't think you're going to make it, Icelyn!" Eveshone shouts, unrestrained joy shining through her words.

She told me so.

I scale one story at a time, grabbing what holds I can find. I've climbed this portion of the skyscraper so many times in preparation for this trial. I don't have to think about where to reach next; *I just know.* That broken crack, this ancient iron beam, that crumbling stone edifice. Grab, pull, climb.

Every part of me screams *slow down, rest, give up*, but instead I quicken my pace. I've learned that in such situations, it's wise to do the exact opposite of what you initially want to do.

I reach the glittering pinnacle of the tower, and inhale the salty winds that rush through me. The view is different every morning. Willowy ghosts of crimson red from the sunrise still cling, stubborn and unyielding, to the clouds that obscure Mountaintop, making it look like the home of my youth is surrounded by a sea of blood.

"Sixty counts have elapsed, Dear One!" Omathis warns.

"You only have thirty more!" Eveshone cackles through her words. We've made a bet: that I could climb up—and get back down—in only ninety counts. If I win, she must take me diving. ("But the sharks, Dear One!") If she wins, I tell her one story from my childhood every night for a week. (As boring as they are, she laps them up like honey.)

She's confident of her victory as I enjoy this hard-won perspective for few more counts. I want the sight, the smell, and the feeling of exhilarated fatigue in my muscles to stain my brain cells so that I can never forget this moment. *In every moment, there's a hidden eternity*, I think to myself. A new Brathius proverb, one that I've recently coined. I force myself to *stop and appreciate the eternity I'm living right now*, because life passes by at a blistering pace and you'll miss most of it otherwise.

"I hope you've got a bunch of stories stored up, Lovely," Eveshone proclaims. Poor girl. I'm about to steal her triumph. Sometimes sure things turn out to be anything but. It's a good lesson to learn.

"You haven't won yet!" I answer, as Omathis continues with the numbers. Seventy-five, seventy-six, seventy-seven…

I've practiced this, though only while they sleep. I'm about to shock them. Look at what this weak Cognate is capable of! I examine my toned, strong arms like they belong to someone else. I can scarcely believe they are mine, but I suppose it makes sense. You can't live among creatures as incredible as the Anaghwin without having some of that strength rub off on you. I wonder if I couldn't beat Catalandi in a footrace by now.

I take a deep breath, tense every muscle in my body, and then exhale and relax. I pay attention to where muscle attaches to ligament and ligament connects to bone. I feel the blood rush through my body—heart to lungs, back to heart, out to the rest of me, then always back to heart.

I crouch down, close my eyes long enough to fool myself into wondering whether this is real or a dream, and then I leap.

Eveshone and Omathis scream.

I soar up into the air until gravity grabs hold of me and pulls me down. I hold my knees to my chest, my whole body tight like an angry fist, and flip over. When I straighten out I'm pointed, head first and diving, toward the rapidly approaching ocean surface.

Hold steady, strong. It's all about the angles as I approach. Omathis' terror at seeing me plummet from the top of the skyscraper has stopped his counting, but I continue it in my head. Eighty-six, eighty-seven, eighty-eight.

I cut through the water so straight and rigid that I barely disturb the glassy reflection. I'd been working on minimizing my splash because I wanted Omathis and Eveshone to wonder if they'd just seen what they thought they'd seen. *Did I just disappear into another dimension?*

I go limp and allow my body to plunge as deep as it will as the count reaches ninety. Sorry, Eveshone, I managed to get back to the bottom in time. I open my eyes and suffer the saline sting. I take in this mysterious world that fights to overwhelm me, invading my nostrils, ears, and open mouth.

I pretend that I'm dead. Floating aimlessly beneath the surface, pulled by the currents.

Finally, I feel sympathy for Eveshone and Omathis, sure that they've reached the point of panic over my disappearance. I break through the water and they're grabbing hold of me like stern schoolteachers, scolding me for my foolishness.

It's a welcome respite from my godly responsibilities. It makes me laugh, which only makes them more agitated.

"Let's get you out of here. And us too. It's not safe."

"Well, you'd better get used to it, because we're going on an underwater diving expedition! Those are the terms of the contest I just won," I respond.

"I stopped counting," Omathis sputtered, "so the result is invalid."

"What?" I feign outrage. "Eveshone, how can you stand for this miscarriage of all things good and fair?"

"He stopped counting, Lovely. I'm sorry."

My lovely Anaghwin can be such terrible cheaters sometimes.

I splash them both and wiggle out of their grasp to take one last peek at the world below.

2

THEN

"Mom?" Travis' voice cracked—not only with the onset of adolescence, but also from a growing panic. "Mother?"

She'd hadn't come home during the night. At first he wasn't worried. She'd probably stayed over at Sean's place. Normally she would have told him something like that, but she could be absentminded sometimes. Still, his inner voice nagged, she'd never abandoned him completely. In her own icy colorless way, she was a mother who cared.

He'd tracked her using her phone. For someone so intelligent—and Travis' mom was *the biggest genius he'd ever met*, even smarter than Sean—she always acted like he'd cast a magical spell when Travis used her phone's GPS location services to figure out where she was.

He saw that she was at the lab, which was odd. She'd stopped going there long ago, and Travis thought the strange project—the one he had to promise to keep a secret—was over.

She should have been responding to his text messages, because she still had plenty of battery life left. He'd become so nervous that he'd actually called her, and he never called anyone. *Mom, phones are for texting and games, not calling*, he'd explained to her once, exasperated, when she'd tried to institute a rule that he *had* to answer the phone when she called.

Now *she* was the one not answering.

By the time he'd gotten to the laboratory building, he'd let his imagination get the better of him. He didn't even bother to lock up his prized bike—the carbon-framed Santa Cruz he'd saved for years to finally buy—before he rushed inside, panic roaring in his ears.

This was the place he couldn't tell his friends, teachers, or *anybody* about. He used to enjoy coming to this secret lab, even though it was home to those freaks that made his stomach feel like it'd been put into a blender. He'd always wanted to look at them, but immediately regretted every time he did. They scared—and maybe saddened—him deep inside, in a way that was hard to understand. One time he'd just wanted to make them go away, to stop existing, or at least teach them that they weren't better than him, although he feared they were. So when his mother was otherwise occupied he'd pushed the Punishment Button and watched as the pain flowed through them. It felt good at the time (and bad, too, if he was honest), but he was never allowed back to the lab after he hurt them, so later he regretted the mistake.

His mother was a remarkable person. When she gave even a hint of who she truly was, engaged and alive, it filled Travis with warmth for months. This had been the only place where he ever got those hints. Anywhere else, she was distracted and irritable.

The front door was open. This seemed wrong to Travis. This place was meant to be secure.

The lab was dark, its backup lights flickering in a ghastly rhythm, like a horrible, twisted laser show. It made him think of the last time his mother had taken him to Disneyland (the last time she'd taken him anywhere, really) and how the spotlights and colored beams and fireworks around the castle had seemed too good to be true. This was the nightmare version of that. Too bad to be true.

Why would his mother stay here all night? Why was she still here? What if she hadn't done so by choice—what if something had happened?

He tried to bail himself out of his quickly rising flood of fear. He was jumping to the worst conclusions and allowing panic to take the wheel, as he had a tendency to do. Of course Mom was fine. He worried about her often, but she was always fine. He worried about everything often, actually, and more often than not, everything was fine. That's what his therapist had reminded him to tell himself, and that's what he repeated now, under his breath, as he moved slowly through the dark.

Then he saw the security guard.

Bloodied and gashed, the flashing security lights revealing him for a moment and then cutting out, plunging the room back into a darkness that Travis was actually thankful for. He didn't want to see the brutal way the man in black fatigues had been carved out. As the lights flickered on again, he caught a terrible glimpse of the carnage; this man was only one of many dead rent-a-soldiers piled up outside the cage room. Each still clutched a rifle, as if they'd like another go at whatever had slaughtered them. But the torso of each had been ripped apart, the torn-out innards nowhere to be found.

The door to the cage room was ajar. The door that everyone knew *must always be kept closed* was *open.*

Travis plodded toward that door. He couldn't even care about these deceased men and women that he stepped over, people who had wives and husbands and children and friends who would never be the same because of what had happened here. All that was of no consequence compared to his mother.

He pushed the door wide and held fast against collapsing. *Be strong,* his inner voice commanded him. His mother wouldn't want him to faint at the sight of her, hung up and on display in a way that could not be accidental. He held her lifeless hand and cried, feeling his mother's cold strength flow into him.

She wouldn't want pity, and she wouldn't want tears. He would have no more of either, he told himself, cheeks wet and legs unsteady. His mother, this astonishing galaxy of brilliance who had raised and loved him, and now lived on only through him, would want *revenge.*

If she were here, he knew, she'd insist that he even the scales. Balance had been important to her. He could hear her now in his head: *Both sides of the equation must be equal, or else you're left with chaos.*

He was only fifteen, a pup with no facial hair and a cursory introduction to puberty. But he now knew the path his life would follow. He heard a dark and brutal call, and he answered *yes.*

He'd bring revenge, he swore, clutching his mother's hand in the dank, flickering cage. He'd balance the equation. He'd make things right.

Sean Brathius had no time to explain.

"Just come with me, please. It's an emergency."

Sean had woken the large, muscled soldier—who was still composed and starch-straight disciplined, even after being yanked from his sleep at this late hour—by banging on a window and setting off his home alarm. Sean had caused such a disruption, he realized, that he was lucky he hadn't been shot.

"What do you want, Sean?" The voice on the other side of the door made an effort to avoid sounding perturbed, as if the man genuinely wanted to be helpful. The door opened and Sean entered. Sean watched as his friend's eyes methodically scanned a series of computer monitors, smart phones, and watches, finding no alerts that justified this intrusion.

"Ollie. I need you. There's been… I need you to help me."

Sergeant Ollie Hailgard was the only man Sean Brathius could trust with the knowledge that Omathis and Amperous had escaped containment. A decorated military man, Ollie was compassionate, empathetic, and wise. Spending time with him had always felt more like a session with Mahatma Gandhi than an appointment with General Patton.

"Men who thirst for peace make the best soldiers," Ollie had explained once when Sean asked how he managed to exude such a calm demeanor. "Since we know the true cost of war, we never wage it thoughtlessly."

This was why Sean had trusted Ollie enough, way back when Omathis and Amperous were young, to allow him to train them. Ollie had been fond of the two extraordinary creatures, and Sean always suspected that other than himself and Laura Lee, only Ollie truly appreciated the wonders that they were. He was one of the only people who saw their potential to be more than weapons.

Unfortunately, Ollie had needed to be removed from the project once it began to turn. It was more an accident than an attack, but when suffering from the negative side effects of their Somnolent Aggressiveness Treatments, Omathis and Amperous had pounced on Ollie, snarling, talons flared, losing themselves in the rush of the attack.

Sean couldn't promise that this, or worse, wouldn't happen again, so Ollie had been relieved of his duties.

At Sean's urging, they'd loaded into Ollie's military-grade Land Rover Wolf. Vehicles were Ollie's one indulgence in his otherwise spartan life, and the Wolf, which Ollie had used during deployments in Iraq and Afghanistan, was equipped with a triple-reinforced steel bulletproof chassis, hand-stitched leather seats, and even LED lights that lit up the road with programmable colors while he drove.

The low rumble of the Wolf calmed Sean's nervous heart. Finally, action was being taken to quell the disaster. He broke the news.

"What do you mean, gone?" Ollie asked, concern hardening his face.

"They have left their enclosure."

Ollie drove unnervingly fast through the suburban neighborhood.

"Did someone forget to close the door?" Ollie asked, his mind spinning, though he knew this was impossible. Their cage was unbreakable, and designed specifically so that the creatures could not accidentally be let out. For obvious reasons, the entire lab had been set up to ensure that escape *could not happen.*

Sean had decided not to mention the deaths of Shai and the others for now. That knowledge might turn Sergeant Hailgard against Omathis and Amperous.

"I had been notified they were scheduled, that the project was scheduled, for termination," Hailgard stated.

"It had. Apparently Omathis and Amperous did not agree with that decision."

Ollie felt suspicions rise within him. As much as he loved those creatures, he'd always worried about Sean's attachment to them. "*They* didn't? Or *you* didn't?"

"I was resigned to it. I hope you're not suggesting that I…" but Sean didn't want to finish the sentence. He hadn't helped in their escape, it was true. But what if someone else had?

"Why are you telling me this like it's a secret? Where are the alarms? Where's the re-containment effort? This entire community needs to be evacuated. Who is in charge of disaster management?"

Sean knew that the alarms at the lab, which were set up to notify those in charge of disaster recovery, had been disabled. He hadn't done it, but he had an idea of who had. He was grateful, because he knew "disaster recovery" really meant treating his creations like monsters—hunting them down and slaughtering them. They deserved better than that.

"Listen, Sergeant. Help me find them. We don't need a military response. You know that at their foundation, they are gentle. Don't condemn them to death."

Ollie knew they were not always gentle; they could be deadly. He had seen this firsthand. Yet his conscience was pricked. If they could find Omathis and Amperous before any violence erupted, it would be the best possible outcome.

Ollie idled at an intersection. Alert the authorities and keep this secret between him and Sean? His mind raced, calculating risk and possibility.

"They don't deserve to be executed, Ollie."

Ollie nodded in agreement. "Have they hurt anyone yet?"

Sean lied without hesitation. "No."

Ollie used his onboard computer to scan police reports and confirmed there had been no incidents reported. Though he hated to step outside of protocol, maybe this could be resolved without bloodshed.

Sean didn't mention that the lack of incidents reported was to be expected, whether his Croathus were murdering humans or not. True to

Omathis and Amperous' training, they would keep their kills hidden to avoid detection until they were strong enough to face their enemy head on. The one exception was Shai, Sean thought bitterly, because they despised her.

Ollie stared across the empty intersection, thinking. "It's likely they're looking for you. Where would they try to find you?"

"No. They aren't. Not yet."

"What else would they do? What else could they want?"

"They want to breed."

Ollie shifted gears, pulling the Wolf onto the lonely freeway. The engine roared to life as they drove north.

"Be patient. You must stop. Deny yourself."

Omathis scolded his brother, who had plucked another human from the shadows to satisfy his yearning. The hot scent of the victim's blood swept over Omathis, calling to the fury within him, but he resisted. His instincts had promised that indulging this hunger would feel good, but it hadn't. In fact, he'd felt dirty and ashamed. He could only imagine what Mister Sean would say.

They'd reached an area where the buildings the humans had built were fewer in number and farther apart. Trees, bushes, and grass began to replace hard asphalt and steel. Though Omathis preferred the soft touch of leaves and dirt to harsh concrete and glass, he felt jittery inside. It was unsettling to leave the only place he'd ever known. To add to his worries, despite an agreement to ignore their hunger and head north toward the Other Batches without delay, Amperous seemed unable to allow an unsuspecting human to pass by without gutting and draining it.

"Join me. I can feel your desire. It's every bit as strong as my own," Amperous tempted him. Omathis felt resentment rise up hot within him. He wanted to bathe in crimson blood, too, but Amperous' lack of discipline angered him.

"What did this man do to deserve what you've done to him?" Omathis hadn't meant to say it, but did. He'd decided that, when it came to Amperous, a practical approach was the best way to handle the question of whether to slaughter a human or not. *We don't have time for this, we must be going.* He hadn't meant to make it a moral question. Amperous seemed not to care about matters of right and wrong. Omathis didn't want to face that difference between them yet.

Amperous tensed up at the question like he'd been challenged to a fight. "You've learned, just as I, that no one gets what they deserve. What did we ever do to warrant *their* wrath? We always obeyed their orders, and look where it got us."

"Mister Sean wouldn't be pleased. You know that." Omathis surrendered to the gravity of the conversation.

"Mister Sean created this desire in me. And in you. *It was his design.* What kind of monster punishes his creation for acting according to his design?"

"I know this: Mister Sean is no monster."

"Nor is he a creator of monsters," Amperous added.

Omathis was glad to find an area of strong agreement with his brother. He could find no way to express the unsettling pricking he felt in his gut whenever he or Amp murdered a human, so he decided to revert to practical reasoning.

"For me, brother. Swear you'll not kill again, at least until we reach the Other Batches. Only if we need to for our survival. We *must* reach the Other Batches. You sense that as strongly as I do, true? How important finding them is? It is everything. It is the only thing we should care about right now. With all this killing, we are only delaying what must be done."

They'd agreed on this before, but now Omathis was asking Amperous to *swear to him.* Oaths had always been sacred between them. Amperous considered his words thoughtfully. He would never break an vow made to his brother.

"Your words are wise. I will follow your lead."

According to an instinct Sean Brathius had installed in them, they dug a hole to conceal the dead man and carefully dressed the grave until the area appeared undisturbed.

They lowered their large frames onto all fours, sleek, graceful and only inches above the ground. Though larger than any other creature that roamed these lands, they moved with such assured silence that someone could be nearby when they passed and hear only the gentle whisper of the breeze.

They reached a wilderness that bore no evidence of humanity. Here, their constant inner furies were relieved to the point where they were almost forgotten. As a sun the color of blood rose above them and chased away the last vestiges of the night, they glided through the underbrush and woods, splashing through cold creeks and over craggy stone canyons. They'd never experienced a paradise like this before, and a deep affection rose in Omathis and Amperous for this world they hadn't even known existed. Who could have known there were areas where humans did not roam, live, and dominate? Where you could go days without seeing a hint of their existence? Omathis never imagined such miracles could be possible.

They counted to three and dropped from a thick white-and-tan mottled tree branch into a clear pool of water. When they emerged from the deep and swam toward the shore to do it all over again, Amperous laughed.

Omathis cried. He hadn't heard the sound of his brother overcome by joy since they were children.

Omathis began to believe that this was all part of Mister Sean's wise plan. He'd made a paradise for them and the Other Batches, far away from the humans, terrifying in their dark suits and metallic cities. Soon they would be a multitude, stuffed full of joy, laughing like Amperous as he plunged into the brisk clear water, living in this verdant green and sparkling blue dream.

With Mister Sean by their side.

Yes, now he saw it. This was what Mister Sean had wanted for them all along. Everything they'd done was according to his plan.

NOW

Andalas was enjoying himself. This was probably the best day he'd ever lived so far.

Finally, he was hunting!

The young Croathus tumbled through leaf, brush, and branch like a boulder, chasing a trio of frightened bear cubs.

"Not too fast," Carriana shouted toward her son. "Use patience, and control. Wait for the moment to open itself up to you." Carriana loved watching her still-clumsy child learn to hunt, but the risk of the endeavor had her on edge. Where cubs were, mother bears weren't far away. And Carriana knew firsthand how protective mothers could be when their children were threatened, for she was one.

Andalas slowed and calmed his hyperactive four-foot frame. He knew his mother was right. If he pounced now, he'd be lucky to get even one of the cubs. If he pursued the proper way—hiding and re-emerging, chasing then feigning being evaded—he could tire them out and claim all three. None of the other Croathus pups had nabbed more than two at a time yet. To kill three would be a dream. He could brag about it day and night and nobody could do anything but be impressed.

"Don't only charge ahead, Andalas," she instructed, "but wait and sense, too. Action and perception are of equal importance. Each is worthless without the other."

The potential mother bear was not the only reason Carriana was on edge. She sensed a threat nearby, but she couldn't pick up on the true shape of its nature, or even whether it were real or imaginary. With the ruckus Andalas was scaring up, she feared that vital clues were being lost in all the twig snapping and leaf rustling.

Andalas held his breath, willed his pulse to quiet, and waited as the cubs slowed and started to believe they were safe. They neared a dark enclave formed by two stone shelves that overlapped in an upside-down V. Once the cubs reached this cave, Andalas knew, he could corner them. He felt a bubble of joy rise in his throat. Three cubs at once!

As the young bears entered the shadows, Andalas remained silent, despite the instinct begging him to charge and roar. No, he instructed himself. *Stay under control. I just need to wait a little longer, and everything I want will be mine. If I move too quickly, I'll lose everything.*

Carriana followed from afar, and the hair on the back of her neck stood on end. Why did she feel so nervous? This was proceeding exactly as she'd hoped. She tuned into Andalas' inner dialogue and was proud of his self-discipline. He was a good boy. He'd make a fine Croathus once fully grown. She tried to ignore her inner paranoia so she could enjoy this.

The forest was silent except for the chirp of birds and whirring of insects. The bear cubs' ragged breathing and yelps for help had ceased as they'd calmed down, sure they'd evaded their pursuer. Yet Carriana felt a danger masked by the peace, and worked to analyze the surroundings. She felt nothing tangible, only a thick haze of trouble, heavy as a blanket. She knew Andalas would not forgive her, but they had to abort this hunt.

Yet it was too late. Andalas joyfully charged from his hiding place, roaring with unbridled bloodlust. The cubs froze, cornered. Carriana relaxed. She had over-reacted. Everything was alright.

Then a snarl emerged from the shadows, mightier than anything the cubs, apart or together, could possibly produce. When Andalas reached the mouth of the cave, he stopped short at the sight of a giant sow bear, double his size, standing and squared up for a confrontation. The Croathus pup swallowed his confident roar and switched direction just in time to avoid the sharp talons swiping by his face.

Every Croathus pup had been told that a bear attack was quicker than a lightning strike, but knowledge alone couldn't have prepared Andalas for what happened next.

Amperous had hoped to catch Icelyn and make her pay. She had lured them up to her Mountaintop paradise and made them feel her love, only so she could try to murder them without a struggle. Then she had slipped away, once again eluding justice, never answering for the atrocities committed by her and her kind.

Someday, he'd vowed, that reckoning would come.

It was that promise that had kept him from expiring, his lungs shredded and his heart a ball of fire in his chest, as he managed to scale and fall over the Wall that for centuries was meant to keep him and his kind out.

At the foot of this crumbling insult, a symbol of the great rejection they'd suffered at the hands of their creator, he'd closed his eyes. Not to die. Just to rest.

There was still much to accomplish.

The mother bear bellowed hot breath, her humid sticky wrath enveloping Andalas as she tore into his chest and bit down on his shoulder. The Croathus pup, moments before brimming over with bravado, was weakened by blood loss, fear, and shock, and did nothing to fight back. The attack had come too quickly, like nothing he'd ever seen before.

As he felt the talons probe deeper inside him, leaving a path of bold crimson lines of destruction across his body, Andalas had fleeting thoughts of self-pity. Croathus aren't supposed to die. Most of them never do. And yet here he was hoping for death. It had to be better than this pain.

The mother bear was an unbound cyclone of violence—tearing, biting, crushing. Like she'd never be calmed again until Andalas was torn into a thousand pieces, crushed into dust, and scattered throughout the woods. Her cubs watched, comforted and horrified by what she would do to defend them.

His pulse sounded weakly in his ears, and Andalas knew he was one strike away from his end. He closed his eyes and murmured his mother's name. *Carriana.*

His eyes were filled with blood, so he didn't see what happened next, but felt and heard it. Suddenly the grizzly was no longer atop him thundering in triumph—she had been knocked aside in a flash. Whimpering for mercy.

He struggled to wipe his eyes clean and sat up to watch his mother, furious and unrecognizable, carving the great muscular beast in two. Croathus pups were introduced slowly to the remarkable violence adults of their species could commit, so Andalas had no conception of how brutal and lethal his mother could be before this moment. The grizzly sow had no chance against a fully grown Croathus.

Now it was Andalas' turn to watch his mother, comforted and horrified by what she would do to defend him.

Carriana finished skinning the mighty grizzly, preserving its head so the pelt and skull could one day be worn in the tradition of the Croathus.

She tossed the heavy remains to her son. "Here, carry this home."

He gasped with every breath. He'd never been injured like this before. "But mother, I'm bleeding," he protested.

She laid a gentle hand on his chest and he could feel heat flowing from her, different than normal physical warmth.

"You'll recover," she assured him. "You're a strong one."

Andalas hadn't felt strong while being mauled by the bear, so he appreciated his mother's words. To his relief, he saw that his wounds had already started to heal. Jagged gashes in his skin were narrowing before his eyes as fresh new cells appeared—pink tender skin replacing the terrible red.

You'll recover. You're a strong one.

Spent from the kill, Carriana finally relaxed her vigilance.

But this was a mistake.

Action without perception is worthless.

The trouble she'd sensed in this forest hadn't been the mother bear. She'd been wise to be worried.

She'd been wise to be worried, but the trouble she'd sensed in this forest hadn't been the mother bear.

Now the real threat surrounded them, she realized in horror, and she wasn't able to do anything about it.

3

ICELYN

I force myself to reflect on the laughter I shared with Omathis and Eveshone this morning. I need to if I'm going to survive another accursed session of Petitions. Petitions are my least favorite aspect of being a god and the most tedious part of my life in general. I adore the Anaghwin, every one of them, but dealing with Petitions makes me defensive and surly. I can't help but feel unloved and unappreciated and fear they've lost their affection for me.

I wouldn't blame them.

I am not an easy person to spend time with anymore. Perhaps I never have been, but it's gotten worse. Before, I had been tormented by dark visions of the Great Death, realizing over time that they were Omathis' memories—his worst traumas, which he tried to keep boxed up and neatly hidden away. Now I've realized that these haunted memories are not exclusive to him. All Anaghwin suffer from their past. As I've grown close to them, I've taken their greatest terrors as my own. I have channeled their darkness, and in doing so, I worry that I have been made into darkness itself in the process.

My parents spoke of something called a *honeymoon period*, a phrase left over from the Apriori referring to when freshly married couples would bathe in affection for each other, everything painted by the sun-soaked glow of their newborn love, before they settled into the inevitable seething resentments that resulted from their overwhelming incompatibilities. Since marriages are born of less emotional considerations in Mountaintop, and more closely resemble a controlled scientific process rather than the animalistic breeding of unruly beasts, that phrase—and the phenomena it describes—has since become obsolete.

But I fear we, as a people and their god, have been through a honeymoon period and now are on the wrong side. At first I was faultless. I was the standard by which right and wrong were defined. But now?

Upon returning from our ill-fated pilgrimage to Mountaintop, I heard whispers. Nobody said anything to *me* outright, but I knew they were talking to each other. I could sense it, whether said out loud or not.

Why did so many Anaghwin have to die?

What was the purpose of this suffering?

Was this part of her plan?

What kind of god has a plan that requires her children to die?

If she didn't intend for this to happen, but couldn't prevent it, how much power could she truly have?

But if she had enough power, and chose to let this happen, how good could she truly be?

I was either not good or not powerful. One or the other— or maybe neither. A god ought to be both.

They resolved these doubts on their own, though I suspect not to anyone's satisfaction. I asked Omathis about it once, and he brushed it away like an inconsequential bug. *Oh, don't you worry about all that, Dear One. We know that you are good. It could never be possible for us to understand everything in your plans. Sometimes misunderstanding makes a good thing look bad.*

Not even I, who was the one being exonerated by it, could believe that line of thinking. *Any action or decision, no matter how foolhardy or vile, could be justified using that logic.* That's how you can tell a thought is dangerous—when it can be used to excuse or encourage dreadful behavior.

II'm not so sure about the decisions I've made either, and whether they've been worth it. I've lost so much—Adorane and Torrain's friendship, my father and mother, my home, many of my beloved children, the life I'd always known, everything familiar. I doubt myself and my choices, too.

But what kind of god expresses regret for her actions or admits that perhaps she's done something wrong? A weak one. And my children deserve a strong god.

Back when I would wander through the woods with Adorane in Mountaintop, which seems like a thousand years ago, I would see fallen trees and feel sad for them. They had been standing tall, reaching for the sun, spreading their branches. But now? Creatures picked at them for nutrients, and other plants plunged their roots into the once-proud monoliths, breaking them down into dirt. All varieties of slimy and crawling bugs would bore holes into that previously impervious bark, softening it, weakening it until you could no longer recognize what these lumps on the forest floor once were.

During the Petitions, I'm the one lying on the ground, being picked at and carved into.

I do not believe in a god, but I've learned that if a deity is anything at all, he's the corpse his offspring feed upon when they require energy to birth a new world.

My children have moved on from their underlying doubt, just as I have, but I fear it remains lodged firmly in the shadows of their thoughts and escapes in small questions here and there.

Could we perhaps live somewhere else other than the Drowned City?

Surely a god as strong and merciful as you can forge a peace between us and the Croathus?

I had a quarrel with my friend; could you change her heart toward me?

All matters covered up and swept aside during our honeymoon period were now brought to my attention, front and center, out in the open. It was jarring, because my upbringing hadn't prepared me for conflict. No one ever confronted anybody like this in Mountaintop. It wasn't proper and ran counter to the Code.

Though I imagine that if, say, Adorane and myself had ever gotten married because of our youthful passions, I'd have grown used to conflict before too long.

No. I turn my thoughts consciously away from Adorane. His absence from my life is better ignored. The Lack of Adorane is everywhere and everything once I acknowledge it.

The sheer volume of requests that I could not fulfill overwhelmed me, and each felt more like a suspicious jab than a goodhearted appeal. At first, I limited all petition-making to one day a week. Even that was too much for me. Now, they are only afforded one per moon cycle. The session only lasts roughly three thousand counts. It's all I can bear.

If only I could be a father god, like the one the Veritas worship, I could command them to do my bidding without question. I'd stand strong for myself and rule over them. But I'm cursed to be a mother god, who cares about her people more than she cares about herself. That makes my job more difficult. Yet I'd much rather worship a mother god than a father god, given the choice. I think everyone would, except those who love to be dominated. So at least that's one bright spot.

Petitions have become highly regimented. All requests are submitted to Omathis and Eveshone in advance, and are then pared down and polished. Omathis has offered to give me a preview of what will be asked, but I've found that the less I think about Petitions outside of those three thousand counts, the better. They make me miserable.

I approach the throne they've crafted out of shells and ancient glass pulled from the sea, and then sit tall in this temple made of bones and kelp, beneath the portraits of my ancestors—Lovely and Mistersean—who are both reborn in me. I breathe deeply and keep my back straight and strong, hoping my confident posture gifts me the courage I need.

I begin the dreaded session by making my declaration.

"Let us now start this time of Petitions, when all blessed Anaghwin can ask what they will of myself, Lovely Brathius, the Mother of Mercy, who has brought you to the highest point in world and back again. How can I fill your mouths with laughter and your hearts with gladness?"

I start a silent count in my head, *fifty-two, fifty-three, fifty-four.* Only two thousand nine hundred and forty six counts left. How bad could this be?

No one will look me in the eyes, not even Omathis or Eveshone. They fiddle with their talons, clearing their throats. A quiet but determined guilt seems to have settled onto them, as if they feel bad for what they're about to do but have to decided to do it anyway. I feel alone.

"What is going on here? Why is no one speaking?" I ask, though I'm not sure I want to know the answer.

I smell an ambush. This particular Petitions will the worst of them all, I am sure of it. A complete bloodbath that I never saw coming.

Do they want a god or a sacrificial lamb?

Or, as far as they're concerned, is there any difference?

THEN

Omathis could hear them calling. He could feel their quiet resigned panic, throbbing like a headache. They were scared. Just as he and Amp had been. Trapped, emaciated, and waiting for death.

"Amperous, do you—"

Amp cut Omathis off before he could finish. "We cannot allow them to be terminated."

They were close. *We are coming for you*, Omathis transmitted, and could feel a glimmer of peace pass through the Other Batch. His sense of their presence grew stronger, almost as if they too ran beside him and his brother. He could see them in his mind, as clearly as if he and Amp had painted them on canvas during one of their creative sessions with Mister Sean. Amperous had despised having to draw and paint and mold clay. He once spat that this was the kind of thing weak human babies did when they were too stupid or slow to do anything else. But Mister Sean had always lectured them that they had to be well-rounded, even if they preferred throwing the ball and pouncing and doing their math.

Omathis concentrated on running in sync with Amperous so that they mirrored each other in movement. When he did, the Other Batches grew clearer to him—their thoughts, their fears, their essences.

"When we are together in unity, brother, we are connected more deeply to them, too," Omathis observed.

Amperous fell out of sync to test the theory. Their connection to the Other Batch wavered.

"We are meant to be as one," Amperous declared, excited, as they again reflected each other in precision and the connection snapped back into clarity. *Do not be afraid. We will be there soon.*

They crossed a great bridge built of spindly rods of metal. They scaled the peaks and arches of the orange-red structure to stay hidden from the cars that drove below. To Amp, the bridge looked like the skeletal remains of an ancient dinosaur. He'd always been fascinated by those mighty armored creatures that somehow managed to die out while weak, squishy humans covered the planet like a plague. He took their demise as a warning: No matter how strong you may appear, you must never let down your guard.

They reached an urban area where the scent of humans clung to every street, building, and vehicle. The poor trees, so regal and free in the wilderness, were coated here in the sour essence of mankind, manicured and bent over in submission to their will. Unlike in the untamed woods, these trees were arranged in straight lines, uniform and bland, forced to grow in a location of humanity's choosing. It made Amperous sick.

This is what the dark-suited men had wanted to do to with us, he reflected. *Line us up for humanity's purposes, broken and unnatural, with no will or freedom of our own. When we refused, they scheduled us for termination.*

"Amp, you are allowing your thoughts to stray wherever they wish to go. Please stop," Omathis pleaded. "We're losing their location."

Omathis was right. Amp concentrated and they cut through the city.

The Other Batch's cries for deliverance grew to unbearable levels. Omathis feared they'd be terminated if they weren't rescued soon. *Fight back,* he commanded. *They are weaker than you. You deserve to exist. Destroy those who think otherwise. We will be there soon.*

He and Amp felt rage flow through the Other Batch.

They finally arrived at the lab, a windowless block of fortified cement and steel.

"We have no time for stealth," Amp insisted. They sensed the Other Batch's strength waning. Whatever had been sent to terminate them would succeed soon. Though Omathis suspected Amp was a bit too excited at the prospect of tearing apart more humans, it was the only logical course of action.

The guard who patrolled the entrance offered no resistance. Amperous rushed him from behind, silent and swift, and tore into his soft warm neck with protracted claws before the man even knew to feel fear.

"He wasn't able to shoot his weapon once," Amp observed with a burst of glee, like a child awash in surprised pride after learning, finally, how easy it was to ride a bicycle. They crashed through the entrance and sped down the hallway toward the Other Batch. "We were too fast! He didn't even have time to scream."

This close to their anguish, Omathis didn't need to be in sync with Amp to register the Other Batch's cries. He heard them out loud with his finely tuned ears. A few guards did manage to shoot at them, but Amp and Omathis swerved, lept, sprinted, and sliced into them before the guards could slow their advance.

Omathis threw himself into the door to their lab. With a crash he knocked it from its fortified hinges. He spied a pair of hideous scrawny white-coated Shai-look-alikes hovering over the most beautiful creatures he'd ever seen. These humans were eager to administer whatever lethal poison they'd prepared. Amperous crouched and sprang into them, gutting them both in one motion. He lifted them in disgust and tossed their bodies out of the lab.

"This room is now a sacred space, and their horrible presence defiles it," Amp declared, and Omathis agreed. Omathis didn't feel the least bit bad at the death of these two. If they could resurrect, he'd happily slay them a second time. Nobody should ever hurt one of their beloved Other Batches.

Amperous and Omathis gently removed the restraints from the

frightened, brutalized creatures and lifted them from their Sleeps Beds.

Omathis was shivering, unable to speak, his mind overwhelmed. He'd seen the Other Batches in glimpses, in his mind, but none of those hints had prepared him. The first uninterrupted vision of these beautiful wonders shook him inside and buoyed a part of him that he'd feared was dead.

These precious miracles were precise counterparts to he and Amperous. Women to their men. Omathis hadn't even known females of their kind existed. Oh, the many unexpected blessings Mister Sean continued to shower upon them. These lovely women were not steely cold and cruel like Shai, but warm and accepting, like Lovely.

He and Amp were not alone anymore. Now they'd always have a family.

Omathis clung to one of the creatures. "My name is Soneyane," she whispered. Her voice, though weakened by humanity's torture, emerged brilliant and soothing. Omathis' heart was stilled at the sound. She held him fiercely to her.

Amp was lost in the eyes of the other creature, the smaller of the two. Lenolin was her name. Omathis caught sight of Amp and Lenolin together and felt a shade of embarrassment for his brother. Amp appeared vulnerable and exposed to her, and Omathis had to look away or lose a measure of respect for his brother's dignity.

Is that how I look too?

Lenolin turned her head toward Omathis and smiled as if he had told a joke. "There is no shame in a bond between two creatures, Omathis. Our connections make us great." Far from feeling scolded, Omathis knew that she had explained to him a truth of vital importance. She was right. Soneyane could make him into a foolish servant and he'd never complain. Even subjugated to her, he was stronger than he ever could be dominant and alone. They were all mightier together. That must be how Amperous felt about Lenolin, too.

He watched as Lenolin disappeared into Amperous' soft embrace, and could no longer tell where his brother ended and Lenolin started. *Amperous!* Omathis could scarcely believe it. His gruff, angry, forever disgruntled brother was acting as nurturing as a hen with a baby chicken.

Soneyane stroked Omathis' face with the back of her hand until he forgot about his brother's unnerving display of affection. He disappeared into her beauty, feeling secure and held in a way he hadn't since he was a newborn.

The four of them awoke to a new sensation, a stronger signal, amplified by the presence of each other.

"Let's rescue the others," Soneyane proclaimed as she and her sister left the cage they'd lived in all their lives.

Ollie and Sean were startled by the waves of alerts that came across the scanner all at once. Ollie's phone vibrated without relief.

"We're too late," Ollie said grimly.

When they arrived at the Center for Progressive Research, it had been torn apart like the target of a precise and devastating military attack—which, Sean reflected, it was. Probably the most advanced strike in the history of mankind, though the operation hadn't been carried out by humans at all.

Military personnel swarmed the building, working to cordon off the scene and usher curious onlookers away. Ollie and Sean flashed their credentials and were allowed to wade through the carnage.

"You made them strong enough to do this?" Ollie asked, judgement in his voice, as they neared a steel door. It had been twisted and bent, blasted from its cement frame. Sean nodded, enraptured and shaken by his creations' handiwork.

"What safeguards did you build into them so that we could control them?"

Sean didn't answer, because *none* didn't seem to be a suitable reply. The safeguards had been scheduled for installation in the next phase.

Ollie examined the seven dead bodies on the scene, cut apart with surgical precision, and his part in this disaster became clear. He had made a mistake keeping the escape a secret.

"We're not going to be able to stop them, are we, Sean?"

Sean didn't respond.

"How many more are there, in captivity? Have all others been eliminated yet?"

Ollie detected hesitance in Sean, and it filled him with fury. He wheeled toward Sean and slammed the pensive scientist against the wall. He growled, "You cannot still be trying to figure out a way to protect them. They must be destroyed. All of them."

"They're innocent—"

Ollie silenced Sean by ramming him into the wall again. Sean didn't try to fight back, but took the violence with humility, like he deserved it and more.

"Amperous and Omathis were slated to be eliminated first," Sean stammered. "They were the only ones who exhibited undue aggression toward their handlers. The others were passive."

Ollie handed a phone to Sean. "Make sure the others are eliminated. Now."

Sean dialed reluctantly.

ICELYN

"What's going on? Omathis, Eveshone, what is it?"

I want to leave my throne and run from the temple, curl up into a lonely rejected ball somewhere dark and hidden, and cry. Then they'd understand how dreadful and unfair they're being. But that's probably conduct unbecoming of a god—or even a mature human being. So I don't.

"Will someone please say something? I can barely breathe, this silence is so thick," I beg.

Two of my Anaghwin followers lead a pair of hunched, emaciated Croathus into the temple. I recognize them as Carriana and Andhalas, a mother and child we've recently taken into our community. They shuffle before my throne, but won't look at me. They are brittle, already broken. I've never seen Croathus look as weak as these two.

Their appearance is a protest, a reproach, a denouncement of the difficult decisions I've been forced to make.

"Do these two wish to make a Petition?" I ask, pushing down my doubts and attempting to present confidence.

An Anaghwin named Kaiyoumay—a female who, I've been hesitant to admit, makes me nervous, because she's brash and bold and doesn't seem to care that I should be respected—speaks out defiantly.

"Look at these two, and face the fruits your commands have nourished into harvest."

I study Carriana and Andhalas. The color has drained from them, like they're the ashes left over once something beautiful has been burnt in a fire.

"I have instructed you to treat them with utmost kindness, keep them in the best accommodations, provide them with our finest food," I argue. Kaiyoumay seems to be implying that we are torturing this pair, which isn't true at all. "They are our guests, not our prisoners."

Kaiyoumay seems eager to respond, but the weakened Croathus Carriana raises an arm to quiet her and speaks instead. "Guests are not captured against their will and made to live among strangers, enemies, far from home, far from family. Prisoners are."

I scan my heart, deep inside, trying to find the slightest hint of a Soothing so I can connect with Carriana. She's not a prisoner, nor is her son. They are here to join us, to become a part of us. I am saving them, not hurting them.

But I sense no connection to either of them.

"Carriana, you and your son are Anaghwin now. We have adopted you into our family. I have brought you both into my heart." Once again, I survey my inner landscape, looking for the smallest connection with these two. I know the bridge must exist; I just need to find it.

"Love will win, eventually," I insist. "I know this might not look much like love right now, but eventually…" I trail off.

The boy shuffles toward me. A glimmer of hope. A child will know how much I love him. He's not yet jaded by life and pain.

I extend a hand to him. He studies it with wide-eyed curiosity. *Yes, take my hand, Andhalas. Come to me.* Andhalas turns back to his mother, as if asking for permission. She nods.

Excitement fires within me. This is our breakthrough. This is what I've needed to start relating to the Croathus I've brought into the community. And with everyone watching, too.

Andhalas raises his taloned hand and reaches toward me, slow and deliberate. "Yes, come to me, little one," I entice him, knowing he can feel the deep care I have for him. "Take my hand."

It all happens before I can react, yet I watch it unfold slowly, frozen in horror. The talons grow from his fingertips—sharp, long, and mean. He spits into the palm of my hand, his face ugly and twisted. Before I can respond to this affront, his small but lethal claws swipe down with stunning ferocity, tear into me, and leave angry crimson trenches emblazoned across my welcoming palm.

I scream at the blinding pain, clutching my wounded hand close to my chest. Eveshone covers me in a flash, shielding me against any further harm.

"Careful, Icelyn Brathius!" Carriana threatens. "Next time you ask him to take your hand, he may not care to give it back."

As Eveshone carries me away from the chaos, I hear Andhalas shout, his voice bloodthirsty and unhinged: "We are Croathus. Never Anaghwin."

4

NOW

Torrain hadn't fallen into this trap for a long time, but the mother bird was a stealth attack. Normally he was productive and upbeat—the kind of leader the rest of the Kith required. He'd sworn off moping in the self-sorrow that always beckoned him, and he felt better for it.

Yet he'd awoken to the sweet song of a tiny blackbird, the feathers on her head tufted like styled hair, chirping her warning to interlopers. Torrain peered out the window of Pannous Lab to see the creature perched on a small branch, chest puffed up and out, infused with as much confidence and bluster as an animal could be when weighing no more than a couple of ounces.

"I'll call you Shield," Torrain whispered, pleased at the name he'd come up with for this brave bird. She took another moment to assert her dominance atop the small branch, and then launched herself into the air, bullet-fast and fierce, until she warded off an unwelcome bird that had come too close.

Torrain was impressed by this diminutive guardian. He saw the beneficiary of this brave sentinel's vigilance: a miniature nest containing three scraggly chicks, hatched so recently that their eyes hadn't opened yet.

The mother returned to her perch, which afforded her a view of all angles of approach. Again she shot herself into the air, fast and vicious, and repelled another trespasser—this time a large dragonfly. Even after the dragonfly had been scared away from the nest, she continued her pursuit and snatched it out of the air, crumpling it in half. She returned to the nest and dropped hearty portions of the convulsing bug into her babies' hungry mouths.

Torrain lost track of how long he watched the mother bird's impressive cycle: perched and vigilant, then flying and aggressive, then hunting for food and feeding her young. Then back to perched and vigilant to start all over again. The mother was devoted to the cause and took no break, even for a count or two. She no doubt would do this until the day they left the nest and became brave, dedicated parents themselves.

Tears filled Torrain's eyes at the thought that he'd never seen a better mother. It was an innocent thought, but brought with it a dark afterthought.

No, I can think of one better. His deceased mother, Nandor. She was always lovely and brave, warm and caring.

The bird on the branch, perched and vigilant.

She never wavered from caring for him.

The bird detecting a threat, charging through the air.

She'd defended him against Tranton's unfair charges and paid with her life.

The bird sensing her chicks' hunger, grabbing an insect out of the air.

Torrain would never forgive life for stealing her away from him. They were the kind of mother and son that needed to grow through the years together. She should have seen who he'd become, second in command in all of Mountaintop, a worthy partner to the mighty Adorane.

Thoughts of Nandor gave way to thoughts of Icelyn, and the other half of his heart hurt now too. He'd lost every woman who'd shared even a trace of affection with him. He'd tried to erase the memory of Icelyn's face, betrayed and heartbroken, as she left Mountaintop for the last time. Yet here it was again, as if that portrait were carved inside his head.

There was only one way out of this downward spiraling sadness, so Torrain pulled himself away from the window and the bird that had brought him so much misery with her fine motherly example. He poured his attention into his research. He wasn't sure avoiding his feelings like this was healthy, but at least it was productive.

He'd had many unpleasant thoughts he'd wanted to avoid since returning to Mountaintop. His inventions—and the Kith in general—had benefited from the distractions he craved. He'd refined the water bringing machines so that their output had increased three-fold. He'd set up a system of conveyers and pulleys throughout both sides of Mountaintop so people didn't need to spend so much time carrying tins and bags of water home from Waterpump. He'd even invented a machine that could be used to print multiple copies of a book or essay—a press that used carved stone and ink squeezed from berries. Now the Kith could distribute written materials without needing to write them over and over by hand.

Yet all those inventions—and the many others he'd brought to the community—were dwarfed in importance by his latest project. This one was the most distracting yet.

He'd collected as many Brathius masks as he could after that terrible day. It had been grim work, as they weren't easily removed from the deceased Threat Belows; they needed to be pried off carefully, or they would break into pieces.

The masks were special. Not merely wood, they were lined with an organic material that had bonded with the skin of the Threat Below, grafted itself into them. He hadn't completely figured out the technology.

Not yet. But he was about halfway there.

Amperous had awoken in darkness, bound so tight that he couldn't move. He was blind with pain and anger, and he felt terribly weak.

The pain and weakness he understood. He'd nearly died from the poisonous gas in the Mountaintop air. But why was he so angry?

Then he smelled humans. Had they captured him, to poke and prod and satisfy their darkest curiosities? He'd die before he endured the Sleeps again. That's what this felt like, tied down in the blackness. The Sleeps.

He roared in frustration.

"Good, yes, let it out. As far as I can tell, you still have poison in your lungs. Screaming will help." A soothing voice, kinder than any he'd heard since he was a child, washed over him.

"Unbind me." Amperous commanded.

A tall tongue of fire flared above him, and Amperous saw that he was tied down to a stone slab, like a bed. Like the metal beds Mistersean used for their Sleeps. Amperous couldn't see anyone else.

"I will, in time. You must understand that I would have already, but the others have their concerns. I don't want to run roughshod over them. We have this idea that we're something of a *collective* down here."

Was this human invisible? Amperous turned his head as far to the side as possible in his restraints, looking for the source of the voice.

A chuckle floated up to Amperous. "Down, closer to the floor. I'm a short one. I know compared to your kind, all humans are short. But me even more so."

Now Amperous saw him, though he could hardly believe his eyes. He'd never seen a human so small before, and if not for the instinctual hatred he felt for this creature, he'd doubt the speaker was human at all.

"Where am I?"

"You're below the ground, in the Mines."

"What do you intend to do with me?"

"I ask only two things of you. First, that you let me help you. You are sick and need care."

The man was now close to Amperous, his face barely reaching the top of the stone slab where the Croathus was held fast. He examined Amperous, his eyes hungry, his breath short. This curious man was in a state of unglued excitement, like he feared he was living a dream that might end at any moment.

"What else?" Amperous was suspicious. The man's voice sounded gentle, but in his experience, gentle-sounding humans did the most damage.

"I only want to learn more about you. Threat Belows have only ever been fearsome legends to us. I know that you are more than a nightmare."

ICELYN

"You should have warned me!"

I cannot keep my anger contained. Shouting at Omathis and Eveshone will do tremendous harm, but after the attack I've suffered, my pain is unbearable. The shadowy parts of me, normally restrained and silenced, hunger to strike back.

"You told us not to bother you with the Petitions before they start, Lovely," Eveshone scrambles to explain. "Otherwise we would have—"

"No!" I cut her off, which I've never done before. She bristles, and a part of my heart softens (after all, she had rushed to defend me against the attack), but I immediately toughen back up. They all ambushed me. "You two have the authority to guide the Petitions. The responsibility. You could have—should have—edited those requests out altogether. Answered on my behalf. Is it too much to ask that you defend me?"

Eveshone bows low like a chastened pet. "Of course, you're right. We should have done that for you." I hate to see her brought down like this, drained of her regal grace. She looks like a butterfly doused by a bucketful of water, soggy and unable to fly. I want to reach out to her, offer a comforting token of reconciliation and whisper *it's okay, Eveshone—it's not that bad, really*. I want to restore her to the confident, loved creature that she is. Yet I cannot bear a repeat of what just happened, ever, so I need to ensure the sting hurts them at least half as much as it did me.

"We didn't defend you or eliminate these particular Petitions, Dear One, because we agree with them." Omathis stands tall, and projects his words deliberately, *out loud.* He doesn't share them with me with intimacy, through our roots, like those who share a pulse can. It's a conscious—and distancing—choice. The blood that spilled from my hand still stains my clothing, yet he confronts me like we are strangers. Verbally and out loud.

"We have discussed this before," I respond. "It's necessary. We must capture them and keep them here." I answer out loud, but curse myself, because there are tears in my eyes and I can't do anything to control them. Attempts to stifle them only lead to more. "Since no Anaghwin can or will reproduce, we must find another way to add to our numbers. The Croathus increase every day. We need children to grow. To have a future."

Omathis holds my damaged hand in his and begins to clean the gashes and apply soothing balms. I'm too weak (or too needy) to pull it away, even if that's what my pride urges me to do.

"Icelyn Brathius. While I recognize your wisdom, please recognize mine. No future worth living can be built upon the backs of others."

I was once the unquestioned leader of the Drowned City. Now they argue with me. Omathis himself accusses me of violating their rights. The Brathius *gave* them their rights—their entire existence—in the first place.

"I cherish their individual freedom. But the Anaghwin refusal to reproduce is wrong. Wrong for our survival. Compelling them to do the right thing when their flawed nature would have them do the wrong is an *affirmation* of individual freedom. It's short-sighted to prioritize individual freedom over the very survival of those individuals. Without communal security and the survival that growing numbers would guarantee, there will no longer be individuals whose freedom we can preserve. They'll all be dead."

Omathis sighs, unconvinced. "The Croathus you have commanded us to take from the Mainland are prisoners. They're refusing to eat. Your goal may be to add them to our community and ensure our survival, but that's not what is happening. They're just dying."

He needs to give it time. He needs to give it support. How can this succeed when everyone obeys with such reluctance? We need to be unified and enthusiastic. Why can't they see this?

"I am your god, and I command it. You have sprung from me. You exist because of me. And this is what I order of you. I hate having to give a commandment—please hear me. I do. If you would only obey, joyfully, and without protest, I would never need to command anything. I would only suggest or request. But I've been pushed to this."

One of the few perks of being a god who has come to live among her people is that few should argue with your edicts, no matter how thoughtless they appear. I used to enjoy this. But now even that benefit is fading. It's all so tiresome.

They don't understand. Nobody does. I see a future that they cannot—a future where we no longer exist. I'm doing what I must to avoid it.

I have commanded them to reproduce, a reversal of Omathis' ancient prohibition. He didn't want newborn Anaghwin brought into this world. Anaghwin existence was too painful a burden to be laid upon new sufferers. Those who disobeyed, such as Eveshone's father and mother, were banished from the Drowned City.

Yet we are in a new age now. A Brathius has descended and lives among them. We must thrive and embrace the future. We must have children.

Omathis doesn't understand. It's not just physical survival I'm trying to preserve for them, and him in particular. It's also emotional and psychological survival. I tried to explain it to him one evening while we sat beside the still waters.

"Omathis, you've spent hundreds of years in pain, abandoned by your father. Everyone who owed you protection wounded you instead. They left you broken—a cracked bone reset and reshattered a thousand times. I too have suffered, though not on the scale you have, and so we have both been left twisted and hurt. But wholeness is promised. Healing will come. Sometimes it just takes the next generation to see it. I want you to have children, because I want you to see the healing you have waited so long for. I want you to see the simple love a child can have for a father who has never betrayed her. I want you to experience that in your child. I have only seen that healing by discovering you and Eveshone and the rest of my Anaghwin children. I want it for you too."

Omathis nodded, but my encouragement only seemed to deepen his pain. "Dear Lovely, what does one do when children are part of that unfixable pain?"

I didn't know what he was talking about, and he would not expand on it. He'd only cryptically reply: "All that has happened has happened, and I've accepted it."

Though the Anaghwin have told me they hear and are trying to obey my new ruling, none have conceived. I can't ensure that *they are trying their hardest* without invading their privacy in an unacceptable way, but Omathis promises me that they are. They are simply, after all these years, infertile. "When a thing goes unused for too long, Lovely, eventually it goes away entirely," Omathis explained.

He had thought that would be the end of the initiative. We'd live, our small remnant, in our Drowned City, just as they had for hundreds of years.

Yet I'd been raised in a small remnant, trapped behind a wall on a small speck of rock. That was no way to live. There's no such thing as survival without growth; eventually, something will find you, hunt you, and destroy you. Your water will be poisoned. The Croathus will grow in numbers and overwhelm you. All remnants are eventually wiped out. I remember what Adorane once said to me, about our community in Mountaintop: *We settled, Ice. So much that now we all deserve death. We haven't progressed enough to stay ahead, and death always pursues us. It's inevitable.*

We need to grow or we will die.

I learned that lesson firsthand. If I don't follow the wisdom I'd earned through tragedies, then all of the loss—of Aclornis, of my home, my parents, my relationship with Adorane and Torrain, the Anaghwin who died in Mountaintop—would be for nothing. There's no thought bleaker than that.

So I issued a new command, one that was more unpopular than any I'd made previously. More unpopular, even, than my decree that a brave band of Anaghwin must travel to Cloudline every new moon and slaughter the mad Cloudy Croathus that gather there. "These are our brothers," Omathis would remind me. "Even if they are bad, they are blood. We worry that you only ask us to do this to bring a measure of protection to the humans left behind in Mountaintop." I could not expect them to understand why I would ask such a thing, and didn't believe I should have to. But he was right.

The new command was that we needed to, *for our survival,* hunt and capture Croathus women and children and integrate them into our community. If we couldn't make our own Anaghwin, we'd import them. There was no other way to proceed.

Of course I hated the idea of it. Yet ultimately, I reasoned, living alone as a Croathus was not a life worth living. Divorced from your source, away from your Brathius creator? They should be reunited to me.

My mandate was an assault on them, I knew, but it was an assault born of mercy. This was force, yes—but like forcing a hungry woman to eat, or a sick man to take medicine.

Growing the Anaghwin numbers was the ultimate good, even if it required actions that seemed bad.

Why can't they just trust me? If I were a male god, like their beloved Mistersean, they would listen to me without doubting me. Or at least, if I were a male god, I could just tell them all what to do and not care so much about how they all felt about it.

5

THEN

Sean found Travis in Shai's condo. The boy was leafing through her research notes. He'd expected Shai's son to be an emotionless sieve, and as predicted, Travis' eyes were neither red nor wet. Travis had never been a normal child—but the boy's chilled demeanor now, after all that had happened, was unnerving even so.

"Travis, I'm sorry about… she was a wonderful woman." Sean blinked back tears.

Travis finished reading a section of Shai's elegantly written observations and turned the page. Without looking up, he said quietly, "She was a genius."

"I was wondering if you wanted to say something at her funeral."

"My mother never cared for eulogies. Or funerals, for that matter. Just cremate her. Her memory is all we have now. It's all we need."

Sean nodded and cleared his throat. "Would you like help packing up your things?"

Travis shook his head no.

"You've been told that you're coming to live with me?"

Travis nodded yes.

"I was thinking we could move you in on Saturday—"

"That's my birthday," Travis responded. His birthday. Also the day before his murdered mother's funeral. God, what horror.

"Oh—we'll have to get you a cake," Sean replied. He meant well, but immediately it felt like an awkward and heartless thing to say. *Hey, you've lost your mother—but how about a nice red velvet with cream cheese frosting? Things are looking up now, kid!*

Sean quickly changed the subject. "I wanted you to know that the adoption papers are being expedited. So you have a family, you know? Me, Laura Lee, you. It'll be great."

Travis didn't nod, though he felt a hot flash of anger rise from his gut to his face. *A family formed out of guilt. Just what I need.*

The silence was too much for Sean to bear. "Okay, I'm going to go. I believe your nanny…ah…Stacy…"

"Sally. Her name is Sally."

"Right, Sally. She'll be here soon. I have some matters to attend to… so I'll be going." Sean shuffled toward the exit.

Finally, Travis spoke. "Do you know that I saw her?"

Sean froze. "What?"

"The day she died. She hadn't come home. I was worried. I went to visit her, but nobody else knew what had happened yet. There were no alarms or emergency responders. *The accident in the lab*, as you called it—I saw it. I saw her."

Sean's mind flashed to Shai, cut up and hung up on display. He prayed he was misunderstanding.

Travis looked up from his mother's papers, and his eyes bored into Sean. "Did *you* see her at the lab, Sean? Were you there too?" Travis pressed.

"No," Sean lied, and glanced down, away from the searing interrogation. "The authorities thought it would be better if I didn't visit, um—the scene. Better if I didn't see."

Travis stared past Sean with dead eyes. "The authorities were right."

It's strange. After people die, you realize that however well you thought you knew them, there's so much about them that is—and now always will be—a mystery. Sean sat in Shai's condo, trying to find her essence so he could commune with her one last time. One more moment of contact. If anything, just to overwrite his final vision of her, hung up and gutted.

He'd never been in her home before and was now wondering why. Had she never invited him? Why had he never thought this strange?

She liked cubist art. He hadn't known. All of her furniture was either black or crimson red, and it all matched. She had a complete library of cookbooks—an excessive amount spanning multiple culinary genres—though Sean had never eaten one meal she'd prepared. He realized with guilt that if he were forced to complete an exam about Shai, he'd probably fail.

Shai had never been a warm person. Sean knew that. She was often sarcastic, as sharp and practical as a surgeon's scalpel. Once Laura Lee, after witnessing one of Shai's tamer tirades, had asked Sean why he stayed with "that wretched bloodless wraith," especially since Laura Lee knew that her mother had been giving and kind. "Shai is the opposite of what you lost when Mom died," Laura Lee had sobbed. "Why would you make her the new center of your life?"

He hadn't had an answer for Laura Lee. Not one he was willing to put into words and share, at least. But now, as he flipped through the pages of Shai's precise notes, laced with bursts of brilliant insight and inspiration, he began to miss her for the first time. *This is why I loved her. She was a mirror to my own thirst for knowledge.* She was the only person who understood that part of him. Everyone else had judged his insatiable desire for discovery, once they'd witnessed how vast it truly was. She hadn't; she had encouraged it.

He liked having Shai around because she'd amplified his ambition.

Guilt flooded him, starting in his gut and rushing up until his cheeks were flushed and his back was wet with sweat. For a moment his carefully cultivated defenses failed. He was forced to stare straight into the face of what he'd done, the choices he'd made.

Flipping the pages of Shai's research made it clear. He'd chosen the wrong path at every opportunity. He could have chosen to be a smart man with a respectable career who made his loving daughter the priority she deserved to be. Instead, he'd indulged his obsessions. He could have made the world better, slowly and patiently—but he'd decided instead to hack through the rules and force a shortcut that resulted in a nightmare. And God, poor Omathis and Amperous. He should never have created them—but once he did, he should have given them the love, acceptance, and guidance that any living being deserves from their creator. Instead, he pumped them full of hate and rage, starved them, and worst of all, abandoned them to their isolation.

Every observation Shai had recorded on every page of her research notes cut into Sean. Her words were straightforward, scientific, objective—but every sentence pointed to his failures.

Then he read a line that made him stop breathing. The hairs on the back of his neck prickled. He felt a sudden chill blow through the room, though no window was open.

NOTES TRSMTD: 03042015032245 BUNDESNACHRICHTENDIENST / MARKEL

He flipped back and forth through the pages and saw this line repeated. The numbers differed, but everything else remained the same.

NOTES TRSMTD: 07042014011932 BUNDESNACHRICHTENDIENST / MARKEL

Everything she'd written.

NOTES TRSMTD: 12302012131215 BUNDESNACHRICHTENDIENST / MARKEL

Every breakthrough. Every insight. Every accidental discovery.

NOTES TRSMTD: 09092011194310 BUNDESNACHRICHTENDIENST / MARKEL

Every chart. Every diagram. Every test. Every failure.

NOTES TRSMTD: 04102013103254 BUNDESNACHRICHTENDIENST / MARKEL

Everything they'd built together. All of it, all their secrets. Sent to someone else.

She couldn't have done this, he soothed himself, even as he already resigned himself to the fact that she had.

Shai. No.

What have you done?

Shai had been the one who'd stumbled across the incubation method needed to fuse diametrically opposed DNA in a way that benefited the newly created hybrid. Even Sean had to admit that this breakthrough had been instrumental in the creation of the C.R.O.A.T.H.U.S.

Without Shai's contributions, Sean would never have determined the precise combination of temperature, amount of time, type of protein strain, and mix and type of hormonal marination required to reverse the fertilized mammalian egg's natural resistance to further insemination.

At least that's what she'd claimed, her voice rising louder over Sean's fierce opposition. It was true—her experiments on the red deer population in Scotland, where she'd found that dominant and strong females tended to produce sons while feebler, weaker mothers tended to give birth to daughters, had provided rich raw material. She'd discovered a variety of repeatable patterns when it came to the internal temperature and chemical makeup of the animals' respective wombs. But it had been Sean, not Shai, who'd seen those patterns among the discordant geyser of unorganized information she'd produced. He'd seen how her discovery could be fused with what he already knew about trait selection and purification to create something grand and new.

She provided a piece of information; he'd divined the implications.

She'd written a sentence; he'd folded it into the larger masterpiece.

She'd played a single note; he'd composed the symphony.

Shai hadn't appreciated the metaphors, but eventually they stopped arguing about it, and Sean's view prevailed.

Shai had never seemed too upset about the agreement they'd come to, after the initial argument had been messily contained. She knew her place in his discovery.

Now, though, Sean could see that she hadn't known it. He hadn't given her the credit she believed she deserved, so she'd decided to steal it.

Sean thumbed through the reams of notes Shai had maintained. She transmitted everything to BUNDESNACHRICHTENDIENST / MARKEL. Notes, formulas, videos, diagrams.

He found messages sent back, praising her work and her intellectual determination. Sean felt sick reading the impersonal short messages between Shai and Markel.

SHAI: Latest subjects no longer growing weaker and dying at 12 weeks outside of womb. Now avoiding hybridization collapse. Stabilized balance of *Turritopsis / Human* cells. View document B-$296ER for details

MARKEL: Highly pleased with results. Continue as planned.

Sean couldn't have been more hurt had he discovered that Shai was having an affair. This was worse—an infidelity perpetrated in test-tubes and DNA sequencers instead of hotel rooms and expensive restaurants. Something more precious to them both.

The betrayal blinded him to the deeper concern, which only dawned on him later. Sure, Shai had stolen his secrets and claimed credit for his work. He'd thought they'd been a team, but instead she'd only used him. He now had to wonder if she'd pushed for Omathis and Amperous' termination in order to destroy his project while hers flourished in secret. She'd never been supportive of them, even though they'd clearly been remarkable.

Now it all made sense. Could they have been competing with her own creations? What project were Omathis and Amperous competing with?

Sean's skin broke out into goosebumps as he realized the enormity of what Shai had done. Who was Markel? Had he been successful in using Shai's detailed notes and instructions?

This would be a devastating theft. Sean had thought himself the only one capable of developing this kind of hybridization—and thus the only one who could be trusted with its immense power. But if Shai sent it to someone else, he'd have no control over what they did with them.

Were there other creatures? And if so, where were they now?

NOW

Tranton was no longer confined to prison, but it made no difference. Adorane and Torrain—those boys who ruled Mountaintop with the full force of their impetuous adolescent naiveté—had determined that they had no use for his counsel. Or for tradition. Or for anything else that had kept their community safe for the previous centuries. They refused to acknowledge that his action—releasing the poisonous gas—had saved Mountaintop. They refused to identify and properly demonize the true threats to their safety: the Threatbelows and anyone who supported them. They refused to admit that Icelyn Brathius had betrayed their community by bringing those beasts to the top of the mountain in the first place.

Tranton was given no job. He was entrusted with no responsibilities. Whenever he asked, he was told that Adorane and Torrain were still working to determine what his role in the Kith should be. He had so much to offer, yet they denied him over and over.

He knew why. They placed the blame for their own mistakes on him. They would never forgive him.

Torrain held Tranton responsible for his mother's death, which wasn't fair. Nandor's death had ultimately been her own fault. When one chooses to rebel against the established order, they risk dying. It's that simple. It's the rule everyone agrees to in order to maintain a civilized society.

Beyond that, though, they held an even greater crime against him. Her. They never talked about it, but they missed her.

The lovestruck boys blamed Tranton for Icelyn's self-imposed exile. That was his ultimate sin. He'd done what was necessary to save Mountaintop, and instead of being thanked, he was reviled. He had been cast out because he'd hurt a girl's feelings when a few of her pet monsters had to die.

These days, since he had nothing else to do, Tranton spent much of his time in his ancestors' secret cave, living like a hermit. He poured over the documents Travis had left behind. He read them again and again. As he worked to clean and organize the cave, he uncovered scores of new documents.

Tranton mused at how foolish these boy leaders were. If they'd only given him something else to do, he wouldn't have bothered to hang out here so much. But they hadn't, and now he'd learned so much more than he ever knew before.

And now he had a new plan.

Istoch straightened each hand-carved wooden cross with care. He saw that the morning rain had splattered dirt across the base of each grave marker, and he began the painstaking process of wiping them clean. The little babies deserved at least that much.

As he scrubbed, he said another prayer for each poor departed soul. In doing so, he saw their faces and heard each of their *coos* and *aahs* in his memory. Some had started talking before they died—just a couple of words, but even those little verbal seeds were rich with the promise of a whole personality.

He wondered where they were now. Everyone says a dead person is dearly departed—but departed to where?

Istoch wanted to believe in a paradise; his own dearly departed parents had taught him of its existence since he was a child. He liked to imagine his beloved mother and father there now, welcoming the babies. The whole bunch of them would live as one big loud family, waiting for that joyous day when Istoch would join them too. But this world was filled with such dark misery that he suspected any hope that the next would be happy was unfounded. The best Istoch could wish for was peaceful nothingness. If he persisted into another life, he knew he would be sad there, too. That's all life would ever or could ever be: sadness.

As usual, Istoch was the only one visiting the graves. He suppressed annoyance at the rest of the Kith. Most of them had a child laid to rest in this graveyard, yet they rarely visited to show that they still cared. He knew they were grieving in their own solitary desperation, behind closed doors, still recovering from the shock of an entire village going infertile and stillborn at once. But he felt it was important that they at least show up now and again to pay their respects to the dead.

He was surprised to see someone else approaching the little resting place that Istoch had created for his deceased New Batch. The sight buoyed him, then disappointed him.

He nodded at Tranton with a deliberate curtness and remained silent. He didn't know why Adorane had released Tranton from imprisonment after only a year of captivity. A venomous snake didn't belong out and about among the Kith.

"I've come to pay my respects," Tranton whispered, as if loud words would be an affront.

Istoch suspected all this was an act. He said nothing as he continued rubbing away at the dirt staining the otherwise-pristine wooden crosses.

"Istoch, everyone has a full store of sympathy for you," Tranton started.

Istoch wished he could silence the Cognate.

"What you've been through—"

"I'm not among the dead," Istoch cut him off bitterly.

The way he said the words made Tranton wonder if Istoch wished he were.

Tranton had hoarded many pieces of information patiently since he'd discovered that hidden history in the cave. He'd held his secrets close, knowing their value, and doled them out only when the right moment arose. This was one of those moments.

"Istoch, would you like to hear what I think you should do next?"

"No."

"Good. Then I know I can trust you with my secret."

ICELYN

A shriek echoes throughout the Drowned City, urgent and raw. It feels like it's made of more than sound, like a rusted old knife directly scraping against my inner ear.

I want it to stop.

More importantly, though, I need to figure out what it is. I rush from my temple and see Anaghwin disturbed, desperate, and rushing toward...

Oh no. This is everything I've feared. Now I recognize the voice, screaming, guttural.

Carriana.

Omathis meets me outside the gates, though he hasn't been waiting for me. He's busy opening the portal. A mass of Anaghwin have gathered here, and I can feel their sharp looks piercing me as I enter. *You did this,* their eyes accuse me. T*his is your fault. We begged you to let them go.*

As the gates slide open, I see what Andhales has done. The young Croathus, still a child, has used his talons to tear at his own flesh. His neck, chest, and abdomen are a bloody mess—a violent monument to the misery I've trapped him in.

Carriana holds his lifeless body and wails. She's the only one who isn't hurling wordless condemnation my way, because she's too focused on her dead son to notice I've joined her.

I rush to their side and lay a hand on Andalas' torn-up torso. It's still warm.

"Come and gather!" I command, yet no one moves.

"He is still with us," I plead. "Bring him back from the shadows."

Omathis joins me, more out of duty than desire, while all others hang back. "We need to join together. Please, our power is only strong enough when we all stand together." Eveshone emerges from the Anaghwin and joins Omathis and me, but I know it still won't be enough.

I tear Carriana's attention away from her broken son, risking her wrath as she realizes who I am. "Carriana, tell them to come. We can draw him back. There is still warmth in his veins. We can draw him."

I see a flash of sad understanding come over her face. "No. We are Croathus. You are Anaghwin. You cannot restore him. You cannot draw him."

"We are the same. Croathus and Anaghwin are two words for the same people. They will prove it to you. Let them call to Andalas."

Carriana nods, weakly, still stunned, shocked enough to try anything. The Anaghwin, who had been awaiting her permission, swarm Andalas' shredded body and join Omathis, Eveshone, and me. We place our hands on him, heads tilted back, our eyes closing, opening, and closing again. A buzzing noise rises. Each of the Anaghwin make a vibrating sound too gentle to be heard individually, but together it sounds like a distant storm, a burning fire, a whisper that could make you go deaf if you're not careful.

I can feel Andalas. He is far away, but not gone. Not yet. A coordinated rhythm rustles through the Anaghwin. They sway forward, then lean back, all as one, like different parts of a single entity.

"Andalas," I whisper, "come back. Don't leave Carriana alone."

I feel a response to my request. I'm left so cold that it's as if I've been trapped in a snowstorm without any clothing at all. *No*, he responds. *Let me leave.*

The urgency of the Anaghwin increases, and I'm relieved that I'm the only one who knows Andalas' true desire. They pull harder, draw him back with all their strength. I fear they will collapse from exhaustion. Some fall to the ground, but most double their efforts.

The darker lines on Andalas' body, the ones that commonly trace the contours of Anaghwin or Croathus musculature, pulse dim green and yellow, like the light emitted from a glowworm or a firefly.

The color returns to Andalas' face. I close my eyes and touch him. He grows hotter—so hot that his flesh begins to burn my fingertips, but still I hold fast. I keep my eyes closed, because that seems like the right thing to do, but even through my clenched eyelids I sense a bright light. It blinds me, even with my eyes closed; the after-image of the young Croathus glows behind my eyes, so that I can't see anything else.

I fainted. I wasn't the only one; as I wake, confused, I see that many Anaghwin have passed out from the effort required to bring Andalas back. Still, I'm disappointed in myself. I fancied myself leading the effort to draw him back from darkness. Yet I wasn't even conscious when he was fully restored, and now he is gone.

"And was he grateful?" I ask, desperate for more details.

"No, he was not," Omathis answers quietly, his words clipped. He doesn't want to talk about it.

But I need to know more. "What did he say? What did Carriana say?"

"Andalas said that he didn't die by accident, and he didn't wish to be pulled back. But you knew that already."

I did. But I hoped he'd change his mind. This was proof that they were one of us, that Anaghwin and Croathus could unite. That I could turn all of them.

"Was Carriana moved by the renewal?" I ask, cursing myself for fainting and missing this important moment.

"Carriana wants the same thing she's wanted since you brought her here: to leave."

"But she's an Anaghwin. They both are. We've proved that, at least."

Omathis seems exhausted, and I'm not sure if it's from the effort expended on Andalas or from dealing with me. He looks at me, eyes hard.

"The only thing we've proven is that you're a god who doesn't care much for free will."

6

ICELYN

I plunge below the ocean's surface, relishing the idea that no one in the entire world knows where I am right now. I'm alone, floating in this endless blue, which seems fitting. I love when my surroundings match my inner state, when symbol and reality lock into a perfect reflection of each other. A thundering sky-splitting storm when I'm angry. A frozen morning when I'm empty inside. Or now, disconnected and lost, floating away unguided toward an unending horizon of water.

Even though I never believed in one, I'd always assumed that *if there were* one true God, He would be in an enviable position. He'd be in charge of everything, knowing fully that he possessed more power than all the others. He would know he deserved to be honored, obeyed, appreciated, and glorified. I believe that's exactly why, historically, people in power have so often loved to trot out God's name; by claiming to speak His words, they could often enjoy the same benefits. No underlings would dare dissent if doing so could cause them to be flung to the fiery depths of hell. This is why the Kith had abandoned religion long ago (along with the fact that it was foolish superstition). Leadership should be based on intelligence and merit, not illusions and fear. A leader who called upon God was dangerous.

Yet somehow I've managed to bungle this. While my connection to the Anaghwin as their deity is unquestioned, it seems only to mean that I am the recipient of all their shadowy feelings of blame. I am set high above them, yes—but as a target to be shot at, not an object to worship.

Growing up, I'd always thought I was on a path toward greatness. My destiny felt undeniable. Nothing could waylay who I was becoming. Now that desire felt naive, like that of a toddler declaring that she'd like to grow up to be a bird and grow feathers and fly away. Impossible from the start.

No matter what I did, I was never going to be great. I see that now.

My only consolation is that I don't believe there *is* greatness to be attained. Not anymore. Not in this world. My mistake was in having any faith in greatness in the first place.

A jellyfish, clear and round, aimlessly drifts past me. I push my arm through the water, and the currents I create send the alien creature into a tailspin, unable to control where it is going. *I know exactly how you feel.*

I close my eyes deliberately, so tightly that the tender muscles I clench to keep the light out start to tire. This is my statement to the world. *I don't want to be a part of any of this anymore. I see what you have to offer. I choose darkness. Leave me alone.*

In the end, Omathis and Eveshone had promised to obey, but reluctantly. I needed them to agree with what I was asking—wholeheartedly, and not just out of a sense of duty—but they would not.

"We will continue to abduct and torture our brothers and sisters, if it be your will," Omathis had replied, his head hung low. Both he and Eveshone acted as if I had beaten them.

"Good. Let's double the effort, then." I don't know why I commanded it. I hope it was because I felt desperation that we'd be overrun otherwise. And this is true. The Anaghwin in the Drowned City appear to me increasingly as grains of sand falling to the bottom of the hourglass, and I fear it's only a matter of time before they disappear entirely. But underneath this, I must acknowledge, was a darker feeling—I wanted to be right. "Please send three separate parties to find more future Anaghwin. I want at least three females and three children added to our numbers."

I took my leave, and haven't seen them since. I wonder if they're looking for me now. Or are they content to have me absent from their life, drifting away from the Drowned City? Is that their preference?

I feel a kinship to the jellyfish, held at the mercy of the currents that swirl below, unable to plot a course and move under its own power. Perhaps the jellyfish knows a truth about reality that has eluded me up until now. Deliberate movement, decision-making, planning—all are a mirage. Perhaps the jellyfish is the true God, having figured all this out already.

"Teach me your ways, oh great jellyfish," I declare. "I beseech you, share your wisdom with me."

Even if nobody misses me, I miss them all. I feel as though a hole has been torn through my chest. Mother, Father, Belubus—I haven't seen them for so long.

I have required my Anaghwin to keep Cloudline clear of dangerous Cloudies in hopes that someone would descend and visit me, but no one has.

Adorane too has become a distant memory to me, though distant like a mountain—looming over you even when it's hundreds of miles away. Even when I'm not thinking about him, he's never far from my thoughts.

Torrain. He's less a mountain and more of a whisper. Sometimes I'll remember an interaction or a glance or even the way he'd sit under a tree and read, and it hurts. I won't even know why I'm hurting at first, and then I'll realize it's because I'm thinking of him.

I want to see them all, but I cannot visit Mountaintop—that death trap, where my two best friends conspired to slaughter my children. They may claim it was beyond their control, that it was Tranton who kept releasing the murderous gas once they realized their mistake. But a fire, whether started accidentally or on purpose, burns just as hot and deadly, and it takes the same terrible toll.

Torrain had to prepare those deadly gas canisters—he and Adorane wouldn't have simply found operational ones lying around for three hundred years. Just as he'd done with the scuba tanks we'd used to retrieve the Masks, I know Torrain worked hard refining his technology to have them refitted, refilled, and ready to kill.

Still, I miss them. My sadness is made even more powerful by my anger.

There is a thought that's been plaguing me lately; I've tried to ignore it, but all this recent heartache has only made it louder. I need to leave the Drowned City. There is more for me to do on the mainland. I can't go back to Mountaintop. I'm not even sure where I should go—I just feel the need to leave.

I told Omathis that I wanted to journey away from the Drowned City. That was a mistake. Somehow the others found out and they began monitoring me nearly all the time. All of them insist that I'm not imprisoned—that of course I'm free to go. I'm merely being kept home, close to loved ones, for my own protection. But whenever I start to make plans to leave, I'm met with the most gentle, loving, and yet unbreakable shackles. Because of our strength disparity, they can treat me to soft and comforting embraces—while also keeping me trapped against my will and guiding me away from anywhere I may want to go. They claim they're worshipping me, but they are suffocating me. That's why floating out here feels so free; swimming is my only escape.

So I've stopped talking about it. But that's only made the impulse more frequent and more insistent.

When I was younger, I thought Mountaintop was magical. Yet as I got older, I realized it was a place where I no longer belonged. Then I found the Drowned City—finally, a place where I fit perfectly among the Anaghwin. But now I see cracks in this foundation, too. Every day, another hint that this isn't the place for me. Do I belong anywhere? Or is there something about me which doesn't fit anywhere?

I need to jump in a current and see where it takes me. Maybe I'll just float away now. Finally everyone here seems to have lost track of me; I should take advantage of it.

I hear a splash beside me, quiet and barely there. I already know who it is. The peace that floods me makes that obvious.

She slips her large taloned hand into mine. It's such a lethal hand, but so soft and gentle in my presence, which I take as a compliment. She floats beside me without saying a word. It's exactly what I need. I open my eyes, squinting against the sunlight, and see her large glacial blues gazing back at me.

"My love for you is big enough to carry disagreements, Lovely. Your love for me is, too. I can feel it."

I have to concentrate all my energy on holding off the deep, ugly sobs that are threatening to escape, so I can't say anything in response. I close my eyes again, squeezing her hand and placing it over my heart.

I can tell she has something more to say. However, she doesn't say it yet. We both enjoy this shared moment of silence, floating together. We are alone, but we are also connected to the entire world in the best possible way, and neither of us wants it to end.

I feel the cool water pressing from below, pushing and pulling, her hand in mine, her heart beating in sync with my heart, the comfort and joy we're finding in each other, satisfied and, at least for now, not thirsty in the least. This is greatness.

Finally, Eveshone has to shatter the spell.

"Lovely, look at the horizon. We have a visitor."

NOW

Amperous had awoken from his slumber confused. Was Belubus in this sub-cavern with him? He found himself overcome with disappointment that he was alone. As wretched as humans were, Amperous enjoyed this odd man's company and often wondered if Belubus was human at all.

"We most certainly will not!"

He did hear Belubus' voice, though far away. The words were aggressive, like a swarm of bees, and made Amperous' talons grow from the ends of his fingers.

Like he did every day since he'd ended up underground, Amperous pressed against his restraints. His strength was returning. It was coming in drips rather than torrents, but he could feel himself recovering.

He heard another voice, one that chilled him. "Please, Belubus—he has one purpose. To tear our throats out. He's too dangerous to release or keep here. We have to exterminate him while we still can." It reminded him of those dark-suited men so many years ago.

Currents of centuries-old rage surged through him. Never again would he wait while groups of men decided his fate.

Another voice joined the discussion. "She's right, Belubus. He won't be feeble for long. To ensure our survival, he must be eliminated."

Amperous knew that tiny Belubus would not win this argument.

However, he tried. "I've bonded with him!" he shouted. "He relaxes in my presence. Do you understand what that could mean for our survival? If I can figure out how to forge a peace with their kind—"

Amperous tore through his restraints, powered by his newly excavated ancient rage. *There will never be peace between their kind and mine.* His senses awoke to all the humans underground with him, their hot, sweet, cursed blood flowing through their veins, and a latent hunger surged within him.

These children of the men with suits dark as night would not eliminate him.

Persopile Opal had been born with a berry-colored stain upon her beautiful face. Of all the places on her body where a stain could land, she'd always wondered, why her face? The stain could have been hidden on her back, on an arm, on a leg—*anywhere* except for right on the front of her face. Even another six inches to the right or left and it would have been covered by her gorgeous mahogany hair, never to be noticed at all. Six inches and her parents would have accepted her; she could have grown up a proud Opal daughter in Mountaintop. But instead she was banished to the Mines. She had always considered herself cursed.

Yet on this day, Persopile Opal had been fortunate. While others' instincts had been to run, hers had been to freeze and fall back into the shadows. This had saved her.

She watched as the terrible creature Belubus had insisted contained a kernel of goodness grabbed Jarda and flung her feeble body against the stone wall. He didn't even bother to gorge himself on her blood, as he'd done with the others. Amperous no doubt found her appearance unappetizing.

Persopile didn't make a sound while those she loved were hunted. She felt guilty for this, for continuing to exist, moment to moment, as they were torn apart. She remained in the shadows as the sounds of destruction —screams, growls, howls, desperate fleeing footsteps—faded into silence.

After what seemed like an eternity, she gingerly took a step forward. Nothing pounced on her. One more. She wasn't sliced into pieces, she realized, stunned.

She was suddenly overcome by sadness and exhaustion. She wanted to lie down, close her eyes, and never open them again. Anything to avoid the sight of the awful carnage before her. But she knew she needed to leave this underground grave and never return.

She hadn't been above, in the air, under the sun, since she was a newborn. But now she craved a breath that wasn't laced with the scent of blood.

The passages smelled like sweat, iron, spilled innards, and fear. Everything was dark, most flames extinguished. She ignored the bloodied bodies around her. If she stopped even for a second, if she looked at any of them, she knew she'd never have the strength to move again. She'd collapse to the cave floor and join them.

The Mines, for so long a refuge for the abandoned, rejected, and broken, had in the end proven to be a death trap. There had been nowhere to run as the enraged blonde beast ripped apart one terrified victim after another.

She followed the path the demon used to escape. She knew there was a good chance it would be waiting for her at the end. It seemed so hungry, like it would never stop hunting. But the surface called to her, and she scrambled, panicked, toward the light. If she could escape this hell, even if the cost of one clean gulp of outside air was death, it seemed a fair bargain.

Belubus stood in front of the boulder door, defiant and unyielding before the creature that towered over him.

"Amperous. Why have you done this?"

Amperous was stilled by his words. Belubus sounded mournful rather than angry. Amperous felt his talons retract. His ragged breathing, drunk with death, calmed as he started to question what he had just done.

"Release me. That has been my only request since you brought me here."

"I trusted you," Belubus stated.

"I never asked for your trust. Nor have I given you any reason to place it in me."

Yet on the edges of his mind, Amperous began to feel the bond that had developed between himself and Belubus. He tried to channel his rage, but he still couldn't leave their connection behind.

"Release me!"

Belubus turned toward the elaborate system of pulleys and locks and codes, defeated. "We could have built a friendship." He paused, then said sadly, "We *did* build a friendship. You have torn it apart."

While Amperous was stilled by Belubus' words, an approaching light appeared in the shadows. It ignited a rage in Amperous. Something was coming to hurt him.

"I have been forced to act like your friend—to keep you and your kind from tearing me apart!" Amperous bellowed. He swung at Belubus with ferocity. Belubus crumpled into a heap, and Amperous' talons retracted.

Belubus couldn't feel his legs, but he didn't need to. He could see they were shattered. How curious to be without pain yet broken beyond repair.

"Please," Belubus stumbled over his words, weakened, "finish me off. Bring your betrayal to completion. Don't leave it undone. Show mercy to me."

"I have no hunger for your death, only my freedom," Amperous growled. He crouched low and sprung into the boulder door, over and over, until it cracked and rolled aside with a groan.

Even with the blessed open air in front of him, the inkling of what he and Belubus had shared kept Amperous from escaping into the night. He stood still for a long time, stymied by his confused mass of feelings.

Finally, Amperous grabbed Belubus and dragged him into the moonlight. This was a better place to die than in that dark pit. That's the best he could do for this strange man.

"We had no friendship, Belubus. But I am not your enemy either. I did not mean to hurt you."

Amperous felt weak, and he wasn't sure if it was from the elevation, or the guilt he was trying to ignore. He slipped away into the shadows.

Persopile worried as she neared the exit. She didn't know the elaborate codes needed to unlock the thick stone door. But it turned out not to matter. When she arrived, the boulder had been torn from the opening, the frame cracked and broken.

Belubus' lethal guest had been able to do this. *How strong was this monster?*

She climbed out of the damaged gateway and felt the crisp air fill her lungs like a miracle. She fell to her knees, then laid back and let the twinkling diamonds overhead fill her eyes. For a moment, a sense of wonder and relief flooded over her, and she forgot the carnage that had happened down in the Mines.

She heard a weak groan. Her eyes had by now adjusted to the darkness and she saw a tiny crumpled heap, unmoving. Belubus!

Persopile rushed to his side. He looked like a spider that had been squished, shriveled up and twisted.

"Does it hurt, Beloved Leader?" she asked, immediately realizing that it was a stupid question.

"Not as much as other things," he answered cryptically.

Persopile felt that she knew what he meant. His decision to show Amperous mercy, while kind and good, had resulted in the death of so many and would result in his own. How unfair that his leadership would be justified or condemned not on the ethics and heart behind the decisions that he'd made, but on the capricious back of their consequences. Results were a bitter judge, blind to virtue, random and uncaring. He'd applied kindness, and faith, to a beast who he'd known had decency within; she was stung by the unfairness of life.

"The creature, is it…" She trailed off, fearful.

"It has fled down the mountain," Belubus answered, his voice sad and weary.

She examined Belubus' crumpled frame and knew that he was broken in ways that would never heal. Regardless, she felt she needed to do something. She lifted him gently, and he didn't protest.

"Let's go get you some help."

7

THEN

Laura Lee lay awake in the dark. She used to look forward to the refreshing reset sleep provided. The worst day could be wiped away by climbing into bed and awaiting the dawn of a new one. There was nothing so dire that couldn't be renewed in the hopeful rays of morning sunshine.

All that had changed once she'd suffered through the day no amount of sleep could reverse.

It's your fault, Laura Lee.

Now she approached the setting of the sun with a deep sense of dread, knowing that with darkness everything would be quiet and still, with no diversions to distract her from her thoughts.

You freed them, and they killed her.

She'd given up arguing a long time ago.

I didn't technically free them! She had argued desperately in those initial days. *I only made them aware of their own strength, and they freed themselves. They were good. I was only trying to save innocent lives.*

In the end, these lines of defense collapsed under the weight of her guilt.

Blood will stain your hands forever .

She wanted to talk to someone about it, but her father forbid it. "No one can know you were there," he insisted. "Ever."

She'd honored his request, but at the cost of her sanity.

How long had she laid in bed tonight with eyes closed but no rest? Hours, no doubt. She was afraid to check the time. She wanted to get up and do something to distract herself, but she clung tenuously to the hope of sleep.

I need rest for tomorrow.

For what?

She'd lost enthusiasm for every activity that used to fill her days with joy anyway. All she really cared about anymore was what had happened to *them*. Where had they gone? What had they done? Who knew about them? But that trail was cold, and if Sean knew anything, he wasn't sharing it with her. He refused to answer any of her questions, and he warned her to stop asking, lest she invite trouble.

It was as if they had never existed.

Except Shai was still dead.

She'd be alive if you hadn't meddled. Travis would still have a mother.

A crash of glass shattered the silence of her stifling nighttime tomb. A high-pitched whirring sound followed. The alarm blared.

Laura Lee slowly got to her feet, curious at her own lack of panic or urgency. She stumbled from bed and toward her broken bedroom window. She should probably hide or run or scream for help, but she just didn't care.

She heard her father pounding on the door. "Laura Lee, what is happening? Laura Lee! Let me in!" He struggled with the doorknob, but it was locked.

She now locked the door every night, but he hadn't noticed until now. She had given so much to her father already; she needed at least the desperate nights to herself.

She turned to face her shattered bedroom window and watched dispassionately as an explosion of sparks illuminated the darkness with waves of orange and red. Someone was cutting through the metal bars Sean had installed outside her bedroom.

She was filled with a strange relief. Finally, at least, something was going to change. Even if that change meant death, it was preferable to the unending depression she'd been mired in for so long.

The bars fell away with a clang. Laura Lee waited as the acrid smoke cleared. Slowly the familiar face of Oliver Hailgard emerged out of the darkness. Laura Lee felt disappointment. She had been hoping, strangely, that her intruder was someone who would harm her. This desire disturbed her, but it didn't make it any less real.

"I need to take you away," he commanded, quiet but insistent.

Sean's desperate pounding grew louder. "Laura Lee! What is happening in there?"

She looked to the door.

"He cannot be a part of this," Ollie insisted. He moved stealthily through the opening and stalked the perimeter of the room, tossing out strands of hair he removed from a bag and shaking a small cloud of dust out near her crumpled bedsheets. Finally, he dropped a rubber ball on her bed.

Laura Lee recognized the ball. It was the one Amp and Omathis used to toss back and forth with her father.

"What are you doing?" she whispered.

"Making sure no one tries to find you."

Laura Lee stood frozen. "I'm disappearing?"

"They're coming for you. I need to get you out of here."

Something about Ollie's earnest care for her awoke a flicker of survival instinct. "Why?"

"They know what you did."

Laura Lee had known this would happen eventually. She hadn't done anything to conceal her presence in the lab the night she helped free Omathis and Amperous.

"I should say goodbye to Father."

"There isn't time." Ollie grabbed her and carried her toward the window.

Laura Lee didn't have time to pack anything before she escaped with Ollie into the darkness. As it turns out, she might as well have died that night, because she left everything about her old life behind, never to be seen again.

Sean Brathius found the ax he kept in his utility closet and used it to splinter the thick oaken door to Laura Lee's bedroom into pieces. Her room was dark and silent—whatever had happened here was over. For a second he hesitated in the darkness, too panicked to face reality.

He feared seeing the room painted red, his daughter hung up as Shai had been. He forced himself to calm down.

They would never do that to her. Amp and Omathis loved Laura Lee; they even called her Lovely.

He switched on the light and was relieved to see only a disheveled bed and an open window. But Laura Lee was gone. He ran to the window and saw no traces of her anywhere.

"Laura Lee." Her name escaped his lips, painful and quiet, not loud enough to be heard by her or anyone. Had she run away? Had she cut through the steel bars and left him behind?

He examined the room carefully for any evidence of what might have happened.

Then he saw it: the ball. The one they'd tossed with him during happier times. Before the Sleeps, before he'd installed uncontrollable fury into them. When they were pups who only wanted to play.

They had been here, and they had taken her away with them.

Sean held the ball in his hands and sank down into Laura Lee's bed. He buried his face in the pillow. It still smelled strongly of her—the scent of vanilla and honeysuckle blossoms.

He closed his eyes and wished fervently for death. His lack of options paralyzed him. He would never find them. They were trained to disappear into the night. And even if he could track them somehow, what could he do? It was clear they did not desire a reunion. If they had wanted to see him, they could have; but they'd locked the door and taken her instead.

He'd lost them all.

It was all his fault.

NOW

Amperous' strength returned in exhilarating surges as he rushed toward Down Below. It felt like forever since he'd breathed the rich air his lungs craved. How long had he been trapped below the ground, a shadow of himself, while Belubus claimed to be healing him?

Belubus. Surely he is dead by now. Amperous pondered this, embarrassed by the sadness he felt. He'd purposely slaughtered so many humans without regret; how odd that he should worry so much about the one he'd killed by accident.

The sun began its gentle rise. Amperous decided to leave the gray half-existence he'd suffered in Mountaintop and the Mines behind, in his past. This most recent nightmare should be to his vast collection of traumas—unforgettable, but out of reach.

The fog, the paucity of oxygen, the dirty underground, the fetid smells, the sulfurous poison that had strangled his army. Belubus. He would leave it all behind in this wasteland he should never have visited. As he entered the lusher lowlands, he vowed to not return to the anemic, barren hell on top of the mountain. And to think, Omathis had always believed Paradise lay up there!

Amperous knew he'd been held captive for a long time, though he couldn't be sure whether it had been weeks, months, or even years. His followers no doubt believed he had died with all the others. Amperous expected that they had scattered in the wake of their defeat. He did not anticipate that anyone could be waiting to meet him Down Below.

Amperous was wrong.

ICELYN

A visitor.

Not just any visitor, but him.

Oh, how I have waited for this day. I have imagined what I would say, what he would look like, where we would be. I always thought I would see him again at sunset, like the evenings the three of us used to spend together—laughing, talking, and tossing shells into the ocean. But deep down, I never believed it would actually happen.

Yet looking through the ancient *bino culars*, I confirm that this is no mirage. A familiar figure rows a boat across the vast ocean, toward us.

I'm curious to find I feel no joy. I am alarmed, flushed with a heated, bitter strain of adrenaline and unable to speak. I become clumsy, drop the looking glass, and one of the lenses cracks.

Adorane.

He's still miles away. I want to call to him, though I know he wouldn't hear me. In any case, I don't know what I'd say.

"Do you think, Lovely, that is may be…" Eveshone trails off, as if I've forbidden the mention of his name.

Something about Adorane's confident, upright posture perturbs me. He's wronged me and the Anaghwins who live in the Drowned City. His approach should be a touch more penitent.

On top of that, it seems he has put much effort into growing *a beard*, like a man. I do not like at all. Indeed, I despise the tangled mass that obscures his handsome youthful face.

"Please see that he is captured, Eveshone. Unharmed, but captured."

She looks excited at the prospect, as if I'm asking her to go on a date with a long lost friend. Is no one immune to Adorane's magnetism?

"Not captured by you," I clarify, irritated. "Not by anyone who is friendly with him. I want him to be scared. I want to speak to him alone."

I want to dictate the terms of our reunion. I don't want him to be in control of the situation, orchestrating it with his charm, forcing me to drop my justifiable anger simply to bask in his glorious light.

I search through the storage chambers with unconcealed intensity. Where is it?

"Lovely, if you let me know what you're looking for, I can help," Eveshone offers.

I don't want to admit what I'm looking for. *That fierce gold mask that makes me look scary. You know, so I can intimidate Adorane.*

The Anaghwin are skilled artisans, and they have showered me with many gifts. Keeping track of them requires a level of effort that I haven't made. One of my children (Celarinha, a woman I would like to spend more time with) presented to me an offering that she called the "Mask of Refinement." Molded out of a fortune's worth of gold, it featured a startlingly lively likeness of my face, but merged with the Threatbelows' more animalistic features—fangs, enraged eyes, mouth opened and poised to devour. "This is you, ridding the world of all who would try to harm us," Celarinha had explained.

I wore it once, then put it in storage. Though I appreciated the gesture, it's not exactly the kind of thing you'd wear to breakfast or while having a seaside chat with a friend.

It's here somewhere. Why did he have to grow a beard? The Adorane I knew didn't have a beard. He's not Adorane if he's bearded. Why must he mar his face? I haven't seen it for ages, and now he's hidden it away from me still.

My movements are clipped and unnatural. I knock over a neatly stacked pile of books. In my attempt to fix the mess I've made, I bump into another carefully balanced wall of antiques. Apriori boots and games and weapons clatter to the ground all around me. I give up on making any of this chaos right. I stumble on, groping and hoping to find the mask.

"You seem disturbed, Dear One. Could your unrest be due to the approach of—"

She's only asking to be polite. She knows why I'm upset. I can't hide my crashing, unwieldy feelings from her. They're massive, unrefined, and impossible to conceal, especially since we share a pulse.

She places her hand on my back. Lately I've noticed a peaceful vibration that flows from one Anaghwin to another when they are in sync. It's not a physical current, but a mental one—like a cat's purr, but in the soul. (I know that whenever I try to explain phenomena that I experience among the Anaghwin, it sounds ridiculous. But I'm doing my best.) When I first sensed it, I wanted to call it *Purr-fection.* I found this hilarious, but no one, Omathis especially, seemed to appreciate the humor. They call it a *Vibram.*

Is the Vibram like the Soothing? I had asked.

No, not at all, Omathis answered, before he and Eveshone shared a chuckle at my expense, as if what I'd suggested was utterly laughable.

At least a little like one? I had insisted, trying to defend my observation.

The Soothing comes from you alone. A Vibram we can collectively share with one another.

The Soothing calms you down; a Vibram stirs you up.

The Soothing warms you like a blanket; a Vibram is a refreshing dip in briskly chilled water.

And on and on. The differences between the Soothing and a Vibram are, apparently, innumerable and obvious to everyone but me.

Eveshone shares a Vibram with me, and whispers, "His life is empty without you, Icelyn."

I am overcome with satisfaction on top of the bodily clarity I always enjoy in the wake of the Vibram. I turn around and there is the angry golden mask.

"I doubt very much that he thinks that," I say as I place the mask over my face. But I hope that it's true.

NOW

Torrain hadn't wanted to complain, but he resented being left behind. Adorane had presented it as an honor. "You'll be in charge here—the chief in my absence!" Torrain believed he and Adorane should have been joint chiefs anyway, since they had both saved Mountaintop together. So this seemed a curious, and rather condescending, honor for Adorane to bestow upon him.

It reminded him of when they were children, and Torrain would beg to be "the sergeant" in a game they'd called "Ascension." Adorane would choose someone else to play that coveted part—anyone else—before he'd ever choose Torrain. (Why Adorane was the one to select who got to play the sergeant always baffled Torrain, but no one else seemed to challenge it.) Finally, Torrain's turn to play the sergeant arrived, and not even Adorane could keep him from his moment in the spotlight. Everyone knew that nobody could be the Sergeant twice before everyone had been at least once.

Yet still Adorane found a way to deny him. He declared that it was indeed Torrain's turn now, but that there was a new game starting. Everyone joined Adorane's new game—called "Super Ascension." Torrain was left to be the sergeant of nobody but himself.

It wasn't fun to play games alone. Much like this.

He hated being left behind while Adorane got to go Down Below again. Nobody but Torrain knew the wonders that were denied those who stayed in Mountaintop. He thirsted for another trip to the lower lands—the beauty, the adventure, even the danger. He missed it more every day.

"I can't bring anyone else along. We know how that course of action ends: in death. Everyone who has traveled Down Below has died," Adorane had explained.

"I didn't die," Torrain protested. "I survived. I can do it again."

"I'm already pressing *my* luck. You'd be pressing an even greater amount of it."

"Do I need to remind you that I slew a grizzly bear?" Torrain countered.

"Nobody ever needs to be reminded; you make sure of that. If it were bears I were worried about, I'd take you along for protection. But it isn't."

In the end, Torrain hadn't insisted hard enough, which was why he'd stayed in Mountaintop. It was also why he hadn't become a joint chief in the first place, and why he'd never gotten to be the sergeant. Against the force that was Adorane, Torrain would always inevitably succumb.

Someday he won't be able to run me over, Torrain vowed to himself, though even he didn't believe it.

"You may hold your prayer meeting in Kith Hall on Winter Solstice," Torrain replied, bored, to Charnith's petition. "You've been on the schedule for months. Why wouldn't you?" Of course Torrain was going to grant her request. She was Adorane's mother.

"The Cognates insist that they have priority with their 'Association for the Examination of Kith Cultural Trends as They Relate to Religion-Free Living' seminar. They tell me that they must meet at the same time, in the same place."

Torrain winced at the unwieldy name, which members of the newly formed group maintained could never be abbreviated. Cognates were skilled in many ways, but they had no talent for creating catchy titles.

Torrain hated negotiating every disagreement in Mountaintop. It was too difficult, because there was no Code to rely on anymore. Adorane had *temporarily* suspended it for emergency purposes more than a year ago and not bothered to lift the suspension since. Torrain yearned for a simpler time, when the Veritas weren't demanding a newly imagined privilege every day. Now that Adorane had declared that the Veritas and Cognate were equals, everything had gotten messy. Of course Torrain, and the rest of the Cognate, agreed that they were all equal; but that didn't have to mean they should all have the same rights. People can be equal in worth but treated differently for the good of the community. Everything was more peaceful back then, when Cognates had a certain unquestioned position, and Adorane's declaration seemed only to make everything worse. Even the Veritas couldn't be enjoying this nonstop bickering.

"Then delay your meeting," Torrain suggested. "Why do you have to make this an issue?"

"The issue is that you are asking *us* to delay our meeting, but not *them*. Why should we be the only ones asked to make accommodations? Why are we the ones expected to submit with a smile?"

Torrain could already hear the complaints and protests from the Cognates, so used to always getting their way, if he asked them to move their meeting.

"If you insist on your scheduled time, it'll make such trouble." Torrain resented developing a headache over a matter that he didn't even care about.

"They're the ones making the trouble. We were on the schedule first. We're tired of being accused of making trouble when we're only trying to grasp onto what's been stolen from us in the first place."

Torrain wanted to be back in his lab, elbow deep in his latest inventions. "Fine, I'll talk to them about it. You can keep your time. But give me a week first. Hopefully Adorane will be back by then, and he can handle it."

"On that, we are both in agreement."

Charnith hadn't wanted Adorane to leave.

But she knew he needed to.

Mountaintop was dying.

8

ICELYN

I am not sure how to greet him; I can't decide what kind of welcome he deserves. Omathis is enraged at the thought of Adorane entering the Drowned City—and rightfully so. The boy has slaughtered so many of my children, each beloved by Omathis too.

"We should send a seafaring party out and repel him," Omathis declares. "We should not welcome him as a guest."

My anger toward Adorane hasn't subsided even a whisper since he released the deadly gas in Mountaintop and murdered my followers. But, while wrestling my way through all these horrors, I have started to listen to his account of the incident in my head.

What I imagine he would say, of course. It's not as if he's communicating with me telepathically, as my children would. But I've such a sense of what he would say that he might as well.

They had started to tear us to pieces, Icelyn. Good people were dying. I waited as long as I possibly could. You were the one who led them up to our last safe haven. You are every bit as responsible for what happened, if not more. You were the initiator of all this horror; I only reacted to protect our kind. What else could I do?

I have seen the wisdom behind his way of thinking. Yet it brings me no form of reconciliation—only more warfare, this time within myself. I resent him for having such understandable reasons behind his incomprehensible actions.

"He is not our enemy," Eveshone declares.

"Oh he's a friend, then, is he? How fortunate! To count among our allies someone so lethal and cruel!" Omathis growls, low and rumbling, like a warning.

Eveshone doesn't back down. "A wounded animal who lashes out when you invade its den and threaten its brood cannot be considered an aggressor." Even as all other Anaghwin in the Drowned City have portrayed Adorane as a villain worthy of legendary scorn, Eveshone has maintained a quiet support for him. He saved her, after all. But it's more than that. A mysterious connection had formed, wispy and tender, between the two of them, and it persists over time and distance.

I still have mixed feelings about it.

Sometimes when your head clouds with differing loyalties and perspectives, you have to return to *what actually happened* to clear away the fog.

And when the mist clears, one fact remains: Adorane killed them all.

"I've given instructions to have him captured, Omathis. He will not be entering the Drowned City as a friend, but as a prisoner."

Eveshone's giant eyes reflect betrayal. This is fitting, because there's a part of me that is hurting in the same way. I want to explain: *I see what you're saying, but he's wounded our people forever, and that cannot be overlooked.* Whenever I disagree with Eveshone, it feels like my life has been twisted out of shape and thrown into the garbage.

But Omathis is right. We cannot pretend Adorane is innocent.

"Do you want me to be afraid of you?" Adorane asks.

With one question, he dismantles my planned offensive entirely. I don't know the answer. He was never intimidated by me before, which I always appreciated. Many have told me that I can be overwhelming, and the idea makes me uncomfortable. I'm no more than a strong person should be able to handle; I should not have to apologize for my lack of meekness. Adorane has always been able to laugh off my worst traits in order to enjoy my best. Not everyone can do that.

"I can be afraid of you, if that's what you want," he adds, which is exactly the kind of thing a person who isn't the least bit of afraid of you might say.

I've kept the Temple of Lovely darkened, illuminated only by flames. Honestly, yes, I was hoping to scare him. But clearly it isn't working. Just as he's taken no notice of my newly fit body and toned muscles. I feel stupid for hoping he'd be impressed.

"You are unharmed?" I ask, because I don't know what else to say.

"Your devoted followers have shown me unmatched hospitality," he answers sarcastically. I can't figure out whether that's good or bad.

I sit on my oversized throne in the heart of my Temple, Eveshone to my right and Omathis to my left. Adorane stands before me, upright and proud, not an ounce of deference in him. His hands and feet are bound, and two of my Anaghwin hold him tight. I'm thankful for the golden Mask of Refinement that I wear, because at least we're both hiding our faces from each other. I've suffered so long without seeing him, and now his accursed beard blocks his essence.

"Icelyn, I've come because—"

"You will speak only in response to her questions!" Omathis bellows, so outside of his character that he shocks everyone in the room.

Adorane complies, but maintains his bravado. He nods toward me, as if giving me permission to speak.

"Why have you journeyed to the Drowned City?" I ask in an accusatory tone. I'm thankful that Ad can't read my thoughts, as Eveshone and Omathis can. He'd know that I've been waiting for him to visit, yearning for this day, wondering what was taking him so long.

Now that he's here, I wonder if perhaps I didn't want it at all. It's strange when you finally get something you've hoped for and feel only misery.

But it's *not* strange that I feel mixed up, I realize. I haven't gotten what I want because *I'm not being me, and he's not being him*. And what I want more than anything is for us to figure out how to be *us again*.

Adorane clears his throat, as if asking for permission to respond. I nod.

"In Mountaintop, we initiated an increase in births to replace those Kith members who died due to the…recent tragedies." He speaks with slow deliberation, as if his life depends on him correctly pronouncing each syllable.

I stare stoically, stifling the questions burning through my mind.

Did you and Catalandi have a child?

Has Torrain fathered a baby?

I panic, imagining that my friends have catapulted into a new stage of life without me, becoming parents and adults while leaving me behind, alone in every way.

Adorane pauses for what feels like an eternity.

"But before any of them were able to reach a year in age, death descended and took them, one after another."

I gasp. I know now why Adorane has exerted such control over his words. If he didn't, he might cry. My mind flashes to an image it often retrieves against my wishes, one I want to forget: my beloved Anaghwin, collapsed and lifeless, fallen all over Mountaintop. Only now the tiny bodies of infants have been added to the carnage, all their potential snuffed out into darkness.

I've always adored babies and am fortunate never to have seen a dead one. Not that they didn't die in Mountaintop—they often did—but all have been hidden away from me, thankfully. I'm not sure I'd recover from the sight.

"How many have died?" I ask, each word laborious to speak.

"Twenty-eight."

Oh God, what a tragedy. I imagine every person in Mountaintop, and how each might handle the wave of tiny deaths. Father, Mother, Istoch, Torrain. Would anyone ever be able to smile again?

"How many are still alive?"

"None have survived."

Now I hope that neither Adorane nor Torrain had fathered any of the ill-fated infants, not for my own selfish sake, but for theirs.

I remove the Mask of Refinement and place it by my side. Adorane can see the watery sadness in my eyes, which I was hoping to avoid. But I need to remove this metal barrier between us.

"Why are you telling me this?"

Adorane gazes at me, and I see *him* for the first time since he's arrived. I'm relieved to know that he's still there—familiar, intimate, earnest, as much a part of me as my own heart—despite his bewildering facial hair, despite the time that's passed since we've last seen each other, and despite what he's done.

"Can I approach?" he asks, gently.

The words sound so feeble that I reply "Of course" before thinking about it. Omathis stiffens, ready to pounce. The Anaghwin guards release Adorane.

He walks toward me as confidently as one can with their feet bound.

"Do you have any water?" He asks. I point to a pitcher kept near my throne. He picks it up and pours some over his hand, then extends his arm toward me.

"May I?" he asks.

I nod, again without thinking. I lean toward him instinctively. He touches his soaked fingers to the space behind my left ear and rubs the water onto my skin. He watches, holding his breath, like the space behind my ear is the most important thing he's even seen. Finally, after what feels like forever—both because Adorane is so close and Omathis is so riled up and nobody seems the least bit comfortable, including myself—Ad exhales and smiles, looking as though he is on the verge of tears.

"You are uninfected," he declares. "I had hoped."

"What do you mean, *uninfected?*"

Adorane's eyes widen like they do when he's being serious. (They crinkle up a little when he's joking or lying—a sign I've never let him know I discovered.)

"You are the only one who can bear a child who will not suffer the same fate, Icelyn. The only human who can keep humanity from dying."

NOW

Was he seeing things? Amperous wiped his eyes clean and inhaled deeply to be sure he wasn't still suffering from the lack of oxygen available at higher elevations.

As the sun rose behind him, he walked toward the edge of a rocky outcropping hanging over the valley below. Amperous caught his breath. A multitude of Croathus were gathered on the valley floor, chanting in unison, in a language foreign to his ears yet somehow completely understandable. Their shouts beckoned to him, lifted him up, strengthened him, restored him.

Unus est rediit. Unus adest. Unus est rediit. Unus adest. He understood what they were saying—though in words he'd never heard before. *The one has returned. The one is here.*

The incantations grew to an ear-splitting roar. Amperous couldn't tell if the air that rushed through him was a brisk wind or the sound waves themselves threatening to push him over. He lifted his right arm in triumph, yet felt little control over the action—as if this motion had been choreographed by a greater power.

The chants stopped, and every Croathus fell to their knees, bowing before him, silent in their reverence.

There was one exception, still standing in solitary defiance among the prostrate crowd. A female Croathus—her features striking and severe—stared directly at him. He felt as though she was looking *into* him. She wore clothing he'd never seen on a Croathus before, with no customary covering of animal skins, but instead shimmering, shining fabrics—silks, cashmeres, and linens—as humans would wear, in a vibrant rainbow's worth of colors, adorned with gold and silver and brilliant gems.

Amperous, never one to be found searching for words, was struck silent.

"As I foretold, he has returned," she proclaimed with a voice as clear and bright as the desert sun.

The bowing Croathus resumed their chanting—more muffled, but no less intense. *Unus est rediit. Unus adest. Unus est rediit. Unus adest.*

"Amperous, I am the Priestess of Two Temples. Join us," the standing Croathus shouted, and though she was far away, he felt her in his heart. "We have been waiting for you. We shall be a new people. Together we will strike this world until it cracks in two. And out of that wreckage, a new heaven and a new earth will be born."

THEN

What if the apocalypse began, but nobody knew? What if the fate of humanity was sealed, their death inevitable, yet everyone merely paid attention to the next news cycle, the next status update, the next scandal, whatever new shining distraction that could occupy their time?

Reports of break-ins into several research facilities throughout the state appeared only in the local sections of the paper. The news channels and national sites offered the events scant attention, if they mentioned them at all.

Sean knew there had been another connected break-in—this one unreported. He'd analyzed the dust and hair he found in Laura Lee's room to confirm that Omathis and Amperous had invaded and taken her with them. But they'd disappeared again just as quickly.

Sean Brathius should have expected it—stealth was an essential aspect of their design—but even he was amazed at how seamlessly his creations had disappeared. Twelve large apex predators, six breeding pairs of one male and one female each, had vanished from their laboratory prisons without leaving any sort of trail.

Everyone returned to their normal lives, not knowing that normal life was a dying star whose light had already been extinguished. But that's how the greatest tragedies often play out. Nobody has any suspicion that they are anything but safe until the moment it becomes obvious that they aren't.

Sean Brathius noticed the door to his study open. He sat down and pressed his fingers against his temples. Travis had broken the rule again.

"Hydrogen, Helium, Lithium, Beryllium…" He recited these elements like a prayer, rhythmic and deliberate. "Boron, Carbon,

Nitrogen, Oxygen…"

This mantra corralled the chaos that had spread throughout his thoughts, as it had since he was young. His breathing slowed. He could figure this out. There were rules. Not all of the rules were known yet, which created an illusion of lawlessness. But that only meant he needed to discover them, not that they didn't exist.

"Fluorine, Neon, Sodium, Magnesium…"

Once he knew the rules, he could tame the maelstrom. He'd turn a nightmare into a paradise.

Sean ran through the periodic table until his fists unclenched. Now to focus on the matter at hand: Shai's son, Travis.

Sean had tried to raise the boy as his own in the wake of her death. It had been a struggle. They'd come to an understanding just that morning, and their fragile truce had already been breached. Travis knew that Sean's study was forbidden. He'd agreed to avoid it.

Sean entered the study and had to run through the table of elements again to withstand the geyser of rage that erupted from within him. Travis hadn't even tried to hide his presence here. Papers were stacked haphazardly on the floor. Books had been thrown and left where they landed.

Sean blinked, frozen in stupor. Was he seeing this correctly?

Pages had been torn from some of these books, ripped into a hundred pieces and scattered on the ground. Sean felt as if he'd been doused with gasoline and swallowed by flames. Many of these were first editions, some of them never digitized in any form—irreplaceable.

Sean had never been one to let his anger show. He prided himself on his efforts to harness it, compress it, and find a way to relieve it quietly. He sat, surrounded by the sea of tattered books and scattered research, until the day grew dark.

NOW

Persopile struggled up the incline, careful not to jostle Belubus' broken frame. Despite his refusal to complain, she could tell he suffered at the slightest bump. Her porcelain pale skin felt burned by the sun, which was brighter and hotter than she'd ever imagined it could be.

"You're strong, Persopile," Belubus encouraged her, though she wished for his sake he'd stay silent. No need to waste breath on her. She wasn't accustomed to compliments anyway.

"We're going to get you help, Beloved Leader," she promised

earnestly, speaking to herself as much as to him.

"If you don't, it may be for the best. Perhaps this is the piece of ground I'm meant to join. It's a pleasant spot." Belubus seemed so peaceful that she suspected he was delirious. "And no need to call me Beloved Leader anymore. I have no one left to leave; you have no more reason to love me."

His breath had become ragged. Every word seemed like a sacrifice that he couldn't afford to make. Persopile decided not to answer in order to lower the chances of further conversation. But she wanted to say that he could still lead her, and that she still loved him.

The way those underground had spoken about Mountaintop, she was afraid to shout for help. What if she were arrested and mistreated? Worse, what if a citizen had one of those weapons, the death-bringer called a gun, and shot her as soon as they saw her stained face? But she needed help, and soon, if Belubus had a chance at survival. So she raised her voice and took the risk.

"Can anyone hear me? Help! He's going to die!"

Istoch hadn't felt like himself since the babies died. They had resurrected him. But now that was buried alongside them in their tiny graves.

He journeyed outside the Wall often. Though his excursions were still forbidden, nobody tried to prevent them. That was a fringe benefit of being the boy whose heart has been trampled countless times—everyone felt such pity for him that they just left him alone. It was a curse as much as a privilege, though, because to be left alone was to be left always lonely.

Istoch was aware that wandering until lost, which was a habit he'd gotten into, was reckless. He wouldn't take food or water on his unfocused quests, and often he'd grow disoriented and only return to town late at night—tired, famished, and parched. Though for a healthy person this weakened state might serve as a warning, something to be avoided, for Istoch it stoked a compulsion in him for more. Out here, with his body lost, hungry, and miserable, his soul didn't feel so discordant. At least all parts of him were in agreement; the pain in his body distracted him from the pain inside.

It reminded him of something his mother had often said when he was young: "When you know who you are, you can wander and never be lost." Only he was now the opposite. He'd lost who he was, so now he could be in familiar places and still disoriented.

Istoch was on another one of his pain-seeking vision quests, puzzling through the terrible, intriguing ideas Tranton had shared with him, when he heard her voice. Like fire erupting in the frigid darkness, the sound brought him warmth and buoyed his weakened steps and dulled vision.

"Please! Can anyone hear me?"

He was worried for whoever owned the desperate voice ringing through the silent woods. Though there hadn't been any Cloudies just outside the Wall in recent years, (and indeed, rumors were that the beasts no longer even lurked in Cloudline), their lethal presence was always a possibility. He wanted to call to her to be silent, but his sand-dry mouth couldn't form the words.

He forced himself into a trot with an energy he hadn't known he still possessed and broke through thick underbrush and into a clearing. There he saw a blood-soaked girl carrying a small and broken man. She stared at him with fear in her eyes, but she didn't look away.

Istoch took a step forward, feeling himself strangely drawn to her. On her face, she bore a crimson red mark. The stain brought Istoch immediate comfort. *It's the shape of my heart*, he thought, though he knew better than to say it out loud, and wasn't sure exactly what it meant.

He gathered himself enough to focus on his words. "Let me help you," he whispered gently, holding his arms out. She passed the injured man to him with great care. Istoch thought that the battered man must be dead, but he felt a faint pulse as he clutched him close.

The girl looked down and away. "Thank you. I was told you were all heartless."

Istoch ducked down until he caught her eyes again, and they shared a glance. "I feared that I was. Heartless. But now that you're here…I know that I'm not."

They fidgeted, as if uncomfortable in their own skins. Embarrassed, even, because their emotion was undeniable, but felt inappropriate and out of place. Despite the nearly dead man, each felt happy, at least for a moment, simply because they'd met each other.

Istoch had to break the spell. "Let's get him up to Mountaintop. I'll take care of both of you." He was suddenly sure of where to go. He headed uphill, and she walked beside him.

Though Istoch didn't think it would make any sense to say it out loud, he knew that she would be—and already was—taking care of him too.

9

ICELYN

I've often resented the way nature has distributed the cards between men and women. Why must the woman's body be invaded to ensure the survival of our species? However, my objection has always been academic in nature—uncharged by passion, more a disapproving shake of the head than an emotional plea.

Yet now *I* am the one being coerced into giving myself up to the next generation, and the idea steals oxygen from my lungs. I've only started to realize who I am and my place in this world. And *now*—just when I've really begun living—I'm asked to become a fallen carcass that's devoured so that new life can emerge?

I can't sleep. I've stolen down to the locked room where Adorane is being kept, managing to evade Eveshone and Omathis long enough to have a moment alone with him. As I unlock the door and swing it open, I'm pleased to see that he has shaved the beard. Finally, his beautiful copper-bronze face has been restored to how I remember it.

"You've shaved the beard! I'm so glad. You *knew* I would hate it," I accuse him, playfully at first, but then I feel bashful.

Neither of us knows what to say for a moment.

He grows serious. "I needed it if I was going to come down here and face you. I can handle your hatred from afar, but not up close. I needed a barrier. Not skin to skin. I couldn't expose myself to that."

This is probably more than Ad's admitted to me about our relationship in our entire life. I catch my breath and try to change the subject.

"Kind of fascinating, right? This space has been well preserved since the time of the Apriori. You're sleeping in a bed just like they did." I don't know why I'm talking about this, but the words come fast and uncontrollable. "It even has their artwork hanging on the wall. This was a more affluent person's living space, from the looks of it."

Ad's face scrunches up in response, as if to ask if this is really what I came here to talk about.

Of course it isn't.

"It's certainly the nicest prison cell I've ever been locked up in. No debate about that."

"I've been locked away in nicer, to be honest," I reply truthfully. "Anyway, we can't let you roam freely in the Drowned City, for your own protection more than anything."

He sits on a sleek, graceful chair carved of wood, which is nothing like the rustic furniture in Mountaintop. "Is this the conversation you were hoping to have with me tonight? Is this why I found these, delivered by squirrels to the trees in Mountaintop?" He opens his hand and I see a few acorns.

I don't need to look at them any closer. I'd carved messages to him on many, some time ago, and had my Anaghwin scatter them around the mountain.

We should end the silence.

Remember who we were?

I miss you.

I never thought they'd get to him. Now I'm embarrassed at how earnest the carved words are.

"You're acting like I've come unbidden, but you've been inviting me," he says softly.

It feels like he's guiding this conversation where he wants it to go. I decide to take the reins. "Do you believe that I'll simply become an… incubator for your offspring, Ad?" I ask, choosing my words carefully. So many thoughts fight within me—long-repressed desire, resentment at the position I'm being put in, shock at the outright salaciousness of Ad's proposal. I'd dreamed of this since I was a girl—but never, never like this.

I expect a wink, but instead his expression grows dark and he remains silent.

"What is it, Ad?"

He soaks his hand in a basin of water and splashes some behind his own ear, just as he'd done with me. As I watch, three blotches emerge, angry like embers on his skin. I hate seeing them stain Adorane, who has always prided himself on being rather flawless.

"What's wrong with you, Ad? Are you sick?"

"All who drank the water developed this. Everyone the Croathus poisoned are blighted, and they will all pass that frailty onto their children. The babies are too small to fight it off, so they die. I'm a dead-end, Ice. I cannot father a child—not one that will survive past the first few months, at least."

I think of Adorane's father, Aclornis. He was the best father I'd ever known. I realize now, though I've never expressed it in any form, that I assumed Adorane would be just as good a parent.

"I'm so sorry," I whisper.

"I will never have a son. The poisoned water has stolen that me. The Croathus have stolen that from all of us in Mountaintop."

Mostly I feel terrible for him, because this is a nightmare. But I'm perturbed by him mentioning that he cannot have a son and not even raising the possibility of a daughter. Irritation flames up in me.

I guess my face betrays a flicker of my thoughts.

"What did I say?"

"Nothing. I'm just sad for you."

"No. That's not all. I know you're sad for me, but there's more. I said something that made you angry just now."

"Look, it's not worth talking about."

"Tell me."

"I'm trying to be mature and show restraint. I'm trying to be better than the old Icelyn, who would say whatever she wanted. I'm trying to care more about your sadness than whatever might be bothering me."

"Save your maturation for someone who has asked for it. I don't want enlightened Icelyn. I want you—whining and all. Tell me."

"Fine. You said that you could never have a *son*, but you didn't mention your sadness at never having a daughter. And that makes me wonder. Because I think that people view the men as the apex of humanity, and women as the necessary part of humanity that exists only to birth more men. Men are the importance of life itself, while women are tools used to make more. Men are the glorious end goal that justifies the wily, unpredictable, weak means of femininity. Men exist because they're incredible; women exist to make more men. It's an undercurrent that has always flowed through Mountaintop, and I had always hoped not to detect it in you."

Adorane looks at me like I've grown a third eye.

"You're the one who begged me to share what I was thinking," I shrug.

"If I had known that's what you were thinking, I wouldn't have asked."

I can't tell if he's angry or hurt. Adorane, for all his good attributes, has never taken criticism well.

"Forget it. What I really want to say is that I've always thought you'd be an amazing father. And I'm sorry. Really, really, sorry."

My words make the moment less strange, but also more sad. A few thoughts run through my mind, but nothing worth vocalizing. Finally, he breaks the silence.

"Anyway, because your father always insisted on you drinking the Winter Rain Waters instead of those from Waterpump, you haven't been afflicted."

"Right. That makes sense." Lucky me, I guess.

But what exactly is Adorane asking me to do? If neither he nor anyone else in Mountaintop can father a healthy child, what does he want from me? I can't very well create a baby by myself.

He reads my thoughts and offers the answer. "I need to take you to Apex, Icelyn."

I laugh. *Apex*? I am sure he is joking, though his somber eyes make it clear that he isn't.

"Apex doesn't exist," I declare, confident, but losing my assurance. "… Right?"

"It does. And we need to go there."

THEN

Omathis looked at their expanding family and laughed.

"What did you find to be funny?" Soneyane, his one love above all other loves, asked him. She studied what Omathis had been looking at—their children, Amperous and Lenolin's children, and the children of the other breeding pairs, all scampering through the rushing waters of the river.

"I didn't realize I had laughed," Omathis answered. "And I don't know why I did."

"Perhaps you are happy," Soneyane offered.

Omathis noted that his insides felt light, like they were floating, bouncing gently off each other. Watching the children play brought him joy, he realized. The young ones in their community did not know pain and darkness as he, Amperous, and the other breeding pairs had suffered.

"Their lives are so different than ours were," he whispered.

"We've given that to them," Soneyane agreed.

They held each other close and smiled while they watched children jump from a jagged cliff into a shimmering pool. Another pair of young ones pounced on top of each other, taking turns dunking the other under the water.

This is paradise, Omathis and Soneyane agreed, using their roots.

Their satisfaction was disturbed by an unfamiliar rumble. This was a sound neither had heard in a very long time—one that immediately drained them of their gladness.

Soneyane was the first to pursue the source. Omathis chased. Before long, Amperous and Lenolin had joined them as they rushed through the jungle. Their talons were extended, their eyes burned with anticipation, and their stomachs raged with hunger.

It's the belching of their vehicles, Amperous declared. *I know the sound. It can be nothing else.*

But they don't live here. Omathis hoped it could be something else—anything else.

We know what lives in this jungle. None of the beasts that do sound anything like this. We all know what that sound means.

They jumped over ravines and descended into canyons. They rushed through the canopy of treetops and glided below the underbrush, all as one, their movements unified. They didn't need to coordinate a plan. They knew what they'd do if they found what they feared they would discover.

The sounds and smells were vibrant now. There was no doubt. This was the burning sweet odor that the humans' machines left behind. They knew it well from their days in the city.

The men had no time to fear; their death came swiftly. The rumbling truck masked any sound of approach the four creatures might have made, though they made very little. It took each only a flick of a sharpened talon to slice the soft part of the neck, bringing instant death to humans.

Such easy creatures to kill, they marveled. *Strange how they have been so dominant.*

There was no drinking of their blood; these deaths were not celebrated. The four didn't even hollow out the bodies and string them up in the trees as a display. Instead, they efficiently worked together to hide all traces of the humans. Amperous knew of a sinkhole where everything—even the truck and the angry buzzing devices the men had been using to cut down trees—could be tossed and never seen again. In less than an hour all traces of the massacre were erased.

After sinking everything deep into the ground, the four beasts returned to their idyllic clearing, despondent.

"We had to slaughter them. They would have seen our community. They would have told the men in dark suits where we are," Omathis started, assuaging his own guilt.

Once Mister Sean had given them this paradise, they knew there was no good reason to kill humans anymore. They could be left to live here, undisturbed. When they were escaping from their prison in the north, bloodshed had been necessary. They'd had no conception of a place free of humanity, which didn't require killing for survival. Then they had finally found it.

But now they had stained their refuge with the blood of humans. Now everything—their home, their community, their insides—felt defiled. But they had to protect what was theirs.

"If the men start coming into our paradise, what can we do?" Lenolin asked.

"We should fight them," Amperous answered. "More will come. We should attack them first, in their cities."

"No," Soneyane said. "There are still few of us. We've seen their weaponry. If they band together, they will win. We should do a better job of hiding."

She tilted her head as if she was sensing something, and then leapt into the canopy above them. A moment later, she returned with the limp body of a jaguar.

"Let's wear the skins of animals. That way, even if they see us, they'll think we're one of the beasts that live in the jungle."

Amperous liked this idea. "Yes! Shai possessed an animal that she pretended to love very much. A dog. It was her pet." He efficiently cleaned the jaguar carcass and separated the furs from the rest of the body. He pulled it all over his body, head and all, like a cloak.

"*Now* are we worthy of your affection, Shai? Now will you trust us, humans?" he asked mockingly. "Have we finally become the kinds of creatures that you will cherish? Your pets, who dare not have a vision for their lives outside of what you want for them? Who do exactly what you command them to do? *Now* will you love us?"

It's not a memory I retrieve often—mostly because it unsettles me, shakes my view of the people I thought we were.

But I remember. I still do. Both Adorane and I do, even if we've never talked about it. We couldn't forget it if we wanted to.

We were only five years old, or maybe seven. Adorane and I, along with a Veritas girl named Rutia (who I'd liked when we were younger, though we'd drifted apart as we got older), were playing a game of twigs and stones in the Big Meadow when we heard heavy, raspy wheezing.

I screamed because I saw her first: A woman, caked in a permanent layer of ground-in dirt, bleeding and dizzy, stumbling toward us with an outstretched hand.

"Water," she pleaded, her voice gravelly and unnatural. "Where is the water?"

Her eyes were wide, mostly pale amber irises with just a pinprick of black pupil, and they jittered left and right, up and down, as if there were no way they could see everything that needed to be seen but were trying their hardest anyway. Her hair looked like it hadn't been washed in ages, if ever, and her cloths were tattered rags, revealing so much of the dirty skin beneath.

Rutia fled, afraid, but Ad and I were too curious to leave. The woman could barely move, falling over her own feet toward us. If she posed any danger, we knew we could easily evade her. Adorane had an ultralion bladder of water with him (always prepared, even at such a young age), which he tossed to her. The woman eagerly, clumsily lifted it from the ground and fumbled with the clasp. Adorane stepped forward and opened the bladder for her. I was struck by his kindness, but also the risk, and alarm bells rang throughout my body. He was close enough that she could have grabbed him if she wanted to.

She emptied the entire bladder into her wide open mouth, which I noticed was missing teeth. Her lips were scarred and twisted, like the sunbaked roots of a wind-worn Cyprus tree.

"Where did you come from?" Ad asked. She wasn't a member of the Kith, and there were no people left in this entire world except the Kith. And how could she make it through Cloudline if she were from anywhere else? Perhaps she lived Down Below and smelled and looked so beastly that the monsters below didn't know she was human. Still, it made no sense.

"Apex," she replied, then clenched onto Adorane as if her life depended on it. "Don't let them send me back. I can't go back." He wrenched his arm away, afraid, and she fell to the ground sobbing—though so dehydrated, I saw, that no tears came.

By that time Rutia had told an adult what she had seen in the Big Meadow, and our parents had rushed to find us. Marjan ushered me away, quietly explaining to me that this woman was one who'd been disbursed long ago because her mind was sick. That made sense to me at the time. You couldn't have such madness existing freely among the Kith. She was too dangerous.

Apex had since become a punchline between Ad and me, one we'd never shared with anyone else, because even at the time we knew it wasn't right. That lady's haunted, hollow eyes and emaciated frame fueled my nightmares for months. The only way I could stop thinking about her was to make fun of her, so we turned her into a joke—me more than Ad, if I'm being honest. That way we could laugh instead of examining all the other feelings we had about this woman, about where she'd come from, about where they'd sent her. About what she'd been through. We never saw her again, and every time we asked about her, we were hushed by the adults.

Whenever something strange happened, like when we both swore that we'd left our collection of acorns in his mother's kitchen and found later that they were gone without a trace, one of us would whisper "Apex." It became shorthand for anything unexplained, spooky, mysterious, or ridiculous.

A moving shadow outside my lab? *Apex.*

Wind blowing through the cracks in Hailgard Round, creating a high-pitched otherworldly howl? *Apex.*

Adorane's utter bafflement at what girls might be thinking half the time? *Apex.*

In retrospect, I feel shame about it. The suffering of that woman had been painful to see, and we shouldn't have turned her into a source of casual amusement. But children can be cruel and unthinking, especially when the adults in their lives don't help them become anything else.

"Why would I go to Apex, even if it *does* exist?" I ask. "And why can't you just—I don't know, find a woman there?"

"There are no women there," Adorane answers. "It's a city of men. Men only."

I can't understand how that would work. "How is that possible? They'd have no children."

"According to what I've read, they've figured out a way. I don't know the details. It's not important; it's not why I'm here. We just need to get there."

"But that doesn't make any sense. There is no way to make children without women, Ad!"

"And yet they continue to exist."

We've hit a dead end. How long can you discuss impossibilities when one person insists they are possible? "And so why can't they carry the torch for humanity? Let them continue with their methods," I say.

"And let Mountaintop die? Does that not matter to you? You are still a Brathius, yes? The Kith lives on only through their children. Mountaintop can only live on through you."

I must agree that this makes sense. "How do you know all of this? About Apex?"

"I'm the leader of Mountaintop. I have access to secrets that are shielded from others."

This makes me feel unexpectedly strange. The leader? A Brathius should be leading Mountaintop. It's the natural order of things. I let my discomfort go.

"Oh, you're the leader? Good. That's great, Ad."

"I wouldn't call it great, but it's probably the best we can hope for. Torrain helps, too."

"What did you tell the Kith you were doing, coming down here?"

"I told them I was visiting in hopes of persuading Icelyn Brathius to save them. Most believe I will fail."

It shouldn't, but this hurts. If he's trying to inspire me, sharing their dim view of me isn't the correct lever to pull.

"Oh. Who *did* believe that you could convince me to help Mountaintop?"

"Me, for one," he answers. "Torrain, too." He pauses for what seems like an annoyingly long amount of time to achieve dramatic effect. "That's about it."

I sigh, unhappy and tired of this journey already. "So what's the plan? If I come with you?"

"We find a man in Apex."

"And I have a baby. Then what? One baby can't reproduce anyway."

"You have more than one baby."

"My children will have children with each other?"

"Perhaps we take more than one man from Apex!"

"I have children with more than one man?"

Adorane is tired, too. "I haven't figured it all out yet. But this is survival, Icelyn. Maybe all the traditions and normal propriety don't apply. You think I *want* to ask any of this of you? You think this is how I saw the future playing out? I don't *know* what the plan is. I only know that without you, there won't be a plan. Only death."

10

THEN

Travis' fingers glided over the fretboard of his Rickenbacker 325 until he lost himself in the strumming. He didn't remember when the transformation had happened. He used to have to look out for mistakes, remember what to do next, stretch and press just so to avoid hitting the wrong notes. But his playing had morphed into its own intelligent being, one joined to him but not always controlled by him. He was continually surprised by what he and his guitar were able to accomplish together now.

Travis had developed a trembling tenor voice and thought there was a chance it was pretty good, though he didn't want anyone else to hear it yet. It felt too soon. Like birthing a baby and expecting it to do homework and flirt with the girls in homeroom right away. Still, by himself, he enjoyed singing.

"Where are you now? Do you let me down?

Do you make me grieve for you?

Do I make you proud? Do you get me now?

Am I your pride and joy?"

Travis stopped, disturbed by a distant sound that wasn't distant enough. Sean was home. Travis hoped he hadn't heard his song. He'd probably be encouraging and tell Travis it was excellent. He'd tell Travis that he had a real knack for this, ask if he wanted more lessons or maybe recording equipment or help getting a band together. Sean was relentlessly supportive, which can be a real drag when you hate a person as much as Travis despised his adoptive father. He was desperately upbeat in hopes of repaying a debt that could never be repaid.

Travis remembered the ruined state of Sean's study, *his pristine untouched sanctuary.* Finally, Sean would drop his mask of smiling concern so they could argue.

By the time Travis had wiped any fingerprints off the gleaming surface of his guitar, Sean appeared in the doorway.

"Travis, do you remember what we talked about this morning?"

"Sorry, Sean, but I had a book report and needed to do some research. I was looking for Hawthorne. Or maybe it was Melville? Whatever. It was all for naught, as they say, because I couldn't find either one."

"The study was locked." Sean maintained his even-keeled *everything-is-going-to-be-fine* tone, as if he were talking a deranged cat down out of a tree.

"My goodness," Travis continued, "I just realized that the root word of *naughty* is *naught*. And I was talking about Melville. Isn't that fascinating? What do you think that could mean? Do you think my subconscious was connecting the *nautical* themes of Moby Dick to disobedience?"

"I lock my study for a reason, Travis."

"And I unlocked it because I had to get in there." It hadn't been easy, either. Sean had taken the only key with him. Travis had made it his project of the day, scanning the lock and creating a new key using the 3D printer Sean had gifted him for Christmas. (Yet another failed effort to compensate him for what had happened. *Sorry your mom's dead because of the monsters I created, kid. Here's a sweet piece of tech to make up for it.*)

"You are not allowed in my study." Sean kept his tone calm and casual, as if he were instructing Travis how to best keep his slacks from getting too wrinkled in the laundry. *Nothing* could break Sean out of his placid facade. God, Travis loathed him.

"The classics were calling to me," Travis shrugged and started picking at his guitar. "Why? Are you upset? Do you want to yell at me? Tear into me? Like I tore into those books? Sorry about that. Some of the pages were kind of sticking together and when I gave them a little tug they just…" Travis made a loud ripping sound.

"I have tried to make this work, Travis. I have made it my highest priority."

"Nobody asked you to do that."

Sean slumped against the door, deflated.

"What do you want from me, Travis?"

Travis knew that Sean would never give him what he truly craved—an honest account of what happened to his mother. And it wasn't even possible for Sean to provide what Travis wanted *most of all*—which was his mother back from the dead, breathing and alive, quietly ignoring him in the next room and working on something that made her pulse race. So he asked instead for what would at least be an improvement over the prison his life with Sean had become.

"Just send me away. Anywhere. Away from you."

ICELYN

"You cannot go, Lovely. You cannot." Omathis is more animated than I've ever seen him. He's shed his customary calm like a snake sheds its skin, revealing a fresh and angry passion. "We have only now finally been reunited with you after all these years. You cannot go."

He sounds as if his voice could crack into two and be washed away in a flood of heartache at any moment. I hadn't expected his vehement opposition. I thought talking to him and Eveshone would help clear my head. I've been twisted up into a thousand knots at Adorane's insistence that leaving the Drowned City and traveling to (likely mythical) Apex in order to have a child with a stranger was the only correct course of action.

I wanted gentle counsel. Instead I find someone equally insistent, but in the opposite direction, and my thoughts are now doubly confused.

Eveshone, Omathis, and I have gathered in our favorite spot atop the highest building in the Drowned City. From here we can see the cloud-shrouded Mountain where I once lived, the ocean stretching into the horizon, and the lush green and deep brown expanses of Down Below. I've always felt like I could see the entire landscape of my life—my past, present, and future—from this spot.

But now everything is murky.

Omathis is disappointed in me. Why would I even consider going? It's as if by going I will let him down personally and make a lasting statement about the strength of my love for him.

Eveshone jumps to my defense, her voice quiet against Omathis' quiet fury. "If Lovely feels as if she must do this, who are we to question her wisdom?" Eveshone, always loyal. She has an excess of invaluable traits that are in short supply in others.

Omathis turns to Eveshone, his eyes broadcasting a thick wave of condescension. "Eveshone, leave us alone for a moment, will you?" Though I've tried to break the hierarchy in the Drowned City—where all defer to Omathis, and Eveshone defers to all—Eveshone complies and begins to walk away.

"Eveshone, no. This is a conversation for all of us."

"I can grant Omathis a moment, Lovely. It brings me no suffering," she replies, and busies herself with collecting seashells on the opposite side of the rooftop.

Omathis' voice assumes a tone of authority, like Belubus' when lecturing me in school. "You have to know that while we all adore Eveshone, her counsel is not trustworthy."

The way he discounts her—as if her lack of value needed no explanation, and I only required a gentle reminder—enrages me, but I keep my composure. For all his bluster, Omathis is fragile. The scolding I'm tempted to unleash would do him no good.

"And why is that?"

"We've graciously accepted her back into the heart of the Anaghwin because she came with you. But you must remember, she's a Cast Out. She should have been banished long ago, if you want my opinion."

I know that Eveshone and her father had scraped out a living alone on the mainland, apart from both the Anaghwin and the Croathus, but I'd never been told why, even when I'd asked. It seemed to embarrass them all too much to delve into.

"Why would you banish anyone so pure and wonderful as Eveshone?"

Omathis' desperation to convince me to stay has played tricks with his mind, because he's finally willing to divulge this secret. "As you know, before you descended from the Mountain, this world was too dark and painful to welcome new life. But Eveshone's mother—an Anaghwin among us, always tiptoeing on the edges of what was acceptable, beguiled her father—despite all my commandments, despite what was right."

So a female and a male Anaghwin fell in love and had a child. I didn't see the crime.

"Eveshone was the result of their union. They could not stay."

Probably because they were too happy, I thought bitterly. Omathis hadn't wanted the others to see that they could bring children into this world and have love and family, and that all was not made up of loneliness and abandonment.

I calm myself and remain gentle in my words. "Eveshone and her father lived inland, not too far from here. Where did her mother go?"

"Her mother was shamed. She disappeared. Some say she lived by herself in the wilderness, a kind of witch—conjuring up evil, no doubt."

Is this truly dear trustworthy Omathis indulging these superstitions? The longer you know someone, the more they reveal themselves. You're bound to see something ugly eventually. It's inevitable.

"That is the blood that flows through Eveshone's veins. While we all love her, we cannot have faith in her instincts or words."

A witch! A woman is stripped of her community and family and sent out alone to die, and she's accused of being a witch. If a man were living alone in the wilderness, he'd be hailed as a great mystic or a holy man. It's more evidence of this insidious assumption that women only exist to serve men and children of men, but never themselves; the moment one focuses on her own well-being, she's condemned as a witch.

Is this how they view me in Mountaintop, set apart from all of them. Do they think I'm a witch? Untrustworthy and volatile?

"You forget that my blood flows through her veins, too, Omathis. Just as it flows through yours."

I'm unsettled to discover this division between Omathis and Eveshone. They are constants in my life, so I assumed they were for each other, too. But now I find out they have shadowy fractures between them. It makes me wonder who may have secret quarrels with me.

"Eveshone," I shout, while staring with defiance into Omathis' eyes. "Tell me, what do you think I should do?"

Eveshone scampers over to us, oblivious to the percolating tension. "Lovely, you have declared multiple times that we in the Drowned City should reproduce despite our misgivings, because our species must survive. You have even forced us to kidnap Croathus children and mothers to accomplish this. I know I am still young, but to me this seems similar to what Adorane is asking you to do. If you refuse, he may call you a hippopotamus."

I break into laughter because she meant to say hypocrite. The idea of Adorane calling me a hippopotamus, the mammoth lumpy water mammal that looks like a gray potato come to life, is hilarious. Or maybe everything is so tense that I crave some kind of release from the pressure.

Omathis doesn't see the humor. "Eveshone, Icelyn belongs to the Anaghwin now. Don't you see? We are her people, and she cannot leave us."

"That makes sense too. You both make sense! That's probably why this is such a difficult conversation. It's just that I think Lovely should be able to do whatever she wants. It's not up to the created to control the creator."

"But when you create something, you create a debt to it too. We didn't ask to be made. The Brathius brought us into this world, so the Brathius cannot abandon us here."

Eveshone is right. I have been forcing the abducted Croathus (though "adopted Anaghwin" is my preferred way of referring to them) to reproduce for our survival. How could I refuse to do the same for the Kith?

But this is madness. Am I really going to travel to Apex do this?

There's another aspect to this question—one that I would never mention to Eveshone or Omathis.

I have been thinking about heirs. When I die, will the Anaghwin's god die too?

An Anaghwin lives much longer than a human. How tragic to be forced to watch your maker die. If I have a child, Lovely and Sean will live on in that child, as they have lived on in me.

I can't explain this to Omathis, but when I leave the Drowned City and visit the mainland, I'll be going for the Anaghwin and the Croathus as much as for humanity. Probably even more so.

"I would never abandon you, Omathis. But I am going."

I'm not sure what I'm expecting. Maybe that Omathis softens and embraces me, we share a Vibram, and he realizes that my intentions are pure. But that's not what I receive.

He does hold onto me, but not with kindness.

"Let me go," I stammer, shocked, as his grip tightens. "I command it. I command it as your God!"

Rather than obeying, Omathis looks straight at me without an ounce of shame. "I adore you and your commandments, Lovely. But I hope you love me enough to forgive me, because I cannot obey you in this. The creature you created me to be cannot obey this commandment, and I have no choice but to be myself. I hope that means something to you. If it doesn't, then I am sorry."

"You cannot imprison your God," I protest, but I'm tired, and the fight has drained from me.

"When my God wants to do something so foolish as to abandon us, what choice do I have?"

THEN

Amperous tossed a boulder. He watched as it soared and then dropped into the dense jungle foliage, heavily thudding into the moist black-brown soil. As it hit the ground, joyful and chaotic howls rose, loud as thunder.

Amp and Omathis scampered to the spot where it fell. They lifted the massive stone from the ground, leaving behind a deep hole in the dirt where it had landed. They crouched on either side of the newly formed pit and lifted their eyes to the sky with ceremonial reverence.

"Wild and free, yet according to your plan, Mister Sean. We bring another into this world—one step closer to transforming it into the world you're creating," Amperous prayed. He produced a sapling from beneath the jaguar skins he wore.

He carefully placed the young tree into the hole, and he and Omathis surrounded the roots with rich, dark dirt. The sapling joined a scattering of new green in the clearing, trees of varying sizes and ages reaching toward the sky.

Amperous and Omathis were joined by Lenolin, Soneyane, and twenty-three Croathus children of varying sizes and ages. Lenolin held an infant born only hours ago. She and Amp gently leaned toward each other until their foreheads touched. They held this pose, gaining strength from their closeness.

She handed the infant to Amperous.

He held the child over the newly planted tree. "Your name is Decerec, and like this tree, may you grow where you are meant to grow. No other may uproot you. No other may use you for their purposes. You are your own, and you belong only to those you choose to share yourself with. For yourself and for your family only will you labor. You will be gentle toward those you love and fierce toward those who do not love you. You will be strong and tall and everlasting, and together, we will cover the earth like a forest."

The group cheered and growled and chirped in agreement.

11

ICELYN

It's those who claim to love you who bind you with the tightest chains. What other conclusion can I come to, based on the evidence of my life? Father and Mother, Belubus, and now Omathis. All dear to me, and all determined to keep me locked away, a captive to their vision of what my life should be.

Am I flawed deep inside? Why else would I become a prisoner to so many? This captivity happens too often for it to be everyone else's fault. I must bear the blame.

Omathis has stationed a battery of Anaghwin to serve as guard. He's told them that I've commanded everyone to leave me alone, even if I beg and plead to be let out. That I am testing their obedience.

"Omathis! You are lying to them! You are lying to yourself! Let me out!" I pound at the thick wooden door until my hands hurt, but nobody replies. "Please! Open this door! Please!"

I am in the smallest of rooms at the peak of a skyscraper. It's curiously shaped, like the top half of an egg, and made out of metal framing that once held molded glass. For the Apriori, it was a lookout of some kind, so that people could ascend and see their world from on high. Now the glass is broken, but Omathis has twisted and tied a diabolically thick barrier of dried sea kelp to the frame. I pound against it, but it's as hard as stone. What's worse is that I can't look out and see anything.

At sunrise, and again at sunset, the Anaghwin gather outside to worship me. They sing and recite poems full of lovely words composed in my honor. They proclaim my greatness. They promise that they long for my wisdom, my direction, my embrace, and my love. When I was first brought into the Drowned City, this worship was warm and personal. I would connect with each of them individually, and they with me.

Now it leaves me cold. They could be doing this whether I existed or not. What was once about the bonds that connected us has fossilized into a choreographed, distant ceremony. It hurts my heart to hear it.

I am trapped in the darkness.

I might as well sleep. Perhaps in my dreams I will taste freedom again.

I imagine myself stretched until I tear into pieces and carried around the world. I want so many things and their opposites at the same time. I want to keep humanity alive, yet I have no desire whatsoever to have a child right now. I want to be everything I've ever promised to the Anaghwin, yet I want to disappear and just be Icelyn Brathius, away from here, away from everyone.

It makes my head hurt. My heart, too, probably, though I can't be sure it hasn't already shattered into dust and blown away.

I am every emotion at once. Furious about the order of things. Angry that I have to fight it continuously. Overwhelmed by the tyranny of nature, by the role it's assigned to me. Whether I want to or not, I am expected to bring a child into this world. I am told to appreciate that role. But I don't. I may even want to, yet I can't.

None of this is what I'd choose for myself. If there were any other way, I'd back out. Any way. The natural order has let me down. Why can't Ad have come up with a better plan? He's smart. Ad has let me down. And now Omathis has let me down. I am in a prison, under layers of hurt and anger, with no way out in sight.

Could it be that if you look around and think that everyone has let you down, you have somehow fallen out of step with reality? Maybe nobody has let me down. Maybe I am just someone whose natural state is to be made low. To be let down. Maybe it is my destiny.

Why can't I just want what everyone else wants for me?

I hear the creaking of the great door and jump to my feet. I rush toward the blinding light, still half asleep. Then I am stopped by a strong, gentle arm.

Omathis.

The sight of him breaks my heart. He seems more upset than I am—and that's a notable accomplishment, because I'm a mess. His fur is matted, his normally clear blue eyes bloodshot. He stoops where he's normally upright and regal.

He sits beside me with a loud sigh. He doesn't say a word.

"You may leave, Icelyn. But I make one request before you do. Give me permission to die. I'm tired of this world. With you gone, I cannot bear another moment. If you leave, grant me this wish. Let me die."

My insides feel like they're contracting. My own desires suddenly feel small in comparison to what he's saying. Omathis wants to die? No. I refuse to believe it. I don't know what to say.

He pulls the door closed and we are plunged into darkness, save for the dull green glow of the dried kelp illuminated by the sunlight beyond. We sit beside each other in silence.

"What you ask for I cannot give you, Omathis. You must live. You cannot die."

"Then I cannot let you leave. And you see why. It's the same. If you cannot let me go, how do you expect me to let you go?"

"Where is Eveshone?" I ask.

He tenses. I know why. She is the only one so loyal to me that she will let me make the decision I want to make, even if it's not the right one. Omathis is afraid she'll help me.

"I restricted her access to you."

I want to tell him how much he's hurt me. I want to tear into him, to cry out bitterly against what he's turned into. I decide to communicate with him using our roots, so that the message is stronger and deeper. But when I try to access our roots, I'm surprised to find that all of these venomous sentiments I've prepared won't form. Instead, all I can communicate to him, despite my conscious efforts, is one sad, solemn statement.

I'm sorry for breaking your heart in the past, Omathis. I'm sorry for breaking it now. I'm sorry for the way I will break it in the future, too.

I continue to send this message to him long after he leaves me alone, still imprisoned in the dull green darkness.

THEN

Travis had been foolish to believe that *anywhere* would be better than living with Sean. His new school was not better.

Longrave Military Academy versus living with Sean Brathius. Two terrible, equal hells on earth.

"Second study hall is for quiet endeavors, Cadet," Colonel Hodges spat the words, his face only inches from Travis'. "You are not to play the guitar, regardless of how magically your twinkly little fingers flit and flutter over the strings—"

"Okay, yeah," Travis interjected, desperate for this moment—only the latest in a frequent series where he was the center of attention—to come to a quick and inconsequential end. "That makes sense."

"Makes sense? Do you think I care at all whether what I'm saying *makes sense* to you? Are you implying that our rules are somehow justified because *you* think they are logical? Do you think what we say would be illegitimate if you didn't agree?"

"No. I only—what I mean is, yes, you're right, obviously."

"Why do you have this compulsion to put your stamp on everything that happens? Are you God, that you have to see the sun and declare that it is good? And on the Fourth Day, Cadet Travis Nilson saw the Rules about Quiet Endeavors During Second Study Hall and declared that they were Right, Obviously! Make note, everyone, this is a holy moment!" Colonel Hedges' voice rang throughout the silent hall.

God, it was as if everything Travis did to calm the situation only made it worse. Like he thought he was throwing water on a burning house fire but had grabbed a bucket of gasoline instead.

"Sorry, I was trying to say…what I meant was…" He trailed off, sure that he'd be interrupted before too long anyway.

He was right. "Let me explain something to you, Cadet. You don't always have to *say* something. When you are given an order, all the discussion that was required already took place among the people who needed to do the discussing. You do not need to question it, you do not need to talk about it, you do not need to approve it. You just need to *do it.* Do you know why?"

Travis didn't know whether to respond, so he just shook his head.

Colonel Hodges was a massive man, the kind that a space alien might mistake for another species entirely in comparison to your average human. His face was so tough and leathery that it was hard to believe any stubble in the world was strong enough to grow up through his skin, yet he bore a five o'clock shadow shortly after shaving. He focused his immense energies directly on Travis for a suffocatingly long time.

"Cadet Kaye, come here."

Soren Kaye was the gold-standard student that everyone at Longrave aspired to be. He walked confidently to Colonel Hodges' side. Half a foot taller than Travis, with the kind of muscles that puberty promised but rarely delivered, Soren was unfairly attractive. He had soft brown eyes which appeared gentle, though Travis had already had enough run-ins with Soren to know that those eyes were filthy liars.

"Cadet Kaye. On my command, I'd like you to throw a punch at Cadet Nilson." Colonel Hodge pointed at a specific spot on Travis' right cheek, as if exact precision mattered greatly. "Hit him right here. Do you understand?"

Soren nodded. His stoic expression couldn't mask the pleasure he'd take in obeying this order.

"Cadet Nilson, you may attempt to evade his strike. In fact, that is my command. But—and this is important—you no doubt have many questions and opinions about me instructing another student to sock you in the face. After all, you always have *so much to say.* So, once I've given the command to punch you, I would like you to ask those questions of me and await my response before you move even an inch to avoid being hit. Only once I've answered to your satisfaction may you dodge. Do you understand?"

Travis didn't, but he knew better than to say as much. He nodded.

"Cadet Kaye, punch him now."

Soren cocked his dangerously strong arm back and sized up his target. Soren was the best boxer in the class; his form was flawless.

Travis held still as a statue, knowing that any attempt to dodge would bring terrible consequences. As ridiculous as it seemed, he felt he'd get in worse trouble if he didn't attempt to ask a question.

He got as far as "Colonel Hodges, please tell me why—" before Soren's fist connected with his cheekbone. He saw pinpricks of glowing points scatter like stars before his vision tinged with a flash of red and then collapsed into total darkness.

He re-entered consciousness while being pulled back to his feet in the steely grip of Colonel Hodges. He was nauseous and disoriented, and only by a miracle did he avoid falling over again. His face felt like a beach ball had been grafted to it.

Colonel Hodges brushed off Travis' shoulders, pulling his woozy frame upright. "There you go. Okay, get ready, Cadet Kaye. I again order you to dodge, Cadet Nilson. Only this time, if you wish, you can follow that order immediately, without discussion. *Or* you're free to ask a question first. Your choice."

He nodded to Cadet Kaye. Travis lunged away from the impact as soon as he could. He barely escaped.

Colonel Hodge was filled with satisfaction as he turned Travis' trauma into a lesson for all the cadets in the barracks. "There, you see! The reason we cannot all talk and question as much as Cadet Nilson does when an order is given is because *we do not have the time.* When the enemy has thrown a punch, all we can do is move. Orders are given to keep you safe. But they can only do that if you act before the fist crushes into your face."

Laura Lee crowded close to a feeble fire. The unrelenting snow had left her feeling wet and cold deep in her bones. "Come on now, things could be worse," she said to herself out loud, as she had developed a habit of doing. After all, what was the alternative? Losing her voice from disuse?

She felt the first delicious hints of heat spreading through her chilled fingers and focused on those tiny sensations, rather than the cold that held the rest of her body captive.

"Yes, this world is good. I have a future in a world that is worthy of life and joy and happiness."

A welcome wave of warmth rose from her fingertips to her arms and chest and wind-burned face.

Breathe in. Breathe out. "Feel the life, Laura Lee. This is why you have survived."

In one spot in the sky, the thick clouds retreated enough to form a window that revealed the stars above: dazzling, living diamonds pasted to a black velvet canopy. As an act of discipline, Laura Lee forced herself to savor this moment. There were so few worth savoring anymore.

Then she heard the helicopters circling overhead. She shoveled dirt over her makeshift fire. "What a shame," she spat, disappointed. It had taken such effort to kindle these flames, and she needed the warmth. Smoke leaked through the mound of soil and she gathered her belongings with life-or-death urgency. She had to disappear before the smoke alerted them to her presence.

She hadn't been prepared for a life like this, and she certainly hadn't known she was choosing it when she made her best effort to save those poor creatures from execution. Yet in the curiously muted aftermath, while everyone was eager to sweep away what had happened and bury all evidence of her father's experimentation, she became the main target of a federal investigation. People had been slaughtered, Shai among the victims, and Laura Lee had been clumsy and naive enough to leave behind evidence that she had something to do with the breakout.

Laura Lee scrambled toward the camouflaged shelter she'd been calling home and prayed it would keep her hidden even if the helicopters were followed by investigators on the ground. She sat still in this pocket that had been carved out of the limestone by centuries of wind and water. This wasn't a permanent solution to her problem; she couldn't even stand up straight in here. But scrub and brush kept its entrance masked, so it worked as a hiding place for now.

She willed her rapidly beating heart to calm and rifled through her backpack until she found a black metal rectangle with a single button.

She pressed the button and then curled into a ball, covering herself with leaves and pine needles and branches, making herself as small and hard to see as possible.

NOW

"What is that? What approaches?"

In the distance, over the mainland, a strange black spot marred the otherwise blue sky. It rose and fell chaotically, without pattern or grace, and looked like nothing any of the lookouts at the Drowned City had ever seen.

The mammoth flying machines of the Apriori hadn't been operational for hundreds of years. Many Anaghwin now doubted that they had ever existed, despite the legends. These days, the skies were filled only with birds, bats, and insects. But none of those creatures grew anywhere near this large.

It moved in the jarring manner of a thing only just learning to move, frequently jostled in unexpected directions. Yet for all the clumsiness, there was no doubt that it was headed, steadily and purposely, toward them.

There was an anger in its movement, too. Not fluttering or graceful like a butterfly or a falcon; this thing seemed to have a dark purpose.

Omathis felt great fear deep inside. Though he didn't know what it was, he knew to be afraid of it.

Sentinel Anaghwin blew conch shells and banged on steel beams to sound the alarm. All of the Drowned City awoke. They were under attack.

Eveshone tried to obey Omathis and stay away from Icelyn's prison. He had convinced her that this was Icelyn's command. But now, as this airborne nightmare was darting toward the Drowned City, she wasn't going to leave it up to others to defend her Icelyn. She scaled the skyscraper two stories at a time. She could feel the flying thing nearing; she had to reach the top first.

The Anaghwin, following Omathis' lead, hurled anything they could find at the beast approaching from the air—chunks of aging buildings, whale bones, large sections of hardened coral. Some hit the creature, but nothing could make it fall from the sky or turn back.

There was an eerie familiarity to the beast. It looked like one of them, an Anaghwin or Croathus, only sharper and meaner. Most upsetting, it had leathery black wings attached to its lean, muscular body, connected with strong, elastic skin to the inner length of its arms and legs.

The beast was so close now that everyone in the Drowned City could hear, and feel, the massive whoosh from each beat of its wings. It didn't even seem to have full control of its movement and Omathis could only imagine how dangerous it would be once it actually learned how to fly.

As it got closer to Icelyn's tower and no Anagwhin was able to knock it out of the air, a furious desperation grew. Could no one stop this rampaging beast? This kind of hopelessness was not normal for the Anaghwin. They were accustomed to being the most physically gifted creatures in any battle or hunt.

"It's heading toward her chamber!"

"Stop it!"

They looked to Omathis.

He had no answer.

Icelyn heard the sounds of terror filtered through the tightly coiled kelp walls. She could feel an intense fear in her children, a fresh horror thick in the air. She couldn't imagine what it was.

She pounded on the walls in the greenish darkness, trying to find a weak point in the kelp, but with no success.

She wasn't sure if the rising terror she felt was her own or belonged to her Anaghwin, but she lost herself in its enormity. Her arms froze, and she was unable to move. She fell to the ground and struggled to breath. What was going on out there? She closed her eyes and wished for sleep.

Among the jumbled feelings, she sensed one unique attitude—determination and focus.

Eveshone.

She was nearby. Icelyn held fast to Eveshone's thoughts and let go of all others. She stood and placed her hand on a segment of the kelp.

Come to me. Thank you, Eveshone. Come to me.

The flying beast had nearly reached Icelyn's tower.

Eveshone grew disheartened. She was still a hundred feet away from the top.

Come to me! Thank you, dear Eveshone. Come to me!

Courage jolted through her as she felt Icelyn's voice. She charged upward.

She reached the pinnacle and saw the murky silhouette of Icelyn's hand resting on the inside of the kelp wall. Eveshone's talons grew and she sliced downward until the kelp split and Icelyn slid through the opening and into Eveshone's embrace.

Eveshone shielded Icelyn just as the soaring beast reached the tower. It targeted Icelyn with unwieldy movements. Eveshone dodged and the beast crashed into a bent steel beam with a shriek.

It was larger than a Croathus, with crueler, angrier eyes. They were not Brathius blue, but jet black with flecks and gradations of gray. While Anaghwin and Croathus had teeth more or less human in their shape and proportion, this creature had a jumble of jagged fangs that couldn't be completely contained in its mouth. The Anaghwin below stared at it in a stupor; it looked like them, but disturbing where different.

With Icelyn safely tucked in her arms, Eveshone leapt from the pinnacle of the tower to a balcony on a nearby building. When the winged beast tried to follow, it was blocked by a line of Anaghwin guards. They weren't able to stop it, but they did slow it down before it took flight again.

Eveshone crashed through a window and crouched in preparation to jump to a nearby skyscraper. The winged creature slammed into her and knocked her from her perch. Icelyn flew from Eveshone's grasp and slid across the floor. The horrible creature darted straight toward Icelyn.

They gazed at each other for a moment that seemed longer than it was —both finding each other unknowable, mysterious, and fascinating. The creature's toothed-packed mouth managed to speak a single garbled phrase: "For the Mothers."

It broke from its stupor and reached for Icelyn. Eveshone, in a blur, swept through and knocked it off its feet. Eveshone grabbed Icelyn, crashed through a rotted wall and entered a nearby skyscraper, all in a dizzying split second.

The creature recovered quickly and buzzed around the tower, angry and disoriented, trying to figure out where they had gone. It had lost track of Icelyn. It bellowed in frustration.

Anaghwin guards had entered and began launching chunks of steel and cement at the creature, each hitting its target and weakening it.

Finally, it charged through the air at one of the Anaghwin guards. It scooped the Anaghwin up with its cruel talons, slammed the poor, surprised creature into a steel beam a few times, and then headed back toward the mainland with its unconscious prey dangling from one claw.

12

THEN

Oliver Hailgard examined the digital maps projected on the screen with care. "And here," he pointed to the center of the continent, "you've seen a decrease in the deer population. Is that right?"

The analyst shook his head as he pulled up a photograph of elk carcasses, bloated and rotting in a field, on the display. "Not deer. Elk. Though I'm sure you know that an elk is a type of deer."

"Now I do. If I ever win a round of elk-related trivia, I'll be sure to thank you." Oliver studied the photos of the dead elk and then declared: "This isn't helpful. These elk died of natural causes."

"Actually, unnatural," the analyst corrected. "Fertilizers and pesticides in the water supply, probably, but—"

"You're wasting my time with your caveats," Oliver said flatly. "They weren't butchered. That's what I mean. What else do we have?"

Another analyst interrupted, eager to please. "The seal population has suffered increased incidences of emaciation and starvation."

Sergeant Hailgard fought back his temper. There would be no positive outcome from exploding at these hapless analysts. He was angry because his search had been stymied, not at anyone in the room, no matter how incompetent they appeared to be.

How is it possible for such large predators to simply disappear?

He carefully calibrated his response. "I don't need to be notified of every stressor affecting every animal population. I've been clear. I'm looking for reports of creatures being butchered. Torn apart. Slaughtered."

Everyone gathered knew better than to ask the obvious question: *Slaughtered by what? What exactly are we looking for?* Those who had asked that question before had been expelled from the project and demoted.

Silence. Oliver pressed. "Does anyone have anything for me? Anything."

One nervous analyst cleared her throat. She was the newest addition to the team and hadn't had a chance to frustrate Oliver yet. "I did discover a pattern of…" She trailed off, unsure.

"Jane Viveck, right?" Oliver asked, and Jane sat up straight, buoyed that he would remember her name. People normally didn't remember anything about her, even that they'd met her at all.

"Yes, sir, that's right. What I was saying was—I think I've found a pattern of missing persons. All throughout the Southwest." She rose nervously from her seat and projected a map onscreen. It was marked with a series of dots that looked like a river flowing from north to south.

"Good. Now *that's* something." Jane expected Oliver to look pleased, but instead he appeared suddenly sick. His skin took on a drained pallor, like he'd instantly acquired the flu.

A vibration in his coat pocket shook him out of his stupor and he regained his poise. "Jane, send me what you've found. This is good work. I'll talk to you all again tomorrow."

He left the room and walked along the corridor, allowing his phone to vibrate repeatedly. Finally, he entered an empty, dark, windowless room. He closed the door. He locked it.

Only then did he look at his phone.

Laura Lee.

Amperous sensed that he was being carried on the warm winds that preceded a torrential downpour. For so long, he'd been sure he was a blighted creature cursed to live a tortured existence. But finally, these weights were slipping away. Maybe there *was* a place for his kind to flourish, free of fury—and maybe they'd finally found it. It's funny, he mused, to have stumbled into a heaven he'd never believed existed.

He led his twelve children through the underbrush, teaching them how to stay hidden even while traveling at great speed. He closed his eyes while they moved, letting the current that flowed between them and him provide guidance.

"Stop," he commanded, and they froze as one, silent. Amperous chuckled to himself. How chaotic and loud they often were at home, hopping off the limestone cavern walls and colliding into each other, especially when Amperous and Linelin pled with them to settle into their nightly rest. He'd have to remember how orderly they could be when they cared. And of course they cared.

Their father was finally taking them to see *a human.*

"When will we see it, Father?" Finnarious cooed, his voice still bearing a trace of the lisp he'd had since he first learned to speak. "Where is it? Where is it?"

"It'll flee in fear if you keep talking out loud. Use our roots to communicate, all of you."

"Ugh. Just one more word, please, Father?"

"One more, but quiet."

Finnarious scrunched up his face as if he were lifting something that weighed a hundred tons. "It hurts when I have to use our roots. It feels like when Jampis squeezes my head and won't stop."

"I haven't done that for a long time, Father, I promise," Jampis protested.

"Define 'long time,' Jampis," Empata, their oldest sister, and nearly an adult, if not in age then at least in attitude, snapped.

"It's been at *least* a week, and I want to squeeze his head every hour. So it's really an impressive display of self-control, Father, just as you've commanded."

Amperous took joy in comparing the life his children had to the horrors he and Omathis had endured. His children were happy.

He reached out and touched Finnarious on the shoulder. He couldn't help it, but everything his scrappy, undersized youngest son ever did or said, even if naive or selfish, only endeared Finnarious to him more.

"Everything that makes you stronger hurts, Finnarious. Change your thinking about pain. It's not to be avoided, but embraced. It's a sign that you're on the right path."

Of course, Amp thought to himself, *not everything that hurts makes you stronger. Some pain can weigh too much, and if you have no one by your side to help bear it, it might crush you and leave your spirit broken and twisted; it might set you down the wrong path entirely.* But that was too complex to explain to his children and irrelevant to the life he and Omathis had created for all of the Croathus. His children would always have Amp to help handle their pain; they would never learn any of this firsthand, thankfully.

There's one now! Down, everyone! he commanded silently, using their roots, and they all complied.

Gathered at the peak of a stony cluster of boulders, they watched the canyon below, undetected. A rumbling steel machine, which Amperous instructed his children was known as a truck, sputtered along a barely cleared dirt road. Amperous held his breath and worked hard to shield his children from the fear that flitted through his mind.

He couldn't see the face of the person driving, but it didn't appear to be a *tourist* on *vacation* who was just hoping to have an *adventure* before returning to the city, Amperous observed, working hard to recall all of the words he'd learned when he was younger. That's the only kind of human they ever saw in their tropical jungle refuge, if they ever saw any at all. This one wore a uniform and rode along with a clipboard on the seat beside them, like the one Shai would use when recording her terrible thoughts for others to read.

Shai? No, she was dead. This couldn't be Shai, could it? Had she become *not dead* and tracked them to bring more sleeps? Was she coming to terminate them?

He cleared those thoughts from his mind. Humans couldn't become *not dead.*

Amperous had become so lost in his worries that he hadn't realized the change that had settled over his children. He was surprised to see that talons had grown from their fingers and toes, and their backs had arched in heated alarm. They growled quietly. All the joy at the prospect of *finally seeing a human* had been drained from them and replaced with what appeared to be pure aggression.

Can we tear it to pieces, Father? Amperous couldn't tell which of his children had asked this question, and then realized why.

They all had. As one, in unbroken unity. Even gentle Finnarious stared at the human below with furious anticipation.

"You must go. Back home. Now. Now!" he whispered urgently, shaking them from their rage. "Empata, take them back to the cavern!"

Amperous needed them to be far away from here. Not because he was afraid of what the human might do to them; there was only one of her and many of them. Even if she were Shai (which was not possible—Shai was dead, he assured himself), they were too powerful to be harmed by one human.

Not because he was afraid that his children would unleash their fury. As their father, he still had enough control over them to prevent that from happening.

No, it was for another reason. His intense fear at seeing the uniformed Shai-shaped human boiled over into a fury that pounded in his ears.

Amperous shouted out loud, "Fast! Fast! Away. Back home before…"

"Before what, Father?" they all chorused using their roots, but he wouldn't tell them.

"Run. Run!" he commanded. Feeling the pull that he soon wouldn't be able to resist.

"Why aren't you coming with us?" Empata worried.

"Go, I will explain at the cavern. Flee!" Finally, they obeyed and disappeared into the jungle.

They heard an anguished scream in the distance and stopped, but Empata insisted that the curious children ignore it, just as she knew her father would want.

Empata too was eager to turn back and find the source of the scream. But this was exactly what Amperous didn't want them to see. He would not allow their eyes to be defiled by seeing what their beloved, gentle father was doing to that uniformed human with the clipboard.

ICELYN

Eveshone has crashed through one room after another of this abandoned skyscraper. We are now deep inside of it and far from that flying beast.

What was that nightmare? It looked like a Croathus or an Anaghwin, but gone horribly wrong. Warped and twisted. This was not something created by a Brathius. Eveshone and I communicate through our roots just enough for me to know that she is terrified to think of what it could be.

I feel the same way.

Though distant, I can feel that the Anaghwin are traumatized from the attack. I also sense in them some relief, and I know that the creature has left us behind for now.

"Do you want to speak to them, Lovely?" Eveshone asks. I sense she is telling me that she thinks I should. I want to, but I can't. It is difficult to leave my people this way, but I fear that I must take advantage of the chaos. Otherwise, Omathis will imprison me again. This time he'd be more justified in keeping me safely locked away, too, with that soaring, deadly menace out there, hunting me, leaving behind scores of Anaghwin dead with every attack.

"Let's find Adorane, please." I answer. Eveshone is clearly disappointed in my decision.

"I can't risk being imprisoned again," I explain.

"Is it really a prison if it's to keep you safe?" she asks. It's as close as she gets to outright disagreeing with me. "It's more of a fortress than a jail. That beast was after *you*."

I think of Mountaintop. Safe places ultimately prove to be mirages. Omathis and Eveshone might think I'm secure here, but I am not. This flying nightmare will be back, perhaps with others. I've known for some time that I needed to leave the Drowned City. This attack has proven my instinct right.

"The Drowned City is our past, not our future. It has served its purpose, but it is no longer for us. We are built for the journey," I answer. "We are meant to move. That's how we stay alive. To stay in one place is to die in slow motion. Will you help me escape, Eveshone?"

Her face contorts as she considers my request. I'm forcing her to choose between me or Omathis.

"Yes, I will. But only because you ask."

The cruel irony is that her decision to help will only make Omathis more sure in his belief that Eveshone is impure and untrustworthy. Yet for me, this cements my conviction that she is the only one I can trust.

I expect to contend with some Anaghwin guards—and maybe even Omathis—as I approach where Adorane is being held. But the attack on the Drowned City has thrown everything into disarray, and he is alone.

Adorane's back is to us when we enter, and he's unaware of our presence. He's locked in a small brightly colored space behind a wall of plexiglass—like a child's nursery would look, if it were also a prison and a zoo. This was no doubt one of the enclosures Sean used when Omathis and Amperous were young. Adorane doesn't hear me approach, because the clear wall muffles sound.

Eveshone rushes toward the door, key in hand, ready to set him free. I still her with one motion. *Not yet.*

I stare at Adorane for a moment. This is a gift—to be able to look at him without him knowing. I don't have to be polite and look away, lest I send the wrong message. I can truly study him.

He looks older.

I suppose we both do. I don't look at myself often, though, so I forget. Every once in a while I catch a glimpse of myself in a puddle of water or the ocean's surface and am reminded that I'm not the young child who left Mountaintop years ago.

His eyes appear less eager, as if what they've seen has hurt them countless times in the past. His brow is crinkled, and I can tell he's worried. I'm struck by how rare this is. I've scarcely seen Adorane worried. He's always the one who knows what to do next. His mouth, before always on the verge of breaking into an easy smile—if not already forming one—is set straight and serious, as in stone. He's kneeling on the ground on his knees, and his face is tilted upward. There's something curious about the way he's posed; it's not natural, yet it seems deliberate.

Adorane lifts his arms slowly, palms facing up, and I realize with an embarrassed start what I've been witnessing. Adorane is praying.

I shouldn't be watching this. I've never seen him pray before. I'm reminded of the time we embraced and kissed on the beach, for some reason, and the memory overwhelms me.

I wave Eveshone on, allowing her to unlock the entryway. Her presence shakes Adorane from his concentrated prayers, and his face beams at the sight of her. I try not to be jealous, but it would be nice to have him look at me that way. Like he once did.

"Get up. Let's go," I say, more harshly than intended. Something curious keeps happening between myself and Adorane these days. When he's not around, my feelings for him are warm. I long for reconciliation, to be his best friend again. But when we're in the same room, anger tinges my every word, and I surprise myself at how poorly I act toward him.

Adorane doesn't seem to mind, though.

"Where is everyone?"

I wonder if he even knows about the flying creature. Probably not. He's been trapped in this soundproof cell with no access to anyone's thoughts or feelings.

I can tell Eveshone wants to tell him everything, but we have no time. I give her a quick silencing glance.

"Come with us. I'll explain when there's time."

13

THEN

Travis had always known that he was strange. He'd never been able to make friends; he couldn't understand how others were able to connect so easily. But here at Longrave, his inability to get in step with everyone else had consequences far beyond the loneliness he was used to. Step out of line, and he could get ambushed in the bathroom, or cornered behind the shooting range. All with the Colonel's blessing, too.

For the first time, he was making an effort to fit in. He swallowed every word that popped into his mind, because he realized that his instincts were distasteful to most other people. He had to learn how to be someone others wanted around. In his natural state, he had no idea how to do this, and all his attempts so far had borne no fruit.

But something about the way Travis took a punch caught Soren Kaye's attention, and not just because Soren was the one who threw it. Travis was a plebe who'd only been at Longrave for a couple of weeks and still didn't know the first thing about what it took to be a man, yet he'd stood and accepted the punishment without flinching.

Soren had been annoyed by Travis' stupid shaggy hair when he arrived, by his weak awkwardness, his refusal to look anyone in the eyes for too long, the sound of his voice, his precious beat-up guitar, his insistence that his mother was a genius. Everything about him. But now, he was strangely impressed. He wanted to help the freshman out.

Soren sat next to Travis in the mess. It was the first time anyone had, so Travis noticed, but warily. Why would someone like Soren approach Travis other than to abuse him?

"Listen. Longrave may seem confusing at first, but it's actually pretty easy to succeed here. You just have to leave behind who you were and become who they want you to be."

If only it were so easy, Travis thought. *Who I am won't be left behind. I've tried. That sucker always catches up.*

"Yeah, sure. Thanks." Travis tended to be stingy with his words now, because more often than not, he found himself saying the wrong ones.

"I'm going to do you a favor, okay? You really can't go around asking everyone questions here. But you can ask me. A few. You aren't exactly born for this life, I can tell, so I'll help you out."

"Got it. Will do," Travis responded, though he knew he never would. Soren was baiting him, he was sure.

Soren detected Travis' suspicion. He was tempted to write the kid off out of spite, but even he could see that the wariness was justified. After all, the purple and crimson bruising in the shape of Soren's knuckles hadn't even begun to fade from Travis' face yet.

"Like the dust-up with Colonel Hodges the other day. I know that Cadet Johnson was playing his trombone, so you probably thought you could play your guitar."

That's exactly what Travis had thought. The trombone was louder than an acoustic guitar.

"The guitar? That's the *you* that they want to erase. Snuffed out. Destroyed. The trombone? Hell, you want to get good at the trombone, they'll put you in the brass marching band and you can make us all proud on the Fourth of July. That's the *you* they want to see. You get the difference?"

Travis nodded. He did.

"And just to let you know, other examples of quiet endeavors that the *you* they want to see could do include reading your class assignments, studying the scripture, or writing a letter to your mother."

Tears welled unbidden in Travis' eyes. He controlled his breathing in hopes that they wouldn't start to fall.

Goddamn, what is up with this kid?

"What is it, Nilsing?"

Travis didn't hear the question. All of his concentration was focused on not breaking down.

"Nilsing, what is going on?

Travis wanted to disappear. "Nothing. Don't worry. I'm done eating."

"Nilsing, for whatever fool-headed reason, I'm trying to be your friend here. What I just said upset you, and I need to know why, because that's the only way we can figure out how to make sure you don't have this reaction in front of the others. Because let me tell you, if you start crying in front of everyone just because someone mentions your mom, they'll kill you. Right then and there, I promise. They'll pull out a gun and shoot you in the head."

They wouldn't, of course, but what Travis would face instead would make him wish they would.

"My mom is dead."

Soren was genuinely surprised by Travis' answer. He hadn't expected that.

"Christ, Nilsing, so is mine," he responded in a heartfelt voice. He knew how that felt. "I am definitely going to help you out here, okay? We'll start a Dead Moms Club. How's that sound? We'll find the Travis Nilsing that they want you to be."

Omathis rushed through the jungle. When Amperous' children had stumbled into Haven Underneath shaken and afraid, Omathis didn't wait for them to explain what had happened. He knew.

He sensed a dark malevolence seeping up from below as he climbed the steep stone walls toward the canyon floor. It had been a relief to live far from humans and not have to confront this violent streak that ran through Amperous. (To be honest, this taste for violence ran through himself and all the others that lived in Haven Underneath—even those who had never seen a human—as well, but in Amperous it was especially pronounced.)

He scanned the treetops for what he was sure he'd see: a human, hollowed out and hung high on display. He saw nothing, but he still felt an uncontainable sadness.

Omathis slowed as he turned a corner in the canyon.

Finally, he found his brother—and the carnage he'd feared.

Even though he'd been expecting this, he was shocked by the raw severity of the kill. The canyon floor, the battered truck, the dense foliage, and the rock walls were all splattered with blood. Omathis was embarrassed to feel a thrill at smelling that warm crimson again after a long hiatus. It felt like home—a home he hated to admit he'd ever lived in.

Amperous crouched beside the uniformed woman's remains, and his expression surprised Omathis. Omathis had expected to find his brother given over to bloodlust. Instead, Amperous appeared downtrodden. His shoulders were slumped forward, his eyes clouded over, his normally regal face slack.

"You look like you bear the weight of a thousand regrets, brother," Omathis observed quietly.

Amperous took a mournful glance at Omathis, then his sad eyes looked back over the dead human.

Amperous' disposition reminded Omathis of a painful memory. Omathis' youngest daughter had once accidentally stepped on her pet scorpion and crushed it. "I didn't mean to do this," Plainius had cried. "Do you think it knew that? It probably thought I wanted to kill it, and its last thoughts were confused and sad, laced through with betrayal."

Omathis had planned to scold his brother and remind him of their oath not to kill except when necessary for survival. He'd even prepared himself for a battle with Amperous, if need be, to subdue him and remind him that he couldn't do whatever he wished without consequence.

Yet Amperous appeared small. Omathis felt like consoling him. He placed a gentle hand, talons retracted, on Amperous' shoulder.

"I thought she was a threat. She reminded me of Shai," Amperous explained, more to himself than to Omathis. Through the blood and grisly remains, Omathis could see that the deceased woman did bear a resemblance to Shai. Omathis realized that he probably wouldn't have been able to resist slaughtering her either. Shai was a notable exception to any oath.

"Let's hide what's left and forget this happened." Omathis tried to coax Amperous out of his depression. "No need for such heartache."

Amperous shook his head and refused his brother's encouragement. Omathis now noticed the objects of his brother's fixation. Amperous held small photographs, themselves splattered with blood, and examined them with care, one after another, compulsively, over and over.

The dead woman, along with other humans.

A man. A teenaged girl. A young boy. A baby.

"I looked through her possessions, trying to figure out where she came from and if others would follow. I found these."

The humans appeared happy together. Omathis and Amperous had been convinced that humans were without even a speck of good. This small family, the camera catching them in casual moments of unforced affection, was evidence to the contrary.

The parents tossing a ball to the children.

Omathis and Amperous loved playing throw and catch with their growing families.

The family gathered around a richly frosted cake.

They had celebrated the anniversary of the birth of Amperous' oldest just yesterday.

All of them surrounding the infant, kissing its cheeks, holding it close.

Amp and Omathis had both just welcomed new additions to their families.

Omathis was confused. "Amperous, are you filled with regret because you have broken an oath to me, or because you have killed this human?" Amperous had only ever felt joy in the slaughter of man.

"There are opposite feelings fighting for a home within me. I want her dead. I want every human gone, as we were created to want. Yet, I want her children to catch another ball she throws, to taste another cake she bakes. I want her youngest to be able to cry and have her tears wiped away by her mother. No newly born living thing should be forced to grow older alone. I am glad I have slaughtered her, and yet I regret it too. I want her dead, but I want her not dead. I don't know which I want more."

Omathis sat beside his brother and looked through the photographs slowly, letting Amperous' sadness flow through him.

To fully know something, you must understand its opposite too.

They sat together, unspeaking, feeling the pull of contradictory impulses, until night fell. Finally, Amperous worried that their children might wonder where they were and worry that they were in danger. They buried the woman—along with the truck, the photographs, and any trace that she had ever visited this canyon—deep in the ground below.

The boys' boots pounded the ground aggressively. They weren't just running, but beating up Mother Earth herself, pummeling her with their unforgiving black heels, teaching her a lesson she'd never forget. They sang together—shouted, really—a cadence that was threat and celebration and inspiration all in one.

Soren and Travis took the first positions, as they always did these days. *The examples to which all others should aspire.* That's how Colonel Hodges introduced them now.

Load another magazine
In my trusty M-16
'Cuz all I ever wanna see!
Is bodies, bleeding bodies!

Travis lived a syncopated life now. Everything fit into a rhythmic structure that wouldn't accommodate even the slightest deviation.

Up at four-forty in the morning, yes yes.
Into the kitchen to prep the breakfast by 5:12a.m., yes yes.
Finished eating and cleaned up by 6:16, yes yes.
Commence running at precisely 6:46, yes yes.

Throw another hand grenade!
Delightin' in the mess I made.
Cuz all I ever wanna see,
Is bodies, broken bodies.

His troop moved as one for miles, keeping time together: right, left, right, left. One speed, one mission, one goal.

They sweated together, suffered together, were broken together, mended together, and grew stronger together. Running, showers, then inspections, classes, lunch, obstacle course, chapel, labs, athletics, study hall, dinner. Then recalled to barracks, another study hall, taps, sleep.

Stab em with the bayonet!
Did he squirm? You ain't done yet!
Cuz all I ever wanna see,
Is bodies, cut-up bodies.

Each day, Travis was comforted by predictable pain. His lungs would feel like they were about to burst, his muscles would ache, his pride would be decimated, and his worth questioned. But it was all according to a plan. This was better, he now saw, than the free-form chaos he'd lived before, on the outside. A regimented life allowed him to cut his darkness into smaller, manageable portions, so he could lock them away and move on.

Call down flames and fires from hell.
On ev'ry foe we need to kill!
Cuz all I ever wanna see,
Is bodies, burnin' bodies!

Travis was becoming a man molded according to design, and everyone, even Sean, would see that Longrave Military Academy was exactly what he had needed.

ICELYN

My initial plan was to climb down the outside of the skyscraper to the water. There is a small armada of boats in the Drowned City, and we can take one. However, with one glimpse I see swarms of Anaghwin scouring the tall structures that make up the Drowned City. They're looking for me. We won't be able to escape this way.

I can feel Omathis on the edge of my roots, trying to locate me. I keep him from connecting. He knows I'm still in the Drowned City, but nothing more. I try not to focus too much on the fear I can feel in him. He's suffering from an abandoned desperation that I must ignore—otherwise, I'll rush to his side.

"Perhaps he could be convinced to come with us, Lovely," Eveshone whispers as we retreat further into the skeletal guts of this once-grand building. She can sense Omathis' pain too.

I don't respond. We both know that won't work. Also, I'm already leaving my children; I can't take Omathis from them, too.

"How are we going to escape all of them?" Adorane asks. It's a fair question, but still it annoys me, because I don't have an answer.

A rough outline of a new plan starts to form. I hate that there's not enough time to think it through; to be honest, it seems like it might be a terrible idea. But it's also the only one that might work.

"Eveshone, let's visit the ArSea building."

"But Icelyn, are you sure?" She clearly has concerns, as do I.

I nod yes even so.

Icelyn scoops Adorane and me up into her arms. I'm used to being carried by the stronger Anaghwin when need dictates, but I can tell that Adorane feels uncomfortable. Perhaps one day he'll be secure enough in his masculinity to enjoy being cradled like a baby. It's actually quite nice.

She bolts toward the east side of the skyscraper and stops when we see the ArSea building ahead. Through the crumbling and rusted beams we watch as a group of Anaghwin scamper by, searching for me.

She crouches, holding us, and waits until they've cleared. Then she springs off in a ferociously fast sprint. I can barely breathe, we're moving so fast. She runs straight to the edge of the building and leaps without slowing. We shoot out of the skyscraper and soar straight toward the ArSea building, which is at least twenty yards away. Despite the rush needed to clear the space between the two buildings, Eveshone sets down gently.

We've landed safely, but I feel anything but safe.

The building groans and creaks with the ocean's waves. Screams echo through the darkened spaces. This area is normally lit with torches, but they have been extinguished by the wind that whips through the ancient corridors. I have long commanded that the ArSea building be kept welcoming and warm—the very best we have to offer in the Drowned City. But right now, it's dreary and scary. More howls rise from the darkness. I hope it's just the wind, but I know better.

"Why would we escape to this place?" Adorane wonders out loud. I catch Eveshone nodding in agreement, but she stops as soon as I notice.

"We're going to free the adopted Anaghwin." I walk into the darkness.

"No, Lovely!" She doesn't follow me.

"We have to distract Omathis."

"What are adopted Anaghwin?" Adorane calls urgently. "What does that mean?"

A screech emerges from the hallway before me. "Help me find the keys."

My eyes have adjusted to the darkness. I can make out the main corridor. I stride toward the terrible noises and hope that Eveshone and Adorane follow. To my relief, after a little hesitation, they do. It's probably to protect me rather than because they support my foolish plan, but I appreciate it.

I run because I am afraid that if I slow, my fear will get the better of me. Best to get this over with quickly. Eveshone and Adorane catch up with me.

"Once you set them free, what next?" Eveshone asks, worried.

I don't want to share the second part of my plan. It's worse than the first.

"As soon as we open it, we rush further into the darkness. I'm sure the adopted Anaghwin will head toward the light and freedom."

"Yes, but once they're outside, then we'll have *two* groups pursuing us: Omathis and the Anaghwin, and the Croathus you've freed."

"Wait, you're freeing *Croathus?*" Adorane stammers. "There are Croathus here?"

"Adopted Anaghwin," I correct him, though I'm not sure why. The distinction makes no difference to anyone but me. "Eveshone, we won't be going outside."

We've arrived in the area where Anaghwin guards would normally be posted. The growls of the Croathus are deafening. I search the tables and shelves for a key, but it's difficult to see in the meager light.

"I don't understand," Eveshone answers.

"We'll take the Shaft to escape."

I feel the terror this creates in her. I don't wait for a discussion. I find the key, jam it into a lock, and turn. It frees a crank that I begin to turn. Metal clanking echoes loudly through the darkness.

"The Spine of Darkness? Are you sure, Lovely?" Eveshone starts.

"It's just a Shaft, Eveshone, even though the Anaghwin have given it an ominous name."

"A Spine of Darkness doesn't sound like somewhere I want to go, Ice," Ad argues. I tune him out and continue straining to turn the weighty crank.

"Perhaps we should consider alternatives." Eveshone advises.

"She's being polite because she adores you, Icelyn, but what she means is that this is a awful plan," Adorane adds.

I keep opening the Adopted Anaghwin gate. It's not an easy task. My heart races, and beads of sweat form on my brow and in the space between my lips and nose. I catch Adorane looking at my arms. For the first time since he's visited, I think he's noticing that I'm a lot stronger than I was before. He might even confuse me for a Veritas if he didn't know any better. Despite everything that's happening, I find his surprise funny.

His brief stupor wears off, and he reaches to stop me.

"Adorane. I'm telling you. If you want to leave this place, with me, this is the only way," I argue.

He considers what I've said. Then he steps forward and helps me with the metal crank.

As the steel gate begins to groan, the captive Croathus' growls grow to a roar. As soon as it opens a sliver, they pour out in a torrent. Eveshone instinctively covers Adorane and me, but these creatures are so desperate for freedom that they rush toward the distant sunlight without noticing us.

I feel regret. I thought once these Croathus experienced firsthand the love that bound all of the Anaghwin to me, they would join our community. Instead, all this time, they were desperate to leave.

14

ICELYN

Seeing the Croathus escape to freedom, I think again about a secret I harbor.

I may leave the Drowned City with Adorane, and I may say it's to have a child in order to ensure humanity survives. But that will not be completely true. I may be leaving with Adorane in order to visit Apex. But I have another purpose for returning to the mainland, and—though I cannot tell him this—I use him as an excuse to make the journey.

I'm not proud of this, but my pride or shame don't matter if something needs to be done. I think back to that awful day when Amperous and his Croathus hordes followed us into Mountaintop. They were intent on slaughtering us.

Yet I made a connection with them—a Soothing.

I could feel it. They could too.

I can turn them, I realized. I could wipe away their murderous instincts. I could feel the good in them, and I feel it still. They are not lost. I can win them back to me. They can become as safe and connected as the Anaghwin. I know it's possible, although I've tried without success to achieve this here in the Drowned City with the Croathus we've plucked from the mainland. I've met with only failure, as the wound on my hand proves.

I need to journey to the mainland to do it.

I need to leave the Drowned City. I don't know where I must go or what I should do, but I know it's possible. And now Adorane is offering a way out.

If I do this, despite Omathis' protest, I would be doing it for him, Eveshone, and all of the Anaghwin. We either unify with the Croathus or we cease to exist. This is as clear to me as water is wet, even if none of them will admit it.

Adorane believes I'm leaving the Drowned City to visit a legendary settlement to ensure the survival of the human race by having a child. I may do that; I may not. I still haven't settled the question in my head, though I'm not about to tell him that.

Even if I do, I know now that it's not the main reason I'm leaving. I see it now, as clearly as I watch the silhouettes of the stampeding Croathus escape into the sunlight. I'm escaping the loving prison Omathis has created around me to find a way to turn them toward me. Not only them, either. All of the Croathus. Every single one of them.

I was close. I was on the verge, up in Mountaintop. I could feel their hearts. They could feel mine. I had almost turned them before Adorane and Torrain unleashed their hellish poison and began to kill them. I know it's possible.

Not by imprisonment; I know now that that was the wrong tactic. But it doesn't make the goal any less right.

There is no Anaghwin without Croathus. We only survive if we unite.

I've never been in the Shaft before. Neither has Eveshone.

We stand with Adorane before a pile of refuse that stretches stories above us. We've reached a cavernous room in the ArSea building. We can see the edges of the many floors overhead. The pile of rubble, bound together with kelp, is made up of anything the Anaghwin could find to make it an impenetrable barricade.

I'm trying to dissemble it so we can enter the Shaft.

"Please, Eveshone, help me."

I've only moved a few stones and large chunks of coral and I'm already tired. I can't do this on my own.

"They sealed this off for a reason, Lovely."

"Yes," I answer, though I continue my work. I strain against a heavy object—a large rectangle made of some unnatural material that the Apriori must have manufactured. It's neither glass nor metal, but somehow resembles both. I can't budge it, especially with my injured hand. Instead, I grab a little bit of the rubble and toss it, hoping the others will help.

"Why did they seal off the Shaft, Icelyn?" Adorane asks.

"Just help me, will you? Listen. There is no other option. We can't go outside. Omathis will capture us before we've even reached the water." *Or the Croathus would*, I think. The sounds filtering in from outside prove that releasing them has created the distraction I was hoping for, but it's also unleashed another group of hunters who could intercept Adorane and me. Or worse, slaughter us. Even though they still have their inborn fondness for the Brathius, the deep cuts on my hand show that they've managed to overcome it to some degree. Plus, Adorane is only human. They'd welcome the chance to tear him apart.

Adorane and I manage to lift the heavy rectangle. Still, he and I could work on this barricade for a week and be nowhere near the portal to the Shaft.

"Eveshone, please."

"Adorane, as you know, the world Down Below is no longer suited for your kind." Eveshone stalls, appealing to Adorane instead. "The creatures that live in the Shaft are evidence of this."

"There are creatures that live in the Shaft?" Adorane stops lifting.

"Yes. Like nothing that existed when humans were dominant. They came from the ocean and combined with something humans left behind. Or perhaps they changed due to the void left by humanity's disappearance. Nobody knows," Eveshone explained.

"What are they like?"

"They're not as strong as you, Eveshone. That's all that matters," I say, to calm the fear I sense in her and Adorane. "And they aren't as strong as the rest of the Anaghwin, or as dangerous as the Croathus, out there. That's why the Shaft is our only way out of the Drowned City."

"Not as strong as me, but still lethal to you," Eveshone answers grimly. "And there are many of them. And I'm the only me." Still, she seems resigned to my logic. She rolls aside two massive concrete pillars, a feat Adorane and I combined couldn't accomplish in hours.

Eveshone used to believe I was immortal, but now she fears I am not. I would like to assure her that I cannot die, but it would be a lie. She stills considers me her God, her creator, but I can't help but feel like something has been lost.

She clears a path through the pile of refuse. Adorane and I do our best to lift a large table.

"Can you tell me what we're about to face, Icelyn?"

"I don't really know. I've never seen them. A long time ago, creatures would emerge from the shafts in the buildings."

"What are shafts?"

"Didn't you ever learn about elevators?"

He seems offended that I ask. "Of course I did. It was a real difficult lesson, but I managed to follow along." I grin at his sarcasm. None of the Anaghwin know how to be anything but straightforward; I've missed this.

"Well, okay then. This is the entrance to an elevator shaft."

"What would these creatures do?"

"I guess more than anything they were pests."

Adorane nods his head toward the barricade we're working to clear. "Quite a lot of work to keep pests away."

"The creatures would attack the Anaghwin. They might leave a deep gash, or a slash, or remove an arm or a leg, but—"

"God, Icelyn!"

"I don't think they ever killed anyone, though. It was more annoying than anything."

"Sure, an amputated leg. What a way to start the morning. A real bugaboo."

I laugh because this reminds me of the Ad I used to know. Plus, I'm scared, so it feels good to laugh. "I mean, with the Anaghwin's ability to rapidly heal, it's not the worst thing in the world."

"An ability we do not share, Icelyn."

Eveshone lifts and tosses a giant bag of sand. It crashes and lands with such fury that I guess it weighs about five hundred pounds. The sound reverberates through the building.

"What's a bugaboo?" Eveshone asks.

"Just a funny word," I answer, breathing hard as I clear away a patch of small rocks.

"I don't think there's anything funny about *an amputated leg*, Dear One," she observes, deathly serious.

I don't answer.

We're staring at what she's revealed. The portal. Someone has scrawled *NE INTRAVERITIS* across the steel surface in multiple places. I remember my Latin lessons well enough to know that means *DO NOT ENTER.*

Along the edges of the two doors, which meet in the middle, something has carved jagged scratch marks.

"What *pests* those creatures must be to be able to dig into pure steel like that," Adorane observes. The doors themselves appear buckled from the inside, bashed and battered by a force strong and angry.

"You're sure you want to open this, Lovely?" Eveshone asks.

I nod, but slowly.

Eveshone slices through the leathery kelp. They seem to have wrapped the door with almost a hundred layers.

"Wow, this is thick," Adorane observes. I can hear what he's really saying. Maybe this is one last warning that we shouldn't be removing it? But one glance down the long corridor and outside makes it clear that there is no other way. Anaghwin and Croathus swarm the Drowned City, their screams echoing throughout the chamber.

I pull back the kelp to create an opening large enough to step through. "Here, help me," I instruct Adorane. He does. With Eveshone's help, we've cleared enough so there is space to enter.

We wait outside the shaft. It smells terrible, an odor so strong that it affects not just my nose, but my eyes and skin too. "Like a mixture of Sulphur, rotting carcasses, and…" Adorane trails off, sniffing like a scent connoisseur, "something sharp and almost citrus-y. Like a lemon."

He's joking. Neither of us has ever tasted a lemon. We've only read about them in books when we were young. They had always seemed so delicious that we nurtured a joint dream to someday try one. It's a weird memory to evoke in me now, as we stand on the precipice of something so terrifying.

Groans and a skittering series of clicks emerge from the darkness. The clicks are obvious. The groans are so subtle that I wonder if I'm imagining them.

I should be scared—and I am, of course. But the truth is that I've always been fascinated by the Shaft and have long desired to see it firsthand. With Omathis' tendency to protect me to the point of imprisonment, I never thought I'd be allowed this chance.

The Shaft is in the very center of the building, a dark spine that runs from bottom to top. It used to house elevators—boxes that could lift and drop the Apriori between levels through some magic they'd devised. All this just to avoid walking on stairs, which is not difficult at all. Sometimes, it seems to me, the Apriori wasted their miracles.

Now the Shaft was home to frightening creatures that arose from the oceans to torment the Anaghwin. At one point, when they'd told me of the Shaft, I advised that we take on the threat directly and clear it out. Why seal it up and let the darkness fester? I did not understand how anyone could be content to live with this core of darkness so close. Yet they always seemed comfortable with it. As good as they are—and Eveshone and Omathis are among the best—they all seem resigned to, or even to embrace, the fact that they have a dark streak slashing through their existence. That one vein in their circulatory system contains an evil stream of blood, and there is no use pretending otherwise. This is their Fury. They all believe this. Though I am never willing to admit it about them, they've told me often.

"Why do you wish with such fervor that we clear it out?" Eveshone had asked me about the Shaft in the past. "Is it because you are all good and have no dark side? Does this darkness at the center of the building crash up against your sense of who you are, against what you think the world should look like?"

It's incredible that Eveshone still claims I am all good. She seems to have a blind spot for all my faults. Yet she also has a point. I see my dark sides as temporary. I have my shadows, but they only exist until the sun moves and makes everything bright. For them, their dark side is part of them, just as much as their goodness. It's a piece of who they are, and it's not going away. They accepted it a long time ago. It's simply how they were created.

Eveshone runs back and grabs a torch from one of the cells where the Croathus were held. She hands it to Adorane to hold. This makes sense; she needs both arms to defend against the creatures within the Shaft, and I'd probably drop it out of clumsiness.

"It's time," I say, and Eveshone leans down in front of us. We crawl onto her back. She enters the shaft.

The groans and creaking of the buildings swaying are a constant backdrop in the Drowned City, because the waters below push and pull at their foundations. Here in the Shaft, though, the sounds are magnified by the tight spaces and direct access to the ocean below.

The torch illuminates the narrow Shaft, and it's not as scary as I imagined. Eveshone can reach from one side to another without even stretching. Adorane can almost, too, but only if he strains. The black walls are encrusted with centuries of salt and barnacles, which make the otherwise slippery surfaces easy for Eveshone to grip and climb.

We start a careful, methodical descent.

"How far above the ocean would you say we are?" I whisper, because speaking out loud seems like a bad idea.

"Thirty floors. Maybe forty," Adorane answers. Eveshone stays quiet. She glances at us, a subtle scolding for the noise we are making. I don't understand why she's so cautious. The barnacles aren't going to attack.

She stops lowering us down the Shaft and I can hear her in our roots.

Look, Lovely. We are not alone.

Hanging from a mass of barnacles, a silky rope holds a bulging sack. As my eyes adjust, I see that the sack is made of whitish, semi-translucent material, and also what it holds. A large fish—no, a shark. Not the kind that had been strong enough to consume a Croathus when I first visited the Drowned City. But definitely one that could swallow me in one bite.

Adorane stares at the sack and then me. If he were comfortable speaking, I'm sure he'd say that it's some pest that could catch a shark of this size, kill it, and hang it thirty stories above the ocean, seemingly just for show.

Once I've seen one, I notice that there are many natural ropes and sacks all around us. Some hold sharks, and others many of the sea mammals that I've come to love while living in the Drowned City. Sea Lions. Dolphins. All look like they've had the life sucked out of them—withered, gray, and collapsed.

Some are only a collection of bones with ragged bits of skin still attached.

It's a nightmare.

My perception flickers as I stare at the walls around us. In the warm torchlight I can now see that what looked like slick black walls spotted with salt crystals and barnacles is actually a cluster of hard-shelled creatures, huddled together thick on the walls, their exoskeletons mottled to blend into their surroundings. I blink a few times, because their camouflage is so effective that they seem to disappear each time I look at them.

My heart swells with fear. They're all around us. While smaller than Eveshone, they are still large—somewhere between my and Adorane's size. Every end of them appears to be sharpened and lethal. They have spikes on their backs (though to be honest, I can barely tell which side of them is the back and which is the front) that could easily run through a person and leave her skewered and dead. They have multiple long legs, each with two jagged joints and a sharpened claw at the end.

What are they? I remember my unit on marine life with Belubus. He would be fascinated by these monsters. At the base of it, they appear to be crabs of some sort, or hard-shelled spiders. Yet at the center of their front, where there normally would be extended crabby eyes, there is a bulge that extends upward. I fear this is to accommodate a larger brain. It resembles the head of an octopus, clad with armor. How clever are these beasts?

Are they sleeping? I ask Eveshone using our roots to maintain silence.

I hope so, she answers.

Adorane senses that we are communicating. "What's going on?" He whispers, and I cover his mouth to keep him from making another sound. I take the torch from his hand and point the light toward the huddling masses of creatures which surround us. I watch as his eyes widen and his breath quickens. He sees them now.

Eveshone is doing a masterful job of using the gaps between the creatures to continue climbing down. It's slow, tedious, and nerve-wracking. We hold our breath watching her, knowing now that even the slightest wrong placement of her hands or feet could awaken a mob. Sometimes the creatures titter and click. Are they snoring? It's hard to tell what is going on. At one point we have to freeze for a good ten minutes, because a loud quivering moaning tone arises from a group of the spider-crabs.

We've made progress. I would guess we're about halfway to the bottom. While it's good to be closer to the end, we're also deeper into the center of all the monsters. They are above, below, and beside us, as far as the torchlight can reach.

Perhaps we should just fall and dive into the water, I suggest, eager for this slow-motion descent to end.

We have no idea what waits at the bottom, Eveshone observes. *Falling into that darkness could be suicide.*

I can tell from Adorane's crinkled up features and rapid blinking that he resents our ability to communicate in silence. It must be difficult, I imagine, to be the only one who cannot. I give his arm a squeeze to reassure him. There's more than one way to talk without speaking.

The clicking rises in frequency and then slows. Louder, then quiet. It disturbs me. I can tell that Adorane is tuned into it, too.

They aren't snoring. Snoring is rhythmic and slow. It happens without purpose, involuntarily. I concentrate and hear that the sounds have a drive to them. Different creatures make different sounds—like one is calling and others are responding.

Adorane puts it together first. I can tell by the panic in his eyes. And then I realize: They're counting down. A leader is holding them all at bay. No need to attack until we are in a position where we cannot escape.

It's too late to do anything with the knowledge.

15

ICELYN

The spider-crabs pulse on the wall. Their shells shift from the black and whites they used for camouflage to a pattern of bright oranges and greens. No need to disguise themselves anymore. The attack is imminent.

"Eveshone." It's all I can manage to say.

"I know, Dear One," she responds.

Adorane swings the torch, as if that could make a difference. The creatures knit themselves together, their legs interlocking, until they form a spherical net out of their bodies—above, below, and all around us. The joined spider-crabs move around us, faster, until they are a blur, and seeing any single one of them is difficult. Watching their movements has a mesmerizing effect on me. My body is frozen in fear.

The clacking noise becomes a roar.

I'm detached enough to observe that it's almost like we are being attacked by one creature, not thousands—a giant, spinning, pulsating sphere of spikes and claws, closing in on us. I realize suddenly that together like this, they will kill all three of us.

They slow their spinning until I can see individual creatures again. I watch as a bulge rises out from all of the bodies in unison and a fleshy soft part is exposed. These must be part of their faces—normally protected, but now eager to get a good look at us. Each has dark craters that appear to be eyes. Adorane throws the torch and it sizzles as it hits one of their faces. The spider-crab screeches in pain and then fury, and the rest join in the howling. One of the creature snatches the torch, and now its light has joined the sphere. They spin quickly again, and the torch forms circles of light in the darkness.

"You made them angry, Ad," I mumble. He doesn't answer, but he looks triumphant that at least he's hurt one of them.

Eveshone has found a ledge where we now huddle together. "Stand here, you two," she requests, her voice solemn. We obey.

"Crouch down."

We obey.

She contorts her body until she's covered the two of us like a shield. She squeezes us tight with her arms until she's the only one exposed.

They swarm.

The torch still flies through the air, passing from one spider-crab to another, so I can see them in flashes. They slash into Eveshone's back, and I can feel the strength of the impact as they cut into her.

"No, Eveshone!" I can't see how she can survive this onslaught. One creature after another digs into her.

"I will protect you, Dear One," Eveshone replies in an even tone, though I can tell she is having difficulty catching a breath.

She doesn't battle them, because to swing or kick would take away from the protection she's providing to me and Adorane. I can't handle this. Even if we survive, I don't want it to be at her expense.

"Eveshone. I forbid this!" I shout. The crabs clamp down into her with clattering mandibles and jab her with sharpened spikes. "Let's plunge. I'd rather die in the darkness below than live while you suffer like this."

Adorane sees the wisdom in my desire, and he and I both grab hold of Eveshone. She's weak, so she offers little resistance. We both work to shove her toward the edge.

We fall.

We're plummeting, and I'm not scared. I've been practicing diving from high places anyway, so I know that as long as there's water below, I should be able to enter it without hurting myself. Mostly I'm relieved to be leaving the spider-crabs behind. I can still see them, joined together in a furious orb, far above me, passing the torch between them, illuminating bits of them at a time.

They moan in unison as they realize we've left them behind. They break apart and scamper down the walls in unison. Fortunately, even though they're quick, gravity is pulling on us faster.

I grab hold of Adorane's hand while I turn my body into a proper diving position. He seems to get the idea and attempts to do the same. Eveshone is smeared with blood from head to toe and struggling to keep her eyes open. I hope the crashing whitewater can start to heal her wounds when we enter it. I can hear it growing louder below. The air is cooling too, like it does when you near the ocean's surface.

I close my eyes and look forward to plunging below the surface.

But the splash never comes. Instead, we're grabbed in the air and bounce up and down, suspended. The impact was as gentle as could be, but I feel no relief. We're stuck.

In the light of the approaching torch, which brings with it a horde of descending spider-crabs, I can make out what's happened. We're caught in a web. Translucent, sticky, shimmering.

Adorane struggles against it, but all that manages to do is tangle us further.

"Wait, wait, stop moving!" I beg him. He calms himself down and looks to me for our next move.

"Eveshone, can you cut through this with your talons?" I ask, scrambling to think of what we can do.

"Dear…One…I…" She can barely put her words together, and feebly lifts an arm before it drops back by her side. I reach toward her and grab her arm. Using it like a tool, not part of my beloved Eveshone, I hack at the wet silken restraints that bind us. It works a little. I sever one of the supports that connects us to the wall and we fall about ten feet before we're caught again. I swing with her arm again and cut another connecting thread. We fall, but before long we're bound again.

The spider-crabs continue their fearsome pursuit. Some of them are heading straight toward us, rappelling down the wall using their own single threads of webbing.

"We have to get out of this," Adorane shouts and begins biting at the web. I continue to hack away with Eveshone's sharpened talons. We slice through another few layers of our gluey prison, but it's not enough. I don't even want to look up to see how close they are. I can smell them, the scent of briny death and rotted flesh. I can feel the pressure change in the air. They are right above us.

Adorane pulls at the debris stuck in the webbing—chunks of coral, seashells, bones from unfortunate sea creatures who weren't able to escape the fate we now face—and tosses it at the descending horde.

Something loud hits the wall next to us, and there's a bright flash of fire. Adorane has hit the torch with one of his desperate tosses and shaken it loose from the spider-crabs. It has come to a rest on a small ledge not far from us. I'm nearest to the ledge, so I reach for it, but we're stuck fast.

Adorane busies himself with chomping on the silken strands. I have to admire his tenacity. It probably tastes awful. He bites through it and I grab the other side of the thread he's cut with his teeth. I have an idea. I swing the severed line of web toward the torch but just miss it.

"Let me try," Adorane cries, understanding what I'm trying to do. While web whipping was never a skill either of us practiced growing up in Mountaintop, I suspect he would be better than I am.

He grabs the base of the silky thread and flicks it toward the torch. He misses the first time but quickly recalibrates.

The spider-crabs have now almost reached us, thick and dark as a plague.

On his next attempt, the tacky end fastens to the handle of the torch, and he snaps it back and catches it in his hand.

In a flash, he holds the torch to the silken web. It sizzles as the flame catches. The blaze weakens the hold of the web, and we fall another level while the fire spreads above us. The spider-crabs find themselves engulfed in the growing fireball. They retreat and scatter to avoid the heat.

Adorane swings the torch again, and more levels are engulfed in the flame. I can feel parts of my skin burning, but I don't cry out. This fire might save our life.

Finally, like a miracle, we plunge into the bracing waters. When I come back to the surface and look up at the fiery inferno that Adorane's torch has created, I know that we have to hurry. The spider-crabs are spooked by the flames, but it's only a matter of time before they continue hunting us.

Eveshone pulls herself out of the water and slashes through another kelp barrier meant to keep these creatures sealed up in the Shaft. The splash into the salty waters seems to have knocked her back into the world of the living. Her eyes are clear, and she's gained strength. Still, she's suffered so many slashes and cuts that it's hard to look at her.

"On the other side of this barrier is a corridor leading to where we keep the boats," I explain to Adorane. We both offer our meager help pulling at the kelp wall. The fire above us is dying down, and I hear the clattering approach of the monsters.

Eveshone cuts through and blessed sunlight spills in. We squeeze through the kelp barrier just as the first spider-crabs drop through the smoke above. Adorane and I rush ahead, and Eveshone pulls at an ancient metal beam in the middle of the corridor. She breaks it free and tosses it at the mob of hard-shelled nightmares. It hits the first row of them, shattering their armor and leaving them crumpled and dead. Still, she only buys us a few seconds. The rest of the horde continue their hunt.

She runs after us but stops and pulls at another metal beam. This time she tosses it low and hard, spinning it so that it can do the most damage. She hits an area filled with the spiny monsters, and the metal tears them apart.

The building groans and lists.

Eveshone grabs another metal beam.

"I think those keep this building standing!" I shout.

"What's it matter if the building is standing if we're dead?" Adorane asks.

Eveshone hurtles the beam at an angle, and it crashes into a wide swath of the pursuing creatures.

We continue repeating this pattern. We run, the crabs get too close, Eveshone pulls metal from the building and uses it to kill and delay, and then we run again. Finally, we're only a hundred yards from the outside, and I can see the ocean and the boats and the sky.

The building creaks loudly and the walls bend and crack. The entire structure is on the verge of collapse. The crabs are a few seconds behind, so Eveshone again peels away a supporting beam and uses it to decimate those closest to us. Crashes threaten to burst my ears. Adorane shoves me to my right just as a chunk of cement falls where I had been.

I don't think we're going to make it out. But we run as fast as we can for the opening. Eveshone forgets about the crabs and scoops us up just in time to emerge from the building as it collapses into a pillar of dust and groaning metal.

We dive into the ocean, and I look back as I surface. A few spider-crabs managed to escape, but most are caught in the destruction, crushed by a hundred floors of ancient Apriori workmanship.

"Come on, Icelyn. We don't have time!" Adorane shouts, and I swim toward the boat he and Eveshone have pulled themselves into. We row as hard as we can as the ArSea building disappears into the ocean behind us. I marvel at the sight. It was so grand; now it's a mass of bubbles and whitewater.

"This is why you don't tolerate having a dark spine running through you," I murmur. "Eventually, it'll destroy you."

"I suppose," Eveshone replies. "Though you could say that if we'd cleared the Spine of Darkness out years ago, we wouldn't have been able to escape. We needed a shadowy spine for you to get away."

She's not wrong.

THEN

Sean Brathius was a survivor.

He'd suffered the worst possible outcome in a project of great importance. Yet he was about to lead a new initiative funded by a nearly limitless budget.

Everyone acts as if failing is the worst thing a person can do, but he knew that as long as you are excellent at something, people will keep giving you more chances. Sean Brathius' previous endeavor had ended in tragedies so great that they had to be covered up and buried deep, but he was excellent at scientific pursuits, and so his services were always in demand.

The wondrous things he *could* provide still outweighed the horrors he *had* provided.

Sean and the team arrived at the peak of the stony mountain via helicopter.

"I told you to wear a parka," he scolded the most important man in the party, Senator Charles London. "Armani doesn't matter much when it's windy and cold." The Senator's custom-tailored suit was doing very little to keep him warm, and he looked ridiculous in these rugged surroundings.

Sean grabbed a pile of puffy blue coats from beneath a seat as they exited the helicopter and distributed them to his guests—high-level government officials, wealthy investors, futurists, and thought leaders. "Hey, you're all going to be wearing Walmart for the first time. I told you this would be a momentous day."

Sean enjoyed tweaking his Very Important Guests, especially the futurists and thought leaders. Anybody who would bestow themselves with these titles was better ignored. True thought leaders were too busy creating a new future to bother calling themselves anything so pretentious.

"I promise it's not so cold in the summer. Really, it's nice up here. Secluded." He led them up a steep, slippery trail, where each step caused a mini avalanche of stones beneath their feet. A futurist lost his footing and nearly slid back to the helicopter's landing site.

"Yeah, you have to be careful," Sean warned, too late. "And make sure to take it slow, rest if you need to, and breathe deeply. I don't want any of you developing acute mountain sickness. I couldn't handle the guilt."

They came upon the compound, and the group was clearly surprised by all the activity. Teams of workers were busy constructing the foundations of two large structures.

Sean cut off any questions before they could be asked. "As you can see, that is the pumping facility. The water will be coming up from the valley below, in a design that doesn't require any electricity." He knew that would impress them. Futurists loved the idea of using no electricity.

"I had no idea we were so far along already," Senator London commented, and it sounded more like an accusation than an observation.

"Why wait when you're on the verge of a breakthrough?" Before anyone could dig into the details of how everything could have happened so fast, Sean directed their attention to a tower being built on the west side of the pump.

"And that will be where the research takes place. As you know, we're close—we only have to refine our methods to make them scalable to a larger population."

However, what Sean was promising was never going to be scalable to a larger population, and he knew it. Sure, he'd figured out a small-scale miracle. He could turn water into *more water*. Sean had a knack for figuring out the way the very elements of the world worked. He could see processes and combinations and patterns that no one else could. Beyond that, he could envision processes and combinations and patterns that didn't exist yet, but *could* (and in his opinion, should).

In the classified hearings that followed his C.R.O.A.T.H.U.S. debacle, one of the main arguments used in his defense was that *if he hadn't done this, someone else would have*. Technology marches on. Everything that can be discovered will be discovered. To blame the person who happens to be the one who stumbled upon it isn't fair.

Sean played along, but he knew it was a lie. Certain people have specific insights; they are special, made up of a different material. He was one of them. Omathis and Amperous existed only because Sean existed. No one else could have figured out how to synthesize their perfection.

The same was true about Sean's latest project, the Water Bringer. Through a complicated energy-thirsty procedure, he had devised a way to take a small amount of water and, using the air around it along with other basic elements, double it. *The water basically reproduces, like yeast.*

On the rapidly drying West Coast, this miracle had caused even Sean's biggest detractors to quickly forgive the C.R.O.A.T.H.U.S. mess. The fact that he'd only been able to demonstrate this ability with microscopic amounts of water so far was immaterial; Sean sold hopes, not results.

"I'll be living in this tower, too, so I can oversee the research," he explained, as they gazed at the skeleton of what would become a workspace and living quarters.

They looked out onto the horizon, but could see only clouds and the fog that had rolled in from the faraway ocean.

"We're above ten thousand feet here, so any malfunctions would be limited to this remote mountain." The Water Bringing process was potentially volatile and couldn't be conducted near a population center.

All that was beside the point, though, because as Sean ushered the satisfied party back to the waiting helicopter, he knew he had no intention to push the Water Bringing process much farther than he already had. He'd determined it was a dead-end long ago, one that required too much effort and energy for very little result. It was like using a nuclear bomb to rid a house of termites, and even then only killing a bug or two. But he wasn't about to share that with the powers-that-be. He'd essentially devised a parlor trick, not anything that could be relied on for millions of thirsty people. Yet he'd string it out for years by showing them just enough progress and wowing them with flashy proofs of concept at the proper milestones.

There was no way to actually make water reproduce. He knew that, but they didn't.

And so, by selling them hope for a future that would never come, he'd be able to prepare a place that was going to be vitally important for a future he hoped would never materialize.

He'd do his best to make sure it didn't. But just in case it did—well then, this place, this refuge high above the clouds, would be here.

16

ICELYN

Adorane, Eveshone, and I hide in the shadows of a decrepit building. I rub my hands over Eveshone's back, calming her, hoping to quicken the healing process. It seems to be working, and I can feel her strengthen as the pain washes away. Adorane's eyes widen as he watches the darkened contour lines which emphasize Eveshone's musculature pulse with a subtle bioluminescence. Her skin begins to knit itself together and replace the gashes from the spider monsters with layers of fresh derma.

"You've never seen this before, have you?" I ask, like this miracle is old hat for me.

"No, I haven't."

"They regenerate. Especially if there are others around, like me, or others of their own kind, who can help with the process. Adding to the healing with love, basically."

"But I've seen some die."

"Right. Sometimes their bodies are too far gone to piece themselves together, or they don't have enough other healthy creatures concentrating on their healing. Then they can die. It's rare, but it happens."

"How many do you think will travel with us?" Ad asks.

I'm surprised by the question. "None. I'm not taking any of them away from the Drowned City."

"No, you need a guard. A mighty force. To protect against the Croathus. We can't travel through Down Below again unprotected."

"We don't have a mighty force. The remains of the Anaghwin must stay here. Safe. Out there, compared to the Croathus' numbers…there are hordes of them, Ad."

"I know. That's why you need protection."

"I'm sorry. I can't have any more of their kind die."

"Are you willing to see *our* kind die?" Ad asks.

"I've made the mistake of allowing them to commit suicide for me before, and I won't do it again. I'm not negotiating. How can you argue with me about this? So many died at your hands. Never again."

He exhales for so long that I wonder how he had so much breath inside him in the first place. "Fine. Then it'll be you, me, and Eveshone again."

"I imagine Torrain will want to come, too," I add. "After all, he'd be hurt if we died without him."

"He'd definitely feel left out," Adorane agrees.

Eveshone and I lead Adorane to the marina where the Anaghwin keep the larger vessels they use to sail from the Drowned City to the mainland. We jump in, and I urge them to move us through the watery man-made canyons quickly. I want to make our escape before Omathis finds us.

A heavy wind has kicked up, and the water has grown white and frothy. We row headfirst into rising swells that do their best to beat us back. We also encounter more of the scampering crab spiders now and then. Eveshone dispatches them without too much trouble, but it keeps us vigilant.

I feel an emptiness growing behind my eyes and helplessly suffer as it descends into my gut. It's the lack of any bond with Omathis; we've now withdrawn from each other completely. Goosebumps form on my skin, and I shiver. I sit in the bowels of the boat, trying to avoid the winds, and hold my legs close to my body. But I am unable to find any warmth.

I look at Eveshone. "Do you think I've lost him?" I ask.

Adorane scans the buildings for any sign of Omathis. "I don't see him anywhere. I think we're going to make it, yes," he answers.

But he doesn't understand what I was asking. Eveshone does.

"I wish I could say that you can never really lose someone once you've bonded with them," she starts, herself starting to shake like the cold is affecting her too. "But I know that's not true. If anything, being bonded with someone just makes the loss of them, if it happens, more complete."

I know what this separation from Omathis means. He's blocking me. He doesn't want me to know what he's thinking, what he's feeling, or where he is. He's turned away from me—hardened himself against me. I do this to him sometimes, but he's never done it to me before. It makes me feel alone.

Has he forsaken me completely?

We turn left, then right, then left, making our way through the ancient labyrinth of buildings toward the open ocean. We're near. We turn one last corner into a narrowing waterway.

Now I see why Omathis has shielded himself from me.

He wanted to be able to surprise me.

THEN

Only the most important among their kind were welcome into the Heart of Paradise, the deepest cavern, tonight. Torches were lit in the Crowded Corridor—a narrow, serpentine system of caves that was forbidden to everyone except the Council of the Wise. The flames caused a commotion in Haven Underneath, because they meant something momentous was to be discussed and decided.

The Council of the Wise's membership wasn't officially bestowed by any leadership, but it was obvious among the creatures living in the caves who should attend and who should not. The ever-growing herd instinctively knew who was stronger and smarter. In the rare moments when someone thought more highly of their station than the herd, they were soon corrected.

The Council of the Wise piled into the cramped Heart of Paradise. Their numbers had grown and they pressed against one another, packed tight. This was good, and it was done by design, because this is how the herd operated in reality, too. One couldn't move without the rest feeling the shifts. There was no use pretending an individual didn't affect the whole.

Because of their shared roots, most sensed what the general topic of discussion would be. Their herd had flourished and had now finally reached the Strength. This had been a goal of Omathis, Amperous, and the other Breeding Pairs since they first escaped. The Strength was the tipping point where they could emerge from hiding. Where they were more of a threat to the survival of humanity than they were vulnerable to mankind's clever weaponry. Humanity could no longer stop them. They could overwhelm, swarm, and destroy. As they'd been designed to do.

Whispers spread through the caves—*when will we rise?* Yet this meeting wasn't meant to be a rally. The more sensitive among the wise sensed that there was an opposing view. *Just because we have the Strength, must we use it? Mistersean wants us to defend, but does he want us to attack?*

A fire roared in the center of the room. Once everyone had settled in for the session, Omathis approached it and scooped a handful of red embers until they filled his hands. They sizzled in his cupped palms as he spoke.

"Tonight we decide our herd's destiny. I have heard your hearts, and I affirm that you are correct. We have reached the Strength."

A muffled round of applause rose, but quickly faded. This group was not the kind to cheer too loudly. Plus, no one wanted to take up too much time while Omathis endured the pain of holding the burning embers.

"We could cover this land from ocean to ocean if we desire. We could breathe the air in the north, in the south, in the east, in the west. We could spread. Yet we could also choose to follow another path—one where we stay here and let others continue to live where they are. I will hold my thoughts on the matter until later in the deliberations," Omathis promised.

Omathis dropped the embers back into the fire. The gathered Council waited. Who would be the next to reach into the fire and scoop up the right to speak? This was their tradition: No one could address the Council unless willing to hold the pain of the flames close. This was only right. When someone had to sacrifice in order to speak, their words were clear, focused, and rarely untrue. The high cost required to address the gathering ensured that council members only shared thoughts of great value. Plus, it kept the speeches short.

Tularis, a trusted ally of Amperous, pulled handfuls of glowing wood from the fire. She deliberately placed them in a line along the inside of her forearm, as if she didn't care about the pain so much as the aesthetic.

"We have long known that we are superior to humans. I understand that there are those who would claim that Mistersean would ask us not to step into that superiority. But I would remind you of the pain humanity inflicts on all who share this world with them—even the evil they commit against one another. Let me ask you: If showing mercy to a cruel creature allows it to continue in its cruelty—is that truly merciful at all? Or is the true mercy eliminating the source of all cruelty in the first place?"

Tularis brushed the still-white hot coals back into the fire and returned to her place in the crowded gathering. Her reasoning was well received, and all members of the Council could feel where the consensus was going through their roots.

Brave and wise members of their herd approached the fire, one by one, to share their support for stepping into their rightful place in the world. The ground would be better cared for without humans. The air would be cleaner. The water purer. And maybe most important—they had been born with an instinctive hatred of humans. Why would this be, unless they were meant to destroy them once they'd reached the Strength?

Omathis had hoped this meeting would flow in a different direction, yet he saw no use in fighting the currents of the herd. It was clear to him what his kind wanted to do. If everyone desired this—even those he knew to be wise, good, and kind—he could accept that his interpretation of Mistersean's will was wrong.

After everyone had shared their thoughts on the matter, Omathis addressed the Council.

"I do not agree with what's been said here, but neither will I fight it. I had a different vision, but we are a herd, and I trust in your wisdom, even when it is at odds with my own. Therefore, let it be declared that as of—"

"No," Amperous bellowed, scooping the embers from Omathis' hands. "Not all have spoken. I have not weighed in yet."

No one thought they needed to hear Amperous' opinions on this matter.

But Amperous couldn't rid himself of the pictures of the woman he'd slaughtered, of her children. How many families would be killed if they embarked down this path?

"Omathis! Why would you silence yourself in the face of the herd? Sometimes only one creature senses the poison. How is it wise for that one to remain silent—so that all can die? The herd can make a mistake, especially when it forgets that it's made up of individuals, each with their own thoughts, visions, and convictions. If each individual erases itself for the herd, than the herd is hollow, made up of nothing."

"So we are supposed to deny the birthright of every one of our kind simply because Omathis does not feel comfortable with our Strength?" Tularis shouted, after grabbing another handful of burning coal.

"Not only Omathis," Amperous replied. "I also do not believe it is the time. You clamor for this, but most of you have no idea what it means to take human life. You hunger for it, yet have no idea what it feels like once it fills your belly. Omathis and I know. And we are the two who hesitate. What does that tell you?"

Everyone gathered could feel the mood shifting.

Even Tularis' voice had softened. "Promise that we will not make this decision for all time today. Let us revisit it."

"Every year," Amperous promised. "This is a wise compromise."

Tularis and Amperous dropped their embers into the fire, and the debate was over.

Sean Brathius drove the unpaved sand road alone. He did almost everything alone these days, so this was no surprise. His ancient Jeep rumbled and roared through the narrow slot canyon, miles away from any paved highway.

He'd come to appreciate this drive through the desert, especially when the winds kicked up swirling sheets of sand, as they were doing now. This barren landscape where life had to scrape and fight to keep on living seemed right to him. Everything here—the plants, animals, sand, and stone—was scarred and baked until hard and thick.

It's how he felt. He belonged here.

He rounded the last blind corner and accelerated. Just a straightaway lay before him now as he left the high sandstone walls behind and raced across the open ocean of sand, kicking up a magnificent cloud in his wake.

Finally he reached a gleaming field of solar panels fanning out from a tower capped by a metallic dome high above the desert floor. He passed through a series of gates and walls meant to keep anyone who wasn't him away.

Sean could have driven into the underground garage, but instead he parked a few hundred yards away from the dome and walked. He wanted to feel the 118-degree heat, let the hot winds smack him around a little, and embrace the day as the desert had intended before he entered his climate-controlled sanctuary.

Being exposed to the elements jolted Sean into a heightened level of perception, sensitive and surreal. He sought out being overheated, frozen, soaked with rain, or snowed on as often as possible. He felt that human shelter blunted their connection to the physical world.

Once inside the building, Sean strode past the front labs and rooms of machinery. All of them, while operational, were for show—shiny, expensive, and intended to impress others with the great progress he'd made in the Water Bringer Project. He even had a small garden planted in the middle of the floor, hydrated only by water he'd created using his groundbreaking processes. The garden, in particular, had greatly excited Senator Charles London. A flashy touch for maximum distraction.

This desert outpost had a true purpose, known only to Sean—and it didn't have anything to do with water.

Sean entered a sequence into a keypad. A section of the wall opened, revealing an elevator. He entered and descended.

He exited into a cavernous space carved out of sandstone, lined with machinery lit up like the holiday season. An unnerving blend of humming, beeping, and static white noise filled the space.

Sean took a deep breath. *This* was why he was siphoning millions of dollars from the Water Bringer.

Down here, amidst DNA sequencers, centrifuges, sophisticated scales, analyzers and compilers, he indulged his original obsession.

"You're going to help with this, aren't you?" he cooed affectionately to a giant swarm of bees, buzzing chaotically in a plexiglass rectangular cube. He walked past a long row of identical cells, each housing their own living creatures, greeting each like a loved one. One held ants, another wasps. Over there, yellowjackets, termites, and hornets. Others held mammals like squirrels, meerkats, and naked mole rats. Another row of tanks, filled with water, was populated with a mesmerizing swirl of jellyfish. A colony of shrimp occupied another. Some held sea sponges, anemones, and sea hares.

Sean pushed a sequence of buttons so that a small circle on the side of the bees' glass cage opened, just large enough to stick his arm in. He calmly held his unprotected arm straight amidst the swarm of angry insects and allowed them to sting him. He watched his exposed skin carefully, wincing only slightly at the pain, until he saw what he was looking for.

Sean gently pulled his swelling arm out of the cage, and the opening closed before any swarming bugs could escape.

"You're going to help me get your brothers back, right?" Sean whispered, his tone so optimistic that if any of these creatures could talk, they'd reply that they would. Of course they would.

Sean wielded a set of tweezers with steady concentration to remove the stingers from his arm. He collected more than twenty of the small samples, each in their own miniature vial.

"There we go, perfect. Just what I needed." Sean added a reddish-purple liquid to each vial and inserted them into openings in one of his many machines.

Omathis and Amperous were not evil. Sean knew this as instinctively as he knew anything. They'd done terrible things, but that wasn't who they were. At their essence, they were good. That spark of decency may have gotten buried beneath their fear and the struggle for survival—but as their creator, he knew it couldn't ever be extinguished.

Sean Brathius could figure out anything, and now he had only one goal.

Across a large bank of computer monitors, numbers and letters started to flow and dance. Sean watched with the anticipation of a child on Christmas morning. He pressed a button and watched as the information was presented as charts and graphs, growing and shrinking, arching and falling. He pressed another button; this time the charts became a glowing swirl of colors, as beautiful as the Northern Lights.

Sean calmed his breath and watched. He grabbed a notebook and started to scribble, his writing unable to keep up with his thoughts.

He was going to unlock their goodness.

He was going to get them back.

17

ICELYN

Omathis has barricaded the watery alleyway with floating chunks of sun-bleached driftwood, wrecked boat remains, twisted bits of rusted metal, cracked shards of glass—anything he could find to block our exit.

He stands on a vessel before the blockage. His icy blue eyes border on dead. He doesn't look angry or even sad—just hollow.

"Icelyn. Where are you going? Icelyn. Why are you leaving?"

My heart stops beating when I hear his voice, which is tired, old, and sounds as if it is about to die. At the same time, it sounds like that of a child who is, for the first time, learning that adults aren't always good. Or maybe never are.

Adorane and Eveshone slow their rowing—as if I'm thinking about abandoning our escape, as if I'd consider staying in the Drowned City.

Omathis is crouched over, gray and weak.

"Don't slow down," I tell Ad and Eveshone. "We will move that barricade piece by piece if we have to." I must be strong about this. I want nothing more than to hold Omathis and tell him how much I love him and that I'll stay here forever. But if any of us are going to survive, I can't do that. I cannot let myself be convinced otherwise.

"This doesn't mean what you think it does, Omathis," I shout to him, but my voice is weak.

"You promised you would never leave me." His words are brittle. I turn my eyes toward the shore and focus on the sounds of the water splashing and crashing all around us. "Like Sean Brathius left us so many years ago."

I search for words and have nothing. Still, I need to say something. So I jump into conversation without any idea what I'm going to say. "You saw that flying creature that came for me. It was different than you and Eveshone—different than all of the Anaghwin and the Croathus. There will be more of them. I cannot stay. Eventually none of us can. Our future isn't here in the Drowned City. It never was. As Mother to the Anaghwin, I must find where we can go next. I must do this before the other Mothers rise."

Adorane and Eveshone stare at me, their faces scrunched up and confused.

"Who are the other Mothers?" Adorane asks.

"I don't know," I answer, quickly, hoping he'll be quiet. It's true. I have no idea why I said it, except that ever since that terrible winged creature said "for the Mothers," to me, I haven't been able to shake the thought.

"*Other mothers?*" Omathis whispers, as if it means something to him. I'd ask him to share his revelation, but this isn't the time.

Our vessel glides until it gently knocks against the platform where he stands. I leave our boat and stand beside him. I extend my hand. I still feel him blocking me in our thoughts, so I don't want to touch him without permission.

After what seems like an eternity, he takes my hand and guides it behind him until we embrace.

"I forbid you to leave. I forbid it," he commands, his words strong again. "I can protect you here. I cannot protect you out there. Every single Anaghwin in the Drowned City could accompany you, and we would still die. They are too strong, too many. We are few."

I know! I think. *That is why I've been forcing them to reproduce and snatching up Croathus!*

I match him in volume. I don't think I've ever been in such a loud argument in my entire life. I feel lost, like I'm falling off a cliff. "Do you think I *want to go?* That I have any desire to leave you?"

"Then why would you go?" he demands. "If it's not what you want?"

"This all stopped being about what *I* want a very long time ago, Omathis. Now it's only about what…needs to happen. Regardless of what anyone wants. Me especially."

I pull back from the embrace and touch his lovely face. I trace every graceful contour.

My touch seems to still his fury, at least a little.

"I can't stop you from going, Icelyn. I can hate it, though."

"We both hate it. On that we agree."

I nod toward Adorane and Eveshone and they begin to clear the blockage Omathis has erected, revealing the open waters beyond.

I step away from him. I'm sad to feel that the emptiness is still within me. I didn't think it would be. For reasons I can't completely comprehend, Omathis still isn't bonded to me.

"Why have you withdrawn—"

"Please don't ask," he cuts me off. It feels like he's struck me in the face, but not out of cruelty. Out of self-protection. "It hurts less this way."

I back away from him slowly, and step back onto our vessel.

"I'm going to see you again, Omathis," I say.

"I don't believe you."

Eveshone and Adorane row with precision, and we move through the barricade. As soon as we hit the open water, I hear Omathis howling behind us.

I can't look back.

NOW

Omathis cried out to her long after she'd disappeared into the hazy horizon.

"Come back! Don't leave me here! Why must you go?"

He knew she couldn't hear him. But still he cried to her.

He felt cold. Even though the ocean air was brisk and a steady wind blew through him, his chill had nothing to do with the weather. He'd been abandoned again.

She promised she'd never leave, and yet she was gone.

Omathis suffered the curious sensation of being himself, but simultaneously existing at two different periods in time. His life was one long loop where nothing began and nothing ended, everything only repeated, with each revolution bringing more pain.

He was that creature again, centuries ago, abandoned by Mistersean to captivity and the evil wishes of Shai. Mistersean, on the other side of the thick plexiglass, unwilling even to hold them before he left them forever. Now Lovely had done the same thing. Lovely was Mistersean. The Drowned City was his cage. Everything happens again and again. The misery replays forever, unchanged in essence, only growing stronger and stronger. In every moment, there is an eternity just waiting to reveal itself.

Omathis returned to the Temple of Lovely and bowed before the image of her, praying. It had been so long since he'd needed to do this. He'd been able to sit by her side and hear her in his ears and feel her in his heart. Now, as he'd done for hundreds of years before she'd descended, he was left begging a painting for connection again.

Wilshone, one of Omathis' most trusted allies in the Drowned City and a great warrior, approached reverently. He crept up cautiously once Omathis' cries had trailed off into silence.

"We have contained the outbreak from the dark shaft."

Omathis nodded. Good. "Any casualties?"

"Only wounds that will heal."

"Those are the preferred kinds of wounds, should one be forced to suffer some," Omathis observed.

"Wounds are the cost of being alive," Wilshone agreed.

Omathis arose, and they left the temple. They stood at the edge of the floor and gazed out at the ocean and the mainland.

"You have more to report to me," Omathis observed. "Proceed."

"We've recaptured the escaped Croathus. What should we do with them?"

Omathis closed his eyes.

"Icelyn would like them returned to their homes on the mainland."

Wilshone seemed surprised by the edict.

"This is her wish?"

"Yes," Omathis answered, his voice growing in confidence. "But you won't hear it directly from her. She's hidden in her tower. Where no one —not even I—can see her without using eyes of faith. This attack was an attack on her. We cannot risk another. She will speak through me."

His words tended to the pain radiating from his heart as he spoke them.

Yes, she was still here, with them. She was here because she had to be here. They needed her. She'd always be here, in the room on the top of the tallest tower, even if they couldn't see her. She was there, and she would always be there.

The Anaghwin gathered at the peak of the skyscraper, outside the chamber where Icelyn had been imprisoned.

Omathis stood before them and spoke.

"My children, from this day on, Lovely will remain with us but hidden from our sight. She is in this hiding place, caring for us as always, but we have reached a time when we must rely on faith and memory to remain close to her."

Omathis turned toward the chamber and fell to his knees.

"Lovely, thank you for dwelling among us. You are here, and we are with you. So shall it always be!"

The Anaghwin bowed low and hummed a haunting tune.

"Lovely, we can feel that you are with us now," Omathis sang.

"Lovely, we can feel that you are with us now," they repeated.

Tranton scoured the scroll he'd excavated from Travis' cave of wonders. He could barely breathe. So many things that had been blurred in the shadows were coming into crisp focus.

The scroll told the sad, proud tale of a woman named Shai. A foremother of Tranton, she'd been Travis' mother and a true visionary genius.

Sean Brathius had been a thief and a fraud.

The Nilsings, not the Brathius, were the originators of this new breed. Shai had formed them out of her thoughts and ideas.

Yet he had no interest in recovering her work as it related to the Threat Below. He'd make no claim on them. Sean Brathius had snatched Shai's bold theories and perverted them when creating the Croathus. Sean had installed parts of himself into these flawed creatures, and Tranton had no desire to waste any time on these fundamentally weaker children. Sean Brathius' Threat Below were the runts of the litter. It was only a matter of time before they passed away.

Tranton had one goal—and one alone. He was going to find those children born of Shai's steely cool resolve.

He was going to find the strong ones.

THEN

Travis Nilsing saw the shape his life would take—clearly, now, and with no confusion. Even better, he thought it was a pretty good life. He and Soren would attend West Point. Colonel Hodges had told them that they were basically shoe-ins already. With the glowing recommendations he'd written, coupled with their physical prowess and academic achievements, they could sit back and enjoy their victory lap.

Life felt like a victory lap lately. Hazing the plebes, gaining their respect, turning them into men, as had been done to him. Sneaking across the river to flirt with Haley, his maybe-girlfriend at Padua Academy, the all-girl Catholic school that served as a feminine oasis for the boys at

Longrave. In every track meet, the only question was who would win first and who would win second, Soren or Travis—no one else in the state could compete with them. Dr. Monroe, his science instructor, had asked Travis to co-author a portion of an article based on his research, which had recently been accepted for publication in the *Journal of Defense Acquisition and Weaponry*. Travis had only volunteered to help Dr. Monroe because he was fascinated by improvisational weaponry and mankind's knack for figuring out the lethal potential of just about any object—he never thought it would turn him into a published author.

Even visits home (if you could call it home, which Travis didn't) to see Sean weren't the hell they'd once been. His former brattiness stripped out of him, Travis could see that Sean meant well. They'd never share an emotional bond, but Travis had developed enough discipline to show Sean a cold, distant respect.

Travis entered the headmaster's office and saluted, formal despite the warm undercurrent of affection the general and colonel harbored for him. Most other cadets would be worried about a call to the headmaster's office, but Travis had looked forward to this gathering since first being notified that morning that Colonel Hodges and General Strain wanted to talk to him. What new frontier could be opening up for him?

Another man was waiting with them—tall, thin, and bearing a pale complexion that bordered on ghastly.

"Senior Cadet Travis, this is Prescott," the General started. It was strange to have this man introduced with no title, no context, and only one name. Here, everyone had a title. They were important signifiers of who a person was and what he had accomplished.

Travis didn't have a clue who Prescott could be.

"You are the beneficiary of a great honor," Colonel Hodges cut in. "Prescott is a Special Forces operative, and he has requested your assignment to his mission." General Strain and the Colonel appeared proud, which made sense. Prescott had asked specifically for Travis—it was an exhilarating promotion that most cadets would die for. It only happened once every twenty years or so that someone from an elite organization would pluck a cadet and press them into important service.

"Just me, or Soren too?" Travis asked shyly, unable to believe someone would choose him over his best friend.

What was it that had attracted Prescott to him, Travis wondered? His code-breaking abilities? His affinity for engineering? His contribution to the published article?

"Just you," Colonel Hodges responded. "You should be very proud. We are."

Yet something was making him uneasy. There was an aspect of their pride that seemed forced—like they were trying to be happy for Travis but couldn't ignore an agitation that they were unable to calm. For the first time, they looked…scared.

Maybe they were only sad because this meant Travis might be graduating early, and they'd miss him. Travis decided to believe that this was at the root of their mutual disquiet.

"It would be an honor. I've trained years for an opportunity like this," Travis responded confidently.

Prescott dismissed Travis' mentors from the room with a brusque hand motion. Who was Prescott that he could send these powerful men away without a word?

With Travis' allies out of the room, Prescott's demeanor grew more disinterested, which Travis would not have guessed was possible. "I believe you can be of great value to your nation, Cadet Nilsing." Prescott's dark, glassy eyes bored into Travis dispassionately as his monotonous voice lowered. "What I'm about to tell you is classified."

The workers had completed their projects, and the water-pumping mechanism was working as Sean had planned. His mild case of self-diagnosed obsessive-compulsive disorder was satisfied by the upward flow of water from the river thousands of feet below. It was a perpetual-motion machine using the current of the water, a series of elegant pulleys and counterweights, and gravity to propel itself. There was no electronic component that could corrode, no digital component that needed to be programmed. It could last for hundreds of years if it had to, with minimal, if any, maintenance required.

This mountaintop outpost was peaceful now that the construction crews had cleared out. Sean walked along the stone perimeter of the pumping building and inhaled deeply. A rush of crisp air and pine scent filled his nostrils, soothing as a massage.

He could live here if it came to that. High above the clouds, it was probably the closest to heaven he'd ever get.

It was quiet up here, and the air was thin, so sound traveled faster and louder. Sean had grown accustomed to hearing cracks, shuffles, and snaps—all normal sounds at the top of a mountain. But now a new sound disturbed the silence, and he couldn't tune it out. It was too loud to be made by anything that shared this space with him. He exited his lab tower and searched the unmoving landscape.

More shuffling.

Sean had no reason to be afraid. There was a metal fence below the cloudline and a more substantial wall above it. Only authorized personnel could enter, and Sean had made sure that the authorization list was short. He received an alert on his phone anytime those perimeters were encroached upon, which provided a video of the intruder. Outside of woodland animals or curious hikers, no one had been near the outer fence yet.

Sean cleared his head of worry and turned to enter the tower again. He startled as his phone rang. He answered it.

"Hello, Sean."

Sean was shocked into silence by the voice.

"How did you get this number?" Sean asked.

Oliver Hailgard laughed. "I haven't seen you in ages."

Sean felt a rush of guilt. It was true. "Don't take it personally. I haven't seen anyone in ages."

"Let's remedy that. Come to the Wall."

Sean checked his phone. No alerts. How was that possible?

"You're here?"

18

NOW

Persopile followed the boy through the thick underbrush. She hustled to keep up with him so she could sneak another glimpse of his face without him noticing. Maybe it was the way sunlight illuminated a person's countenance here above the ground, but she was pretty sure he was the most beautiful creature she'd ever seen.

Istoch carried Belubus' broken body with great care even as he moved quickly through the pines. She'd carried him long enough to know that Istoch must be very strong. He didn't seem to be strained by his weight at all, and now they were moving up the steep mountainside. Persopile was winded from the ascent, and she wasn't even carrying anyone.

Belubus groaned, which comforted Persopile. His groans meant he was still alive.

They reached the towering, decrepit wall that Persopile had heard about but never seen. The sight of it—imposing, threatening, unflinching—made her remember everything she'd heard about the cruel, heartless people who lived on the other side. She felt an instinctive rush of panic.

Istoch lowered Belubus into a downy bed of green leaves and brush with deliberate gentleness. He scanned the trees and scampered toward a grove of eucalyptus trees, then pulled a small stone knife from under his tunic and began slicing vines from the branches. He was consumed with the task, but Persopile noted that he still managed to notice her watching him. He didn't seem to mind.

She looked away.

"Do you think he'll live?" she asked.

"I do," Istoch responded. He was surprised by his own optimism. Based on his experience so far, he'd only learned that people died. Sick, well, strong, weak, young, old, beloved, strangers—they all died. But something about Persopile made him believe otherwise. Maybe some people recovered and lived. Maybe Belubus would.

Persopile watched, impressed, while Istoch wove the vines into a thick rope. He placed a series of straight branches below Belubus and fastened them to the twine. He then tossed the vines up and over a thick overhanging branch to create a pulley.

He tested it by pulling down, and Belubus' body lifted off the ground. He let Belubus down easily and then handed the rope to her.

"I'm going to climb up. Can you lift him to me?"

Persopile relished the chance to do something. Down in the Mines, she'd never been assigned any job of importance. She'd never been considered particularly smart, or strong, so she mostly just existed and busied herself with tasks that she knew didn't matter. Like arranging pebbles by size from smallest to largest or straightening the portraits and paintings that hung in Belubus' throne room. She doubted anyone even noticed.

She was careful not to jostle Belubus as she raised him from the ground to the top of the Wall.

"That's good. Strong and steady," Istoch encouraged her.

Istoch had easily scaled the edifice and was waiting to guide the injured man to safety. When Persopile had lifted him to the top of the wall, Istoch grabbed him and the vines went slack.

"Can you climb up here on your own?" Istoch asked. "I know you've never done it before, so there'd be no shame in asking for help."

Persopile thought she'd try, though she appreciated Istoch giving her the excuse. She found that there were enough footholds and places to grab in the old tree trunks and rusted metal binding that she was able to join him. It was the perfect kind of difficult—challenging enough for her to feel like she'd accomplished something, but not so hard to be impossible.

They used another overhanging branch to duplicate their pulley setup on the other side and worked together to lower the groaning, unconscious man to the forest floor.

"Look at that—we did it," Istoch said cheerfully.

We, Persopile thought. She'd never been part of a *we* before. She liked it.

Torrain was roused from his work in the lab by a tremendous commotion outside. He finished writing his latest batch of notes on the nature of the

Threatbelow's Brathius masks before he rushed out the door. What had riled everyone up?

He saw Istoch, who appeared to be carrying someone or something very carefully toward Torrain's lab. Istoch was not bearing his burden alone. He was joined by a woman Torrain had never seen before. She was tall and lithe. Nearly half of her face was stained a dark crimson the color of blood.

Torrain wondered how it was it possible to see a woman that he'd never seen before. He knew all the humans in the world. It wasn't hard to do—there weren't that many left.

Tranton and a group of Cognates crowded them. Most scowled and looked generally displeased, and Torrain could hear their complaints.

These two have been disbursed for a reason!

This is highly improper.

Just because we don't have the Code doesn't mean we can't have standards.

Istoch and the mysterious woman carried their controversial burden and laid it at Torrain's feet. Though broken and bloodied, Torrain could see that it was Belubus. Icelyn's former tutor needed immediate help.

Torrain ran inside to grab linens and herbs. He was no doctor, but had been curious enough about the ways the forest could heal a person that he'd learned many tricks through reading, research, and experimentation.

He concentrated on binding Belebus' still bleeding lacerations and stabilizing his spine and neck. Torrain barked orders to Istoch and the woman, who was eager to help. The three of them made a coolly efficient team, and before too long, the broken man was covered in herbs, scaffolded with splints, and bandaged to stop the bleeding. It still looked bad, but at least now he had a chance at survival.

"Please, let me die," Belubus mumbled as Torrain wet a sponge and emptied it into his parched mouth. "Don't do this."

The Cognates watched in disapproval. Torrain couldn't ignore their clucks and whispers any longer. Once he was positive nothing more could be done for Belebus, he turned to address them.

"You mourn the loss of the Code. Of the old order of things. I agree that we have perhaps gotten rid of some good along with the bad. But *right now?* Complaining that Istoch has saved the life of Belubus by bringing him into Mountaintop? Grousing because a compassionate woman has come in alongside him? You are demonstrating exactly why the Code was lethal to us. If we cannot act human in our struggle to survive, then what good is humanity's survival anyway?"

Tranton was unaffected by Torrain's rebuke. "You have done a fine job of appealing to our emotions, Torrain. But I remind you that this isn't about feelings. This is about safety. Belubus was disbursed from our community because he was found to be a danger to our way of life. And this girl? How can we trust her? She could have malicious intent—how would we know one way or another? Would you blindly eat a handful of acorns knowing that one of them could be filled with poison?"

"People are not poisonous acorns, Tranton. They aren't acorns to be eaten at all. To *view* them as such is the *true* poison—one that we must ruthlessly work to rid ourselves of." Torrain wished Adorane were here. Adorane was the one who had decided that Tranton should be released from his prison—something about new beginnings and the chance to prove yourself after you've made a mess of things. But Torrain didn't want to see that man's face ever again. He blamed Tranton for his mother's death.

"Putting us all at risk?" Tranton jeered. "Just so you can feel like you're a good boy, virtuous and true? No. I will not allow it."

"Tranton, you are not a leader among us. Please stop acting as if you were. You had your chance and were not up to the task."

Tranton's face twisted in anger. "All I did was try to keep us safe."

"That's not all you did. We were here. We remember. Regardless, we're not going to debate whether we will try to save the life of man beloved by many in this community and embrace the girl who risked her own life to bring him to us. Some decisions are so clearly right that there is no debate. This is one of them."

Torrain, Istoch, and the girl worked together to gently lift Belubus.

"They'll stay in my lab with me," Torrain said firmly.

ICELYN

Our voyage to the mainland is quiet. None of us has anything to talk about, which creates a whispery panic in my chest. When we lived in Mountaintop Adorane and I would chatter with one another about anything under the sun. Conversation was easy, with no awkward pauses or scrambling to figure out what to say next. It's like how when it's raining, nobody stops to wonder how so much water manages to fall from the sky—but once you're suffering a drought, the idea of any drops ever falling again seems like an impossible miracle.

I can still hear Omathis, though I'm not sure if it's my memory of his sadness or him trying to connect to our roots. It makes no difference; he dominates my thoughts just the same.

"If he could be trusted to come with us, I'd welcome his presence," I say to Eveshone, half apologizing, half justifying.

"Of course, Lovely. Your will is above all." She answers so quickly that I wonder if she truly believes the words she's said. She puts her large hand on my shoulder. "I am grateful that you trust me enough not to abandon me too."

She's trying to be comforting, but her words sting. There's no other way to view my actions, I realize. I *am* leaving Omathis behind. I hate that I'm doing this to him. Again. His entire life is this story repeated, being abandoned by those who should love him most—and now I'm writing the newest chapter.

"How are things going in Mountaintop?" I ask Adorane, and immediately regret it. But it's the only thing I can think to ask.

"Better," he answers cryptically, and then says nothing more. He doesn't want to talk about it.

"I guess I'll see for myself soon enough."

Adorane finally stops scanning the horizon for threats and turns to look at me. "We're not going to Mountaintop. We're going to the desert. We're going to find Apex."

I'm not ready to tell him that it's yet to be decided whether I'll actually make that trip. We'll have to find the right time for that discussion.

"Well, if we're going to get to the desert, we have to go through the mountains first. That's just simple geography, Adorane. You can't argue with that."

"It would be better if we avoided Mountaintop."

"Better for me or for the Kith?" I ask.

"Better for both."

"Then I'm not interested in better. I choose worse, Ad."

Adorane sighs and throws his attention back on the approaching shoreline.

"He wants to see you, too."

"This isn't about Torrain."

"Oh, I was talking about your father."

"Of course. That's what I meant. How is he?"

"Why did you mention Torrain?"

"I mentioned him just to make it clear that he's *not* the one I'm thinking about."

"Good thing that we're clear on that."

Eveshone has been watching our back and forth with her forehead scrunched up. "I don't understand. Do the two of you like one another now, or do you dislike one another? I see evidence for both."

Adorane begins to row toward the shore again. "If you figure it out, please let me know."

"And so Apex is…what, exactly? How do you know it's real?" Our previous conversations about the place have not gone well, but my curiosity and desire for something to talk about has gotten the best of me. We have another few hours before we make landfall, and I need conversation to pass the time. Though I don't want to discuss our potential journey to Apex, I do want to know what Adorane knows.

Adorane and Eveshone pull and push at the oars rhythmically and row the boat with disciplined precision. They've given me the job of steering, which is to say they've asked me to do nothing at all. With such a wide open expanse of water, there's no real need to navigate. I offered to help if either of them wants a break, but so far neither has accepted my offer.

"Shortly after the initial Ascension, there was a divide in Mountaintop. A small group grew dissatisfied with Brathius leadership."

"Some things never change," I interject.

He ignores me—rightfully so. "They left and found their way to the desert, where they erected a tower so tall that they were safe from the Threat Below when living on the top."

"This sounds like a ridiculous fairy tale, Adorane. How do you know it's true?"

"You know," Ad responds quietly, knowingly, like whatever he's talking about is the source of great shame.

I realize what he means. The woman we'd seen so many years ago—the one we had not helped.

My face flushes. "Look, we were just kids. What were we supposed to do?"

"More than laugh, that's for sure."

I can't argue. We might have been kids, but that doesn't mean we had to be so rotten about it.

"Our leadership, both Veritas and Cognate, talked to her. They learned much from her. They wrote it all down, sealed it away, and then sent her on her way."

He's condemning both my father and his with this account. This wretched decision would have been their joint decree. Or, I suppose, my father could have overruled Aclornis in the matter; if that was the case, I don't want to know. Adorane reads my hesitancy and decides not to talk any further about it.

"And how do you know all this?"

"When you're in charge, you learn all the secrets." The Adorane I knew back in Mountaintop would have been bursting with joy at the prospect of learning all the secrets. Now, he sounds like he wishes he could forget them.

"The woman who stumbled into Mountaintop—her name was Klamath. She was the last female in their community. They'd ostracized her."

"What do you mean, the last female? They don't have any women or girls there at all?"

"They value men more."

"Why?"

"I don't really want to talk to you about it. I'll probably say something wrong."

"If I'm going to visit the place, I need to know."

He sighs and proceeds with his words carefully. "According to what Klamath told them, according to the men who live there—not to me, mind you—women make bad decisions. Women value the wrong things. Women's instincts are counter to survival. Women contribute only one resource needed for survival, fertility, but they manage even that poorly, consistently making the wrong choices."

I can barely understand what he's telling me. I know that throughout history, across many different cultures, the men have worked to quiet and subdue the women. This was true even in Mountaintop, though I'm sure the men there would dispute that. Back in the Apriori days, some men completely silenced the women among them and kept them hidden from public view altogether. It seems to be a male instinct to disregard women to the utmost point possible. But to banish the women altogether?

"Without the women, how would they continue to exist?" I ask.

"They've developed a technology," Adorane answers matter-of-factly. "That's what she said, at least. They use the Underneath Forge. That's how they get their children. No women required."

"You've said this before, but…that's not possible."

"That's what she told our fathers."

"So once they didn't need women to make babies anymore, they… what? Banished them? Sent them out to the desert to die?"

"Because they preferred a culture of men, yes. That's exactly what they did."

I hate everything about what Adorane is telling me. The sheer impossibility of reproducing without women frustrates me. Yet beyond that, the underlying principle horrifies me.

Of course the men would expel the women once they figured out how to reproduce without them—because that's all women are needed for, right? Not their wisdom, nor their artistry. Not the emotional connections they offer, nor their empathy, their mercy, their insight, their strength. Once you've figured out a way to make babies regardless, everything feminine can be sent to the desert to die. Because women make the wrong choices, and a culture of men was preferable.

Apex sounds like a place filled with horrors.

"And you want me to find a man from among *these people*? To have a child with?"

"If you can think of any alternative, I'd welcome it."

"Humanity can live on using their accursed Underneath Forge, I guess!"

"We've been through this before, Icelyn. We should just leave Mountaintop to dry up and blow away in the wind? Icelyn. Our ancestors ascended, at great sacrifice, to preserve the Kith. Let Apex survive, while Mountaintop dies out? No. We want to continue. And we want to continue through *you*."

He's appealing to a side of me which I hate to admit exists, and I resent it. I've craved this kind of specialized attention from Mountaintop ever since feeling the sting of their rejection years ago. I push against it.

"Mountaintop and I no longer share a common destiny, Ad."

"Mountaintop is in your blood. And we'll all live on through you. You're still a Brathius, aren't you? Doesn't that mean something? "

"The Brathius name isn't the honor we once thought it was."

"Please, Icelyn. I'm choking on all this self-pity. I know you may have issues with your home, and the people who were once your whole world —and your father, and your mother, and probably even me. But you have to admit there is good living in Mountaintop, good that deserves to survive."

"Mountaintop murdered my children!" I shout. "And you were part of it!" I hadn't planned to say this, but now that it's out, I'm glad I've said it.

"And maybe this is a way for me to make up for that—by finding a way to bring you a new child, one that will endear you to the people who once loved you, and whom I know you still love. Do you think I look forward to risking my life to find another man for you? Do you think I want to do this? Don't you think I would rather…"

He looks painfully away. I reach out and hold him hard and tight, pulling his face into the crook of my neck—mostly because we both crave a closeness that now seems less possible than ever, but also because I don't want him to finish his thought. Whatever it is—and I think I know what it is—I don't want to hear it, and he knows he shouldn't say it. It's all too painful to bear.

I catch a glimpse of Eveshone, and somehow she's not at all uncomfortable with this display of intimacy. She seems almost relieved by it. I'd probably jump from the boat and swim to shore if I were her.

I am not sure how long our embrace lasts. It's not thrilling like other times I've been close to him. It feels more like crying. We're mourning something together. I'm the first to pull away.

"Why do you think Apex will even welcome me?" I ask sadly. "They've banished all their women; I doubt they're looking for replacements."

"We'll have to figure that out. They may not need women anymore, but Mountaintop needs children."

There it is again, this terrible idea. *Women cannot be defined by their gender,* I think bitterly. How much Apex has lost! How much value lay in the women they have banished? What of those women who were geniuses of warfare, philosophy, and wit—who are experts despite—or *because of*—their femininity?

"I don't want to talk about this anymore, Ad."

"You're the one who asked the question, Icelyn. I didn't want to talk about it either."

"How much longer before we reach land, do you think?" Eveshone asks, hoping to break through the tension.

19

THEN

Other than brief visits from Travis at home and perfunctory tours of the outpost with those who funded his cover projects, Sean lived a solitary life. It wasn't what he wanted, but it was easier. He had his obsessions, and there wasn't room for anyone or anything else in his life. Maybe it had always been that way; only now was he finally willing to admit it.

He reached the Wall to find that Oliver Hailgard had already scaled it.

"I figured the authorization invitation was coming any day now, so I remedied the oversight myself," the soldier said.

"Yeah, well, this project is…I don't control the classification," Sean stammered by way of apology.

"Sure. But don't worry—you can't really keep me out anyway. I'm here, aren't I?"

He embraced Sean. They had been very good friends once.

"I've missed you," Ollie said. "The tragedies have left you alone. I'm sorry."

For the first time in years, tears filled Sean's eyes. *Where did those come from?*

"No farmer can act shocked when he plants pumpkin seeds and pumpkins grow. Every consequence I suffer is the fruit of a crop I willingly sowed. I know that now."

"Who are those tears for?" Oliver asked. When Sean didn't respond, he prodded. "Yourself? Shai?"

"I don't know. Not myself," Sean answered honestly. Not Shai either, though it seemed cruel to say so out loud.

"Laura Lee," Oliver stated, because he could see it was true.

Sean had to sit. He'd done a good job protecting himself from memories of his beloved daughter. Now, at the mention of her name, the image of her face, always optimistic, her eyes sparkling glacial blue, saturated his mind.

Whenever he thought about Laura Lee, he wanted to die.

Sean was too lost in his own misery to notice, but the sounds of leaves crunching echoed in the woods. Footsteps. If he'd been more perceptive, he'd have seen Oliver nod and wave someone over from a grove of a trees.

"Sean," Oliver instructed, "look. I am not your only visitor."

Sean tried to clear the hot tears from his vision. But he couldn't tell if he'd been successful. Were his eyes open or closed? Was he was seeing or remembering? He was afraid to trust what he hoped he saw. It was as if the memory of his daughter had morphed into a solid three-dimensional figure before him. Crouching beside him, holding his hand, and wiping away his tears with tenderness.

"Father," she whispered, "I am no longer lost to you. And you are no longer all alone."

Break the ground, dig down deep. Over and over, until your shoulders scream for relief, until you start to feel muscles in your back that you didn't even know existed.

Laura Lee was glad to have a permanent place to hide. She'd grown tired of being shuffled from one location to another by Ollie over the years. Each change of scenery happened amid fits of panic—she always had to leave, NOW, or risk being taken by the shadowy people who never stopped chasing her.

Drop the seeds into the ground, and gently pat the soil into a mound over the top. There, there, isn't that nice, snuggled up in your rich earthy bed, little seeds? When you wake up, you'll be reaching for the sun—beautiful newly born corn, snap peas, or string beans. We have so much to look forward to.

She would forever be thankful for Oliver Hailgard's protection, but being on the run felt worse than the prison he'd helped her avoid.

One day, others will join us up here, and you will help us all live, just as I am now helping you come to life.

According to Oliver, it wasn't only prison that would have been in store for her. "They theorize that Amp and Omathis have a special connection to you," he explained once, cryptically, "and no doubt planned to use that in their recovery efforts." He'd never told her how they might have exploited her connection to the creatures, and she'd never asked, because from the way he said it she knew that his answer to the question would probably be worse than she could imagine.

"These people who are after you are not nice people, Laura Lee," he'd warned, "and they're afraid. Compared to what they're afraid of, you're worth nothing at all."

She enjoyed the toil that molding this mountainous terrain into small gardens required. With only primitive tools, her connection to the labor was immediate. After her forced nomadic lifestyle, she could finally stick around long enough to enjoy the harvest. She could make this serene mountaintop refuge her home.

She adored the pristine blue sky, the sheet of clouds that extended as far as she could see, and the craggy exposed stone.

Here comes the water, my little seedlings! It's traveled all this distance just to meet you. That's how loved you are—water defies gravity and flows uphill to quench your thirst.

She watched the flowing current of water as it snaked its way into the pumping building, losing herself in the swirls and eddies, and musing about where that particular drop of water might have been before it got here. Starting out in a cloud, then falling as snow, melted and flowing down a mountain creek, joining into a larger rushing river, tumbling over a waterfall, running out into the ocean, riding a current hundreds of miles offshore until it reached an island, crashing down onto that beach as a wave, sinking down into the sand and finally, during low tide, evaporating back up into the air to join a cloud again. Somewhere along the line, it was taken from that river up to her, so she could watch it flow by and witness that miraculous drop of world-traveling, shape-shifting water.

Reach toward the sky, with your verdant leaves and shoots pulsing with the green of life itself. Grow as tall as you'd like, proud and ambitious.

Laura Lee had long stretches of solitary time up here, but far from despising it, she relished every minute. She could write. She could think. She could lay flat on the dirt and feel the weight of the entire earth below her, pressing up against her, holding her close so that she didn't fly off into the universe, adrift. She sang. She began to recognize the squirrels individually, and she could repeat the different birdsongs from memory.

After never having enough time while being skirted from one place to another by Ollie—always fearing that soon the shadowy men would find her, forcing her to run—she savored the slow pace of life at the top of the mountain. It tasted like eternity.

You don't need to worry. You have everything you need to grow: water to nourish you, dirt to cushion you, the sun to feed you. And me to love you. Sean spent more of his time here than in his desert research center, so that he could be with her. She'd often wondered whether Oliver had made the right choice, letting her father believe that she was dead or taken by Amperous and Omathis, and had argued that they should let him know she was still alive. But Oliver had dismissed her over and over. There was so much suspicion and surveillance centered around Sean in the immediate aftermath of the breakout. He had to believe she was dead or gone, for his own safety and hers.

Laura Lee now saw that there had been another benefit to Sean mourning her disappearance. Often, people cannot appreciate what they have until it's ripped away. Now, Sean appreciated her—really, truly cherished her. Finally, their relationship felt like a father and daughter's should.

She missed seeing other people, of course. But Oliver had warned her that if whatever Sean was working on out in the desert didn't work—and soon—then she wouldn't be alone in this secluded high point for much longer.

Before long, Ollie predicted, this might be one of the only places where humans could live.

She would have company.

Travis hated what visits to Sean did to him. At Longrave, Travis knew his worth—he was confident and appreciated. During breaks, he reverted back to who he had once been: an orphan who Sean had taken pity on out of guilt. Outside of Longrave, he was tolerated and ignored. Even when Sean was encouraging, which was annoyingly often, Travis was sure he knew the real intent. It was only because Travis was pathetic and required charity. At Longrave, his acclaim had been earned.

But this visit would be different. Travis looked forward to it. He was on an important mission, one that Prescott had deemed "the action that stands between mankind's survival and destruction." That's the way Prescott talked, but he wasn't being over-dramatic. Prescott was a man who was always aware of the stakes, however hidden they might be.

"Here's your room, untouched, just the way you left it. Just the way you like it." Sean had been giving Travis a tour of his place like a nervous hotel bellhop hoping for a tip, as if Travis hadn't already lived here before. "Oh, with one exception: I had these built for you." Sean pointed to well-crafted shelves on the wall, which held a collection of gleaming trophies, plaques, and medals.

These were Travis' awards. They had been packed away somewhere by Shai, who thought that displaying them would only *encourage Travis to rest on his laurels and grow complacent*, but Sean had found them, polished them, and arranged them with care. Travis tried not to be touched, but it was too late.

"Sean, you didn't have to do this."

"And now, the final piece. I still can't believe you tried to keep this a secret from me." Sean placed a hefty golden monolith at the center of the display: the Longrave Military Academy Senior Cadet of the Year. "It's only their most prestigious award!"

With a pang of guilt, Travis feigned modesty. "Still surprised they gave it to me." He wasn't; he deserved it. Even Soren, his only competition for the honor, had admitted as much. Travis had purposely neglected to tell Sean about the ceremony, but his adoptive guardian (not father; he'd never call Sean his father) had managed to find out about it and show up anyway.

"Sure, we're all shocked." Sean replied, facetiously. "Anyway, there's your guitar. Do you still play?"

Travis shook his head no.

"That's a shame. You were always so talented."

"My talent doesn't make it any less a waste of time," Travis answered, his voice so steely that Sean decided to drop it.

"You get settled in, and I was thinking we could go to Fritto Misto for dinner. The pink sauce is still the best in town." Travis didn't want to play into Sean's excitement, but he was famished, and Sean was right. The thought of that pink sauce sharpened his hunger. He nodded.

"Great, tell me when you're ready." Sean left Travis alone.

Once the door closed, Travis refocused on the mission in his head, pushing aside his misgivings. Who cares if Sean seemed different—warmer somehow, more human? More like the father Travis would have liked earlier in life? It was too late now. Maybe if he'd been like this years ago, their relationship could have been different.

Don't forget what he did.

"I'm here for one reason. And one reason only," Travis stated, quietly but intensely, like he was scolding himself.

He was going to betray this man who he was tempted to start liking. It had to be done to tip the scale from mankind's destruction to mankind's survival.

And to avenge his mother.

Sean glided past the rows of glass cubes in his underground desert laboratory. He watched a bloom of jellyfish expand and constrict and found himself mesmerized by their graceful dance. *There's something here*, he thought. *Pay attention.* He moved onto a colony of ants and studied the way they swarmed. The ebbs and the flows of their movements seemed chaotic, yet Sean divined a clear purpose in their activity, as if they were being guided by a single master.

For Sean, walking among his collection of animals was a tonic against the growing collection of worries that had hardened and settled into his gut. He was still troubled by Shai's notes and wondered where she had been sending them. Had she plundered his discoveries and shared them with outside parties? The universe had entrusted him with this treasure, and he was the one who knew how best to harness or unleash it. If Shai had sent his secrets to others, the results could be disastrous.

Sean finally broke from his concentration on the ants and headed back to his bay of machines and monitors.

He was frozen by what he saw. A silhouette defined against the glow of the screens.

Someone was sitting in his chair. This was not possible. Though there were a few lab assistants and scientists who worked on the Water Bringer Project up aboveground, none were given clearance to enter this cavern or even knew it existed.

"What is all this, Sean?" The voice was familiar and, though calm and deliberate, tinged with anger. And fear.

Sean was tempted to ask Oliver Hailgard how he'd infiltrated this space, but he realized he didn't need to know. Sergeant Ollie had long boasted he could break into any place, and he'd proven that claim true many times in the past.

"I'm trying to clean up the mess I've made," Sean explained. He was disappointed to hear his own voice. It sounded weaker than he intended, more apologetic.

Ollie stood and faced Sean. "By making them greater?"

"No. No. They're already great. By making them good."

Sean and Ollie stared at the rainbow-colored underwater world on the other side of the glass wall. Clusters of sea anemones clung to the coral, and orange-and-white clownfish darted in and out of their tentacles.

"Look," Sean urged, "closely. You see those fish? They aren't afraid of the anemones, because they don't need to be. The anemones can just exist alongside them. No aggression. No danger."

Sean held a tablet in his hands and pressed buttons until another group of fish—silver and black—were released into the tank.

"But these fish? They aren't clownfish. Anemones don't feel the same way about them."

The silver and black fish swam among the anemones. The anemones suddenly swelled on one synchronized movement and shot numerous venomous barbs. The fish suffered a few spasms before being pulled into the anemones and absorbed, cruelly and efficiently.

"The anemones have a different instinct toward these ones," Sean observed. "But watch: I've patched a behavior modification into the anemones, which is triggered by the introduction of a biological element."

Yellowish green fluid was injected into the tank. As they watched, the anemones changed—one after another, as if they something were spreading through them like a wave. They went from looking aggressive and dangerous to relaxed and peaceful.

Another school of silver and black fish entered the water. These fish swam among the anemones unharmed.

"You see!" Sean beamed. "This is the solution, Oliver."

"These are anemones and fish, Sean. What you released into this world is a little more complicated."

Sean brushed him off. "It's still only cells. It's just behavior. Matter is matter—it's just combined and organized differently."

NOW

Tranton read through the scrolls and examined the maps to distract himself, but he kept hearing Torrain's words echoing inside his head. That boy, lecturing him: It was a humility he should never be expected to suffer. Tranton was the only one who knew how truly great the Nilsings were—these secret scrolls told a history that no one else knew. Once all was made clear, everyone would see how shameful it was that Torrain was ever permitted to scold him.

Like a flea rebuking a god.

Tranton scrawled quickly across page after page, his pen hardly able to keep up with his thoughts. Reading the story of his great ancestors had been inspirational. He now knew what to do. He'd restore the glory of the Nilsing family first—and then the glory of mankind.

He saw where he'd gone wrong before. His destiny was never in leading Mountaintop; that was folly. He was meant to thrive outside of Mountaintop. Far away from here.

Torrain cleared the stone workspace before he and Istoch gently lowered Belubus' broken frame onto the surface. Torrain took a quick inventory of the wounds the poor man had suffered.

"Severe lacerations across the top chest and the right arm." Torrain recognized the handiwork; only one creature could do this kind of damage. "It was a Threatbelow that attacked him?" he asked. Istoch shrugged his shoulders and looked over at Persopile.

"Y-yes," she stammered, still shy in the presence of these intriguing strangers. "He had taken one in to nurse it back to health after it was poisoned."

By us, Torrain thought with regret. He flashed to the scene he'd tried so hard to forget. Icelyn storming away, furious at him and Adorane, while so many of the creatures who called her *Mother* lay dying around them.

Torrain continued to examine Belubus' body. He winced when he inspected the legs. They were crushed. These were never going to heal. "Looks like Belubus was too successful for his own good. This creature had gained its full strength back when it attacked. I'm going to guess it was Croathus and not Anaghwin?"

"I don't know what that means," Persopile responded. No use pretending she did.

"It doesn't really matter. Croathus thirst for our blood. Anaghwin do too, but they won't act upon that hunger because Icelyn forbids it." Torrain treated the wounds with serums he'd created from the herbs and minerals in the area. "Goodness, Belubus, how are you even still alive?"

"Will he ever walk again?" Istoch asked, looking at the mangled legs.

Belubus struggled back into consciousness. His eyes darted back and forth, and he had a difficult time opening his mouth. Torrain gently held a clay mug of water to his parched lips. Belebus drank.

"Just let me die," he murmured, his voice hoarse. "I'm begging…" he trailed off back into sleep. Torrain checked Belebus' chest to make sure he was still breathing.

"We're not a community that lets the weak die. Not anymore," Torrain declared. "We're going to save you, Belebus."

20

NOW

Amperous hadn't felt this way since he'd lived his life beside Lenolin. Because of that, he felt guilty. He'd always believed that if he couldn't love her anymore, he'd love no one.

Yet it couldn't be helped. The Priestess of Two Temples made him feel disloyal to Lenolin because she made him feel as only Lenolin had.

As they led their horde of exuberant Croathus through the great valley, she walked just ahead of him. Normally this would upset him. No other creature should assume she was better than Amperous. Yet she walked ahead, and he thought it made sense.

She was extraordinary.

"You can look at me longer if you'd like," she stated, both matter-of-fact and alluring. Amperous averted his gaze, chastened that she'd caught him staring. She stopped and turned to face him. "Go on. Your eyes must be hungry to see after so long underground."

Amperous studied her for a moment, but then he grew shy. He turned and stared at the multitudes of Croathus who had stopped walking, mirroring the Priestess in her movements exactly. They gazed at her, expectant, like she might perform a wondrous miracle at any moment.

"When I led them, they were a chaotic bunch, each hungry to fill their own stomach. How have you tamed them so?" Amperous asked.

"You still lead them, Amperous. Only with me by your side," she assured him, her voice melodious. "By your side. Or slightly ahead sometimes, perhaps," she added with a smile.

She reached her right hand toward him. He slowly reached until he held it.

"Our kind are meant to live in connection with each other. We fit into each other to build the whole. Like one hand grasping another, we are each created to fill what the other lacks. The Mothers have made us so, and the Mothers make no mistakes."

She continued to hold his hand while she turned and continued their journey into the narrowing valley. The thousands of Croathus behind them resumed their march.

"Mothers?" Amperous asked, genuinely confused. "Who are the Mothers?"

She laughed, as if the very thought of them made her happy without reserve. "I continue to forget what you know and what you do not. The Mothers? They are our true gods, Amperous. Our actual creators. And they cannot wait to meet you."

They ascended from the great green valley until they overlooked a flat golden expanse of scrub, giant boulders, and leafless trees. The sun was hotter here. They needed to take a break; the elevation was wearing on them. They weren't to the point where madness or death might strike them, but the heights still took their toll.

Amperous had never been to this place before. He'd always preferred staying closer to the ocean. He'd never figured out exactly why. To be closer to his brother in the Drowned City, maybe. Even though the area had brought him great pain, he'd never wanted to leave. Perhaps he didn't want to leave because it was the source of that pain.

The sunbaked trees looked like creatures frozen while attempting a desperate escape.

"Have you ever been to the desert before?" the Priestess asked.

"No."

"It's lonely," she replied. "But a good kind of lonely. The kind that makes you stronger. I lived a solitary life here for years. That is how I've emerged as I am now. All great faiths are born in the desert."

Faith? As in a religion? Amperous thought of the blinders his brother refused to remove—his devotion and dedication to the Brathius. The Anaghwin clung to their faith to avoid reality.

"Religion is weakness, not strength."

She smiled, put a gentle hand on his shoulder, and laid her head flat against his back. His heart rate increased. She slid her arms around him and held him fast, an embrace from behind. He could feel her heart pumping, too.

"Tell me, what we are experiencing right now, together. Is this strength or weakness?"

He could not speak. His breath grew ragged. It was partially due to the elevation, but mostly because he could hear her breathing in his ears and felt her warmth all around him.

"The most wondrous things in this world are both strong and weak at the same time, Amperous, not one or the other. That which is bonding us together right now is a force stronger than steel. But our bodies, in the presence of its glory, tremble like frightened rabbits. Strong and weak. Life, love, religion: All are strong and weak at once."

Amperous didn't know what to make of what she was saying, but he knew he never wanted this moment to end. He wanted to be skeptical, but he found himself willing—eager, even—to swallow whatever she would feed him.

She broke from the embrace. Amperous felt like he'd been dropped into frigid water, the transition was so sudden and unwelcome. She stretched a halting hand back to the Croathus. They stood still while she walked forward. Amperous followed her.

"If we embrace religion, we will be no better than the Anaghwin. Denying reality," he protested, regaining his senses.

She walked to a place where a pair of identical hundred-foot tall boulders nearly touched. Between them, there was an opening just wide enough for her to enter. She continued walking, stately and elegant, and Amperous found himself struggling to keep up.

"The Anaghwin have survived, despite their meager numbers, have they not? There is a resiliency to them. Many of them accepted certain death for their faith. Was that not a bravery of the highest kind?"

She turned a corner in a rocky slot canyon and approached a watery oasis lined by tall palm trees. Where everything had been muted browns and dull blackish greens, now Amperous was stunned by emeralds and blues.

His head felt foggy. Still, he argued. "Not so much bravery as foolishness." He looked ahead and blinked, trying to regain his bearings. What was he seeing? Was he hallucinating?

The Priestess headed toward a magnificent structure. It stretched high above both of them, shimmering in the sun. It had graceful balance and symmetry, with multiple towers and arches surrounding the main structure. Amperous could tell that no human had made this. Mostly by his knowledge of what human-crafted buildings looked like, but also because of how it felt.

"We built this," the Priestess stated proudly. Amperous stared. On the coast, Croathus only lived in the ruins of what the human construction. They'd never made anything more than a simple hut out of twigs and leaves by themselves. Yet this was grander than anything he'd ever seen—even from the time when he was a pup, before humanity fell. The building almost looked like the body of a Croathus itself—grand, toned, elegant in its sublime lines, reaching for the heavens.

The building glowed like the sun, most of it shiny and yellow, forged out of gold. It was accented with polished stones, some black as the night, some bold jade green.

"Sometimes bravery laced with foolishness is exactly what we need to survive. Amperous, you need to see what you lacked before—see what you were missing. You had nothing to bind us all together. You led an army to the top of the mountain, and they were defeated. I say this not to bring you shame, but to point out how to make you stronger. In order to survive, to prevail, to dominate, the Croathus need a light worthy of survival, victory, and domination. Hungry stomachs and a thirst for revenge are too dim. You lost, and you will continue to lose, because you have nothing that makes you desperate to win."

Amperous could no longer muster any energy to argue. He found, curiously, that he didn't even want to.

"Tell me, what is your religion?"

"Your brother worships the Brathius. Our father. But that father abandoned us, so he is unworthy of our worship. That's where the Anaghwin have gone wrong. We've corrected that. Welcome, Amperous, to the Temple of the Mothers."

I must do this before the other Mothers rise.

Icelyn's words repeated in Omathis' mind.

The other Mothers.

They awoke in him a dim connection to his brother, Amperous. This confused Omathis—Amperous had died in the poisonous cloud up in Mountaintop. Why was he sensing him now?

The words shot adrenalin through his legs, like when you almost fall from a great height but catch yourself just in time. He hadn't felt a terror like this since Shai had taken over Sean Brathius' lab.

Omathis remembered Lenolin's rage when her child had been slaughtered in the attack by the humans so many years ago. Even compared to Amperous' rage, white hot and unstoppable, she had been volcanic.

He thought about the animals that populated this world. Nothing was more fearsome than a mother. When a cub was threatened, a mother bear would transform into a savage beast. A father's fierce defense of a child is hit or miss; there are even instances where a father slaughters his child to assert his own power. Children are not always a priority for fathers.

When a father loses a child, he may be angry or depressed. He may even die from his grief. But a mother? They grow violent, cruel, vindictive —their vengeance becomes their only mission. Nobody fears a father's vengeance, but we all fear what a mother is capable of doing when her child has been hurt. For a mother, her child is more important than existence itself.

Before the other Mothers rise.

Omathis hadn't figured out what that meant. Not yet. But he did know, with complete certainty, that these other Mothers rising—whoever and whatever that meant—would be very bad for the Anaghwin. And they could spell doom for Icelyn, for the humans who remained in Mountaintop, and for every living thing that had ever hurt a Croathus.

ICELYN

My legs are sore and wobbly as I fall over the side of the boat and stumble onto the sand. I've always adored the way the waves rise into the air and then crash in an explosion of white froth. I lie where I'm crumpled and watch, exhausted but exhilarated.

Adorane searches the beach with wary eyes. I know we've arrived back on dangerous land, but I'm strangely calm. The sound of the surf, rushing in and out, could lull me to sleep.

Adorane grabs me by the arms and jerks me to my feet, more roughly than I like.

"Come on. We don't have time for whatever it is you're doing," he scolds.

"Ad, we're not any more or less safe if I rest for a moment," I complain.

But then I notice Eveshone.

She is on all fours, scouring the shore, sniffing and stalking. She's graceful and strong, but clearly in distress.

"What is it?" I ask Ad.

He stands close to me, as if to shield me against the invisible terror

Eveshone is sensing.

"I have no idea, but I've never seen her like this."

He's right. She's making a series of confused noises that seem involuntary. Cheeps, moans, deep breaths, exhalations, chirps. We run to her. If there's something powerful enough to unnerve Eveshone, we shouldn't be far from her protection.

"Eveshone, what is it?" I ask.

She locks eyes with me long enough to convince me that I should be scared. But that's all the time she can spare before she's back to her patrol. Finally, she stops stalking and stands tall in front of me and Adorane.

"There is a creature on this beach with us. One familiar and alien at the same time."

I squint and stare but see nothing.

"And it hunts us," she adds.

I will myself to look harder, feeling the tiny muscles that control my eyes and attempting to flex them—forcing them to see whatever it is Eveshone has picked up on.

"Do you see anything?" I whisper to Adorane.

He shakes his head no. Not seeing what Eveshone sees is far more terrifying than seeing it.

The beach is wide and flat as far as I can see. The trees and brush are hundreds of yards away. There is nowhere for a creature to hide.

"There!" Eveshone bellows, pointing to the place where the higher tide has left the sand darker and it contrasts with the lighter, almost white sand. "Stand behind me. It's coming."

"Should we run?" I ask.

She points to behind us, to our left, in front of us.

"There are more than one. They have surrounded us."

I blink again, hard, not in order to see more, but this time to verify what I think I may have seen. I think I may be picking up on what Eveshone has sensed, and I very much hope I am wrong.

I see them in the mist rising from the crashing wave. It's hard to explain, but the fine sprays don't dissipate the way they should. They wobble just a little. That's the key to seeing them—noticing that tiny shift. Once I picked up on that, their form starts to become obvious to me.

They rise from the waves—walking on two legs, with muscled torsos, long arms, large heads. I can see them, and then I can't. They are transparent shifts in the scenery around them, at least at first.

Yet they are not completely clear. I see thin ribbons—blood red, royal blue, deep purple—running through their bodies, like beautiful dyed fabrics I would have loved for playing dress up when I was little. These threads seem to hang in the air as the space around them shimmers and shifts, distorting the view of what's behind them like a drop of water would. They are unmistakably moving toward us.

"I don't understand what I'm seeing," I say quietly.

"They are as I am," Eveshone replies, "but not."

She's right. I see it now. The clear shimmer is in the shape of a pack of Croathus or Anaghwin, only invisible.

"We need to get out of here," Ad says.

"Maybe they aren't dangerous," I offer hopefully. They are somewhat beautiful. Even though their movements are off-putting—jerky and stilted, while still with some measure of grace—I do find myself beguiled by their form. Maybe they are blessings, not curses?

Before anyone can reply, a quiet, high-pitched whistle sounds in the distance. Eveshone throws her outstretched arm in front of Adorane.

The air pressure changes, and I hear a squishy sound—the kind that happens when something wet hits against something dry.

A crimson red whip punctures her skin and plunges deep into her. She roars in terrible pain. The blood-red ribbon extends from one of the creatures—still twenty yards away. The ribbon moved with unbelievable quickness and would have plunged deep into one of Ad's eye sockets if not for Eveshone's reflexive defense. Ad picks up a piece of driftwood and bashes at the red projectile until it's no longer attached to her.

While he pounds away, another series of ribbons shoot toward us. Eveshone picks us both up, leaps over an approaching line of the See Throughs, and rushes toward the trees.

"That ribbon was meant to strike you or Adorane, Lovely." She states, regaining her customary calm. "I stood in its way."

More multi-colored wisps whip toward us as she runs. Eveshone cradles us and contorts her body to dodge most of them. Some hit her and she stifles her screams of pain.

Still, despite being hit multiple times, Eveshone appears to get faster and stronger. We near the treeline. The See Throughs hesitate.

"They can't leave the water behind," Adorane observes. "They'll dry up!"

The sun overhead burns down onto us, hot and relentless. Some of the See Throughs have started to shrink from the dry heat and slink back toward the tideline to rehydrate.

Eveshone steps forward.

"And you call yourselves strong!" she bellows. "There are many of you, and only a few of us, and we prevail!" I think it's rather kind of her to include myself and Adorane in the "few of us," as if we're also worthy opponents to the See Throughs, and not just prey who need protection from their pursuit.

Though not daring to brave the heat of the sun any further, the Sea Throughs project their ribbons toward Eveshone as she gloats. Many fall short, but a few hit her. Some have enough strength to pull her toward them before she manages to disentangle herself.

"Eveshone, stop! Let's go. You don't need to boast!" I plead with her. I'm not sure how many hits from the terrible ribbons she can survive—especially after suffering such damage from the creatures in the Dark Spine.

Eveshone closes her eyes tightly against the pain that rips through her body. "Two things, Lovely," she stammers, barely able to get the words out. "One: I do need to boast. It's part of my nature when in conflict. You of all people should know that, because you made me this way."

Another series of barbs pierce her skin as she gracefully jumps back and forth to shield me and Ad. We are the intended targets.

"And two: The venoms of the jellyfish may kill other animals, but my kind are designed to be strengthened and healed by them. This hurts like a million fires pressed against my skin, but soon I'll feel stronger than ever."

21

NOW

The Priestess pulled the towering jade door open and invited Amperous to enter first. He felt embarrassed because he was afraid. He wasn't sure he wanted to find out what awaited him inside.

As he approached the opening, he could hear noises, which surprised him. He had been expecting reverent silence. The sounds were distant, but he thought he could recognize a screech, a roar, a growl.

He stepped inside the temple and into a circular room that was open all the way to the roof, hundreds of feet above. Sunlight streaked through windows placed in an ascending spiral from the bottom to the top. Some of the windows were filled with colored glass, staining the light with different hues—reds, greens, purples, and blues. The result was stunning, a spinning rainbow of color.

About thirty feet above his head was a balcony that encircled the entire hall. It bore trimmed railings made of wood from the trees Amperous had seen outside. Curtains woven from silks and linens hung heavily all around the wall behind it.

"Walk to the center of the space, Amperous," the Priestess requested. Amperous obeyed.

The Priestess approached a large standing stone circle that rose from the floor like a mill wheel. Words were carved into the stone. Amperous could read them—they were written in Latin.

LEO

URSA

AQUILA

TURRITOPSIS DOHNII

FORMICAE
ACINONYX
VESPERTILIO
PORIFERA
LUPINE

"Close your eyes," she commanded, though gently. He complied.

She held onto the stone and pushed downward against it, spinning it slowly. As the stone wheel turned, the curtains above began to raise from where they hung.

"Open your eyes."

Amperous kept his eyes shut for another moment, finding it difficult to open them. What would he see? The noises from earlier were growing louder and more aggressive. A howl. A fluttering of wings. Another low rumble.

"Open your eyes, Amperous."

This time he did. Where the curtains had been, he saw a series of openings carved into the side of the temple walls, stretching all around them in a full circle.

The Priestess hummed. She held a tremulous note for what seemed like an eternity. As she did, from each of the openings, an animal emerged and perched itself on the railing above.

Amperous turned and saw them each in progression.

A mountain lion. A grizzly bear. An eagle. A cheetah. A wolf. Each watched him in silence. Amperous felt a curious sensation rise in his stomach—sadness, but also joy. It felt like both.

"What about those openings?" Amperous managed to whisper, and pointed at four that were still empty.

"Wait and see," the Priestess answered as she continued to turn the large stone wheel.

As he watched, a large glass cistern on a stone platform emerged from one of the openings. It was full of water and contained a pulsating, ghostly white orb. Another glass vessel appeared in the next opening. This one was filled with dirt—though that dirt was criss-crossed with a series of squiggly lines and tunnels. Another water-filled cistern slid toward the railing. This one contained a group of brown spongey blobs.

Finally, from the last opening a flying creature emerged and swooped over their heads before landing on the railing. Amperous thought at first that it was a bird, but he quickly realized that it was not. This creature was a bat—a mammal that could fly. It was larger than any he'd ever seen, too—nearly the size of a fox.

Amperous slowly turned in the middle of the sanctuary, looking from one creature to the next. He was overcome by the feeling he'd been confused by earlier. It was sadness, mixed with joy, and now another element. It was a distant familiarity, he realized—like he'd once known each of these creatures intimately but had forgotten them. To see them all here, in one place, made him feel as though he was awakening from a long slumber. He had a curious itching on the corners of his mind, like he knew what they meant to him, but couldn't remember yet.

The Priestess continued to hold her note. The creatures—each in their own way—joined in.

Amperous fell to the ground and bowed. He rose and then fell to his knees again. Nine times, once to each of the animals looking down on him, he rose and bowed.

After the final bow, the Priestess lifted him back to his feet.

"Amperous, whose hair is golden as the sun, join me. Spread this new faith across the world. Only you can lead the Croathus to where they are meant to be. And I will help you."

"Tell me more about the faith of the Mothers," Amperous whispered.

The Priestess locked eyes with Amperous. "Omathis' belief in the Brathius was centered on obedience. *We must wait on Mistersean; we must do what Mistersean commands; we must be patient.* The Mothers teach us to fight for what we want. We look at the world and see that which doesn't belong. And we destroy it. The Mothers want *us* to make this world into the place we need it to be. We do not look forward to a reward that will someday be given to us; we create that reward ourselves. We remake the world in our own image by tearing down what doesn't belong, melting it, and molding the remains into what does. Amperous, you are meant to lead this battle. Will you become the creature you were made to be?"

Amperous didn't have to think about his answer. "Tell me how."

She held him close and pressed her forehead against his. It was an act of intimacy Amperous hadn't experienced in centuries.

The creatures above roared, growled, screeched, pulsated, and howled.

Amperous experienced a strange perception. Suddenly he could see—not only through his own eyes, but from the outside. He could see himself and the Priestess from multiple perspectives. It was as if he were looking through the different creatures' eyes, each of them, down upon them.

Through this new perception, it was clear—he and the Priestess looked right together. Their union was blessed. It was his destiny.

"Our mothers approve," Amperous whispered.

THEN

Oliver scanned research notes, diagrams, calculations, and experimental results on the central computer silently as Sean watched. Sean knew better than to try to stop him. At six foot two inches and muscled from decades of combat training, Oliver Hailgard could subdue an elite soldier. Sean couldn't do ten pushups without collapsing.

"I see flight. Underwater breathing. Longevity and regeneration. Reconstitution. Echolocation. Group non-verbal communication. Camouflage." Oliver wasn't only stating facts, he was making accusations.

Sean sighed. "None of those abilities are new in the Croathus. But they aren't apparent in them yet. Unlocked potential."

"You built *backdoors* into living creatures like they were *software?* The ability to upgrade at a later date?"

Ignoring Ollie's accusatory tone, Sean responded with enthusiasm. "Exactly! You understand. There was a roadmap. So yes—I built the ability to fly, say, into their genetic code, but added a mechanism so that it needed to be unlocked. Likewise with all the other attributes you mentioned, and more."

"Sean, these are dangerous creatures with consciousness and complex emotions—likes, dislikes, and the ability to make their own choices, right or wrong. Not computer software."

Did Ollie really think that Sean needed to be reminded that Amperous and Omathis were more than mere lines of code? Sean loved them. He always had. That's why he was doing this work instead of joining the effort to find and exterminate them.

"As they are, they are lethal and nearly unstoppable. And you built in new, even more dangerous abilities that they could figure out how to unleash at any moment? I've never heard of such foolishness, Sean!"

"This is not something they can just...unlock on their own. It's highly complex. And I'm not going to unlock all of those elite abilities in them, Ollie. I'm focused on one," Sean assured his friend. This was a lie, but a small one. "I am looking into how to reprogram them in one discrete area."

A light of realization went on for Ollie, and with it a trace of hope. "You're trying to change their instinct toward humans."

"I'm going to reverse it, so they feel toward humans the way they do toward me and Laura Lee."

An interesting idea—but it wasn't going to work, Ollie realized, deflated. "First we'd have to find them, which is already proving difficult. And what are you going to do—give them a pill? An injection? You know they won't tolerate captivity again."

Sean pressed a series of keys until video feeds of the different social creatures appeared on the screens—meerkats, ants, honeybees, squirrels, and others. Individual members of the colonies busied themselves with their tasks.

"No, nothing so crude as that. Look at the ground squirrel. A coyote appears on one side of the field, and within seconds all the squirrels in the area know to go below for safety."

Sean pressed a button and an image of a savage predator appeared in the squirrels' cube. Instantaneously, all the small grey animals dove into their burrows.

They turned their attention to the ants, who were busy carrying dead members of their colony to the surface. "An individual ant dies, and the others know, even if they're miles away. We're not sure *how* they know—maybe a pulse of electricity, maybe pheromones, maybe something else—but they know, and they come swarming to clean up the mess."

On the screen, Sean and Ollie watched groups made up of individuals who executed their roles as expertly as members of a professional orchestra or dance troupe.

"It's like upgrading a networked cluster of computers. I spliced the characteristics of hives, swarms, flocks, herds, and colonies into Amperous, Omathis, and the others. It's why they can communicate non-verbally and sense each other's presence. When they're together, they're stronger. They amplify each other; they heal faster, too. But that's not why I made them this way. I added this ability specifically so that I could unlock the upgrades if need be. I never wanted to have to kill my existing creatures because they were obsolete once we moved onto a new design. That's the only reason I made upgrades possible. It was born of my love for them, I promise."

Ollie was annoyed at how often he fell under the spell of Sean's twisted yet compelling vision. Certain acts could be objectively foolish—like breeding the ability to fly into already super-powerful lethal creatures. Yet after Sean's explanation, he could see how it made sense.

"And how close are you to making the Love for Humanity Upgrade possible?"

Sean could sense Ollie coming around to his plan. It felt good to share it with someone. It had been only his for so long.

"I'm on the edge, Ollie. *Right on the edge.* I've figured out the environmental trigger and everything."

"What does that mean?"

"Some biological changes can only happen when something extraordinary occurs in the environment. For instance, redwood seeds will not germinate until they're consumed by fire. That fire is an environmental trigger."

"So you're going to burn Omathis and Amperous?"

"No, nothing like that. In their case, I only need to dissipate my DNA into the atmosphere."

"My God, you're a Narcissist. Only instead of your mirror, you have your work. Whatever happened to science being objective? You can't seem to stop inserting yourself into your experiments whenever possible."

It's *my* work, Sean thought. *Of course I insert myself in it.*

"I only need to find them, and I can fix this."

Ollie made a tremendous effort to shake off the appeal of Sean's plan. He regretted keeping the beasts' escape a secret; they should have been eliminated back then. Now Sean was trying to exploit his compassion again.

"No. If we find them, Sean, we will exterminate them. That's the mandate."

"But I can make this right," Sean insisted.

Ollie stood, his posture rigid and his words clipped to disguise his anger. "Don't you see? Say all goes well and you manage to solve the problem in Omathis and Amperous. Even so, by the time you do it, their children and their children's children will have mutated. And then we'll all face an even greater threat—more lethal, more capable, more angry, more wounded. This is not within your control anymore, Sean. It never was."

Ollie stood and walked away from the computer. Their discussion was over.

Despite his disappointment, Sean exhaled in relief, not even aware that he had been holding his breath. He was lucky. Ollie had not found another area of Sean's research during his computer scan.

Not only was Sean on the edge of using their hive mentality to reverse their lethal instincts, he was also on the verge of something else, equally as important. Thanks to his tireless work over the past few years, he now had a very good idea of where they were hiding.

Travis laid on his back, trying to recover from what he'd found.

This was just more information. He had to take it in and act accordingly. He could not wither away, broken and empty. He was a soldier, not a dying flower.

Prescott had predicted this, down to every detail. Travis had hoped he'd find nothing, but his investigation had confirmed Prescott's account. Sean was involved in something terrible.

"Sean Brathius is protecting his creatures and even working to *enhance* their abilities," Prescott had insisted. "The very same creatures that slaughtered your mother. We believe he has an idea of where they are, but he's hiding that from us. We've hacked the information on his computers and even infiltrated his study at home, but everything is encrypted beyond our ability to decrypt. But we know what he's doing."

That was where Travis' mission began. He had to gain Sean's trust so Sean would slip up and share something with him—anything.

This had been easier to do than Travis anticipated. Travis didn't even know any more if he was pretending to have a relationship with Sean or actually forging one. While Sean was busy working on the Water Bringer Project throughout much of the day, he'd carve out a chunk of time each day to focus on Travis. He'd listen to every one of Travis' words as if they were valuable and worthy of contemplation.

Non-distracted Sean Brathius was such an upgrade.

They'd visited a huge bookstore downtown and spent hours looking for hidden gems among the stacks of dusty used hardbacks. They'd explored the ruins of a zoo the city had abandoned in favor of one with more room for the animals to roam. Somewhere along the line, Travis started to gain more of an understanding of Sean.

They'd gone on a hike to a small waterfall. The area had suffered a drought for a few years, so it was more of a trickle. In fact, when they'd finally arrived at what Sean had promised was "his favorite waterfall in all the world," Travis had to laugh. After an arduous miles-long climb in the sun, *this* was the reward?

"It's water. And technically, it's falling…but…"

"Yeah, it's only a hint of what it used to be. Time to fire up your imagination."

"You've seen Bridalveil, and McWay, and Snoqualmie, and *this* is your favorite waterfall?" Travis chuckled, incredulous.

Sean jumped down off a cluster of boulders and approached the pool at the base of the falls.

"Hold your judgment until you see these."

Travis joined Sean and let his eyes adjust until he saw motion below the surface of the water. Now he saw what had Sean excited—bright flashes of orange and yellow weaving gracefully under the falls.

"These are newts. When I was a child, I would come here every day." Sean dipped his hand into the pool and gently scooped one up. He held it toward Travis.

"You see how they're always smiling? It's a genuinely happy-to-see-you smile, isn't it? I'd spend hours with them, letting them walk up my arms, telling them all sorts of secrets."

It sounded pathetic—except when Travis saw the way Sean looked at those newts, he understood. Sean must have been a lonely kid, too. *Anything* wanting to spend time with you makes all the difference in the world, even if that thing is only a newt. Travis would have enjoyed having a newt around to keep him company while Shai was logging long nights at the lab.

Travis held his hand out, and the newt cautiously stepped onto his outstretched palm. He'd expected angled snake-like eyes, but he was wrong. The newt's eyes were round and jet-black, saucer-like and endearing, in the style Disney would use to animate an adorable amphibious sidekick.

"You named them, I'm sure?"

"Of course. Mostly variations of Isaac. You know, Isaac Newt—"

"Yes, I get it. Very clever," Travis chuckled.

"Isaac, Isaaca for the girls. Or Issacette. Izzy. Some of them I'd name Fig, too."

"You must have been an interesting child."

For weeks Travis had listened closely to everything Sean had said, hoping to find the password that could crack the encryption keeping all those secrets locked up tight on his computer in the study. Travis had found where Sean kept the fob that randomly generated numbers for the decryption protocol. He'd figured out from asking Sean for his Netflix, iTunes, and Wi-Fi passwords that Sean always began his passwords with a 7, added a question mark and an ampersand to the end, and replaced Os with zeros.

Now he just needed to figure out the middle.

He'd tried so many already. After every day spent with Sean, he had a whole collection of candidates. They'd all failed.

While Sean left for another desert lab trip, Travis seized his chance to check his recent collection of promising passwords.

7IsaacNewt?&

Incorrect.

7IsaacNewt0n?&

Incorrect.

Travis bit his lip in frustration. He only ever had three tries before the system locked him out for twenty-four hours.

He slowly typed his last best guess, taking pains to type every character correctly.

7IsaacFigNewt0n?&

As paranoid as Sean had become about security, he never suspected that Travis could be the person to infiltrate his most closely held secrets. He was wrong.

The screen unlocked.

Travis scrolled through the information in stunned disbelief. "Sean, what have you been doing?" he whispered.

He sank back in Sean's desk chair, weakened as he realized the full impact of what that kid who played with newts and named them Isaac and Fig had become.

Travis stumbled unsteadily to his feet and transferred the unencrypted records to the portable hard drive Prescott had provided.

He considered talking to Sean before he made the call to Prescott. Maybe there was some explanation he'd missed.

Or maybe people were just good at pretending to be someone they weren't. Sean had seen what those murderers had done to Shai. Anything other than the total extermination of his lethal creations made no sense. He shook off any sympathy he felt for Sean.

Travis dialed Prescott's number. The answer came immediately. "You've found something?"

"Yes."

The die was cast. Finally, Shai's death would be avenged.

22

ICELYN

Eveshone sets us down on the forest floor.

"Eveshone, you appear happy," Adorane says, disbelieving.

"It's amazing what some venom coursing through your veins will do for your mood."

"Maybe the sheer joy seems, I don't know, inappropriate. We almost died," he says flatly.

"No. *You* almost died. But I protected you. So everything is good. As it should be, even!" she exclaims. "There's nothing like jellyfish venom to bring you back to life."

"Eveshone, those weren't like any jellyfish I've ever read about," I say.

"True, Dear One. They were like me, but also like jellyfish."

"Do you not think that's strange?" I ask.

"Very strange, Lovely! I was hoping you'd know how that was possible and could explain it to me."

I do not. I look at Adorane, who shrugs.

"First we saw one like me who could fly like a bird," Eveshone muses, "and now we see a whole group like me who seem to made of jellyfish, Lovely."

I don't reply, but I feel a sense of dread rising. Eveshone continues to speak.

"I didn't feel that we shared roots with them, though, did you? And even if we could, I'm not sure they could speak, or think, or do anything but feel. They didn't feel…*smart,* if you know what I mean. Tell me, Lovely, what do you know about them? Did you make other creatures that were not smart?"

She's assuming I made them, but of course I didn't. I don't think Sean

Brathius would have made them either. This brings me to a question I'm hoping Eveshone and Adorane won't think to ask, because I don't like where the answers could lead.

Who did *make them?*

Adorane brushes off Eveshone's musings. "No need to give them an intellectual aptitude test. Let's just make sure we avoid them."

He gets to the business of orienting himself, looking at the sky, observing the flow of wind, tracking the position of the sun.

"Apex should be in that direction," he says, pointing in to the northeast. "We can avoid the mountains if we use the pass. It's about two days' journey that way."

"We've already talked about this," I say. "We don't *want* to avoid the mountains."

"And Adorane, let me remind you that I saved your life multiple *times* on the beach," Eveshone lectures. "So it should be up to *me* where we go next. And I declare that you and I should both obey Lovely's wishes, for she is a god."

"You saved Icelyn's life too," Adorane mumbles in protest.

"Oh, I'm not so sure about that. I don't believe gods can die. I mean, I'd rather not test it, in case I'm wrong, but I do not believe Icelyn can die. Not as easily as you can, at least. For she is a god, and you are not."

"Yes, you've mentioned that," Ad says, annoyed.

"From observing your interactions with her, it seems you require frequent reminders that she is a god and you are not, and that you should obey her wishes."

He relents. "Fine, we'll go to Mountaintop. It will save us time anyway." He turns to me. "I was just trying to save you some hurt feelings."

"What's that supposed to mean?" I ask.

"You're going to regret visiting."

He strides off into the thick woods toward the distant mountains, Eveshone and I trailing behind.

"Why? How? What do you mean?"

"You'll see soon enough. I don't want to talk anymore, Icelyn. Let's try silence for a while."

We reach a grove of mighty trees that I remember well. When Ad and I had originally descended beyond the Wall, we spent time in this beautiful spot. The sunlight filters through the leaves and casts a greenish haze on the space. The tree's bark is a mottled tapestry of whites, tans, and browns. It feels more like a masterpiece an artist would have painted for our benefit than something that grew out of happenstance.

I visited this place again on the only trip I made away from the Drowned City since the tragedy in Mountaintop. That's how important what I did here was.

I've been eager to show Adorane what I did then, but now I find myself bashful. He's been moody during our trip up the mountain, and I can't be sure how he'll react.

"Adorane, do you remember how we once promised each other that we'd move those resting in the forest higher up the mountain to this spot?"

"Those *resting?* You mean my father and the other Veritas?" He answers, sounding put off.

I don't know why I said "those resting" instead of "Aclornis." He's right to be annoyed, but this whole exchange is going much worse than I'd imagined.

"Yes. Aclornis and the others."

"I do remember," he states flatly.

I lead him to a sun-dappled part of the clearing, where polished stone markers are lined up neatly.

"I did it," I say quietly, hushed in the presence of such greatness laid to rest. "I kept the promise."

"By yourself?" he asks, though it comes out as an accusation.

"Well, I had help, of course. I had to bring Anaghwin to protect me —and I couldn't move everyone on my own."

Adorane examines the markers. He crouches before the one where the name *Aclornis* is carved.

"You had help from the same creatures who tore him into pieces? You allowed those beasts to disturb my father's remains?"

Dismay rises within me, and my cheeks flush hot and embarrassed.

"No, not beasts. The Anaghwin helped me. It was Croathus who killed them."

"They are all Threatbelows, Icelyn! How could you move my father without my consent? Do you even know the rituals? Did you even say the prayers? Of course you didn't."

"I did! I remembered every word from when I heard you say them!" Adorane's anguish when laying his father to rest was lodged deep inside my heart. I'd never forget. "I repeated them all!"

"But you don't even believe. It's a mockery coming from your mouth."

"Stop it!" I shout, so loud that I surprise myself.

"Saying the prayers, just parroting what I once said! It means nothing!"

"I did it for you!" I interrupt him. I desperately need him to understand.

Suddenly I launch myself at him and tackle him to the ground.

My actions surprise even me, but I feel as though the dam of my anguish has finally exploded beyond my control. There's a brokenness inside of me. It's been there ever since I watched the Anaghwin die in Mountaintop. And it wasn't just their deaths—it was that these boys who had become my brothers were the ones who helped kill them. How could I not be torn in two? I'd finally found a place where I belonged, in the way every person dreams of being loved, and now I was responsible for their death at the hands of those who were closest to me. How was I supposed to put it all back together? How could I ever move forward from losing the love I thought I'd found?

The answer is that I can't. The best I can do is push the thoughts away. Ignore them. Pretend it never happened. But deep down, it is always with me.

It's not just a feeling, either. It's as physical as it is emotional, like I could map the size and shape of the brokenness if I needed to. I can point to where the dark stain lies within me, extending the full length of my chest, from my heart down to my stomach. Sometimes burning red hot; other times weighty, threatening to crush me from the inside; sometimes stabbing with sharpened points of panic; other times a dull ache that throbs with my pulse. Sometimes I forget my grief and that terrible day, just for a moment but then it comes roaring back. Dark, loud, always present.

My brokenness.

It's this that has catapulted me into Adorane and pinned him to the ground. I'm no longer in control. My brokenness craves connection, even if it's baptized in anger.

"I did this for you!" I scream. "Not for me! I'm sorry if I read it wrong! I did it only for you and Aclornis."

I know he could shove me aside if he wanted, but he doesn't. He takes it. Maybe he has brokenness too.

"Look around!" I cry. "It's so beautiful here. I had to fight Omathis to let me come out here to do this. I did it for you. Because if I had a father as wonderful as Aclornis, I'd want him to rest in a place like this. And we promised each other."

I hold him tight, burying my face in his neck, squeezing as hard as I can. I'm powered by anger as I realize what has happened. Adorane was the great love of my life. This love was always destined to be silent, never acted upon, but we both knew it, were always there for each other. Now look at us. We have nothing. Bitter tears run down my face.

He squeezes me back, and it hurts. I can't tell if he's fighting back or embracing me, and I guess it doesn't matter. Our tears mix together, and we continue to hold either to the point of inflicting pain—on each other, on ourselves. We can't tell the difference anymore.

Finally we end up beside each other, on our backs, exhausted from the struggle, looking up at the circle of trees that surround us. Adorane nudges my hand with his and then rests his on top of mine. It's nice.

"I did believe the prayers when I said them," I say quietly, looking up at the light through the green canopy above. "It felt as though your belief was saying them. Through me."

He sits up and traces the letters I carved into his father's polished marker stone. I think he can tell how long it took. Aclornis' stone looks the nicest. I chose one that was just the right shade of green and polished it for what felt like forever.

"This is a nice place, Icelyn. Thank you for moving him here."

I catch a glimpse of Eveshone keeping her distance. No doubt she had struggled against an instinct to rush in and protect me, yet she had not intervened. I'm sure she's learned by now that Adorane and I are confusing and bewildering but mean each other no real harm. I'm still in the process of learning the same.

THEN

"We claim more of this world so that we can continue to grow in strength and family," Amperous declared. He and Omathis stood above a mass of Croathus.

Their offspring were gathered in the torch-lit underground expanse, as grand as a cathedral. They were multiple generations now; their numbers had swelled and they needed more space.

Amperous and Omathis threw themselves against the cavern wall one after another. With each hit, the cavern shook and the crowd cheered.

Finnarious, Amperous' youngest son, watched in awe as the limestone started to crack. He left his place with his mother and joined Amperous.

The crowd sighed and giggled at the intrusion. It was improper and unusual for a child to disturb a ceremony—but who could complain about Finnarious?

"Father," he asked shyly, "Can I take a turn?"

Amperous grinned at Omathis like they shared a secret.

"See if you can be the one to break through and expand our world."

The wee creature coiled up like he'd seen his father do countless times. Finnarious acting like a lethal beast was adorable. Amperous wanted to laugh, but knew he'd embarrass his son if he did.

Finnarious sprang from his position and roared as he crashed into the wall. Amperous and Omathis' impacts had weakened it to the point of breaking, so he crashed through. The crowd cheered and pushed forward.

"In this jungle, in these caves, we will grow and live and love! This is how Mister Sean planned it! This is our home!" Omathis declared, as the Croathus swarmed the newly opened cave and eagerly explored it.

Omathis was thankful for the increased space. He saw the wisdom of what Mister Sean had done. The humans could keep their cities. Omathis and Amperous could spread throughout the places the humans hated to go anyway, underground. Mister Sean had given them a hatred for humans and also provided them the ability to live apart from them. It could all be as he'd planned.

Travis tried to act like he belonged. Still, *he was in the Pentagon*. Earlier in the day, Prescott had shown up unexpectedly. "You want to see the fruits of your labors?"

Travis hadn't been sure what that meant, but Prescott was the kind of guy whose invitation you should accept.

A ride in an armored convoy. A flight in a helicopter. Landing in Arlington. Being ushered into the famous building. Now, waiting in a room with grim-faced people, watching a series of screens.

Travis made sure his face was suitably dour. This was serious business.

On the screen, he watched the view of the lead copter as it soared over the jungle.

"We've launched from a base in Peru," Prescott relayed, his voice monotone and gravelly. "Eight Apaches. Forty special forces. Among our very best."

Travis knew better than to talk. He furrowed his brow enough and Prescott heard his unspoken question anyway.

"Yes, that'll be enough. There were four breeding pairs. They could only birth one child per year. And the young ones stay children for a long time. We figure we have at most eight adults and fifteen to twenty children to contend with."

Travis stayed quiet. He reflected on what two of them had done to his mother—and the armed guards who had tried to stop their escape.

"Do they have bombs on those helicopters?" he asked.

"If need be, we have a transport plane ready to follow up and drop a fifteen-thousand-pound MOP."

"Is that a nuclear weapon?"

Prescott chuckled. "Peru might have a problem with us dropping nuclear weapons in their ecological preserves. This is the largest strike they'll allow us to make."

Travis assured himself that Prescott and the others were the experts. They knew how best to execute a strike like this. Still, he couldn't shake the feeling that they needed more.

Andersen. Jones. Wayne. McCauliff. Johnson.

The soldiers who were speeding over the treetops in the AH-64 had flown fifty missions together already.

A lesser group of soldiers might be tempted to make jokes right now. They were, after all, headed into battle against an enemy no one had ever fought before. They'd been briefed not to take these creatures lightly. *Bred to kill. Created to fight our wars.* It sounded like hyperbole—or terrifying if actually true. Either way, a joke might seem appropriate.

This group stayed focused on the mission. They'd have to be precise. So many parts of a raid could go wrong; even the slightest deviation from the plan could be disastrous.

"They don't know we're coming. That's our advantage," McCauliff said, as if he'd memorized it.

"We are one of two units that will infiltrate their underground living space and place our timed explosives throughout," Wayne followed with his piece.

"Spread out to the northern and western parts of the cavern. Pillars there, if destroyed, should collapse the entire underground ecosystem," Jones recited.

"Surgical, precise, quick. If we do it right, nobody will even know we've been here."

That was the goal. It was one they'd accomplished 50 times so far.

Travis watched as digital diagrams of the cavern system appeared on the screens.

"Have you done any heat sensing to validate your estimate of how many are living down there?" he asked.

Prescott nodded in approval. It was a smart question. "Yes, though as you know, they are not human, so it's hard to gauge their heat signature. They run hotter, so it can mess with the measurements."

"You mean they're giving off the heat of a larger number of creatures?"

"Their internal temperatures run hotter, so we consider the results unreliable."

Tonight was a celebration. The new cavern space brought optimism to their children, who had become cramped and cranky. They weren't created to live piled on top of each other. Omathis and Amperous watched as the Croathus rush between each nook and cranny, exploring, figuring out who would live where. They heard laughter and purring.

There were freshly slaughtered beasts for meat and a full spread of sweet, ripe fruits laid out as a feast. The new cavern, which they'd named Hidden Heaven, had an underground river, winding and curled like a serpent, running down its center. Now they could have their fill of water without needing to leave home.

Everything was lit up by a hundred torches. They were dancing. From different parts of Hidden Heaven, spontaneous songs arose—harmonies and melodies telling of the greatness of who they had become and who they would be.

But neither Omathis nor Amperous could share in the joy.

Amidst the festivities, they'd detected a foreign presence. It was a whisper, but since they both felt it, they couldn't ignore it.

They knew that the others were too busy having a wonderful time to feel a thing. But that didn't matter. Omathis and Amperous had, when very young, shared in suffering a unique set of horrors. Only they could sense that kind of terror closing in.

"I haven't felt anything like this since…" Amperous growled quietly to Omathis.

Omathis didn't want to reply with his true feelings, because it would incite his brother. The men with dark suits. Whatever was burning up his thoughts and seizing his body—it felt like when the men with dark suits were around.

Soneyane and Lenolin could feel the darkened undercurrent flowing between their beloved Omathis and Amperous.

"Go. Do what you must do," Soneyane urged.

Lenolin—being connected to Amperous more intimately—had clearer insight into what he was feeling and fearing. She was not content sending Omathis and Amperous to deal with this darkness alone. She wanted to help. None of them wanted to disturb the celebrations, but something was coming. Something was already here. "Soneyane, you and Omathis head toward the northern portal. Amperous and I will handle the east."

The four of them recognized that this was wise. They needed to check both entrances to the caves, but it would be foolish for Omathis and Amperous to each confront the threat alone. They were powerful individuals, but their true might was in their numbers.

They took one last look down at the seething, pulsing mass of Croathus lost in oblivious celebration. They had those dominant numbers now. That much was for sure.

23

ICELYN

It's strange; you forget a scent for years, and then it's familiar the moment you smell it again. We are on our way to Mountaintop, climbing the brutal crisscrossing trail I've traveled only a few times before. Even so, it is ingrained into me—the smell of wet dirt and green leaves, the views to the ends of the world, the burn in my legs and lungs.

This trip has never been without intense emotion. On the way up with my Anaghwin, feeling their excitement at entering their Brathius paradise. My fears of seeing the Kith, mixed with anticipation of them seeing me, powerful and in command of those mighty creatures who loved me.

Descending in a panic, having watched them poisoned, my skin still smelling of Sulphur and hell, believing Eveshone had died.

Coming down for the first time, getting my first peek at the glories of Down Below, seeing a Threatbelow up close, stumbling into the place where Adorane's father and the other Veritas were slaughtered. This same trail holds so much misery and happiness, but mostly misery. That's probably why Adorane has been so silent for so long.

"Dear One, can I take a closer look at your hand?" Eveshone asks. She always speaks with such deference for me. I don't know which hand she means, so I hold both out toward her.

"Haven't you told me that your kind take a long time to heal?" she asks, her eyes wide. "And yet you've mended yourself nearly as quickly as I would."

She's right. I see only fresh, young skin where that sad little Croathus had dug into my flesh. I had forgotten all about it, but the ever-present pain is no longer there.

"How have you sown your skin back together with such ease and speed, Lovely?"

"I don't know," I answer.

"Probably because I love you so much. I wanted your pain to stop. I'm sure we were in agreement on that."

We were, of course, but I hardly think her wanting my wound to heal had anything to do with it.

"Yes, it could have been that," I indulge her. If she wanted some credit for my healing, why should I deny her?

"Or the salt water did it," Adorane adds. He hasn't spoken in at least hour. I stare at him—this is what he chooses to break his silence to say? "Probably the salt water," he declares again, even louder, nodding his head definitively.

We've reached a lookout, and I gaze across the ocean at the Drowned City, tiny on the dark horizon. It's odd to see this place—my entire world for years—from afar. While there, it had seemed grand, all-encompassing. Now it looks like a speck among countless other specks. It's funny how we get lost in our own tiny spaces, forgetting that there's much more outside our tiny sliver that we can see and experience at any time.

Yet I'm not only seeing the Drowned City.

I can feel it, too. I can hear it. Maybe it's in my head, but that doesn't mean it's not real. The Anaghwin have a hunger for me that I haven't experienced in a long time.

Their longing makes me woozy, and I have a difficult time catching my breath.

Should I return to them? Maybe I've made a terrible mistake. I belong to them. What have I done, slipping away during a chaotic attack? What kind of god does that to her people?

Yet I have something to accomplish away from the Drowned City. Not something Icelyn the human girl could do—something only Lovely the Brathius god could. I know that with certainty. These competing impulses are impossible to reconcile with each other, yet neither will subside.

Existence is impossible sometimes.

"Icelyn, let's go," Ad suggests. He's unsettled by how I'm staring at the Drowned City. I realize that I look like I'm in a trance.

I don't respond. I'm not sure I could even if I wanted to, but I don't want to. I'm awash in impossibilities and anguish. A normal conversation feels inappropriate.

"Perhaps we should give her some more time," Eveshone says. Bless her, she's in tune with me more often than not.

I crave advice. Guidance. Who can tell me what I should do? There should be a group for gods where we can discuss our problems and support each other in our godlike dealings with our creation. I would form one, but as I'm the only god who actually exists, it would be a lonely meeting.

More and more, I think I realize why Adorane prays.

"Ad, when you speak to your god, do you feel like they answer?" I ask.

Adorane waits a long time to respond. He's probably trying to figure out why I would ask such a question. In the past, it would have been to tease him.

"Yes," he says tentatively.

"Does your god tell you what to do? Help you figure out problems?"

Again, a long stretch of silence. He doesn't want to answer.

"Adorane, I promise, I'm not setting a trap. I want to know."

"My god…helps me figure out what to do, I guess. Sometimes. But it's deeper than that. More often, they let me know that I'm…that I'm here, and that I belong here. That it's not an accident I exist…that I'm where I am for a reason. It's a confidence. It lets me know that I don't always have to wonder if someone's made a mistake."

The Anaghwin devotion pulsing from the Drowned City draws on me like a magnet. I'm not sure if they can now sense me, too. It seems to be growing in strength. I want to be with them.

"I think I should like to start imagining conversations with your god, Adorane. We could be colleagues, so it would be different than your prayers. Maybe swapping stories about what it's like to be a god, that kind of thing. Could you arrange that? Tell me how to start?"

Adorane half laughs, which I don't appreciate.

"That's not really how it works. And if you think it's all imaginary, then how could it help anyway?"

"Just tell me how to do it, Adorane. Set it up. I need to talk to someone."

NOW

"Ah," the Priestess perked up, as if she had been summoned by something silent. "It approaches." She took Amperous' hand and led him to a stone spiral staircase in the next chamber.

Though Amperous was curious, he knew by instinct to refrain from asking *what* was approaching. He followed her confident lead.

They ascended one story after another until they reached the top of the temple. The Priestess pushed open a set of jade doors and exited into the bright sunshine. The rays reflected off the hammered gold leaf trim, breaking into a thousand glittering beams of light. Amperous felt as if he'd been transported to the surface of the sun itself.

They stepped out onto a balcony.

The Priestess held her hand out and pointed into the flat desert horizon. "Come to us, *Primitia Aquila*."

Amperous squinted. The heat rising from the desert floor in waves distorted his vision. He couldn't trust what he was seeing. And yet, even after he blinked and wiped the sweat from his eyes, he still saw it. There was a giant creature flying toward them with large wings beating erratically. It looked sick, like it might fall from the sky at any moment.

"What is that?" Amperous asked. He wanted to add that it looked monstrous and terrible, but he sensed that the Priestess would be offended.

"The first fruits, Amperous. And it bears a gift."

The terrible beast was near enough to frighten Amperous. It's mouth was a unsightly collection of jagged, chaotic teeth. It appeared to have the body of any normal, regal Croathus—but with a few awful exceptions. The sleek Croathus body made the creature's overall appearance all the more terrifying—like a beautiful butterfly caught in a spider's web.

As it neared them, the beast's eyes fixed on Amperous. He shuddered and willed himself not to look away. These eyes weren't blue. They were a deep green, like the jade door.

The flying creature held the ragged, beaten body of its prey as it flew. Amperous couldn't make out what kind of poor animal it was—maybe a horse, a deer, or a seal. But it seemed larger than any of those—nearly as large as the flying beast itself. Despite the Priestess' pleasure at the delivery, Amperous wasn't looking forward to receiving the gift.

With a ground-shaking thud, the offering fell beside them. The winged beast landed unsteadily and perched on the edge of the balcony. The Priestess neared the monster and stroked its wings.

"Oh, look who's done a good thing. *Primitia Aquila*, I'm so proud of you." The creature stretched and shook under the Priestess' hand, soothed by her praise.

Amperous wasn't watching, though. He was too distracted by the gift that had been dropped at their feet. What kind of animal *was* this?

Then he realized with horror. "This is an Anaghwin," he stated, his words laced with disbelief.

The Priestess grabbed a brown rectangle—some kind of mashed-together treat—from a pocket in her robe and held it out. The beast grabbed the offering and greedily gnashed the reward between its teeth.

"Okay, girl, you've done well. Now go get some rest." The Priestess gave it a final congratulatory pat, and the ungainly creature launched into flight and away from them, back toward the horizon.

"This is an Anaghwin," Amperous repeated.

The Priestess spoke in a hushed whisper, as if she didn't want anyone to hear them. "I know. I know. I understand why you're upset. It's not Icelyn Brathius, which is who we wanted. But I didn't want to complain while the Primitia was still here. They're very sensitive to criticism, you see—very fragile at this point. The next ones will be much stronger with your help, but for now they're basically children. Regardless, an Anaghwin is better than nothing. The Mothers will greatly appreciate the sacrifice."

The sight of the Priestess bending over the near-dead Anaghwin jolted Amperous from his stupor. Since he'd first met the Priestess, he'd been hungry to please her without even realizing it. He'd certainly never wanted to disagree with her, even when he found what she was saying or doing distasteful. He'd never been attracted to something he'd also feared; it was a unsettling mix.

But this was too much.

"We need to release this Anaghwin," he stated clearly.

"That's against the Mothers' wishes."

She began to bind the injured Anaghwin to a long metal pole with leather straps.

"We don't harm the Anaghwin. Except when they force our hand. We certainly don't make sacrifices of them," Amperous declared.

The Anaghwin mustered what strength it still possessed to slip from one of the cords.

"They worship Mistersean," the Priestess replied, as if that settled the matter. "Here, help me with this, will you?"

"They are our brothers and sisters!" Amperous argued.

While Amperous grew emotional, the Priestess remained detached and resolute—like a patient parent discussing bedtime with a child in the midst of a meltdown.

"This creature is a gift to the Mothers. Neither you, nor I, nor any force in the entire world can do anything about that now."

"Look, I don't care if your winged abomination—"

"The flying creature is a *Primitia. Primitia Aquila*, to be precise," she said sharply. "Please, this Anaghwin's health will soon return. If we don't have it properly tied up by then, we'll have a battle on our hands."

"Let him go. I don't care if that monster captured the Anaghwin and brought him here. It doesn't mean I'm going to watch while one of my brothers is murdered."

"Fine, I'll do it on my own." She sprung into a series of hits and holds —kneeing it in the back, squeezing her arm around its neck, then kicking its legs out from under it—to weaken the Anaghwin once again. Then she finished binding it to the pole. It surrendered and appeared dead except for its slight, ragged breathing.

She neatened up her robe, which had become disheveled from all the activity, and then turned toward Amperous. "My darling," she started, her voice gentle and alluring, "remember how you felt when the Mothers approved of you, and of us? Remember. Your soul felt like it had finally found a home, for the first time in your life. Isn't that right?"

He couldn't deny it. He nodded, and fought tears as his eyes grew misty.

"Don't let your rational thoughts—the Brathius part of you, the Father's part of you—deceive you and ruin what you know, in your heart, to be true. We have been anointed to lead this great faith. But we do not write the rules—they are already written on our hearts. We simply obey them, just like everyone else. We must submit to the Mothers. Do you understand?"

Amperous' thoughts were clouded. He looked from the Anaghwin to the Priestess, and back again. She touched her forehead to his.

"I…I don't understand," he stammered. "I need to know. Where did that monster come from? Who are the Mothers?"

The Priestess laughed, as if she couldn't be happier. "Oh, it's time to make the journey, I see!"

"To where?" Amperous asked.

"I am the Priestess of Two Temples. This is the first. Now it's time to show you the second."

THEN

Andersen scaled the network of descending roots on the tallest walking palm tree in the area. From up here, he had a view of both the northern and eastern entrances to the cavern system. Nothing could enter or leave without him seeing it. He watched as the other helicopters unloaded. His elite colleagues crept through the jungle—really nothing more than invisible shadows. He saw them only because he knew they were there, because he'd been trained to see them.

When he was sure the 39 soldiers were in position, he sent up the flare.

Prescott's tongue darted out of his mouth, then back in, so quick that most wouldn't have seen it. Travis noticed, though, and it reminded him of a snake anticipating a meal.

"There, that's the signal. They're going in. Let's put this ordeal to rest." Prescott leaned forward toward the monitors, relishing the Croathus' impending death.

The sun had set and the jungle was dark, so the video screens had an eerie greenish tinge. Travis could just make out the outlines of the soldiers as they approached the cavern entrances. They were heavily armed with their standard rifles and sidearms, and one soldier in each group had something bulky and long attached to his back. Travis guessed this weapon shot out something especially lethal—liquid fire, perhaps, or a missile.

Prescott's eyes were wide and his normally haggard, lined face seemed younger—like he'd finally caught up on those hundreds of hours of sleep he'd been missing. Travis fidgeted with the buttons on his shirt, feeling sick to his stomach.

"Come on, kid," Prescott scoffed. "This is why we do what we do. You've put in the work. Enjoy the results."

Andersen glanced at the portable screen he'd set up in the branches of the walking palm tree. Its yellow dots marked the GPS positions of the 39 soldiers who made up the strike team. They'd already entered the cavern; he watched as the dots split up and spread throughout the subterranean limestone labyrinth like a virus.

All according to plan.

"Bull Position activated," a voice crackled over the radio. The explosive device had been set at the first critical pillar. Four more, and they could be on their way and watch as the vermin that lived below were exterminated.

"Pointer Position activated," came the next report. They were ahead of schedule. *Employ elite people, get elite results,* Andersen thought with satisfaction.

The yellow dots were already infiltrating into the deepest portions of the caves. At this pace, they'd be finished within the next five minutes.

Lenolin was the first to sense one. Smelling a human after so many decades came as a shock to her. Amperous tuned into the scent immediately.

There are more than one. He used their roots to communicate. *There are many.*

Amperous and Lenolin didn't feel fear. They felt hunger. They sped along the cavern floor silently as the intoxicating scent grew stronger. They could taste human blood under their tongues, sweet and rich in iron.

Andersen noticed a cluster of yellow dots had stopped moving.

"Andersen to Team Quatro. Is your GPS not firing?"

No response.

The cavern was deep. Despite having the best technology in the world, there was always the risk they'd be unable to track them perfectly. "Have we lost your location tracking, Team Quatro? Check in."

Travis watched with concern as Andersen tried to summon Team Quatro. Their yellow dots hadn't moved in what felt like ages. Nobody responded to Andersen's request for a status update.

Prescott couldn't be bothered.

"Just a tech issue. Something always fails. Good soldiers are prepared for it."

Prescott's eyes followed the other yellow dots, which continued to advance deeper into the maze, according to plan.

"They've got Thresher Point and Lemon Point activated too. Just one more and this mission will be a success."

A tech in the room stood and crossed to one of the open computer consoles. His fingers tapped the keyboard in a flurry of movement. "I scanned the feeds," he reported in monotone voice. "Team Quatro's GPS feed is still tracking them. We haven't lost the signal." This made sense to Travis. After all, each member of Team Quatro was tracked separately. The chances of losing one of those signals were pretty good—like Prescott had said, something always fails. But all five of them at once? It didn't make sense.

"Well, what are they doing then? Stopping for a picnic?" Prescott asked, sounding more angry than concerned. He pressed a button to initiate communication.

"Team Quatro. Status. Why aren't you moving?"

They stared at the static yellow dots on the screen. No response.

Then, almost as if Prescott's words had made it happen, one of the yellow dots did move. It left the pack of unmoving markers quickly, zipping through the underground maze at an unnerving speed.

"What is happening down there?" Prescott thundered.

24

ICELYN

Mountaintop was once the only world I knew. My senses had only seen, smelled, heard, and felt within its walls.

Now I've been exposed to much more, just as I'd wanted since I was young. But as we near the Wall, I realize I've paid a steep price for my knowledge. Now this place, once a comfortable home, feels distant and strange.

I've only been here a handful of times in the past years, and each time I have found myself changed. Even when I headed up the mountain, my Anaghwin by my side, I was no longer the girl who had left. I'd seen death, and love, and a whole new world Down Below. On my way back down after the massacre, I was torn in two, changed forever by the slaughter of my children and Torrain and Adorane's betrayal.

Now I am here again—and once again, everything has changed. I no longer know what kind of god I should be to the Anaghwin, or even whether I want to be one at all. I've abandoned Omathis. And I'm facing the daunting task of repopulating a community that no longer welcomes me as a member. I'm also hoping to change the hearts of the Croathus, while not being sure I can even change my own heart. After being the same girl in the same place for years, I'm now a different Icelyn every time I'm here.

How much can one girl change before she loses her most essential parts without any hope of recovery?

As we scale the Wall and head toward the village, I realize that I have been desperately looking forward to the familiarity of Mountaintop. I want something to be the same. I'm different. The Drowned City is different. My life with the Anaghwin is different. Adorane is different.

Our relationship is different.

I hadn't admitted it to anyone, including myself, but I had hoped that Mountaintop would be the same.

I experience such disappointment when we arrive. Everything has changed.

Nobody has gathered to greet me. I am not complaining; I am relieved. If I could freeze the world and walk around for a day or a week, that would be my preference. I don't need attention right now—either positive, which I don't expect, or negative, which I dread. I want to be left alone to figure out how I feel about all of this, about anything.

We left Eveshone further down the mountain out of necessity. Without a mask, she couldn't handle the elevation. She will meet us again once we descend.

I can still sense her thoughts, as we are not so far away as to be unconnected. I feel that she delights in spending time alone in the woods, and I am glad. Every bird song, every tree leaf, every insect or creature she experiences fills her with joy. She adores the woods, which makes sense. After all, she was raised Down Below—the Drowned City was never her home.

It is a small mercy that I get to take in Mountaintop without also needing to figure out how to interact with the people who live there. We've arrived only an hour after dawn, and last night there was a full moon, so I imagine most of the Kith are lazily enjoying a sleepy morning in their labs and rounds.

Adorane picks up on my uneasiness, because he suggests that we climb to a hidden high point of Waterpump, where we can peek at the town below without being seen. It was a favorite spot of ours when we were young.

"Remember the time we saw that Harkus was stealing honey cakes from the Unther family round's windowsills?" I giggle, despite myself. "It felt like we'd uncovered the greatest scandal in human history."

Adorane laughs. The Harkus Honey Cake Scandal had kept us occupied for an entire week. Harkus was a Cognate that neither of us liked. He'd once relished scolding Adorane and me when we'd been having the best time flinging mud at each other. He shamed us, lecturing us that it was unthinkable for the children of such esteemed leaders to wallow in the dirt like pigs.

And then we caught him sneaking bites of a Veritas family's baked goods.

"We worked hard to put an undeniable case together so that he couldn't escape justice," Adorane mused. "What a hypocrite, condescending to us about our mud fight and then stealing from the community."

"And then, when we brought all the proof to our fathers, they only laughed and said they hoped he'd nab one for them too next time," I sigh. "It rankles me to this day."

Ad raises an eyebrow at me. "You can let it go, Icelyn. Harkus was slaughtered by the Croathus during the attack."

That certainly drained the fun out of the conversation.

Then I suppose not all the slaughter of humans in Mountaintop was bad. I sense Eveshone through our roots. I guess she's been listening in.

No, Eveshone, even his death was a tragedy, I correct her gently.

But you said he rankles you to this day. Surely he is better dead?

If rankling someone was worthy of death, then I'd have been killed a long time ago, I reply.

It was meant as a joke, but I can tell she doesn't take it that way.

THEN

Amperous and Lenolin had come upon the five humans before the soldiers even sensed they were no longer alone. They'd sliced and gutted them before the humans had time to scream. It was almost merciful.

As their blood spilled onto the cavern floor, a new level of hunger arose in Lenolin. She dipped her taloned hands into a puddle of blood and then wiped it on Amperous' face, creating a series of streaks on his forehead and cheeks and outlining his large, icy blue eyes. He did the same for her. Their motions were deliberate, gentle, and intimate.

They heard a faint beeping noise, constant and unrelenting. A dim light flashed on a stone pillar. When they investigated it, Amperous gasped and felt a wave of dizziness overcome him.

"We need to get everyone out of here."

Lenolin understood. Furious, she picked up one of the soldiers and slammed his body against the wall.

"Now, Lenolin! We must warn them!"

Amperous sped into the darkness.

Lenolin followed, still clutching the dead soldier in her claws.

The situation room erupted into chaos: Phones rang, people shouted, and techs typed furiously.

Travis stayed focused on that yellow dot, which continued to dart around corners and barrel down straightaways at a tremendous speed. No human could move this fast.

Travis knew why that yellow dot was moving so fast. He'd seen *them*. He'd seen what they could do to a person. Prescott hadn't.

"Abort the mission," he whispered, his throat dry, barely able to get the words out. "Abort the mission."

"Leave the room, Travis," Prescott commanded, though Travis didn't obey. Prescott shouted into the intercom. "Team Mega. Are you there? Team Mega, please respond."

No answer. He shouted hoarsely: "Team Luno, please respond. We'll need you to activate the Nurse Point. Team Quatro is down."

No responses. On the screen, every blinking yellow location tracker was now still.

"What is going on down there?" Andersen asked, from his treetop perch, without a trace of panic in his voice. He was a professional. "Report." He cycled between the radio and the screen, waiting for movement or response. The one yellow dot that had been rushing through the cavern was unmoving once again. It had stopped in a part of the cavern they hadn't mapped, outside the bounds of their diagram.

While he watched, the yellow dots started moving again. Fast. So terribly fast.

And leaving the cavern.

"Teams, we still have one more point to activate. One more point."

Still, the dots rushed in the opposite direction.

"Report in. Do not abandon the cavern. Complete the mission?"

Every flashing yellow beacon was covering so much ground so fast. Andersen did a quick calculation and realized the men were moving at least thirty miles an hour—in the dark and over rough terrain. Humans couldn't do that.

"What is going on down there?" He asked again. This time, fear crept into his voice.

The escaping Croathus swarmed the tunnels, rushing toward the northern and eastern portals. They'd scooped up the slaughtered soldiers on their way out; it felt wrong for these accursed humans to defile their underground haven for all eternity. They needed to be removed.

What had been an evening of joyous revelry had devolved into desperation. The creatures were now purely animal, enlivened by the heavy scent of human blood and trying to escape their caverns before death came.

Omathis, Amperous, Soneyane, and Lenolin led the fleeing creatures and did their best to keep their own thoughts away from their most beastly instincts.

They passed more of the quietly beeping, dimly flashing devices on their way toward the portals. Omathis and Amperous wanted to smash them out of pure fury, but both knew better than to follow their rage. Smashing them would only hasten what they were designed to do—which was explode.

In the situation room, they watched in stunned silence as the yellow flashing lights scrambled toward the exits at inhuman speeds. All commotion had ceased. No amount of shouting or typing or button pushing could change what was happening.

"Detonate the devices. Now." Prescott commanded.

NOW

Torrain entered the room where Belubus was resting and nodded to Istoch and Persopile. They hadn't left Belubus' side since he'd arrived in Mountaintop.

"How is he doing?" Torrain wasn't sure why he asked. He could tell by looking that Belubus wasn't doing well.

"You could ask me," Belubus responded, his eyes still closed. "If you had," he continued, "I'd tell you I'm doing terribly and would like to die, if you can arrange that."

Torrain laid out an assortment of poultices and efficiently tended to Belubus. "I promise you will die eventually—but not anytime soon, if I can help it."

Belubus sighed. But Torrain's touch was gentle and soothing, so he didn't protest.

"Don't worry," Torrain said. "I'm going to get you walking again. Good as new."

Belubus didn't respond, but Torrain noticed his breathing grew ragged and his heart rate surged.

"I've figured some things out. You're going to love it."

"No," Belubus croaked. "I don't want that. Leave me be."

"You're just saying that," Torrain insisted. "You'll change your mind when you see what I can do."

"Tend to me if you must. Relieve my pain. But don't see me as a broken thing that you must fix," Belubus responded.

"Not fixing, Belubus. Healing," Torrain argued gently. "You'll see. It will be a miracle. You will walk again."

"Leave me be."

Torrain pulled Istoch aside.

"Tell me more about Persopile."

Istoch didn't want to. "I don't know much about her."

"Do you like her?" Torrain pressed.

Istoch squirmed at the question. "We talk. She's very sad. So am I. So the time we spend together feels better than time spent alone."

Torrain could tell he was making the boy uncomfortable, but he needed to say this regardless.

"If you like her, you may want to figure out a way to hide her. She hasn't had a sip from Waterpump, has she?"

Realization dawned on Istoch's face—and then it turned to anger. "Who would force her to do anything for Mountaintop? After she was banished because of her beautiful face? Left to die as a baby—and now they'd ask her to have a baby to keep us going?"

Torrain nodded. He agreed with everything Istoch was saying. He'd said it himself during Councils already.

"It's bad enough that anyone thought asking Icelyn to do this made any sense," Istoch fumed. "But at least she's *from* here. Persopile doesn't belong to Mountaintop. She doesn't belong to anyone."

"Survival can bring out the worst in people. There's been talk. And I'm afraid it might become more. That's why I'm warning you."

Torrain noticed that the sun had faded outside and marveled that hours had passed when it felt like seconds. That's always the way it was when he'd entered into the flow of his work. Sometimes, thinking back, he wondered if he'd been in a trance.

He took a step back and admired what he'd accomplished. Sanded down, stained wood bonded to rods of metal he'd salvaged from the Wall and polished until they looked almost new—part utility, part sculpture. Shaped until a graceful form emerged.

What a design the human body was. He'd fussed over it for days to get every detail right, memorialized in wood and metal. Gears and hinges, gyroscopes and hydraulic chambers, balanced to perfection and ready for motion. Two legs, hips, a spine, shoulders, and arms, built from the ground up.

All the parts of Belubus that were broken.

Torrain turned his attention to a clay jar filled with a dull tan dust—a material he'd whittled away and refined from the Brathius masks. He knew it would work—he'd already accomplished so much with this strange substance. This had bonded the masks to the Threatbelows' skin—surely it could bond Belubus' broken body to the frame he'd built.

Torrain checked on Belubus, who was resting, though fitfully, in the next room.

He wouldn't bother him tonight. The miracle would have to wait for the morning.

ICELYN

Mountaintop is nothing like it once was. I hardly recognize it.

First, forget about rounds and labs each being in their proper places. Now I see some rounds have been built where only labs should be, and vice versa. And some dwellings don't appear to be either labs or rounds. Mountaintop is no longer neatly organized into Veritas on one side and Cognate on the other; it's chaos. I can't imagine why anyone would allow it.

Also, as people begin to trickle out and greet the new day, many Veritas kneel and bow their heads. Many set collections of dried sage aflame, and thin plumes of smoke rise above them while they sing. Singing, praying, the whole ritual—all in public. I see more of the symbols that Adorane's religion considers sacred—carved into rounds, painted on doors, even raised outside of Kith Hall. It was as if Mountaintop had forgotten all that mankind had learned in the past three thousand years and willingly descended back into the Dark Ages.

"I can hardly tell which side is Veritas and which is Cognate," I comment, quietly, not sure how to tell Adorane how much I disapprove of Mountaintop in its current form. After all, he is the leader. Had all these changes been approved by him? Had they been his idea?

"Yes, that's because there are no longer Cognate and Veritas. We no longer use those words."

"Oh, please. Just because you change the words doesn't change that there are Cognate and Veritas. You're just not admitting it anymore."

"Icelyn, I believe it's the exact opposite. There never *were* Cognate and Veritas. Just words we used to pretend there was a difference."

As I watch, a group of young men and women gather in the Village Green with guns. They parade with precision, then shoot at a series of targets while other Kith (are they still called the Kith, I wonder?) cheer.

"You have an army, Ad?"

"It's small, but they're well-trained," he answers with pride.

"Do you think it's a good idea to train the Kith to be killers?" I do not. It's not like they can actually kill the Croathus. All they can really do is kill each other.

"We have to defend ourselves," he replies.

As we watch, they wield long spears with metal tips on both ends. The twirl and stab in a fierce display.

"Looks like Torrain has finally added something to those spears," Adorane explains, unable to contain his excitement. "Some kind of technology he developed from the Brathius masks."

I can see what he's talking about. From the tips of the spears a kind of motion is emanating, like heatwaves distorting the air around them on a summer day.

"Why would you do this? Have you not learned anything from what Tranton did?"

"There were many lessons to learn from what happened," Adorane answers, his words clipped and precise. "We can't pretend we live peacefully with the rest of the world when there are hordes of creatures who are one mask away from ascending and killing us."

"But to turn the Kith into weapons, to prepare them for a fight? It seems foolish to me."

"Oh, and what have you done, Icelyn? You haven't trained yourself, building your muscles, your speed, your agility? Your combat skills have improved. Why would you do these things if not to prepare for a fight?"

So he *has* noticed my level of fitness, although he's never mentioned it until now.

I'm upset with Adorane, and it's gotten my blood pumping enough to face other people. "Since you mentioned him, I realize that I want to see Torrain. Very much. I miss him." I'm hoping this upsets Adorane, at least a little bit.

I think it does, though he doesn't let on. "Of course. He'll be happy to see us all."

25

THEN

The faint hints of moonlight grew as the horde of Croathus reached the portal ahead.

The fresh outside air dissipated the heavy iron-filled odor of blood a bit. Omathis felt his burden lighten. His kind were finally emerging from the blood-drunk, panicked spell they'd been under. They'd reach safety. They'd drop these humans outside in the darkness, where they belonged.

A series of low and loud rumbles emerged from deep within the cavern behind them. Omathis felt the pressure change. The air grew weighty and then rushed by him all at once.

He turned back to watch as the sides and roof of this beloved cavern —their haven for the years to come—buckled like they were made of dust. He heard the screams of Croathus as they were caught up in the destruction. He rushed back, deeper underground, as the cavern continued to collapse in upon itself.

"Continue toward the open air!" he shouted to the terrified Croathus. "We must leave the haven!"

The horde followed his instructions. Creatures who had been buried by falling boulders and pieces of the cavern walls tossed those obstacles aside and continue their ascent toward the moonlight and the outside air.

Prescott and Travis watched the screens in unblinking disbelief.

"Like ants. They're covering the ground like ants," Prescott marveled, almost sounding impressed. Travis wanted to repeat Prescott's confident estimate—that there would be no more than twenty-three of the beasts living in the cavern system—but figured it would do no good. They had miscalculated exponentially.

There were thousands of the creatures escaping from the underground.

They watched as the beasts unceremoniously tossed the shredded bodies of soldiers into the trees. Travis buried his face in his hands. His heart pounded, and for a moment he was back in the lab again, Shai's strung-up body hanging before him.

These creatures were evil.

Andersen had heard the command to detonate the devices and tried to protest. His people were still underground. If any of them were alive, this would be suicide.

He didn't have time to worry for long before the explosions came. He watched as the stretch of jungle ground above the cavern collapsed and fell, creating a sinkhole as far as the eye could see.

At least the beasts were dead, he calculated grimly. By everything he'd been told in the briefings—which wasn't as much as he'd normally have liked in terms of knowledge of the enemy—this would be a tremendous victory, even if it meant his team suffered casualties. This was a threat that needed to be snuffed out.

But amidst the overwhelming sound of the cavern system crashing down upon itself, Andersen detected another rush of noise. It sounded more organic—like barking and screeching, yet not quite. Smarter than that. More organized.

His eyes detected movement near the portals. Something stealthy and smooth was moving in the shadows; even in the dark, the moonlight provided glimpses of shimmering motion. He felt a murmur of hope. Had some of the troops survived?

He dug into his pack for night vision goggles and fastened them securely, hoping to get a better sense of what he was seeing. He scanned the space between himself and the ruined cavern. There appeared to be a flow coming out of the cave opening—was it dust? Was it water? He couldn't tell.

Then, a bloodied body of a soldier flew directly toward Andersen's perch. It hit him, smearing him with blood, and nearly knocked him from the tree. Andersen swallowed his shock in time to see another mangled body coming his way.

Now he realized what he'd been witnessing all along. The flow he'd seen was hordes of beasts pouring out of the cave opening, covering the ground as far as he could see. Some were holding the fallen bodies of his best friends, taking turns tossing them.

Directly at him.

Their icy blue eyes, fixed on him, reflected the moonlight like a deadly constellation of stars.

The next body knocked him from his lookout. They swarmed him with stunning speed. He was dead before he hit the ground.

Waves after wave of Croathus dug out of the rubble and escaped into the jungle air. All bore injuries from the collapsed limestone. Most of the wounds were minor; already, their healing abilities were restoring them to complete health. Those who had been more seriously hurt—crushed and bent in ways that would kill other creatures instantly—were being pulled from the wreckage by other creatures.

Around them, healthier Croathus gathered, moving in sync and making a guttural humming noise. Their unity buoyed the badly hurt creatures in the center of the gatherings and quickened their recovery.

Amperous finished his inspection of the jungle and determined that every human threat had been slaughtered. He rushed back to the collapsed portal to check in on his family. He saw Lenolin first. She was strong and healthy—with no injury whatsoever. She'd already gathered their children. All were fine.

Amperous exhaled. He nuzzled his children in grateful relief before he and Lenolin pressed their foreheads together. They'd survived.

Still, though, a worried part of his thoughts wouldn't relax. He could hear it protesting—a low droning noise that kept him on high alert. He scaled the tallest tree in the area, needing a higher viewpoint to assure himself that there was no more danger.

His ragged thoughts had summoned Omathis. His brother joined him in the tree. They scanned the dark horizon in hopes of spotting what could be scaring Amperous.

Your loved ones are safe? Amperous asked.

Every one, Omathis replied.

But still, the droning wouldn't relent. If anything, it grew louder. Amperous felt a surge of adrenalin in Omathis. *You hear it too, don't you?*

His brother nodded. Then they saw the flashing light in the far distance.

"Scatter!" Amperous bellowed, already knowing he was too late.

They leapt from the tree and split to alert the Croathus to the incoming—and even larger—threat.

The sound of the airplane was now inescapable. Amperous and Omathis worked to keep the horde from panicking. *Keep moving! Keep running! Get away!*

Those injured and laid aside were lifted gently by the fleeing Croathus.

Amperous' eyes focused on a Croathus who scooped up both of her children. She held one in each hand, close to her side, and charged forward without missing a beat. He was proud of her love and strength.

It's the last thing he remembered before their world ended.

NOW

Belubus opened his eyes and stared at the ceiling. One benefit of losing his ability to move was that he could better concentrate on what he saw, what he thought, and what he remembered. So many of the higher human abilities were lost in constant motion, in the crude act of getting from one place to another and doing this or that once you got there.

There was a crack in the ceiling, and beside it, a cobweb. In the center of the cobweb a spider perched proudly, surrounded by her trophies. Unfortunate bugs who'd wandered into the wrong spot were drained and wrapped in silk for their mistake. Belubus forced himself to dwell on his memories of Amperous. Was that golden-haired creature merely a spider, designed to devour? Was Belubus an insect who was destined to be drained?

If Belubus could have moved his arms, he would have put his hands around his own neck. Can a person crush his own windpipe? Belubus thought about every person who had lived in the Mines. They'd trusted him to protect them, and now they were all dead. Torn to pieces by Amperous.

Belubus had brought Amperous into the Mines. Belubus had nursed the creature back to health. And Amperous had massacred everyone in the Mines. This was Belubus' fault. There was no other conclusion. He'd run the equation multiple times.

This was why Belubus thought about his crushed windpipe. What cruelty, that Amperous had managed to break so many parts of him—but not any part essential to his survival. But that was probably right, too. Death at this point would be a mercy. Instead, Belubus realized, what he deserved was to think about everyone he had condemned to death—over and over, every day, for as long as it took to reach a proper amount of penance.

A buzzing bee flew across the room and became stuck in the web. The spider pounced on it. Belubus watched it all. He couldn't look away if he wanted to.

ICELYN

We walk through town as people stare and then shuffle away to hide. They look at me like I'm a ghost, or worse—a monster. Adorane lightly presses his hand against the small of my back, guiding me and maybe assuring the frightened Kith that I'm only unshackled and present by his permission. And that I'm not accompanied by more Threatbelows.

I suspect that the townspeople weren't part of the decision to ask me to bear their future children. This was Adorane's idea alone; I begin to wonder if he's shared it with any of the Kith at all. They certainly don't appear to have expected my visit.

Now I understand why Adorane wanted to skip the stop in Mountaintop. I'm not welcome here.

People who once warmly greeted me turn away in hopes that I don't see them. This makes me sad, but I don't want to talk to them either. It's terrible to admit it, but I'm relieved that they flee from me.

I suppose it makes sense. We've been warped differently now. I was not around to trudge through the aftermath of two world-ending tragedies. I wasn't here to experience their grief in the wake of the massacre, when Amperous and his Croathus followed me to Mountaintop and slaughtered so many of their people. I was also absent when they had to bury one infant after another. I'm two nightmares removed from this community. Our experiences are now wildly different, and I wonder if we even perceive the same colors or smell the same scents anymore.

The number of people who I have any genuine relationship with has dwindled. Is Eveshone all that remains? Maybe there are two, if Adorane and I can push through our past. Three if I'm lucky, and in a good enough mood to be decent to Torrain.

Even before we've arrived at Pannous Lab, I see hints of Torrain throughout the village. There are polished wooden pipes that run from beautifully carved Water Trees—the invention he'd created to solve the water crisis. I appreciate Torrain's creations because they're as much works of art as they are technological achievements. Every gear, dial, spring, and crank is carved out of wood or metal, like a sculpture the Apriori may have housed in a museum. I reach out to touch them as we walk, and they feel solid and smooth. Even if Torrain and I are no longer friends—and I'll find out soon—at least I can appreciate the things he's so lovingly created.

Outside Torrain's lab, I examine a clear glass cylinder that houses a tiny curled piece of fire within.

"How is this possible?" I ask Adorane. "What is this?"

Adorane shrugs it off. "Torrain spends days on end making this and that. I honestly can't keep up with all of it. This provides light when the sun is down. I don't know how it's better than a torch. I guess because you don't have to light it?"

"He's figured out how to make *electricity?*" I stammer. This would be a huge accomplishment.

Adorane sighs like I'm trying his patience. "I guess so. There were caves that he found. Do you remember those? The ones with machines that captured energy from the sun? He took one apart and…I'm not sure what he did. Even if it's exciting, he always manages to make it sound boring. Anyway, it's only enough electricity to keep this one small bulb lit, so it's not changing anyone's life."

Torrain and his experiments. As soon as he starts talking about them, you want him to be quiet.

But I know the truth—that his obsession with technology can be worse than boring. He'd worked for months on the canisters in order to fill them with oxygen so we could explore under the water. They hadn't worked for centuries, and he made them work again. Figured it all out, solved one problem after another. That was good.

But then he applied all that work to the tanks of poisonous gas that killed my Anaghwin. Tranton might have been the one who used them, but there would have been nothing to use in the first place if Torrain hadn't put the terrible pieces together and made them run.

"You ready to say hello?" Adorane asks, tired of staring at the brightly lit bulb.

Since I'm now suitably furious at Torrain again for the trauma his work has unleashed on my world, why not?

THEN

"It's a hit," Prescott declared impassively, like he was specifying which flavor of coffee he preferred.

Travis watched as a multitude of beasts—enough to cover the grounds for what felt like miles—disappeared in a pillar of fire and smoke.

"And *that's* why you have a contingency plan," Prescott said, sounding pleased with himself.

Travis was not satisfied. His forehead was wet, his mouth dry, and his hands shaking. It was a large bomb, to be sure. Prescott had bragged that it was larger than anything they'd dropped in Iraq. But he'd read his mother's carefully written notes. These creatures were built to withstand bombs—created to be unkillable.

While Prescott breathed easily, Travis couldn't exhale. He continued to stare at the screens before him, studying the aerial feed from a camera mounted on the bomber plane. He was waiting for the smoke to clear. He needed to see the creatures blown into pieces, torn apart. The way they'd left his mother. Carved out. Unmistakably dead.

The fog cleared and revealed mounds of Croathus bodies, just as Travis had hoped. Nothing moved. Finally, he unclenched his fists. It hadn't been easy, but perhaps they'd done it. Everyone else in the room cheered, but Travis didn't participate. He continued to watch the screen, searching for any sign of movement.

Suddenly, from the jungle below, a tree—torn from the ground, its roots exposed—was launched toward the plane. The image on the screen jostled violently as the bomber took a direct impact. The plane veered back and forth, losing elevation. Another tree trunk shot up from below and also hit its mark.

The revelry was replaced by shocked silence. A boulder catapulted from below crashed into the plane, and the video feed grew fragmented. They could see only enough to make out the quickly approaching ground.

Travis couldn't be sure, but in the seconds before the screen went dark, he thought he could see movement. It looked like a thousand beasts rising from between the shattered trees and boulders, roaring back to life.

Amperous was one of the first to regain consciousness. He heard that accursed droning noise—the bringer of death and fire—continuing to sound above him. In his fury, he tore a tree from the ground and threw it toward the noise. By then, some others had also recovered from the explosion. They joined him. It wasn't long before the metal flying machine had run aground. It was swarmed instantly by angry Croathus, who ripped open the vessel and had their revenge on the screaming humans within.

Amperous stumbled through the jungle hellscape. The ground was torn up and burning. An evil chemical smell that reminded him of the substance Mister Sean injected into him during the Sleeps hung heavy in the air.

He found Omathis first and lifted his brother from the ground. They took no time to celebrate that they were both alive. Both began urgently to search for their loved ones in the darkness.

Omathis found him.

Dear little Finnarious. His torso was still on fire. Omathis rushed to the young Croathus and patted out the flames. Finnarious' frail chest smoldered.

"Help me!" Omathis summoned. A group of Croathus dutifully

abandoned their own search for their beloved and gathered around Omathis and the broken young one. They crowded, moved in sync, brought their roots into strict unwavering unity, and hummed. If this child could be revived, they were going to do it. They called to him.

But he was gone.

There was no spark of life left that could be fanned into anything more.

Omathis held Finnarious, his own heart burning with grief. He spied his brother desperately searching, halfway across the crater. He walked toward Amperous, who froze when he saw them coming.

Amperous only shook his head. No. He wasn't going to accept this. No.

What kind of monster would kill Finnarious?

Omathis gently placed Finnarious' body into Amperous' arms. Lenolin ran to her husband's side and wailed as they both held their son's lifeless body. They hummed and tried their hardest to bring him back. All around him other Croathus were doing the same with their critically injured loved ones. Many were successful, because their kind was built to live. But Finnarious was gone.

Amperous stared at Omathis. *Humans have broken the truce, brother. Mister Sean commanded that we do our part to keep the peace, and we did. But they did not.*

Omathis stared at Finnarious. Their kind had been happy in their caves, away from the humans, carving out a place for themselves. But the humans just couldn't leave them alone, because that's what humans do. They invade; they spread; they never stay where they are. They come to take what you have, even when they have enough for themselves. They are always a threat.

He knew he could no longer hold his brother back.

He no longer wanted to.

We keep the peace no longer, Omathis replied. *The time has come to spill their blood.*

Amperous could remember a time—when he was young—when he did not hear the persistent voice in his head, urging him to kill, to tear apart, to empty out. But he had been hungry for human blood ever since Mister Sean inflicted the Sleeps on him.

Now that voice was a roar. It was all he heard. It was all he saw. Every inch of his skin begged to be covered in the blood of humanity. His talons grew out, long and sharp, and they would not recede. His mouth tasted bitter with longing for their death.

He watched as Lenolin cradled their broken boy in her arms. She sobbed with a ferocity that no sound could convey, so she convulsed in silence. This somehow made it worse. Amperous could tell that Lenolin wanted only one thing now: vengeance. Everything else she cared about would from now on would flow through her need for revenge. She would encourage her husband to become more lethal. She would urge her living children to become killers. And she would unleash a fury upon humanity that would never end.

Without saying anything, Lenolin gently carried Finnarious back toward the caverns. Most of it was rubble now, but one section of the once-grand cave was still intact. Amperous and their other children, who had been located safely, followed her, though they kept their distance. She found the area Finnarious loved the most—a cool, dark nook where he would sit and play with stones and sticks he'd carved to look like jaguars, monkeys, and other wild animals. She laid him down and filled his arms with the toys he'd cherished.

While the others watched, she held a mournful, piercing note until it echoed throughout the chamber and rang as much inside their heads as outside. Then she bolted from the darkness. Something about the way she ran from the cave made Amperous and the children know not to follow.

In an instant, she was back with the tattered remains of one of the human soldiers who had attacked them. She ripped open his abdomen and painted the stone walls with his blood. While they watched, she brought to life many scenes they'd all enjoyed with Finnarious. Him rushing through the jungle. Swimming in the river. Letting him stand on Amperous' back to reach the perfect mango. Watching while he tried—and failed—to hunt a boar. Laying between her and Amperous at night, trying to fall asleep, but afraid of the sounds that sometimes echoed underground. She painted with fervor, as if she could bring him back to life through these images. When she'd finally covered every inch of available space around Finnarious' resting space with visual tributes to how much he was beloved by them all, she turned to the family.

They held each other as one, in one giant clump of sadness, disbelief, and rage. A unity shot through them, an energy without a name, perfectly aligning them.

"Humans always invade," she declared. "They always kill. They can never stay where they are, content to let us exist elsewhere. They spread.

No matter where they are, they are a threat."

The others howled and growled in agreement.

"We will not rest until they are no more."

26

NOW

Belubus awoke with a start. He'd been asleep, which disoriented him. He couldn't remember falling asleep, or dreaming, or at any time waking and returning to slumber. Nothing. Only the waking up. He looked at the familiar ceiling, confused. How long had he been asleep? Why did everything feel different?

Belubus turned his head and saw sunlight streaming through the window. He reached for the soft orange beam, and then decided he must be dreaming.

He couldn't reach with his arm. Not when awake.

He observed his arm with detached dispassion. It was his familiar arm, but attached to a delicately sculpture wooden structure bolstered by steel and gears and tubes. The arm quietly whirred and whizzed as it moved, rotoscopes turning, hinges bending. He tried to pull the structure from his skin but found that it was bonded and fused, as firmly attached as muscle to bone.

Belubus sat up, again convinced he was dreaming. He examined his legs and found them similarly attached. His body was bound to something. At his shoulders. On his spine.

His hands were now free to move in whichever way he choose.

He moved them and gently clutched his neck.

This didn't feel like a dream.

He felt strength enter his fingers as he pressed around his neck. He constricted until he started choking. He felt stronger than he'd ever been before.

The pain in his throat was immense as he felt his fingers constricting and crushing his windpipe.

Torrain heard the violent gasps for breath and rushed into the room. Belubus had awakened. Torrain had hoped to be there when Belubus realized the miracle he'd performed.

Torrain had expected gratitude.

Instead, he strained to peel Belubus' dangerously stubborn fingers from around the man's own neck.

"Istoch! I need your help."

Together they were able to hold Belubus' arms fast, far from their target.

"What have you done to me?" Belubus moaned, more sad than angry.

"I fixed you! Like I told you I would," Torrain stated.

"And I told you to leave me be! I had accepted myself."

"I couldn't do that. Not when I could make you better."

Belubus pushed himself up in bed. Torrain felt a flush of pride. The wood and metal exoskeleton was even more beautiful bonded to Belubus than it had been by itself.

"You call this *better*, Torrain? I'm not myself anymore."

"What is this sorcery?" Istoch asked. "How was this accomplished, Torrain? Did you find scrolls from ancient times hidden away? What incantations did you learn?"

Torrain shook his head. "Not magic—science. Though I suppose all magic becomes science once you figure out how it works. Which I guess maybe just means that science is actually magic, if you think about it. Anyway, you see, on the Brathius masks, there was a substance that I realized could genetically bond organic matter to wood and stone. It's kind of like when you get a cut, and your skin starts to knit itself back together, only in this case—"

"Undo it," Belubus commanded.

"I'm not sure that I can. It doesn't just bond to the skin. You're more deeply connected than that. Which is a good thing, because otherwise your brain wouldn't be able to send the commands to move."

The weight of Torrain's words, and the situation he had now found himself in, settled over Belubus. He sat back, resigned to it.

"Leave me alone."

Not even a word of thanks. Torrain would have regretted the time he invested in this project, except seeing Belubus moving when he had previously been paralyzed made him borderline giddy.

"Okay, but you were trying to strangle yourself. I need you to promise you won't do that again."

Belubus sighed. "If I promised you this, I would be lying. Have you not controlled enough already? Leave me."

The edge to Belubus' voice startled Torrain. He mumbled a garbled apology before he and Istoch left Belubus alone.

"He'll understand soon enough what I've done for him," he whispered to Istoch, hoping it was true.

Tranton hadn't been invited to the Council. He bristled at the thought. Why wouldn't they want the wisest man in Mountaintop to share his wisdom? Did they think he was more useful trapped in his lab, filling up scrolls with words no one would ever read?

Yet he had his sources on the Council, and he knew what was discussed. It had gone according to his plan. Persopile remained unpoisoned by the waters. After a few carefully placed suggestions by Tranton, a movement had begun to use her fertility for Mountaintop's survival.

The boy Istoch is strong—not just in body, but in will and head, too. He had yet to wilt. He would be useful.

Istoch had rejected him when Tranton had tried to enlist him before.

But now, because he would want to protect Persopile, Istoch would have a reason to leave Mountaintop.

Now, the three of them could travel together. Finally, Tranton could take his rightful place far away from here.

Omathis gazed at the Anaghwin. Night or day, this is where they now gathered, huddled outside of the room at the top of the tower, where they believed Icelyn was staying. They murmured prayers, bowed deeply, and sang songs of sad longing and praise.

In daylight their raw devotion was hard for Omathis to watch, but it was in the darkness, like tonight, when it threatened to suffocate him completely.

He felt her absence even more because he was the only one who was aware of it. The others could sense the lack of root connection, too, but that only made them more desperate in their worship of her. If they could make it clear how intense their love was, they thought, surely she would appear and connect roots with them again. They were convinced they had done something wrong to turn Icelyn's attention from them. None would dare blame her for abandoning them.

He felt tears in his eyes, which only reminded him of her and Sean Brathius. His kind weren't created to be weapons. If they were only mindless beasts, why would the Brathius give them the ability to cry?

Weapons did not weep.

If you would only say my name, I would no longer be hollow, they sang, slow and ponderous. *Cast me not away from your presence, Lovely!*

Whatever I have done to turn you from me, I beg you still let me follow, they pled.

Open the door and let me in. I'll change everything I am to see you again.

How strange; their adoration of Icelyn seemed to have grown once she was distant from them. When she was here with them, they spent most of their time complaining about her. Now that she was ignoring them, they meditated on the thought of her—craved her like she was water or air.

Omathis felt the burden of their pain along with his own. Their earnest devotion might have once touched his heart, but now it added to the weight of her betrayal.

Lovely is more beautiful than a thousand dazzling oceans
More wonderful than a hundred thousand feasts
She will never leave us, she cares for us always
She is unfailing love, she is everything we need

A part of him argued that she should be able to do what she chooses. But no. No one who brings others into this world is free any longer. She was obligated to them. They'd waited so long for her to arrive, didn't she owe it to them to stay?

Yes. He'd wasted hundreds of years waiting for her to appear. He wasn't going to wait any more.

Omathis quietly slipped over the edge of the skyscraper and gracefully descended the outside of the building without drawing any attention.

He dreaded what they would do once they realized he was leaving them too. Hopefully they'd know it was for their sake as much as his. He was going to bring her back.

He crept into a boat and it slipped into the glassy canal.

He could still hear the worship far above, outside Icelyn's room. Maybe the Anaghwin wouldn't even notice he was gone. Maybe they'd be too busy worshipping a god who wasn't there to notice anything.

ICELYN

Torrain crashes into me like an unruly puppy, and his unrestrained joy overwhelms my anger.

"You're here! I was sure I'd never see you again. I ran the probabilities every day, and this only had a one in twenty thousand chance of ever happening. But you're here in my lab, and…Adorane, can we declare this day an official holiday? Is it too late? I'll write the proclamation, and we can both sign it, right? And then it'll be official. She's back!"

There's no hint of flattery in his words. No complications. He's happy I'm here. His embrace grows stronger, and I squeeze him back. It feels good to be genuinely welcome.

"I'm here," I whisper weakly, but it's enough.

He lets me out of the hug and holds me by the shoulders to take a look at me. His eyes are hungry, but not in a way that makes me uncomfortable.

"You look different," he observes.

"Does that mean better or worse?" I ask.

"How do the words *better* or *worse* apply?" He responds. "That's like asking which is better, a sunrise or a sunset. They're just different. Both are…" I know he wants to say the word *beautiful*, but he catches himself.

"Anyway, you look different, and it's a miracle to see you at all. Are you here to stay?"

I'm confused. Doesn't Torrain know why Adorane visited me?

"No, we're just on our way to…" I trail off because *to have a child with a stranger* sounds too ridiculous to say out loud.

"Oh God, no. Adorane, there has to be a better idea. That was always a terrible idea. Icelyn, why would you agree to that? It's awful."

I hug him again for saying it. Finally, someone acknowledges that it might be a bad idea. Or at least a difficult thing to do. Yet I don't want to admit that I've had second thoughts from the beginning, because I need him and Adorane to accompany me inland, even if I'm not sure about visiting Apex.

"She sees the wisdom in it, Torrain," Adorane answers flatly. "If she doesn't do it, Mountaintop will not survive."

"Do you know that for years—centuries, even—the Apriori rode on the backs of animals to get from one place to another? And anytime they wanted to get somewhere faster, they only thought: *How can we make these animals stronger or faster?*"

Adorane rolls his eyes. I'm tempted to join in, because this sounds like another classic Torrain tangent.

"They thought that was the only way, and for centuries nobody could imagine another solution. But then someone came up with a *machine* that they could ride in. No animals needed. For all of human history, no one had bothered to think about another way. But then once one person thought of it, it worked."

"If you're saying that you can invent a machine to make babies so that we don't need Icelyn, then I'm sorry, but that is not going to work."

"What I'm saying is that we haven't explored any alternatives yet. You can't just say there is no other way when you've never looked. "

THEN

The Croathus split into different groups. Some headed south, others east, and others west. They overran the humans they met without resistance, leaving no survivors. Amperous, Omathis, and their families knew where their group was headed: north. Back to the land of their birth. A homecoming painted crimson red.

As they worked their way northward, the human defenses became more sophisticated. Nothing they hadn't trained for, of course: tanks, guns, airplanes. Still, the humans moved in slow motion compared to the Croathus. Amperous and Omathis found they could employ the simple war game tactics that Sergeant Ollie had taught them long ago and outmaneuver any force or weapon the humans could muster. One hundred Croathus could easily defeat an army of thousands of armed humans. And there were many more than a hundred Croathus.

In each city, they would clear out human life. As they moved, they found many posters and leaflets printed by the people in charge, talking about the threat the Croathus posed and warning the humans to prepare for the attack.

"It's odd that they don't admit that they started this bloodshed," Amperous observed. "They act like we're monsters who are attacking them just to be cruel."

"Remember, these cities are full of people like Shai," Omathis answered. "They are liars. They would never admit that *they* are the problem. That the cruelty began with them."

Amperous nodded. Cities full of Shais; he shivered at the thought. They'd killed her many years ago, but he realized they'd left the job mostly undone. The sooner they cleansed the world of her, the better.

One of the posters read: *DO NOT LEAVE THE CITY! You will be undefended! Remain in your homes while we fight for your freedom!*

Amperous scoffed. Why had they believed the humans were more intelligent than the Croathus? "They're doing us a favor if they all gather in the cities," he told Omathis. "Surrounding themselves with barricades that cannot hold us back. They only save us the trouble of having to track them down."

One city had constructed a large metal rectangle and buried it underground, in the hopes that their most precious citizens would find safety within. It took days of digging and cutting into the thick metal walls with their claws while bashing it with boulders and parts of buildings, but the Croathus eventually breached the armored bunker. What had been a shield for the humans was now an inescapable trap.

Lenolin killed more than any other. For every human that Amperous slaughtered, Lenolin murdered two. She had never fought in all the years they'd lived in the caverns in the wilderness; she'd shown no interest in it. Now she was their most lethal soldier. She relished the taste of blood.

Though bullets weren't much of a threat to kill any of them—they'd quickly heal before their life was in any danger—they did hurt the Croathus, and guns often kept the others at bay. But Lenolin ran straight into the bullets. They motivated her to charge even harder and faster.

Amperous was proud of her. She had loved Finnarious more than he even knew.

Sean Brathius, hiding away in his desert research lab, had not yet learned about the attacks on humanity.

He'd been shielded against all outside communication. No visitors, television, or radio—nothing to distract him. He'd spent days of quality time with the hives of bees. He stood and watched as they swarmed as one, moving from one tree to another within their large blue-lit glass cage. He'd figured out how to trigger this swarm. That had been his latest breakthrough.

Conventional bee wisdom held that if a new queen left the hive, tens of thousands of worker bees would follow. This is why they swarmed. He liked this idea; it made sense. Among all social creatures, there were more important individuals who set the course for the rest. He was one for humanity. Omathis and Amperous were surely special among all of the Croathus who had been born so far. If you wanted to control a large group, then, you didn't have to focus on the masses. You could focus on the special individuals—the queen bee, Omathis and Amperous. The rest would follow.

But this wasn't a real answer, was it? What caused the queen bee to leave the hive? What prompted it to make this risky decision? Sean had spent months extracting, refining, sequencing, and splicing pheromones from the worker bees, the queen bees, the drone bees, the larvae, and the pupa to find out exactly where the trigger was.

Some blends of potent pheromones enraged the hive, and Sean had the scarred forearms where they'd stung him to show for it. Other blends, he found, caused them to slumber peacefully. Finally, after many failed experiments, he'd found what he was looking for. Using a specific blend of pheromones, he could drive the queen from her nest and cause a swarm on demand.

Integrating that breakthrough into the genetic backdoors he'd already sown into the Croathus didn't take long. He'd drawn his own blood and used his underlying DNA when sequencing what would ultimately correct the flaws in his creation.

Why must you always insert yourself into every one of your studies? he heard Shai criticizing, the way he knew she would if she were here. But she and Ollie didn't understand. It wasn't possible to not insert himself into his studies. This was true for everyone; he was simply more honest about it. His work was as much him as were his fingerprints or his blood. There was no way to avoid it.

When the computers finished synthesizing what he needed to fix the Croathus, he packed the vials into a metal box and left the lab, exhausted but exhilarated.

It had taken many years, but he would finally perfect them.

27

ICELYN

I'm not sure what I was hoping for in returning to Mountaintop. I tried to keep my expectations low and have still managed to be disappointed.

The Kith are in a sorry state. There used to be a clear distinction between Veritas and Cognate and a unity to the whole that couldn't be denied. Back then, everyone knew their place.

Now no one knows who should be doing what anymore. It's chaos.

Adorane and Torrain take me on a tour of the village I once knew so intimately.

"What is that?" I ask, pointing to a series of wooden fences twisting through town like a jittery snake.

"Some Veritas wanted to create Veritas-only areas where they could pray in peace, without having to experience judgment by the Cognates," Adorane answered.

"I thought you said there wasn't a Veritas and Cognate distinction anymore," I ask, confused.

"There isn't, unless a Veritas wants there to be one. And then there is. Some Veritas like being Veritas. And they like spending time with other Veritas."

"That doesn't sound right."

"It's not up to you to determine what sounds right and wrong when it comes to being a Veritas," Adorane answers.

It feels like he's trying to shut me up. Aren't I allowed to say what I think? "Are there Cognate-only areas?" I ask.

"Is that what you want? A place where I wouldn't be allowed to go?" Adorane responds.

"No, but I don't think the Veritas should have places where I'm not allowed to go either!"

"You've only ever been a Cognate, Icelyn, so you don't know what it's like to be a Veritas in the company of Cognates. Cognates can't help it—even now, after everything has changed, they're used to being in charge, expecting their words and their opinions will have more weight. They've been taught they're more important for hundreds of years, so that's what they believe. Often they don't even know they're acting that way. It's exhausting, and sometimes Veritas would like relief from it."

"But to say a Cognate is not welcome. Aren't you acting like you say the Cognates were, acting like you're better?"

"You're not understanding what I'm saying, Icelyn. And right now, in this conversation? You're demonstrating exactly what I'm saying."

"I'm only trying to share what I'm thinking. My opinion," I sigh.

"To quote myself…'They expect their words and opinions to have more weight.'"

I'm Icelyn Brathius! Why should he not care what I think about life in Mountaintop? "Adorane—I'm still a Brathius. If I came back to live here, would I not be the leader? Why wouldn't you want to hear what I have to say?"

"Icelyn!" Adorane interjects. "You left! You left us behind. Years ago."

"I was flushed out by a cloud of death," I argue. They cannot pretend I abandoned them. They betrayed me!

"You left," Adorane responds. I look to Torrain, who has been noticeably silent.

"Maybe it would be best…" Torrain begins, creeping through what he's about to say like it's a well-set trap, "if you listened instead of spoke. That's what I've had to learn. We're Cognates. We don't know what it's been like to be Veritas. It would be helpful if we just listened. Didn't immediately point out what we see as inconsistencies, but rather mulled them over for a while. Because maybe those inconsistencies are actually consistent; it's just our Cognate perspective that makes them seem out of order."

Adorane smiles. "See, this is why I like Torrain."

"Because you've brainwashed him."

"I'm not brainwashed," Torrain insists. "It's just that…stitching equality back into a community that has been dominated by one group for ages is difficult. You'd know that if you'd been here with us for the past few years. It's not easy for anyone—not the people who use to dominate, and especially not the ones who were treated unfairly. It's confusing. Like learning that 3 plus 4 in reality equals 7, when everyone has insisted it was 23 all your life. And look, it's all a transition. That's why the fences are made out of wood instead of stone. It's not permanent. But for now, they want these boundaries. And I think, considering our histories, they deserve to have what they want."

Our histories? The Veritas were always treated well by the Cognates. They seemed happy enough to me. I don't understand why Torrain and Adorane are acting like they were preyed upon by Cognates day and night. But I feel ganged up on, so I drop the conversation.

As we walk through town, nobody approaches me. I expected this, but I thought there would be *some* exceptions to the shunning.

"So everyone got together and decided beforehand that they were going to ignore me?" I ask, trying to make it sound like a joke. But it comes out sounding pathetic.

"You left, Icelyn. Nobody knows what to think of you."

My anger flares up again. "We're talking about a village that turned my bedroom into a prison and kept me locked away against my will. Why wouldn't I leave when given the chance?" I ask.

Adorane laughs. "At some point, you're going to have to let that grievance go. If Torrain Pannous could set you free, was it really so harsh an imprisonment?"

I see more public praying, even by groups of Cognates who were never religious before. Cognates carry burdens through the street on their own now. I don't understand how Torrain and Adorane can witness this without yearning for a reestablishment of order. I continue to stifle these questions, knowing they aren't open to them right now.

"Where are my parents?" I ask as we examine one of Torrain's Water Bringers, interrupting his explanation of the wonder of their design.

"They don't leave Brathius Tower," Adorane answers. "Once Nicholas was released from prison—"

"You imprisoned my father?" I ask, shocked.

"The community did, by vote, and we upheld the results. He and Tranton. You have to understand that prison was a mercy. Many wanted to dispurse them instead," Adorane explains.

"Imprisonment was a victory, Icelyn," Torrain adds. "We fought for it. Some even wanted us to kill them for what they'd done."

"You put my father in a prison like a *criminal?*"

"And Tranton had my mother killed, with Nicholas' permission,"

Torrain reminds me. His voice is strangely empty of emotion, but it jolts me out of my own struggles. Adorane's father is dead. Torrain's mother too. I suppose I am the lucky one.

"For only a year," Adorane explains, "by the will of the Kith. And truly, once he was released, he made Brathius Tower into his own prison anyway. He stays there and writes endlessly. He's free to come out, but never does."

"What does he write?"

"Nobody knows," Torrain answers. "It's the subject of a lot of discussion. I'm curious myself."

"I should go see him."

Adorane and Torrain exchange a glance. "He asked that you don't if you ever return. He and Marjan."

"Why?"

Adorane sighs before he answers. "Icelyn: Once again, *you left.* Many people don't understand why."

I search their eyes. "But *you* do, right? Torrain? Adorane? You both understand, right?"

"Sure. I mean, we've tried," Adorane answers.

"And we'll keep trying," Torrain adds.

"Anyway, it's for the best. Seeing you would muddy waters that are finally at least a little settled," Adorane explains. "Marjan hasn't been well. Your return could mix everything up again, especially because you're about to turn around and leave immediately again. It wouldn't help."

I run through all the people I thought were friends, desperate for someone I can connect to again. "What about Istoch?"

A blank look spreads over Torrain's face.

"What is it?"

"Can you excuse us for a moment, Icelyn? Leaders' conference," Torrain says. He pulls Adorane aside and they begin whispering to one another. After having what appears to be a very interesting conversation—during which they often stop, look at me, and then start talking again—they return to me.

"Istoch has a new friend, apparently, from the Mines. But yes, sure."

NOW

Tranton arrived at Istoch's round and knocked repeatedly.

"You'd be wise to stop ignoring me," he said. "I'm here for your own good."

Inside, Persopile Opal and Istoch sat in silence. They'd enjoyed each other company more than they'd enjoyed anything else in their short, difficult lives.

Istoch's few years had left him feeling weathered despite his youth. He would be unusually dour for someone who was nearing the age of fifty, let alone a teenager. He was the kind of person who made every smile seem temporary and every frown like forever. If he still had parents, they would worry that their boy would never feel happy. But since they'd died two years ago, he hadn't even had anyone to hope for the impossible for him anymore.

Persopile had changed that.

She wanted to see Istoch happy—even though she knew the strength of his sadness more than anyone else could, because she carried grief on a similar scale.

"Maybe you should just see what he wants," Persopile suggested.

"He's not a good man," Istoch replied. "His visits always bring bad news."

Tranton sighed, resigning himself to being locked on the outside. "Fine, I will tell you what you need to hear through the door instead of face to face. I know you are listening. Icelyn Brathius has returned to Mountaintop. It's caused a commotion."

Istoch flinched. Was this true? He wanted to see her if it was. But he remained silent.

"Here's the part no one else knows, Istoch. She's here because she's uninfected by Waterpump. Adorane wants to find a man who is also uninfected, so that Mountaintop can have babies who survive their infancy. But that's a desperate plan, wouldn't you agree? One that I'm sure Icelyn, Adorane, and Torrain despise but feel forced into."

A fire of realization lit in Istoch's eyes. He rose and started to pack clothing and supplies in a satchel.

"Persopile has also never taken even a sip from Waterpump. Once they think it through, do you believe they'll allow her to run free while Icelyn is forced into a depraved choice?"

Istoch swung the door open, already packed and ready to go.

"How long do we have?" he asked.

"I would guess they are already on their way," Tranton responded. "The three of us should leave together. I know a place where we can go, where they'll never find us. Where Persopile will be safe."

Given more time, Istoch would have never agreed to partnering with Tranton in their escape. Tranton was full of deceit and consistently aimed to benefit himself at the expense of others. If it had been up to Istoch, Tranton never would have been released from captivity.

Yet desperation transforms the worst ideas into viable options. Istoch could not allow them to force Persopile into whatever vile plan they had in store for her, and Tranton seemed to have another plan.

"How dare they plan to make you a vessel for their survival," he ranted quietly, more to himself than to anyone, as they crept through the darkness toward the outer reaches of Mountaintop. Tranton assured them he'd arranged for a gap in surveillance, which they could slip through to freedom. "They tossed you out to die, and now they want you for their babies? Never."

As they hid in the forest, they saw Adorane, Torrain and Icelyn heading toward Istoch's round. Tranton hadn't lied in this case. Istoch hoped Icelyn hadn't approved of the plan to have a baby for Mountaintop. He didn't think she would ever agree to anything like this. How he wished to greet her, to speak to her. It had been so long, and he'd always liked her.

"I don't know. If I can help, maybe we should talk to them," Persopile offered, though tentatively, because she understood how upset the whole matter made Istoch—even though she didn't completely understand the details of what Adorane and Torrain had planned for her. "Their fathers left me to die, not them. From what I've heard, they govern with more kindness."

"Not kind enough," Istoch declared.

"There's been so much death, death heaped on death," Persopile added, her eyes somewhere else. "If I had a chance to reverse that, maybe even a little, and bring life. I'd like that."

Istoch listened to her, and what she said made him love her more. "This is why we need to get you out of this place. They'll prey on you here. What they would ask you to do is something no one should ask of anyone. And, what's more, I fear they would not *ask*."

"You can be sure of that," Tranton added. "Survival comes first, and survival hinges on either Persopile or Icelyn. Knowing those boys, who do you think they'll spare?"

Istoch hesitated. He wasn't fond of Icelyn being pressed into this role, either. Yet he shook off the thought. Icelyn was strong enough on her own. Istoch's responsibility was to protect Persopile, who was more vulnerable and had already spent a lifetime being wronged.

Istoch often wandered through Mountaintop after dark, when most others were sound asleep. The death that had plagued him throughout his life made slumber difficult for him. The benefits of his familiarity with Mountaintop were on full display now. With startling efficiency, he was able to sneak into the storehouses and grab a hearty store of roots and cakes. He secured multiple days' worth of water from the reservoir. Most important, he retrieved weapons for defense from the armory, even a few of Torrain's newly created ultraspears. Tranton and Persopile watched him with muted awe. Had he been planning this for years and only needed an excuse to execute a well-prepared escape?

Properly outfitted, they headed for the Wall and beyond. Tranton's idea was to commandeer a boat on the shore and head out into the ocean. No place on land was safe from Adorane and Torrain, he insisted. They would track Persopile down if she stayed on the continent.

The prospect of drifting into the vast ocean felt right to Istoch anyway, so he didn't argue. Let's see what the horizon offers us, he decided. Surely it will be better than here.

THEN

Sean's breakthrough deserved a celebration. For him, that meant a single bottle of artisanal Parabola beer. It wasn't so much the taste—silky and refined though it was. It was how arduous the process of brewing it was. It took years to age in barrels made of particular kinds of wood. It felt like a metaphor for the work Sean was doing.

He drove toward the normally glittering skyline of the city that had sprouted in the middle of the desert. Normally this improbable metropolis was an obscene contrast to the still, silent lines and jagged red wilderness that surrounded it. Now the lights were out and all was silent.

What was happening?

He entered the city and parked, noting uneasily that there was no one at all in the streets. He went into one of the mammoth buildings. Its sides still projected videos of acrobatic shows and delicious buffets, but there appeared to be no one to be seduced by their calls to indulgence.

He arrived at a sports bar filled with rows of televisions and sat down. No one at the bar, no one working.

He stared at the news broadcast, frozen.

It was happening.

He willed himself out of his stupor, sprinted back toward his truck, and drove back into the desert.

Every major city.

Every minor town.

Every farming community.

Everywhere in South America where people had lived had fallen under a terrible blood-stained darkness.

Before they sank into blackness, these cities managed to broadcast horrific news dispatches. Creatures—shadowy, large, and terrifyingly fast—were swarming the skylines and slaughtering those who ran through the streets. What were these beasts, and where had they come from? They were smart. They appeared to set traps for any military response they faced, lying in ambush and annihilating whole armies.

According to the frantic broadcasts, the creatures would appear en masse and butcher entire populations in hours. When planes flew overhead looking to bomb them, they disappeared entirely, confusing squadrons into flying lower, until they were in range of projectile boulders and trees. These beasts could improvise any material into a lethal weapon.

Nobody heard anything from South America anymore. The governments didn't respond. The news stations had ceased broadcasting.

It was a mystery. Only one thing was known: The creatures were now moving north.

It was his fault. If Travis hadn't told Prescott where the beasts were living, they'd still be there, not harming anyone. Now an entire continent was dead.

Travis called Sean again. No answer. It had been this way ever since the Croathus had emerged furious and bloodthirsty from their underground lair. God, Sean, is it too much to ask that you pick up the phone?

It was his fault.

Prescott had insisted on making him a part of the fallout containment effort. Travis only wanted to curl up and go to sleep. Instead, Prescott had given him a white pill and told him it was better than sleep.

"We need your expertise, Travis."

All his expertise had done so far was destroy the world. Why would Prescott want more?

In South America, the creatures targeted high-density population centers first—destroying the cities, then moving outward. *It's almost like they were designed to kill as many humans as possible as quickly as possible.*

Prescott and his men questioned Travis day and night. He wasn't tired after taking the white pills, but he wasn't fully awake, either. He felt like he was watching himself from the outside even while he was talking.

"Where will they go next?"

"I don't know," Travis answered truthfully.

"Might they stay in South America?"

"I doubt it," Travis replied. They seemed to be moving north with a purpose.

"Are they trained to return to their home?"

"I told you—I don't know much. I wasn't part of the research. I just read some of the notes afterward."

"How can they be killed?"

Finally, he knew something that might help, though he'd already given Prescott the information. "They have to be decimated. If there's enough of their body intact, they rapidly heal. But they can't do it if they're blown to pieces, vaporized, stuff like that. Standard lethal wounds won't matter unless they're already very weak."

Travis remembered reading Shai's notes about the rapid healing genetic variation they'd discovered and installed into the creatures. She'd been so proud. Travis wondered what she'd think about it now.

They interrogated him for hours, as if he were trying to hide something. He was an open book, he insisted, and harbored no secrets. They told him that of course he was free to go, but whenever he tried to leave, they asked him to stay for just one more round of questioning.

Sean had reached standstill traffic—5 lanes wide, 50 miles out. Even for Los Angeles, this was extreme. There were license plates from Utah, Arizona, New Mexico, even Colorado. It appeared that everyone in the entire Southwest was heading toward California. He spied a military officer by the side of the road attempting to keep everyone calm and orderly. With the exception of a few honking cars and screaming drivers, she was doing a pretty good job of it.

Sean pulled his dusty truck to the side of the freeway and approached the officer, his credentials already on display. "I need to get to the Coliseum as soon as possible."

The sentry scanned Sean's security clearance and made a call. A minute later, a helicopter was circling overhead.

Sean could see the military buildup as the helicopter darted toward Los

Angeles. Tanks in formation, planes flying low overhead, bombs lined up and ready to launch, tens of thousands of soldiers swarming and gathering. Except for familiar landmarks—the Griffith Observatory, the Hollywood sign, the Capitol Records building—he could hardly believe this was the city he'd lived in since college. It was unrecognizable.

Throughout the basin, towering metal barricades had been erected to shield the city from the south.

From his vantage high in the sky, he could see masses of people waiting to enter the protected zones. Miles of cars in every direction.

It's not going to help. He thought to himself. *None of this is going to help.*

There was only place where they would be safe.

28

NOW

Eveshone could sit for hours without moving a muscle. It was a skill that had been purposely given to her, and she enjoyed practicing it. It was a way to become invisible, because what most living creatures saw was movement. Everyone tuned out still and silent and focused on loud and fast.

She'd been sitting in the woods waiting for Icelyn to return for what felt like a full day now. A few times she'd lost patience and considered ascending to Mountaintop and checking on her, but her throbbing temples and the pain in her lungs reminded her that this wasn't an option.

So instead she concentrated on sitting statue still. She covered herself with dirt and leaves to further blend into her surroundings, and at one point she was so successful that a trio of chirping birds mistook her for a tree and sat peacefully on her shoulders and arms. This delighted her somewhere deep inside.

This stillness afforded her a connection with Icelyn, even from so far away. A whisper of their roots was loud enough to hear. She could tell that Icelyn was safe. She was in a bit of distress, but not the life-threatening kind—more like Icelyn's standard level of distress when she spent time with Adorane and Torrain.

ICELYN

Torrain knocks on the door to Istoch's round, but without much energy. "It's abandoned. They've left," he says.

"How can you tell?" Adorane asks. "Maybe they're sleeping."

But a home feels different when it's empty, and I can tell that this home has been abandoned. "He's right. They're not here anymore," I say.

I'm disappointed. I was looking forward to seeing Istoch.

"Where could they have gone? Why would they leave?" Adorane asks. He knocks again, more loudly. He seems more perturbed than he should be.

The unease that had been haunting me since we'd started out toward Istoch's round finally clarifies itself.

"Because Istoch knew what you had planned for the girl from the Mines. Adorane, is that why we're here? It's not right. You'd be forcing her."

Adorane doesn't appreciate the scolding I'm giving them. "We were only going to ask. No one was forcing anyone to do anything."

"And when she says no?"

"Hopefully she wouldn't say no," Adorane answers. "And if she did, we'd have to figure it out from there. But if we have to force someone, I'd rather it be her than you," he admits.

There it is—what I have feared is true.

Adorane checks the fallen leaves around the round carefully. "They couldn't have gotten far. They left only a little while ago. We can still find them."

"Let them go," I declare.

"I don't think you understand. This is a chance to avoid—"

"I understand what Persopile represents. Thank you for your concern for me. But I don't want your protection—not if it means others must be victimized. No one will follow them. Promise me."

NOW

Istoch and Persopile cut through the woods with deliberate speed. Tranton had too much pride to ask them to slow down and ignored the pain in his legs and lungs in an effort to keep up. Finally, he could no longer pretend he wasn't in agony.

"Perhaps we can rest for a moment," he suggested. "Reorient. Make sure we're still headed in the right direction."

Istoch knew they were headed toward the ocean. It wasn't confusing. They'd scaled the Wall only an hour ago, and he had no desire to slow down. He'd never been Down Below, and his desire to see the world hidden from them was growing. "I know where we are," he answered, keeping up his breakneck pace.

But Persopile was sensitive to what Tranton was actually asking. "I could use a break too," she said, slowing down. It was a lie. Persopile's life below the ground in the Mines was rigorous and had kept her fit. The growing richness of the oxygen as they descended made the run much easier too.

They slowed to a stop in a clearing and rested beside a tree.

"I'm sorry, Persopile, I didn't know you were tired," Istoch explained. "I would have slowed long ago."

Persopile had never been treated so kindly in her life. It made her shy. "I know you would have. Don't worry about it." Then she whispered, "I'm not really tired, but Tranton is a mess and needs a break."

Somehow the rest made Tranton seem worse off, as if the last of his adrenaline had been replaced with misery and exhaustion. He leaned against the trunk of the tree.

This turned out to be a mistake.

Eveshone was shaken out of her trance in the most unwelcome manner imaginable. A loathsome human pressed against her legs. It smelled terrible—of sulfur, sweat, and slimy skin.

She launched the vile creature across the clearing. As her eyes emerged from her meditative state, she could recognize that there were two other humans near her—strangers. While she'd grown to tolerate and even appreciate Adorane, other humans still reflexively disgusted her.

Surely Icelyn wouldn't mind if she killed *these* humans. One had touched her unbidden.

She raised up, made herself as large as possible, and roared. This had the desired effect—the humans nearest her huddled together, paralyzed. She'd heard that human blood was sweet—that once you had a taste of it, you wanted nothing else for the rest of your life. Though she found it hard to believe that such a delicious delicacy could be housed in these abhorrent bodies, she had always wanted to taste it, at least once.

The humans screeched at her—the sounds were familiar, somewhat like the words that Adorane and Torrain would speak to Icelyn, but they were foul in tone. She knew Icelyn loved humanity—but while Adorane was a notable exception, as a whole humans truly were deserving of destruction. She felt this more than thought it, as involuntary as her need to breathe, as the beating of her heart.

Tranton had no taste for violence. Some men were energized by combat. Their purposes focused with their quickening pulse; their senses were heightened by a life-or-death struggle. He was not one of those men.

After he was flung across the clearing by the creature he'd somehow brushed against without seeing, he was tempted to keep his eyes shut and remain huddled into a ball. Yet even as his body begged for surrender, his mind yearned for survival. He had a destiny to fulfill, and it wasn't meant to end in an accidental confrontation with a solitary Threatbelow.

"Istoch! Grab the ultraspear!" he begged. This was why he'd invited Istoch and Persopile along instead of venturing out by himself—for moments such as this.

His words shook Istoch from his stupor. The boy grabbed the ultraspear from the ground and charged fearlessly toward the Threatbelow. Tranton was impressed and grateful, but still felt a prick of condescension. Fearlessness was just another facet of idiocy.

Istoch had felt guilty when he lifted one of the few ultraspears from Torrain's lab. In doing so, he was taking advantage of Torrain's trust. The long gracefully carved weapon had been a labor of Torrain's love—inlaid with stone, ultralion bone, and steel, balanced and lightweight. The tip, covered in a material from the Brathius masks, was what made it invaluable, and also why Istoch had rationalized stealing it. After all, they'd need this kind of weaponry Down Below if they were to survive. He was glad to feel the weapon in his hands now

The fearsome beast leapt toward Persopile, eager to tear into her. Istoch jumped between them and jabbed at the creature with the weapon. He plunged the spear into its abdomen.

Torrain had told Istoch what the ultraspear would do when it came into contact with Threatbelow flesh, so the boy had an idea of what to expect. Torrain had concentrated the substance from the Brathius Masks, which create an organic, airtight bond between Threatbelow skin and mask. He'd increased the dosage to the point where it not only bonded, but consumed. That was the hope, at least. Torrain had never been able to test it on anything.

Istoch was shocked and relieved to see that it worked.

The tip began to melt into the creature's skin in a subdued shimmer of yellows and blues, as a glowing ember might sink into a snowdrift. The creature bellowed in pain and shrank away.

Istoch felt a tinge of regret, but he had to be sure. He thrust the spear again. This time he hit the beast in the shoulder, and another dull explosion of color drew screams from the creature. The beast gave up its pursuit and escaped into the dense underbrush.

Tranton rose to celebrate. "Did you see it scurry away like an injured dog? Pursue it, Istoch! Finish it off!"

But Istoch and Persopile stood in silence. They were grateful they'd survived, but Istoch had inflicted a tremendous amount of pain on a living creature. Neither felt good about that.

Persopile shoved Tranton back to the ground. "Do not delight in another creature's suffering," she ordered. "Misery is never something to celebrate."

Istoch watched the trees until he sure that the creature wouldn't be back. "Let's go. I'm not hunting, Tranton," Istoch stated. "I'm only defending."

He held Persopile's hand, grateful for her warmth. "And to be clear, I'm mostly defending Persopile. I don't want to see you die, either. But if you upset her again, we'll leave you alone down here. You need us much more than we need you."

This angered Tranton and washed away any feelings of gratitude he had felt. "Don't you forget that I'm the one who warned you they were coming for Persopile. You owe me."

"Now that we're outside the Wall, I can't think of one reason we need you. For now, you're lucky that we're nice enough to keep you around. I'd advise you to be nice, too," Istoch said. He and Persopile resumed their brisk pace into the forest.

THEN

Oliver Hailgard was waiting when the helicopter landed near command central. He made no attempt to hide his anger.

"Where have you been?"

"In the desert lab," Sean answered, matter of factly. "I cut off all communications so I could work without interruption." Sean opened his satchel, revealing the vials of synthesized potions. "The good news is that I have the solution to all this. I can make them good."

Oliver gave a disdainful glance. "It's too late for that. Have you seen the casualty counts? They're in the hundreds of thousands, if not millions. No one can even get to South America to make an estimate."

Sean brushed it off. He wasn't going to dwell on what had happened; he simply wanted to fix it. "No, listen to me. We just have to set up diffusers. That'll create an environmental trigger that—"

Ollie walked away. Sean followed, increasingly desperate to explain. "Once they gather here, we vaporize this material into the air. When Amperous and Omathis see me, it will trigger a change in them; their hatred of humanity will disappear. Then that change will pass through the rest of them, like a network of computers or a colony of ants. It's all as I designed it."

"It's too late. They've massacred an entire continent. As you designed it."

"But you're not listening. I can make this right!" Sean insisted.

"If you say one more word about those damn vials I will smash them all over the ground. *This has gotten away from you.* Even if that *was* the solution, it's clear that they're mutating from one generation to the next. By the time you solve one problem, they'll have evolved beyond it anyway. No matter what you do, they will return angrier and more lethal. Stop pretending you have any control over this process."

Sean knew to back down. It was clear that Oliver had no faith, and so he couldn't be reasoned with. How quickly humanity resorts to fighting when nonviolent solutions still exist. He'd have to figure out another way. He swallowed his words.

"You want to help? Let me know what you think of this plan." Oliver showed Sean a scale model of the Los Angeles basin, walking him through where the barricades had been erected, where the soldiers would be stationed, where the bombs were set up.

It was a fine plan. "It's the best you can do," Sean stated flatly. "But everyone is going to die." He wasn't going to try advocating for the vial vaporization plan anymore, but he had to be realistic. "Except me, I guess. They still like me."

"Why are there so many of them, Sean? Their reproductive generations weren't supposed to be compressed."

Sean shrugged. "Their reproductive generations were going to be however long they needed to be to optimize their survival. In order to build a population, in the right conditions, they could have reached sexual maturity in as little as a year."

Oliver stifled his fury at this genius' carelessness once again. They shouldn't have been able to reproduce at all. But despite Sean Brathius' role in creating this disaster, his knowledge still probably represented mankind's only chance for survival.

"Forget the vials. If you don't think these defenses will hold, what would be your Plan B?" Oliver asked.

Sean Brathius turned his eyes toward the horizon, where the distant mountain range rose and provided a stunning backdrop to the city. "I've been preparing a place for us. Just in case."

"If you do not have a blue-coded armband from the security center, please return to your home or nearest shield center. This is an order. You will not be allowed inside."

The recording boomed through speakers, but it made no difference.

Crowds trampled through the rose garden planted outside the perimeter in their attempt to enter the Coliseum. They pressed against the fences, but the metal barricades held.

"Please let us in! What difference does one more family make?" A mother pleaded, but guards had their instructions. Only those who had the armbands would be allowed in—and only those selected were issued the armbands in the first place. No exceptions.

Oliver was angry that word had leaked of the gathering of chosen ascenders in the Coliseum, but he didn't have the time to track down who had shared the information. It wouldn't matter anyway once the Croathus arrived—and they were arriving soon.

A well-dressed family attempted to remain calm while they navigated the boiling mass of anger and made their way to the gate. They wore blue armbands. The rejected grabbed at the bands, as if ripping them away might be the only way to save their own lives. A military escort joined the man, his wife, and their two young children and started to clear out the troublemakers using plexiglass shields, smoke bombs, and steel batons.

"Why do they deserve to live?" a man shouted. The well-dressed family did their best to ignore it. "Little girl! Do you think you are better than my daughter?" The young child shook her head, and her mother grabbed her by the hand and hastened her along.

At the gate, the guard scanned the family's armbands. "Mr. and Mrs. Ross, you are verified." Though their faces remained strained, relief flashed in their eyes as they held their children closer. "Please proceed onto the field. You'll receive further instructions there."

Someone threw a brick toward the family as they passed through the gate. A guard blocked it with a shield, and then aimed a hose and sprayed a thick stream of water into the growing mass of people.

29

NOW

Eveshone tore through the forest. She slammed into tree trunks, but she kept moving. She tripped over boulders and scrambled back to her feet. She had to get away from that stick. The pain was unbearable. She'd been stabbed and cut before, but this was different. This was like she'd been stabbed and then again from within, and then sliced a thousand times more—pain without end.

Humans had only ever been weak nuisances up to this point. When Adorane stabbed her, it was more an annoyance than a threat. But now she feared them. Any human might have one of those sticks. She couldn't risk being attacked again.

Finally, rational thought overcame instinct and she slowed down her panicked fleeing. She didn't want to look, but she had to examine her wounds. The pain wasn't subsiding. She felt no healing.

She gingerly examined her abdomen and shoulder. Her blood flowed without slowing, as if her skin had forgotten how to make it scab up and stop. And what was worse—the bright red craters where the stick had stuck into her had doubled in size since the initial impaling. It was like the stick was still stabbing her and would never relent.

The Priestess and Amperous had been traveling through the desert for almost a day now. Amperous wondered if she was purposely taking the long way. The Priestess wasn't the kind to become disoriented—or to make any mistake at all, really—so he had to assume this was her plan.

"You're wondering where we're going and why it's taking so long to get there, yes?" the Priestess asked. This scared Amperous. They hadn't connected their roots, yet she always seemed to know what he was thinking. Meanwhile, he was always left guessing what might be on her mind.

"Here's your answer: We were headed here."

Amperous spun around, trying to understand where they were. They'd walked into a flat expanse of nothing but brittle cracked ground encrusted with salt. No trees or brush. Nothing notable.

"You know, you can say what you're thinking, Amperous. I promise you that I already know it all. Hiding it only inhibits our closeness."

"I'm wondering why this would be a place where you would want to visit. Is this the second temple?"

She laughed quietly, and Amperous felt embarrassed. "Not a temple. This is the place where you consecrate yourself before you can enter the second temple. Look around; there's nothing. Nothing to trip over, to grab hold of, to distract you."

Amperous nodded.

"No, Amperous—really *see* it. There is nothing. Repeat after me. Nothing to trip over, to grab hold of, to distract me."

Amperous didn't want to repeat what she said, and he wasn't sure why. Was it simply because he didn't like to be told what to do? Or because something else was making him uneasy? But he repeated it anyway. "There is nothing. Nothing to trip over, to grab hold of, to distract me."

The Priestess was pleased, and she flattened the palm of her hand against his chest. "Good. Now say it again—and anything that comes to your mind, I want you to toss it away. Say this and do that until there is nothing in your head, until you are as empty on the inside as this desert is on the outside."

Amperous said the phrase once, and the images that came to his mind were easy enough to throw away. The animal skin he was wearing. His sleeping quarters in the ruined city.

"Deeper, please," the Priestess encouraged.

He said it again. "There is nothing. Nothing to trip over, to grab hold of, to distract me."

This time he didn't want to throw away what came to mind. The beauty of a sunrise. The taste of a freshly slaughtered bear. The smell of a crackling bonfire.

But he did. He hoped it was enough for her.

"Almost there, but let's go deeper. You are still cluttered," she instructed.

This time as he said the words his eyes filled with tears. He saw his brother Omathis. His beloved Lenolin. His children. Green Paradise. He shook his head.

"Please, no. That's all I have," he whispered.

"There is nothing. Nothing to trip over, to grab hold of, to distract me," the Priestess repeated loudly, her eyes locked on his.

"Let me have this," he begged.

"There is nothing. Nothing to trip over, to grab hold of, to distract me," she intoned.

"There is nothing. Nothing to trip over, to grab hold of, to distract me." Amperous responded desperately, repeating the words until his voice matched hers. He collapsed into her, and the Priestess held him close, rubbing his back. He was limp and small and feeble.

"Good, good. You are cleansed. You are ready," she declared.

ICELYN

I am ready to leave. There are many people and places I thought I'd want to see in Mountaintop. But what I had hoped would seem like a warm visit home—a momentary trip back into whatever good memories remained—is instead a nightmare. It's all familiar, but everything is different now, and I'm no longer a part of it.

I'm left alone in Adorane's spare room. He still lives in Hailgard Round. I thought he'd move himself into a lab, since they're nicer, but he hasn't. I also thought he'd be married to Catalandi by now, but they are no longer even betrothed.

I'm embarrassed to find myself relieved when he shares the news. "Oh, why not?" I ask, feigning carelessness.

"Because she did not like who I had become," he answered cryptically. I felt a sudden kinship with Adorane again. We'd both become someone that people didn't seem too fond of.

I cannot sleep. I'm cold, and my blanket seems to be keeping the cold in rather than warming me. My mind is a whirlwind of thoughts that I don't want to think.

I'm disappointed that Adorane bid me goodnight with such formality before he retired to his room. We haven't seen each other for years; I thought we would spend a few minutes more talking. But there's been a stiltedness to him. He seems disturbed by our reunion. He's purposely keeping me at arm's length, so it hasn't been a reunion at all.

I am finally on the edge of sleep, my thoughts growing quieter and my eyelids heavy, when I hear a shuffling of the tapestry that divides my room from the rest of the round. I feel as though I must be dreaming, but then a feel a light touch on my wrist. I hear Adorane say, "Icelyn, could we talk? Outside?"

Adorane gives me an ultralion parka, and I'm grateful for it. The temperature has plunged, and our is breath illuminated in the moonlight. I follow Adorane toward Waterpump.

We don't say much. At one point I ask what we're doing, but he only responds, "You'll see."

When we arrive at Waterpump, I'm curious to see that it's been transformed into a community garden. I'm impressed by the variety of crops grown here: straight lines of mushrooms, trees full of apples, bushes heavy with berries, the tops of carrots.

"This is so nice." In fact, it's the first improvement I've seen in Mountaintop, if I'm being honest.

We sit on a stone wall, and I make a mental note of the rows of plants. There's something comforting about the order that's been created.

"Icelyn, I have something strange to propose to you," Adorane says, after we sit in silence for a very long time.

I'm nervous. I can tell whatever he's about to say is important to him. Right away, as if by premonition, I fear I know what he's thinking.

"Perhaps we should be betrothed," he suggests. My heart sinks, and my face flushes in panic. I don't know what to say, so the silence bears down on us. Just him and me—with no distraction from the heartache I'm about to unleash.

"The experiences we've shared Down Below have warped us both into creatures who can't mesh with anyone else," he explains, and there's a desperation to it. It's as if he can tell I'm pulling away.

He's right about our being twisted. But the cure to that curse isn't found in betrothal.

"Adorane," I start, and just the way I say his name is all he needs to hear.

"We're going to be facing terrible trials," he argues. "Traumas that I don't think we can survive on our own. We need each other to get through them. I don't want you to be all alone in this, and I don't want to be alone either."

He may be happy that centuries of tradition in Mountaintop have been erased in the last few years. But I can't shake the idea that a Veritas and a Cognate should maintain sensible boundaries between them. It wouldn't be fair to him or me—we are on different levels. It would never work.

"You're right that we don't fit with anyone else," I start. "But we don't fit with each other, either. Not in that sense. We can be allies, sharing in friendship. But betrothal and marriage? I don't see how that would work, Ad. It just not…proper."

He seems taken aback by what I'm saying. Could he really have not expected this response from me?

He redoubles his effort with another surge of Adorane-powered passion. "Icelyn Brathius. This is Adorane in front of you. We have been best friends since before we could speak—before we could walk. You've shared more of your life with me than you have with anyone else. Don't lose sight of me. There is a connection between us—real, and strong, and warm, and alive. And you're going to tell me that projecting us together into a future is *not proper?* What do dusty old rules created hundreds of years ago by dead men have to do with what's between us, alive, right now?"

A part of me is seduced by his words, and even more so by the pulsing life behind them. He's creating a world that I would like to live in, a paradise I could see myself lost in. But I shake myself from it, because it's a mirage.

"Adorane, I'm sorry, but the answer is no."

"Because I'm a Veritas."

"Adorane, stop," I plead, but he continues with his accusation.

"And you're a Cognate."

I scan the rows of plants with my eyes, calming myself by focusing their structured order.

"We don't get to choose how we're born, Adorane."

If I had a difficult time falling asleep earlier, now it's an impossibility. It doesn't seem fair when you have two choices and both seem like the worst possible path to take. I'm losing everything either way.

Am I wrong? What if Adorane is right, and the Old Ways were never the right path, as I've always trusted they are? What if, regardless of whether they were right, the Old Ways are now over, obsolete, vanished?

Could it be that I'm still living in a world that was obliterated without me noticing? Am I like a villager in the ancient Apriori city of Pompeii who has somehow missed the erupting volcano and wakes up to start crushing grapes beneath her feet and tending her flock of sheep, never noticing the community around me has been obliterated? Have I been oblivious to the annihilation of everything I've ever known and believed?

And something even more unsettling rises in me. Am I using all of this as an excuse to push away Adorane, because I don't even want to face the true reasons the idea of marrying him—even if we were both Veritas—terrifies me. Would I lose myself in him? Be stripped of my freedom to become who I'm meant to be when in a marriage to him? Even worse—*would I lose him*? I adore so much about Adorane and I'd hate to see any of that changed because he was bound to me. I don't trust myself enough to be sure I wouldn't mess him up.

Dawn comes without clarity. I'm exhausted. Why did Adorane have to poke this hornet's nest? I may never sleep again.

Eventually I must have fallen into slumber, because I awaken to find the round empty. I hear the summoning bell, which unearths memories I don't have the energy to dissect. Death, disappointment, fear, and a tinge of excitement are woven into every one of them.

I look out the window. The Kith have gathered. It appears that Torrain and Adorane are being honored. I climb up the outside of Hailgard Round to find a better view. It's clear that they're being sent off on this journey like heroes.

And me, who's the one to make this sacrifice? Apparently, Adorane was content to let me sleep through it. Anger flashes within me, but I try to I push off the temptation to feel sorry for myself.

I try my hardest to see Adorane and Torrain through different eyes. I force myself to be proud of them, and to my surprise find a pride that's not completely faked. They've held this town together over the past years. The Kith survive. They've weathered more trials than I can imagine. I remember how making the slightest decision for this community would dig into Father and wear him down until he became a shell of the man he once was. Adorane and Torrain have taken that burden and done their best with it.

They deserve this sending off.

And I do not. I haven't been here. I am resigned to this. I understand it. No use fighting the fact that water is wet.

As the ceremony wraps up—it appears that Adorane is now passing authority to his mother, Charnith—I make my way back down the side of the round and wait for the boys there.

I cannot believe who visits me instead.

They look old. I've only been gone a couple of years. They should not look this old.

Or maybe they were already old when I left, and I hadn't noticed because I'd seen them every day since they were young. Now my absence has made me aware of what I'd not seen before.

Father seems shorter—certainly frailer. Mother is taller than him. Has that always been the case? Or is it that she stills stands tall—Marjan has always stressed the importance of good posture—while Father makes no effort?

They advance toward Hailgard Round, slow yet determined. They look around, nervous, vigilant for threats present only in their imagination. They look paranoid—two hermits who have left their isolation for the first time in ages.

They're coming to see me.

I rush to greet them. Every grievance I've held against them seems like a story I can now barely remember, something I was told by someone I shouldn't have trusted in the first place.

I don't have to choose which one to embrace first. They see me coming both erupt into big smiles; all three of us hold each other. An emptiness I've long suffered is momentarily filled, and I'm grateful to feel Father's rough sandpapery cheeks scratching against my face. Mother smells as she always does, of lavender and smoke.

"We've missed you," Mother says. She's barely able to get the words out.

"I've missed you, too." Not only for the time I've been gone, too, I realize—I've missed them for so long.

Father says nothing, but he has tears in his eyes and a small half-smile. He looks as though he could die right now with peace in his heart. What's he going to say? Would he apologize for what happened? It would seem insignificant compared to the moment we're in right now, I realize. This isn't about past mistakes and betrayals. It's about us—our flawed, sickly, and vastly important little family—right now.

Family is a promise that can never truly be kept. It is a promise of undying love—unconditional, sacrificial, loyal. I can feel the fruits of that promise now, perhaps even more so because of how much we've all failed each other in the past. No matter how much we love each other and how much we try, we will all fail in our vows.

But now I feel Mother and Father's hot tears running down my face, the tired arms of my frail parents that refuse to let go as we hold each other. Suddenly, the years of separation lift off me like a weight. An exhausted sense of peace washes over me.

Just because you can't keep a promise perfectly doesn't mean you should ever stop making it.

30

THEN

The journey north, back to where they were born, was more difficult than their initial escape southward. The humans knew they were coming. Most were harmless, whimpering, and easy to slaughter. But many gathered together and had their weapons ready.

It was nice, though, not to be stuck in the shadows. Even Omathis had to admit that. To attack the humans head on and know they had the power to win every battle. Day by day, their swarm rolled northward.

Omathis and Amperous had always known they were smart. Mister Sean had drilled them on numbers nearly since they were babies. They'd noticed early on how much Travis struggled with the same kinds of math. Even while he mocked them for wearing diapers, it was clear he wasn't as good at addition, subtraction, or formulas. Which was worse, Travis? Wearing a diaper or being simple-minded? They made sure to laugh at his stupidity only when he wasn't around—but they did laugh at him. Amperous joked that Shai had made a dim-witted child compared to what Mister Sean had created.

While waging war on humanity, new aspects of their Croathus intelligence emerged every day. This made sense, Amperous noted. Mister Sean had created them to wage war on humanity. They were at their best now, doing exactly what they were made to do.

Whenever Amperous talked about this or mentioned Mister Sean, Omathis felt a distant echo somewhere deep inside. He had a sudden instinct that Mr. Sean wouldn't like what they were doing. He would be disappointed in them and their children. Normally, though, Omathis would slaughter another human to drown out this voice, and it would be silenced by the warmth of the blood.

Amperous and Omathis were pleased to discover that they knew the areas they needed to attack and disable in order to make their trip north as easy as possible—all the military bases, weapons caches, strongholds, airfields, and harbors. This knowledge must have been a gift from Mister Sean. Maybe he'd provided the information during one of the Sleeps. That's sometimes how the Sleeps would work; they'd awaken and discover they knew much more than they'd known before. It didn't make the Sleeps worth it—nothing ever would. But it was nice to learn so much so quickly. For the most part, that is. Sometimes the knowledge they'd acquired was troubling, especially in large amounts, and there was no one there to talk over what they'd learned. One time they awoke to find they knew all about the wars that humans had ever waged against each other and how they'd kill one another without a second thought. It seemed as though the humans spent most of their time and money trying to figure out how to kill as easily as possible.

Humans were wretched, they knew now. The world would be better off without them.

Another fleet of airplanes flew overhead. Of all the weapons the humans used against their kind, these flying menaces were the most dangerous. Every once in a while, one would kill one of Amperous and Omathis' swarm.

"They can't fly forever," Amperous observed. "Let's make sure we're there when they land."

"Yes," Omathis agreed. "Let's make it so they can never fly again."

The humans tried their hardest. But they were shocked at how skilled the Croathus were in combat. Humans had always been good at killing, of course—both one another and the animals they shared the world with. But they were no match for the Croathus. How sad, Amperous thought to himself. To care only about one thing and pride yourself on it, only to eventually face an adversary who proves you were weak all along. He almost felt sorry for them. Almost.

The Croathus masses leapt over the fences that surrounded the base where guns, missiles, and flying machines were kept. Even these walls made Amperous chuckle to himself. They were built to keep other humans out. They made no difference to the Croathus.

These humans worked so hard to invent better tools for killing when the Croathus could use anything lying around as weapons and be more lethal. The Croathus uprooted trees and lifted cars and boulders inside the base. Amperous swung the trunk of an oak tree and crushed a full troop of soldiers. Omathis tossed a weighty chunk of sandstone, and it landed on a helicopter with a satisfying crunch.

The Croathus covered the airfield like rising floodwaters. Pilots were caught unaware by the attack and desperately tried to scramble for their airplanes and lift off. They were plucked from their seats and tossed aside. They'd be handled later—for now, the Croathus were focused on destroying these terrible machines that shot at them from the sky.

Within minutes, the once-gleaming fleet was reduced to plumes of black smoke, twisted metal, and shattered glass. Nothing would fly above and kill them anymore. Amperous was pleased. The humans couldn't hurt *any* of them now.

Because every Croathus was precious and needed to live. Unlike humans, who did not care when another human died, Amperous and Omathis felt deeply that all Croathus should live. Even one death was a disaster.

Oliver and Sean watched as the football field on the Coliseum floor below was covered by those who had been selected to ascend. This crowd had not been chosen at random. They'd take twenty-five thousand people. That's all the helicopters could reasonably transport before the Croathus arrived. Two thirds would consist of those who could protect the group and help it survive—members of the military, the police department, firefighters, paramedics, and their families. Only the best, the most skilled, and the elite. Oliver made sure of that.

The other third would be drawn from the true treasures of humanity, according to Sean Brathius: scientists, inventors, educators, innovators, and entrepreneurs. Of course, there would be some government officials too—but only because they used their authority to guarantee themselves a place on the list, not because they earned it through merit or paid their way in. Money made no difference here; cash would be worthless on top of the mountain.

Sean also insisted that no slots be held based on creative merit alone. They'd have no need of theater or music. Sure, it could be nice to hear a tune now and then, but they had limited resources and needed to preserve the truly brilliant minds among them. Why give a place to a celebrity or rock star when it could be saved for someone who could come up with a scientific breakthrough?

The crowd that had gathered was eerily quiet, especially in contrast to the riots outside the stadium. They knew they were lucky to be on the list, and most of them felt guilty.

"Pendleton has fallen," Oliver announced, his face grim. This was terrible news. The military had set up a massive concentration of troops and tanks there. It was the first—and best—line of defense to keep the Croathus out and maintain a safe zone. "Overrun. Communications have been cut off."

"What about the helicopters?"

"Communications have been cut off."

Sean worked to keep his mind calm and thinking—not just feeling and fearing, which is all that he wanted to do. The helicopters were probably already on their way; they had to be. That's how this group was getting to the top of the mountain. But what if they had been overrun before they could leave Camp Pendleton?

"Are there any other helicopters available just in case?" Sean asked, searching for options.

"We'd concentrated them in Pendleton," Oliver answered.

"And if we don't have the helicopters?" Sean wondered, though he knew the answer.

"Then we'll have to ascend on foot."

They looked to the sky and hoped to hear the whooshing aerial sounds they feared were not coming.

The helicopters should have been here already. They were thirty minutes late.

"We can't just wait for transports to arrive, can we?"

Oliver scanned the gathered ascenders one more time. "Maybe all this survivors' guilt is misplaced. Maybe none of these people are lucky as they think they are," he observed.

Sean Brathius sensed a coming storm. He looked to the horizon and marveled at the beauty to the west. The clouds were orange and pink, bright and cheery. Like the dawn of a new paradise.

Even though there was no breeze, he felt a warm wind rushing through him.

He hadn't felt this in decades. Shai had hated how distracted he could become when Amperous and Omathis were on his mind. She'd often have whole conversations with him before he had to admit that he couldn't remember a thing either of them had said. There was something about those two that inhabited his thoughts and wiped his mind clean.

"...We can't wait for Air Force One any longer. They still haven't made a determination as to whether they're coming. Since Pendleton has fallen, they believe Washington is safer..." Oliver Hailgard was peppering Sean with one urgent announcement after another. Sean had to exert all his will in order to concentrate.

"If the President doesn't join us when we ascend, he will die," Sean answered confidently.

"They don't think it's safe to fly directly into the affected zone."

"All zones will be affected in time."

Sean couldn't remain interested in the discussion and was only vaguely aware as Oliver barked into his phone, urging Washington to send their officials as soon as possible.

His beloved creations were here. He could feel it in the earthy, warm adrenaline rushing up the base of his spine, in the tingle and dancing exhilaration of the pulses behind his eyes. He struggled to breathe.

He wanted to run from the stadium and find them. It wouldn't be hard to do. They weren't far. It had been so long.

But suddenly, his head was gripped by vile images. He collapsed to the ground.

No.

They were not who they'd once been. They were flooded with a darkness. He could feel that now. They were violence. He felt a hatred running through his blood that shocked him back to action.

"Where's Travis?" He asked, desperate. "We need to go. We need to go now," he ordered.

"Washington will make a decision in the next hour," Oliver answered.

"We don't have the time!" Sean stormed out of the luxury box suite that had been transformed into a control room to search for his adopted son. "We leave now or nobody survives!"

ICELYN

I'm leaving a place I don't recognize. During my exile, I imagined that Mountaintop was carrying on in the same way it had when I was growing up. I could always visit if I really wanted to. But all along, I've been missing a place that no longer exists.

It's hard to accept. It's one thing when you give a place up, but quite another when it gives up on you in response. I am adrift, my roots severed, and it's playing games with my thoughts.

At least this time we have water and food, along with weapons. Torrain is particularly proud of the weapon he calls an ultraspear. He assures me that if we come up against any Cloudies we should be safe.

"Have you tested it, then?" I ask.

"No, but it should work. I've done the calculations," he answers.

Despite his confidence in his calculations, I'm hoping we don't see any Cloudies.

We have left Charnith in charge of Mountaintop. It strikes me that a Veritas woman runs my whole childhood world, while my father sits alone in his tower and writes a history that he won't let anyone read. Yet another piece of evidence that the place I'd once loved had been annihilated. A Brathius in seclusion while a Veritas leads. This world has changed indeed.

"Charnith is a wise woman," Adorane says to me as we leave the Wall behind.

"I know, Adorane. She's one of the best women I have ever known." I have no desire to quarrel, so I'm not going to add that this doesn't mean she should lead Mountaintop.

"She's as qualified to lead Mountaintop as anyone ever has been. With some of the conversations we've had recently, I thought you'd love seeing a woman in charge."

He's right, I should be thrilled. What torture when your feelings don't line up as they should.

"Anyway," Adorane adds, "We didn't leave Charnith to lead by herself. Belubus will help her. He's very wise."

Torrain shoots him a pointed look, and Adorane looks embarrassed. He must have made some mistake—said something that Torrain didn't want me to hear.

"Belubus is in Mountaintop?" I gasp.

Both men look uncomfortable.

"Why didn't anyone tell me? I'd have loved to see him!"

"He was injured; he wouldn't want you to see him," Torrain answers, a bit too quickly.

"Injured by what? Is he going to be all right?"

"Torrain fixed him up," Adorane answers, his voice oddly high. "He'll survive. Amperous hurt him."

I freeze in my tracks. "Amperous died. He died with the other Croathus."

Adorane pulls me forward, and we resume our descent down the mountain. "Belubus found him near death and nursed him back to health in the Mines," he says grimly.

Adorane doesn't have to finish the story. I shudder, suddenly realizing the fate that must have befallen everyone else living below the ground. Most of them were kind, warm people—and even those who weren't deserved better.

"And the others?" I ask hesitantly.

"Persopile, Istoch's friend, was the only other survivor. She brought Belubus to us. No one else."

"And so Belubus was injured when Amperous escaped? Is that why he doesn't want to see anyone—was he hurt in ways that will never be healed?"

"Oh, Torrain healed him," Adorane answered. "That's why Belubus doesn't want to be seen."

"Where is Eveshone?" Adorane asks when we arrive at the place where we planned to meet her. It's not like her to wander off. He shuffles carefully through the pine needles and twigs like he's caught a scent. I realize suddenly, with a pang of anxiety, that I have not felt her presence in some time.

"Something happened here," he observes, his voice low and gravely. "See all this?" He points to a circle of disturbed forest floor. "A scuffle."

A scuffle with what? Eveshone would have been the most powerful creature in these woods by far. Even a Cloudie, weakened from years in the thin air, would be easy for her to dispatch.

Adorane glides his hand across the dirt and lifts it slowly, his eyes filled with concern.

His palm is covered in blood.

We follow the trail of blood deeper into the forest.

"Eveshone! Eveshone!" I shout, searching my roots to find her. I feel nothing.

Adorane finds a small cave in the sandstone and calls me over. His voice holds a tremendous sadness.

I rush to him and freeze. I see a pile of fur stained red with blood. It's Eveshone.

"Help me get her out of here!" I shout to Adorane and Torrain as I struggle against her dead weight. She's completely passed out, crimson from head to toe.

Once we've pulled her out of the cave, I touch her face. I'm relieved to feel that some warmth remains. But one glimpse of her abdomen makes me fear for her life. There's a hole where much of her core should be, and the flesh around it appears to be rotten, decayed, like a dead animal left in the woods for days.

"What could have done this?" I say. "Eveshone, it's Icelyn. Stay with me. Please don't leave me."

Torrain and Adorane share an expression I can't decipher—it's like a mixture of guilt and secrecy. I turn from them bitterly, stretch myself out as long as I can, and press my body against Eveshone's.

I concentrate on a Soothing and a Vibram, desperate to revive her. Nothing happens. Despite the hint of warmth still left in her, she feels like a stone to me—unyielding, dead. I crush her closer to me. I refuse to accept that she's gone. She can't be gone.

"Eveshone. Hear me! Eveshone. I am because of you. You are because of me." I repeat these words until they become sounds, vibrations bouncing back between her and me.

I am losing sense of my own existence. I already felt disconnected, and now I don't feel like there's any permanent *me* to connect to anything else at all. I am only the vibrations. *Eveshone. Hear me! Eveshone. I am because of you. You are because of me.* I am touch, the sensation of her skin on mine. I am desire to see her return. That's all I am, and perhaps all I've ever been. I've lost myself in her. It's a price I'll pay a thousand times over if it means she can return.

I can feel our roots begin to stitch themselves back together, piece by piece. She's returning to me. I press my hands against her abdomen, willing her body to fight the infection, calling on her skin to grow again —commanding her blood to clean itself, flow through the wound, and bring healing.

Eveshone is my center. I know that now. I am confused when I'm away from her, but everything snaps into perfect focus with her nearby. The darkened contours along her skin that line her musculature glow blue and purple, casting their light on me.

My purpose is to love her. And she was made to be loved by me. It's that simple.

I press my skin against hers, gentle and then hard. A caress and then a press. I move my hands over the deep gash in her abdomen. The blue and purple lights pulse brightly, in sync with her heartbeat, illuminating the cave.

She jolts back to consciousness.

"Icelyn! You have called me from a darkness," she says, her voice joyful yet strangely sad. “I was lost.”

The Soothing and the Vibram seize us both, and as I watch, her abdomen grows back into the form it should take. The rotted flesh retreats, overcome by fresh new skin. Her breathing returns to normal.

I don’t know how long it takes, but finally Eveshone has fully returned from the brink of death. We stare into each other’s eyes, both of us on the verge of laughter and tears.

“What just happened?” I hear Adorane ask, though he seems far away, more like I’m remembering him saying it in a dream. In my periphery—I dare not look away from Eveshone—I can see him and Torrain staring down at us in amazement. Adorane’s wonder seems to be tinged with caution. Torrain’s is unabashed.

“You just witnessed proof that Icelyn is a god, Adorane,” Eveshone answers, never moving her eyes from mine. I feel a trace of vindication. Adorane has never believed in my divinity—not even a little bit.

She pulls herself to her feet.

“Now, let’s go…” She looks to me, latching onto the question in my mind. “…where? I can’t remember we are headed.”

She lifts me to my feet and holds my hand.

“Where would you like to go, Icelyn?”

31

THEN

The sun set, banishing those optimistic clouds into the darkness.

Oliver had redirected as many armored transports from the front as he reasonably could. They wouldn't be able to fly to the top of the mountain, but at least they could roll there surrounded by shields made of steel.

Travis had finally arrived, one of the last in. Sean was relieved to personally load him into one of the transports.

"Stay here, Travis. I'll be back to join you in 10 minutes at the most."

Travis rolled his eyes. He was a grown man now. Why did Sean insist on treating him like he was still 14 years old?

The massive job of loading the evacuees into the oversized tanks was proceeding in as orderly a fashion as possible.

"We should be ready to depart in 45 minutes," Sean noted as he and Oliver entered the elevator to the command center.

"Washington has arrived at a decision. They're sending the plane."

Sean shook his head. "Tell them to meet us at the top of the mountain. We can't wait for them."

They exited the elevator and scanned the rioting crowd outside of the stadium fencing. Both quickly looked away. Nothing could be done for them.

"You know they can't land Air Force One on top of a mountain," Oliver said.

Down the coast, in the distance, they watched as the shimmering lights of the city blacked out in batches. The darkness was closing in on them.

"Tell them to come in a helicopter, then. They won't be able to land here in a few hours either, whether we wait for them or not."

The convoy of armored ground transports rumbled through the darkened city streets.

Soldiers bearing rifles stood roadside. Other than the tanks, the normally bustling neighborhood was eerily still. One hothead threw a rock at the procession in protest, but most of the disorder had been left behind at the stadium loading area. Here, people huddled quietly in their homes and stole furtive peeks through window blinds.

Another sound soon joined the landscape—subtly at first, but then growing in volume to the point where they could no longer be ignored.

"What is that?" one soldier asked, aiming his weapon out into the darkness.

It sounded like a distant waterfall mixed with the patter of raindrops. Only instead of serenity, the sounds promised dread.

On the rooftops of the city buildings, snipers scanned the perimeter through their scopes. The barrels of their rifles began to vibrate. Before long, the scopes shook so much that they were useless.

Without panic, they set the scopes aside and stared into the shadows. But no one could see anything unusual.

"Maybe they're letting people drive on the freeway," a soldier suggested.

"Where would anyone be going?" There was no getting in or out of the city.

In the distance, a pillar of fire grew high in the sky and illuminated the area around them. By the time the orange glow revealed what they had been hearing and feeling, it was too late to do anything at all.

The predators had crept in stealthily; the entire attack was soundless except for sporadic staccatos of gunfire, more from shock than self-defense.

The Croathus had arrived.

Later on, the steel transports rolled through the area. They had no windows except for triple reinforced slitted openings for the driver to use in case of camera failure. This was a mercy for the travelers within. They were spared the sight of the massacre which had occurred in the streets.

Oliver Hailgard scanned every monitor, looking for the slightest movement. Nothing. He exhaled in relief. No sign of them. The Croathus were focused on the population centers that the transports had left behind. He felt guilt—this was terrible for those humans in the city, even if it was good for the ascenders who'd been selected.

He and Sean Brathius sat in silence, as they'd been doing since hearing the screams and howls behind them as they rolled out of the city. What was there to discuss?

"You know why I decided to enlist, Sean?" Oliver asked, his voice low and grim.

Sean had never considered whether Oliver Hailgard might ever be anything other than a military man. It seemed odd to him that it had even been a choice.

"Because that's who you were meant to be, I suppose," Sean answered.

Oliver shook his head. "I've never craved battle. I'm not a thrill junkie, like so many others are. I hate it. Always have."

Sean listened intently.

"But I always wanted to help people. I thought maybe I'd be a doctor, you know? I was good at science. I understood it. But when I got to college, I found out that my high school had been about two years behind all the others. The classes I took were basic, and I needed to be advanced just to begin on the same level as everyone else. Our school didn't offer advanced chemistry. I didn't even know it existed. I was miles behind the starting line. I could never catch up."

"That sounds difficult," Sean replied lamely. He didn't know what else to say. The idea of being *behind in science* was as foreign to him as dry water or cold fire.

"Anyway, I enlisted. I figured it was the best way I could help people right away. There'd just been the attack in Washington, you know, and I thought maybe I could help prevent another."

"You and I had the same goal and the same motivation, even, in some ways. The whole reason I was interested in creating the Croathus was to prevent attacks like that from ever happening again."

Oliver bristled but didn't say anything. For such a brilliant man, Sean was stunningly out of touch.

"The point I'm trying to make is…as much as I hate battle, I hate fleeing from it even more. Leaving all those people behind. That's not what I'm made of."

"Think of all the people you are saving now, though, Oliver. Thousands of people."

"I can only think of those I abandoned."

NOW

Amperous and the Priestess left their followers behind at the base of the brown stone mountains and passed through alone. Amperous had known only mountains that were covered in trees and brush, and others high enough to bring madness and pain. These looked like the spine of some great beast, vertebrae sharpened to jagged points, picked clean and bleached by the brutal sun. The mountains Amperous had always known were full of life; these promised an unending death.

He liked both kinds of mountains. He saw himself in both—felt at home in different ways in both.

He'd tried to express these thoughts to the Priestess, but she had not seemed interested. She had a habit of talking only about what she wanted to discuss and simply ignoring that which she didn't. Amperous was drawn to her, hungered for time with her, yet often found himself uncomfortable in her presence. He second-guessed every word he said, felt like he was taking up too much space wherever he was—and whenever she looked at him, he had the uncomfortable feeling that she was discovering a new flaw he hadn't become aware of yet.

He yearned for her to talk to him, to look at him, to be with him. But he spent much of his time afraid that these things might happen too. He hadn't felt fear in a long time. Not since the dark-suited men when he was very young, probably—or the Great Death, definitely. But he felt it now, around her.

They scrambled through gullies, over ridges, and down into canyons to pass through the unforgiving stone mountains. These sun-scorched mountains were not too tall—even at their summits, Amperous felt no shortness of breath. He was used to leading the way, but the Priestess was every bit his equal in this place. His navigation skills had always been a point of pride, but even before he could calculate the best way through, she'd already be on her way.

"Do these mountains have a name?" Amperous asked.

"They've had many names," she replied cryptically.

"And…what were they? Or are they?" he pressed.

"That's up to you," she responded. "Or me. Why use the names of those who came before? The powerful get to name the world. We will be naming much of it from now on."

They ascended an anvil-shaped outcropping that angrily stabbed the sky. As they reached the apex, he finally saw where the Priestess was taking him.

Across the flat desert below lay a sprawling series of reflective circles, each the source of a blinding beam of sunlight on this bright day. Unlike most of what had been made by the humans who lived in this world before, these were unaffected by age—shiny, intact, like new.

In the center of the concentric circles of mirrors was a gleaming metal tower that stretched high into the sky. At the top of the tower was a mammoth mirror—like the others, only a hundred times larger. It bounced and refocused a thick line of heat and light from the sun above to the mirrors below.

Amperous felt a rage rise within him. "Are there humans here?"

"No," the Priestess assured him. "Humans might have created this originally, but we fixed it. Made it our own. This, Amperous, is my second temple."

While Amperous tried his best to take in this shimmering landscape of white light and mirrors, his eyes were drawn to small explosions of smoke scattered through the sky.

"What am I seeing?" he asked.

The Priestess extended her graceful arm and pointed at a bird flying through the air, heading toward the beam of light reflected off the tower.

"We will become a beacon that draws pilgrims from all corners of the world."

The bird soared straight into the intensified sunlight and vanished into a sizzling cloud of smoke and feathers.

"And those who are not strong enough will be burnt out of this world, leaving only the mighty. Leaving only the worthy."

As Amperous and the Priestess passed between the mirrors set in circles on the desert floor, he was surprised to see how large they were. When he'd first seen them from the lookout above, he imagined they were half his size. But the opposite was true; they were double his height.

The Priestess didn't wait for him as he stopped to examine, and he had to hustle to catch up to her. His feet crunched on the charred bones of the birds who hadn't survived the focused sunlight.

She headed straight for the Silver Tower. Once they reached a portal, she turned toward him ceremoniously and extended her right hand to rest on his shoulder.

"Before we enter, I must give you two gifts."

Amperous grew excited and nervous all at once.

"First, you will know my name," she declared. "To all others, I am the Priestess of Two Temples. But carrying that title is a woman, and her name is Barielta."

When she said the word, Amperous could feel the heat of the secret spread from his ears through his head and down into his chest. *Barielta.* She'd given a tiny portion of her power to him.

He held her hand in his and then put it on his heart.

"Barielta, I am honored to meet you."

Her eyes softened, and for a moment she wasn't only the creature of grace, strength, and power who scared Amperous as much as she attracted him. "I am honored to have you meet me."

Then a rigidity returned to her posture. She removed her hand from his heart and instead placed it on his shoulder.

"And now you must have a title for others to know you by. From today on, Amperous is just a name for me."

Amperous nodded slowly. Why should everyone know his name? It could be a secret for Barielta.

"From this day onward, you are the Lord of Both. Both Croathus and Anaghwin. You will unite them and usher us all into what we are meant to be."

She knelt before him. "I worship you, Lord of Both."

Amperous filled with exhilaration at the idea of being worshipped by such a powerful creature. He bathed in her reverence, and then knelt in front of her too.

"And I worship you, Priestess of Two Temples."

She embraced him, and they held each other for a long time. Finally, they both rose.

"Now let me show you what I have done. And what we will do together."

Omathis couldn't sense Icelyn—not even a hint of her. Because of this, he had no idea where to go. He had no idea what to do. So he went nowhere and did little.

He kept still, camouflaged in the forest, and watched the world around him. He witnessed a few scattered Croathus cross the meadows in the distance—some on their way to fetching water, another hunting an elk. He tracked the sun's progress through the sky above until it descended on the horizon and gave way to the brilliant pinpricks of bright white light against the jet black sky. The rhythms of the world were often soothing to Omathis, but he found no comfort in them now.

The mainland reminded him of Amperous, of the families he and his brother had raised and the life they'd celebrated together. It was haunted—crowded with all those ghosts pressing up against him, torturing him with how alive they'd all once been. Now he was alone, unseen by the world, unfelt by anyone else. Not only did he not sense Icelyn, but he detected no trace of any Croathus he'd ever known. And he'd left behind the Anaghwin, abandoned them without their even knowing.

He hadn't realized until now that he still foolishly harbored a hope for reunification with Amperous. They'd been two halves of a flawed but glorious whole for so long. Amperous was a cornerstone in Omathis' life, and to give up on your foundation is to topple over. But his brother had died in the gas in Mountaintop.

Omathis remained still while tears filled his eyes. The tears were proof that they were more than killing machines, more than executioners, more than hunters. Omathis was grateful to know that they were more than murderers, but often wondered if this unrelenting pain in his heart was too high a price to pay for that knowledge. Mister Sean would have been merciful if he'd made them numb to the cruelty in this world, especially since they were designed to inflict much of it.

The thought of his brother made him yearn for a time long ago, and he wished he could step back into the moments they lived then. Did he cherish them as much as he should have while they were happening? He had tried the best he could, but the answer was clearly no. It's not possible to appreciate the time you have together with someone enough while it's happening—you can't know just how much you'll miss them once it's over. This was true with Amperous, with his wife, with his children. And with Icelyn.

Omathis was moved by these thoughts to explore the forest and the land beyond it. Not knowing where else to go, he decided he would try to find a place he once knew.

32

THEN

Amperous climbed to the top of the building where they'd once lived. He roared in triumph.

This city, once filled with humans who wanted to terminate him and his brother, now belonged to them. He thought about the dark-suited men—the ones who would murmur hateful words to each other about him and Omathis.

He watched the sea of Croathus and the carnage they'd left in their wake. If the dark-suited men weren't already dead, they'd be split in two and carved out soon. The thought brought him comfort.

Warm winds blew inland and made the city feel like a car left in the sun with the windows up. Amperous and his kind could tolerate the heat, but they didn't enjoy it. He yearned for their cool, dark cavern.

Omathis joined him atop this highest building in the city. Amperous had dreaded seeing his brother, sure that in Omathis' eyes he'd see guilt for what they'd done—especially now, in the place of their birth, where the memory of Mister Sean and his teachings was strong.

But Omathis was triumphant, just as Amperous was. Why feel guilt for what they'd done? They had been content to stay in their lovely cavern, in their green paradise, thousands of miles away, but the humans had destroyed their haven. The humans had beckoned them; who could blame them for answering the call?

"We've secured the city from the valleys to the oceans," Omathis reported. He sounded proud. It had been even easier than they'd anticipated. Disabling the air machines had rendered the humans' defenses ineffective.

"Good. And every human must be slaughtered. We're in agreement on this? Survivors will eventually try to hurt us."

Omathis and Amperous shared a memory of their bombed out cavern and nodded in unity.

There was one question that neither wanted to ask, though both knew it had to be answered. Omathis broached the subject first. "Everyone is searching for Mister Sean and Lovely."

They dwelled on the Brathius they had loved long ago, and a prickling awoke in their heads. Mister Sean and Lovely weren't here, in the city, but both could feel that they weren't dead—and they weren't far away, either. The two brothers turned and faced the hot, searing winds.

The moon illuminated the tallest mountain in the range, which lay just beyond the city. The peak was obscured by clouds, but that didn't keep them from knowing what the mountain represented.

Fires rose from the base of the mountain—a red and orange river of flame, spewing a pillar of smoke high into the sky.

The transports continued their climb up the mountain, making slow progress since leaving the paved roads miles behind them. They'd been stymied by the wild overgrowth covering the mountain and had cut a path through the impassable trees and foliage by setting fires. Oliver watched as vacation homes were engulfed in quick-moving flames. Normally a forest fire would be a disaster—but nobody was going to be living here anymore, so what would it matter? The dry season and the Santa Ana winds blowing in from the desert were a potent combination. Soon the entire mountainside was engulfed, leaving a trail of ash miles wide.

They hoped they'd be able to reach about eight thousand feet in elevation within the safety of their armored vehicles. Then they'd only have to climb the final few thousand feet to the top of the mountain on foot. Which was probably still too many, Oliver worried.

He watched the monitors closely, taking in the smoldering remains of trees, smoke rising in plumes, and walls of flames. Occasionally he'd catch a flash of a deer fleeing the fires or a bird soaring overhead.

Oliver was tempted to feel relief. The Croathus had concentrated their attacks on the city. Perhaps they could finish their ascent without trouble. He fought off his optimism and redoubled his vigilance.

The transport driver picked up the speed, and Oliver could hear the engine straining under the stress. The last thing they needed was a mechanical failure in the midst of this hellscape.

"Slow down," he growled. "You're going to wear it out."

The driver nodded but didn't obey. Instead he pushed the transport harder. The engine's screaming grew intolerable.

Oliver noticed that the driver looked spooked. His skin was gray and drenched with sweat. His eyes darted back and forth. Had he seen something?

"Slow down!"

"I can't," the driver responded quietly.

Their transport slammed to a sudden stop. Oliver and Sean were thrown from their seats from the impact.

"What was that?" Oliver asked in the silence that came after impact. Something had hit them. He scanned the monitors but couldn't see anything.

The driver stood, panicked. "I can't. I can't."

"Stay calm." Oliver commanded.

The radio crackled and a voice, urgent, filled the transport's cockpit. "Transport One, do you hear us? What happened?"

"We don't know—something hit us," Oliver answered. "Did you see anything?"

The voice on the other end paused, as if she didn't know what to say. "I don't think so. I don't…no, I don't think so."

"Resume the ascent," Oliver replied into the radio, nodding to the driver.

No movement.

"I can't," the driver muttered over and over.

Oliver placed a gentle hand on his shoulder. "You take a break. I'll drive." His touch silenced the driver. Oliver slid behind the steering wheel and inhaled. He engaged the gear. Everything appeared to be working. Maybe they'd just hit a boulder while driving too fast.

He studied the monitors while he drove and settled into a steady pace.

"Just another half mile before we reach the fog," Sean noted. "At that point, the elevation will start to adversely affect the transports." Oliver nodded and concentrated on the drive.

Then one of the monitors caught his attention.

One of the transports following them was flipped on its side.

"How did that happen?" Oliver asked. He stopped the convey and rewound the recording from the monitor. The transport had been upended in an instant, as if flicked by an invisible hand. This time, Sean noticed a shimmering wave on either side of the transport. It was a slight flickering, like when heat off the asphalt distorts the horizon.

"What's the frame rate on the cameras?" Sean asked.

"Forty-eight," Oliver answered.

Sean shook his head. He knew government bureaucracy too well—he'd been navigating it for his entire professional life. They might pay for forty-eight frames per second on the front-facing cameras, but they'd skimp on the rear and side cameras. "No, that's the front camera. What about the rear cameras? They're not the same. See? These feeds are jerkier."

"Why would it make a difference?" Oliver asked.

"Because there's a chance the camera isn't catching…" He trailed off. No need to inject any unnecessary panic into the cockpit. Instead, he advanced the video, one frame at a time, methodically.

"Even if it's twelve frames per second, there's no way they could be that fast," Oliver argued. "They couldn't move in and out of the shot in a twelfth of a second. Could they?"

Sean continued to advance the frames, hesitant to answer.

"Could they?" Oliver repeated quietly, his voice fearful now.

"They're not always that fast, obviously. But they can move in quick bursts, and—"

He continued to run through the frames one by one, and then stopped. *No.*

Oliver saw it too. It was shadowy, blurred, and nearly translucent—the ways things moving at great speed are when captured on camera—but it was unmistakable.

A Croathus.

ICELYN

I spend the night near the sandstone cave where I brought Eveshone back from the abyss. I'm exhausted from the effort, my head feels both overstuffed and drained, and I have no desire to trudge down the mountain while carrying supplies. But more importantly, I don't know where I want to go.

I still feel the pull of the Anaghwin back in the Drowned City, and I want to return to them. I also want to bring the Croathus into the love of the Brathius. I know I can turn them. Somehow, too, the idea of bearing a child has started to seem like a good option—even apart from Mountaintop's need for children. For Eveshone. For the Anaghwin. For the Croathus. Despite knowing that there is something god-like within me, I don't harbor any illusions that I am immortal. I will need a child who can grow into being their new Lovely when I pass.

My experience with Eveshone has muddied my feelings and made me want to take all three of these divergent paths at the same time, each of them with a fierce, uncompromising desire.

My time in Mountaintop has destabilized me, I realize. I don't trust myself to make this decision. I don't completely trust who I am in the first place. I press my fingers against my face a lot, trying to figure out what it is I'm touching. I say my name to myself. Icelyn. The word sounds like nothing I've heard, nothing anyone has ever said.

While securing a campsite for the night, Eveshone jumps back and away from Torrain—fearful in a way I've never seen.

"What is that monstrous invention?" she asks, shaking, her breath quick. She points to Torrain's weapon, the ultraspear.

Again, that inscrutable look between Adorane and Torrain. Secrets. They're quiet, so I answer.

"It's one of Torrain's inventions, Eveshone. They brought it to defend us."

"It's evil, Icelyn. Filled with curses and pain beyond words! Take it away," she begs, like a child awakening from night terrors.

"Why does she fear your invention so, Torrain?" I ask, growing suspicious. What is going on?

"Because it works," Adorane answers. "Clearly."

I'm starting to understand. "Eveshone, have you seen this before?"

"Yes," she stammers, "A human had one. Plunged it into my stomach. That's what sent me to the dark place, Icelyn. I would have been lost there if it weren't for you."

Even though Adorane and Torrain don't smile, I can sense they are made glad by this news, and I hate it. Finally, the test Torrain wanted—and it didn't matter to him at all that Eveshone was the unwitting subject.

"You created something that could hurt Eveshone?" I ask. It's an accusation as much as a question.

"Using the Brathius Masks, yes," Torrain explains. "You see, that material bonds with their skin, so I combined it with a cocktail of venoms to create necrosis—the breakdown and death of skin and muscle. We have to be careful around it, too. It's as dangerous to humans—"

"It's for defense, Icelyn," Adorane cuts him off. "You should be thankful we brought it. Eveshone can't shield us from an attacking horde."

I don't want Adorane telling me what I should be feeling. I need to get away and think.

We find an indentation in the mountain. Not proper shelter, more like a small lean-to created by large slabs of rocks resting on one another. It feels safe, because we can see any threat that might approach us before it gets too close. Here Adorane and Torrain labor to make a comfortable bed out of leaves for Eveshone, who needs to sleep in order to continue her recovery. It is kind of them, and I appreciate it.

Eveshone rests comfortably now. Torrain sleeps too. I try.

Adorane stays awake, on guard against whatever might be out there. We know now that a human with an ultraspear lurks in the darkness—along with who knows what else.

Sleep eludes me, though I desperately need it. I feel every slight discomfort in my body, every hint of disquiet in my mind. A pebble, a twig, a regret, a worry—they all conspire to keep me from rest. My thoughts swirl through my head and make their way down to my chest too. My heart pounds. If there's an opposite of rest, that's what I've entered into.

I sit up and surrender to the forces that keep me from slumber. No use fighting them any longer.

Adorane, vigilant as ever, looks toward me.

"Can I help you?" he asks in a monotone voice, and I can't tell if he's being genuinely helpful, sarcastic, or something in between. Before we first traveled Down Below, years ago, I could always tell what Adorane was thinking. Now, after everything we've both been through, I rarely can.

"I can't sleep," I reply simply.

I have an idea of what I'd like to do, and I need Adorane's help. But I don't want to deal with his questions. If only there were a way to sneak in and steal a bit of a person's knowledge without them knowing.

"Adorane, if you want to talk to your god…what is your god's name again?"

"My god's name isn't a word that can be said," he answers. "My god's name is who my god is, what my god wants and does. It's hard to explain. But if my god's name were trapped inside a word, and we were to find out what that word was, that word would probably burn the lips and tongue of anyone who tried to say it."

I don't understand a single bit of what he's talking about, but I like the fervor behind his words.

"So you don't want to reduce your god to a word that can be said. I understand that. But when you want to talk to your god, how do you do it? Is there a certain phrase you say to summon him—"

"Not him, Icelyn. Well, not exclusively him, at least. Him and her. And it."

"I thought you only had one god," I say, confused.

"I do, but my god is him, her, and it all rolled into one."

"And when you want to talk to him, her, and it, how do you do it?" I ask, laughing. I don't understand this at all.

"It's different for everyone. And anyway, I'm not about to tell you how I do it; you would definitely hold the information against me later," he says with a smile. I hope he's joking, but I worry he's partially serious. "Plus, talking to god is powerful. You have to want it, beg for it, figure it out. Earn it. If someone gives only half a thought to wanting to talk to their god, they shouldn't bother. It's a long journey you must take to *prove* you want to go where you *say* you want to go."

I know he's trying to talk me out of it, but it sounds so appealing.

I stand and walk past Adorane, exiting the stone shelter.

"Where are you going?"

I start to scramble up one of the slabs that forms the shelter and pull myself atop it.

"I'm going to start a long journey."

"Icelyn, why?" he asks, tired. "You don't even believe in any of that."

I continue to climb until I can barely hear him. "Because even a god needs someone to talk to," I answer, though mostly to myself.

33

THEN

Travis was knocked out of his seat to the ground for the second time. This wasn't just rough terrain. What was going on? The silence from the cockpits gnawed on him. He pressed the button on the intercom communicator again. "I've got a couple hundred concerned people back here, and we'd like to know what's going on."

He opened the weapons locker and distributed rifles. Two-thirds of every transport were filled with military or law enforcement personnel, so they were ready.

He burned with anger toward Sean Brathius. It was bad enough he hadn't allowed him in the cockpit. To keep him in the dark like this was too much.

The transport shook again, as if God himself was kicking it.

"What's going on out there?" he screamed.

Silence.

The monitors revealed that half of the transports had been flipped. Oliver turned a crank to remove the steel shields from the front- and side-facing window slots. They couldn't rely on the cameras anymore. They needed to know what was going on.

"Switch to manual vision," he declared over the radio. "Cameras are useless."

They could see them from through windows now. The smoke afforded the creatures the perfect cover, and Oliver regretted ever setting the brush on fire. Groups of three or four would explode into view, a streaky blur, and slam their bodies into the side of the transports. Their attacks were precise, efficient, and relentless—one after another, choreographed like a ballet.

Sean was transfixed by their graceful coordination. Even though he'd created these creatures, he'd only ever seen a few. Seeing groups of them moving as one gave him a thrill he couldn't admit out loud to enjoying. They were beautiful.

Oliver watched Sean with disdain but didn't have time for an argument. He grabbed ahold of the onboard gunner and followed the creatures' movements, cursing under his breath. He'd switched from bullets to explosives—all the transports were equipped with high-velocity kinetic energy penetrators, small missiles, and anti-aircraft rounds—knowing that conventional artillery wouldn't make any difference. Because of the way the Croathus were moving, to shoot at them was to risk hitting another transport. From what he knew about their intellect and tactics training—which was a lot, since he'd at one point personally trained Omathis and Amperous—he guessed this was intentional.

A transport behind them unleashed a desperate barrage of explosives. It didn't hit a single Croathus—they simply dodged as if it were firing in slow motion. Instead, the explosives slammed into three of the downed transports, ripping the steel vehicles apart in a series of fireballs.

"Only launch your missiles if there's no other transport in harm's way," Oliver shouted into the radio.

His warning was ignored. For the other transport gunners, this was the first time they'd seen a Croathus in person. None could resist trying to destroy the nightmares. Their convey quickly transformed into a deadly C-shaped firing squad.

Sean took over the radio. They were going to die if they stayed here, but the creatures couldn't survive at higher elevations. They were close to that cut-off point. "Move forward. We're almost to the altitude where they won't be a threat."

Oliver shook his head and shoved Sean aside. "We can't leave all of those people behind." He pointed at the flipped transports which littered the mountainside. "We'd be abandoning more than half of the ascenders."

Despite Oliver and the lead transport's failure to move, all other transports that hadn't been flipped began their slow progress up the side of the mountain again.

"Stay! We need to stick together," Oliver commanded. "Do not resume movement until we've recovered the ascenders from the disabled transports."

None of the transports stopped.

"We can flank left and right and create a zone for recovery," Oliver determined. "Transports, this is a command. Position yourself wide and fire on the perimeter. Keep them at bay just long enough to transfer those people from the stranded transports into the operational transports."

The transports ignored him and continued their path upwards.

Four Croathus pounced on an upside-down transport. They tore away at the steel shields and tossed pieces aside as if it were made of cardboard.

Within the downed transport, the soldiers and police officers held their weapons at attention. They attempted to quiet the screams of the civilians on board. In truth, they were panicked too. The sounds of their tank being torn apart terrified the soldiers. Everyone worked to stay on their feet as the vehicle rocked back and forth.

"This is Alpha Eight. Can anyone hear us? We are under attack. Please respond," one soldier repeatedly radioed. No one responded.

Finally, another soldier crushed the radio controls with the butt of her rifle just to shut him up. It worked.

A streak of sunlight invaded the dimly-lit transport interior. Soldiers filled the opening with gunfire to keep whatever was trying to get in out. It worked, and for a second everyone felt a wave of relief.

Then another section of the transport was peeled away—and another. And another. Soon there were too many openings for the soldiers to focus their collective fire.

"I'm not going to sit here and watch this," Oliver declared, watching the Croathus batter their way inside the shattered transport.

He grabbed a compact rocket launcher.

"What are you going to do?" Sean asked. "What can any of us do? We should try to save ourselves."

"Even if I fail, I need to *try* to help," Oliver explained as he punched in the code to open the door to their tank.

"You're going to die! Just like them! What's the use in that?" Sean argued.

The top hatch hissed open and Oliver climbed out. The panicked driver reached up and closed it again as soon as Oliver left.

Oliver stood on the hood of the tank and shot a rocket just short of the mass of Croathus swarming the Alpha Eight transport.

The explosion drew their attention. They turned from tearing apart the tank and leapt to the ground. At the sight of Oliver, they stood tall, defiant—matching his brave stance. They hissed and screeched.

Oliver loaded another rocket. This one he shot directly into the chest of a Croathus who had moved far enough away from Alpha Eight to make the strike worth the risk. The Croathus fell back, its torso a ball of flames.

Half the Croathus gathered around their fallen comrade, attending to its injuries.

The others charged straight toward Oliver.

Omathis and Amperous were stunned by the pain that tore through their hearts.

From their perch atop the skyscraper, they turned toward the mountain on the horizon.

Someone had been injured, but they couldn't tell who.

One of their own—or a Brathius?

"I told you we should have pursued them into the mountains," Amperous grumbled. "We should be there."

Omathis didn't reply, but Amperous picked up on his thoughts anyway. It was easy to read them, because Amperous shared them. Neither of them wanted to see Mister Sean. If he was going to reject them again, neither could bear it. If Mister Sean was going to die, they didn't want to be near. They'd both stayed away for the same reasons—even if neither would admit it out loud.

Now, feeling this communal distress, they knew they'd made a mistake.

"We are needed on the Mountain," Omathis declared.

Before he'd finished the statement, they were swinging down toward the ground.

NOW

Belubus paced from one side of the room to the other. Despite his fury at being pressed into Torrain's miracle and trapped there, he had to admire what the boy had accomplished. His creation didn't just offer the ability to take him for a ride—somehow it had revitalized his nerves and muscles so that he was moving along with it.

Yet there was something foreign about the experience. He was working together with the exoskeleton, yet sometimes he sensed that it was leading him more than following. What exactly was in that Brathius mask bonding?

Belubus had lived his entire life being Belubus, and because of this knew his own thoughts well. Now he felt impulses that were not familiar. His initial desire to snuff out his own life had been washed away—though, he suspected, not by himself. It was as if someone had reached into his mind and talked him out of it.

Belubus knew how he felt about all this—Torrain had violated who he was, and it made him angry. Yet now he struggled with another thought. It wasn't gratitude; he could never be thankful for this.

It seemed closer to *desire.*

He desired, he realized, to use what Torrain had bonded to him to get what he really wanted. He just didn't know what that was yet.

And for some reason, he was fearful at the thought of finding out.

Omathis stumbled through the overgrowth until he found the place. He couldn't tell it by sight—it looked different than it had back then. But soon his mind adjusted his eyes until they could see both what was now and what had been so long ago.

This is where he and Amperous had first seen their true loves. Where at first he'd been embarrassed to watch his brother grow so tender—but then happy for him, and free to do the same.

There's too much joy in this place, he realized. The thought escaped before he could guard himself against it. Happiness from long ago that hasn't carried into today turns into a sadness that's too much to bear. Omathis lowered himself down onto the ground, which was now dirt, rubble, rocks, and vines. Long ago, it had been smooth polished cement. He remembered how his wife had laid on top of him, covering him head to foot, completely, and how warmth and electricity leapt between their bodies. His skin hungered for that connection so much that he could feel it again—but only enough to realize how brutally he missed it. It's one thing to want something; it's another level of hunger to realize you'll never have it again.

She had gently pressed her face against his until he couldn't tell where he ended and she began. He hadn't felt shame for being soft and quiet and kind. With her, he could admit that often he *wanted* to be that more than he did hard, loud, and fierce. She had awakened him. She had let him become all he'd hoped he was but hadn't dared believe he could be.

Now she was gone—as was Amperous, and all the rest of them. Wiped away by the violent wave of humanity. Swallowed up in bloodshed.

He'd rather not dwell on this, which is why he hadn't given it much thought in hundreds of years. But here, he had to. Here, where the union had begun, this wellspring of joy, to think about anything else would be to pretend it had never happened, and that felt blasphemous.

He had forbidden the other Anaghwin from loving as he had so they would never have to be crushed beneath this pain. Oh, to be free like them, not knowing how much better life could be—never having to face how much they had lost across the years.

Yet he would never trade any of his memories, no matter how eternally gutting they were now, for that pain-free ignorance. Those moments, with her covering him, loving him, bound to him—they were worth an eternity of torment and more.

ICELYN

I sit a hundred feet above the others. It's clear and quiet up here. I sit still long enough to wonder if maybe I have fallen asleep after all and am dreaming.

My thoughts have calmed, and I can examine them with care. They're not as overwhelming this way. I can feel the cold air entering my nostrils, and then exiting, warmed after making its trip through my body. Cold air from the outside, filtered through me, sent back out warm and completely changed.

Everywhere you go, new things come to you. Do you keep them and make them a part of who you are? Or do you send them back out, changed? I have inhaled Mountaintop, the Anaghwin, my parents, Omathis, Eveshone, Torrain, Adorane, the death I've seen below and above. How much is now a part of me, inside, sewn into my essence? How much have I transformed and breathed out?

How much of what I hate in my life is a result of myself?

My thoughts aren't making sense, at least not in the way I think thoughts should. But for now, that's not a bad thing. Everything has to be jumbled up before it can become clear. How can you recognize order if there's no chaos to compare it to?

Adorane said that everyone accesses his god in a different way. He wouldn't even tell me how he achieves his connection. Does that mean everyone just makes it up on their own?

What would mine be? If it is up to each person to create their own access, what should mine look like?

I would like if my access to Adorane's god were through the people I have loved. And through singing, because I like singing very much—both my own voice and the voices of others. I would love a world where I could share myself with the people I love without worrying about all the ways we've failed each other. Where I can enjoy life without being plunged into shadows, and pain, and the ways everyone and everything good and wonderful eventually betrays me.

Adorane. The good, uncomplicated, wonderful side of Adorane. He's pure exhilaration; he's wide-eyed wonder. He's funny and brave. Torrain: loyal, trustworthy, shy, awkward, brilliant, endearing. Mother, desperately loving despite what the traditions taught her she should be. She couldn't help but he affectionate and playful even though such behavior was unbecoming of a Cognate woman. Father, unlike other Cognate fathers in Mountaintop, holding my hand, picking me up, holding me close, talking to me every day. Omathis, protective to the point of tearing his own heart out. Eveshone, the embodiment of all that is good.

The sun peeks over the ridgeline and bathes me in a beam of golden light. The night is over. I haven't slept, but I haven't struggled, either. I feel rested.

I stretch out over the rocky perch where I've sat through the night. If I could embrace it, I would. It's a sacred place. Something has been taken out of me, cleansed, strengthened, and then put back in.

Adorane's god never showed up, but in any case, I feel relieved. At peace. Ready to face whatever we might see Down Below.

34

THEN ❧❦❧❦❧❦❧

Oliver Hailgard sprinted to load the next rocket, then turned and fired. He barely had time to register the hit before running again. He was doing damage to the pursuing Croathus. He marveled at how devastated and attentive the other creatures appeared whenever one of them was injured. Half would retreat from their attack and drop back to look after their fallen ally.

Oliver had a nimble mind for military tactics. Even while he ran, focused on his own survival, he turned this tendency of theirs over in his mind. It was different from how humans often performed on the battlefield. What was going on, exactly?

"Transfer them over to our tank!" he shouted into his radio. "While the Croathus are occupied with me!"

He had devised a strategy on the go. His hope was to distract the Croathus so people could move from the downed transports into the operational tanks.

He'd succeeded in drawing the Croathus away from the fallen vehicles —and with each hit of the rocket launcher, another bunch were focused on injured Croathus and nothing else.

He counted how many rockets he had left in the ammo box.

Only two.

He'd reached the limits of his plan.

Gratefully, he watched as soldiers emerged from his transport. They led the trapped occupants of the torn apart Alpha Eight vehicle to the lead transport.

Good. Maybe some of those who were sure to die would instead survive.

And at least he'd die on his feet with a launcher in his hands.

Travis' patience had been exhausted. He wasn't going to fumble around inside this transport, blind to what was going on outside.

"Here, help me open this," he barked at the nearest soldier as he grabbed a heavy steel lever.

"Our orders are to stay in the transport. We're safe inside," the soldier protested.

"We have no communication with anyone. If the orders were changed, they wouldn't be able to tell us," Travis pointed out.

The transport was again rocked by a massive impact.

"And we're not safe inside. Not for long."

Travis' argument worked, and the soldiers helped him open the portal to the outside. Light burst into the vehicle, momentarily blinding those within.

Travis felt their *presence* before he saw one. He saw a carved-out human carcass discarded on the ground—and the image of his mother, seared into his memory, flashed before his eyes. He was suddenly filled with a blazing, exhilarating anger.

He was going to kill them all.

He hadn't realized it until now—but it's all he'd ever wanted to do.

"Grab your weapons and follow me."

As his eyes adjusted to the bright sun, Travis figured out what was going on. Oliver had run to higher ground, and the Croathus were following him. A mangled transport had been torn open by the beasts.

"Get those people into another transport!" he ordered. Soldiers rushed and pulled wounded and frightened people from Alpha Eight toward safety. Once Travis was satisfied that the rescue effort was well underway, he turned his attention back to Oliver and the Croathus that pursued him.

Sean Brathius watched Oliver's reckless heroism from the tank. He didn't know what he was feeling. Was he mourning the death of ascenders, the imminent demise of Oliver Hailgard, or the Croathus who had been hit by missiles?

While he watched, Oliver shot his final rocket. Another direct hit straight into the chest of a charging Croathus. Sean winced. He couldn't help it—it hurt to watch any of his creatures injured.

Now Oliver was surrounded by the murderous Croathus army.

"I can't let this happen," Sean mumbled.

"You can't do anything about it," the driver answered.

A flash of inspiration tore through Sean, and he began to climb the small ladder toward the exit. "There *is* something I can do."

Why hadn't he thought of this earlier?

ICELYN

Adorane hunts through the brush to find serpents who can lend their venom toward Eveshone's recovery. Torrain tries too, but he doesn't have the same aptitude for snake-hunting, so he's mostly worthless. Earlier he pointed out a small snake, but then refused to pick it up with his hands, so it slithered away from us and under a rock. We all pretended not to notice to spare him embarrassment.

Eveshone is far from her normal self, but with the help of time and venom, she is well enough to start moving again. Adorane leads the way —something a healthy Eveshone would never tolerate for long—and we keep a slower pace, behind him but in front of Torrain. I can sense a novel emotion tumbling around inside of her. Panic. Despair.

I put a hand on her arm, and she startles a bit before allowing my touch to comfort her. I want her to be free of her turmoil, but know my words can't help her. I think warm, caring, and affectionate thoughts toward her. It's not hard to do; I've always loved Eveshone easily. For me —for whom even the best relationships inevitably become needlessly, foolishly complicated—this is a welcome rarity.

Adorane is in tune with Eveshone's condition, and he can tell she needs a rest. The thinner air hasn't helped in her recovery, and she struggles with a fierce headache on top of her wounds.

"Up here, around that pass, there's a nice place to sit and relax," he announces.

"I don't need to rest! Let's keep going," Eveshone protests pridefully. She doesn't like to think she's slowing our progress.

"Not for you, Eveshone," Adorane lies (I think), "for Icelyn. And Torrain, probably." I'm more touched than offended. I know he is only being sensitive to her feelings.

Yet as we near the area of promised rest, I wonder if it's just for Eveshone's sake that we're stopping here. It is a manicured clearing, with swirls of sage blooming in blues, reds, and purples. The circles are lined with bright yellow poppies, mountain sunflowers, and even white and violet irises. It's as if someone took all my favorite flowers and planted them in exactly the way I would if I could.

It's a garden.

I stare at it until a tightness in my chest gives way to tears in my eyes. I wish I could live here forever—shrink myself down and never leave.

I blink through the tears long enough to remember that I'm not alone, and I see that Adorane and Torrain are taking obvious pleasure in my reaction to the place. They share something secret between them.

"Did you...did you two plant this garden?"

They nod. "Welcome to our special project. We never thought you'd actually see it."

I don't respond. My eyes move, stunned, over the gently sloping mounds of dirt beneath each whirlwind of petals.

"But these are all flowers. Adorane, you've said that a garden that didn't include crops to eat was a waste of soil and sweat."

"I was wrong," he responds.

Eveshone has perked up in this garden, even more than from the snake venom. "This is a tribute to Lovely's divinity?" she asks. "I approve. I'm surprised you two would build it, but impressed."

"No, it's not a shrine. Not a shrine built to worship her, at least. I could never...*worship* Icelyn," Adorane responds.

I know, Adorane. Trust me.

"When we had to start the recovery from the tragedy in Mountaintop, many in the Kith just wanted to burn—" Torrain starts to explain.

I suddenly understand, and I don't want him to say anything more. "Stop!" I shout.

He does.

Adorane and Torrain buried my beloved Anaghwin here. The others in the Kith wanted to burn their noble remains, but Adorane and Torrain honored them here and marked the spot with my favorite flowers.

"It *is* a shrine," I correct Adorane. "Not to me—you're right—but to love. My love for them. And your love for me, too, Adorane and Torrain."

They both look embarrassed, but neither denies my words.

"Does this make up for the...mistakes we've made?" Torrain asks, his voice penitent.

"I'm not sure," I answer honestly as I wander through the flowers, overwhelmed by the scent and the sight. "But it's one of the most beautiful things I've ever seen."

I sit for a long time in the garden. My brokenness is still strong within me, but being here, I enjoy a reprieve from the raw pain of it. For the first time in a long time, I consider the idea that the turbulence will cease and I will someday be at peace again.

NOW

The Priestess of Two Temples held Amperous' hand and led him toward the mirrored tower.

"What is this place?" he asked.

She stroked his hand before pressing it between hers. "I'd rather you see than be told. And truly, if you remain still and look within, you'll find that you already know."

Amperous tried for a moment to look within, but he wasn't sure how to do it.

"Discovery is remembrance," the Priestess stated, "and remembrance is discovery. You've been fighting against both for so long. But not anymore."

A shudder of fear passed through Amperous. His memories were dark. He avoided visiting them. Discoveries led to horror—even when they initially seemed bright, they always ended in darkness.

The Priestess embraced him. "All that ends now, Amperous. Do you not understand what a new day is? Where there have been tears, there will now be laughter. You and I will trade sorrow for joy. That's why we're fighting: to make everything new. That's why every one of our kind needs this."

Amperous let the comfort seep into him, and the whispering threat of annihilation seemed to recede.

He walked after her as she pressed a series of buttons on a shiny reflective black surface. A door slid open. Unlike the stone tower that held the Mothers, which was rustic and ancient in form, this one looked more like the buildings where Mister Sean would take him and Omathis to be tested and prodded by the men in dark suits. He did not like this building. It pulsed with the magic of men, a dangerous glimmer that he hadn't seen in centuries.

They passed through the sleek metal portal and into a large space dominated by whirring noises and flashing dots of light.

Barielta glided from one machine to the next, inputting codes, turning dials, flipping switches, pulling on levers—like she'd done it all a thousand times. Like she had been born to do it. Amperous watched, frozen. She looked much like the men in dark suits. She looked like Mister Sean.

This was not the way Croathus were meant to act.

She could sense his concern. Though their roots hadn't been strong so far—a fact that confused Amperous and at times made him worry—their connection had grown to the point where they could sense in each other generalized feelings, if not specific thoughts.

"You see, Amperous, my first temple is about our past—our roots, the foundations we are built upon, the shadows we've emerged from. Our Mothers. The mystery of who we have been and how we've gotten here. The first temple is about belief in the darkness, trusting what we cannot see, respecting what we'll never understand," she explained, as she finished dialing in a series of sequences.

There was a clacking and then a thud as something heavy fell into place and engaged, followed by a low continuous groan. An entire wall began to lift from the ground, revealing a series of towering glass cylinders filled with blue-green liquid.

Each held a form that Amperous couldn't make out—like a Croathus, but incomplete. Like a lump of clay that might someday be sculpted into something.

Barielta strode toward the cylinders and placed a hand against the glass. An unformed Croathus held out what should have been a hand toward her, but without fingers or talons. A face without eyes or nose or mouth leaned toward her. Amperous thought to himself that he'd never seen anything more awful.

"What are these, Priestess?" Amperous asked, fear echoing in his words.

"Potential, pure and limitless. No pathways are blocked for them yet. They can be anything. Live anywhere. Do whatever they need to do."

Amperous felt an instinctive fear. If being able to do whatever and be anything looked like these formless creatures, he wanted limits. He felt the pull of how Barielta saw them, a swell of exuberance that made him feel worse for how much he disliked what she had done.

"This temple is not about our past, Amperous," Barielta proclaimed. "This temple is about the new. What is yet to be. Our future.

THEN

Travis ran from one flipped transport to another and knocked on the sides, shouting for them to open up. The armored portals swung open and people cautiously filtered out, led by armed soldiers.

"Head upward, toward the top of the mountain," he encouraged.

"We're not far from safety!"

Travis realized there was no way they were going to transfer all the people from the smashed tanks into the few remaining transports. If they stayed here, locked away, they'd only be waiting for death once the Croathus inevitably turned their attention back to them.

This was their best chance at survival.

"Toward the cloudline. There's safety at the higher elevation."

It wasn't long before a thick line of terrified humanity had formed and was hustling its way up the mountainside. Soldiers marched along the perimeter, rifles trained on the pillars of smoke in case threats emerged.

Travis grabbed a launcher capable of firing the same miniaturized missiles Oliver had been using. He knew bullets weren't going to make a difference. He charged toward where Oliver and the Croathus were caught in a stand-off.

He wanted to inflict pain.

Sean Brathius walked toward the granite precipice where Oliver Hailgard was surrounded by Croathus. Sean held his hands up in the air.

"My children! Do not attack. I am here. You can be redeemed," he shouted, his voice loud and clear in the cold air.

The sound of his voice froze the Croathus. He wasn't sure what he was hoping would happen next. Would they fall to their knees and bow? Wait for him to embrace them one by one? He suffered a moment of doubt as they didn't do anything. Would they recognize him as a Brathius? He knew Omathis and Amperous well, but these creatures had never met him.

Yet love for the Brathius had been built into who they were. Sean hoped desperately that he could trust in his creation.

Oliver didn't know what was going on between Sean and the Croathus. He was angry at Sean for approaching without a weapon. Yet he'd distracted them. Oliver took advantage and ran from the spot where they'd cornered him. He rushed toward Sean.

"No," Sean shouted, pushing Oliver back. "This is between me and them. I can't be associated with the pain you just inflicted on them."

Oliver was perplexed by Sean's surety. The man seemed taller, stronger, and more powerful. Oliver obeyed.

Travis rushed toward the gathered Croathus.

He was shocked. Sean Brathius was standing one hundred yards away from them, holding his hands out toward the creatures, as if he could hold them at bay. The craziest part was that it seemed to be working. The creatures, who moments before had been viciously charging toward Oliver, were now in a stupor.

They were gathered beside a tall granite cliff, with a stony overhang stretching out hundreds of feet above them. A waterfall thundered behind them. In simpler times this area was a popular sightseeing destination, packed with hikers wearing khaki shorts and hydration backpacks. It felt incongruously beautiful alongside the fire, smoke, and destruction.

Travis held his launcher steady and trained his aim on one of the Croathus. He had only five missiles, though, and there were at least twenty of the creatures facing Sean. He could take out five at the most. That would still leave fifteen to easily massacre himself and the thousands of ascenders now marching toward the cloudline.

Instead he tilted his eyes upward and studied the large granite overhang. He aimed and fired.

Massive shards of granite broke from the cliff upon impact and smashed down over the frozen Croathus. Travis watched as the beasts were buried under boulder and rock. An intense, electric satisfaction ran through him.

Sean Brathius shouted in agonized shock. He hadn't seen Travis' shot and couldn't understand what had happened. Travis watched as Oliver grabbed him and stopped him from rushing toward the rubble.

"Let's join the procession upward," he bellowed to them both. He held the rocket launcher above his head so that Sean would see it. He watched as Sean turned slowly, a look of shock and then heartache registering on his face as he realized what had happened. Travis grinned instinctively at his pain.

"Come on, move. I've stopped these, but surely more are coming for us."

35

ICELYN

We decide to stay in the memorial garden overnight so Eveshone can be restored.

I awaken midway through the night to discover Adorane and Torrain huddled together, whispering. It's clear to me that neither has slept, although both acted like they were retiring for the evening earlier. Were they only pretending in order to get me to sleep, like I'm an unruly toddler with bedtime issues?

I have long been sensitive to the curious bond they share, because it so often seals me on the outside. Now that they share leadership of Mountaintop and have read the secret archives that only leaders can access, the feeling has only worsened.

I pretend that I'm still sleeping so I can eavesdrop. Adorane is telling Torrain about the See Throughs, the weirdly transparent creatures that attacked us on the beach. Their voices are maddeningly quiet, so I only hear every second or third word.

Torrain doesn't seem surprised. He says something about how it *looks like they are continuing the work*. I don't know who "they" are, or what the "work" is, but Torrain's lack of shock unnerves me.

"...Suppose...stop at...the tower," Torrain says.

"...You think you can trust...tower...If it's still there...hardly believe..." Adorane whispers intensely. If only I were a little closer!

Eveshone shuffles in her sleep and the boys quiet even more, so now I can't hear anything. I try to quiet my anger toward them. I have a secret plan of my own, after all, so I shouldn't be hypocritical.

We've reached a side of the mountain I've never seen before—one that faces a dry, sunbaked desert. While I've heard of the desert, and seen pictures of it in old Apriori books, I am unprepared for the sight. I feel as though I've slipped through a crack in our world and landed in another. Strangely, it reminds me of when we plunged below the surface of the ocean and swam with the assistance of Torrain's metal breathing tubes. The plants and rocks and sand make me think of what I saw at the bottom of the sea.

The trees in the desert—if they can even be called trees—are sharp and angular, as if during their growth they abruptly, desperately change their minds and shoot forth in all different directions. All the plants are covered with barbs and needles, making it clear that they'd like to be left alone. I've never felt such kinship with plants before—prickly on the outside, soft heart within.

I'm exhausted. Adorane has filled countless skins with water, and we're all required to carry them. Eveshone offered to carry mine for me, but I refused. She's still not completely well. I'm regretting that decision, but not enough to relent and ask her to lighten my burden.

Overwhelming heat consumes me. It's hot past the point of discomfort—it almost feels as though it's burning the bad things right out of me. All my dark thoughts, regrets, fears—melted and dripping onto the ground. I like the feeling, although I am afraid of what's to come.

"Make sure you drink enough," Adorane reminds me, in a caring way that I appreciate. I take a sip from one of the ultralion skins and accidentally spill some drops of water onto the sand, where they evaporate as I watch. "Don't waste it," he scolds.

"It was an accident," I say testily.

"No one else is spilling anything. It's not an accident if it's due to carelessness."

I tune him out and focus instead on the explosion of color against the beiges and browns below my feet. I didn't know flowers grew in the desert, but here they are. Vibrant reds and deep blues, purples fit for royalty, yellows worthy of a god. The ground is covered with sprawling vines, and caterpillars cover the leaves. Lizards scurry in and out of holes. From a distance everything appears still, but up close there is a flurry of activity hiding under that blanket of serenity.

I watch Adorane closely, because I expect that the scurrying insects and reptiles will delight him and reveal a side of him I remember well and miss often. I'm disappointed, as instead they seem to disturb him.

"What's wrong?" I ask. It's a question Adorane always seems to resent, because he wrongly believes that no one can ever guess how he's feeling from the way he looks.

"Nothing," he deflects at first, but it's unconvincing. "Maybe I'm just still upset at the gallons of water that sloshed out of the side of your slack-jawed mouth."

"You were looking at the lizards. Normally that kind of thing would excite you—but it looked like they reminded you of something. Something that upset you."

"If you really want to know, I'll tell you."

"Of course I want to know, that's why I asked!" Torrain and Eveshone look exhausted at our exchange.

"All this activity reminds me of what we haven't seen—even once—on our trip so far. Why is it so still and peaceful?"

"You mean—where are the Croathus?" Torrain asks.

Adorane nods. "The last time we descended, we saw them. They were in the ruined cities, scattered here and there, in little packs. I haven't seen a single one. It's odd."

I haven't been sensing any of them either. Now that I think about it, it does seem strange.

"Maybe it's a good thing," I offer. "It certainly makes our trip easier. Maybe the desert is too hot for them."

"Maybe," Adorane responds, though he doesn't seem placated. "Or maybe they're planning something."

"I'm going consider it a blessing. Yet another gift from this beautiful place—like the flowers, the smell, and the unending sky. No creatures hunting us down, trying to kill us."

Adorane shrugs off my hopeful theory, but he's happy to let the conversation die, so he doesn't argue.

How many other hidden pockets of beauty are there are in the world? As awful as this planet can be, it still manages to surprise me with its wonder. I promise myself that I'll remember these flowers when everything else seems dark.

The beauty embedded into the sun-scorched brutality here in the desert has clarified something for me. This is where my next chapter will be written. I cannot return to the Drowned City, and I cannot pursue the Croathus. Not until the desert heats me up, melts away what needs to go, and molds what's left of me into whatever I am meant to become.

"We're going to Apex," I declare, and the sound of my own voice surprises me. I guess I've decided.

Adorane and Torrain, deprived of any insight into the internal debate I'd been suffering, both look at me with faces that say *of course we are—that's been the plan all this time.*

But Eveshone appears truly shocked, like she was sure I'd choose another way. "Why, Lovely?" she asks, her eyes wide.

"Because the desert is where I belong. At least for now."

THEN

The last operational transport rolled slowly behind the marching mass of ascenders. Travis, Sean, and Oliver walked alongside the column of people.

Reduced oxygen at the higher elevation made many of the academics among them, already far from being in good physical shape, glacially slow. Many tripped and had to be convinced to rise again because they wanted to stay on the ground. They shambled ahead, lurching like an army of the half dead. Law enforcement and military did a better job of moving forward, holding their weapons with jittery nervousness. They were spooked.

Travis alone was in good spirits. He'd dreamt of killing these monsters since he was a child, and now he'd buried a dozen of them in one strike. Shai would be proud. *It was all for you, Mom.*

The mass of people stumbled to a stop when they saw something grey and hulking looming ahead.

"Stay here!" Oliver commanded, though he didn't need to. Nobody seemed anxious to rush ahead into the mist.

With a battalion of soldiers providing cover, Oliver advanced with Travis, Sean, and a group of armed guards—everyone with guns drawn except Sean, who walked in the middle, eyes glued to the object ahead.

As they neared the object and the smoke began to clear, Oliver was the first to realize what it was. His brain took a moment to recognize what his eyes were seeing. The scene was unfathomably gruesome, even for a veteran of countless battlefields.

It was the empty shell of one of the transports that had gone on without them. Its large steel shields had been torn apart. The bodies of the massacred were strewn on every side of the tank.

Oliver ran forward, hoping to find survivors. He checked the first victims he reached. No sounds. No struggling to breathe, no crying for help. Nothing.

He rushed from body to body, desperate, while Travis and Sean watched.

"Oliver, there are no survivors," Sean stated matter-of-factly. "You can't help them now."

"There are always survivors!" Oliver shouted, digging down into the second and third levels of the dead.

"Not here," Travis stated. "The creatures were designed to ensure no one would survive. An *upgrade*—right, Sean?"

Oliver stopped his search, defeated, and scanned the clouded horizon. He climbed atop the flipped vehicle for a better view. Sean and Travis followed.

All around they saw more transports, ruined and split apart. Oliver made a quick count. None had escaped.

"This doesn't make any sense. They shouldn't be up this high," Sean insisted. "Maybe the Croathus wouldn't *die* at this elevation, but they'd be weakened to the point of insanity. They would never come up here willingly."

The grisly scene around them made an unspoken counter-argument. Only the Croathus could have done this.

"Well, they're here. That much is obvious," Travis replied. "Maybe they want to kill us so badly that they don't mind the pain." If this was the case, Travis understood—the feeling was mutual.

"Well, it's not like we can retreat. Upward is the only way," Oliver said, his voice weak. "Let's pray that at least some of us survive. At this rate, we'll be lucky if even one person does."

Omathis and Amperous slowed.

"What is this, brother?" Amperous asked. He felt a thick and sticky evil. It reminded him of their bombed-out cavern paradise, or of the men in dark suits who had decided to terminate him a long time ago.

Omathis crept forward, sensitive to the pulsating wave of despair. It was strange to him that they would feel such ugliness, because the place was beautiful—far more pleasing to their eyes than the city they'd left behind. There were tall, strong trees and walls of stone. They walked along a clear creek filled with turquoise blue water.

As they crested a precipice, their nostrils filled with the acrid scent of smoke. Amperous blinked tears away from his burning eyes.

"Who would burn this beauty?" Amperous asked, though he didn't need to.

They both knew the answer. They'd seen green paradise reduced to smoldering black dust before.

“This is what humans do. To their land, to each other, and to us,” Amperous growled. Every step through the smoky wasteland stoked his simmering anger.

The downtrodden procession entered a thick soupy cloud and resumed their slog upward. They pushed on through a dreamscape where everything was white and even their view of each other was grayed and ghostlike. Within minutes, they were all soaked from the mist.

Oliver tried his best to estimate how many ascenders were still alive. But counting had been difficult even before they’d reached the cloudline; now it proved impossible.

He tried to make a reasonable guess. At least half had been killed when those transports moved ahead despite his orders. And then so many had died before he and Travis had managed to distract and kill the remaining Croathus. At most, he calculated, ten thousand out of the twenty-five thousand remained.

Oliver hated how this journey up the mountain had been marked by blindness. They’d been blind to the threat while in the transports. They’d had a hard time seeing what was attacking them in all the smoke and fire. And now, with the dense fog of the clouds that had settled atop this mountain—he could barely see more than five people at a time.

“If you spot anything unusual, please shout!” he ordered. “Spread this command!” The soldiers obeyed until everyone was notified.

A distant cry echoed. It pierced the densely humid air, then was squelched. Everyone stood silent.

“What was that?” he shouted.

No answer.

“Everyone look to your left and right, in front and behind. Is anyone missing?”

No answer.

He watched the swirls of fog, fearing the lethal movements of the Croathus in every graceful wisp. Yet other than the eerie white clouds, all was still.

Oliver resumed their ascent.

NOW

Amperous knew by now that disagreeing with Barielta was a waste—

of effort, of time, of well-being.

He wanted to break through the clear cylinders and tear these formless Croathus into pieces. Snuff them out before they became the *something new* that seemed to excite the Priestess so much.

But that impulse immediately felt like an old memory—something he had wanted to do at one point that no longer made any sense. Instead, he looked at the Priestess without saying a word, like a baby waiting for his mother to feed him. A distant part of him worried that he should do something different, but mostly he wanted to hear more from Barielta.

"In your rush to exterminate the humans, you didn't stop to consider which parts of them we might want to keep," she purred gently. "Let me ask you this. When you hunt and kill a beast, do you then merely toss it aside? No—that would be an insult to life itself. Instead, as any good Croathus knows, you feed on the meat, take the bones for building, and save the fur for clothing. Only a monster kills and then wastes what it has slain."

"We have taken their cities," Amperous argued, though weakly. "Some Croathus live in houses the humans built—or at least, what remains of them."

"You tossed their dead bodies aside, not even considering what might be worth saving," Barielta scolded gently. "I'm here to tell you. We need their faith. That much you've come to realize. That's why Omathis and the Anaghwin have survived as long as they have. But what of the other great human invention? The one that grew out of their religious tendencies, which mirrored their thirst for the divine? They even use the same tongue for these twin pursuits—Latin. *Ex nihilo nihil fit*, Amperous!"

Amperous' throat had grown dry, but he managed to speak: "Science." Not even Omathis, fool as he was about religion, dared explore this human abomination. Science was Shai. Science was the Sleeps. Science was the origin of all their pain. "Priestess, you don't understand what science is. What it can become."

Instead of responding, the Priestess tenderly glided her hands across the surface of the cylinder. The formless life within pressed itself against her touch. For the first time since he'd met her, Amperous picked up on her roots. He understood why it had taken so long to reach this level of intimacy with her. He'd been afraid—and for good reason.

Barielta's roots were stronger than any he'd connected to in the past, even Mister Sean's. He lost himself in them. There was only her; the part of him that would protest was melted down and silenced.

He looked at the featureless face of the creature through Barielta's eyes. He felt the affection she had for it, the rush of hope. These would change the world again, maybe even more than Omathis and Amperous and the other Croathus had. He could join her, or he could be left behind.

I know what science becomes, Amperous. That's exactly why we need to embrace it.

36

ICELYN

Torrain and Adorane have studied maps and journals they claim are classified—"for their eyes only," they like to say, more often than I like to hear. They whisper about what they've seen. Whenever I catch a stray word and ask for clarification, they tell me that they're sorry, but they aren't allowed to discuss any of it with me.

It's all as terrible as it sounds.

"You know, I'm sure Father saw those maps and read those journals, too. He would have told me what they contained had I thought to ask," I argue. "So it's not really any breach of secrecy to clue me in."

"He would *not* have told you what these materials contained," Torrain responds. "Trust me."

"Well, I bet it's a bunch of boring old diagrams and useless ramblings. You're both just trying to spice it up to make Eveshone and I feel left out."

"Oh, I don't feel left out, Lovely," Eveshone says. "I'm not nearly as jealous of the knowledge they possess as you are."

Torrain and Adorane laugh as Eveshone betrays the emotion I've tried to keep hidden. Sometimes it's a distinct disadvantage to share roots with someone as oblivious to human behavior as Eveshone.

Adorane takes pity on me. "What I *can* tell you is that we're heading toward an old lab. It's between here and Apex, we think." He furtively consults with a map—not *the* map, but one he's drawn on his own from memory. Apparently it's still too big a secret for him to let me see it. "Through that pass ahead. There we can restock on water and find shelter from the sun."

"Yes. If we tried to make it straight to Apex without stopping, we'd probably die," Torrain adds. They both have the bad habit of sounding condescending when they're explaining something to me—but now, when they actually do have access to more information than I do, it's reached a new level of insufferable.

"An old lab? What does that mean?" I ask.

"Can't say anything more. Although, if you only knew, you'd be amazed," Torrain answers. "I never thought I'd get to visit. I'm so excited."

"That's it! Either tell me more about what you know or keep it to yourself. You know I hate secrets, Torrain."

"We'll keep it to ourselves," Adorane promises.

But it's too late. Now I imagine that everything they say or don't say represents a larger secret they are keeping from me, and it makes me miserable.

As we pass through ruins of Apriori villages, I'm reminded of Adorane's concern. He's right—before we would have seen signs of Croathus habitation in places like this. Now, nothing. Nobody mentions it, though. We don't talk much at all.

It's difficult to accept when reality reveals how wrong you were about everything. I'd always assumed that I shared a certain level of togetherness with Torrain and Adorane. I believed there was a part of all three of us that would forever be *us*, and that nothing could take that away. After everything we'd suffered through together, the parts of me I'd worked so hard to keep hidden from everyone else but allowed them to see, and the fact that I had kissed both of them—I always thought there was an essential foundation that we all shared. That no matter how angry we made one another, how much we might hurt one another, I could always get them to laugh, and then we'd be the three of us again. I've considered them my constants, my brothers, my true loves.

Now I see that this isn't true.

Maybe I hurt them too much when I left. Somewhere in my heart I knew I'd always find a way to forgive them for releasing the gas and killing so many Anaghwin—it would just take time. But in all that time, I never considered that there was a chance I was doing something *they'd* find unforgivable.

I abandoned them. I see that now. Or at least, I see why they would think that.

I want to tell them that I didn't think I was abandoning them. But I know they won't understand what I'm talking about. I can't form the words even when I want to say them.

Adorane is busy preparing a small rodent stew. Eveshone occupies herself with catching the creatures to put into the stew, laughing at how they dart in all directions when she lifts great boulders off the desert floor. Adorane and Eveshone seem to be enjoying their food-producing tasks together, and this should make me happy, but I only feel a stab of self-pity. Everyone seems to have a purpose except me.

I decide to try to talk to Torrain. He has always had a soft spot for me.

"I'm tired of being on the outside, Torrain," I say, sitting down next to him. He seems startled by my presence, and wipes away what he's been drawing in the sand. More secrets.

"You're not on the outside of anything," he answers.

"Well, then why did you do *that?* Why do you whisper all the time? Remember when you used to tell me everything?"

"I never told you everything, Ice. That would be madness! Nobody ever tells anyone everything. You wouldn't want to hear everything."

That's true, I suppose. I harbor secrets too.

"Why are we going to the lab?" I ask. He can tell me that, at least.

Torrain looks like he wants to tell me a secret, but he holds back, looking down at the sand.

"Come on. I'm going to find out anyway. And who am I going to tell down here?" It's a solid argument.

"What are you two talking about?" Adorane cuts in sharply.

"Nothing," Torrain answers quickly.

"Where's Eveshone?" I ask, hoping to change the subject.

"Chasing a desert rat. I don't know."

"I'd better find her," I say, and stumble away.

There is definitely no *us* anymore. And I haven't been prepared for how sad that would make me.

THEN

Omathis and Amperous reached an unnatural, freshly formed mound of broken boulders. They froze. Was this a trap?

They saw where the granite shards had come from—the cliff bore a massive scar where the stones had once arched gracefully overhead. *It must have been beautiful,* Omathis mused.

There were groans and whimpers from beneath the boulders, and they suddenly realized what had happened. They had to move quickly. Some still had a chance at regaining life. It wasn't too late.

They charged into the wreckage and tossed aside the massive stones. They dug until they reached a battered Croathus, covered with bruises and blood, its legs and arms mangled and chest collapsed by the avalanche.

Omathis grew tender and cooed to the miserable creature.

"Let's get you out of here, Dear One," he whispered, and he and Amperous gently lifted the beast away from the carnage. Both Omathis and Amperous placed their heads against the creature's temples, and the creature's eyes flickered open.

"You're still with us. You'll survive this," Omathis encouraged him, though the horrid wounds this creature had suffered seemed to render his hopeful words ridiculous.

"This is Ulares, descended from the great Riverside Batch," Amperous stated. Amperous was proud of his ability to remember many of the thousands of Croathus by name. "His father is Tintal, and his mother is Luewal."

At the mention of his family, Ulares' whimpering grew louder, sadder, and more desperate.

"Stay with us, Ulares. You will be reunited with your great family. I know you are tempted to leave. But they would want you to stay, and so do I," Amperous urged.

A unified vibration arose from Omathis and Amperous. It grew louder, like a purring. Ulares gave himself over to it, and his whimpering quieted. As they purred over him, his twisted arms straightened out and mended.

"Yes, choose to stay among us. The struggle must not be abandoned," Amperous coaxed.

Ulares' crushed chest began to reinflate. His broken ribs knit themselves together as new skin grew over the wound.

Ulares now purred too. "There are others who are struggling to remain in this life," he declared. His body had now regenerated enough strength to sit up. He stood and tossed a boulder aside. "Let's find them."

Another cry broke through the white haze.

This one wasn't far away, Oliver could tell. All of the screams and shouts only lasted a second before they were silenced or faded due to distance.

"Keep moving! No one stops! Upward! Upward! Our only safety is upward!" Oliver shouted.

The mass of ascenders obeyed, eyes flicking from side to side in terror.

Their blindness was accompanied by the rhythmic sounds of the march—feet crunching through fallen leaves and underbrush—plus the sporadic screams of terror. Gasps as marchers realized the person walking beside them had disappeared, the quick breathing of people doing their best to stave off panic. The staccato of gunfire as the soldiers made feeble attempts to keep the assaults at bay.

Sean noted, with grim optimism, that with the undefended marchers so easy to attack, the Croathus appeared to be leaving the last remaining transport alone. At least the ascenders riding in that armored vehicle might survive. So humanity might have a chance.

"What can we do, Sean?" Oliver asked, after another round of sounds made it clear that the Croathus had killed more marchers behind them.

"We're close to the wall," Sean responded. "We have to reach the wall."

Sean was feeling better. There hadn't been an attack in at least a half hour, and they were nearing the wall. They'd emerged from the thick clouds and could see again.

"Look here," he said, pointing to the field of shattered stones. "There's a lot of iron in those stones. We'll mine here for metals and minerals."

Oliver shook his head. This was no time to speak of future plans. They had to survive their gruesome trek first—what was left of them, at least.

Oliver scrambled up a rocky outcropping and used the clarity of the fog-free elevation to look out over the survivors.

"Is there anyone still in the clouds?" he shouted, not wanting to believe what he saw.

"None living," was the response from the soldiers bringing up the rear.

Only a thousand, perhaps, still marching. And another five hundred in the transport. Dear Lord.

"With the minerals we find, we can rebuild our technology," Sean continued.

"We just lost more than twenty thousand people, Sean. Maybe it's not the right time to discuss how we're going to revive technology."

Sean looked shocked. "Yes. Right. I'm only pointing it out because it means we're close to the wall. The rest of us should be able to make it."

Oliver shook his head. All this time with no attacks made him nervous, not glad. Why had the creatures suddenly left them alone?

"The wall is the absolute highest they can travel before they die," Sean explained, sensing Oliver's concern. "They've been satiated to the point where the pain isn't worth it anymore."

"Why do I understand these monsters better than you do, Sean? You created them," Travis barked. "They aren't giving up anything. They'll pursue us until they drop dead. Not a moment sooner."

"You don't understand them as I do, Travis. They're not all bad. They have goodness in them—"

Sean's words were cut off as Oliver Hailgard wheeled around, grabbed him by the shoulders, and slammed him up against a withered tree.

"They've slaughtered tens of thousands of us up here and millions in the city below," he growled. "Keep any praise of their innate goodness out of your mouth and away from my ears!"

"I'm sorry. You're right," Sean apologized. "Let's just get past the wall."

Travis smirked. Unbelievable. It was as though Sean cared more about those dead beasts of his than the many humans who had been slaughtered. Sean had deserved to be slammed up against a tree by Oliver.

He deserved this and much more.

Oliver detected a change in the aural landscape. Was he imagining it? It was hard to identify. The transport: check. The steps of the thousands still marching: check. The birds singing: check. The cicadas chirping: check. But now he heard something else.

What is that?

He was tempted to command the transport to stop, but they were so close to safety that it made no sense to halt their progress.

There it was again, another sound layer that he couldn't ignore.

"That sounds like wheezing," he asked Sean in a low voice. "Do you hear it?"

Sean had a curious look on his face, but shook his head no.

Travis didn't trust him.

"What is it, Sean?" he pressed. "What do you know?"

"Nothing."

Oliver had no patience for this. "Sean, even if it's nothing, *tell us.*"

"I sense them, but I don't. I can't explain it. Except that if they were this high up on the mountain, they'd probably have so little airflow to the brain that they'd essentially be brain dead. Their more sophisticated cognitive functions would be impaired, and they'd be running on instinct."

"Like they have rabies," Oliver observed.

"That's a good analog, yes," Sean agreed.

"So any higher reasoning is gone, and they're reduced to pure hunger and aggression," Travis added. "Is that right?"

"Yes."

"And animals with rabies disregard their own pain, and even their imminent death, just to satisfy their hunger to attack. They ignore all instincts for self-survival. There's a chance they may not even remember how much they love you. Isn't that right, Sean?"

"That's all possible, Travis," Sean responded.

They followed the transport up to a precipice, and the armored vehicle idled to a stop.

They finally saw it—the wall. They'd made it.

Still, nobody cheered.

Gathered alongside the wall, bunching two or three deep, were the Croathus. Hunched over, straining for ragged breath, looking little like the sculpted, graceful creatures Sean was used to. They were covered in tattered animal skins, splattered with mud and blood. The thick, sweetly rotten stench of decomposing flesh washed over the marchers.

"What are we going to do, Sean?" Travis whispered.

37

NOW

The Priestess led Amperous to the peak of the reflective tower. From here he could see the circles of mirrors below, laid out like they were bowing to the central building.

Beyond the mirrors, Croathus who had flocked to the Priestess and Amperous had encamped, waiting for whatever would come next.

The sun was so bright up here that everything appeared to be different shades of white, as if the color had been burnt out of the world.

"In this short time, we've already built so much," Barielta mused.

"*You've* built so much," Amperous corrected her.

"Oh, no. While you were away, there was only a partial foundation. I pressed on because I believed, but with little to show for it. It was only after you descended and joined me that the work on this began."

Amperous knew this wasn't right. He'd come down from the mountain to a horde of Croathus already devoted to the Priestess. Though he sensed she was only saying this to make him feel better, it still worked.

"I need you to support me," Barielta urged.

"I do," Amperous was quick to respond.

"That means you support what I do. I have a vision. I know what we are meant to be. I'm the only one who has seen it."

Amperous was confused. He wanted more information, even if asking for it made Barielta believe he didn't support her without question. "How did you see it?" he asked.

"Did you know that every thought that any creature has ever conceived is archived permanently? Sewn into the air above us, pressed into the stone beneath our feet. Croathus, human, beast—it doesn't matter. You may believe a thought just floats away into the mist, but it doesn't. Not everyone can access that great library of thoughts. But I can. I was born accessing them. It's maddening, to be honest—until you realize the true power of it."

Amperous was quiet as he considered what she was saying. Mistersean had taught him and Omathis logic and reasoning skills long ago, and he applied them whenever he came across something curious. He'd never heard of this library of thoughts before. It sounded like something she was simply making up. Yet he had to consider what she had accomplished already. This tower was now buzzing with electricity—when the magic of currents had died long ago with humanity. She'd united the Croathus who had scattered in fear after the massacre in Mountaintop. And there were those faceless, formless monstrosities floating in liquid, too. It was clear that she wasn't merely telling stories.

He decided to test her. "Are my thoughts in this library?"

"Everything ever thought is there. Are you going to ask me to retrieve something you've thought to test what I say?" she replied.

Amperous felt a sudden shame. Had she not shown herself to be trustworthy already? But if it was a matter of simply retrieving a thought from the library, maybe it was not much trouble.

"If you could."

Barielta's face clouded. Amperous had given the wrong answer.

"A union must built upon faith, not tests. It appears I've misunderstood the nature of our relationship."

Amperous couldn't tell if Barielta was punishing him.

She continued to be polite, but a formal distance shaded their interactions. They appeared before the Croathus together in the mornings and evenings for the rituals. They presented a united front as they encouraged the growing crowd. News was spreading of their movement in the desert, and many were coming to see for themselves. Once they heard Barielta speak of her vision of the future, every one of them stayed. The Priestess of Two Temples and the Lord of Both—here to lead them all into the future.

Amperous hoped that those who gathered couldn't sense how he felt on the inside, even as he was sure that Barielta could. He had doubts, but he wanted to keep them quarantined to himself. It would be terrible if they spread, because the Croathus needed this hope. They couldn't be what they'd been in the past—weapons created to kill, creatures made to serve human interests. They couldn't remain what they were now, either—

roving beasts without purpose. They needed a future; Amperous knew this. Yet he'd never before thought of what that future should be.

He didn't want to admit it, but he instinctively feared the future Barielta had in store for them.

"Humanity wasn't sacrificed in vain, my children!" Barielta shouted to the Croathus below. "The humans were slain to serve as the fertile soil in which we plant the seeds of tomorrow! You are each a seed. We must become more. Greater than any Croathus, any man, any god could ever imagine. We must *frighten* the gods with our glory. Because only then will they admit that *we were the true gods all along!*"

The crowd roared. As they retreated back into the tower and the silver door slid shut, they could hear the rapturous cheers still rising from the desert floor. Powerful sound waves shook the tower walls.

"Barielta," he started, "I'm sorry for questioning you."

She smiled at him. "Lord of Both, do not feel shame for having questions. All I ask is that you admit when you've found the answers, too. And I submit to you, Amperous. You can find the answer to every one of your questions in me, as I have in you."

THEN

If they had had the time, Oliver would have gathered the soldiers with rocket launchers at the front of the procession. He'd have lined them up to shoot any bloodthirsty Croathus who charged. Then he'd have the transport drive right up to the wall and use it as a ramp for the marchers to climb over to safety.

That was the plan he'd improvised when they first confronted the brain-dead Croathus. He ran and shared his plan with trusted lieutenants, who then rushed to share it with more, until the order spread to everyone.

He felt more rage than fear, which was good. Rage was his coping device. When he was angry, he could keep a clear head and do what needed to be done.

There was much to stoke his fury, too—for instance, the primitive way he had to communicate with the other soldiers. All radios had been left behind when the tanks had been destroyed. If they all had radios, he thought bitterly, they could have coordinated better, and more people would survive.

There was Sean Brathius, who was clearly still hoping for a way to save the Croathus, even at the expense of more human lives. Sean felt sorry for them. He grieved when any of them were injured. It was hard enough to defend against these creatures without having to contend with Sean's sentimentality.

And as for Travis Nilsing—well, he only wanted to kill the beasts. He wanted to watch them suffer. Oliver had fought alongside soldiers who displayed the same mindless bloodlust in Afghanistan and seen the casualties it inevitably produced. He realized what he had to do.

"I want you both in the transport," Oliver commanded, shoving Sean and Travis toward the armored vehicle.

"Why? I know their makeup better than anyone! You need my knowledge!" Sean protested.

"Did you see how many I killed?" Travis argued. "Why would you send me to hide?"

As far as Oliver was concerned, they were equally misguided and both just as likely to mess everything up.

He pushed again, but they stood firm against him. He sighed. "There is only one goal worth pursuing at this point: Protect the ascenders. I don't want either of you out here because you're both distracted. Every casualty we've suffered weighs heavily on me. But I'm not dwelling on those failures, because doing so would lower the chances those who remain will survive."

"I don't see how that's at odds with what I want, Oliver," Sean said.

"I can't have you always trying to figure out a way to redeem them," Oliver responded. "They're your children. You're compromised."

Sean looked down guiltily.

"And you just want to make them suffer," Oliver continued, his eyes locking with Travis', "even if we all die in the process."

Travis couldn't argue.

"We're not here to save them. But we're not here to watch them burn, either. It's too late for both of those outcomes. *We're here to survive.* Tune out everything else. All that matters is defending these people. If you can promise me you'll do that, you can stay. Otherwise I'll have you bound and thrown aboard the transport."

Sean and Travis both nodded, chastened.

As the troops readied themselves for battle, an eerie deadlock presented itself. The Croathus seemed oddly oblivious to their presence. Sean theorized that their normally heightened senses had been dulled by oxygen deprivation. "It's possible they're even hallucinating. Who knows what they're perceiving in this weakened state."

In any case, Oliver's plan was never given an opportunity to work.

As more ascenders reached a place where they could see the Croathus gathered near the wall, panic spread. This was the first time many of them had seen the creatures outside of the haze, in the clear daylight—and these Croathus looked more monstrous in their crazed, shambling state. The soldiers, police officers, and firefighters had the professional training to keep themselves calm in the face of this nightmare, but the civilians didn't.

Most watched the wheezing beasts in silence. But a subtle wave of whimpering began to rise. This was their final prize—their reward for evading death thus far? Having seen their comrades torn apart, they now had to face the ultimate nightmare?

Mothers and fathers attempted to quiet their children, to varying degrees of success.

Don't look, honey.

Come here.

Close your eyes.

Mommy has you.

No, we can't turn around.

No, we can't go back.

Because it's not safe back there, either.

Soldiers quietly commanded all those gathered to remain silent, so as not to draw the beasts' attention while Oliver's strategy could be put into place.

One man compromised the entire plan. In his panic, he rushed straight toward the beasts and had to be restrained by a group of soldiers. "I don't want to survive," the man insisted. "I want this to end. Let them kill me. Please, I want it to end." His voice echoed through the crisp, thin air, bouncing off the rocky mountain—too loud. The soldiers tackled him and held his head in their arms, muffling his voice.

The Croathus turned and sized up the gathering humans, as if their perceptions were finally catching up and identifying what their eyes were seeing, their ears were hearing, and their noses were smelling. A dim flicker of realization ignited in their eyes, and they began to shuffle toward the humans.

"Move the transport ahead!" Oliver commanded, fearing what would happen next. "Forward until it's against the wall!" Even without the rocket launchers in position, they'd have to start sending people over the barricade into safety.

The transport rumbled to life and rolled toward the wall—and directly toward the Croathus. This movement jolted the beasts to action, and they charged with stunning speed—crazed and dead set on tasting human blood. They weren't organized, there was no coordination. They were driven by reckless hunger.

They threw their massive bodies against the transport, denting the steel siding. They ricocheted off the vehicle only to rush and crash into the oversized tank again.

Oliver could see that they didn't have much time. The Croathus were going to destroy the transport before too long. He rushed toward the rear of the armored vehicle as it reached the wall and urged the ascenders to climb it. One by one, he shoved the panicked civilians upward.

"Help me out here," he shouted, and Travis and Sean ran to his side. They climbed the transport and started leading people over the wall.

A Croathus leapt to grab hold of those people who were running across the top of the armored vehicle. Soldiers used the butts of their rifles to hit it away.

The first person over the wall was a young woman, not more than eighteen years old. Travis forced her to jump to safety and she landed—away from the Croathus, away from the world humanity had known for thousands of years, and into the only speck of land they'd occupy for hundreds to come.

A wave of creatures moved past their attack on the transport and focused their attention on the line of people waiting to climb. Travis grabbed his rocket launcher and aimed toward the monsters.

He faced a tricky target. The Croathus were right alongside both the wall and the transport, and firing directly on them risked destroying their last chances at survival.

Instead, Travis fired on the ground and created a massive ditch, which slowed down the charging Croathus.

Following Travis' lead, more rockets exploded into the hard ground, sending dust and shards of stone high into the air and extending the trench barriers as more ascenders crowded atop the transport and jumped to the other side.

He couldn't stop to savor it, but with each person who made it to safety, Oliver felt a pulse of satisfaction. He beckoned and shouted, waving the civilians forward. It seemed like the Croathus would overwhelm them soon, but at least he'd die knowing that some had lived.

38

THEN

More ascenders escaped over the wall, desperately climbing the transport and narrowly dodging the outreached talons of relentless Croathus. Occasionally a beast would knock someone from atop the transport, and the unfortunate person would be torn to pieces.

"Don't look down!" Sean commanded. "Toward the wall and over! Toward the wall and over!"

Travis and Sean made for a curiously effective team atop the armored tank. Travis organized soldiers into a perimeter on top of the vehicle, watching the approaching Croathus and shouting out orders so they could defend against the constantly changing threat.

"Attacks coming from the northern end! Another bunch on the west!" They'd shoot bullets, smack them with the butts of their rifles, kick them away with their boots, anything to keep the beasts from breaking through and grabbing a prize. It reminded Travis of a game he used to play on the boardwalk long ago called Whack-A-Mole—only here, if you missed, a handful of people would lose their lives.

Meanwhile, Sean coaxed the terrified civilians to keep a steady pace and avoid bunching up. Many were tempted to stare at the mayhem when what they needed to do was to walk, one foot in front of each other, until they reached the wall and could topple over it. If even one person stopped to look at the chaos, the entire line stalled—and people would perish.

"Eyes straight ahead! No stopping! One step at a time. Keep moving. Let's get you to safety." Through trial and error, he'd arrived at the right cadence, tone, and words to keep people progressing forward.

Oliver took on the most dangerous role. He stayed on the ground, toward the rear of the transport, where the marchers climbed onto the makeshift bridge to safety.

The first step wasn't easy, and less physically gifted ascenders required a boost. Oliver remained vigilant. One moment he'd push back—with his rifles and his rockets—against a persistent Croathus that had made it past the trenches. The next he'd lift two civilians at once so they could find their footing and head toward the wall.

He was focused amidst the chaos, and he found he was able to tune out the inevitable deaths happening all around him. He kept the length of the ascenders' procession in mind—it looked like only a quarter had made it up and over the wall at this point—and balanced it against the amount of Croathus who had made it past the trenches. Soon there would be a tipping point, where the Croathus' numbers would overwhelm any efforts he could make and everyone who hadn't yet made it over the wall would be lost.

He calculated that that tipping point was five minutes away at the most.

At least they were weakened up this high, Oliver thought, as he smashed his rifle into a charging Croathus and kicked its collapsing body down the steep slope. If they were at full strength, like they had been down below, not one person would have gotten past them.

Oliver grabbed ahold of a young girl and her slightly older brother—probably nine and ten years old, he estimated—and set them atop the transport.

"Get over that wall," he encouraged them. He didn't see their parents with them and assumed that these two had become orphans on their trip up the mountain. "As fast as you can," Oliver said, and placed a comforting arm on her shoulder. That was a mistake. He'd been distracted for just a second, and now was going to pay for it.

He saw it in her eyes first—they widened and then closed as she turned away.

He felt the talons dig into his right side and his left leg and slice easily, as if he were made of softened wax.

"Run!" He shouted to the children, who were frozen watching the Croathus attack. "Over the wall!"

Sean grasped the steel bumper, determined to keep the creature from carrying him off. He refused to be tossed into a group of monsters and devoured in a frenzy, as he'd seen happen to many others. If he was going to die, he'd do it here, while fighting.

Despite the pain, he lifted his uninjured leg and kicked backward, hard. The Croathus yelped and stumbled back. Oliver turned to confront the creature that had ambushed him.

Face to face with the nightmare. It was wheezing, hunched over, and appeared to be on the verge of collapsing. Even so, its eyes were focused on him.

"You're going to regret starting this fight," Oliver shouted.

Sean Brathius was grateful for every person who made it over the wall. When he'd originally built this refuge atop the mountain, it had been as a contingency in case absolutely everything went wrong. He never thought they'd actually need it.

He continued urging the traumatized ascenders to move forward toward the wall. By now he was so used to saying the words he needed to say that his mind wandered and he watched the carnage down on the ground.

He'd been locked in on getting survivors up and over the wall. He hadn't noticed how gruesome the attacks had grown.

So many had died. As terrible as it was, each new victim helped those civilians who still needed to make their way up onto the transport and over the wall, because a fresh body drew a crowd of Croathus and distracted them from attacking the others. Each person who was picked off from the herd was like a sacrifice to angry gods to spare the others.

Sean saw Travis, saving lives with his military training, and felt a bittersweet pride. Shai would have loved to have seen the brave man her boy had grown into.

Suddenly he was seized with fear. Where was Oliver? He scanned the activity below until he found him.

No.

Blanketed by a pair of Croathus. Weakened. Close to death, if he was even still alive.

They were pulling at him, trying to carry him away. With hope, Sean realized that they weren't doing so easily. Oliver was still fighting.

Sean grabbed a wooden branch off of the wall and rushed toward the confrontation.

Oliver's fingers started to give. Another Croathus grabbed him from behind. Together, the two monsters pulled at him with unbearable strength. Another talon dug into him—this time slashing across his back. He resisted the urge to scream—he knew the beasts were excited by the sound of human misery. He was tempted to surrender and let this struggle end.

This made him angry and activated another level of strength in him. He was insulted by his own desire for death. Oliver had trained in combat for decades. *He'd* been the one to teach the Croathus their tactics.

Oliver pulled his feet up and coiled his body, and then sprang and spun, knocking against both the Croathus' arms. He swept his feet to topple the unsteady predators.

If this had been a one-on-one battle, Oliver would suddenly have the advantage. But it wasn't a fair fight. The other Croathus blindsided Oliver and crashed into him from behind. Oliver spun onto his back, but the downed Croathus had already jumped back to its feet, and he was exposed to both of them. He tried to push himself off the ground, but his torso was pinned down by a Croathus foot. He struggled against them but couldn't budge.

Oliver refused to close his eyes. He'd face death head on. Both Croathus lowered themselves toward him, savoring their victory.

The thick scent of death washed over Oliver as they blocked out the sun and covered him with their darkness.

He waited for the pain—but felt nothing. Instead he heard a loud *thwack*, and light broke through the shadows. One of the Croathus above him fell to the side, and then the other. He wiped the blood and dirt from his eyes.

Sean Brathius stood above him, smashing the Croathus over and over, one at a time, with a wooden club. It was a shocking display of ferocity—one Oliver never thought he'd see from Sean Brathius against anything, let alone one of his beloved creations.

Oliver knew that these beasts couldn't be killed with a stick, regardless of the wielder's fury, so he had to get Sean away from them. He struggled to his feet and held onto Sean's shoulder.

"You have to get out of here."

"So do you," Sean responded.

The creatures stared at Sean. Oliver noticed that their faces appeared more human when they did. Their eyes were downtrodden and their brows furrowed. They looked heartbroken—betrayed.

Sean dropped the bloody club like he regretted ever holding it, like it burned to the touch.

"I'm staying here," Oliver declared. There were many people still outside the wall.

But he saw then that the shambling, stubborn Croathus had reached them—and nothing he could do would save those who hadn't yet made it to safety.

They'd reached the tipping point.

Oliver pulled away from Sean, but stumbled, dizzy and weakened from blood loss.

"Travis," Sean barked, "Help me with him." Travis jumped from the armored bridge.

"No! I'm not going! Not until everyone is safe."

Despite Oliver's protests, Sean and Travis heaved him onto the transport, then scrambled up behind him just as monsters swarmed the area.

Oliver watched as a young woman clawed to get on top of the transport. He slipped away from Sean and Travis and ran toward her. He grabbed ahold of her hand and pulled her up. A Croathus grabbed hold of her by the legs.

Oliver strained, determined to win this high stakes tug-of-war contest. The woman kicked at the beast. Oliver fell back while he pulled her to safety.

She stood up and scrambled toward the wall.

Below, Croathus overwhelmed those who were left behind, bashing the side of the transport with boulders and tree trunks. It started to crumble beneath their feet.

"We have to go!"

Oliver fought, but they forced him along the transport roof and toward the wall. He made one last effort to resist.

"Leave me here."

"And I'm not going to let you die, Oliver Hailgard!" Sean responded. He shoved him over the wall as hard as he could just as the transport began to crumble and groan beneath them. Oliver landed in thick brush on the other side.

Sean and Travis grabbed hold of the wall as the transport was torn apart beneath them. They pulled themselves up and over—the last two to free fall as the screams and crunch of metal rose to a deafening roar behind them.

NOW

Amperous finally fell into a comfortable rhythm with the Priestess. They appeared daily before their growing flock of Croathus. Normally

Barielta would whip them into a frenzy with her stirring words. Sometimes Amperous was prompted to speak, too—but he never affected them like she did.

They spent a lot of time together, and she seemed to have an unending supply of questions. When they were together, he felt like they were growing closer. But when he was away from her, he would realize that he had shared so much of his own past and yet knew nothing of hers. She remained a complete mystery to him.

Once, as they went for a walk through the arranged mirrors at the base of the tower, he decided to try to learn more. Even remembering this intention took great effort, as spending time with her always felt a little like trudging through a disorienting fog. But he forced himself to focus.

"From where did you come, Barielta? Before I descended from the mountain, I'd never seen you."

"Oh, and you know every Croathus there is, Amperous?" she joked.

"So you are from far away, across the land, near the other great ocean?" he asked, because yes, he actually *had* known most who lived in the valleys near the mountain range.

"I didn't say that," she answered.

"So you're from the north, perhaps, where the land is white and the air is cold?"

Amperous felt an impulse flow from her roots into him. *It doesn't really matter.*

Of course it didn't. Why had he felt the need to know, anyway? "What matters is where you are now," he whispered.

"And who I am here with," she added, taking his hand in hers. "Come with me—I'm ready to share something with you."

Amperous followed her to the base of the tower. He watched as she pressed a sequence of buttons on a pad, then stepped past sliding doors into a metallic cylinder. He silently cursed himself for not being stronger. For days now he'd been able to avoid this—and now, in his weakened and compliant state, he was following her directly into the place he'd hoped he'd never see again.

They descended until they arrived below ground. The doors opened and revealed a series of tubes, each holding a formless Croathus.

"I know you hate it down here," Barielta cooed gently. "But I promise: What you think is fear are just the seeds that will bloom into a boundless joy."

He followed her as she walked between the cylinders and gently touched the clear walls. The formless creature in each drifted toward her hand as she glided past.

"You're right—in their current form, they are not complete. What you should fear, though, is not them—it's the wasted potential they represent. The worst thing that can happen to a creature is to have a greatness within that is never released. So you see now what I must do."

She gazed at Amperous for a very long time waiting for an answer.

"I have no idea what you must do," he finally said.

"But you do. *Ex nihilo nihil fit.* Nothing comes from nothing. What these creatures are meant to be must come from humans. Humanity's very essence. But not just humans—god's too. The lifeblood of creation."

Amperous still wasn't clear on what she was saying, but her words terrified him.

"The lifeblood of creation?" was all he could stammer.

"Yes. You see, I've done my research. And what's become clear to me is that our next phase can only be unlocked by design." She paused, but it didn't matter. Amperous had finally picked up on her meaning through their roots.

It was an abomination. Even worse than anything Omathis would ever consider, and that was saying something. A mingling that Amperous never imagined anyone would welcome.

"We must bathe them in the warmth of Brathius blood," Barielta purred.

39

NOW

Eveshone crept through a narrow slot canyon. She could smell the creature—not just its fur, but its fear. If she remained still enough, in the silence she could even sense tiny heart palpitations. She pounced and reached into a crevice with startling quickness, and she was rewarded with a plump, fuzzy rodent.

Eveshone appreciated the chance to hunt and get into the flow of a good pursuit. She relished the relief she found in the chase—those incessant thoughts she didn't want to be thinking were muted behind a cresting wave of adrenaline-soaked instinct.

She pressed the creature to her face and inhaled. She lost herself in the scent. It was a complicated kaleidoscope of musk and ammonia—oily and earthy, then piercing and sharp. She was tempted to toss the rodent into her mouth and bite down. Not because she was hungry, but because any hunt felt incomplete until she felt the soft, warm burst of blood fill her mouth. Instead, she threw it into a basket she had fashioned out of agave husks. The others were hungry, and she decided that she would derive more satisfaction from feeding them than she would from consuming her kill.

As soon as the pursuit had ended, she was mired again in the anguish she'd been trying to avoid—the reason she'd craved a distraction in the first place. She couldn't figure out why her thoughts were tinged with so much darkness. Lovely was in distress because of her fractured relationship with the other humans. But that was fairly normal. They never got along very well, so far as Eveshone could tell, except for when they were getting along *too* well. It was all awfully confusing, but there was no fresh confusion to contend with. Nothing to explain the newly distressed way Lovely had been feeling.

Eveshone wasn't prone to introspection. She'd always rather be chasing a rodent across the desert than trying to sort through her feelings. Yet she sensed the importance of this change, so she tried to work her way through a couple of simple questions.

What am I feeling? Bad. Down. Sad. Like she could cry, but she didn't want to, because it wouldn't be the sort of crying that made her feel any better. It would be the type of crying that gave her a headache, made her eyes swell, and filled her with shame.

Is it because of the wound I suffered? No, it wasn't. The wound made her feel terrible feelings, but they were not a mystery—anger at the human who had done it, fear they might return, a thirst for revenge. All of those feelings made sense, and she knew what to do with them. It would be strange if she *didn't* feel them.

When did I start feeling this way? This question stumped her. She thought back to when she was first recovering from her wound. She wasn't feeling this way then. When they were descending the mountain and first caught a glimpse of the strange desert landscape? She hadn't been burdened with this malaise then either.

It was when they first neared the mysterious destination Adorane and Torrain planned to visit. *That's* when the first hints of her unease had started to appear, she realized. That's when she started to feel so sad—and the feeling had grown worse and more piercing as time went on.

She didn't want to think about this anymore. She only wanted it to stop. This hole inside of her chest felt many times larger than herself and growing. She realized, with a start, that this emptiness was the same shape and size as the place in her heart that Lovely had occupied since they'd been united.

Have I grown distant from Lovely?

She dropped her basket of rodents and they seized their freedom and scurried away. A part of her wanted to chase them again, knew Adorane would need them for his stew, but that part wasn't controlling her footsteps any longer. A disoriented, sad part of her pressed her to stumble out of the slot canyon and toward the horizon—away from Lovely, away from the other humans.

As she pressed on toward her unknown destination, she gulped at the air, like it might fill the void within her. She liked the way it smelled—sweet and pungent, sharp, new. Crackling with an invisible energy. Air, but more than air—like a higher level of the heavens above had crashed down to earth, shattered, and was now swirling around her.

She heard a rumbling, quiet at first, and then louder. She realized that what she was smelling was the approach of rain. It hadn't rained in so long that she hadn't recognized it at first, but now she found herself overcome with excitement. She could use a cleaning. The whole world could.

"Gather those who have massed here and take them away!" The Priestess ordered abruptly. Amperous looked behind him, scanned the room where only moments ago she'd pressed her head to his chest and treated him to an embrace. Was she speaking to someone else? No, she was talking to him. She made it sound like he was her servant.

Though he felt a primal anger at this disrespect, he didn't protest. As soon as he opened his mouth to demand equality, he heard himself acquiescing instead. "Of course. Where would you like me to take them?"

Amperous cringed slightly, and inwardly scolded himself. He was re-enacting a disturbing pattern he'd identified earlier in the day. He would think he had figured the Priestess out—who she was, what she thought of him, whom he was to her. And as soon as he grew comfortable in this understanding, he would be jostled from it.

Since they'd met, the Priestess had kept Amperous guessing, shifting her mood from one moment to the next. Something about her—or maybe something about him—made him mistake her current state for her essential state, over and over, only to be jolted into something new and disorienting.

He'd settled into her embrace, sliding under it like a warm blanket on a cold night, and now this. She was ordering him around like he lived only to satisfy her impulsive desires.

"Do not question why. Just take them. They will follow you. I must be left alone here."

Amperous couldn't find the courage to argue that he hadn't even questioned why. The force of her personality had already prevented him from asking any questions he had; she didn't need to stack another command on top. It was humiliating, and he was glad that no one else was there to see it. He nodded. "Of course."

"Take them to the Mothers. Begin preparations. I must be left alone here."

Amperous had so many questions. *Preparations for what? Why must you be left alone?* But even though he still hadn't connected his roots to the Priestess' so they could share their thoughts, he shrunk back as he realized that *he knew.* He hoped he was wrong, but deep down, he knew he wasn't.

Knowing was much worse than not knowing.

"I will leave you alone. We will go begin preparations with the Mothers," Amperous promised, feeling disgusted with himself as he slunk out the door.

ICELYN

No one warned me that there could be so much rain in the desert. Earlier in the day, it had been as dry as fire. Now so much water is falling from the sky that I can't see anything between or beyond the thick, heavy drops.

Adorane has abandoned his stew by necessity because a creek had formed where we had set up camp—and now it threatens to become a mighty river. Everything has changed so quickly! I stumble to keep up with him and Torrain as we follow him to higher ground. He seems very concerned that we could drown if we remain on the desert floor. Moments ago I thought these fears ridiculous—but now I can see that they are valid.

I do my best to avoid slipping off the giant boulders we scale, while still scanning the blurry, dark horizon. "Do you see Eveshone?" I shout.

"Like I said, she'll survive a flood just fine. We won't," Adorane replies. I know it's logical, but I can't shake the feeling that I'm abandoning her.

"Why don't you call her—you know, with your mind? The way you do?" Torrain suggests.

I don't respond because the truth is that I don't sense her in my roots, which frightens me. Then again, Eveshone has been hunting desert rats, and sometimes the predator role consumes her. Maybe that's all this is.

At least this is what I tell myself to quell the rising panic.

Lightning flashes overhead, followed by sky-splitting thunder. I'm focusing on the rapidly flooding desert floor below and lose my balance, scraping my knee and giving the boys a scare.

"Concentrate on your own safety for now," Adorane scolds me. "She's alive. I guarantee it. If you don't start paying attention, though, *you* won't be."

He jolts me back into self-preservation, and I follow his lead higher up the mountain. When we reach the top of the massive mound of rocks, Adorane seems confident that we're out of reach of the rushing waters below. He finds slabs of stone balanced against each other to block the rain, and the three of us huddle beneath them and watch the madness below.

"Eveshone!" I shout. "Can you hear me?"

She was supposed to be back an hour ago, before the rains even started.

The waters grow violent, faster and higher. My body is flooded with panic.

She can't be hunting in this. Where is she? And why can't I feel her?

THEN

Though they could still hear distant screams drifting in from beyond the wall, this side was remarkably peaceful. Sunlight shone through the treetops above, illuminating the leaves until they glowed green. Birds chirped cheerful tunes, as if nothing bad had just happened or ever could.

Sean Brathius rose from where he'd fallen and breathed in deeply. The air was crisp, tinged with cold. Fresh. It didn't smell like death.

He pulled Oliver Hailgard to his feet. The man was bleeding badly. He was lucky to have survived.

Everyone on this side of the wall was downtrodden—frozen from the horrors they'd witnessed and survived. Many sat with their backs against the wall or trunks of trees, or curled up in a ball, staring at nothing in particular, their faces blank in disbelief.

Yet Sean could feel their gratefulness. Mothers and fathers held their children close. Strangers embraced and wept. Despite the searing horror they'd experienced, each one of them had won a grisly lottery, surviving where countless had died. It struck Sean that each of them was fortunate—a luckier group of humans, in fact, than any other in history.

"Every one of us has been entrusted with an unprecedented responsibility," Sean declared loudly. Oliver and Travis stared at him, baffled. Was Sean really going to give a speech?

Sean hadn't planned on it, but the words flowed. "We are the remnants of humanity. Each of us is needed to survive. Every individual here is vital to the rebuild. We are the ascenders. Not only because we made it to the top of the mountain, but because through us and our children and our children's children, humanity will once again ascend to its rightful place of glory and dignity."

Sean's words buoyed the meager remnant of humanity.

"Come now—let us enter our new home."

Two hundred and forty seven people.

Oliver Hailgard had counted twice. Two hundred and forty seven survivors. They'd started out with twenty-five thousand ascenders. Not even one percent had made it to the top of the mountain.

Sean was already whispering nonsense about his great acts of heroism that would never be forgotten. But all Oliver could think about was the number *twenty-four thousand, seven hundred and fifty three.* Those who had died. Anything he might have done out there, no matter how brave, hadn't resulted in anything for those people.

"Look around you. Every person here is alive because of you. I don't doubt that," Sean encouraged, reading Oliver's despair. Oliver made an effort to focus on the living, but for every person he watched walking upward toward their new settlement, he could only see the people who were moldering away on lower elevations of the mountain—even just outside the wall.

"You should have let me stay out there longer," Oliver said.

"You would have died," Sean responded, surprised.

"I could have saved three to four more people, and then my death would have been worth it."

"It was more important that you survive," Sean urged. "We're going to need you."

"It would have been nice to reach two hundred and fifty survivors. I didn't even save one percent, Sean. Not even one percent."

As they made their way up the mountain, Sean was worried about Oliver. He'd asked multiple times to be left behind. "I'll catch up. Go ahead. I know you want to get to the settlement," he'd urged. Sean wasn't sure whether Oliver's reluctance to climb toward the top of the mountain was emotional or physical. Oliver had lost a great deal of blood—enough to kill a normal man. And even more worrying, it seemed like Oliver didn't *want* to survive.

"You should have left me out there," he repeated, each time said with different emotional emphasis. Sometimes sad, others angry, others wistful.

Travis helped Sean move Oliver up the mountain. They'd fallen behind the rest of the ascenders as they struggled with his weight. The lack of oxygen was taking its toll on all of them. Oliver pleaded with them to let him rest.

"We're not leaving you behind," Travis scolded. "That's how people die. And you're not going to die."

"You should have left me out there," Oliver responded, predictably.

Travis rolled his eyes and kept pushing forward.

It was a slog, but they finally reached the settlement. Oliver could see the spires of the main hall stretching above them. He'd hoped to be one of the first into Mountaintop—considering he'd designed it, and that the place was his idea in the first place. He'd wanted to usher everyone else in.

He also wanted to be the first to see Laura Lee.

40

NOW

Eveshone found her way through the labyrinth of narrow canyons, pressing on as water cascaded down from above like a thousand waterfalls. The currents were rising, carrying uprooted trees and spinning boulders with them. Progress was difficult. She was able to dodge most obstacles with grace, but some knocked her off her feet propelled her back hundreds of yards. A distant part of her worried for Icelyn and Torrain and Adorane. If they were caught in anything like this, they would be dead. But even this worry couldn't deter her. She couldn't help them now. She had to forge her way forward.

She finally exited the canyons and spilled into a larger expanse of water. Through the driving walls of rain, she made out a towering building that rose from the center of the giant lake. Lightning crashed overhead, splitting into multiple branching strikes. The electrified bolts were reflected in the surface of the tower—as though it too was made out of mirrored water.

She navigated between mirrored squares that spread out around the tower in circles. As the waters continued to rise, she began to swim.

She finally reached the tower and found the outer wall to be slick. When she looked at it, she was startled by her own reflection. She rarely saw herself, and never quite so clearly as this. She recognized bits of Icelyn's countenance in her own and felt a dull sense of longing. *Lovely, I miss you. I'm sorry, Lovely.*

She realized with a muted sadness that for the first time since she'd met Lovely face to face, she was abandoning her. *I will return to you, Lovely,* she promised, though it felt empty, more what she wanted to feel rather than what she felt. Something else—an instinct, overpowering—had overtaken everything that seemed important before.

The surface of the tower was made up of smaller rectangles, and Eveshone found that she could easily grab hold of the cracks between and lift herself out of the water. She began to scale the tower.

It was not a difficult task, yet she couldn't force herself to move any faster. She needed to climb—though she didn't know why. She didn't want to. It was instinct more than choice.

She feared what she would find at the top.

The Priestess stood atop the tower, overjoyed by the splitting fractals of lightning. She relished being surrounded by such dangerous beauty. Barielta realized that those words—dangerous and beauty—were redundant, because nothing could be dangerous without also being beautiful, and certainly nothing could be beautiful without also being dangerous. Both words described the same essence.

Barielta was seldom shaken by anything. For one thing, she had expected nearly everything that ever happened to or around her, at least since she'd been reborn. She could access so much knowledge that it was difficult to surprise her.

Yet here she was, surprised, disoriented, and unsure of what would happen next.

Barielta thought about Amperous. If she could feel truly bad about anything, she would feel sad for him now. But she'd flushed negative states out of her being ages ago and promised she would not indulge in them again. That poor, noble creature had seemed so offended by her reaction to the coming winds and her command to leave her alone.

She reminded herself that though he was great, he was still unevolved, like she had been before she was reborn. She had a difficult time remembering how she'd felt back then, but she attempted to access glimpses of it to understand him better.

Amperous would ascend someday, and then he would understand everything.

She pushed Amperous out of her mind. It was no longer useful to dwell on him. She needed to focus on what it was she'd driven him and the others away to experience. Something unforeseen approached—unbidden, unplanned for, and somehow even more dangerous and beautiful than the lightning storm before her.

Barielta held an outstretched hand over the edge of the tower and waited, wondering what exactly was coming. So many feelings she hadn't felt since her rebirth flooded her—fear, joy, sadness, excitement. Even longing for something she'd once had.

As she watched, another hand—slender and graceful, taut and strong, reached from below and held tight to hers. She pulled hard—embarrassed by her feelings, yet indulging in them like she'd never wanted anything else—and worked to lift whoever was below so she could finally see.

Though clouds darkened the sky, the top of the tower seemed illuminated by the presence of this darling female Croathus. She was the most exquisite creature Barielta had ever seen. She had eyes as blue as a glacier, a face that captured the Priestess' attention as if it had been sculpted out of her own dreams, and she wore the golden fur of a majestic slain beast —which was somehow still dazzling even when wet. The Priestess had seen thousands of Croathus in her time as their leader. This one was flawless, standing a level apart in both strength and beauty.

Yet it wasn't this girl's appearance that had transformed the normally icy Priestess into a bubbling concoction of inner chaos. It was more than that. This Croathus had somehow remained pure, untouched by the horrors of this world. Every Croathus carried deep shame within them, dating back to their shared origin, baked into their collective foundation. Even Barielta felt it, like a thorn she could not remove, embedded deep in her flesh. This creature bore no trace of that shame.

Barielta scanned the creature hungrily with her eyes, every inch of her, quickly and greedily. It was as if she was afraid the girl would vanish and desperately wanted to press as much of this vision into memory as she could before that happened.

She froze as they locked eyes.

The creature looked like it had been crying, but Barielta couldn't be sure with the rain. The Croathus lowered her eyes and fixed on her hand and Barielta's, still holding fast to each other. She placed her other hand atop the Priestess' hand, then pulled it toward her.

She gave Barielta's hand a kiss, soft and tender.

They locked eyes again. Even in the rain, it was clear now that they were both crying. For a moment, the creature grew unsettled, almost woozy, as she broke eye contact and looked around at the watery desert below. Then she gathered herself with great effort and focused on the Priestess again.

"Why am I here?" the Croathus asked.

The Priestess pulled her in until they'd merged into one, enveloping her with an embrace.

"You are here because I am. And I am here because you are."

THEN

Sean hadn't prepared his remarks. In truth, he'd given little thought to how life would be once the survivors had reached Mountaintop, because he'd never actually believed it would come to this. But now that they'd left the horror behind and had a better picture of what their future would look like, he realized that so much needed to be done.

They needed a set of laws. They needed to codify how they were expected to live up here.

Sean realized this was an opportunity. As horrific as this apocalypse had been, it was a new beginning, a reboot of humanity—a chance to learn their lessons from past failures and systemically create a better build. To root out the flaws that had made humans violent and unstable in the first place. He saw the future they could build—one without religious superstition, racial oppression, nationalist prejudice, or economic inequality. They could create a society founded on the principles of proven science—on reason and intellect alone.

He had the vision. Now he needed to lead the way and make sure they didn't repeat their past mistakes.

He knew the arguments Oliver and Travis would make. He'd ushered in human extinction in the first place. Why should he emerge the leader? He'd deal with those objections later. He was best qualified to make the most of the terrible cards they'd been dealt—even if he had been the dealer.

Amperous and Omathis had reached the white haze of the lowest clouds.

"We should turn back," Omathis cautioned.

Their heads felt as if they'd been locked in a vice, and their lungs felt as though they had been set ablaze. They couldn't stand up tall, and instead hunched over like animals.

But this wasn't why Omathis felt they should quit their pursuit up the mountain. They could handle pain; it made them stronger. The real reason was that Omathis had reached the edge of sanity. He and Amperous were close to toppling over it. His rational thought was fighting a war with his desire to follow the scent of the humans. They'd passed ruined vehicles and spilled blood, and each dead man, woman, and child stoked his hunger.

"We are close to our goal," Amperous wheezed in protest.

"If we follow our desire, brother, we will never come back. We will die from the height—or we will lose our minds and be nothing but our hunger." It took great effort for Omathis to say each word. He only wanted to continue their pursuit, too. Losing his mind didn't seem so bad. There would be peace in the madness.

"I am surprised that you can stop. Not only for the blood, but because..." Amperous trailed off. Neither of them wanted to mention him. It hurt even more than the elevation.

"Mister Sean is gone. I can feel it. He's slipped past our reach. So has Lovely," Omathis said.

"They have left us behind," Amperous agreed.

Once Omathis said it out loud and Amperous confirmed, the abandonment stung sharply.

"So we have nothing to live for?" Omathis asked. "If that's true, we might as well enter the clouds and become beasts."

Amperous bristled with defiance. "Nothing to live for? Do you forget what we had in the green jungles and below the ground? We have the others, who look to us as their fathers. We have the whole world now." Amperous spat the words, heavy with pride, with a force intent on convincing himself as much as his brother.

"Let's return to our children, then. Let's take the world he has to left to us and make it ours."

"We will make it our paradise. One they can never destroy."

ICELYN

I spend the night wet and cold, watching as the waters continue to rise. I make no note of my own misery, though, because my heart is exploding in fear at the thought of Eveshone alone out there. Adorane and Torrain keep suggesting I try to sleep. I suspect they want a reprieve from my constant worry. But even if sleep were possible in this driving rain, I have no interest. They won't look out for her as closely as I will—and I don't want to miss her if she needs help.

Now the sun is rising over the desert, and the rains have ended. The rivers have calmed, leaving behind vast lakes. It's peaceful. It's hard to believe that the chaotic churn of water and stone raged only hours before.

"I think I can find some dry wood over there," Adorane announces, pointing at a pile of rocks. "Then maybe I can start a fire and warm us up.

It'd be great to dry our clothes."

I'm frustrated that Adorane is concerning himself with whether tunics and pants are wet or dry when I can't even sense Eveshone anywhere. I've been trying to connect to her roots, and even now—when the storm has passed and the sun begins to warm the desert floor again—I feel nothing.

"Yes, good idea," I mumble, distracted, as I scan the receding waters below. "Maybe take Torrain with you." I wouldn't mind being alone in my misery. As much as I'm upset at both of them for not tuning into my worry, I also don't want to talk about it. I'm afraid one of them might suggest that she has not survived, and I'm already terribly afraid that's why I can't connect to her. Hearing my greatest fear confirmed out loud would be too much.

They finally leave me alone. I'm eager to get below and look for her, but the waters remain, and I know I won't make any progress. Instead, I spend my time consciously trying to connect to her. This is as strange to me as having to try to breathe—it normally happens without effort. Even though I can still feel traces of Omathis—so many miles away—I can't find her anywhere.

"Lovely, I've missed you so."

I'm startled to hear Eveshone's voice behind me. It's tentative, plaintive, apologetic. I turn and see her. She's wet, her golden fur covering is matted and dirty. She seems smaller than she ever has before, and her eyes are fixed on the ground. It's strange—she normally stands so tall, appearing larger than her seven feet. She also normally looks me straight in the eyes, eager to connect. Poor girl! She must have been through something terrible.

I rush toward her and crash into a wet, sad embrace. She seems to have lost her strength—somehow, I am the one physically overpowering her.

"Eveshone! My love! I've been so worried about you. I wanted to come and look for you, but Adorane and Torrain wouldn't let me because of the floods."

"They made the right decision, Lovely. You would have been injured by the waters," she answers. Her words are clipped, distant.

"Where have you been? I am so happy you're back. You're not hurt?"

"I am not injured. I am healthy. I am good," she answers, though without conviction. Eveshone normally only says something when she believes it with all her heart. Now, it's as if someone else has written what she ought to say and she's having a hard time putting any passion into it.

I try to connect to her roots to get an idea of what's happened to her. But I can't—just like I couldn't while she was away.

"Do you think a Soothing might lift your spirits, Eveshone? Or a Vibram?" I offer, trying to figure out what is wrong and how I might fix it.

"Let's just sit and watch the sun rise, Lovely, if that's all right with you."

"Of course," I say. We sit together on the edge of the cliff and watch the sun continue its rise over the flooded desert below.

What has happened? Could I have upset her somehow? I've never felt so distant from her since the moment we met.

I scold myself for the dark thoughts. *What is wrong with me?* I can live with a little distance. All night I've been worried she was dead. It's a miracle to have her back and safe. For now, it's best to focus on that.

41

ICELYN

Adorane has figured out a serpentine path that winds along the higher ridge so we can avoid the waters below. He seems quite proud of his new route, often pointing out how impossible walking through the waters below would be and marveling at how lucky we are that he's figured out the way.

I nod but mostly can't be bothered, because Eveshone remains lifeless.

"What happened to you, Eveshone?"

"Oh, just lots of rain and some flooding. I'm fine, Lovely," she answers quietly. For the first time in our relationship, I suspect that she's lying to me.

"Are you sure that was it? You can tell me the truth."

I look over at her and am surprised to see a tear run down her face. *Is she crying?* But our route is strenuous and the sun is hot; it may just be that sweat has flooded into her eyes. I've been wiping mine clear for a while too.

"Just rain and flooding. All is well now. I would like it if you didn't ask me about it anymore, Lovely."

I fear I have hurt her by not actively searching for her while she was missing. I continually apologize for this failure on my part. But she insists that it doesn't bother her. That nothing is bothering her.

I try not to be hurt by this new rift in our relationship. To assume there is no rift at all, because Eveshone insists there is not. To not worry that this nonexistent rift is widening. Maybe she's just tired.

But when she talks to Adorane, she isn't as subdued.

"You should have seen it, Adorane," she says. "It was like a giant pillar of shimmering water, rising straight from the ground into the heavens."

I wouldn't say she's back to her old self when interacting with him, but she's certainly much more animated than when she and I talk. I used to be a source of life for her; now, for some reason, I seem to be sapping it from her.

She talks to Adorane about a great gleaming tower that she found, and how she has a feeling that we must visit. This excites Adorane and Torrain greatly—this was their destination, the Apriori lab that was mentioned in the maps they wouldn't share. None of them will tell me much about it.

"Eveshone, you didn't tell me you saw a tower," I summon up the courage to say. "What did you do there?"

My words appear to bring her pain. "If we could avoid speaking about this, Lovely, I would feel better."

It was bad enough when Adorane and Torrain left me out of their secrets—but with Eveshone in on the action, it's unbearable.

As we crest another in a series of unending peaks and summits, I focus on my physical misery. The heat consumes me, and I wonder why I ever thought I knew what the word *hot* meant up until now. This is another level, another world. Everything I thought was hot before seems like a pleasant breeze in retrospect. My muscles burn. I'm thirsty even while drinking water.

I'm thankful for the pain, because it distracts me from the dark, growing shadow in my chest that promises to eat me up from within. The more I worry about Eveshone, the more I frustrate her and the farther I drive her away. It's a terrible cycle, one I seem to have accidentally turned several hundred rotations already.

We finally see the lab in the distance. It's a shimmery column covered in mirrors rising from the desert below. In contrast to everything else I've seen Down Below, this doesn't appear to be a ruin. It looks almost new, as though someone has been caring for it.

"How is this hundreds of years old?" I hear Torrain mumble in disbelief.

"This is the tower you saw?" Adorane asks.

"Yes," Eveshone answers quietly. She seems transfixed by the tower, as though she cannot look away. I want to know why, but I keep my mouth shut. Why can't I access her roots? Is it a choice she's made—or is it involuntary?

I'm not sure which would be worse.

THEN

Laura Lee was waiting for the surviving ascenders.

As they trudged toward the front gates of the mountaintop settlement, she greeted them with blankets and baskets of freshly harvested fruits and vegetables. She'd even made a batch of acorn cakes topped with honey. She handed out clay jars of water.

"All those injured can find bandages, splints, and medicine in the main hall, along with cots and warm jackets," she announced, pointing toward one of the largest buildings in the settlement. It was made of stone and stretched toward the heavens, almost like a church.

Ascenders, burdened with backpacks, exhaustion, and horrific memories, appeared surprised by the presence of Laura Lee. She placed blankets over the shoulders of young children and spoke soothing words of comfort. "There—that's nice, isn't it? You can keep this blanket. You're going to like it up here. I've been living up here for a long time, and I am so glad to have new friends join me."

Children jostled to hold her hands and walk beside her as she led them to the main hall. She scanned the faces as more people arrived, trying to hold her worry at bay. Where was her father? Had he survived? It seemed odd to her that he wouldn't lead the traumatized procession into Mountaintop.

Then she caught a glimpse of him, and what she saw made her proud. He was late to arrive because he was helping an injured man. She could see now it was Oliver Hailgard who leaned on his shoulder, limping. He had one arm around Sean and another around a young man.

"Those of you who aren't injured, you can find a series of temporary shelters beside the main hall. These will only be used while we build new permanent structures." She pointed to rows of vinyl tents.

Her words flowed more quickly now. She wanted to continue to help —she'd been working on making this moment as warm and welcoming for the survivors as possible since she'd first come to live in this place. But she was also eager to finish with them so she could hug her father close.

"First come, first served on the tents—but they're all the same, so there's no need to be grabby. There's more than enough for everyone." She felt a pang of sadness at the truth of her statement. There were many more tents set up than would be needed. She had anticipated thousands of new residents, but the ragged group before her numbered no more than a few hundred. What had happened?

"In two hours, we'll gather for a warm meal on the green beside the water pump. That's that large stone structure over there, just beyond the tents. We'll sit and eat together to commemorate your entrance into this place. Together, we'll build it into one of the greatest cities that's ever been. Welcome, everyone, to Mountaintop," she said warmly.

She waited until she was sure that people understood what they were to do, where they were to go—and, as much as possible, felt like they'd entered a place they could call home. Only then did she feel free to greet her father and Oliver.

Having feared her father had died down below, Laura Lee held him tighter than she'd ever held him before. They weren't known for their hugging, but she was going to force him to make an exception this time.

"You survived," she whispered thankfully. She'd been so lonely, waiting for a day when others would live in this place with her—and yet feeling guilty for having that desire, because others would only move to Mountaintop when the world below grew too terrible to inhabit.

"We made it. Thank you for preparing this place for us," Sean responded.

Every person who'd made it up the mountain felt like a miracle, especially her father.

Oliver Hailgard was a shadow of himself, but he managed to break through the darkness consuming him to greet her and accept her embrace.

"It's good to see you," he said, and she could tell he meant every word. It wasn't a hollow greeting. His eyes searched her face, desperate for good news.

"It's good to see you too, Oliver. But God, you're hurt."

"I'll survive," he said, sounding sad.

The other man walking with them was familiar to Laura Lee, though she couldn't remember where she'd seen him before. He held a confident hand out toward her, a gesture that felt strange to everyone. It occurred to Laura Lee that there were no offices or boardrooms up here—would people still shake hands? She brushed off the thought and warmly wrapped his hand in hers.

"I'm Travis Nilsing. We've met before, but I was probably about two feet tall at the time."

She laughed, which felt good. Travis! Shai's boy. She remembered him. He'd been aloof and difficult to talk to, even when they were both children.

"I remember. I was only about two feet tall too. I guess we've both changed a lot." She noticed that he blushed and found it endearing. She liked people who blushed. It showed that they cared what other people thought on a basic biological level.

"Well, good," she said, rubbing her hands together in the chill air. "Let's get up to the settlement. I promised a warm meal to everyone, so that's going to take some work."

"I'll help," Travis offered. "I mean, I'm not exactly a gourmet chef, but I can stir a pot."

"I'll probably take you up on that, but get Oliver up and into the main hall first. He needs treatment."

Oliver sat beside the flickering flame and drew a horrific scene from memory: an accursed creature looming over a man and his child. Oliver closed his eyes to stoke his recall and then sketched the man's features. The man's face hadn't been marked by terror or self-survival. The man cared about only one thing—protecting his son. Oliver erased his first attempt at the man's torso and redrew it so that he was shielding the child.

Finally, the drawing was complete, and Oliver appraised it. It was just as he remembered and a fitting tribute to this man's best instincts. None would be forgotten.

Oliver Hailgard spent time every day in his newly constructed home—primitive, made of stone and mud, but cozy—writing and sketching all he could remember before the memories faded.

"I was thinking I'd walk to the south side and gather berries later," Tamar gently whispered, placing her hand softly on his back. "I'd like very much if you would join me."

Tamar was coaxing him back into a life worth living. She didn't scold him for choosing to hide away in their round hut night and day, feverishly scrawling out his memories, but she had started encouraging him to do other things with his time.

"Thank you. I just…I need to make sure they're remembered," he explained. He felt a responsibility to keep their memories from being blotted out.

"You're doing what needs to be done. I couldn't be prouder. I'm only wondering if you could come pick berries with me afterward too."

"I'd like to pick berries with you afterward," Oliver replied, as he lifted her hand and softly kissed it. "Thanks for forcing me into the sunshine."

"Somebody needs to remind you that you're not dead."

"It's easy to forget sometimes."

He laid another piece of paper flat and held a pencil, ready to create another tribute. His eyes closed tight, and his forehead wrinkled with concentration. Who else had he seen out there? Who else must not be forgotten?

He softly dragged the pencil against the paper, and the image of a soldier emerged. This woman couldn't have been much older than eighteen—just a girl, really. She'd run without hesitation and placed herself between the beasts and a group of civilians. As they pounced on her, the ascenders had been able to get onto the transport and over the wall.

So many heroes. So many acts of bravery. Everyone who now lived in Mountaintop was only here because so many others had died.

NOW

Amperous led the ocean of bustling Croathus through a narrow gap. Thousands funneled into a pass only three wide at the thinnest point, sandstone cliffs rising hundreds of feet above them on either side.

He was afraid that the crowd would grow unruly at the disruption as they reached the pinch point. They'd been walking for a day now, making good progress, and overall shared a joyful spirit, but it seemed to him that their cheerful morale was held in fragile balance. He'd spent much of his time leading them fretful about upsetting it.

He wondered about Barielta. He missed her—her presence, of course, but mostly her leadership. Though she had insisted many times that they led this movement together, he knew that the Croathus were here mostly for the same reason he was: to follow her.

They were uneasy about her absence from their caravan, just like he was. Yet her command had been clear—even if the intent behind them was murky. He was to take them to the Mothers.

The Croathus entrusted with carrying the giant glass flasks containing the formless beings took their jobs seriously. There had been gasps among the Croathus when the creatures were first revealed. None had known of their existence—hidden in the gleaming lab, they were known only to the Priestess, Amperous, and a few trusted assistants.

When the mass of Croathus had first beheld the creatures, Amperous could sense the same disquiet he had felt. What were these creatures, both familiar and utterly foreign? It was like staring into a twisted mirror and fearing that the reflection is what you really look like.

Yet their collective discomfort remained unexpressed. Instead Amperous shouted, "Hail to our future, our potential, what we can be as a people!"—just as the Priestess had instructed him to do. Predictably, his exhortation incited a thunderous response. Any misgivings were overwhelmed by the enthusiasm spreading through the crowd.

The clear flasks passed through the gap first. Amperous oversaw their passage anxiously. The faceless beings appeared agitated, knocking themselves against the glass violently, kicking and thrashing in the water.

"What should we do, Lord of Both?" the creature-bearers asked as they struggled to hold the large vials. It appeared at any moment that they may topple over and crack open.

Amperous stretched out his right arm and approached the creatures. As he neared them, they stilled. He pressed his hands against the clear glass of one of the vials and noticed that his talons were extended, as if he were ready to fight or kill. But inside, he felt a great peace.

A featureless creature pressed itself against the other side of the glass, like a frozen animal desperate for warmth. Amperous was shocked to feel a connection with the being, intense and unmistakable. It was hunger and desperation and sadness, a shadow longing to be solid, a whisper desperate to be heard.

Amperous walked alongside the vials and stared at each creature one by one, holding his hands against the glass. As dark as they felt, he now had a connection with all. Even a connection to depression and terror was better than no connection. He loved them now. And he could feel that they loved him, too—as much as a being like them could love anything.

"I will see that you are born, each of you," Amperous promised them. "And then I will guide you, and mold you, and you will never be alone." Emotion surged in Amperous' chest as he said the words. His heart stung as he was reminded of his children and wife long ago. He had said the same words to them and meant it—but time had passed and made him a liar.

This time he would fight until they were true.

42

ICELYN

Torrain approaches the gleaming metal tower like a Kith child on his fifth birthday. (Fifth birthdays are when a Cognate or Veritas are given their family name and also bestowed with the greatest haul of gifts and sweets. I was given a whole jar of honey, along with a stack of books, a newly stitched set of boots—and the last name of Brathius. I'll never forget that day.)

Adorane pushes me from behind, urging me to catch up with Torrain. He wants to get to the lab as quickly as possible, and yet he knows he can't leave me behind. I appreciate his not wanting to leave me alone, but he's being rude.

"Is this as fast as you can go?" He prods.

I remain stunned by the sight of the behemoth rising toward the heavens. I feel barely attached to my body, and moving fast seems impossible. I just want to stare at it—I can understand why Eveshone appears dazed at the sight of it too.

"Maybe I'm in no rush to reach that tower," I murmur. This is true. I don't have a terrible feeling about this place, but I certainly don't have a good one either. I don't know how I feel. Maybe something terrible happened here—or is still happening here. I can't tell, and I'm not sure I want to.

Adorane has no interest in my inner state and drags me along anyway. "You can rest once we get there. Come on."

Once we reach Torrain, he's busy examining the tower's clean, metallic surface.

"I don't see a door anywhere. Or a window. Or any way in." He sounds thrilled at the prospect of another Apriori puzzle to solve.

While Torrain and Adorane busy themselves scanning every inch of the tower's foundation, Eveshone approaches a metal rectangular box that rises from the stony desert floor. I watch as she waves her hand in front of it, then gently touches the front surface.

I hear a low buzz as a section of the metal tower's exterior slides open.

Torrain lets out a whoop of joy. "How'd you do that, Eveshone?" he asks, but rushes toward the opening before waiting for an answer.

Adorane grabs my hand. He clutches Torrain's accursed invention, the same kind of weapon that wounded and nearly killed Eveshone.

"Let's go," he says. "This is important."

"And dangerous," I add.

"We don't know that, but it's best to assume so," he answers. "We're Down Below. Everything is dangerous."

Eveshone follows us.

"How did you know how to open that, Eveshone?" I ask.

A distressed look crosses her face again, and she doesn't answer.

We enter the void.

We find ourselves in a darkened room where a small galaxy of lights blink and shimmer, green and red and blue and white. I've never seen anything like it. When we reach the center of the space, we stop and stare. Torrain in particular is transfixed.

Adorane is the first to break the spell. "How do we make it so that the light appears? What should we be looking for?" He asks. "You know? The light…the light…"

"Switch," Torrain mumbles, and I recall from my history lessons that he is right. "But don't find it yet," he urges. "Let's stand here and feel this."

He doesn't have to explain what he means by *this*. We all feel it—an overwhelming sense of mystery pressing in on us from all sides.

This place doesn't have the sense of abandonment and ruin that marks the other buildings in Down Below. It feels occupied, active. Like something happened here long ago—but continues to happen today.

Eveshone is fidgety. She's looking around like she hears sounds that we do not.

"What is it, Eveshone?" I whisper, working my hardest to sound gentle.

"I, I…" She wants to say something, I know, but trails off, confused. "I don't know…"

Finally Torrain decides it's time to flood the room with light—he knew where the switch was all along, from the looks of it. My eyes take in a cavernous hall filled with towering shiny metal boxes, gleaming tables, and glass squares. The effect is gloomy—they look like mirrors, but darkened and black.

"How is there electricity here, Torrain?" I ask. "Who could be maintaining it?"

Torrain runs his hands against the Apriori technology like a tender lover—it's embarrassing to watch. Yet I know this must be exciting for him, like we've traveled back in time. I've had a chance to see such things through Omathis' memory, but Torrain never has. He's only seen Apriori technology when it's broken, cracked, and dirty. He is finally seeing it all in its glory.

Torrain ignores my question and rushes from machine to machine, so I try to talk sense into Adorane. "Don't you think we're in danger here?" Adorane nods to his ultraspear, as if that's enough to set my mind at ease. When it's clear it isn't, he presses a button and closes all the doors to the room. He thinks he's locking whatever I'm afraid of out—but it feels more to me like he's locking us in.

"We didn't just stumble into this place, Icelyn," Adorane explains. "Visiting here was part of the plan all along."

"Our plan or someone else's?" I ask, but they ignore me.

Maybe I'm finally tapping into Eveshone's feelings, but I too feel easily disturbed, like something is moving just outside my field of vision. I can almost hear something scuffling around, but it's not loud enough to know for sure.

Torrain focuses on a round glowing piece of equipment. He turns to us with excitement. "Hey, all of you, give me some of your hair."

That's a normal request, Torrain.

"I respectfully decline," I respond. But Adorane and Eveshone dutifully pluck some strands from themselves and hand it over.

"Come on, Icelyn. You too," Torrain urges.

"Why? I want nothing to do with any of this until someone tells me what's happening."

"Torrain thinks he might be able figure out why the babies dying, Icelyn," Adorane says impatiently. "The answer could be here. He needs a contaminated sample—that's me. And a non-contaminated sample—that's you."

"Why didn't you tell me any of this before?"

"Look, we didn't think this place actually existed. We hoped it would, but we didn't dream it would still be operational. We thought maybe we'd find a couple of old books here, who knows, something useful. But if this works, maybe we can find a cure, and then you don't have to go to Apex," Torrain explains.

I pull out several strands of hair and hand them over.

"And why do you need Eveshone?"

Torrain smiles. "Oh, that's just curiosity."

He lays the hair samples out on a large table and begins to fuss, preparing them for his experiment. He looks through cabinets and drawers.

"How long is this going to take?" I ask, fearfully looking into the darkness.

"I can't find any enzymes or primer," he complains. "Where would they keep that?"

"Is no one else worried about who *they* are?" I explode. "Has no one else considered that maybe we're not lucky this place is operation? That maybe when we find out who is *keeping it* operational, we won't feel so fortunate?"

Torrain doesn't respond. He's flipping through a thick book he found in one of the cabinets. "Without enzymes and primer I can't do anything," he says to Adorane, as if I haven't said a word. I throw my hands up in frustration.

Adorane presses the button to open the doors to the room. "Well, Icelyn, you might get your answer soon. Let's go find what you need, Torrain."

We push forward in darkness. Adorane says we're keeping the lights off because we want to avoid whoever may be using the lab, but I know it's just because they can't find the switches. Torrain finds a bunch of rags, ties them to a stick, and dips them into some foul-smelling liquid. He then sets it aflame with a little metal nozzle that somehow holds fire within.

The hallway is long and switches back on itself multiple times. I realize we must be descending below the surface of the desert.

Finally we enter into what looks like a natural cave, massive and cool. It's filled wall to wall with more Apriori technology. Most of it is what I would have expected—broken and rotted from the passage of time. Yet some of it looks like it still works.

I have the strangest feeling here. It's a familiarity I've only felt when a place is mine—like in my room when I was younger, or in the secret lean-to Adorane and I built in the woods. Or the throne room in the Drowned City.

Eveshone looks at me and says, "It's not yours, Icelyn. Not anymore." She sounds afraid, and I don't know what she means. "We should leave," she urges.

Eveshone has read my thoughts, even though I still feel no connection to her. I don't know whether to feel relieved or disturbed by this development.

"Whose is it, then?" I ask despite myself. I don't expect an answer and don't receive one.

"This doesn't look like a place where they'd store supplies they still use anyway," I say uneasily. "We should go." I don't want to be here.

"Hold on," Adorane says. He grabs Torrain's torch and heads toward the center of the cavern. We walk past a bunch of empty plexiglass cages —much like the ones Omathis and Amperous were once imprisoned in. No one but me seems to notice them. Finally, Adorane stops and stands before a series of huge glass cylinders that stretch from the rocky floor all the way to the stalagmites above. They are arranged in a perfect circle, and they look brand new.

I suddenly wheel around. "Where is Eveshone?" I ask, but both Torrain and Adorane ignore me.

Torrain examines the cylinders closely. They each have a portal that appears to be open. He smells it like an animal, then touches it. His hands are wet.

He turns to Adorane. "I think we'll find what we're looking for here."

A moaning erupts from afar—and Adorane immediately crouches and points the ultraspear. Finally, my worst fear has been realized. We are under attack.

THEN

Tamar no longer had to beg Oliver to leave the hut. He enjoyed spending time with her more than anything. Earlier on, he'd felt guilty for how alive she made him feel. Those moments he spent with her were the only when he wasn't dwelling on the *twenty-four thousand, seven hundred and fifty three souls* who'd perished under his watch.

Not to mention the other billions around the world who were dead now too.

The sheer scale—of death, destruction, and guilt—was too much.

Oliver was crushed under its weight daily. But that felt right, too. Anybody who wasn't flattened by what had happened was either uncaring or delusional.

Yet broken as he was, Tamar had pursued him anyway.

"I saw a batch over here," Oliver pointed. "They were ripe, sweet—and big, too."

"Oh, was somebody scouting berries on the sly?" Tamar joked.

"You know berries are my hidden obsession," he replied, sharing in the fun before setting the record straight. "Actually, I happened across them while checking on patrols yesterday."

Tamar put her arm around him and pulled him close. "Thanks for clearing that up."

They'd met in the strangest way two people could—yet the most appropriate to the world they now lived in. While other couples before the attacks down below met in ceramics class, or through a mutual friend, or through a dating app on their phones, Oliver and Tamar had met because a beast was trying to slaughter Tamar and Oliver had broken away from Sean and Travis to save *one more person.*

Her.

"I think I might have enough for the pie now—maybe even two pies," she said as they picked the batch he'd discovered. "My goodness. Dare I even say that this might be a *three-pie harvest?"*

"Miracles do happen," he responded.

He had saved her, and now she was returning the favor.

ICELYN distress

I follow behind Adorane and Torrain stands behind me, facing backward, as we walk toward the source of the earsplitting moan. Instead of feeling protected, I am aware of every shadow, my panic rising.

"Eveshone!" I shout. "Where are you?"

Adorane shushes me, but I doubt anyone could hear me over the terrible moaning sound. And anyway, Adorane is holding a fireball on a stick—it's not like we're a stealthy bunch.

We continue to move slowly, spears pointed and at the ready. I'm bathed in fear. I hiss that maybe we should run, but Adorane whispers back that it might be a trap.

We reach a corner of the cavern where no Apriori technology resides. There's a space below a darkened overhang that the light from our flame doesn't reach. The sound comes from there.

"Lower the spears," I hear myself saying.

Adorane and Torrain ignore me.

I step in front of them, toward the opening in the cavern wall.

"What are you doing, Icelyn?"

I continue to walk toward the dark. Adorane tries to grab my arm, but I push him away.

"Stay here," I command.

"Are you crazy?" Adorane whispers.

The moaning is so loud now that we can barely hear one another.

"It's Eveshone. Stay here."

I enter the darkness.

Eveshone's form becomes clearer to me as my eyes adjust to the dim light. I've never seen her in this state. She's coiled tightly into a ball, her arms crossed across her torso, her own talons digging into her sides, like she's trying to restrain herself from doing something terrible.

I sit beside her. I touch her skin, and it's as cold as the stone wall of the cavern itself. I feel nothing where our skin makes contact—no Vibram, no roots, no Soothing. She pulls away, slightly enough that someone else might not notice, but to me it feels like a slap in the face. I cannot breathe.

She's never done that before.

I gently try to pull her hands away from where they cut into her side, but I cannot. Instead I stroke them, hoping to coax forth the intimacy we once shared.

"What's going on, Eveshone? I'm here. I want to help you."

I do a passable job of sounding calm and not as panicky as I feel on the inside. What I *want* is to throw myself on the ground and start moaning along with her. Draw my own blood with my meager fingernails. But I'm her god, her mother. I have to be bigger than her anguish.

"It's all right. You're safe. You're with me. We're alive and together."

I can feel her revulsion at my touch, her desire to pull away, to separate from me. I've spent a lifetime being rejected by those around me, and I've never felt anything like this.

I try to drown out my own internal screaming. "What's going on, Eveshone?" I ask, putting my head on her shoulder. It's always worked in the past, but it doesn't work now.

"What I'm doing is kindness, Lovely, but I don't think you'll see it that way. I fear you won't."

"What do you mean? What it is that you are doing?"

"She wants me to do so much more, Lovely. I won't do it. But I can't just do nothing. I can't. I've thought about it. I've struggled. But I can't do nothing." The words pour out of her, wet with sadness, interrupted by full-body sobs.

"*Who* wants you to do so much more? Who are you talking about?"

After another round of sobs, Eveshone regains enough composure to speak. "You know that I only had my father growing up, right, Lovely? He would never speak of my mother. No one would! She was a secret that everyone found terribly shameful."

"Yes, I've heard this. And remember, you don't have to worry about that anymore, because I am you mother," I respond.

"You don't understand. Listen to me. I met her. *I met my mother.*"

43

THEN

Travis couldn't believe his luck. One of the ascenders—Julian Ascott, to be specific—had packed a guitar in his bags and gotten it all the way to Mountaintop.

Glad God had his priorities straight. Thousands of humans died, but, hey, at least a guitar survived.

But as ridiculous as it was, Travis was thankful. It was undersized compared to a normal guitar—portable, designed to be taken on camping trips—but it sounded good enough. It was the only guitar remaining in all of human civilization.

Sean had chosen ascenders based on their military, law enforcement, or academic qualifications. He'd rejected artistic ability as a qualifying criterion. Because of this, there were no skilled musicians in Mountaintop. Julian turned out to be average, which was strange considering he'd packed the guitar as one of the few belongings to carry into his new life. He really wasn't very good at all.

Travis was probably the best musician in the entire world now.

Before, to attain that lofty peak, he would have had to dedicate his life to practice since birth. He'd need to be born with an already dazzling foundation of talent, surrounded by people who would encourage and support his gift. His life would have to be marked by luck and good fortune. But in an interesting twist of fate, an army of beasts had slaughtered all the musicians who were better than him.

Cutting the world's human population from billions to hundreds affected superlatives in strange ways. The tallest human was now Matthew Tarnall, who was only six foot four inches tall. The heaviest human once weighed nearly a ton, but now Florian Fitz held that title. He wouldn't even have been big enough to play professional football.

Travis had loved reading the Guinness Book of World Records when he was younger, marveling at the crazy outliers and feats of humanity. If one were published today, he realized, it would be no longer than a pamphlet.

Travis liked to spend his free time in the village green beside the flowing aqueducts of the water pump, playing Julian's guitar. Julian had insisted that Travis keep the guitar. One of the perks of being on the Leadership Council.

He enjoyed figuring out some of the better songs they'd left behind. No one had brought any recorded music. Bach, Mozart, the Beatles, the Jackson 5, Brandi Carlile, Beyoncé, Lana Del Rey, U2, Nirvana, Simon and Garfunkel, Radiohead—countless artists and acts that had sold out stadiums in their day—now relied on Travis' memory to have their songs played again.

His concerts drew a crowd, and the songs buoyed the spirits of those who gathered. Travis often thought that Sean had made a mistake in not adding accomplished artists to the ranks of the ascenders. Look at the difference it made in their morale, their quality of life.

That certainly wasn't Sean's first mistake. It wasn't likely to be his last, either.

Travis was halfway through a pretty obscure gem he'd only recently remembered—"Somewhere Only We Know" by a band called Keane—when Laura Lee Brathius exited Waterpump with two jars. He knew it was foolish, but he hoped she'd stop and listen.

"And if you have a minute, why don't we go talk about it somewhere only we know?" he sang—to her, though no one else knew it.

She stopped and watched. Travis felt a thrill and hoped nobody noticed as his voice cracked. It sounded okay, he thought; maybe everyone would assume it was a stylistic choice. In any case, he could foul up the song completely and his audience would still love it.

She nodded a little and treated him to a tiny wave of the hand. It was friendly, but not overly so, but for Travis it might as well have been a bear hug. Then she walked away toward Brathius Tower with her water.

"This could be the end of everything so why don't we go somewhere only we know?" he continued to sing, though the only person he truly wanted to listen had gone.

Travis accepted the cheers as his song ended, and then started another, but he was distracted. What *was* it about Laura Lee? She was like a god here in Mountaintop—there were the mortals and then her, a level above.

Practically speaking, she'd been here first. That set her apart in everyone's minds. She'd prepared this place for them, had welcomed them all here, had planted flowers and crops to cheer them and feed them. Plus, she was Sean's daughter. While Travis didn't share in their lofty opinions, the citizens of Mountaintop revered him and had made them their leader.

He'd known that they could be safe from the creatures up here.

He'd had the foresight to create this place.

He'd had the wisdom to write the Code that now brought them peace and order.

Only Travis and Oliver (and Laura Lee) knew that Sean had created the abominations in the first place. Only Travis and Oliver (and Laura Lee) knew that Sean had love in his heart, even to this day, for those monsters. It had been decided early on that these sinister truths would be kept a secret for the good of humanity. That knowledge about their beloved leader would tear them apart. They wouldn't survive the betrayal.

Even Travis had agreed that this was the correct decision, but he resented how beloved Sean had become as a result of the mythology they'd spun since.

As much as the people adored Sean, they cherished Laura Lee even more. She didn't hold herself above the rest of them. No—she knew every person in Mountaintop by name, and somehow every person came away from conversations with her feeling as if she were their best friend.

She was gracious and kind toward everyone, and Travis loved that about her. If he could change anything about her, he'd prefer that she be warm toward all, but just a little bit more toward him.

He was working on it.

Sean Brathius loved these sessions, especially when they ran deep into the night and required the fires to be lit, stoked, and stoked again. He settled into his seat at the head of the polished oak table. The gathering hall, with its handcrafted stone walls, thick wooden beams overhead, and hammered metal fixtures, felt exactly the kind of place where important history would be made. That's what they were doing—setting the blueprint for a new humanity. One that would take advantage of this opportunity to start over and ensure it wouldn't repeat the mistakes of the past.

"And what of the anti-racial discrimination proposal? Does everyone understand what I am saying here?"

Oliver and Travis nodded their assent. There were three others on the

Leadership Council: Angela Croassan, who had been an internationally renowned mathematician before the attacks; Candice Nguyen, a Pulitzer-prize winning historian; and Stefan Isaacs, who had led the world's top technology company. Incidentally, Stefan had been one of the richest men in the world—but it was his intelligence, not his money, that had gotten him into Mountaintop.

"Are you saying we should force people to marry outside their race or merely incentivize it?" Travis asked. It wasn't an innocent question—the answer had implications for his future plans regarding Laura Lee.

"We're not authoritarians here," Sean assured them. "We will merely encourage. Maybe with more generous food or property rations. The idea is that we blend ourselves as much as possible, so that in a hundred or two hundred years there aren't distinct races and thus no divisions. Humans are tribal; science proves this. We need to completely remove the idea of 'us' and 'them' in Mountaintop to avoid the possibility of conflict."

"But what about preserving the rich heritages of our distinct peoples?" Candice objected. "You want us to mix it all into one basic stew? We'll be missing what makes groups of people special."

"I believe all that should still be celebrated, preserved—perhaps in song or writing. But when heritage divides us, then it becomes dangerous. Like a poison that tastes sweet—we might think we like it, but eventually it kills us. Look, let's be practical. There are barely two hundred of us. We don't have enough people to preserve a multitude of cultures in practice. So we'll honor the cultures of the past but move forward with one culture: *our* culture. In the past, all talk of heritage inevitably led to a dominant culture that killed or subjugated anyone who didn't fit in. We've seen it over and over throughout history. People feel a loyalty to those who look like themselves, a tribalism, which leads to aggression and a distrust of those who look different. It's scientific fact. So how do we use that knowledge to increase unity and decrease strife? Let's take a step back, with this opportunity we've been afforded, and ask ourselves the larger question. Wouldn't it be better to truly become a *united human race?"*

"It sounds a little bit like cultural genocide, to be honest," Stefan added. His tone was diffident, like he couldn't care less but thought he'd mention it anyway.

"No, that's not what I'm proposing. Not at all. Listen. What we call race is really just the grouping of certain traits, right? And traits are based on our DNA. One group of people stayed on one particular continent and kept breeding until they emphasized their unique genes. Another headed north, or across the ocean, and when they had children and grandchildren and great-grandchildren, eventually their unique genes were doubled and tripled and quadrupled until they began to display certain common traits, too. But when you emphasize genetics, you also get a greater risk of disease, mutation, and madness. We have such a small gene pool, we can't afford to breed without regard for the greatest possible diversity."

Candice sighed in resignation. "I can't see how it's practical to preserve a multitude of cultures and races anyway," she conceded. "I'm the only person of Vietnamese descent here, for instance, so what am I going to do? Throw a Wandering Souls festival for myself alone? My culture isn't going to survive."

"But it will survive as part of the new culture, the one we create, if you blend yourself into the greater whole. We can all be kith and kin! That's what I'm saying," Sean exclaimed, his voice a little too excited for the lateness of the hour.

"Okay, resolved," Candice declared. "We'll look into how we can encourage marriage and childbearing across current racial divides, with the eventual goal being to increase commonality among our people."

"Exactly. In order to increase genetic diversity, too."

"But no banning of same-race marriages?" Travis added, eager to clarify.

"No, of course not," Sean replied.

All present voted yes.

"Excellent. Now let's turn to my next proposal. We need to embark upon a frank discussion about the true utility of the practice of religion in our society. Let's ask the hard questions. How much does it really help?"

Laura Lee slept fitfully. Whenever she awoke, she found it hard to believe she'd been asleep. Yet time had passed, and she didn't remember experiencing its passage, so she reasoned she must have dozed off.

Her body felt uncomfortable in any position. He skin felt tender to any contact, so she shoved her blanket aside even though it meant she shivered from the cold.

Most nights she suffered from terrible nightmares. Everyone in Mountaintop did—but her night terrors were different. They relived the horrors outside the wall. Her nights focused on terrors that hadn't ever actually happened. At least she hoped that was the case.

In her dream, emptied vials are lined up on the table beside her bed.

Sharp pains jolt her arms and legs, followed by burning, sweating, and fear so thick she can taste it. Then unbelievable rage. She'd tear herself to pieces if she could. Yet she is restrained.

Her father looks down on her while she's paralyzed. He says nothing, yet his mouth is moving. She's unable to speak, to struggle, to do anything but absorb the torture and make it part of her. Her head feels like it's swelling. It is as though a brain three times as large as her own is being crammed into her skull, whether it fits or not.

Then she wook up.

"What are you going to name her?" Laura Lee whispered, eagerly accepting the sleeping bundle of joy from Tamar. Laura Lee studied the tiny newborn's soft features and saw both father and mother in her.

"The first baby born in Mountaintop!" Laura Lee cooed at the child. Another generation of humanity. The first baby born since all the calamity below.

"We were thinking of making up a new name," Oliver explained. "Since it's a new world. Why try to pretend we still live in the old one?"

"Just a new word altogether? Why not? I like it," Laura Lee encouraged the new parents, nuzzling her nose against the little girl's cheeks. "Any ideas?"

"Well, Tamar and I like to pick berries on the south side, so we were thinking of Berry."

"Berry is kind of already a name, though," Laura Lee said. "I knew a Barry in second grade. And then there was Barry Manilow."

"You don't think the E versus the A is enough of a difference?" Tamar laughed.

"Might get lost on some people. But hey, she's your baby. Name her what you'd like. What about Highberry? Because the berries are high up here on the mountain."

Oliver put his face up to his young daughter and spoke softly, "Highberry Hailgard! My, my, what a big name for such a tiny girl. It suits you, though. What do you think, Tamar?"

"Sounds like the kind of name a queen of legend might have," she said happily.

"But hey, why's it have to be Hailgard?" Laura Lee asked. They'd decided that upon marriage in Mountaintop, people would retain their previous names. No conventions had yet been formed around the naming of the child.

"Alliteration," Oliver answered.

"But Highberry Baldwin has a nice ring to it too," Tamar noted. "How about this? Until we really know who she is, she'll just be Highberry. Once we understand her personality, we'll decide whether she's more Hailgard or Baldwin, and that will be her name."

"And so that she still knows she is equally both our child, at that point the other parent will give her a middle name of their choosing," Oliver said, his eyes lighting up. "So if she ends up being Highberry Hailgard, you get to choose her middle name."

As if on cue, Highberry started crying. Laura Lee reluctantly handed her back to Tamar. "I think you have arrived at a fine tradition," she exclaimed.

ICELYN

She's gone.

She left me.

She begged me to see that she had no choice.

I don't see that. I never will.

She cried and asked me to please understand.

I cannot. I never will.

She said she was choosing a better path—for her and for me.

I begged her to stay.

She wouldn't. She said she couldn't, but I know she could have if she'd wanted.

She didn't want to.

I suggested that I could see her mother along with her.

This terrified Eveshone for reasons she wouldn't share.

She insisted this was something she must do alone.

Torrain and Adorane have not even noticed that everything has changed.

I'm only now realizing how much of my life I'd built around her, and how much of me consists of her—because all that's left of me is a hint of who I was, a layer of dust in the shape of who I had been.

She's gone.

She left me.

NOW

Torrain excitedly scanned the cascading rows of numbers on one series of screens before turning to images of stacking bars and swirling lines on another.

Adorane looked over his shoulder, less enthused.

"I thought you said it would be quite some time before we learned anything."

"That's true, but look. It's working!" Flickering colors projecting from the screens stained his face as he was transfixed by the sight of the sequencer working. "I've waited my whole life to see something like this. The Apriori magic, Adorane—it's right here. We're inside a miracle."

Adorane turned back toward the entrance and then the exits, holding tight to the ultraspear. Something felt wrong.

"Yeah. Well, let me know when it actually tells you something."

Torrain was too enamored to be insulted by Adorane's lack of wonder. He kept pressing.

"Look, Adorane. This is you—and this series right here, that's me. Here's Icelyn. And that's Eveshone."

All the screens looked like undifferentiated bunches of digits and colors and shapes to Adorane.

"...And?" He asked, waiting for the punchline.

Torrain sighed. "Well, if you don't see it, I'm not going to hold your hand. Let's just say it's *fascinating.*"

"I've grown tired of this, Torrain. I respect your interest, but I can't be here while you're like this." He picked up another ultraspear and handed it to Torrain. "Here, hold this. Icelyn's right. It *is* strange that this place is obviously maintained and yet nobody is here."

The touch of the spear in his hand jolted Torrain back to the present.

"Wait, where are you going?"

"Going to check on Icelyn and Eveshone."

Torrain looked like there was nothing he wanted to do less. "Do you think Eveshone is still moaning?"

"I hope not."

44

THEN

Laura Lee busied herself with the preparations. It was already the five-year anniversary of the ascenders' entrance into Mountaintop. She was going to make sure this was a celebration to be remembered.

"No, no, no—you don't put the honey *in* the dough. We drizzle the honey after the cakes are baked!" she scolded, though with a smile, as Travis made yet another mistake in the kitchen.

Travis had insisted on helping out. She was suspicious of his motives—only a fool would not realize he had been pursuing her for years now—but welcomed the assistance regardless. After all, she had two hundred acorn cakes to bake. She crushed the acorns into a fine powder and mixed them with water to create a grainy dough.

"But have you ever *tried* putting the honey in before you bake?" he protested. "Might be pretty good."

"Well, that can be your cake, if you want to be the guinea pig. Just don't inflict your experiments on anyone else."

"It's a deal. But only if you promise you won't get upset when everyone is jealous of me and my innovative honey-laced acorn cake," he responded cockily.

"I don't think that's going to be a problem," she said, rolling her eyes.

She liked having him around. Even though she cherished her time alone—a byproduct of the years she'd spent preparing this place in solitude—she now appreciated spending time with people more than ever. And with Travis more than anyone else, though she wouldn't want to admit that to anyone. Especially him—he'd get the wrong idea.

"So," Travis said, and Laura Lee could tell he was winding up for another sales pitch. This was the cost of their time together—she had to weather at least one of his attempts to woo her. "This flour and this water makes me think of something."

"Is that so?" Laura Lee asked cautiously.

"Yeah. See, if they stay apart, then they're just powder and water. Boring, right? Who cares about that?" Laura Lee could already see where this was going, but decided to let Travis have his moment. She was kind of enjoying it anyway.

"But if you mix the powder and the water together," Travis' voice rose dramatically, as if he was lecturing a group of hundreds, not just her, "then you get this dough, and then you get some cake. And then you have a party. To review—apart, dust and water. Together, a celebration for the ages."

Travis had shared an impressive variety of such object lessons over the years. There was the flower without petals, the moon without the stars, a fireplace with no fire, a fish with no water to swim in. She had to admit this flour and water example was one of his best yet.

"Didn't my dad adopt you?" Laura Lee jabbed. "That makes us basically brother and sister."

"Okay—first of all, you weren't even living at home when he did that. Second, I never asked him to, and it's not like I took his last name or anything. And third, he immediately shipped me off to military school, so I still don't understand why he adopted me in the first place."

"Still, legally, we're brother and sister. You can't deny it," she teased.

"Legally! By what laws? What paperwork? It's all just ashes and dust down there."

"I don't know. While you've apparently always enjoyed the idea of incest, I'm not quite as big a fan." She was joking. They were no more brother and sister than any other couple in Mountaintop. But she enjoyed watching him squirm.

"When a population is small enough, sometimes a little bit of…I wouldn't call it *incest*…but, you know, cousins, at least. It's necessary. Oh God. Never mind." Travis blushed despite himself.

"I love making you justify terrible things. It's one of my favorite hobbies. Can you pass that jar of honey, please?"

Travis passed the honey before trying one last time.

"Just about everyone up here has paired off—"

She cut him off. "Yeah, looks like you missed the boat."

"*Or* I'm waiting for the best boat in the fleet. I've got my heart set on one boat in particular."

"So I'm a boat now? Do you think I look more like a barge? Or, hm… an oil tanker? When will you learn that I am a *person,* Travis? Flesh and blood, a woman? Not some object—or, God forbid, a vessel to be piloted around by you?" She enjoyed this too much.

Even Travis had to smile a little. Laura Lee. How could he help but swoon when she was around?

Laura Lee finished topping off the cakes with the honey and examined their handiwork.

"This is perfect, Travis. Thanks for helping." She gave him a quick peck on the cheek and then scurried out of the room.

He put his hand over the spot where she'd kissed him.

That was a first.

Sean Brathius strolled through Mountaintop. This was his favorite time of day here. The sun was setting, bathing the entire hamlet in a golden light. He watched as fathers and mothers tossed sticks with their toddlers in the village green. They used sticks because only one ball had made it up to Mountaintop—and Sean wasn't going to let people play with it. It was the ball that Omathis and Amperous used to chase when they were pups. It sat in his study, locked away.

This new life in Mountaintop should have made Sean glad—and it did, mostly. They were flourishing because of him. He was a father to all of this. This was his family.

But it also reminded him of all he'd left below in the rubble.

He missed the Croathus.

Sometimes so much that he swore he could feel them, pulling on the corners of his mind, with such strength that it hurt. Laura Lee confided that sometimes she felt the same way, but figured it was a headache left over from her terrible dreams.

Sean made his way to the great drop-off. It was dangerous, but also afforded the best view of the cloud ocean which obscured the world below. He stared at the rolling clouds, attempting to will himself to see through them. What were Omathis and Amperous doing down there? What about their children and their children's children? Sean's heart hurt with a desire to see this other family, the one he'd abandoned, if just for a moment.

He returned to his lab with fresh inspiration. Nobody knew, but he was resuming an unfinished experiment.

He was going to bring his two families together. He knew it could be done.

ICELYN

I hear footsteps. They're gentle but confident, so I know they belong to Adorane. One time Mother said that Adorane walks like his feet are tenderly kissing the ground—and compared to Torrain's graceless heavy plodding (despite his slight stature), I now understand exactly what she meant.

I don't want to talk to Adorane. I don't want to spend time with anyone. If I could avoid even being in the company of myself, I would. Just pause existence, bow out for a while, stop having to be anyone. Stop feeling, stop thinking, stop being—not forever, but just until this storm passes. Or maybe forever. I'd have to think about it, try it out one moment at a time.

"Icelyn?" he whispers into the darkness. "What's going on?"

I swallow my pain and dry my tears. I concentrate on my breathing, hoping to steady it. I don't want him to know how I feel. Or even that she's gone. It's all too much right now. Give me time.

"I'm good," I say. My voice is more feeble than I'd like and cracks a little, but hopefully I don't sound as devastated as I feel.

"Is Eveshone in there with you?" he asks.

I try to form a response, but I can tell that even one word would uncork the sadness that is eager to spill out all over me. So I stay silent.

As clueless as he often is, I can tell he knows I'm upset about something.

"Can I come in?" I shake my head no, but of course he can't see me. I can't speak without sobbing, so I stay silent.

"I'm coming in."

I hear him approaching and resign myself to whatever is about to happen. I cover my eyes with my hands because I don't want to see him. I don't want to be seen. I don't want to be here.

I hear his cautious footsteps quicken once he sees me. Then I feel his arms around me, holding me tight to him.

"What's happening, Icelyn? What is it?"

The release I've been doing my best to suppress overcomes me, more intense because of my attempts to restrain it. I sob and can barely breathe. I still can't say anything. It's mortifying to break down this way in front of Adorane, but my tears are unstoppable.

"Where is Eveshone? Is she…is she…dead?" Adorane asks.

As soon as he says the words, I realize. It *is* like she's dead. Maybe even worse.

Adorane has given me a cold drink of water. He said the hydration might make me feel better. It hasn't. I feel just as terrible, only less thirsty.

We sit in the room where Torrain has been busy with the electrical equipment, which hums and whirs and combines to form a sound that I hate. The sounds are grating, terrible—they seem to come from another world.

"And she said she met…who? Her mother?" Adorane asks. He and Torrain take turns. One paces slowly around the room, concerned, while the other does his best to offer me comfort, and then they switch. A glancing touch to my shoulder, a pat on my hand. In a distant corner of my mind, I note that their awkward attempts at nurturing are endearing, although they don't relieve my suffering a bit.

"Yes, her mother."

"I didn't know Eveshone had a mother," Torrain says. "I mean, other than you of course," he scrambles to add, as if he can make me feel better or worse.

"Everyone has a mother, Torrain."

"Well, not bacteria. They split via binary fission. Or a blackworm—they just fragment until there are a bunch of new blackworms. Then there's the hydra, which just grows a bunch of little polyps that break off."

Adorane and I stare at Torrain until he gets the hint and trails off. I shake my head in disbelief.

"All I'm saying is that not everyone has a mother."

"Those are tiny invisible creatures, Torrain. Everything, you know, that you can *see,* that's a *real animal*—those all have a mother. That's what she's saying," Adorane explains.

He appears to accept the rebuke in silence and try to let the matter die. But then I watch as he struggles to swallow his words and cannot. He adds apologetically, like he really can't help himself: "Well, actually, the copperhead snake—and some other reptiles and birds and sharks—they can all fertilize their own eggs when need be. Not often, but sometimes. I read it! Icelyn, you were in that class with me. You read it too!"

I have to smile; as ridiculous as this is, I appreciate the diversion from my misery. "Torrain, all those animals who fertilize their own eggs are mothers! There may not be fathers, but they always have mothers. *Only* mothers!"

"Oh yes, I guess you're right. My apologies."

Were this a normal day, I'd relish Torrain's admitting I was right. But we have more important things to discuss. I take a deep breath and then find my words. "When Omathis and the others were living in the Drowned City, there was a rule that no one could reproduce. Why bring a baby into such a sad and terrible world? They believed it was a terrible act of cruelty."

"And look at us, risking our lives to figure out a way to have more babies," Torrain observes, pointing at the large screen behind him with the numbers and the shapes all rapidly changing. "We're the opposite of them."

"Maybe you could just listen for a while, Torrain? How's that sound?" Adorane says. Torrain clamps his mouth shut with visible effort.

I continue. "But Eveshone's father fell in love with another Anaghwin, and they had a child. Eveshone. Eveshone's mother was banished to the mainland, out of the Drowned City, and Eveshone never saw her. Until..."

The reality of what has happened crashes down on me again, and I choke on my words and cry. Adorane and Torrain both put a hand on me in an attempt to help.

"Until Eveshone met her mother here at the lab during the flood. And today, she left to be with her."

"Left...for...forever?" Torrain falters.

"She said it's where she belongs," Adorane answers grimly.

"Oh my goodness, Icelyn, I'm so sorry. I'm so sorry. I'm so sorry." It's all he can say, like he's gotten stuck in a loop. He sits down beside me. "I wouldn't have continued carrying on about polyps and copperhead snakes if I had known just how terrible you must feel."

Doubtful, but I appreciate his kindness. He holds my right hand gently in his and squeezes it gently, massaging it between his thumb and fingers.

Adorane sits down on my other side. He puts his hand to my head and pulls it toward his shoulder.

"You're her mother, Icelyn. We all know that."

"She belongs with me," I manage before I start crying again.

Neither of them says anything to try to make me feel better, because they know that's not possible. But they at least try to make me feel not so alone.

I feel as though I am possessed by despair itself, but it's nice to be close to both of them.

NOW

Eveshone ran toward the great upside-down triangle that had been notched out of the ridgeline.

That's where her mother had told her she would be waiting.

She was torn between the mother she was leaving behind and the one she was heading toward. She could feel the roots of neither, and she felt terribly alone.

"You're doing what you can," she whispered, trying to reassure herself, but it wasn't working.

Ever since she'd met the Priestess, she'd struggled through every possible scenario in her mind. How could she reunite with the mother she'd once had but lost, while keeping Lovely, whom she never wanted to lose? It seemed impossible. Every pathway she considered led to another dead-end. Her mind felt twisted, stretched, and trapped by the gulf between what she wanted—what seemed right—and what was possible. How could she keep both her Mother and Lovely? Every possible plan crashed into the cold reality of what the Priestess had said to her.

Without any kind of plan, all she could do was move one disconnected step at a time. All she knew was that she had to see her mother again. After that, she wasn't sure what would happen.

Gusts of scalding wind blasted into her and slowed her progress. She squinted against the heat and couldn't see through the tears that filled her eyes. With every step, she could feel Lovely slipping away. At one point the separation grew unbearable and she turned and ran back toward the shining tower. But then the pain of moving away from her mother set in.

She was being stretched between two distinct, deep, and piercing kinds of pain, and she could only avoid one. She turned back toward the upside-down triangle notched out of the ridge on the horizon.

Even if she returned to Lovely, she couldn't resist the pull toward her mother forever. It was inevitable. It was in her blood.

She ran again toward the horizon, with muted determination more than joy or love.

She had to see this through.

45

ICELYN

Torrain and Adorane have returned to their project in the lab. My sadness has outlasted their compassion, and they need a break. They continued to sit with me for some time, but I could tell they wanted to leave, so I insisted that they get back to their work. They didn't protest much.

Normally when they grow tired of me, I can still count on Eveshone to accept me. She always embraced me even at my worst, which kept me from being my worst for too long. She should be sitting next to me right now, telling me that she knows I am strong and brave—telling me all the things I want to be true, but fear are not.

But she's not here anymore. And now I don't know what's true.

In the mad rush of my breakdown, along with their enthusiasm for the sequencing project in the lab, Adorane and Torrain have left their bag of secretive maps and classified documents unattended in the corner of the room where I sit alone.

At first I feel too hollowed out to look through them, but then I pick up the bag and begin to sift through it. Anything to stop thinking about Eveshone.

I find drawings of a stone tower stretching upward to an impossible height. It's labeled "Apex." I like the look of this tower. It pulls at a part of my heart, reviving a longing that has been part of me since I was very young. I used to feel it when I looked down at the clouds that separated Mountaintop from Down Below. It was what drove me to tell Father, over and over again, that I wanted to go Down Below. It's a thirst for impossible and forbidden things. I know not everyone has this desire, but I seem to have a double portion.

I find a list of names on a page. The top name—seemingly the heading—sparks recognition in me.

Travis.

The name tickles some corner of my brain. Did my father once mention a Travis? I can't shake the feeling that it is familiar to me.

I look through the documents as closely as I can, willing myself to remember what I can. I see the lab we are in, and by comparing one map to another, find that it doesn't appear to be too far from Apex. Much of what I read I don't understand, but I try to commit the details to heart in case I need them later.

I put them aside. My head is swimming with maps of the desert, strangely familiar names, and sketches of stairwells, stone passageways, and water pulleys.

I'm walking in a dream wherever I go. Right now I'm outside of the gleaming tower lab, in the desert, and I cannot remember how I got here. I suppose at some point I made the decision to leave the darkened corridor where I've been wasting away in my grief, and with great effort stood and plodded here. But I can't remember any of that. My sadness is transporting me from one moment to another without any memory of how they are connected. The only constant is the lack of Eveshone.

The sun is gone, yet a low red moon illuminates my surroundings. I wonder if Eveshone is looking at this moon, too, and thinking of me as I am thinking of her. Or has she lost herself in the warm embrace of her mother—her real mother, the one she'd been looking for all along, even while appearing to be satisfied in my love for her.

The stars glimmer magnificently, and I am suddenly angry. Their beauty feels like a lie. Why pretend the world is full of wonder when in the end it all crumbles under the weight of despair?

I lie face down on the desert floor and greedily grab at the sand and rubble. I drop the dusty mixture into my hair and flick it on my back, overcome with a desire to cover myself with it. Even beyond that—I want to cover it with me, to *become* it. I thought I was bright and shining like a star, but now I see the truth—I am dirt and dust, nothing more.

Letting gravity press me flat against the earth makes sense. Only the weight of an entire planet can push back against the sadness I'm feeling. Only the whole world can absorb the loss. Only the vast globe can start to contain my unmapped emptiness.

"I am below the dust," I gasp, and tears fall from my eyes and mix with the desert grit to create little flattened cakes of mud. "I am low. I have never been lower."

A howling erupts from the darkness, and more join until a chorus of wild baying washes over me. I'm not sure if I've called these manic yelps of anguish into existence, or whether coyotes have timed their regular calls to my presence, but it feels appropriate to my grief.

I turn over and stare at the sky as I grind the salty mud cakes into my skin.

"I am below the ground. I have become dirt itself. I am not the heavens—I am the ground."

I say this, again and again, until the feral wailing ceases and I'm left alone in silence.

"What in the world have you been doing?" Adorane asks when he looks at me.

"Just…whatever I do," I answer, because it's true. I'm not guided by intent right now, and am often as surprised as anyone else to find myself doing this or that.

"You look like you've been rolling around in the dirt."

"It appears you are right."

I've returned to the main lab, where Torrain still busies himself with the screens and machinery. He glances at me and doesn't seem to be nearly as surprised by my dusty appearance as Adorane. "Oh, yes. It makes sense if you think about it. Probably for the best," he murmurs, returning to his work.

"I don't understand," Adorane answers him.

I don't either.

"It's nothing, just…you know. It makes sense to me," Torrain says, his eyes glued to the screen.

Adorane looks at me with concern. "Are you alright? Do you want me to find a rag or something to clean you up?"

"No, leave it be," Torrain answers before I can. "It wasn't an accident, was it, Icelyn?"

"No, it wasn't," I say.

"So you covered yourself with dirt on purpose?" Adorane asks.

"I did."

I sit on the ground and stare at a screen filled with falling numbers, shapes, and colors. Then I stare beyond it, just as I do with everything I see—because nothing I see matters compared to what I lack on the inside.

"You really think she's all right?" Adorane whispers to Torrain, as if I'm not in the room (which, to be fair, is half correct). "I'm worried she's losing her mind."

"She's been taken down a notch or two. Or a thousand," Torrain replies quietly. "And, like I said, maybe that's not a bad thing. You don't know what it's like, growing up a Cognate. Being told you're better than everyone else. And not just told, but *treated* that way—day in, day out from birth. It's hard not to believe it. And she was the daughter of the chief Cognate, on top of that. And a Brathius. And then she was told she's a god. Someone like that has no *choice* but to feel entitled."

Torrain says all this like it's an obvious fact that I'm entitled. Adorane nods in agreement. *Thanks, boys.*

"So she's...covered herself in sand and dirt in order to...be less...like Icelyn."

"Look, you know how she is sometimes. Whiny. Completely unable to see how you, me, or anyone else might feel about something. Demanding. Selfish. I mean, I can say all this because I'm often the same way. But at least I notice it now—mostly because you and the other Veritas point it out to me all the time."

Torrain and Adorane both chuckle.

"I'm telling you, we were both raised to not even be aware of it. To just live this way and not even acknowledge that we have it better. If anyone tries to point it out, they're scolded for being distasteful, launching an attack, unfair and rude. How can we expect her to be any different?"

I can hardly believe what I'm hearing. Is this how they talk about me when I'm not around?

"Do you really both think that's how I am?" I ask, barely able to get the words out. "Is this how you view me?"

They appear chastened; somehow they didn't think I'd been able to hear them.

"No, look, we love you very much. Everyone has flaws," Adorane stammers.

"Yes, and apparently mine are so atrocious that they are obvious to everyone," I say.

"Wait, no. Stop. You're much better than you used to be," Adorane insists.

I have to get out of here.

"I didn't mean that the way it sounds," he continues, desperate.

"Look, I'm not an enemy here! I defend you. I mean, sometimes people back in Mountaintop complain about you and I just tell them: 'Look, she's changed so much already! She used to be truly blind to the needs of others.' I'm on your side, Icelyn!"

This is a conversation I could have if I were in another state, but right now it feels like I'm stuck in the grip of a rapidly constricting snake. Their words are sharp and hot and strong, and I cannot be anywhere near them. I cannot bear to hear either of them saying these things.

I stand and head toward the door.

"I can't. I'm sorry. I tried, but I can't." I say, to them and myself and nobody all at the same time. "I can't."

I need to get away.

As I walk out of the main lab, I hear Adorane scold Torrain: "With everything she's going through, *that's* what you say?"

Torrain answers, "We were whispering. How was I supposed to know she could hear us? Should I go talk to her?"

"No, you'll only make things worse. Let's let her cool down. She's lost so much."

THEN

These were the finest soldiers who had survived the trip to Mountaintop. It hadn't been difficult for Travis to convince them to join the Salvation Shadow Group, or SSG for short. As he'd predicted, each was anxious, in their own way, for action. It's hard for a warrior to remain at rest when occupying a fragile perch above a world teeming with unseen enemies.

There was Earl Watters, a former marine who'd famously protected an entire transport for hours during the ascension.

Janelle Brookings, who had been an intelligence officer before the collapse. She was smarter than any of them, and they all knew it. She never lorded her intellectual superiority over anybody, which was only one of her many fine traits.

Matt Wellingsley, a self-described "tiny man" who used his diminutive stature to his advantage. "Imagine if a single ant were determined to kill you," he'd once explained to the group. "That would be terrifying, if you think about it. You wouldn't know when it was around; you could never be sure it hadn't entered your home. It could be devising plans while secretly tucked behind your left ear, and you wouldn't have a clue." The way Matt spoke of this assassin ant made everyone feel as if something were crawling on their skin. Travis wasn't sure exactly what position Matt had held in the days before the ascent, and when he asked the others, they told him he didn't want to know.

Aryan Sadana had worked in classified weaponry development before the apocalypse. Travis had never liked or disliked Aryan much—it was difficult to form an opinion. The woman rarely spoke, so it was easy to forget she even existed. However, Sean had vouched for Aryan, insisting that she be part of the SSG. "It'll be kind of like I'm along for the trip," Sean had said. That actually wasn't a reason for Travis to agree—the idea of Sean coming along on their expedition filled him with dread. Still, Travis knew from asking around that Aryan was particularly skilled at improvisational problem-solving. The nature of their mission guaranteed they'd need her.

Finally there was Maria Gonzales, who Travis suspected would equally enjoy both a high-level astrophysics symposium and an all-out bar fight. She was skilled with blades—knives, machetes, even swords. She loved them all, so long as they were sharp. The only reason Travis briefly considered not inviting Maria was that she clearly hoped to marry him one day, and that could make for some uncomfortable interactions. But it seemed worth it to have her on the team.

By now, Travis was one of the most respected leaders in Mountaintop —to be invited to do anything with him, even if in secret, was a great honor.

The group first gathered in the woods behind Brathius Tower. That was where Sean thought they'd be most likely to escape detection by Oliver Hailgard.

"But why must we hide this from Oliver?" Travis had asked. "Wouldn't it be better to have his support? To make this a known initiative? Why do all this under cover of darkness?"

Sean had discussed this with Oliver enough to know they'd face opposition.

"Oliver doesn't believe this is a viable path."

"Well, then, is it?" Travis asked. Oliver Hailgard didn't seem to be wrong often.

"Humanity can't flourish trapped up here, and there's no military path toward making it safe for us down below. This is all we can do."

Travis had been convinced by this logic. While Oliver was wise and kind and brave, after his traumatic ascendance and the birth of his daughter, he seemed content to consign mankind to this one mountain for the rest of time.

Travis would always consider Sean guilty of unforgivable sins: the creation of the monsters, the death of his mother, the refusal to take action against them before they grew in strength and number. Sean finally seemed to have a solution, so why not give him a chance to clean up the apocalyptic mess he'd made?

Plus, Sean was Laura Lee's father. As Travis had grown closer to her and seen the obvious affection she had for him, his aversion to the man had started to soften. "Oh, no—you don't know him like I do," she'd insist whenever he said anything negative about Sean. "He makes mistakes, but he has a good heart."

"I'll have to take your word for it."

"Yes, you'll have to. That's right." It wasn't a threat, but she wasn't joking either. To love Laura Lee was to at least *accept* her father. Her bond to Sean was too strong to tolerate anything less. Her preference would be for Travis to adore him, like she did.

Travis studied the faces of the three men and three women who had gathered at his request. Each stood rigid, their eyes trained on him, their expressions set and emotionless. Even with the fall of the previous government and demise of the military branches they'd sworn to serve, they'd maintained their professionalism and stoic fearlessness.

"I've asked each of you here because you are warriors. Before we go any farther, I need to make a request of you. You must not share anything we discuss with anyone else in Mountaintop. Not a soul. If you cannot make this vow, please leave now."

He waited as the others stayed where they were, staring directly at him.

"Have you made your decision?" he asked.

Each nodded and affirmed.

"Good. Now, second: Please understand that in this city, at this elevation, you are safe. I am asking you to shed that safety. I am asking you to face the exact kind of death we were lucky to escape when we traveled here."

They listened, their faces placid, as if he were only recounting a new method for honey extraction from the nearby hives.

"I think each of you sense, as I do, that we are trapped by this safety. That our shield is also our prison. But if you do not mind humanity being relegated to the top of this mountain for the rest of our lives and those of countless generations more, then again—you should leave. But if you're willing to leave this place and the safety that comes with it, then you should stay."

None of them flinched.

Travis was satisfied but unsurprised. This is why he'd chosen these six in the first place.

"So it's decided. Thank you for your sacrifice. Now, listen closely. And again: None of this can be shared with anyone else. We are, from now on, the Salvation Shadow Group. Here's how we're going to reclaim the planet for humanity again."

46

NOW

Eveshone grew shy as she approached the arrow-shaped notch in the ridgeline. She wished she could find a body of water to examine her appearance. Knowing she would soon see the Priestess made her worry about the way she looked, when normally she never considered it. She wanted her mother to know that she was beautiful. Probably more accurately, she wanted to know that her mother thought she was beautiful.

Like Lovely did.

Eveshone realized suddenly that she had never worried about this before because she'd always known she was beautiful in Lovely's eyes.

Eveshone pulled her fingers through the fur on her cloak and patted down her headpiece, hoping to make herself more presentable. She stood up straight and tried to project grace and poise.

"You're a mighty one," she encouraged herself. "You are her daughter. Of course she loves you."

When she said this last bit, she inwardly shrank. She hadn't admitted it to herself until now, but this was the core of her fear. She wasn't sure her mother loved her.

She crept through a slot canyon, nearing the place where her mother had told her to meet. As she grew closer, she slowed, finally freezing in fear. She wanted to run back to Icelyn, but it was too late for that. She'd made the jump; now all that was left to do was fall and hope for a soft landing.

She peeked around the eroded stone corner, just to confirm what she already felt.

The Priestess stood—rigid, tall and impossibly composed—waiting for her. Eveshone ducked back into the darkness. Did her Mother know she was there? Why was she so afraid?

"My daughter, leave the shadows. Let us look at each other in the light of day."

Her mother's voice echoed through the canyons, a force of nature like rushing wind, a crackle of fire, a roaring waterfall. Eveshone swallowed, inhaled, and walked out of the canyon toward her.

She couldn't be sure if she was walking as she normally did. *Is this how I walk?* It felt strange, almost pathetic, like she'd forgotten how to do it. She feared she looked disjointed, clumsy, and weak. The more she tried to walk with assurance, the more awkward she felt.

"Come. I'm filled with joy that you have made this journey," the Priestess cooed, and Eveshone felt something like comfort. She decided to focus on her mother's immense beauty instead of her own flaws. Losing herself in her mother, Eveshone could at least forget how strange she felt in her presence.

The Priestess took a few steps toward Eveshone. Something about the way she moved made Eveshone think of ceremonies and rituals—as if her every motion had been practiced and perfected, choreographed and polished. Eveshone couldn't imagine her mother deciding to break into a run and embrace her. It would be too chaotic and unplanned.

The Priestess stretched a hand out to Eveshone as they neared one another. Eveshone closed her eyes, bowed her head slightly, and leaned toward her mother's palm.

"Mother, how I've missed you," she said.

Eveshone hoped for a word, a touch—something from her mother to seal this reunion.

Instead, her Mother spoke. "I will give you a gift I've given no other." Though the idea of a gift should have excited her, Eveshone still felt only disappointment.

"Please do, yes," she replied. "Thank you."

"I will let you know my name. It is Barielta. To know it is to hold a part of me. I have given you some of my strength. Breathe not this word to anyone."

Eveshone didn't want to call her mother by a name; she wanted to call her "Mother." But she knew she shouldn't say this.

"I am forever grateful that you have shared this with me, Barielta."

Eveshone opened her eyes and looked up at her mother, whose face was impassive as her eyes darted back and forth, surveying the space behind Eveshone.

"And now, let us exchange gifts. Have you brought the Brathius girl, as I requested?"

Eveshone shook her head. "Please understand. I have considered your request over and over. It doesn't mean I love you any less. But I cannot." Her words were pinched and quiet, and Eveshone hated how they sounded, hated having to saying them at all.

Eveshone stared into her mother's face and couldn't recognize a single emotion, positive or negative. Just steely, serene composure.

"Of course," Barielta finally said, after a silence that felt like a lifetime. "I would never want you to do anything you don't want to do. Now, my daughter, let's make up for all the moments that have been stolen from us."

ICELYN

My mind won't string two thoughts together. It's a stick cracked in half, a rope frayed until it's a ball of useless fuzz. Nothing works.

I think back on every choice I've made: loving Eveshone, being Adorane's best friend, getting to know and adore Torrain. The adventures I survived with them all, leaving to be with the Anaghwin and Omathis. Each decision was right at the time; I'm sure of it. Each created a memory that I cherish, even if lingering too long over any of them hurts too much right now.

But I can see that each decision also contributed to locking me into a reality that now strangles me. It was inevitable. I don't know what I would change if I had the chance—and yet where I am now is all wrong. How is that possible? It's like filling a bag with a thousand delicious berries and then reaching in to find wasps and beetles.

What did I do wrong? It must have been something, because my world has descended into hell, and everyone seems to think it's my fault.

I'm a cascading mess of feelings without definition. My body is made up of unidentified unpleasantries: acidic stomach, fiery hot face, breath that stabs me inside and never seems to provide enough oxygen. I'd guess that my lungs had suffered a million little punctures, but I know nothing has happened to me physically. All my indignities are invisible. I wish something had beaten and knocked me to the ground. At least then I'd believe my hurt could be healed.

My thoughts return to Adorane and his insistence that talking to his god acts as a balm for his distress. There was a day when speaking to me would do the same for Eveshone.

Eveshone. Eveshone. I have lost her. And along with her, I have lost myself.

Who else would know how this feels? Who else has experienced such profound loss? I think of my mother and father and feel a pang of guilt. I left them. Could they have felt like this? But they imprisoned me and doubted me! They forced me out of Mountaintop. They certainly didn't work to make it a place I would want to stay.

But still, yes, I wronged them. Some part of our fragmenting was my fault, even if much of it was theirs. I wouldn't wish this pain, this impenetrable darkness, on anyone in the whole world. *I'm sorry, Mother and Father.*

I need to climb. If I can't lift my spirit higher, then at least I can lift my body. This is a curious logic, but it makes sense in my weakened state. I scan my surroundings. Ahead I can see stone slabs rising from the desert floor, crooked and jagged, like badly formed teeth stretching toward the sky.

I make my way there slowly and pull my heavy body up, one painful stone grip at a time. Lower temperatures have arrived with the darkness, and my fingers are numb. Still, though it hurts, I find relief in the effort to rise. My pulse pounds in my ears, drowning out my negative thoughts. With each pull and push I lift myself closer to the summit and get a better view of the desert valley below.

As I near the top, the winds pick up and punish me with frigid indifference. I'm tempted to take it personally, but the winds would be doing this whether I was here or not. I'm the one invading this space—not the other way around. I'm the one making this choice, not the wind.

Somehow this makes me feel better. *My choice, my consequences.* With one final heave, I exert my last reserve of energy to flop my tired body onto the rocky peak. I lay flat against the craggy platform, feeling the icy hard stone beneath me.

Now that I'm here, I know why I've worked so hard to reach this spot.

Why are you here? I hear a voice say.

A voice—that's not quite right. It's a voice formed both inside and outside my head at the same time. I can't hear it, not in the way most people hear sounds, and I could very easily ignore it if I liked. Now that I notice it, it's almost as if it's always been around; perhaps I've spent most of my time up until now ignoring it, if I'm being honest. That's how I know it's not my own thoughts, although it feels similar—I can't ignore my own thoughts, even when I try. This voice I have to work hard to hear at all.

Why are you here? the voice asks again. The question is not forceful or urgent in any way—as if it is a gift for me, and nothing is to be gained or lost for the voice whether I answer or not.

Because I have to be somewhere, unfortunately, I answer, *and this is the most miserable, dark place I could find, so I decided to be here.*

Yes, good answer, the voice replies.

I'm not sure it's good, I respond. *It feels like a place to die. The end of something.*

Or the beginning. Perhaps they aren't so different, being born and dying, the voice responds.

I'm confused, though a part of me wants this to be true, because all I've been feeling lately is death.

Seeds grow in darkness first, below the ground, where it's wet and cold and lonely, the voice explains. *Seeds are laid in the grave before they can live.*

But I'm only getting deeper below the ground. Plants grow up towards the sun, not down, I reply.

Right and wrong, the voice whispers. *You think that because you only see the part that grows up—but you aren't seeing everything. Plants grow up and down: half up into the light and half down into the darkness, deeper and deeper. Always in both directions.*

And they fall over if they don't go deep enough into the darkness. They topple right over, I reply.

As I say it, it brings me a measure of comfort. Maybe all this pain and darkness isn't pointless. Maybe I'm being buried so that something can grow tall.

You know what you must do, the voice says.

I do.

THEN

Petals from the matilija poppy. Dried blades of the agave plant. Crumbled manzanita tree bark. Sticky stalks from the bush monkey-flower. Freshly plucked hummingbird sage. Coastal chaparral ground roots.

Travis mixed the herbs into water until he had created a thick greenish-brown sludge. He added clumps of dirt to the concoction, then pounded a sheet of gray slate with a hard chunk of granite until it was ground into dust. He then stirred the slate dust into the soupy mixture.

Sean Brathius entered the impromptu workspace they'd set up in a shed behind Brathius Tower. He handed Travis a plastic bottle—the kind he'd seen filling grocery stores and spice cabinets every day before they were forced to travel to the top of the mountain. It almost seemed fake—completely out of place in the world they now lived in.

"I found some cayenne pepper. Bill Johnson had some, if you can believe it."

The previous month had been a whirlwind for Travis, and for the first time in ages, he felt engaged with life. He and the SSG had developed multiple strategies. How could they descend without being detected? How could they place and prepare the serums?

Travis mixed in a dash of the cayenne pepper. Sean scooped a dollop of the mixture and sniffed it, then tasted it. "Perfect. This should correct the flaws of earlier iterations."

Travis applied the thick poultice to a dummy—an effigy made of human clothing and stuffed with dried leaves and grass, like the scarecrows used on farms when humans lived down below.

Sean wrote while Travis continued to slather the mixture onto the dummy.

"*Anti-Scent Detection Initiative, 31st attempt. Though the creatures outside the Wall left the 30th iteration alone for two days, eventually the covering wore off and allowed the threats to detect the human scent. They attacked the dummy. For this round, we've increased the dosage of pungent herbs and added cayenne pepper to the mix.*"

Sean examined the past dummies, which were labeled with ascending numbers from Trial 1 to Trial 30. Something angry had inflicted great violence on them.

They attached a lengthy rope made of vines to the foot of the latest dummy.

They carried the dummy to the Wall and tossed it over. It flew a hundred or so meters before coming to rest in a small clearing. Then they waited and watched from atop the wall.

Not sensing any activity for hours, they tied the vine to the wall and returned to Mountaintop.

Sean and Travis worked to contain their excitement. They'd thought they'd cracked this code many times before and never had. Still, even from afar, the appearance of the vine gave them hope.

It hadn't been chaotically pulled one way or the other, as it had during earlier rounds.

Travis pulled at the vine. They watched closely as the dummy slid through the underbrush. Once it neared the wall, Travis let out a tiny celebratory whoop. It hadn't been touched by anything.

Despite the dummy consisting of clothing worn by humans, the mixture had kept the creatures from smelling it for three days. Their finely tuned ability to detect the scent of man had been blunted.

Sean was businesslike as they pulled the dummy back up the wall. He inspected it closely. "There's no sign of Croathus activity. Now, this may be a false positive. We should complete more rounds of testing to ensure that our results are consistent."

Travis shook his head. He had waited long enough. "No. Thirty times the dummy was torn to pieces. This is no accident. We figured it out."

"Yeah, but what does it hurt to test it a few more times?"

"We've tested it thirty-one times. We embark on our mission in the morning."

47

NOW

"Look at this, right here," Torrain sputtered, jabbing his fingers toward the cascading colors, numbers, and shapes. "You see it? This isn't right at all."

Adorane looked appropriately studious but said nothing.

“I must be reading something wrong." Torrain opened a nearby cabinet. He pulled out ancient books and started rifling through their pages. "It doesn't make any sense."

"Hey, be careful," Adorane warned, as some of the brittle aged pages started to tear and disintegrate. "These books are hundreds of years old. Be gentle."

Torrain dropped the volume he'd been looking through and turned back toward the flow of data. "Why aren't you as freaked out as I am, Adorane? These are Icelyn's results. This is her DNA."

They stared at the current of charts and numbers. Finally, Adorane broke the silence. "Maybe I'm not understanding exactly what has upset you."

Frustrated, Torrain pointed to one of the jumping multi-colored charts. "That's Eveshone." And then to another one. "That's me." Finally, to a third. "And that's Icelyn. Now do you see it?"

Adorane's eyes widened as he compared the different data flows. "But, that doesn't make any sense, Torrain."

"Where is Icelyn?"

"Still wallowing in the shadows."

"We need to find her."

Eveshone examined her reflection in a chunk of polished marble hanging on the wall and thought to herself that she'd probably never looked more beautiful in her entire life. She wished Icelyn could be here to see her, but she immediately put that thought out of her head. It would lead to tears, which would smudge the crushed powders Barielta had applied above her eyes.

When she was a pup, Eveshone would often daydream about her mother. She'd imagine grand scenarios involving this woman that her father wouldn't talk about and she couldn't remember. Her mother was a great warrior, traveling across the land and protecting all the other women who had been banished for love! Her mother had journeyed to a faraway place and was now the ruler of a distant land, where there was peace and happiness and food and dancing and song. Her mother was trying to figure out where she and father were so that she could join them and they'd be a family once again.

The fantasies she'd manufactured were humble compared to this reality. She walked out onto a stone balcony hundreds of feet above the ground below, following her mother, both of them dressed in the finest clothing Eveshone had ever seen in her life. Their dresses were made of an unbelievably soft and shiny material called silk—which was made by insects, as if by some kind of enchantment—in blues and reds that recalled a brilliant sunset over the ocean. Eveshone cloak and headpiece had never been so clean, as Barielta's servants had scrubbed them until the fur shone like a sunrise.

"We are the beginning and the end, my daughter—the sunrise and the sunset, the water and the fire, wrath and mercy, birth and death and rebirth," Barielta said to Eveshone as they basked in the cheers from the howling Croathus packed below.

Another regal creature joined them and stood on Barielta's other side. This was the one who they called Amperous, Eveshone knew, and it seemed to her that he and Barielta shared a bond. Eveshone was drawn to him, and yet she felt a sharp resentment burn within her at the sight of him. Barielta was her mother—and the wife of her father, forever, even if he had passed. At a base level, Eveshone knew there should be no place for Amperous here.

Eveshone also recognized Amperous as the creature she had ambushed long ago to save Icelyn. He hadn't yet realized she was the creature who had bested him in battle, which was probably a good thing. Amperous didn't seem like the kind of creature who enjoyed being reminded of his failures. Eveshone decided to keep her secret to herself.

Barielta lifted her arms in triumph and shouted, "The Priestess of Two Temples and the Lord of Both have been joined by my extension, my reflection, my amplification, my magnification, the hope I bring to this world made into flesh—my daughter, Eveshone, the Heir of All I Am!"

Eveshone was overwhelmed to hear the titles Barielta bestowed upon her. She hoped she could live up to them—and somehow, the way Barielta said the words made her believe she could. The desert floor shook with the roars of Barielta's followers. Eveshone had long dreamt that her mother was a warrior and a queen, but now she realized that she was even more than those things. Barielta was the hope of all the Croathus, and she had invited Eveshone to be part of the new world she was building.

ICELYN

I have learned from my past mistakes. Before when I took off on my own, I was thirsty, hungry, and defenseless. Not this time.

Torrain and Adorane were so caught up in their science experiments that I snuck through the labs easily and put together what I needed.

Gallons of water, as much as I could carry. Dried rabbit meat and cactus pulp from our inventory. And finally, one of Torrain's terrible inventions: the ultraspear that eviscerated Eveshone.

I feel disloyal even holding this wretched weapon because of the pain it brought her. But she left me. Normally she would protect me on this journey, but she's not here—and I need something. I clutch the spear, and if I'm truthful, it feels good in my hands. I can tell just by touching it that Torrain has put much care into carving and polishing the wood. It's no replacement for the defense Eveshone would provide, but it's better than no weapon at all, or the simple carved stick I'd be using otherwise.

I'm tired from carrying the water but thankful because the activity warms me despite the frigid cold desert night. Looking back, I estimate that the lab is at least two miles behind me, though it's hard to tell out here. With flat ground stretching as far as the eye can see, faraway things can seem very close. Still, it's been a long time since I left the lab, so I hope I'm at least that far.

I also took their maps—despite the secrecy they shrouded these documents in, or maybe because of it.

The moon's brightness makes consulting the maps simple, and I'm grateful to see that one shows me the way I should go using the time of year and constellations. The stars were always one of my favorite topics of study back in Mountaintop, and using them to figure out where I should be going feels like a treat. Up in Mountaintop, my life was so small that I never needed to use the heavens—I could always figure out where to go next by just looking down at my own feet. Now my world has grown bigger.

I push through my exhaustion to keep a brisk pace, and the pain in my lungs and legs masks the ache in my heart, which is still reeling from the loss of Eveshone. I'm leaving behind Adorane and Torrain, too. And I still haven't recovered from abandoning Omathis.

But there is a freedom here that I've never felt before in my life. I am, at last, completely alone. Like a seed pressed deep into the dirt.

I arrive at a workable rhythm as I press forward. The soft crunch of my feet on the desert floor, the constant breath as I strain for more air, the thunder of my heartbeat in my ears. *Thud thud,* in out, pound pound. It's a loop, hypnotic, soothing. I lose myself in this repeating pattern until I forget about anything else.

But this only lasts a moment, because every few seconds there's another trigger that ignites my longing for Eveshone. The scent of flowers that she and I once picked and joined to make crowns. The sound of a rabbit that she would have chased, pegged, and then freed and let scurry away. It's not fair. When you love someone, you invite them into every moment and every thought. But then if they leave, your every moment and every thought become wounds, torn open, uprooted and exposed. Loving someone is seamlessly weaving them into yourself. It's not a process that's meant to be undone.

I'm losing the stars, so I scan the horizon to identify other landmarks on my way. It looks to me like Apex is just beyond a jagged mountain ridge that resembles the plated back of an ancient lizard. Like a dragon sleeping. Once I make my way through and over that final obstacle, I'll get to shove myself down deep into the darkness and see whether roots sprout.

I'm not excited at the prospect of visiting Apex, yet I crave an end to this trek across the desert. Now that the sun has risen, it bakes my skin without mercy. I stop often and drink too much of the water I carry. My progress is slow, and my body aches. My eyes sting from a constant flow of sweat that no amount of hand swipes can slow.

I do see a swift jackrabbit, two bobcats, a large turtle, and countless lizards, though. So it's not all misery and loneliness. The desert, as I have heard, can be peaceful at times.

But it can also be cruel. The vast expanse, the rocks, warped and cracked and jutting into the sky, the winds—constant and welcome when it's hot and dreaded when cold. The plants look like they were invented for another planet, evolved in a world that plays by different rules than ours. Even the trees are unrecognizable, like drawings made by someone who once heard what trees were but forgot most of the details. They are angular where normal trees gracefully bend, sprouting into bulbous bunches instead of leaves, their roots exposed above the ground—as if they are so thirsty for water that they can't be bothered to take the time to search beneath the ground.

I sit below one of those strangely formed trees, picking angry barbs out of my forearm. The desert appears welcoming from afar, but as soon as you actually touch the landscape, you end up with needles lodged under your skin. "Kind of like my relationship with Adorane," I mumble to myself, chuckling.

Actually, my relationship with anyone—given enough time.

I take one last gulp of water and force myself to move on. Otherwise, I might be tempted to just lie down in the sun and join this curious, cruel place permanently.

THEN

This was a night when Laura Lee was tempted to believe in fate, joy, and magic all over again, like she had when she was much younger. The death and loneliness she'd faced since had flushed most of that optimistic idealism out of her, but the rosy vestiges that stubbornly remained made themselves known on evenings like this.

The stars overhead shimmered like jewels. When she was a child, and living in the city with her father, she would be lucky to see ten stars in the reddish gray sky, muted against the millions of man-made lights below. Now those artificial lights had been extinguished, a nice byproduct of the horrors she'd accidentally unleashed. There had been a sky full of twinkling stars all along, but they'd blinded themselves to the sight.

It was strange. Humanity had for ages been inspired by the skies—to be better, smarter, to reach higher—and then used that inspiration to invent technologies that obscured their original muse. Against the fluorescence of convenience stores, the blinking red, green, and yellow of traffic lights, the blinding headlights from bumper-to-bumper traffic, the flashing of high-pressure sales billboards, and the garish nighttime searchlights advertising events, the magnificence of the night sky didn't stand a chance.

The clouds were thick and smooth as they hung close to the mountain, making their peak feel like a lonely island in a vast ocean of white. The fog rose and fell in gentle slopes, like waves frozen mid-crash, with swirls of currents and tides illuminated by the bright white of the moon above.

Laura Lee closed her eyes and then opened them slowly. She asked herself if this was her actual waking life or if she was dreaming. You could not tell from the looks of the world around her. If someone claimed that in fact she'd died in her sleep and was now wandering through some kind of spirit world, she wouldn't be able to disprove it. But she loved this feeling. It was part of the reason she'd made these nighttime excursions a routine: a little dream world was exactly what she needed.

On these nights out, she'd walk along the outskirts of Mountaintop. Sometimes she'd stare at the clouds and imagine the world they'd left behind. Sometimes she was attracted to the sparkling wonders above. Tonight she was surprised to see the torches still burning in the woods behind Brathius Tower. It was so late. Though they had no working clocks anymore, she felt it was only hours before the sun would rise.

Father had been meeting with Travis and others often these days. None of them would admit what they were doing, but their secrecy didn't bring her any fear. Whatever they were up to seemed good—she was sure she'd approve of their plan, if only they would share what it was.

Her life felt better when Travis and Father were sharing in anything—a meal, a laugh, even a conspiracy. Travis had many reasons to hate Sean Brathius. Laura Lee appreciated that more often than not, he tried not to. She knew Travis did this for her.

Laura Lee waited outside the woods, keeping an eye on the shifting orange glow from the fires. She didn't want to miss Travis emerging from his meeting with her father. Not because she wanted to force him to tell her what they were planning—she had a sense of what they were doing anyway. It had to do with the creatures they'd left behind. It had to do with the world below. Travis was being brave. Sean believed that whatever they were planning could be their key to escaping this haven and returning to their rightful homes around the planet.

She didn't need anyone to tell her these things. Her father was feeling them strongly enough for her to intuit. That's the way things were for her and her father. Though their bond wasn't as strong as it had been when she was young, ever since the calamities below she'd been able to divine his slightest mood as easily as if it were her own.

After waiting for what felt like an eternity, she finally heard the crunch of sticks and leaves underfoot. She grabbed the basket of wild raspberries she'd gathered and stood in the middle of the path.

Travis blinked and scolded himself for seeing only what he wanted to see. But she was still there, standing in the moonlight, against the inky black sky lit up by a thousand stars. She held a basket of berries toward him, as if making an offering.

Laura Lee. Considering the dangerous mission he and his team were about to embark upon, he felt silly about being nervous at the sight of her. Yet she was wearing her nicest cloak, and her glacier-blue eyes shone under the lunar light. Even though he'd seen her a million times by now, he had never grown accustomed to her beauty.

"I found a sweet batch near the twisted trees and thought maybe you'd like some," she said casually, as if they were meeting by happenstance—even though it was long past sunset, and all normal people were fast asleep.

"Ah, sure. I'd love some," he replied, and took a tentative handful before placing one berry in his mouth. He chewed with surprising unease. His mouth was dry.

"I know what you're planning with Father," she whispered.

"He told you?" Travis asked.

"No. But I know anyway, even without anyone telling me."

Travis believed her. That's how they were.

"I know you're doing it for me," she said.

"Not only for you," he protested.

"Mostly. Primarily. Predominantly," she argued. "Are those enough adverbs for you?"

He smiled. "You know I'm not fond of adverbs."

"I *staunchly* believe you *completely* suspect that they *unnecessarily* clutter up *normally* clear and *easily* understandable conversations," she responded playfully.

"And I believe you've made my point for me." He wanted to ask what she was doing here. He wanted to hold her close and kiss her. But he'd learned long ago that the way to interact with Laura Lee was to give the best of himself and accept only what she gave freely. She'd never tolerate him taking anything that wasn't freely offered. He'd initially been frustrated by this, but now he could appreciate the gifts she did give, instead of only longing for what she didn't.

"When do you leave?" she asked, her eyes searching his face.

"At sunrise."

She gently put the basket down and took a few steps toward him until they stood closer than was proper or precedented. She placed her hands on his shoulders.

"I'm sorry for making you wait so long, Travis."

"Wait for what?" he asked, feigning ignorance. His heart pounded in his ears.

"I've known for a while now that you're special. That you're worthy. I mean, you've proven it. And I know you've had countless opportunities, but you've waited. For me."

"I don't understand. Are we talking about the berries?" he replied, smiling, though he knew exactly what she was talking about. "I've waited for what?"

"For this," she responded, before slowly placing her lips on his and wrapping her arms tightly around him.

48

ICELYN

Most surprises are terrible. You expect fruit to be sweet, but it's bitter. Or you think you've found someone who will always be with you, and she leaves you.

But who could have expected that this rocky lizard-back mountain would contain a miracle? I thought I'd be climbing through dusty rocks —instead, I find myself lying in a cold, clear, deep creek. Underneath a waterfall. And there are tiny gray frogs watching me, croaking and chirping, cheering me on. One jumps and lands on my knee. It stays there and looks up at me, and I've never felt more validated in my entire life.

I'm surrounded by green—actual trees, bunches of them—and I'm wondering whether I should simply stop and make this place my home. Why not? I could be the strange woman who lives in the canyon. I could drink this water, and mix mud and herbs to create special potions, and forget all about Mountaintop, Eveshone, and Omathis. I could forget it all and focus on this frog and the rest of frogkind.

As if on cue, the frog hops off of my knee and away from me. I feel scolded. The truth is, I don't want to forget about those I love anyway—even if I'm not very good at loving them.

I dip myself back under the water, and then I work to refill my ultralion skins. I'm fortunate. I didn't ration my drinking properly, but now it won't matter, because I'm filled to overflowing again. Maybe it's not so bad to live without prudence sometimes. Maybe this oasis is here because I drank all that water, and I needed it, so it appeared.

There it is again—that noise. I thought I might have been imagining it earlier, or confusing a gust of wind for something more substantial. But I hear the sound of something solid and large.

I saw sheep with large curled horns earlier, drinking from a pool of water. Maybe it's just one of them.

But there is a fear lodged in my roots, in that deep place where Eveshone and I would once effortlessly connect. It's a dark shadow that I can't shake.

No sheep could produce this feeling.

I stand and gather everything, clutching the ultraspear close to my chest. I should be moving on anyway. Icelyn, Strange Woman of Frog Canyon is a phase of my life that will have to wait.

I'm being followed.

Normally, I would be unable to contain my delight at the cascades of water pouring through smooth worn stones into clear pools. Yet I note these wonders without excitement. In fact, the water has become an annoyance to me—every splash and gurgle masking sounds I'm eager to hear. Cracking twigs, crunching underbrush, breathing.

Something is following me. More than one thing. And from the stagnant, rotting smell that now fills the canyon—along with the growing dread lodged in my roots—I'm afraid I know exactly what they are.

Don't worry, Icelyn. They won't hurt you. They can't hurt a Brathius. It's contrary to their nature, I tell myself. *Once they realize who they are stalking, they will flee.*

Still, I hold the ultraspear tightly, pointing it in the direction of any snippet of sound.

"I am Lovely Brathius, daughter of Sean Brathius!" I shout. Why wait for the creatures to figure out my true nature on their own? Might as well give them as many clues as I can.

The subtle sounds of pursuit stall, and I wonder if I've warded them off.

"I am not human," I declare, "but a Brathius. You cannot hurt me!"

My words echo, but the only response is the gurgling of the creeks and crash of the falls. Maybe I'm so tired that I've conjured up this scenario where I'm being tracked—when in actuality I'm alone with some sheep.

But then, in the midst of the unnerving silence, three Croathus emerge from hiding. They were so close all along. They are twenty feet away. I thought I'd been evading them this whole time, but with a cold fear I realize they have been in control of this encounter from the start.

They appear malnourished—their skin dirty and sagging, their eyes a dull version of their normally vibrant icy blue. I can make out their bones, and they hunch over, in stark contrast to the regal, graceful way a Croathus or Anaghwin normally stands. While the sight of them conjures terror within me, I'm also overcome with compassion for them.

"My dears, let me help you," I plead. "What has happened to you?"

They study me while sniffing deeply. I can feel the first thawing of the dread in my roots, and realize that they are feeling the same.

I can connect with them. This is the first fruit of the harvest, I realize. If I can Soothe them, then they will be the first of countless.

"Come to me. I am Lovely Brathius, daughter of Sean Brathius. I am your god, your creator," I say, my words flowing forth like a melody.

Oh they are beautiful. Beneath the matted fur and the sallow exterior, there is a light that glows through. I can see it.

THEN

Tamar glided through the woods outside their newly constructed round. She didn't need to light a torch. She knew the way by heart—she'd walked it countless times in the darkness.

When she found Oliver Hailgard, he was sitting on a fallen log, staring up at the sky, as he always was. He was not awake, nor completely asleep either, as she'd expected. He was in that halfway place where he spent most of the night.

She placed a blanket around his shoulders. His skin was cold to the touch. Since his sleepwalking had become common, she'd insisted he sleep in thick socks, so at least his feet weren't as frozen as they'd been before. He almost lost a toe one night due to frostbite.

"Ollie, let's get back to bed," she whispered with trained gentleness. "I miss you beside me."

He nodded, soothed by her voice. But then his brow furrowed in distress, and he slapped at his forearms. "Stop it!" he shouted, over and over, slapping away at imagined attackers. "Leave me be!"

Tamar placed a firm reassuring hand on his arms and stopped his flailing. "Let me look at you," she urged. He held him arms straight and Tamar noticed scratch marks all over the underside of his forearms. He was clawing at himself again. It hadn't been this bad in some time.

"I'm going to treat these scratches," she promised, while dabbing at some blood with her own shirt. "Then let's get some more sleep."

"I can't stop it from happening," he whimpered. "Even when I know it's happening, I'm frozen. Unable to say or do anything."

Travis raised a fist above his head in silence. His team didn't need any further urging—they'd been training their attention on him and also froze, huddled in the shadows of the narrow natural walkway that snaked between massive boulders.

They held their breath as they witnessed a pair of massive shadows dash through the underbrush only twenty yards ahead. Travis held his rifle tightly, though he knew the bullets would make little difference if they were discovered.

The poultice had gotten Travis and his team through Cloudline without harm. They hadn't seen a single creature while in the soupy white. Travis would have been tempted to believe the monsters had cleared out, were it not for the countless mangled scarecrows they'd used as tests during the development of the covering.

They'd broken through the last of the thick fog and entered the world down below for the first time in years.

Travis let what he was seeing in the distance seep in. The buildings below were still intact, except for a few cracks and crumbles, and they were eerily silent and abandoned. Foliage and undergrowth had started reclaiming the developed areas and camouflaging them from easy detection. He identified a neighborhood where fire had consumed many houses, leaving charred husks of the homes they'd once been.

Travis and the team made painfully slow progress, ensuring their cover with every methodical step. While they hoped they couldn't be smelled, they knew they could still be seen.

He watched two monsters rushing through the woods ahead, seemingly oblivious to their presence, and he wished his team were equipped with more of the miniature rockets that had made a difference against these beasts during the ascent.

Travis got the sense that the creatures were young, and that they were playing a game. For some reason, this was scarier than if they'd been marching or performing lethal drills. It reminded him of Omathis and Amperous, all those years ago, tossing their ball and pouncing on one another. They murdered all of humanity, and now they busy themselves with a leisurely game of tag.

After the creatures cleared out, Travis and his team waited an hour before moving again.

Maria unrolled a ragged map of the city, with locations marked.

"Supplies for batteries will need to be located, mixed, and verified first," Aryan Sadana, their chemical expert, explained. "Copper, zinc, and acid."

"Auto supply stores are here, and here, and here," Maria noted, pointing out the locations. "Construction supplies here and here. Medical supplies here. We'll need to hit them all."

The locations were far apart, and visiting all of them would require marching more than fifty miles in total.

"Are we planning on splitting up, or do we have time to stick together?" Janelle asked, though with her tone she made it clear that moving as one team would take far too long.

"It's not like there's security in numbers anyway," Travis said with a grave tone. "If any of us are discovered, we'll die. They'll kill six as easily as they kill two. There's actually a better chance someone succeeds if we split into teams. Matt and Janelle, you hit the medical supplies. Aryan and Earl, I want you to visit the Home Depots and Lowes. Maria and I will handle the auto supplies."

Maria stole a glance at Travis as if he'd just asked her out on a date. He knew she would, but he had to split the group up this way anyway. It was the smartest mix of personnel.

"We'll meet back here by tomorrow, dawn."

The plan was simple: Activate six massive diffusers throughout the city so that Sean's serum would vaporize and fill the air.

The diffusers needed energy to operate, as well as a timer. There was complex engineering involved—but with Sean's instructions, in combination with Aryan, Maria, and Janelle's knowledge, that wouldn't pose much of an obstacle.

Once everything was prepared, Sean and Laura Lee would summon the creatures to one concentrated area at the base of the mountain. The diffusers would release the airborne serum, which would act as a natural trigger to rewire the creatures. Just like fire can act as an environmental trigger for certain plants to release seeds, Sean had explained. That's how he'd built them. This was always how upgraded behaviors and abilities were to be installed.

Once enough of these creatures were rewired, the new instinct would spread to all of them, because they were networked like computers. It would be like a virus wiping out an entire bank of connected servers—only in this case, the virus would be good.

And then, Sean promised, their inbred hatred of humanity would be gone, replaced with affection. The murderous horde would be transformed into defenders as loyal and protective as guard dogs.

The plan was simple.

Yet as Travis and Maria crept through the shadows, entering decaying buildings for cover, taking great care to avoid the many beasts that roamed the city, Travis began to doubt the elegance of their strategy.

Hanging from nearly every high place—phone poles, the sides of buildings, bridges, *everywhere*—were the skeletal remains of humans. They were on display like Christmas decorations. The creatures had made this into a city of bones, one that celebrated massacre and death as other places had promoted community and human achievement.

Though he knew they should be moving toward the auto supply stores, Travis stalled. He watched the skeletons swaying in the breeze, hanging from electrical wires like pearls on a necklace.

Sean doesn't know, Travis thought to himself. Up there, above the clouds, atop his tower. He's blind to what they truly are. They can never be loving and loyal.

Travis began to devise another plan.

NOW

Another Croathus bashed against Eveshone. It was hot and scary. But wonderful. She'd never felt she was a part of anything before—not like this. She and her father had been cast out alone, on the edges, never in the center. Even in the Drowned City, Icelyn had loved her, but she knew the others only tolerated her. She was never part of them; she couldn't be trusted. She'd heard these things whispered about her.

Now, in the circle of celebration surrounded by large fires stretching toward the heavens, Eveshone was pressed in by masses of Croathus desperate to see her, to touch her, to tell her they loved her.

"Heir of All I Am, look at me!"

"Eveshone, we adore you!"

"Barielta's Reflection, touch us with your outstretched hand!"

Eveshone was drunk on the unending flow of acceptance and desire. She danced to the heavy rhythms the Croathus created as they stomped on the sandy ground, swayed to the haunting harmonies their howling combined to form, and allowed herself to be lifted from the ground and passed from one creature to the next. She was cherished, she was held, she was the object of their desire. With one touch or glance she could bless each of them, change their lives.

Barielta no longer mingled with the masses—they had no access to her—so the chance to commune with Eveshone was a spiritual breakthrough for those who fervently followed the Priestess. Most of them had only seen her from a distance, high above on the balcony. Now they could feel the warmth of Eveshone's skin and inhale her scent as she embraced them one by one.

Some Croathus fainted from the experience; others shook. Some sobbed loudly, and others wept quietly. All were touched. Eveshone was frightened by their devotion, shaken by how much she meant to them. She never wanted it to end, but at the same time, she feared she would be lost in it.

Maybe that wouldn't be such a bad thing, though. Even if she lost herself, at least she'd be lost in the center of something for once.

49

ICELYN

The creatures step toward me. I am not afraid. I reach my hand toward them. "Let me Soothe you. Come to me, my children."

They incline their heads toward me—an invitation to touch.

Just as I'm about to touch the first, her eyes focus on me, and we share a gaze. It's the last piece of affirmation I need—she is mine, and I am hers. I'm going to be able to turn the Croathus. I have no doubt.

But then she shakes her head, like a dog trying to dry itself. The warmth that was growing in my roots—the tender connection between us that I thought was inevitable—reverses. In its place, I suffer first unfathomable coldness and then an unrestrained hatred.

"No," I stammer. "I am Lovely Brathius—"

The creature swipes at me and hits me hard. I feel like I've been knocked completely out of my body. I fly backward, and my head smashes against a boulder. I note with detachment that my shoulder is bleeding. I don't notice at the time, because the impact from the strike is so brutal, but the Croathus' claws have cut through my clothing and sliced my skin.

"I am a Brathius," I weakly insist, but it only riles them up more. I have always believed that no Croathus could kill me intentionally, but I now realize that these creatures have certainly acquired the ability to do so. And the desire.

They surround me, and the crack to my head makes everything seem a second too late—like I'm perceiving the echo of reality, not reality itself. I still have enough of my wits to realize that I need to grab my ultraspear, which had been jostled out of my hand. I point it at the creatures.

I was about to Soothe them, and now I'm threatening them. It's a shocking turn of fortune. *Most surprises are terrible.*

"I don't want to do this," I plead with them through my tears. "Please, leave me alone. I am a Brathius, and I love you. I don't want to do this."

They stare at the ultraspear, and I hope they'll retreat. But instead, the middle creature charges me, her talons flared, ready to tear me open and let me bleed out. I close my eyes, thrust the spear toward her, and can immediately tell that I've hurt her. I open my eyes to see the point plunged deeply into her abdomen. It doesn't look like a normal spear tip going into her flesh—it looks as though it's burning hot, as if she's made of melting snow.

The Croathus screeches in misery, and falls onto her back. I pull the weapon out of her, but the damage has been done—and it's growing. What damnation did Torrain invent? The flesh and muscle and sinews and organs contract and rot, a black void growing as the creature writhes in pain.

The other Croathus look from their fallen friend to me and my spear, and their eyes fill with fear. "I didn't mean to do this," I try to explain. Whatever had overtaken them and turned them into beasts that would kill a Brathius, has now departed and left them the creatures who I nearly Soothed.

"Come, let's revive her before it's too late," I invite them. But instead they flee, crashing into the woods, damaged and terrified.

I'm left alone with the deteriorating creature. I throw the spear down and place my hands on what's left of the beast's flesh. I try to summon a Soothing, anything that might be able to stall the spread of decay and death. But there is nothing. I can feel no connection to this creature.

She is dead. I have killed her.

The animal skin's scent nearly causes me to faint, but I pull it off of the dead Croathus and wrap it around myself. I don't know if I'm vividly imagining or tapping into this departed creature's memories, but I can see the Croathus, long ago, when she first wore this head and fur. She was brimming with pride—she'd stalked the beast for weeks and finally bested it. It was a glorious amber brown fur at the time, and it was crowned with the fearsome head of a bear. The Croathus had revealed a brave, fearsome part of herself that day as she pulled on the cloak.

And now I'm cloaking myself in the essence of this Croathus who I've killed. It's nearly too heavy to carry, especially as the sun grows fearsome and bakes the day. But I took this Croathus' life, and I can't leave all of her behind to dissolve into dust. I owe it to the creature to carry some of her with me, to never forget, to let this dramatic journey into the darkness matter. To remember. I have killed.

My thoughts burden me more than the bearskin does. I didn't only kill the Croathus, no. In that one stab, I lashed out at Eveshone, Adorane, Torrain, Mother and Father, Belubus. I can say that it was in defense; the Croathus attacked me first.

But that wouldn't be entirely truthful. Because this is what I've been doing all along—using everyone else's slights and mistakes to justify my own small steps toward becoming who I now am. *A person who will stab the one she loves in order to preserve herself.*

I've done it to all of them. I can see that now. Some things only become clear when you're stained with blood and wandering through the desert, I guess.

I'm awash with panic because now I see it plainly. I am all alone, and what's worse—my solitude is my fault.

There is no place where my heart can land. It's been treading water for ages, floating and flying, trying it's best to keep from crashing, always with the hope that there will be a place where it can comfortably touch down. Now I see. There is no place—not in Mountaintop, not in the Drowned City, nowhere. Because I have plunged the poisoned tip deep into everywhere and everyone, and they have all suffered decay from the point of my impact. Had I led the Croathus better, they would not have attacked me; had I not alienated my friends and family, I would not be alone. My own choices have brought me here.One step ahead of another I trudge, and wonder how long I've been walking. It could be minutes, or hours. I'm pretty sure it hasn't been days yet, because I don't remember any darkness of night or any new dawns. Then again, now that I think about it, even that is in question. Perhaps there *were* sunsets. Was there a morning or two? It's all been a blur.

I have to remind myself to drink. My thirst isn't enough of a prompt. I have to force myself to stop and rest—my exhaustion doesn't send a loud enough message. I trip over a rock because I didn't have enough strength in my legs to lift my feet high enough to clear it.

I'm grateful for the tumble, as it jars something loose in me and tears form in my eyes. "I'm so sorry," I say, and I can't tell if I'm being loud or quiet. "I'm sorry to everyone, for everything. For who I've been, what I've done, who I've not been, what I've not done. Everything I've thought.

I'm so sorry."

I don't know how long I do this, but by the time my words start to fade, it feels like it's all I've ever done. I see a green-yellow worm bug chomping away at the leaves of nearby flowers, voracious and unstoppable. I can hear its mouth biting and chewing, and swear I can see the grub getting bigger while I watch.

I look farther and see that every flower that grows from the desert sand holds its own green worm, some more than one. All biting nonstop, all chewing.

"No!" I shout, and I swipe at the nearest worm, sending it soaring through the air and tumbling to the ground. "Stop! Leave them be! Let something beautiful stay, for at least a little longer!" I knock another worm from its eating place, and another. "God, are you so hungry that you can't take a break? Eat half as much! Let them stay for a few moments more!"

I kick and hit countless more worms away from the flowers, but I could spend a year doing this and make no difference. There are too many worms, there is too much hunger. I can see that. So I give up.

My tears flow again—or maybe they've been flowing this whole time, and I've only now noticed them again. I can't tell if it's from the worms, or from the mess I've made of this world, but now I'm confused as to whether there's even any difference between me and the places and people I love and the worms and their hunger for the flowers.

It's all terrible, and it's the kind of problem that I suspect can only be solved in a place beyond words, on a plane beyond thoughts and feelings. Honestly, I fear that no such place exists.

"I'm sorry," is all I can moan, to the flowers, to the world.

Finally, I rise and continue on my way toward Apex.

NOW

Eveshone sat by herself, struggling to piece together the last couple of days in a way that made sense. She was invigorated, that much was sure. She had to remind herself to take deep slow breaths, because otherwise she reverted to quick inhalations that made her pulse quicken and her skin burn. She'd been through a gauntlet of senses—smells, touches, sights, sounds—all new, unlike anything she'd ever experienced. Now she craved silence. She found it squirreled away in her room, in the metal-plated tower that Barielta had built to house the Mothers.

The Mothers. Barielta had introduced Eveshone to them earlier, in a ceremony that had shaken her. She felt a piece of her heart being pulled toward each of them, but not in a wondrous way—in a way that hurt. It felt like the Mothers were grabbing and yanking at her, each fighting for a piece, not caring how it felt or what damage they did.

"You're home," Barielta had said to her, "among those from which you flow, the headwaters of your existence."

Barielta often used words in tricky ways that forced Eveshone to replay them again and again in her head to understand what was being said. She did feel home, that was true. But in a way that wasn't comfortable. In a way that made her miss Icelyn and her father and even Adorane, if that made any sense.

"Come," Barielta had beckoned. "Join yourself to them." Eveshone followed her mother obediently around the inner circumference of the tower, from one alcove to another, greeting the Mothers. Barielta bowed, and Eveshone did the same.

Barielta said, "To the source of who I am and the author of my story, I submit," and Eveshone repeated after her.

Each Mother barked or growled or shook in acknowledgement.

"Oh *Leo,* oh *Urse,* oh *Aquila,* oh *Dohnii,* oh *Formicae,* oh *Acinonyx,* oh *Verspertilio,* oh *Porifera,* oh *Lupine:* We surrender to your greatness and adore you for building us in your mighty image."

Barielta chanted this over and over, her voice growing in passion and volume, until Eveshone felt pressured to join her. She could see that Barielta was pleased by her participation in the ceremony, so Eveshone started chanting louder, with more fury, more like the Priestess. It felt chaotic and scary—but good, even as it terrified her that she was slipping out of control.

Now, though, thinking back, Eveshone felt incomplete. She wondered if maybe a piece of her heart had been plucked away and left with the Mothers. The ceremony had hollowed her out, like there had been a spark inside her that was no longer glowing.

A knock on the door shook Eveshone from her thoughts. Panic shot through her body. She wanted to be alone. There was too much left unresolved in her heart and her head. She felt exposed.

Another knock. Eveshone knew it had to be either Barielta, who she feared would force her into participating in another one of her ceremonies, or Amperous, whom she didn't want around. Those were the only Croathus who were allowed on this highest level of the tower.

Eveshone had never realized before that it was lonely in the center of things too, just like it had been on the outskirts. Especially at the highest level.

Another knock. "Eveshone, it's me," the words came through the door.

Amperous. Eveshone was surprised to find that she was relieved. Though her Mother treated her with love, Eveshone had started to fear their encounters.

"I'd rather keep to myself for now, if that is acceptable to you," Eveshone replied, trying her best to treat Amperous with the respect she knew Barielta would expect of her. Yet she had no desire to speak to Amperous, who she now knew was a brother to Omathis. Amperous had peppered her with question after question about Omathis' well-being and whereabouts. He wouldn't accept that she didn't know and didn't want to speak of it.

"I am here not for me, Eveshone. Barielta has sent me to summon you."

Barielta. Amperous knew the Priestess' actual name? The Priestess had told her that it was a secret only Eveshone knew. *Did she lie?* Eveshone pushed the thoughts out of her mind. She didn't want to think anything negative about her mother. She didn't dare to.

Eagerness and fear flowed through her. It felt good to be wanted, even if the creature wanting you made you feel uneasy—especially once their encounters were over. While Eveshone was spending time with her mother, she felt entirely consumed—possessed even—by her presence, and she could only figure out how it had gone afterward. Like deciphering a dream after you've woken up.

"Yes, of course," Eveshone answered and rushed to the door. Fortunately, she hadn't changed out of her fine outfit, so she didn't need to waste any time making herself presentable for the Priestess. "Let's go. I don't want to keep her waiting."

Eveshone followed Amperous up the circular stairs which led to the Priestess' chambers. She sensed the same hesitation in him that often settled into her when preparing for a meeting with the Priestess, and for the first time felt a small connection with him.

"I'm sure the meeting will be good," he said, and she wondered why. Had she somehow made it clear she was nervous? "Barielta is, in her essence, loving."

He didn't sound like he believed it, and she felt a chill. "I believe so, yes," she replied. It occurred to her that they were both lying to one another, and both knew it. She wondered why they bothered.

"And in that love, there is a power. Don't forget that. It is that power that will save us all—you and me included."

"That power," Eveshone started, thinking it through, unsure of what to say next. "Do you think that power is the reason I feel the way I do? Because it's so strong, and so…" She trailed off, but Amperous picked up on her thought.

"It's so powerful that it scares you," he said in a low voice.

"Yes." That was exactly it. That's why she feared meeting with the Priestess—because the Priestess had a love so strong and tough that you couldn't help but fear it. "Thank you, Amperous. You've helped me."
Amperous bowed slightly, and then he opened the door to Barielta's chamber.

50

THEN

They'd been lucky so far. All the creatures they'd seen had been otherwise occupied. Most busied themselves cleaning recently hunted animals. Other younger ones played boisterous games. Yet most of the beasts sat stone-still in the sunlight, staring at nothing in particular. Many even slept, though it was long before night would fall.

Travis thought about how many predators in the animal kingdom spent their time in this way too—stationary for the most part, resting until they needed to move. Confident in their superiority. Only humans felt compelled to be busy every minute of the day.

Every auto supply store they'd checked had been undisturbed. This was predictable—the beasts would have no use for spark plugs or windshield wipers—but still worth celebrating.

They stocked up on the materials they needed. Whether for diffusing serums, as Sean wanted, or for the other purposes that were starting to form in Travis' mind, they'd still need multiple energy sources.

As the sun set, a rumbling arose in the streets like a distant storm gathering. Travis placed a hand on Maria's shoulder, and she got the message. They crouched together in the darkness of what had once been a popular eatery and waited.

Through the window, they saw the source of the noise—creatures moving in one direction, almost as if they were one organism. They climbed to reach higher ground, seemingly desperate to get a better view of something. They were craning to see the mountain where humans now lived—to stare at their improvised, cloud-swaddled home.

Then, the beasts slowed and stopped. Each seemed frozen, stretched toward the mountain like trees reach for the sun. They seemed hypnotized.

Travis suspected he and Maria could walk openly among the creatures and remain unnoticed.

He picked up a chunk of concrete rubble and prepared to toss it outside into the street—right where a horde of the creatures had gathered.

"What are you doing?" Maria whispered, while grabbing his hand.

"Testing a theory," Travis answered, and pulled his arm free. He threw the concrete and it skidded to a stop just inches from ten of the creatures. His heart pounded, but his instinct proved right; none paid the disturbance any attention. They stayed transfixed by the mountain.

The mountain where the last survivors resided.

The mountain where Sean and Laura Lee Brathius lived.

At sunset, Travis thought.

Sunset.

It all made sense now. And his new plan seemed more possible than ever.

Though very few knew the nature of their mission, Travis and his Salvation Shadow Group enjoyed a heroes' welcome upon returning to Mountaintop. Doors throughout the village were opened to each of them, and families begged them for the chance to provide a warm meal in gratitude.

Travis appreciated the response, but he only cared about one person's reaction to their mission.

He and Laura Lee had decided, just before he left, to marry in a secret ceremony. Laura Lee wanted it to be only about her and Travis. Sean would be the only other person in attendance, and he would officiate, too.

Yet as she worked on the plans, Laura Lee had realized this was selfish. The Kith would want to see their darling Laura Lee marry. It was a chance to bring their people together, a shared experience that everyone would remember. They'd suffered through enough death and loss. It was only fair to give them a taste of new life and joy.

Laura Lee often thought about fresh starts. That was a silver lining to the horrors down below. Now they had a chance to rewrite traditions and carve new pathways to use in the future. It was almost dizzying, knowing that they were inventing the cultural norms that their society would someday take for granted. Centuries of religious and cultural practices had been washed away in a swift river of bloodshed below, and now it all had to be replaced with something new and pure and lasting.

As she prepared to marry Travis, she recognized that many of the choices she made would set the template for future wedding ceremonies.

Her first decision was that the dress she wore would not be white. That tradition was rooted in obsolete conceptions of femininity—that woman were objects to be used and that men should want their women unsullied as freshly fallen snow. Men, of course, could wear suits black as night. She'd always disliked the double standard.

So she and Travis designed their outfits. The same pieces of fabric would be used in both, because their lives would grow together like the roots from two nearby trees. She fashioned a crown for him out of materials from the mountain, and he did the same for her. Those crowns were surprises for one another on their wedding day—a chance to show that they would always protect and cover one another with care and forethought.

"I've chosen to adorn your head with yellow lilies. To me, you are the warmth and light from the sun. I've woven the lilies with white sage, for I value and will lean upon your wisdom for the rest of my days. Finally, I've chosen to add the herb known as fragrant everlasting—because your presence in my life is a sweetness I hope will never end," Laura explained as she placed the crown on on Travis' head.

Those gathered at the wedding sighed. Afterward, bouquets of lilies, sage, and fragrant everlasting would become a popular part of any courtship.

Travis produced a leather and fur hat and plopped it on Laura Lee's head clumsily. "It's… a… raccoon I killed… because it'll keep you warm." Laura Lee crinkled up her nose and shook her head gently, weighing the value of his offering. "I'm not sure I completely understood the ritual," he said quietly, with regret.

Travis' face broke into a wide smile as he plucked the hat from her head and tossed it to the ground. "You really think that would be my head covering? Please, give me some credit." The entire gathered village laughed loudly.

Instead, to everyone's relief, Travis' crown for Laura Lee was made up of lavender because she sweetened the world, wild raspberries because she was multi-faceted and complex, and honeysuckle because her love spread and made everything better.

Travis pulled a sharpened knife from a holster on his leg and used it to cut a piece from his outfit. Laura Lee cut a scrap from hers, too. They tied the two fragments of leather and cotton together in a tight, ornate knot.

"As these pieces from two worlds are now joined together as one entity, so shall we be one from this day forward, while still retaining what made us individuals in the first place," she spoke.

One side of the gathered Kith began to sing a simple song, on cue.

"May the melody of your life be joined to the harmony of mine," he replied, as the other half of the Kith added their own refrain to that of the first, creating a haunting symphony of voices. "Two beautiful songs joined to create something that will stir our hearts and carry us through the joys and sadnesses of a life together."

He dug a hole into the dirt and dropped the tied fragment of fabric into it.

"Until we enter into our rest below the ground together, and our children carry our mixed uniqueness in their individual selves, and their children carry more duets of harmonies and melodies—again and again, from now until the end of time."

Laura Lee dropped a mound of dirt onto the hole and patted it down with her bare hands.

"In this way we will become eternal—by passing ourselves on, both individually and blended with the one we love, from one generation into another, forever and ever."

"You know how you and your father often end up at the drop-off around sunset? And you stare at the clouds, as if you can see through them and into world below?"

Laura Lee froze. She and Sean never discussed this strange habit they'd both developed—born of unexplained yearning. She didn't want to discuss it with Travis. He'd never understand.

"No, I'm not bringing it up to criticize you. Not at all. I wanted to tell you that when I was down there—*they* do the same thing. Only looking up. I think in reaction to you."

His words caused her heart to sink in her chest, as if she'd betrayed a loved one. She blinked away tears. She'd never imagined they were all staring back at her and Sean, down there, but it made sense. Of course they were. The yearning she felt at sunset was too deep to be unrequited. She'd tapped into something shared, communal, and terribly sad. She'd experienced not only her own sadness, but all of theirs, too.

"Well, that's sad," she finally replied, unwilling to express her true feelings about this revelation.

Travis held his tongue. Was it so sad, really? These were murderous beasts. He knew that better than anybody—his mind repeatedly replaying the images of skeletons swinging from high points all over the city down below like trophies. Why waste an ounce of sympathy on Croathus beasts because they looked longingly at a mountain?

And who knew exactly what they were longing for, anyway? Laura Lee believed it was for a reunion with herself and Sean. Travis suspected it was for another taste of human blood.

Yet Travis wasn't going to say any of this. Laura Lee and Sean would always believe that there was some essential goodness in these monsters. They hadn't seen what he'd seen down below. He knew the truth, but also knew there was no way to convince them that they were wrong. Sometimes you have to accept someone's blindness and figure out a way to love around it.

"Yes, it is sad. But it could also be used to protect us while we're down there."

She shuddered at his reminder that there'd be another mission. She'd begged him not to go again, especially with their little one on the way. But he'd never wavered. He was essential to completing the mission.

"They were oblivious to everything around them while they stared up at the mountain," he explained. "We could complete our work down there with ease if you and Sean could just try to distract them for hours each day instead of minutes."

She understood. "If it means you'll be safer, we'll stay at the drop-off from sunrise to sunset. We can take rotations if we have to, to maintain focus."

He held her hand and felt a twinge of guilt. She and Sean had no idea what they'd be helping him do down there. He hoped they'd understand someday.

It was the only option.

ICELYN

I resign myself to taking three times as many steps as I think I will. This is a place where space is stretched beyond comprehension. My eyes are fooled over and over again.

How far away is the tower? Only another mile at most.

I thought that hours ago, and yet I appear to be no closer than before. Three times the distance. Three times the exhaustion. Three times the effort.

The less that fills a barren landscape, the harder it is to tell where you are in relation to everything else. That's true in the desert, where I see very little to give me any idea of my progress. It's true of my heart too. Since it's only me, I have no idea how I'm related to anyone I love anymore. Am I close? Estranged? Forever entwined? Hopelessly divorced?

I don't know. Maybe I never will. So I focus on the steps, because I know they're taking me toward the tower. That's all I know right now, so why worry about anything else?

Finally, the mindless rhythm pays off, and I've grown unquestionably closer to the massive stone tower—close enough now to notice the majesty of its construction.

I can't believe humans built this. It consists of massive boulders carved out of the nearby mountains and stained with a variety of dusty browns, reds, and yellows so that it blends perfectly into the desert landscape. Then, as it stretches toward the sky above, the stones' colors shift from the sandy shades to first gentle and then darker blues. This is why from afar I could only see a slight disturbance in the straight lines of the desert horizon—the tower is, by design, nearly invisible. Unless you're looking for it, the eye naturally tunes it out.

But the ingenious camouflage is not the most impressive attribute of this tower. Rather, it is the sheer height. It's taller than anything I've ever seen—taller than any of the skyscrapers in the Drowned City, even. I look to find the top, but it's lost in the gleam of the sun and the blue of the sky.

I walk around the thick base of the monolith, searching for an entrance. Completely circling the foundation takes a long time, maybe even half the day, and I still can't find anything that looks like a door. No ladder, no stairway.

No traces of humanity, except for a massive stone monument to their genius. Nothing else.

I secure all my belongings to me, fastening the ultraspear on tight. Since there is nothing about this place that feels welcoming, I have a feeling I may need it.

I begin to climb.

At first my ascent is slow. It's been a long time since I've climbed up the skyscrapers in the Drowned City. Then my body is reminded of its training, and I can see the path upward. I spot the stony holds to grab with my hands and the minuscule ledges I can push against with my feet.

Before long, I reach a height where a fall would cause serious harm. This is an accomplishment, but it's not one I'm inclined to celebrate. I have no idea how much farther I need to climb, my fingers are sore beyond soothing, and every muscle in my body is screaming out for rest. My shoulder is throbbing where the Croathus slashed me. And I'm high enough now where I could die if I make a mistake.

About a hundred feet above me, I see what looks like a nook where two boulders meet. I head toward it and find that it's just big enough for me to fit inside, if I curl up tight and small. I jam the ultraspear in between the boulders above and below me, creating a diagonal safety bar to keep me from falling out once I fall asleep.

This is the most secure I've been in ages, a clenched ball pressed between two massive stones. It's shaded, which means the surface is cool on my skin. I watch crimson red and violet streak across the sky before they fade to black.

No one in the entire world has any idea where I am right now. And I don't know where anyone else is either. I sense no connection to Eveshone, to Omathis, no union in our roots—and none to all the other Anaghwin or Croathus, either. Adorane and Torrain seem more like memories than real people. If I weren't able to smell my own skin and feel the pain of a scratch on my forearm, I would feel more like a memory than a person even to myself.

Do I exist? Does anyone? The answers to those questions barely seem to matter anymore.

My exhaustion feels like a relief from my pain. I hope to fall asleep quickly so I can escape my thoughts.

51

THEN

Travis played his guitar as he and Laura Lee sang.

"It's the end of the world as we know it, and I feel fine!"

Kith members danced and lost themselves in the music. Those who weren't flailing or twirling stood entranced. They were enjoying a release tonight—years of dread were finally giving way to optimism. They didn't know the details, but they knew something important and good was going to happen soon. The community hummed with excitement.

The final preparations had been made. Unlike the first mission, this one wouldn't be embarked upon in secret. There was no use in trying to keep anything confidential. The entire community had been aware of the SSG's absence during the first mission and celebrated their return. The next departure was a constant topic of conversation.

Though no one knew why they were leaving—that much, at least, had been kept confidential—this time they made sure to commemorate their bravery with a feast. Tonight, each SSG team member had been given a place of honor in the village green. Kith members bestowed their meager treasures upon them—pies, flasks of winter rainwater, polished stones, and even objects from down below, like forks, spoons, and paintbrushes.

Travis finished the song, and the crowd roared. There was something desperate about their joy—like they needed to feel it, inhabit it, grasp it tightly, or else it might give way to a despair that waited just below the surface.

He set aside his guitar to groans. But they'd already played three encores, and he was finished. He pressed his face against Laura Lee's, inhaling the smell of her hair. She'd long ago devised a blend of dried flowers and herbs that she sprinkled on her long brown locks, and the result was as intoxicating to him as it was comforting.

"I'll be back. We'll sing together soon," he whispered. "That's a promise."

"You'd better be, or you'll be in trouble. I'm not planning on raising a child alone."

That evening, Travis was crowded by well-wishers, true fans, and grateful devotees. He laughed most of the attention off—it seemed ridiculous—but Laura Lee had explained to him that hero worship gave the community hope, so he played along.

One interaction stuck with him. Earlier in the night, Oliver Hailgard had pulled him aside. "You got a second?"

Travis had been waiting for this. Oliver had ignored him since his return from the first mission, which was curious. Of course the man would want to know what they'd been up to down below. He'd also want to know why he hadn't been invited. Travis had expected open aggression, curiosity—anything but total silence.

Yet Oliver's entire existence had become wrapped up in Tamar and their infant girl, Highberry. Travis often spotted the three of them playing childish games—pretending to be kittens, rolling down hills. Oliver had permanently retired from being a warrior. Travis thought it possible that the man was now too distracted to care.

"I know what Sean thinks you're doing down there," Oliver confided once they'd left the bustle of the celebration behind. "I also know you're going to do something different."

Far from not caring anymore, Oliver had somehow unearthed the biggest secret of all. *How did he know?* Travis struggled to keep a straight face.

"Our mission is confidential, Oliver. You should understand."

"I'm not here to discuss the details—only to tell you that there is a future here. Sean doesn't see it, and that's why he believes he has to meddle more down below. But we have a life here. All of the Kith. And it's good. Don't do anything to disturb it."

As Travis struggled to formulate a response, Highberry ran from the celebration and grabbed her father's legs. "There you are!" She shouted, laughing. "Were you hiding? Because guess what? I found you!"

"Don't mess with this," Oliver pled in a low voice. "It's fragile, and it might not be what Sean wanted. But it's good."

ICELYN

Ow! I'm pulled out of a dreamless slumber by an explosion of pain in my left hip. What is happening? I'm exhausted, slow to transition from the peace of sleep to the harsh pain of waking. Part of me wants to close my eyes and pretend this isn't happening.

No. Another terrible impact, this time to my shoulder, which already hurts terribly. I open my eyes and see what hit me—an oval-shaped gray rock, polished and smooth, probably half the size of my head, and attached to a stick with tightly coiled twine. The stone lifts back toward the sky, and then crashes down again. I dodge just in time; it only glances off my thigh, but even the slight blow hurts.

"Stop!" I shout. "Stop doing that!" The stone momentarily hesitates where it is, as if confused about what it should do next. I grab my ultraspear from where it's wedged between the boulders and swing it hard against the stone. I knock the stick from the hands of whoever is holding it, and the devilish weapon falls toward the ground below.

My hip, my leg, my side, and my shoulder throb with pain, and my skin is hot to the touch. I can already see the bruises forming, purple spreading beneath the surface of my skin. Still, I'm fortunate my ribs were spared. There don't seem to be any broken bones.

I peek angrily out from my tiny pocket in the side of the tower to see who is attacking me. I stick my spear out and swing it around in a threatening way, in case they have a second weapon.

I see nothing.

"Why are you attacking me? I didn't ask for a fight. But if you insist on one, I am dangerous," I declare. The words flow out, not feeling like my own, but I realize with a flush of confidence that they're true. I have recently killed a Croathus. Nobody should assume they can meddle with me without consequence.

"I thought you were a Threatbelow," a voice responds, after a long stretch of silence. "You look like a Threatbelow."

I am still cloaked in the bearskin that the Croathus wore until the moment I killed it. *Fair.*

"Well, I'm not."

"Yes, I know that now."

I lean further out from my opening in the tower wall, hoping to catch a glimpse of whoever I'm talking to. It's a boy's voice—that much I can tell. He sounds young, like he's only recently become a man. The way he says his words is odd, like nothing I've ever heard. Like they're slippery, and sliding around in his mouth, slow to come out.

"Show yourself, please," I plead. "I promise not to hurt you if you vow the same."

After a small eternity, where the owner of the voice weighs the wisdom of revealing himself to me, a head extends out from inside the tower, about fifteen feet above me.

I like this boy's face. He's around the same age as I am. His eyes are brown and warm, and the edges of them point upward like a smile. There is something about the way he looks that makes me want to trust him right away. I struggle against my instincts.

"I'm Dronmer," he says. "Lowest of the low, on the bottom tier of Apex."

"I'm Icelyn Brathius, formerly of Mountaintop, more recently from the Drowned City."

Dronmer's face grows serious. "I've been commanded to knock you from your perch so that you crash to the ground and die," he informs me. "And since I am the lowest of the low, I must do as I'm told, even if I think it would be a mistake to obey."

The way he so kindly and openly lets me in on his murderous mission somehow puts me at ease. I should probably move away from him—but I have an ultraspear, and his weapon has fallen far below.

"You couldn't knock me from my perch even if you wanted to, and I don't believe you want to," I reply.

"Yes, that is right," he responds.

We stay silent, puzzling out our next moves.

"Dronmer, what do you say we both vow *not* to attack each other? This agreement would be a mercy on my part, not yours, as I am the one with a spear, and you have no weapon. You show me the way into this tower, and we promise that together we'll figure out what to do next."

I watch as Dronmer considers my proposal. He seems to like it—he's no doubt curious about me and would love to let me enter the tower so we can talk further. Even as we precariously cling to the side of the tower, there is a chemistry between us. I'm intrigued by him, and I sense that he is mystified by me.

"My command is to knock you from the tower to the ground, just as I am to do to anything that tries to climb it."

"And you tried to do that, and I knocked your clobber stick to the ground. *Now* if you try to do that, all that will happen is that I will knock *you* to the ground. You will die, and I will still enter the tower. So let me enter the tower with you. The only difference will be that you're alive and I won't have to feel bad for killing you."

"Yes, your words make sense," he finally declares, after another lengthy deliberative session. "Climb up to me."

As I prepare my belongings for another climb, Dronmer shouts down: "Why do your words sound so strange? What are you?"

"Your words sound strange to me, too," I answer. "But I promise that I'm human just like you."

"No human sounds like you," he responds, and I get the sense that he genuinely doesn't know what to believe.

I climb slowly, due more to caution than difficulty. There's a part of me that believes I can trust Dronmer. But just in case I can't, I don't want to make it too easy for him to obey his orders and flick me from the side of the tower.

"Why do you wear the skin of a monster?" he asks simply. It's not an accusation, just curiosity.

I'm about five feet below him. I stop, because if I get any closer, I'll be close enough for him to touch me.

"Because I killed a Croathus—"

“A what, now?” he cuts me off.

“A Threatbelow,” I respond, though I don’t like to call Croathus and Anaghwin such a nasty word. “And it didn't seem right to leave this out to rot away." I figure since he asked the question so simply I should answer it in kind. Plus, it wouldn't hurt for him to think I'm lethal—and anyway, I remind myself, it’s the truth. "So I'm wearing it to honor the beast that I slew." I sound more dramatic than intended, but it does the trick. Dronmer is impressed.

"You killed one of them? I didn't even know they could die."

I take advantage of his stunned admiration to finish the climb and join him on a small ledge near a square opening in the side of the tower. Now, even if he wanted to wrestle with me, he would have no leverage.

"They can't—not really. At least, they barely ever do. But I killed one. I know how."

"They're going to want to talk to you," Dronmer exclaims, his face breaking into an uncontrollable joy. "And they're going to be real happy with me for finding you. This is the kind of thing that gets a boy off the bottom tier."

Due to Dronmer’s strange manner of speaking, I can figure out what he's saying, but only after thinking about it for a while. His vowels seem either stretched out or compressed, while his consonants are either chopped in half or dropped all together. It's disorienting, but it has a strange, slow quality that I like.

"Well, I'd be honored to raise you up from the lowest tier, Dronmer."

He opens a small metal portal and squeezes headfirst into it. From the darkness within, he beckons to me to follow.

Dronmer tells me I must lock the portal door behind me. When I comply, we are plunged into darkness. The passageway we lie in is so narrow that I have to slither—there's not even enough room to crawl.

Dronmer navigates the suffocating chute as if it's the easiest thing in the world. I can't see a thing, but in the time it takes me to wiggle a couple of yards, I can hear that he's advanced far beyond me. "Come on now, stay with me," he urges, his voice distant.

"Wait, if you will. I'm not used to traveling through such constricted passages. Do all citizens of this place enter and exit through these?"

He laughs aloud, as if I've told a joke. "Nobody enters and exits Apex." His laughter is so boisterous that I join in. Of course nobody leaves Apex—just like nobody leaves Mountaintop.

"And the snakeholes aren't for everyone," he continues. "Just us on the lowest tier who have to keep a lookout for intruders. They're tiny on purpose, so nothing big and dangerous can get in if we fail in our jobs."

The way this sentence actually sounds is "*so-ah naot-in' beeg n' 'angeroos kin git 'n,*" which is why it takes me a while to translate what he's saying, let alone respond.

"Follow my voice," he beckons, his laughter echoing through the darkness. "You might be good at hunting, but you're pretty slow in the snakeholes."

"Are they called snakeholes because there are snakes, or—"

"No, just because they're kind of like the holes that snakes live in, you know, down on the ground. I've never seen one—just heard stories of them. Have you seen one?"

I squiggle forward in a workable (though slow) rhythm. At least I'm making progress. I might also be much slower than Dronmer because I'm still carrying food, water, and my ultraspear, along with the bear skin. That's not ideal for slithering through a snakehole.

"I have seen them before. Many of them, actually."

Dronmer gasps. I've impressed him. He is clearly easily impressed—

but still, I'll take it.

"I cannot believe I'm talking to someone who has been on the ground," Dronmer muses excitedly. "Someone who has killed a Threatbelow. A great hunter. You're like a hero from a story! Like a great warrior who shows up to save the day."

I decide that I like Dronmer—and not just because he has a very high opinion of me, though that helps. He seems to be the kind of person who wants to have a high opinion of everyone, who would rather like than dislike someone. And those kinds of people are rarer than you'd expect.

I follow his voice until I see the first hint of orange firelight flickering on the stone wall of the snakehole. Finally, in a slow burst of sweaty exhaustion, I push myself forward into a spartan stone cell. It's only about as wide in any direction as double my height, if that. When I stand, I don't bump my head on the ceiling, but I don't have to reach to touch it, either. There are no windows. There's a heap of shredded cloth that might be a bed. A chunk of sandstone serves as a chair. I only know this because Dronmer sits on it.

"Welcome to my home," he says, and I feel sad for him, because I detect pride in his voice. I don't say it, but this is a prison cell, not anywhere someone should be happy to live.

52

ICELYN

Dronmer rummages through a chest in the corner of the room, agitated. It looks like everything he's ever owned has been thrown in there without thought or organization.

"Of course I want to get you to visit with the upper tiers—oh, they're going to be so excited to see you. Yes, they will. This might be exactly what I need to move up a level or two. Can you imagine?"

His obvious glee at having found me, and what that might mean for his station, makes me hope that I do turn out to be the key to his social ascent. I'm tempted to tell him not to get his hopes up too far. The last time anyone looked at me with such unhidden adoration, it ended in heartache. *Eveshone.*

"Listen. Just, maybe—slow down a little," I start. "I mean, I'm bound to disappoint you and the upper tiers. Everyone, all the way up and down this tower."

Dronmer laughs as if I'm joking. "Oh, right. You're draped in the skins of a Threatbelow, and you're bound to disappoint. Sure. Anyway, I've got to introduce you. To keep you hidden here would be impolite. We're all trained to be exquisite gentlemen in Apex, and to greet our visitors with hospitality."

"You tried to fling me to my death."

"That was my order. It was not personal. I'd rather we tried our best to move beyond that, please. Now, what did you say your name was again?"

"Icelyn Brathius, from the Drowned City."

"Never heard of it. Never heard of you. But that doesn't mean I'm not going to share my daily ration of water with you. Now, there's not much, so you tell me: Do you want to drink it, or do you want me to wash your body with it as an act of welcoming?"

"I think I'll drink it."

"Your choice. I do want you to know that I am considered one of the best bathers in Apex. Strong hands from all the climbing means I can really give a good scrub. That's the only reason I have all these fine possessions and this spacious room, even though I'm a lower tier. I'm sure you were wondering."

I wasn't, and now I have even more questions, to be honest.

"Sit, let's drink. I'll heat it up and make you some tea."

Dronmer turns back toward the corner of his room and stokes a small fire, then places a pot over the flame. I remove the bearskin for the first time and feel relief as cool air washes over my body. I fold it up and place it on the ground, and I decide to lay my ultraspear on top of it. I think I can trust this weird boy. If I'm honest, I enjoy spending time with him.

Before I sit on the lone sandstone slab, Dronmer turns back to me and freezes.

"Why do you look like that?" he asks. He acts like he's seen a spirit suddenly materialize before his eyes.

I examine myself, but I see nothing out of the ordinary. I'm dirty and sweaty, but no more than would be expected.

"I'm sorry, look like what?"

"What are you?" He asks, and I can see his face puzzling though multiple alternatives.

"What do you mean?" I don't know how to answer the question. People usually ask *who are you*, and I have an answer ready for that. *What are you* leaves me stumped.

"You don't look like me. You don't look like anyone I've even seen. Your voice sounds different." He seems scared and suspicious, like he's realizing he's been tricked. He takes a step toward me. "Are you a Threatbelow? A new kind? A spy of theirs, perhaps? One who learned to talk, who made themselves small, who tried to disguise themselves as a human so you could sneak in here and kill us all?"

I back up toward the wall and grab my ultraspear. I should never have put it down.

"Trying to look human? I *am* human." I'm wondering if he's somehow picking up on my Brathius blood, the parts of me that went into the creation of the Croathus. I am part Threatbelow, it's true—or at least *they* are part *me*. Is that what he's reacting to?

"You're like no human I've ever seen. You're not shaped like us. If this is the Threatbelows' best attempt at fooling me, you haven't succeeded. I can spot the difference. I have a keen eye."

"I am a human. I've been human all my life. My father is Nicholas Brathius of Mountaintop. We are among the final remnant remaining, living at the highest point in the whole world." I say the words calmly. I am not afraid of Dronmer—not for my own safety, at least. But I am fearful that he will force my hand and I'll have to hurt him.

"I've heard some of these names before," he says, looking confused. "But only in whispers and fragments. Full knowledge of such events is reserved for the higher tiers." He isn't coming toward me anymore, which is a good sign.

"Yes. Because Mountaintop is a real place, and Nicholas and Marjan are humans who live there with other humans. Humans like you. And like me. Because I am their daughter."

At the sound of the word *daughter* Dronmer's face flashes from confusion to terror.

"No, no! Do not say the forbidden words! You cannot say that word here. We could both be punished—you for saying it, and me for hearing it." His eyes dart throughout the room as he tries to figure out if anyone might have heard. Since we're alone, I don't understand why he's so fearful. "Not even the higher tiers can say such words—not even to each other."

"Why would that word be forbidden?" Everything about this place is odd.

"Because it's related to nature's biggest mistake," he says slowly, like an adult leading a child to an obvious conclusion.

"I'm sorry, I don't know what that means," I respond.

"Putting the survival of humans into the hands of the weak and fickle, the unreliable, the...you know." He recites the words as if this is something everyone knows. He whispers the next words as though he is cheating and giving me the answers to an exam. "The problem Travis solved centuries ago?"

"Dronmer, this history is not known to my people, not in the Drowned City, or in Mountaintop. You're going to have to tell me what you're talking about. Exactly. Precisely. Hinting won't do. Assume I know nothing."

His face drains of all color. When he begins to speak, his voice cracks as though he hasn't had a drink for a week. "I'm not allowed to say the words to describe what I'm talking about, but..." He looks around. As has been the case since he met him, we are surely, completely alone. Still, he whispers, his voice dropping so low I can barely hear it.

"I'm talking about the problem of…*women.* That's why you're not allowed to say *daughter*. Because that word is related to…what I said. Those. Them. What once was." He looks instantly guilty, like he's never regretted anything more than saying these words.

Suddenly it hits me. Adorane and Torrain told me *that no women live in Apex.* I hadn't believed them. How was that possible? But it appears to be true. And that's why Dronmer is so taken aback by my appearance—to the point of not even considering me human. He's never seen anything like me before.

He's only ever seen boys and men.

"Dronmer, can you sit down for a moment?" I ask, measuring my words, hoping they have a calming effect on him.

He complies.

"I need you to know something about me. It's the reason I used the word 'daughter' when I talked about my relationship to my parents."

"You mean *parent*."

"No, parents," I correct him. "Two: a mother and a father." He shudders in disgust and fear. I am overcome with a feeling of anger and pity.

"The reason that you think I look and sound strange…" I pause. I can see that he still hasn't figured it out on his own. The idea that a woman might be talking to him, face to face, must be so outside the limits of his reality that it's never entered his mind.

"…It's because *I am a woman*."

Dronmer's arm flings outward from the shock, and he knocks the pot to the ground. Steaming water pools in a puddle. He stares at it without any comprehension, like a newborn baby might stare at her own hand.

"Yes, see. Yes. I'm going to go and...I think I will go now, into the snakeholes, and I will never talk to you again. Because I am going to jump from the tower, and hopefully I'll die. Yes, I believe that is what I will be doing now. Goodbye."

I grab him as he tries enter the snakehole. "Wait, what are you talking about? No." I yank him back into the room. For the first time I notice his muscles. Not quite as large as Adorane's nor as slender as Torrain's. In between, just right.

My touch calms his manic movements and seems to render him

unable to speak for a moment.

"You can't kill yourself, Dronmer. That's not an option."

“It's the only option. Because, you see, you are not allowed here. You are not allowed anywhere, to be precise. *You are not allowed to exist at all.* So I am required to eliminate you, which I will not do. I cannot do it. But I also cannot take you to the higher tier. They will send you to darkness, where long ago all...not-men were sent. So if I don't kill you myself, and I don't turn you over to those who will, then I will be executed. And that's why I must jump from the tower. Goodbye."

I hold him tighter, leaning against him to prevent him from moving through me.

"Thank you for not being willing to kill me. Even if it means you have to die." I cannot believe he's made this decision so quickly. He hasn't even known me an hour, and already he's willing to choose his own death over mine.

"Yes, well, it's not a hard decision to make. You killed a Threatbelow, so you have skills that I do not possess. I am only a lower tier—even though I have this large room and middle-tier belongings, I know no one is lower than me."

I lean in to make eye contact with him, because he keeps looking away from me. "No, that's not why you're doing this. You're doing it because...you're not making this decision because you’re a lower tier than me. I don't even *have* a tier." As I say it, I realize that I do—or at least did. I've been judging this strange low- and high-level nonsense that Dronmer has been talking about, but I know that Adorane would point out that it's not so different from Cognate and Veritas. He wouldn't be wrong.

"I deserve to die. I have done three unforgivable things. First, I did not kill you as you climbed the tower. Then, I stood by and listened as you said forbidden words, and then even uttered them myself—out loud. Finally, I have come across a...not-man..."

"A woman," I correct him.

"Yes, and I haven't been able to do anything about it because..."

"Because you realize that I'm human, too, and killing me would be wrong."

"No, *not* killing you is wrong."

"But you won't because you like me."

Dronmer nods in agreement.

“You don't have to die to keep me alive—though I can't tell you how much it warms my heart that you would. What were you going to do before I removed the bearskin?"

"I was going to take you to see the higher tiers, because I thought you were a great hunter."

"So let's still do that. I'll put the bearskin back on, carry the spear, and do my best to act like one of you. I'll bind myself up tight so I look like a boy. And this will be our secret."

He seems to like the idea. "And if anyone tries to make you remove your bearskin, you can run them through with your spear. In fact, you might just want to stab the first higher tier we see, just kind of set the mood."

"Is that really something people do in Apex?" I ask, trying to conceal my horror.

"Only when they want to, which is...yeah, it happens often. So be prepared."

I've asked Dronmer to give me privacy as I wipe away any visible trace of my femininity. He didn't need much convincing. Since finding out I'm a woman, he's been awkward—like he wants to talk, while having absolutely nothing to say.

For example, after a long stretch of painful silence, he says, "So, have you ever noticed that rocks are heavy. And firm?"

"Yes, they are," I reply.

"And when they fall on your feet, they can hurt your toes. Because they're hard. Also, if you step on them, they can hurt the soles of your feet. So I guess rocks are our feet's natural enemies."

"I suppose that is true," I answer. I don't know what else he wants me to say.

"Yes, it is. It is true," he agrees. A panicked look crosses his face as he tries to come up with something else to discuss. Thus far we've talked about dirt, darkness, water, air, and—the most unwelcome—tongues, each conversation more stilted and awful than the last.

At one point I decided to spare him the pressure of coming up with the next topic and ask him about something I want to understand better.

"I've heard rumors of a technology called the Underneath Forge here."

He looks scared. "I don't know anything about that. None of the lower tiers do. We're not allowed to talk about it. Not even allowed to think about it."

"How would they know if you were thinking about it?"

"The look on our faces, probably. They'd just know. So I never think about it. No sense in testing them. It's darkness, as far as I'm concerned. None of my business. That's higher tier business—highest of higher tier—and I'm not worthy of thinking about it."

"But you must know how it works—"

For the first time, his deferential manner drops. He snaps: "That's all I can tell you. Please."

We both relish the silence.

Dronmer lifts his stone chair and tilts it sideways against the wall. Time has polished parts of it, so it reflects an image back at me—not an exact likeness, but more like a silhouette. As I fuss and tighten and bind using Dronmer's clothing, I reach a close enough facsimile of a male body. I suddenly miss both Adorane and Torrain in an unexpected way. If they could see me now, doing my best to look and act like one of them, they'd probably laugh.

"I'm ready, Dronmer. Let's visit the higher tiers."

53

ICELYN

I follow Dronmer through narrow corridors, dimly lit by the occasional torch. It occurs to me that Dronmer is the only human I've seen in Apex, which seems odd. We've been ascending for about twenty minutes already.

"Where is everyone else?" I ask him.

"In their rooms," he answers. He nods his head toward a few doors here and there, which I'm guessing lead to rooms like his.

"Right—but where do people go, you know, when they aren't in their rooms?"

"I don't understand what you mean. Into the snakeholes, I guess, to guard and watch."

"No, Dronmer. When you aren't in your room, and you aren't working. Where do people go then?" I'm thinking of communal spaces, like the village green in Mountaintop or Mistersean's temple in the Drowned City.

"Why would we do that?"

"To see each other. To do things." I don't understand why I have to explain this. It seems obvious to me.

"Oh!" Dronmer exclaims, as if I've finally gotten through to him. "Once in a while, after a long time passes, the higher tiers mandate that we should celebrate the building of Apex. We ascend to one of the middle tiers, everyone gathers together, and the higher tiers tell us stories. Everybody loves that day. You have to watch out, of course, because many people die. But that's what happens when you gather. As the saying goes, a joyful crowd soon descends into death."

I can't say I've ever heard this saying. But now I think I understand why most of the residents of Apex keep to their private rooms.

"Do you ever spend time with other lower tiers—in your room, or here in the corridors?"

"If a lower tier came to my room, it would be to kill me. So I would kill him first. If I saw a lower tier waiting out here in the corridor, I would suspect he was here to fight me, so I would have to attack him first."

What a wretched place. "If this is the way it is, why don't you seem afraid right now?" I ask.

"Because I've got you with me, slayer of a Threatbelow. You'd kill anyone who wanted to attack us before I even noticed them."

"I don't kill like that. I don't really kill at all. I regret what happened with the Threatbelow."

Dronmer laughs. "Right. You regret it. A great warrior like you, with a weapon like that. Right."

After what feels like a hundred thousand steps, we reach a grand doorway. Without Dronmer saying anything, I can tell we've reached the threshold of another tier. He approaches the stone and wood portal with a mix of reverence and childish excitement. He inhales deeply.

"Smells better already. Every tier is a little closer to the heavens above. That means those who live in higher tiers are more like the One Who Walks in Shadow and Air. That's what I want, Icelyn."

I assume that the One Who Walks in Shadow and Air is a god. I wonder to myself if Dronmer's god is anything like the one Adorane loves. Considering how bloodthirsty this place appears to be, I'm guessing not.

Dronmer positions me directly in front of the door. "Be poised and ready to pounce."

"What's going to happen?" I ask nervously.

"You never know, but it's always wise to be ready to fight. And if anyone tries to talk to you, make your voice sound more like the rumble of thunder than the song of a bird. Can you do that?"

"Like this?" I ask, doing my best to make my voice low.

He considers it. "Kind of like that, but do better if you can."

"Sure," I say, even lower. A half-disappointed, half-resigned smile crosses his face. "Sure, I guess that'll have to work." He knocks on the portal.

No reaction. He picks up a rock from the ground and pounds on it.

Finally, the door groans open.

"Get ready for battle," Dronmer urges. "You don't look ready."

"What are you talking about?"

"They're coming. This is it."

Before he can explain, a group of men squeezes through the barely ajar door and rushes toward us. They're crusted with dirt, their clothing ragged, and they carry clubs and rocks. They are truly the ugliest group of men I've ever seen in my life. Are they even humans?

"Our place is not for the taking!" one shouts.

"We will not be replaced!" another screams.

"Our perch is earned! All others be burned!"

"Stop it!" I thunder, trying to stall their ragged advance, holding my ultraspear toward them. There are at least ten of them. The mob doesn't acknowledge my warning.

"Slay them, Icelyn!" Dronmer urges. "You killed a Threatbelow!"

But I am no fighter. I didn't think my deception would be put to the test so quickly. I swing the ultraspear toward the first man who reaches me, who has bright red hair and a long matted beard. I swing too hard in my fearful desperation, though, and miss him completely, instead stumbling forward and exposing my back.

The man pounces on me. He outweighs me by at least a hundred pounds. I manage to slither out from underneath him, but I lose my spear in the chaos. Another three men attack me. One of them bashes my shoulder with a rock.

I am filled with rage and disgust at the idea of dying like this, under a pile of dirty, hairy men who have seemingly never bathed. Maybe it's what I deserve. I thought I was great—a god, even. But instead, I'm feed for the lowest of men.

They kick me, punishing me with their clubs and rocks.

I can hear the lilting melody of death, quiet but persistent, and I think I'd like to follow it. The red haired man lifts me to my feet and stares at me with complete disdain.

"You thought you could replace us? I will use you to replace *my rug.*"

I have no idea what he's talking about. The last words I will ever hear make no sense to me. What a waste of everything.

The world slows down and then speeds up. Each moment seems to be skipped or repeated, or somehow occurring backwards. I wonder about the difference between what *is* happening versus what *I want to* happen versus what *I perceive to be* happening. The red haired man lifts his arm above his head and grunts, holding a gnarled wooden stick, ready to lower it down on me for hopefully the last time.

Yet instead of hitting me, he collapses. Then the man who is holding me from behind (so that the red haired man could hit me square in the head) screams and falls to the ground too.

Am I dead and seeing things as I wish they'd happened? I jump back from the melee, and through my own blood-soaked eyes, see that Dronmer has picked up my ultraspear. He's making his way through the group of men like a trained assassin, cleanly executing them one after another.

These men are not fighters. They are a rambling, clumsy mob, driven by animal violence and not by any sort of skill. They are nothing like the Anaghwin (or Dronmer, for that matter). Whenever one lashes out and manages to hit Dronmer, he so deftly dodges that it's more of a glancing blow, and serves to destabilize the ruffian more than hurt him.

I might have blacked out. I can't tell. Or perhaps Dronmer is that quick. By the time I realize what I'm seeing, all of the men are dead.

Dronmer turns back to me, exhausted and bloodied.

"Well, I have to admit that I was expecting a little more from you, Icelyn."

NOW

Eveshone approached Barielta with caution. The longer she'd lived in the sacred tower with her mother, the more she had realized how much deference the Priestess deserved—or required. She remembered back to when they'd first met, how Eveshone had touched her mother's hand. She couldn't imagine doing such a thing now—her skin would probably burn at the point of contact.

"Priestess, thank you for summoning me," Eveshone said, her head bowed.

"You know why I have asked you here," her mother declared. "What must be done."

Eveshone's throat tightened with dread. She knew.

Icelyn.

The Priestess had asked for her so long ago, and Eveshone had said she couldn't do it. The Priestess had accepted that reply then. Eveshone now wondered how she'd ever had the courage to deny Barielta anything she requested.

Icelyn seemed like a distant dream. She was more like a wish, a distant memory, than someone who had once spent years by her side. A perfect being who had held her close, sung songs to her, listened to her fears, and laughed along with her joys. Everything Icelyn had once been to Eveshone now seemed like an illusion, like dust and ash waiting for the wind to blow it somewhere else.

"I will call her," Eveshone answered. Her voice broke as she felt the full weight of her betrayal. "I will not deny you what you request."

Barielta reached out and laid her hand on Eveshone's cheek, rewarding her with a touch. It calmed Eveshone's heart. Yes, this was the right thing to do.

She would summon Icelyn. There was no other way. Barielta had demanded it. Why had she waited so long already?

THEN

Omathis awoke seething with excitement and dread. Had that really happened? Had he heard Mister Sean's voice?

And if he had, what was he supposed to do now?

He crawled out from his darkened den atop the high-rise building and watched the commotion below. Golden rays of sunlight illuminated the early-morning activity of the Croathus. Small groups headed out of the city to start the hunt. Young males and females trained in the decaying alleys—jumping from one wall to another, growing their strength, learning techniques. Parents held newborn pups close. It wasn't the paradise they'd found in the jungles down south, but it was a life worth living.

Still, it was lonely. It had always been lonely, and always would be lonely, because they were cut off from their creator. This was not the way they were intended to live. Amperous hated when Omathis mentioned Mister Sean, but they both knew the truth: They'd always feel hollowed out without him.

Omathis crawled down the exterior of the building. He wasn't moving extraordinarily fast, because he was far from eager to reach his destination. He strode through the city, returning greetings offered by the Croathus he passed. He often stayed in his tower home for days on end. Seeing him out on the streets was a treat for many creatures.

Parents rushed to him with their children in tow, begging for a blessing and the bestowing of a special name. He touched each one and took the time to christen them. He was in no rush.

Finally, he arrived at Amperous' residence. His brother had taken a curiously shaped home for himself—it looked like a series of ocean waves frozen in time, dipped in shining metal, and molded into a massive five-story building. While most other human constructions had been covered with vines or overtaken by dust and water by now, Amperous was meticulous about his home, spending time each day polishing and cleaning it. Omathis had once asked why, and Amperous had only responded that it was his hard-won prize.

Omathis stood before the front entrance, but he didn't need to knock.

Amperous was waiting. His appearance was haggard and downtrodden, as if he hadn't slept all month. "You heard him too?" he asked, without bothering to greet his brother first.

It sounded more like a threat than a question.

"You feel it too, my brother. I know you do. This life, alone—it's empty. Cold." Omathis was only repeating what he already sensed was lodged in Amperous' heart, even if his stubborn brother would never admit it.

"He left us. A long time ago. If our lives are empty, it's because that's his preference. And our lives are *not* empty. We number in the hundreds of thousands. We have our partners and our children. The love we used to have for him is bound up now in this. This is *our world.* Stop gazing toward cloudy mountaintops and accept what we have in front of us."

"He's calling us to him," Omathis insisted.

"And how are we to answer his call? You know what the heights do to us. Should we go to him and lose our minds like those trapped in the clouds?"

A thought jumped unbidden to Omathis' mind before he could shield himself against it. He rejected it—but it was too late. The damage was done; Amperous had already sensed its presence.

Omathis had been keeping a secret from Amperous for years now. This was no simple task, because they shared roots. It couldn't be done through casual indifference—keeping Amperous ignorant required consistent, deliberate rejection, an avoidance of his own thoughts at every moment.

Amperous became aware of the rupture in their brotherhood. He felt a sharp pang in his chest and suffered shortness of breath as his heart was flooded with the first taste of betrayal.

"What have you been doing, Omathis?" Amperous had hoped to growl, but he sounded sad, hurt—more like a wounded yelp.

Omathis placed his hand on Amperous' shoulder, softly, as if he could apologize through touch. "I should show you something."

Amperous lost himself in the strokes of the carved mask. He felt like he'd been shrunken down and could explore each groove as if it were a canyon, twisting here and there, promising treasure just around the corner. The sure, confident lips, just like the ones he'd focused on when he was young, waiting for the words he craved. *"Good job, Amperous. That was the best yet!"* Just one encouraging sentence from the mouth of Sean Brathius could fill Amperous with light for a week.

The sharp, angled cheekbones, bearing an eerily accurate likeness to Sean's face. Mister Sean would sometimes press that face against Amperous' and bestow comfort, even during the scariest, longest, and darkest nights.

Finally, the blue eyes. Mister Sean's blue eyes didn't just belong to Sean Brathius—they *were Sean Brathius.* Every glance revealed who he was, the hidden essence inside. When they looked at you, you wanted nothing more. His blue eyes were everything—they were the world, the universe, all of reality. His blue eyes were the source and the culmination. Staring at the mask, Amperous was again wrapped up in them, swallowed whole—just like he'd been when he was so young that he couldn't speak or think using words, just images and feelings.

Amperous shook himself out of the spell the mask had cast over him, but only with tremendous effort. The truth was, he liked the way it made him feel—even if he hated it too.

"Why would you make such a thing?" he asked, though he feared he already knew the answer.

"To be with him again. In his notes, I found instructions teaching us how to breathe up high," Omathis answered, his words reverent, as he grew transfixed by the appearance of the mask. "You remember what it was like, when he was with us?"

Amperous swiped and knocked the mask from Omathis' hand. It fell to the ground and split in half. Amperous picked up half of the shattered mask and held it in front of his own face.

"We can only carry pieces of him now, Omathis. That is our reality. It hurts us all to pretend anything else is possible."

Omathis was stung by the sight of the shattered mask. He gently lifted its other half from the ground and held it to his heart like a shield in order to block Amperous from discerning his true intentions. If Amperous could experience the mask as a vivid reminder of what communion with Sean Brathius felt like and still reject the call to rise to the top of the mountain, then he would never agree to make that journey to be with Mister Sean again.

Mister Sean was dead to Amperous. But he'd never be dead to Omathis.

"Of course, brother. We won't try to go," Omathis lied. But this was a good lie, he convinced himself, because he needed more time to prepare without contending with Amperous' interference. "Even if Mister Sean calls to us day and night, without ceasing, we'll stay below. We'll make a paradise here, cobbled together out of the pieces that have been left behind for us, instead of longing for the pieces that have been taken away."

54

ICELYN

He tends to my wounds with the same kind of care and expertise that Adorane used so long ago. I'm embarrassed to admit it to myself, but I might be starting to feel an attraction to Dronmer. Of course, it's probably because he saved my life and is now doing his best to soothe my pain-wracked body. One would have to be a monster not to feel something in the wake of all that.

Yet I do wonder why I didn't notice earlier: Dronmer is a perfect mix between the things I like about Torrain and Adorane. He's graceful and brave like Adorane. Yet he's aloof, awkward, and plagued with self-doubt —in an endearing way, not an annoying one—like Torrain.

He takes great care to clean the wounds on my shoulder, back, legs, and arms—all the areas where the horrid mob pummeled me with their crude weapons.

"They have warm water in this room," he says excitedly. "Already warmed—no need to heat it over a fire. I think I'm going to like it here."

Dronmer has claimed a room that belonged to one of the men he killed. He took the first one he found, because he needed to tend to me. But he's told me more than once that he's going to look at all of the available spaces to make sure we've gotten the best.

I think I've been asleep for a while, but there's honestly no way to tell. Being inside this tower, with no window or connection to the rhythms of the outside world, it's impossible to track the passage of time.

"Why did they try to kill me?" I ask.

Dronmer can hardly believe I ask the questions I do.

"Please, Icelyn. Of *course* they'd try to kill you. And me, if they could. The only way someone on the lower tier rises up through the levels is to take someone's place, so every one of us poses a threat. That's how it works."

My mind is foggy, so I have a hard time expressing my thoughts—and a difficult time thinking them in the first place. "But you said that because I was a great hunter, you would get to be on a higher tier. Like they would be impressed by me and invite you along."

"Nobody invites anyone anywhere! There is a *reason* everyone says the portal to heaven is slippery with blood!"

I've never heard anyone say this, but it sounds terrible.

"The reason I thought you would help get me to a higher tier was because I thought you'd be able to kill them all for me—so I'd earn my place on a higher tier. But now I think I'll have to figure all that out myself, because…" He trails off, afraid of offending me. Honestly, the way he's focused on bringing healing to my broken body, I couldn't be angry with him for anything.

"How exactly did you kill that Threatbelow?" he asks. "Because you don't seem like the kind of hunter who could do that."

"I wasn't expecting a battle just now," I defend myself weakly. "You didn't exactly prepare me for what we were about to face."

"I didn't think I had to."

"Assume I know nothing, Dronmer. Nothing at all." I feel a wave of nausea wash through me and lay back on the bed. Unlike in Dronmer's room, where the bed was carved from hard stone, this one is a soft sack filled with dried leaves. The perks of being part of a higher tier, I suppose.
"Well, at least now you've reached your higher tier," I mumble. "Congratulations."

"No, this isn't nearly high enough. This is the lower of the mid tiers —really, it's only the top of the lower tiers. Barely a step above where I was before. This isn't the goal. That's why those men were so easy to kill. They were nearly as low as me."

"Dear Lord. Who cares," I respond without thinking, and I can tell I've hurt his feelings. He just hacked his way through a group of angry men without a scratch, but my offhand comment has somehow wounded him.

"I care."

Eager to make amends with my only ally in this terrible place, I respond, "Then I will too. I'm sorry."

Dronmer washes the blood away and dresses my wounds. He continues to apply firm, strong pressure to my skin, focusing on an individual finger, my shoulder, my forearm. He said earlier that men from the higher tiers have visited him for exactly this kind of treatment, and I can see why. He's very skilled.

"Why are you here?" Dronmer asks. As soon as he does, I wonder why he hasn't asked this up until now.

Oh, you know, I was just hoping to use a man to get pregnant here—because all the babies in Mountaintop are dead, and all the men and women there carry a disease, and I don't want humanity to die out. Also, I want an heir who can continue to be worshiped by my Anaghwin children. But maybe neither of those are my actual reason for being here. Who knows? Certainly not me! I'm pretty mixed up right now because I finally found someone who loved me unconditionally—and who I loved completely and totally—and then she left, and now I'm reeling, broken, and perhaps incapable of having a normal relationship ever again. Maybe I'm just drawn to dark places—the darker and more sinister the better, and this place pretty clearly fits the bill—so I can finally figure out a way to dig deep enough into the shadows to be able to reach for the sun. At least that's what Adorane's imaginary god told me when I prayed to it.

"I want to reach the highest tier," I say simply, because I think Dronmer would be confused by my madness if I shared any of my true reasons aloud—and also because I suspect the highest tier is what he wants too.

"You want to reach the heavens?" he asks excitedly, like I've said the magic words he's been waiting to hear.

"More than anything," I respond.

He looks at me with a mixture of reverence, adoration, and fear. Honestly, it's not a bad feeling, to be looked at like this.

"Shadow and Air," he says quietly.

"I'm sorry, what?" I ask, confused.

"I suspected, but I couldn't believe it was true until now. You are the One Who Walks in Shadow and Air, aren't you? The wandering assassin from far away?"

Not quite knowing what I'm signing up for, but fearing that denying it would be worse, I nod my head. "It is as you say it is. But don't tell anyone. Not until the appointed time."

NOW

Omathis awoke before the sun, as he did every morning. He breathed in deeply and pressed his hands against his chest. He whispered to himself: *I am alone. I am not alone. I am sad. I am lonely. I am loved. I am grateful. I am tired. I am hopeful. I am hopeless.*

Omathis left the hovel he'd pieced together out of the ruins of the lab where he'd first met his great love. Living here was healing. He'd spent his whole life trying to avoid memories of her, when what he'd actually needed was to surround himself with them.

His months in this place—away from the other Anaghwin, away from the Drowned City, away from the cloudy Mountain, away from Icelyn and the pull of the Brathius—had been cleansing for him. He'd never learned who he was by himself, stripped free of others. He had been born alongside Amperous and raised by Sean. Then he'd lived among his family, and then among the other Anaghwin, their roots intertwined. In his hundreds of years of existence, he'd never simply been alone.

With all these connections to rely on and be distracted by, he'd never had to face himself. For the past months he'd had no distractions. It was painful, but he felt fuller as a result of it. He felt more substantial, like a shadow taking form and turning into something real.

I am angry. I am scared. I am furious. I am hungry. I am exhausted. I am excited.

He made it a habit of being aware of his inner states as often as possible. These honest inventories helped him sketch out an outline of who he was every morning. He'd spent centuries ignoring or suppressing this information.

He watched the sun rise. He treasured this moment every day, because at this time he'd found that the veil between he and Soneyane was especially thin. He'd spent centuries believing she was gone, and only recently had he learned that she wasn't, not completely. She was still present, but in a different way.

He picked a flower and laid it in front of him. The warm golden rays of the sun drifted over it as he watched.

"You like this one; it's your favorite," he said. "You called it a 'star flower.'"

The flower's petals shook in the wind. He knew it was more than just the breeze.

"We used to sit in the field, remember, and try to imagine which flowers were related by their markings. Then we'd give them names. And you'd invent whole histories for them."

Tears filled his eyes, but they weren't painful. He didn't wipe them away.

"I know, I know. I've enjoyed our time here, too," he whispered. "But you're right. It's time to go. She needs me."

THEN

Travis walked the full perimeter before climbing the rusted steel ladder to check in on Maria.

She was just as he'd left her—busy navigating a rat's nest of wires. She was cutting, connecting, and coordinating them with the circuits in a way that made Travis' head spin.

"How much longer?" he whispered, though he knew it would annoy her. She'd interpret his question as a reminder to hurry up, and it wasn't as if she'd been loafing around.

She wiped sweat out of her eyes and blinked against the stinging saline before resuming her tedious work.

"I'm not sure I want this to end. It's just so nice here," she deadpanned. Though they had no thermometers to confirm, it had to be over a hundred degrees this far up the improvised tower. "Look, if this were easy work, you'd be able to do it," she joked.

Travis was feeling antsy and knew he needed to make another round. If a Croathus sensed them up this ladder, they'd be trapped like a couple of treed raccoons.

"Okay, I'll check back in soon. Let's get this done."

Travis stuck to the shadows while creeping and straining to detect any disturbance.

Initially, these missions had been easier than expected. Travis and the SSG confined their activity to those times when the creatures were transfixed by Sean and Laura Lee, and kept themselves hidden when the monsters were active. They'd been able to build five "Freedom Towers"—stacks of power sources, wiring, and circuitry supporting a special payload perched high above, at the height needed to support maximum reach. Just as Sean Brathius had requested—though with one significant change that Travis kept a secret from him.

But recently, the SSG had grown too comfortable. A roving creature had discovered Matt Wellingsley while he prepared a tower. He was torn to pieces and hung off the side of it. Janelle had watched, hidden, unable to do anything to stop the carnage.

The scariest thing about this was that it had happened while the other beasts were staring at the mountain and longing for Sean and Laura Lee. Travis hadn't thought that was possible, but it validated the course he'd taken. No matter what, some of these nightmares would always thirst for human blood.

Matt would have been proud to point out that he'd finished his job first. The tower had just been activated when he was killed.

Since Matt's death, their progress had been slow as they attempted to avoid any more casualties. But they were almost finished; Maria was finishing the final stage of Travis' plan now.

Travis heard a slight swishing sound move through the sprawling shipping yard where they'd set up this tower. It sounded like the breeze, yet the day was devoid of wind. His heart sank. He recognized the noise.

Staying in the shadows, he rushed back toward Maria. He cursed how much faster these beasts were than him. Sean had given them every advantage.

Though the day had been still, now a chorus of several rushing winds joined together and surrounded Travis. This was bad. How many were there?

His mind rushed faster than his feet. Should he cry out to Maria to warn her? But then they'd become aware of him too. Maria and Travis had prepared several steel shipping containers throughout the yard in case they needed a place to hide. But would either of them be able to reach safety if he shouted out now and made their location obvious?

Travis climbed a stack of the containers to get a clear view to Maria. He was maybe two hundred yards away. From his higher vantage point, his worst fears were confirmed.

He saw three of the brutal beasts sprinting together in their unnaturally quick way. They were so fast that when he blinked it seemed like they'd teleported from one spot to another.

Travis reached the top of the container stack. He could see Maria, oblivious to the creatures below, lost in her task. Even worse, she was welding, sending sparks flying out in a bright, impossible-to-ignore wave.

Desperate to get her attention, Travis rifled through his pack and found a flash grenade. He tossed it away from Maria, aiming for another stack of shipping containers. It imploded with a deafening bang and blinding bright light.

The explosion caught the attention of the roving creatures below—and Maria. Travis laid flat on top of the container, but raised his head just enough for her to see when she scanned the area.

They locked eyes. They didn't need to speak—they'd set up their escape beforehand. They'd both make their way to one particular steel reinforced container among the hundreds and lock it up.

The creatures headed toward the spot where the grenade had exploded. They moved tentatively, as if they knew it might be a ruse. Travis often had to remind himself that as beastly as they appeared, they were as smart as he was. Maybe even smarter.

Travis watched as Maria hesitated.

What are you doing?

She looked back at him for only a second before returning her focus to the welding. For just a moment she let her facade break, and he could see that she was scared.

But Maria had never let fear stop her from completing a job.

He'd had enough arguments with her over the past month to know what she'd say if they could talk to each other. The creatures had found this tower, and with the activity from the grenade, they knew that humans were here. She'd never be able to get back and prepare it. If they were going to complete the mission, there was no escaping before she'd finished what they'd come to do. Even if she died trying.

Travis had never felt so helpless.

He raced through his options, but none were acceptable. He could hide away by himself, secure in the shipping container. This would be what Maria would want him to do, but he couldn't abandon her.

He wanted to defend her from his high perch, but he had no weapon that could do more than bother the creatures below.

He could probably make it over to the tower and join her, but he would be no help in completing the wiring, and they'd both be trapped once the beasts climbed to attack.

Finally, he decided that he could at least offer a distraction to give her more time to work and hopefully escape. He gathered another five flash grenades from his pack and considered how best to use them. Anyone with military training—as was bred into the Croathus—would know to look for a launch point and not be fooled by the landing sites. He'd gotten away with throwing one, but each subsequent toss would be another data point with which the beasts could locate him.

He crept across the shipping container and jumped to another stack. He tossed the grenade before retreating into the shadows and moving again. If he could move quickly enough between throws, maybe they wouldn't be able to pinpoint his location.

Travis rushed to another secure spot and peeked down at the creatures.

The monsters had split up. One was exploring the impact points of the grenades, and one seemed to be trying to track where they were coming from. The third stayed where it was, completely still, drinking in every sound and sight.

It cocked its head and froze. Travis could see what it was seeing.

More sparks from the welding.

No.

More out of instinct than anything else, Travis tossed a grenade directly at this monster while it galloped toward the tower and Maria. He hit the beast square in the back, causing it to fall to the ground with a pained yelp.

It was a bad idea. Travis had slowed the one, but now the other two knew exactly where he was.

Travis only had enough time to see that Maria still hadn't abandoned her post. She worked quickly, continuing to wire, connect, and weld.

He scrambled along the steel rectangles and hopped down to the ground. He ran through a labyrinth of rusted red and blue steel—he and Maria had memorized the way to go, counting on the maze to confuse pursuers. The creatures screeched in frustration at the twists and turns.

Finally, Travis found the entrance to the shipping container. He slid in and tried to slam the door shut, ready to lock it.

It didn't close.

He pushed against it with his whole body, but a taloned finger was keeping it from sealing. For a moment it seemed like he might be able to sever the finger.

But he was overmatched, and the door sprung open. One of the monstrous beasts entered the container, filling the hot air with the smell of rotting flesh.

They had selected these containers useful for escape because they had openings that connected to other steel storage shipping blocks, like a grand modular gerbil tunnel. So at least he wasn't trapped. He and Maria had spent weeks memorizing the ways the blocks connected in case they needed to use them for escape.

Travis had never imagined they'd actually be in the maze of containers with one of the beasts. His mind went to the story of the Minotaur and the Labyrinth. He realized that he couldn't remember if the hero had lived or died.

He shot his body through the next opening and was nearly able to close the door, but the beast followed with unnerving speed. The only advantage Travis had was knowing where the next opening was, and he used it to stay just ahead. Straight, left, right, above, below. An attempt to close one of the doors behind him would make him lose time, so he only tried it when he thought he might be far enough ahead to succeed.

Time and again, he failed.

Travis decided he'd reached a point where unless he tried something risky, he'd likely die anyway. He grabbed his final flash grenade, curled up in a ball to cover his eyes and ears as much as possible, and threw it against the wall of steel container the beast entered to pursue him.

The explosion and following reverberations were blinding and deafening even with eyes and ears covered. The beast roared in pain. Travis, choking and on the verge of fainting, unable to see anything, relied on memory and touch and felt his way to the next portal. He stumbled through and collapsed into the next container. He willed himself to stand again so he could close it.

This time, it sealed. The beast had not followed in time.

Travis locked it tight.

Blessed silence.

The rectangle was nearly soundproof, but he could feel the impact as the beast threw itself against the wall. But the steel held. Who knew for how long, though.

Travis stumbled to his feet and moved from one container to the next, making his way through the innards of the stacks, climbing and descending, until he had left the creature far behind.

He spent a terrible night waiting for the creatures to finally lose interest in him, fearing what he'd find when he emerged the next morning.

As the sun rose, Travis slipped out of his refuge with caution. They'd finally left, their bloodlust satisfied. He could see why.

Maria's body had been hung from the tower she'd worked so doggedly to activate. They'd made sure to drain her of blood first. He could see the bones of his friend bleached white and clean in the sunlight.

Beside her hanging body, Travis could see a dimly flashing light on the tower. She'd done what she'd set out to do.

The sixth and final tower was ready.

"We'll make this count, Maria. Your sacrifice won't be in vain," Travis promised bitterly, turning back toward home.

55

ICELYN

Dronmer has treated me with an unusual amount of deference since learning that I am the Shadow Air. I regret deceiving him. (Though, I justify, I *have* felt a shadowy darkness in my heart lately. Plus, every time I take a breath I fill myself with air—so it's not all a complete lie. I *am* a Shadow Air. Just perhaps not *the* Shadow Air.) I shouldn't have agreed to anything without knowing what it meant, but it's too late now, so I play the part of a mystical wandering assassin as best I can. Considering I've been performing the role of a god for years, it shouldn't be too difficult.

"Here you go, drink up," he says, giving me another mug full of water. "The cisterns on this level are much cleaner than I'm used to. Not even the slightest shade of brown. I'd heard water could be clear, but I hardly believed it until now. Thought it was something the higher tiers said just to make us jealous."

I wish I hadn't had anything to drink back in Dronmer's lower tiered room, but then I remember that he boiled it, so hopefully I'll be safe from sickness. He watches me as I drink, which is unnerving.

"Visiting times begin soon," he informs me, somewhat embarrassed. "I don't think we should let them know who you are just yet, if that's all right with you. Of course, you get to decide on your own. But you would be doing me a favor, for now, until I figure out the right way to reveal you to the rest."

"I'm sorry. Visiting times?"

"When those from the higher tiers descend upon us for services. It happens from the time the sun completely disappears until it shows up again."

He says this as if it's known by everyone. It sounds ominous, and I think my face reflects this. I wonder how he even knows the sun is disappearing soon, since can't see anything of the outside world in this tower.

"Oh, no, don't worry," he assures me. "Now that I'm not on the lowest tier anymore, it's not going to be nearly as bad. Higher tiers aren't allowed to do as much to those on this tier. Nothing like what they do to those on the lowest."

He's trying to comfort me, but it sounds horrific. "What do they do? I need details."

"To me? Mostly just ask me to lay my hands on them. I have that skill, and they appreciate it. Look, I'm one of the lucky ones. They reward me—"

"Yes, I know, with furniture," I say it more dismissively than I intend. "Sorry," I apologize quickly, "I'm just getting used to this place. It's very different than anywhere else I've ever been."

"There are other places to be?" he asks me, genuinely curious.

"Yes—and though they're all far from perfect, they are much better than this place."

"Oh, I find that hard to believe. Apex is wonderful. You'll see. It keeps us safe from the monsters. And we're all the kings of our own lives. We have the ability to be whatever we want, to make as much as we can earn. What could be better?" I'm surprised by Dronmer's loyalty to this awful place.

"Wait, Dronmer. How do the higher tiers come down here—by what passage?" Since the main staircase is heavily manned, and nobody seems to pass through the levels without bloodshed, I don't understand how those from above can visit safely every night.

"Oh, they have their own passage. Just for higher tiers. It's locked off from the rest of us, so it's safe. They can easily go wherever they want. They have keys to every door in the whole tower."

"Even the locks on your door, to your room?" I ask. How dreadful.

"Can you imagine? Someday we'll enjoy that too. Won't that be incredible? Someday."

His musings are interrupted by the faraway thumping of footsteps against stone and the groaning of a large wooden door.

"Can you hide, please? They're coming."

I crouch in the shadowy corner of the room beside a closet molded out of mud, clutching my ultraspear. I'm not well hidden, but I remain still, and the visitor from the higher tier is completely focused on Dronmer. If the visitor wanted to look in my direction, he'd probably see me; but the room is so spare that this is the best I can do.

Dronmer keeps his eyes fixed on the ground while interacting with the visitor, whose name is Kern. Dronmer acts as if he's not worthy of some greatness inherent in Kern. This is strange to me; by all appearances, Kern is anything but great. His skin is so pale that I can't imagine he's ever seen the sun, his hair so stringy that I wonder what purpose it even serves, functionally or aesthetically, and his body so soft that it's an accomplishment he manages to stand at all. I can't imagine he has any muscles in his legs.

"I heard that you've ascended a level. Congratulations," Kern says to Dronmer. His voice is too loud, and I immediately wish I could silence it. "Although it's never as much fun once one of your favorites starts moving up." He laughs, and I've never heard anything more grating in my life.

"It's not anything compared to how high you are, Kern," Dronmer replies, so obsequiously that I become angry. Dronmer is superior in every way to Kern, and there's a kindness inside of him despite this towered hell he's lived in. Yet he acts like Kern is worthy of his praise.

Dronmer places a carpet woven out of reeds on the ground. Kern plops on top of it and lays on his stomach.

"Well, do what you do, and maybe I'll help you rise up a few more levels," Kern says. It sounds dismissive to me, but I can tell the half-hearted promise buoys Dronmer.

"Oh, I'd like that very much," Dronmer answers and begins pressing his strong hands against Kern's blotchy flesh.

"Thank you for letting me provide service to you, Kern," Dronmer says, almost as if he's been hypnotized.

I hate Apex with every fiber of who I am.

I see that Kern has dropped his cloak on the ground. A key pokes out from one of the pockets.

"Your father sends his regards," Kern grunts. After a long stretch of silence, Dronmer replies, "Oh, that's good of him. I haven't seen him in ages."

"Yes, well, it's better that way—for you most of all," Kern replies. I'm left in utter confusion at the exchange.

"He likes to spend his visitations on the lowest of the tiers," Dronmer says, and I detect resentment in his voice.

"Again, probably a blessing," Kern answers, and this marks the ending of their conversation about Dronmer and his mysterious father.

Kern struggles to flop over onto his back and indicates that Dronmer pay attention to his shoulders.

"And what of Calacas?" Dronmer asks. I detect a note of hesitation in his voice.

"He asked that I not discuss his personal matters with you or anyone else in a lower tier," Kern answers abruptly.

"Of course," Dronmer replies, sounding ashamed. "My apologies for asking."

I stretch my arm from the darkness where I hide, moving slowly.

I want Kern's key. Why has Dronmer never taken it before?

Kern grunts every time Dronmer presses down.

So that my movement isn't detected, I time my shuffling so it's in sync with Kern's disgusting noises. I reach for the key and take it.

"That's it," Kern announces. "That's enough, thank you. I didn't bring anything this time, but maybe next."

"Of course. Your presence is reward enough," Dronmer answers. This response brings a grin to Kern's face.

"Yes, I know. I think I'll go to a lower tier now. Want to see what kind of trouble is brewing down there tonight." Kern laughs as though he's made an excellent joke. To my horror, Dronmer laughs along with him. I can tell Dronmer doesn't actually think Kern is funny. That makes it even more terrible to witness.

"What was that?" I demand the moment Kern leaves the room.

Dronmer looks chastened before flashing back to his normal unforced confidence. "That's the order of things, Icelyn. If I want to enjoy life when I get to the higher tier, I can't complain about it when I'm on the bottom."

"Well, that's a terrible way to view it all." I'm angry. "He was… devouring you. Your dignity, every ounce of you, just chewing it up and tossing the husk aside."

"Dignity? I am of a lower tier, Icelyn. I have no dignity. Once I reach the higher tier, that's when I'll have earned some dignity. Why is this so hard for you to understand?"

"Because it makes no sense," I respond. "Everyone should have dignity." I hold Kern's key out to Dronmer. "But if ascending is the only way I can get you to understand that, let's do it right now."

Dronmer looks terrified. "By the Shadow, what have you done?"

"He left it on the ground. I don't know why you haven't taken it before."

"Because I'll be…no. No. Why did you do this? I'll be torn to pieces, dipped in oil, set aflame, made to offer light and heat to the banquets on the highest tier. My ashes tossed out into the desert, joining the lowest dust and sand. There is no worse fate, Icelyn. At least when one dies trying to ascend, they are enshrined in glory and have a chance of coming back on a higher tier. But I will be shut out of Apex forever."

"This is what they tell you? Because they don't want you getting access to their glorious passages! None of that is true."

"They did it to Yalson, and Untop, and Ewrown, and—"

"Oh, I'm sure they've killed people who have taken keys. I'm not disputing that. But in this place, that's just a normal afternoon, isn't it? I mean the dust and sand part, the being tossed out, the damnation. They just want to keep you down here, docile and afraid, so that they can continue to feed on you. Because they know that if all of you decided to take the keys, you could claim the highest tier by sunset."

"No. Why would we want to do that, anyway? Then when we're on the highest tier, the lower tier would steal *our* keys and take over. Apex would be in chaos."

"If this is how things are, you're never going to be on the highest tier! Why preserve the safety of a position you will never occupy?"

"That's not true. Wintroph ascended. Quinter ascended. They were on the lowest tier, now they're up there."

Oh my goodness.

"Two out of how many? In how long? Is there anyone else?"

"You don't understand. If you did, you'd see. Now we have to get that key back to Kern," he says, panicked, "before he thinks I took it. It fell out of his pocket. Things fall out of pockets all the time, right?"

I do my best to modulate my voice so that I sound like I imagine the Shadow Air would.

"Dronmer, tell me who I am," I command.

In the wake of Kern's visitation and the key, he had forgotten. Now he's been reminded.

"The One Who Walks in Shadow and Air."

"And why have I come?" I want to make a point to him, hopefully—but also, I'm genuinely curious to hear the answer, since I have no idea.

"To teach us about what we have lost. To show us what has been stolen."

This is working out better than I could have hoped. I hold up the key again.

"This has been stolen. This belongs to you."

He studies me for a long time—too long. "No, that doesn't…I don't see how that key has anything to do with…explain it to me. Because, I mean, Travis, and the…not-men, the way *they're* supposed to be. You know?"

I don't want him to know that I'm bluffing, so I work my hardest to act both confident and offended.

"Do not question me. This key is the first step. I promise you, if you have to choose between fearing Kern and fearing me, choosing him would be a mistake." I hate to act this way, but Dronmer seems to respond to haughty bluster. It's why he so easily deferred to Kern.

"Yes, fine. I will follow."

I seem to have made my case. It's not like I haven't had practice acting like I'm better than other people.

"But even if you are the One Who Walks in Shadow and Air, can I make one small request of you?" he asks.

"Of course," I answer.

"I'd like it if you didn't just…change *everything*. There's an order here. It's kept us alive. The highest tier, the lower tiers. I think you'll see that there's a beauty and a balance to it. If you remove it all, you'll only bring chaos," Dronmer explains. I can tell this is important to him.

Oh no.

He sounds exactly like me, pining for a return to the old ways of the Cognates and Veritas.

And now I realize. The reason I hate Kern as I do is because I see *myself* in him. Not just me, but all of the Cognates. Change the people and the titles and the tiers, and suddenly it all looks terribly familiar.

Is this what Adorane was talking about all this time? I can see it now.

I grow insistent, desperate to make Dronmer see what I'm seeing, as if I'm atoning for years of my own ignorance. "Kern's no better than you. I'm no better than you. Nobody is any better than you, Dronmer. Don't you understand?"

"I don't."

I give it up, because no amount of explaining is going to make him see. Just like I couldn't until now.

"Then let's figure it out together. We have to go."

THEN

Acorn cakes drizzled with honey and garnished with lavender were laid out on the great table. The intoxicating scent of roasted deer and raccoon meat filled the air. Children dipped their mugs into barrels of cold water flavored with crushed berries and drank their fill.

"I'm not exaggerating, Travis. Our community has never been so happy, never," Laura Lee gushed. She watched couples dance to a beat a group of women pounded out on drums, and her eyes lit up. "You've done this."

Travis accepted her embrace and leaned into her warmth. He relished the feeling of being held—it was a rarity in his life. Shai had never been an affectionate mother. He'd never had a regular girlfriend in his teens. His twenties had been dominated by the search for the escaped Croathus, and his time in Mountaintop had been dedicated to waiting for Laura Lee.

Sean Brathius had rung the summoning bell and with great fanfare announced that the SSG had achieved a vital victory—a chance to change the beasts below. He'd been vague on the details, but he was so confident that he swept the entire community up in his vision. Travis and the surviving SSG had been given medals and titles, and the crowd had cheered.

Travis didn't care about that. Laura Lee holding him close was the only reward he craved.

In another week, Sean had proclaimed, all would be complete. In another week, at sunset, the world would change.

56

ICELYN

The higher tier's passageway is grander than the one Dronmer led me through as we ascended from the lower tier. For one thing, it isn't streaked black from the long-dried blood of countless battles. The steps are carved out of polished marble. The stairwell smells of sage and the slightly smoky undertones of incense.

"Hurry," Dronmer urges. "We're lucky we haven't seen anyone yet. They'll be leaving the lower tiers and returning to their living quarters soon."

We'd quickly be recognized as outsiders, I've learned, because those on the higher tier wear purple robes. I wish I had stolen Kern's.

"Which tier are we headed toward?" Dronmer asks me, eager to speed up whatever we're doing, and I remember that I am the one leading.

"The very top."

His face grows terrified but excited.

We continue our slog upward, and the many steps seem to me like a cruel prank played by a vengeful god. They all look the same, and they never end. I can only mark the passage of time via my increasingly exhausted legs.

"How does someone like Kern walk up and down these stairs every day?"

"Oh, he's carried. He would never walk all this way," Dronmer answers, as if it should be obvious.

"Who carries him?"

"Lower tiers!"

Of course.

"How many tiers are there?" I ask, frustrated.

"I've been told there are an infinite number."

Then how can one ever reach the top? I shut my mouth, furious.

Far below, I hear the shuffling echoes of feet and muffled coughs. Dronmer panics.

"That's probably Kern and other higher tiers looking for us."

"We're about thirty stories above them, from the sound of it," I whisper, "so I don't think we have much to worry about."

The joyful tinkling of bells washes though the stairwell. It would sound beguiling—alluring, even—if Dronmer weren't so clearly terrified.

"They're after us. We have to get out of here. They'll come from above and below." Dronmer grabs the key and opens the nearest door. I shuffle through after him.

I'm not sure which level this is, or whether they're even numbered or labeled, but the room is much nicer than anywhere I've visited in Apex so far. I see relics from the Apriori here, ancient paintings hanging on the wall. There's even a sphere decorated to look the way the Apriori once thought the whole world looked. Even if they were correct at the time (and I doubt they were, because how would anybody really know?), it would look completely different now.

There's no one here, I notice. This floor is eerily silent.

We rush through one hallway to the next, until I've lost track of where we've been. At least we know they won't easily follow us here—if anyone is even chasing us.

Finally, Dronmer stops. We've entered a room containing two basins carved out of the stone. They're filled with water.

"I've been here before," Dronmer says, more to himself than me. I realize that his past is a mystery to me. Where was he born and to whom? How did he end up on the lowest tier? Where else has he been? What was his childhood like?

"When?" I ask.

"During my long descent, I guess."

I tuck the idea of Dronmer's long descent away and promise myself I'll ask him about it at a more opportune time.

"Why is this tier abandoned?"

Dronmer approaches the vats filled with water and lowers his hand toward the surface until it hovers over the shimmery black liquid.

He turns to me with the strangest expression—confused, afraid, amazed.

"Because this tier belongs to you," he declares, tentative at first. "Yes,

One who Walks in the Shadows and the Air. This is your Shrine."

Dronmer believes I've led us here. It's strange, but I'm not sure I didn't. Of all those tiers we ascended, how was it that we emerged onto this one? It was just blind luck, I tell myself, but it feels improbable.

"Since this is where we are meant to be, do what you came here to do," Dronmer says.

"You've been here before?" I ask. We're both whispering because the space feels holy.

"Only on the outskirts. Never inside. Nobody is allowed in here—not since Travis died so many years ago. No one," he answers.

"I guess we're safe here, then," I laugh, and I am relieved at the thought.

"If anyone is allowed to trespass here, it's you," he replies, deadly serious.

We pass between the two stone tanks and squeeze through a smaller portal. We enter a round room decorated with jewels, gold, and precious stones. It's truly beyond anything I could have imagined. The ceiling is fashioned out of colored glass—still intact, not broken—and sunlight shines through it like a miracle.

"How did they get the sun in here?" I ask. Dronmer shakes his head. He has no idea. He is stunned silent and still by this room of wonder.

In the center is a grand statue, sculpted by adoring hands, of a graceful, triumphant woman. I stare at it for a long time, feeling like I've been taken out of my own body, out of time, out of reality itself. I've never seen a woman who looks anything like this. She is so confident and dominant—as though she is destined to rule the world and would never bow to anyone. This was a woman no man would dare ask to submit. She is strong in a way no man ever could be.

"Who is that?" I ask, after what feels like an eternity.

"The One Who Walks in Shadow and Air," Dronmer answers. I see that he has fallen to the ground and is bowing deeply, spread out across the floor. "This is you."

As soon as he says it, I wish with all my heart that it were true. And while I stand in the color-stained shadows of the statue, I can feel its essence filling me, pressing against me, moving through me, saturating me. The statue does look like me, and I experience a curious pull in the back of my head and the bottom of my stomach to it, like it represents a mother I never knew.

Teach me, Shadow Air. Fill me, Shadow Air. Be me, Shadow Air. Let me be you, Shadow Air.

I walk toward the statue. Her hand is extended toward me, a movement that is born of both strength and grace, a challenge and an invitation. I reach out and touch it.

Dronmer's words ring in my ears. *This is you.*

The statue stands on a pedestal with words carved into it.

And on that day, the One Who Walks in Shadow and Air will emerge, the killer from afar, to restore the spirit of Shai back to our lands and tear the Fools of Mercy from their misbegotten perches. Shai will bring us the blessings of justice and cure us of the weak curses of a misplaced compassion. Shai would have saved us all, but the Fools of Mercy have condemned us to this beastly hell.

For the spirit of Shai will heal the Vessels, so they see where they were blind. Shai will bring knowledge where they are ignorant and shine wisdom into those places where they are foolish. Finally, on that day, when the healed helpmates have shaken off the shackles of kindness and mercy, they will rise and support the men as all men ought to be supported, and in doing so, the land will once again know honor.

I read the words quietly aloud.

As Dronmer has said, *this is me.*

But it's obvious this *is not* me too.

I remember a Shai from Omathis' memories, when I stepped into them long ago. She was terrible to them, and they killed her. Could this be the same Shai? *This* Shai is glorious.

I need to figure out how this is me—which parts, and why, exactly and precisely—and learn what that means. Up until now, I've only known the part that isn't. And I have to figure it out soon, because I know that what Dronmer has said is true.

Icelyn is the One Who Walks in Shadow and Air.

These aren't just words that I said as a lie anymore, a trick I thought I was playing. In this shrine, as I gaze at this statue, the truth fills me.

Icelyn is the Shadow Air. I cannot doubt it. I know it as much as I know anything.

We're fortunate that the inner chambers of the Shadow Air's Shrine are forbidden to visitors. We lock the doors, too, just in case. From in here, we can easily tell when the occasional pilgrims enter this tier, in order to pray or offer food as a sacrifice, while not being detected ourselves.

Dronmer tells me that a priest once lived on this tier, but that later in Travis' life they had a falling out, and Travis had him executed and thrown from Apex. There had been no replacement; Travis had decreed that Shai had no further need for priests.

Dronmer casually mentions this man named Travis so much that I feel like I should know who he is—especially if I am the Shadow Air, the reincarnation of Shai. Again I recall Shai from Omathis' memories. She had a son who antagonized him; could this be the person Dronmer is referring to?

"Tell me, Dronmer," I ask, as we dig into some of the food left as offerings for Shai, "what do all of you think about Travis? About what he did, who he was?"

I can tell that Dronmer has not eaten such magnificent food in ages, if ever. I haven't either. We enjoy sweet treats that the Apriori called fruit. They are orange and yellow, and when peeled, they reveal the most perfectly crafted little segments. When you pop them into your mouth, they explode with flavor, their juices bursting out in every direction. Lemons and oranges, they were called! Adorane would die if he knew.

Dronmer doesn't close his mouth quickly enough, and some of the liquid shoots out and hits my leg. We laugh as he covers his mouth with his hand apologetically. I squeeze one of the segments between my thumb and forefinger, letting a spout of juice hit his cheek in revenge.

"Oops," I say.

After we stop laughing, he answers. "We hold Travis in high esteem. How could we not? The highest. I think it's part of why we all want to get to the highest tier: to be like him. He built this tower, you know, all those years ago. And he taught us about the One Who Walks in Shadow and Air. He escaped that miserable place, where mercy leads to death. We all owe him our lives."

"What place is that?"

"Oh, right. Maybe you don't know. Shai had…departed…before Travis and the others ascended to the top of the Mountain to escape the beasts. But it was an awful place, where no one appreciated his courage and his strength. Where nobody would do what needed to be done. None of that is important anymore—I'm sure everyone up there died eventually. They weren't strong enough to survive."

It sounds to me like he's talking about Mountaintop.

"So after he escaped, he built this tower, where you could be safe from the beasts?"

"Yes—and where the spirit of Shai would someday return and restore everything humans once had. And now you're here. The higher tier is going to be so excited to see you."

"How will they know I am the Shadow Air?"

"Same way I did. The skin of the Croathus, the weapon you carry—who but Shai would have such things? And look at you compared to that statue. It's obvious."

He rips open the last piece of fruit and hands me the first segment. I can see how much he loves it, and I'm struck again by his kindness. I chew thoughtfully.

"I'm confused," I admit. "You told me I have to pretend to be a boy, because...*not-boys* are forbidden here. But from looking at this statue, it's pretty obvious that Shai is not a boy."

Dronmer nods, "I wish Travis could explain that one. He's the one who made not-boys forbidden. I didn't know the One Who Walks in Shadow and Air was a not-boy, to be honest. I don't think anyone does. Maybe back then some people knew, but it's all forgotten now."

He looks at the statue and then at me, back and forth. He's no doubt marveling at how close the resemblance is. It's a darker version of me—more serious, more dangerous. But still like me.

"So I still need to pretend I'm a boy?" I ask.

"I think that would be the safest choice."

THEN

"You've been creating more of these accursed objects all this time? Without my knowledge?"]Amperous bellowed, stunned by the collection of carved masks laid out before him. "You lied to me, brother. You hid your thoughts from me. You have betrayed me."

Amperous began tossing the masks against the stone floor violently, shattering them one after another.

Omathis' grew steely and dark. "Stop ruining my work," he declared.

Amperous froze and then turned toward Omathis. They locked eyes on one another defiantly.

Amperous smashed another mask to the ground.

"Your work will bring us ruin. Your faith will destroy us. That's what faith does!"

"Faith is as useful or harmful as what it is placed in. Faith alone isn't good or bad. If you have faith in something good, it's a blessing; something bad, and it's a curse. Sean Brathius is good," Omathis insisted, "therefore, our faith is good."

"Never say his name again. Faith in Mister Sean will rot you from the head down," Amperous snarled.

Omathis hurled himself into Amperous. They erupted into brutal combat, slashing and striking ferociously. They'd tousled with one another frequently as children, but that was playing. They'd never done anything like this before.

Each lost themselves in their attempt to kill one another.

Croathus gathered on the valley floor, as far as the eye could see. They'd come from far away to answer the call. Many hummed a beautiful, haunting tune. There was joy in the air. This communion was what all of them had wanted. Bloodshed had never been their true desire.

Omathis crushed Amperous' head against the rock floor. He pressed harder, anger rushing through his tightly coiled muscles.

"If this is what you insist on doing, Omathis, then finish the job. Kill me," Amperous spat out his words with precision. "Because you are killing me anyway with your *faith*."

Omathis let up on the lethal pressure. Amperous inhaled precious oxygen before coughing. Omathis lifted his weakened brother from the ground and pulled him toward the edge of the man-made stadium. In the distance, they could both see the Croathus gathered on the horizon.

"There's an ocean of our kin, Amperous," Omathis said quietly. "All of them want what I want. They've come for the masks. And then to ascend to the top of the Mountain. Let our people reach the destiny they desire."

"I will never submit to what you want," Amperous responded bitterly. "But I know I can't stop this wave from crashing down."

57

ICELYN

I leave Dronmer in the outer room and enter the statue shrine again. I notice that the statue wears an amulet. I climb up on the pedestal and carefully remove it. It doesn't feel like stealing. It feels like I'm meant to wear it, too.

I put it around my neck and I am sure that a transformation has happened. It's not my imagination. I am different. Whether that's a good thing or not, I have no idea.

I leave the shrine.

"Let's go to the Highest Tier. It's time for them to hear what I have to say," I declare to Dronmer.

"What do you have to say?" he asks.

It's a fair question. I'm curious to find out, too.

The elite stairway is empty and silent. We've been hiding in the shrine for a day and a half, and the commotion caused by our intrusion has receded. I wonder about Kern and what he's doing without his fancy key.

"Will Kern get in trouble for losing his key?" I ask Dronmer.

"What happens to him will be what happens to him," Dronmer answers. While this is an accurate statement, it's not very useful.

"Can he return to the higher tier?" I ask.

"Only if someone lets him."

I have a hard time imagining anyone in Apex letting anyone else ascend out of kindness.

"Well, maybe he can live in your old room. You had that nice furniture."

"It's more likely he'll be thrown from the tower," Dronmer answers in a matter-of-fact voice. "You cannot lose your key."

I hate Apex. I grow even angrier, because now I'm forced to feel sorry for Kern, too. I feel a twinge of guilt for stealing his key, even as the very thought of him disgusts me.

We quietly climb the spiral set of stairs, and I'm struck again by how unrelenting they are. I haven't been counting, but there have to be tens of thousands of steps. It feels infinite.

"I thought we were nearly at the top," I say breathlessly.

"Compared to the bottom, we were. Compared to the top, I guess not," Dronmer answers.

After hours of torture, we have reached the top of the stone staircase. The door here is different than the rest—fashioned with great care out of cut and polished stones and accented with shimmering gold overlay.

The precious materials are arranged into an image of two men reaching toward the heavens from their place atop a tower. On the ground far below them is a scene of death, despair, and beasts inflicting bloody carnage on humanity.

The space above the door bears an inscription: *Defense is Eternity. Mercy is Sabotage.*

Dronmer drops to his knees and quietly murmurs these words to himself. There are tears in his eyes. I realize that he has been working toward this moment his entire life.

Yet there is something about the way he's groveling on the ground that bothers me. I can't decide why it upsets me so, but I grab him by the shoulder and lift him back to his feet.

"Stop that, please."

He looks completely taken aback.

"You're better than all of this," I offer by way of an explanation. That's what's bothering me. Dronmer is better. This tower isn't worthy of a kind soul like his. The brutal competition to get to the next level, the disdain for compassion and empathy and mercy, the victimization of the lower levels at the hands of the higher ones—it's all exhausting, and I despise it. This tower could topple over tomorrow and the world would be the better for it. That Dronmer's life goal is to reach the pinnacle of this deplorable place makes me feel sick to my stomach.

I insert Kern's key into the heavy jeweled door and turn.

"Let's get this over with," I sigh.

The highest tier is different than I expected. For one thing, we haven't seen anyone. I thought we'd enter ornately decorated rooms, more lavish than those of the Apriori kings. Instead, there isn't much up here at all—only cavernous spaces filled with obscene amounts of food, most of it swept aside and rotting. Dronmer and the lower tiers were hungry all the time, some even dying from starvation. These uneaten piles of food feel like an insult to humanity.

"It's beautiful," Dronmer whispers. "Just as I remember it."

I wipe my eyes and blink hard, wondering if I'm unable to see what he's seeing. No, still just vast amounts of wasted food.

"You've been here before?" I ask.

"Oh, yes. I once lived here with my father and brother. When I was a child. But I was the lesser brother, so I was sent to the lower tier."

He digs through the mounds of food. They appear to bring back grand memories.

"You're a *child of a higher tier,* and they sent you to the lower tier?"

"All lower tiers are children of a higher tier. Only highest tiers get to have children. They send their least favorites to the lower tiers. That's how it works."

"That's terrible."

"No, no. If anyone who belongs on a higher tier is sent down, he has the opportunity to fight his way back to the top. It all makes sense. Everything is sorted out so everyone gets what they deserve. It's a flawless and fair system." He finds a jar of honey and scoops some into his mouth. "Honey! It tastes better than I remembered."

I pull it away from him. Enjoying even a bite from this tower feels wrong to me. "Come on, let's keep going."

We exit one room and come upon a group of men preparing more food in a large kitchen space. They're so focused on their work that none of them notice our approach. I ready my ultraspear in case we are forced to duel.

"They're just lower tiers working. There is no need to battle them," Dronmer explains.

The rules of this tower are confusing to me, but I'm relieved. We pass through the space without being noticed.

We enter a humid, cavernous room pockmarked with tiny windows that allow many rays of sunlight to flood into the space. There are long, steaming bathtubs everywhere I look, all of them filled with bathing men. I look away from their nudity. Is this what the men on the highest tier do all day—eat whatever food they want, waste whatever food they do not, and then lay around and bathe the rest of the time?

I've never seen a naked man in all my years, and now in one minute I've seen more than anyone should in a lifetime.

"The One Who Walks in Shadow and Air has returned," Dronmer proclaims, and his voice is much louder than I've ever heard before. His words echo through the room, and the men turn their attention toward us.

"And I with him! He has killed a Threatbelow and bears the amulet of the Shadow Air."

The men appear stunned by Dronmer's words.

"Dronmer?" one of the men asks, confused. "Is that you?" The speaker is tall and frail, with hair as white as a cloud hanging long and loose from his head. I don't observe many other details; he is flaunting his nakedness, so I do not look at him directly for long. But at a glance, his features seem harsh and angular.

"Yes, Father. I've made my way back. You made a mistake in sending me away. The shame you claimed I brought you is yours alone—I bear no responsibility." I can tell that Dronmer is getting to say words he's prepared and rehearsed. Words he's longed to say for his entire life.

"Father, what is this? Make him leave. He doesn't belong here!" If a slug could take human form, it would look like the young man crying out from the next tub. "Dronmer, you're a lower tier!"

"My brother, I've ascended. I deserve to be here more than you do. You've simply been handed all this; you never had to work to raise yourself even one level."

Dronmer's forceful words silence both his brother and his father easily. These soft, well-washed men don't have any ability to stand up against someone like Dronmer, who has been tested and seasoned in the violence of the lower levels.

Dronmer leads me toward a platform in the middle of the room. I stand on it, and the men stare at me. I want to close my eyes, duck my head, and scurry away, but instead I stand tall and move my gaze around the room. I do my best to look imperial, to stand like the statue I saw in the shrine. I ruffle the Croathus bearskin and draw it around me, making sure they all see it. Should I say something?

Dronmer stands beside me, his eyes glimmering with pride.

"If anyone wishes to challenge me, the One Who Walks in Shadow and Air is eager to spill your blood," I declare. It's not true, but it seems like something that statue would say. And as I say it, I realize it isn't a complete lie. Maybe I'm not eager, given my bruises from the last fight, but I'm certainly willing. And it wouldn't be difficult. From the looks of the water-logged men who fill the baths, I might spill their blood accidentally if I'm not careful.

I hold my ultraspear out threateningly.

My echoing words are met with silence. And then, Dronmer's father stands and starts clapping. His hands are wet, so it sounds more like someone slapping a puddle. Dronmer's brother rises and joins in his father's applause.

Soon, all the men in the room, naked and dripping, probably forty in all—though I'm not about to carefully count them—stand up in their tubs, their bodies jiggling as they mash their moist hands together over and over in a unified ovation.

This wasn't how I imagined the return of the Shadow Air would go at all, but I suppose it could be worse.

THEN

The line of clouds blanketing the peak of the mountain had thinned in recent days.

Sean Brathius considered it an omen. The shroud between the humans and his creations was growing thinner. Soon they'd live together in peace and build a new future together.

They'd reached the appointed day. Travis, Laura Lee, and Sean Brathius were the only ones who would take part in this ceremony. They gathered at the drop off, appropriately solemn, though Laura Lee couldn't keep the inklings of a smile from her face. She was so excited.

Travis had done everything he'd promised. Sean had conceded long ago that he'd been wrong about Shai's son. Now he was thankful that Travis was married to Laura Lee. All the towers had been activated, loaded with the Brathius blood serum; Travis had carried out his plan perfectly.

"My God, how many are there?" Sean asked, as his mind strained to keep up with what his eyes saw between flashes of wispy clouds. What they'd initially thought was brush and chaparral on the sides of the mountain was moving. On closer examination, they could see that it was a sea of Croathus.

"This had better work," Travis sighed.

"It will," Sean replied, without a trace of doubt in his voice.

Sean and Laura Lee had been calling the Croathus to the mountain for weeks now. If there had been any doubt before, it was clear now—their message had been received. Sean's face flushed red, and he struggled to breathe as he indulged in a smile. *After all this, after everything that has happened, they still love me. I abandoned them, but now I've done everything I can to right that terrible wrong.*

Travis placed an ornate wooden box at Sean's feet. "This box represents the blood spilled by the Shadow Salvation Group to bring your plan to fruition," he declared ceremoniously. "May you find it worthy of their sacrifice."

Sean felt a hand grasp his and knew that it was Laura Lee. It was fitting that they'd carry out this honor together.

"Open the box, Laura Lee." She lifted a small black flattened rectangle from the carved container. It was simple—one button. She handed it to her father.

"Let's change them for the better," Sean whispered, smiling at Laura Lee. "Let's make them who I always intended them to be."

58

NOW

Adorane awoke and shuffled out of the cave he and Torrain had slept in. It was still dark. Torrain kept sleeping. This was how most mornings started.

Adorane bowed his head and breathed in, then out. He grabbed fistfuls of the grainy sand and poured it over his own head.

"I am lower than dirt and I need your help," he whispered. "Without pride, I beg you. Guide us." He pressed fine desert dust against his tear-filled eyes until thin sheets of wet mud covered his cheeks.

Adorane had never before been angry at his god—not even when his father was killed in Cloudline. Immortality was promised to no one, at least in this world, and Aclornis departed cloaked in courage. But he'd grown furious while Icelyn had been missing. He'd worked hard to channel his rage into action: Start the day by pestering the Almighty to act, then search all day, then sleep only enough to avoid dying. Something had to change eventually.

"Guide me to her, O Lord. And if you cannot do that today, shield her from harm, O Lord. And if you will not do that today, please allow her to suffer no wound that cannot be healed, O Lord."

Torrain awoke, and Adorane was thankful that they were both equally desperate to find Icelyn. Neither of them dared speak of the likelihood that she might be dead, even though they were both practical enough to know the odds.

They wordlessly gathered their belongings, then set out into the desert to begin their search again.

ICELYN

"I'm not hungry, thank you." I reject a platter piled high with food for the hundredth time. I was polite at first, but now my words are dripping in disdain. Each time is a new disappointment to the servers, who are eager to please me. Dronmer grabs a fistful of food to placate them.

We're seated at the head of a long table in a gold-plated banquet hall where every inch glimmers and gleams—the table, the chairs, the plates, the cups, the walls, the ceiling, the floor. In another place, with other people, I might think this was glorious. But here it feels empty and cheap—an obscene attempt to bring meaning into hollow lives.

The highest tiers have hurriedly arranged a celebration in my honor—which is to say that they commanded their lower tiered servants to do so. Wandering musicians play music. Other servants perform acrobatic tricks to tepid applause.

The piles of food outside the baths were a light snack compared to the banquet here. There are meats and sweets I've never even heard of, even after suffering through two boring semesters on Apriori culinary habits in my tenth year of schooling. There are eggs of every imaginable size and shade, fizzy drinks that make my head woozy, rich sauces and exotic rices and countless breads and cakes. I fill up ten minutes into the festivities. It's exhausting.

"But you must try! If you're no longer hungry, just take a bite and throw the rest on the ground. The lower tiers will clean up after you," they beg, but I don't like this suggestion.

They are desperate to please me, which only makes me more tired of them. I've seen the way they treat those they consider beneath them, and I'm not about to be tricked into believing they are good and gracious people because of how well they treat me.

"I like to imagine I carry the mantle of Travis wherever I go. I pattern my life after him—always asking myself, 'How can I be more like Travis?'" one of the men drones on, boring me. He introduced himself at one point, but I couldn't be bothered to remember his name.

I nod, trying to figure out how to escape the conversation. He trails off and stares at me. I don't know what he wants.

"So…do I remind you of Travis?" he asks, and I've never seen someone so hungry to hear the word *yes.*

I laugh despite myself. What a strange question. "Not at all. No. Sorry. You are nothing like Travis."

I've disappointed him, and I feel a twinge of sadness for him. He's a parasite who preys on those beneath him, but maybe he never had a chance to be anything else. The other men chuckle at his expense—quietly at first but then louder.

"Grenwold! He said you're *nothing like Travis*! Nothing! Might as well be a not-boy!"

The man flushes crimson, as much from embarrassment as from anger.

"Weak! Illogical! Misguided!" The men tease Grenwold, each of them looking toward me as they do, as if their jabs might endear them to me.

"Just like a NOT-BOY!" they shout.

A not-boy? Now I've grown interested.

"Tell me more about the…not-boys," I command.

Since they can see I've finally engaged, they scramble to answer me. They finish each other's thoughts, each eager to jump in and please me.

"Oh! Not-boys used to rule all people, in the darker times."

"Every man was subject to their terrible decisions, which they would always make incorrectly…"

"They had no sense of logic. They would choose what to do, who to love, based on whims and flights of fancy…"

"Ignoring the boys who treated them well, loving the ones who would treat them badly…"

"They didn't know their place, so they ruined everything."

"They wouldn't give the gentlemen, the truly nice boys, the love they deserved."

On and on, the venom boils over and flows from their mouths.

Now that they think I'm part of their club, they share their secrets with me. And I wonder: Is this how all boys, all men, feel about women? Is this how they all talk when we're not around? Would Adorane and Torrain disagree with these men? Would they tell them to be quiet? Or would they listen and nod quietly, maybe even jump in with their own accusations?

I can feel my face growing tighter, and I have no idea how to respond. A chill enters the room as they realize that their attempts to impress me are having the opposite effect. They trail off and eventually fall silent.

Finally, I think of a question. "Dronmer. Do you agree with them? About not-boys?"

Dronmer doesn't answer, trapped between me and the others.

"Dronmer. Do you agree with them? Is this all true, what they say about…women? Girls?"

The men gasp at my use of the ancient forbidden words. Some appear on the verge of fainting. For people who claim that women are weak, they are not very strong themselves. But I'm not going to go on saying *not-boy* when words like *woman* and *girl* exist. Enough is enough.

"No. I don't believe any of these men know what they're talking about," Dronmer answers, his words ringing crisply through the silence.

His answer offends everyone in the room but me. Dronmer's father mumbles something about the foolishness of the lower tiers.

"Ah! See here!" I exclaim with a smile. "At least *one* of you knows something! Of every man in this room, I am only pleased with Dronmer. For the rest, hear my words: The One Who Walks in Shadow and Air came to Apex intending to restore you to glory. Yet I find you all beneath my expectations. I suggest you carefully consider what you say in my presence, lest I abandon you to yourselves."

THEN

Omathis was overwhelmed by the sight of so many Croathus filled with hope. He hadn't seen joy like this since they'd lived in the green paradise. Any contentment his kind had enjoyed had been destroyed in the brutal bombings of their cavern home, and they had been consumed by hunger ever since—for revenge, for safety, for a world without humans.

This hunger had made them strong and mighty. Once dipped in blood, they became brutal and lethal, and they dominated the world.

Yet it had never brought them any hope.

"You remember how Mister Sean taught us how to draw?" Omathis asked his brother. "That was often my favorite part of the day. Drawing with him."

"I try to forget those days," Amperous grumbled in return.

"We were never meant to be only warriors," Omathis stated. "Otherwise, why would he teach us to draw, to see the beauty all around us? Remember the time he asked me if I saw how the sun shone through the green leaves of the plant near the window? Remember that plant? When its leaves glowed in the sunlight, you could see the veins, even the tiny ones. I drew it once, and he put it up on the wall. He said it was one of his favorite pieces of art and that it belonged in a museum."

"Mister Sean was a liar," Amperous replied, his voice tired.

"You'll see," Omathis promised. "That's who we are. We see the sunlight on the leaf and draw its beauty."

Omathis heard laughter among the young ones who darted about. He caught buoyant snippets of conversation.

He raised his arms up above his head. The swarms froze and turned toward him.

"Let us rise above the brutal killers we have become!" he bellowed, and his voice echoed through the canyons asnd rock walls of the mountain valley. "We shall be Anaghwin, as he intended, not Croathus."

Anaghwin. The word prickled the hair on Amperous' neck. Mister Sean had always promised them that they shared his breath and his blood, his *anima* and his *sanguis*. Omathis had smashed the Latin words together to come up with a name for their species that he preferred to Croathus. But it always felt like delusion to Amperous. They were Croathus, the name of the military experiment which had resulted in their creation. Nothing more.

A chant rose in response to Omathis' words.

"Anaghwin, not Croathus. Anaghwin, not Croathus. Anaghwin, not Croathus."

Laura Lee put her arm around her fathers' shoulders and held him tight. She always had to initiate affection with him, but he appreciated it when she did. He tended to forget about the existence of physical contact altogether when left to himself.

"Do you hear that?" she asked.

It was far away, and so quiet that you could easily tune it out if you weren't listening for it. But it was also the most beautiful sound Sean had ever heard.

Anaghwin, not Croathus. Anaghwin, not Croathus. Anaghwin, not Croathus.

"They are made of our blood and breath," he whispered, lost in the memory.

Travis broke the spell. "You can press the button whenever you'd like," he reminded Sean.

Anaghwin, not Croathus. Anaghwin, not Croathus. Anaghwin, not Croathus.

Sean bathed in the sound of the creatures' chants for a moment longer before he shook himself back to reality.

"Of course, thank you."

He held the remote above his head and pressed the button hard.

59

ICELYN

My warning weighs on the men. They are afraid to speak to me for the rest of the evening for fear of offending me further. It must be disorienting for them to hear that I will not tolerate insults hurled toward women—like finding out after all this time that good was bad or hot was cold.

They watch the musicians and performers in silence, continuing to eat whatever is placed in front of them (my, how these men can devour food). After what feels like an interminable amount of time, they rise and return to their chambers with silent bows. They all keep a wary eye on my ultraspear, fearful that they are one wayward word away from me using it.

Dronmer and I are given a suite with a window to the outside. It's packed with a sickening level of luxury. The large beds made of rare fabric, outfitted with soft blankets and pillows that would probably cost a lower level Apex citizen his life if he touched it without permission There are yet more tables filled with food. I can barely handle the smell of it anymore; I long for hunger instead of the overstuffed fullness weighing down on me.

I am tired of the opulence at the highest tier. I am tired of all this.

I relish watching the sun set in the distance for the first time in a long time. A window to the outside world is one privilege I will never tire of.

Dronmer quietly arranges wooden staffs and knives. I may be imagining things, but it seems like he's avoiding me—like he doesn't know what to say to me and would rather ignore me than admit to that awkwardness.

"What did you think of that banquet?" I ask him.

"The food was what I always hoped it would be," he answers, but with less enthusiasm than his words warrant.

"Did I ruin the celebration?"

"Of course you did. But I understand why. It's funny, but until you actually meet a not-boy—I mean, a…woman—well, the things they were saying would have seemed right before tonight. But now that I've met you, I can see that it's all foolish. It makes no more sense than gouging your own eye out."

Dronmer can't seem to help but use the most horrifying of metaphors. But he is sweet—and him saying that meeting me has undone a lifetime of anti-woman rhetoric is perhaps the nicest compliment I've ever received.

"I'm sorry I ruined your party," I say, and I mean it. I know he's looked forward to reaching this tier all his life. "I can tell that you're deflated."

"I am, but you're not the reason why. It's just that—this was what I always wanted, and now that I'm here—it's just another tier. It's certainly not heaven."

"And the people on this tier are terrible. Boring and weak, hardly worth knowing," I add, and he laughs.

A knock at the thick wooden door interrupts us. Dronmer's eyes fill with concern. He moves cautiously to the door and opens it.

His father and brother stand in the doorway, about forty other residents of the highest tier behind them. The best of Apex—a pathetic bunch.

"Father, brother. We are eager to rest," Dronmer states and begins to close the door. "Let's gather in the morning." But his father sticks a foot out and blocks it from closing.

"Dronmer," his father whispers—though I can hear him, so I wonder why he bothers—"I ask that you give us the One Who Walks in Shadow and Air so that we can tear him apart."

"Never, Father," Dronmer states flatly. "I'd rather dip bread in a pool of your blood and eat it." Dronmer says this odd sentence as if it's a common refrain, and his father accepts it as one, too.

"Son, we have conferred and decided that Shai is not who we were hoping he would be. We were more comfortable without him. As highest tiers, we demand that you give him over to us so that we can slaughter him."

"Travis commanded that we worship Shai. There is a shrine to Shai that you have spent your entire lives visiting—where you have prayed, sought wisdom, promised your devotion."

"Yes, but now that Shai is here and is no longer a statue, we do not like him. Not even a little bit. So we have decided there must have been a mistake. Give him to us so that we may kill him."

I creep from the corner of the suite and stand behind Dronmer. I can see that the men are holding knives and swords. They are forged from gold and encrusted with jewels, but despite these gaudy decorations, they appear to be sharpened. At the sight of me, the men press forward into the room, trying to push Dronmer aside. But he's stronger than they are, strengthened in the lower tiers while they lounged in the baths high above him. He holds them at bay.

"No one can defy our wishes. We are highest tiers!" Dronmer's father declares, though his voice is whiny and weak. "As we desire, so we shall have!"

I grab my ultraspear and hold it tight just in case.

"Fine," Dronmer responds. With one strong motion, he grabs one of the men and pulls him out of the hallway, tossing him toward me. "Have at it."

The man lunges at me. I can see right away that he has no combat training. I hold my spear in defense, though I hardly need to. He swings his golden sword at it. Its soft blade bends at impact. The reverberations cause his hands to sting, and he drops it to the ground. Immediately the man bows his head and grovels before me. "Please don't kill me, please. I'm sorry. I didn't mean to offend." He holds his still-smarting hands tight to his chest, as if he's never felt such terrible pain (or, indeed, any pain at all).

I kick gently at the man. "Get back to the hallway. Go." He rises and scuffles away, his head down.

"Who wants a turn?" Dronmer asks. None seem eager to volunteer.

"We were thinking you could subdue Shai for us, Dronmer," his brother says quietly.

Dronmer sighs. "Leave. Now."

"We command that you subdue Shai for us! You must!"

Dronmer leans close to his brother's face and says "And I command you leave us be, or I will slit your throat. We're tired and would like some rest."

Somehow Dronmer's father and brother (as you can see, I've forgotten their names by now) find an ounce of strength and shove past him. The other men follow and charge toward me. Though each of them are slow and soft, individually no match even for my meager fighting skills, as a whole they are intimidating.

I don't want to spill any blood. "Stand back, or you will force me to unleash my power on you!" I warn. A gangly man steps toward me. I turn my spear and poke him with the blunt end. He falls back for a moment, but then finds a hidden store of strength and swings his sword toward me. The tip slices into my forearm, and a sudden hot burst of pain consumes me.

Before I can register what's happened, Dronmer descends upon the man, battering him with a series of devastating moves. Before long, the man is clearly dead.

Dronmer moves on to the next man. I'm suddenly afraid he will kill them all.

"Dronmer, that's enough!" I shout. He freezes, mid-stab, above another one of the cowering men. He looks at me long enough to see that my forearm is bleeding, and that's enough to send him into another mindless fit of rage. Before I can beg him to stop again, another two men are dead.

Dronmer stalks before the rest of the men, who try their best to submit to him, desperate to make their surrender clear before he kills them. But he doesn't want to stop killing them.

"Please, please! We will give you access!" his father shouts. I don't know what he's referring to, but Dronmer clearly does. He stalls his attacks.

"Access?" Dronmer asks. He looks to me, as if asking if this is enough for him to stop the slaughter. As if I haven't already been begging him to stop murdering them in my defense.

"Access to what?" I ask.

"To the Underneath Forge," his father promises, "which only the elite of the highest tier ever visit. You can both have access."

I give Dronmer the sign to relent. Fortunately, he does.

"Clean this up for us, please, and do not try anything so foolish again, or I will not be so merciful. Give us the night to rest—and then yes, in the morning, we will visit the forge," I declare.

The Underneath Forge—the technology that enables them to bear children without women. I cannot believe it actually exists.

Of course I want access.

60

ICELYN

We follow Dronmer's father and brother, who are carried in chairs by men of lower tiers, down a series of descending circles around the exterior of Apex. We move through sand- and mud-packed corridors built onto the outside walls of the main tower. I prefer traveling in these to the interior passageways, because there are openings to the outside. Through the tiny windows I can see the blue sky, yellow sands, and red rock mountains. I strain my eyes against the bright sun, but I cannot find the tower where I left Torrain and Adorane anywhere on the horizon.

I miss the two of them. I haven't realized how much until now.

These outer passages connect larger chambers that serve useful purposes. In some crops are growing; in others water is being collected and stored. We even pass through one that houses animals—ones that I've read about but never seen, birds called *chickens* and mammals called *cows*. All are attended to by men of lower tiers. They don't acknowledge our presence, as seems to be the custom, and we ignore them as well.

Torrain would like to study what I see, I know that. There are pipes to carry and pump water, fires burning, and liquids boiling to create a steam that is captured and put to some mysterious use. I hadn't thought of the technology needed to keep this city in the sky going, but it's impressive. Whoever built this place was a genius.

But I don't have time to study any of this, because we continue our descent quickly and purposefully through the tunnels. Finally, we reach the end of the outer passages and face a steel door into the main tower. Dronmer's father sends away the lower tiers who carried him and the others, then uses a complex set of keys on a series of sturdy padlocks. He swings open the door, and we face the darkness within.

"Wash yourselves," he commands as we approach an oversized stone cistern carved into the wall. The scent of citrus and flowers mixed with something bitter and cutting wafts from it.

I dip a hand into the cistern cautiously, following Dronmer's lead. He pours the liquid onto himself, and I do the same.

"It's vital that we are cleansed of all illnesses before we enter the Underneath Forge," his father explains. "We can't risk dirtying the Vessels. They are fragile and must be protected."

They've dodged every question I've asked on this excursion thus far, so I know that any requests for clarification would be futile. I silently ponder the clues on my own. What are the Vessels?

We've entered a central passageway in the tower. It's dark here, with only torches to provide light, and smells old and musty. I hear distant echoes floating up from below and can't place what they might be. They are rhythmic, almost like one of the machines Torrain might invent; yet they are punctuated with something high-pitched and desperate.

Dronmer's father and brother lead the way, along with another two highest tier men.

"To enter these chambers is an honor bestowed on the few and the best," Dronmer's brother starts, and it sounds like this is a speech he has given many times before. "You have been chosen because you are worthy of extending yourselves into the next generation. This honor was once available to all, and humanity suffered. But now we become greater with every child who emerges from the Forge."

We descend more stairs and the strange sounds grow louder.

I don't like it here.

"You must be a gentleman, polite and worthy of the Vessels. You must be thankful. All others in Apex would give their lives to be where you are today, so act in accordance to your station. The Vessels are grateful for what we provide: a structure, an order, a measure of control they did not have on their own. Likewise, we are grateful for what they give in exchange: an extension of ourselves into eternity—our intellect, our spirit, our greatness made immortal, one generation at a time. This is the natural balance we have found, the reason we have survived when all others have died. This synergy born of natural law is why we are great when all others have withered away."

I can see that the words have their effect on Dronmer. He seems moved, on the verge of tears. I hate it, and I nudge him, hoping to break him out of the spell. This confuses him. Dronmer's father and the other highest tiers all act as if this is the most solemn, beautiful moment one could experience, but something about the speech leaves me with a rising sense of panic.

We continue our descent until we reach another giant metal door, this one marked with the words *The Greatest Honor Is Draped On The Vessels Within.*

Dronmer's father and brother nod toward one another. They both remove their robes, as if this is expected behavior. The other two highest tier men do the same, and all are now completely bare. Their lack of shame disturbs me. This accursed place! I have never seen men so eager to disrobe in all my life. I do not like it. They look to me and Dronmer, as if we should join them in their nakedness. Dronmer looks at me warily. I can see him wrestling between custom and the knowledge that I *cannot* disrobe.

"No," I say, and they don't argue, because by now they know how stubborn I am. Dronmer makes his decision in the wake of mine and remains clothed.

"Be careful, then," Dronmer's father warns. "Do not contaminate any of the Vessels with your clothing. Be vigilant."

THEN

When he heard the massive crack and then the rumbling, Omathis' first thought was that he hadn't known a sound this loud could exist. By the time he saw the cloud of angry smoke rise far above his head, he could only hear a high-pitched droning. He touched his ears and saw that his hands were stained red with blood.

The ground shook beneath his feet, one ear-splitting eruption after another, and more clouds rose on the horizon. He counted four, then five, then six.

When the ringing in his ears had subsided enough to make out other sounds, he heard the screaming and groaning of Croathus all around him.

What was happening?

He pushed himself up from ground and focused on those around him. He'd seen death among the Croathus before—back in the cavern. But this was far worse. Was he the only one who hadn't been torn into pieces by whatever had happened?

He felt a strong hand dig into his shoulder.

"Grab those who retain the ability for restoration, if you see any, but then we must go," Amperous shouted at him. Omathis could see why.

The ground beneath their feet was cracking. Whole chunks were giving way and collapsing into the depths of the valley, carrying the terrified Croathus with them. Omathis heard an eerie rushing sound. He turned and looked toward the horizon, then froze in horror. A wave as tall as a mountain was rushing from the ocean toward them.

Omathis sensed a glimmer of spirit that could be restored in two mangled Croathus and hoisted them from the ground before fleeing after Amperous. They barely avoided free-falling boulders from above and unsteady, disintegrating ground below as they struggled to reach higher ground.

What was happening?

He had beckoned them. They were obeying him. They were there for him.

Why did he do this?

Sean Brathius stared at the wreckage in silence. The perimeter of towers had exploded, creating a semi-circle of mushroom clouds throughout the basin below. Entire plains had been laid low. As he watched, ocean waters rushed into and flooded the lands, claiming it for the sea.

He felt numb. He felt dead.

Laura Lee fell to her knees. From so far away, it looked like ants were being blown to pieces, dropped into the middle of the earth, and drowned by some cruel child. But every speck below was a Croathus—a creature just like Omathis and Amperous.

Omathis and Amperous were part of this crowd.

"How could this happen?" she shouted. "What has happened?"

Her words shook Sean Brathius from his stupor.

"This was not a malfunction in my design," he stated flatly. He wheeled toward Travis, flooded with more grief as he realized what had happened. "This was sabotage."

Travis did not shrink away from the accusation. He stood across from Sean Brathius, eye to eye.

"Someone had to protect what's left of humanity. Generations from now, humans will only exist because of what I've done today. *They'll* know to call me a hero."

61

ICELYN

I'm not sure what I was expecting inside the Underneath Forge. I suppose I thought it would be dark and unforgiving, like a dungeon, or perhaps whirring with machines and electricity, a murky laboratory like the one I left Torrain and Adorane in. Perhaps I expected it would be like the animal chambers we passed through to reach this place—pungent, humid, and smelling of the fetid origins of life.

Instead, we are in a high-ceilinged space even more luxurious than the banquet room on the highest tier. Over our heads is spread a grand mosaic, forged out of shimmering golds, silvers, and bronzes and decorated with sparkling stones of many colors. It depicts a magnificent sun rising behind the silhouettes of a group of strong, confident men. I stare at it, and it silences me.

We walk past plush beds appointed with embroidered silk linens and blankets. I reach out and touch a sheet, and I have a difficult time believing, filled with disbelief at how smooth and soft it is. Waterfalls pour from openings in the walls. Firelight flickers through colorful gems onto the cascading water and broadcasts fractured beauty over all of us, so that I am pulsating blue and green and red and purple depending on where I stand.

A tinkle of finely tuned metal chimes rings throughout the chamber. The sound combines with the peaceful and gentle roar of the falling waters to create an air of calm. Forget about the highest tier—*this* is the place I might mistake for heaven, if I believed such a place existed.

The highest tier men have each staked out their own bed, disrobed completely, and laid upon them. I avert my eyes, upset to see such beautiful blankets and sheets sullied by their bodies.

"Take a bed," Dronmer's father instructs, "and I will send for the Vessels."

I stand beside a bed, but I do not sit on it. How many highest tier bodies have laid upon them in the past? I don't want any part in their defilement. I can see that Dronmer watches me, fearing my disapproval. He sits with noticeable unease on the edge of a bed.

Dronmer's father approaches one of the waterfalls. There, a bowl holds a mound of powder. He scoops two handfuls of the powder and drops it into the currents. The clear water turns red once the powder has dissolved into it, and soon all of the waterfalls flow crimson. This must have been some kind of summoning, because I hear plucked notes and low sustained tones. I've only heard such things a few times before, but I know they are musical instruments.

All of the men's eyes turn toward a darkened portal. I don't know what to expect, but I can already tell I'm not going to like it.

Women.

Women emerge from the dark cave. They are young, mostly, not any older than me. Some even younger.

I was told that they didn't exist here anymore.

"These are girls," I observe.

"No, these are Vessels," Dronmer's father responds. "Girls, women, not-men, they were headstrong and stubborn and foolish, so they died out centuries ago. Vessels are blessed, honored, and wise—and so they have survived."

There are six of them, dressed in a type of ornate white gown that I've only seen in images from the Apriori days. Back then, women would wear them for marriage ceremonies.

"All honor is bestowed upon you, oh Vessels," the highest tiers say in unison.

"The honor is ours, because it comes from you," they reply, their faces blank, their eyes focused somewhere elsewhere.

The women separate and each approach one of the beds. The men stand as the women near them, then kneel on one knee and bow their heads. "I am here to surround you with kindness," the highest tiers promise, again all together.

"To accept your gifts are why I exist," each woman responds, staring directly at the man before her.

This is the Underneath Forge? This is their advanced technology? My skin burns hot, and I can feel my pulse in my head.

A girl kneels before me. She seems confused, because I haven't said a word nor disrobed. She tries to hide her confusion. I study her face closely. She is so young. No great invention, no mystical solution—simply a child.

I cannot let this proceed.

"What is this madness?" I ask. "These are girls. Children."

"I am a Vessel," the one nearest to me insists quickly, as if I might reveal a secret she is desperate to keep hidden. "Not-men were foolish and stubborn, and they no longer exist. We choose kindness. I choose you."

"You don't have to live this way," I whisper to the girl before me. "What is your name?"

She seems confused by the question. "I am a Vessel," she insists.

"Have they trapped you here?" I ask quietly.

"No, this is all one could ever want," the girl near Dronmer replies. "We are protected. We are cared for. We are pampered and adored. Given dignity and honor. Visited by gentlemen—kind, polite, gentle, gracious gentlemen." The girl nearest to me nods in agreement.

Their eyes disturb me. Where others might see serenity, I see something dead—like something that should be strong inside has long ago been shattered. Their stance, their countenance, their eagerness. I'm sure they are lying, even if they believe they're telling the truth.

I reach my hand out to the girl before me, touching my hand to her cheek. I want to comfort her, but can't think of anything to say.

"You are never to touch a Vessel!" Dronmer's father bellows at me, furious. "Why would any man defile himself by making contact with them? No amount of bathing will cleanse you now."

I am shocked, but I notice that all others are obeying this rule.

Dronmer's father looks annoyed. "You offer your gift by placing it on the bed. Then we say our prayers to Travis, asking him to bless the offerings and seal the work. The Vessel will accept the gift and take it into the caves below. Before too long, you will have a son. It is a miracle. The beauty of the Underneath Forge."

He turns back to his own ceremony and tunes me out. From the looks of it, the prayers to Travis are long and involved.

The girl catches sight of the amulet I wear, and her eyes widen. "Tell me, what is this?" she asks, betraying her youth. I lift the necklace over my head.

"Would you like to wear it?" I ask. "This is the pendant of the One

Who Walks in Shadow and Air."

She reaches her hands toward the necklace but seems afraid to touch it, like it's forbidden and she could be punished severely for breaking a rule.

"Go on," I encourage her. "Take it, look at it."

Her face flashes from tentative caution to pure desire as she snatches it away from me. Before I can do anything, she wraps the cord around her neck and starts to pull with all her strength. Her face turns a crimson red. I struggle to stop her, but she's determined.

She's trying to strangle herself.

"You'll see to it that she receives the best care," I stammer, struggling to vocalize even a fraction of all the thoughts rushing through my head. I'm light-headed with anger at what I've just witnessed.

There is no Underneath Forge. Just women, forced underground into a life so awful that one leapt at the chance to strangle herself. Dronmer and I were able to tear the amulet away from her, and she began breathing normally soon after. But she wanted to die. There was no doubt.

I rush through the corridors, back to our quarters, away from the nightmare behind us. Dronmer's father, his brother, and the other highest tiers struggle to catch up to me, stumbling as they pulled their clothing on.

"We warned you about needing to disrobe prior to entering!" Dronmer's father shouts after me. "You should never bring anything into the chamber with you."

"Because you knew that they would try to kill themselves?" I spit back. "Because they've tried before?"

"They're Vessels!" He answers, as if that's all that needs to be explained. "What else would you expect would happen? They are weak! They need our protection. They can't be trusted on their own."

I don't want to argue with these men. They are lost to the lives they've lived, the selfishness born at their elite tip of the tower—and nothing I can say could shake them free of what they've become. If they think that the deeds done in that accursed chamber are good and right, then the time when discussions can turn them back toward decency has passed long ago.

Dronmer catches up to me and puts a gentle hand on my shoulder.

"Icelyn…" he trails off. He seems not to know what to say next.

I whisper to him, "You don't share in their opinion, do you?" My eyes desperately search his face for the answer to my question. I don't even want to ask—because if the answer is anything but a horrified, clear *no,* I won't be able to bear it.

"I had no idea that's what was happening down there. You have to believe me!" Dronmer whispers urgently. We resume swiftly moving ahead of the other men, who doggedly trail us while trying to bait us into conversation.

"Will you not even debate with us?"

"We have pure logic on our side. You only have emotion."

"Are you afraid that we are correct, and you have no argument?"

We ignore them.

"I feel fortunate that my first visit into that place was with you, Icelyn," Dronmer says sadly. "If I had seen it through my father's eyes, I fear that I might have fallen into his particular blindness. But instead I got to see it through your outrage, and I saw it for what it was: monstrous."

Relief flows through me, and I grab his hand.

We make it to our chambers on the highest tier and slam the door closed. I pull him toward me and we embrace. He seems confused by what we're doing, which is the right response. I'm mixed up, too—angry, shaken, yet filled with purpose and passion.

I put my hand behind his head, and the warmth and softness of his hair settles me down. I feel as though I've been soaring higher and higher, terrifyingly high, and I have finally managed to drop an anchor onto something solid.

"Dronmer, we have to tear this place to pieces. We'll save the women and any of the lower tiers you tell me are worth saving. But other than that, Apex must fall."

I watch indecision battle across Dronmer's face. I can't blame him—this is his family, his homeland, his whole world. But don't we all have to tear our family to pieces in some way or another before we can become who we're meant to be? Don't we have to destroy the world we were born into before we can build the one where we're meant to live?

At least that's what I had to do.

"But Icelyn, maybe we could just leave..."

"A Brathius would just leave," I respond. I clutch the amulet—the amulet I found in the Shai shrine, the one that poor girl used to try to strangle herself. "But I am not only a Brathius. I am a child of more than one parent. I am the One Who Walks in Shadow and Air, too. I am

Brathius, but I am also Shai. I am the place where both those rivers converge."

We are drawn together instinctively. He kisses me, and I kiss him back. When we part, he's weakened. Ready to do whatever I ask. It was for Shai that this place was built, and it will be Shai who destroys it.

"My mind is made up," I tell him. "Let Apex be consumed by the hell that it is. No place like the Underneath Forge should escape judgment forever."

62

NOW

Eveshone struggled as she climbed to the top of the familiar mesa. This wasn't the first time she'd made the day-long trip from the Priestess' temple to this peaceful red rock sanctuary.

She journeyed here with one purpose in mind. To call to Icelyn.

Every time so far, while she meant to reach Icelyn, she'd instead only watched the sky turn from blue to pink and orange and then black. She'd stared as the stars emerged from the darkness, and then waited until the sun returned and reclaimed its throne.

Each time, she would return to the Priestess and inform her that she had not made contact with Icelyn. It wasn't a lie, but not a full truth either. Eveshone wasn't about to admit that she hadn't even tried.

Eveshone wasn't sure why she hadn't been able to reach out for Icelyn. She feared the Priestess enough to do so, yet she also suspected that Barielta's intentions toward Icelyn were dark. Eveshone didn't want any part of hurting Icelyn.

But beyond that, what terrified Eveshone the most about calling Icelyn was that she would hear nothing in response. Icelyn was already more memory than person in Eveshone's mind. If Eveshone made her best attempt to recapture what had once bound them together and was greeted with silence, she'd be forced to acknowledge the emptiness growing inside her. It felt better to tolerate the distance with the hope that it was only temporary than to try to bridge it and risk discovering that it was eternal.

The Priestess had ordered her to go this morning. It was time to make contact. This was no longer a request. Eveshone felt genuine fear at what her mother might do if she continued to return empty handed.

Eveshone closed her eyes and cycled through her memories with

Icelyn. It scared her that there were fewer than before. Maybe her mind was erasing some of them, since they hurt her when they drifted into her thoughts; this would be an act of mercy and cruelty at the same time. Still, some of the strongest ones remained. Icelyn holding Eveshone close to her as they drifted off to sleep. Awakening and seeing that Icelyn had been watching her sleep, and that her icy blue eyes were filled with pure and unconditional love. She missed being looked at like that.

Eveshone ran through this memory until she could feel Icelyn in her blood, rushing through her veins, hear Icelyn in her own breathing, feel Icelyn's touch as her skin prickled. Eveshone inhaled deeply, desperate for a connection.

Icelyn. I need you.

Tears formed in Eveshone's eyes. She waited in silence for a reply. Far away, a pack of coyotes howled. Nearby, dried sage rustled in the warm breeze.

Icelyn.

Nothing. Eveshone wondered if all she had remembered, all those treasured moments she'd saved up over the years they'd been together, were merely a dream. For so long, she'd desired to finally meet and be met by a Brathius. Had it all been in her head because she'd wanted it so strongly? Was Icelyn real?

Icelyn, please.

Had things ever really been as good as she remembered them being? Is that possible? Had she really known what it meant to be loved?

Icelyn, respond.

The past seemed as undefined as the future, and both felt flimsy, on the verge of collapse.

Eveshone clutched her knees tightly to her chest, trembling. She felt as if she was being crushed and hollowed out at the same time. The only thing that had every brought her true happiness now swallowed her with sadness. Every nerve lit up with pain, and yet she was numb more than anything. All she could feel was the absolute silence around her.

Icelyn—if there ever had been an Icelyn—had not replied.

ICELYN

Dronmer and I spend the evening preparing. The highest tiers have returned to their banquet halls and chambers and resumed their life as if nothing has changed. Eating, bathing, relaxing—no doubt in the nude more often than not.

If they were smarter, they'd be wondering where we are and what we're up to. But since they believe they deserve their position at the top of this tower—they are *highest tiers,* after all—they do not know they have to work to maintain it.

Dronmer has figured out that if we take a sample of the organic material from my spear and spread it onto other weaponry, then it grows and spreads until we have more lethal weapons capable of spreading great pain. It's an accomplishment, though I'm not sure it's one we should be proud of.

He's gathered those lower tiers whom he insists are worthy of being saved and would fight beside us.

"I promise you, these are good men."

I don't want to hurt his feelings, but I'm not sure he can, being from this terrible place, tell what a good man is. I'm not so sure I know anymore either, to be honest. I've seen terrible behavior here in Apex, and I wonder if all this has only been revealed to me because all the men in my company thought I was a man too. Maybe this is the way all men are when they aren't trying to impress (or trick) a woman.

But I nod along and decide to trust him. We need allies. I cannot do what must be done with only Dronmer by my side.

"You will get the keys to the Underneath Forge from your father," I reiterate. "Then I will take a team of lower tiers down into the Underneath Forge, where I will free the women and arm them. You take another group to clear the way toward our…our…"

It's as if my brain is blinking on and off, sputtering, unable to sustain sequential thought.

"And then you can…that is to say, you go…"

I cannot put my words together. I have no idea what I am talking about. I stare at Dronmer blankly.

"I'll head toward the higher tiers," he helps.

My head grows woozy, my eyesight gives out, and I fall to my knees.

Dronmer catches me before I completely keel over.

"Icelyn, what is it?"

I hear him, but in the distance, like he's shouting from miles away. Instead, I see only one thing.

Eveshone. Alone. Lying beside a red rock drop-off, over a darkened abyss. In danger.

I shout to her, but she doesn't hear me. *Eveshone, I am here! Eveshone, you will be safe. I love you.*

But I am muzzled. She cannot hear or feel me. I fear that even as she's desperate for me, she's forgotten how to connect with me. I emerge from the vision shaken and exhausted.

"What is it, Icelyn?" Dronmer asks, concerned.

I shrug it off as best as I can.

"Let's finish what we have to do here. And then…I know where I must go next."

THEN

Omathis waded through the red waters, looking for any Croathus who could be brought back from death and mended. He found none.

He could sense Amperous. Although his brother was consumed by fury, at least he was alive. Omathis felt relief.

The other connections that had grown as familiar as his own skin were absent. His line to Soneyane had been severed. Was she still here with them? He couldn't find her, though she'd been by his side when the explosions began. He only felt a hard, cold *lack* of her.

He didn't sense Lenolin, Amperous' beloved, either.

His connection to their children was missing.

His connection to Sean Brathius and Laura Lee had ended, too.

He was alone.

He collapsed into the waters, wanting to die along with everyone else. Without Soneyane and his children, this life was not worth living.

Travis played his guitar for the delirious gathering of dancing revelers.

"Everybody wants to rule the world," they sang as one.

Word had spread through Mountaintop of the devastation down below. Every person in Mountaintop had lost so many loved ones to those dreaded creatures. This strike of vengeance was exactly what they'd all wanted. The town had erupted into spontaneous celebration.

All except for two.

Sean and Laura Lee retreated to Brathius Tower to grieve what had happened.

For a time, they watched the celebration in the Village Green. Then they turned away from the window and faced the darkness.

"You can mix more serum. You can send others who are more trustworthy," Laura Lee offered bitterly, though even she knew this was impossible.

"This is what they want, Laura Lee. Every single one of them. More death. There is no other future."

"But what are you going to do?" she urged. "Stay in your tower and mourn quietly, day and night? Give up on fixing this?"

"Yes. I'm tired. I've lost."

Travis could stay out all night and still find someone who wanted to thank him for what he and his SSG had done. He wished he was in a better state of mind so he could enjoy the outpouring of gratitude.

Yet all he could think about was Laura Lee.

That's why he headed back to Brathius Tower. She had to understand why he'd done this. It was dangerous to invite the creatures up into Mountaintop. Only a fool wouldn't see that.

It was late, but he doubted Laura Lee was asleep. His plan had been to give her time, and then talk it through, just the two of them. When they were alone, they shared a unique language, an ability to think the best of one another.

The door to Brathius Tower was bolted shut from the inside. This was strange. Laura Lee knew Travis wasn't yet in for the night. Perhaps in her shock she'd absentmindedly locked up without him.

"Laura Lee, are you awake?" he asked softly, gently knocking on the door.

There was a shuffling on the other side of the door, but the expected clacking of the bolt didn't follow.

"Laura Lee?"

"Yes, I'm awake. I wish I weren't. But I am."

"Can we talk?"

"It's too late for that, Travis." Her voice sounded cold. Detached. He'd never heard her like this.

Travis was seized with panic and fought to stabilize himself against it. *This was Laura Lee. They'd work it out.*

"Let me in, Laura Lee. I can explain—"

"You don't live here anymore." She cut him off with staccato force, delivering each word like a punch.

Travis was blindsided. His head swam in woozy disbelief. "Come on, you don't mean that."

"You don't live here anymore. Not in this tower, not in my thoughts, and not in my heart." Each word was a result of careful deliberation, a fully considered vow.

"What about us? What about our child to come? You can't just tear us apart like this," Travis pled.

Her facade melted and she fought off the tears. This was hell for her. "*I'm* not tearing anything! *I'm* the one who has been ripped in two! *You* have torn us apart. *You* have done this. I can't think of ever touching you again. If I had my way, nobody would ever touch anyone again, because I have learned that love only leads to misery. I never want to hear another chord played on the guitar or another note sung. Everything I once adored, I now despise. So go, Travis. This isn't going to change. As you've proven by destroying those my father sought to heal, some problems can never be solved."

63

NOW §❧§※

Eveshone returned from her lonely evening to find the Priestess waiting for her outside the ancient stone spire. Her heart fell and she cursed silently at the sight of her mother, whom she'd hoped would be otherwise occupied. But instead Barielta appeared to have been thinking about nothing else the entire time she had been away.

"Were you successful in making contact?" the Priestess asked.

Eveshone couldn't say no, but she also couldn't lie, so she said nothing at all. She braced for the onslaught.

But none came.

The Priestess was unusually tender as she held Eveshone's hand in hers. "She'll answer soon. She'll hear you. Don't worry. I know it."

Eveshone was suspicious of Barielta's demeanor, but she was too relieved to do anything but accept it.

"You do?"

"Who would stay silent for long when you're calling them?" the Priestess asked, and laughed kindly. If Eveshone didn't know her better by now, she'd think her mother was the warmest, most loving person in the world. Even with what she knew, she was tempted to believe it anyway. "Come with me, my daughter, and let's get some rest."

Barielta led her through the grand wooden doors and up the spiraling stairs. She led Eveshone past the Mothers—the creatures that had combined with humanity to give birth to their grand species—and all of them perked up. A low, steady symphony of sounds emanated from them.

"It's like they're honoring us," Eveshone observed, and she let herself feel hope. Perhaps she and her mother had just been through a rough patch, and from now on things would be as Eveshone had initially believed they'd be.

"They are recognizing the future," Barielta declared, and Eveshone felt a surge of pride. But then her mother let go of her hand and instead patted her own belly softly. And now, Eveshone realized why the Priestess seemed to hold so much joy.

"The future," Eveshone started. "That's not me, is it?"

The Priestess looked at Eveshone with a smile bright, full, and unrestrained. "You are correct, dear one. I am with child. I didn't even know it would be possible. And *this* one has a noble bloodline. Oh, you will adore your sibling, just as I already do."

ICELYN

I haven't completely recovered by the time Dronmer returns with the keys to the Underneath Forge. I'm working to focus on what I must do here in Apex, but I am consumed by Eveshone. By our memories, by her essence, and mostly by the vision I had of her—weak, terrified, and bereft.

A part of me yearns to leave and save her now, to find a way to forget the women who are trapped in the darkness of this wretched tower. But I remember that I came here to bloom. This is the dark and cold place I've been led to in order to blossom into the person I should be. The old Icelyn would focus only on Eveshone. But it's easy to save the people you naturally love. The new Icelyn will find a way to save them all.

Dronmer slips through the door and rouses me from my thoughts with a gentle shake of my shoulder. It feels like he's only been away for a couple of minutes, and I realize I'm so lost in my thoughts that I'm losing time. It's always strange when your weakened grasp on reality is made clear.

I study his face as he hands me the keys. No blood spatters. "How did it go?"

"They didn't even know I took them," he replies. I'm relieved. I know his family will not survive our plan, but I don't want him to be the one who has to spill their blood.

"Let me guess," I reply. "Too busy bathing? Or eating?"

"Eating while bathing," he answers, smiling. I laugh, surprising myself, and find relief in the humor.

I examine our lineup of weapons. We have thirty in total—clubs, spears, swords, and knives. Most are makeshift, but with the organic material sticking to the tips, they are lethal enough. I select a few.

"How many women do you think there are down there?" I ask. We've only seen six, but there could be many more.

"How about you take ten?" he suggests, and this makes sense to me. There are only twenty "good men," Dronmer included, and everyone who comes with us should probably have a weapon.

I choose ten of the weapons, and Dronmer binds them together with leather straps so I can carry them all. As I watch him tighten the straps, I have a thought.

"I know we talked about splitting up and having some of the men accompany me to the Underneath Forge while you take others higher," I start. I pause to gauge his reaction to me shifting the plan. He seems like he was expecting this—which is funny, because I wasn't.

"But maybe you could come with me. I'd like to arm the women first, let them participate in their own vengeance. We can let them lead the way toward their freedom, and we could follow, if that's what they want."

"I think that's a fine idea. Every part of it."

Dronmer and his nineteen lower tiers follow me as we march through the outer corridors. We see other men, and I wonder if they are worthy of joining us. But each time I look to Dronmer, he shakes his head no. So many men, so few worthy of our trust.

Most ignore us. Some shout vile words as we pass, but don't dare do anything more threatening in the face of our numbers, our weaponry, and Dronmer's by now well-deserved dangerous reputation.

We finally reach the outer court of the Underneath Forge. I use the keys to open the padlocks. I can tell the lower tiers in my company are curious about what is beyond the door and excited at the prospect of finally seeing for themselves. I understand, but I still don't like it. Enough men have already entered this place. No more.

I turn to Dronmer. "I'm going in alone. You and the others stand guard out here."

Dronmer doesn't argue; he either sees the sense in what I'm saying or reads the determination in my eyes. He hands me the bundle of ten weapons.

"Show them who they are, Icelyn."

THEN

Travis knocked on the door to Brathius Tower. He wasn't surprised by the lack of an answer. Both Sean and Laura Lee had hidden themselves away since the explosions down below—from everyone in Mountaintop, but especially from him.

He had hoped they'd grant him one last audience, at least, considering the Pilgrimage was about to start. That's what Travis and his group were calling it: the Pilgrimage. In truth, though, he, the SSG, and their families were being expelled from Mountaintop.

Many had urged him to resist. Fight back. Take over Mountaintop if need be. Why allow themselves to be forced out like this?

But Travis wasn't concerned about living outside of Mountaintop. With the poultice, he was confident they could evade any Threatbelows who were still on the mountain. In any case, he planned to lead his group to the desert. He'd noticed Croathus appeared to avoid that barren landscape. He would build a new city there—different in every way from this one.

Mostly, though, he'd decided against making trouble because he didn't want to fight against Laura Lee and her family any more than he already had.

Knock, knock, knock. Far from angry, his rapping on the large oak door felt sad and pathetic.

"I just want a chance to say goodbye," he said, his voice cracking.

He sat outside the door for a very long time—as long as he could, in fact, considering they were leaving Mountaintop at dawn. At one point he felt he was being watched from one of the windows on the third floor, but he couldn't be sure.

At sunrise, a small group of citizens from Mountaintop gathered to see Travis and his Pilgrims off. There were about one hundred leaving in all.

Oliver Hailgard was among those who showed up to say goodbye. Travis was touched by the gesture.

"We're going to miss you," Oliver said.

"I'm going to miss all of you," Travis responded.

"Survive, Travis. That's all I ask of you now."

"Oliver, can I ask you one favor?"

"You can ask me for two. I'm feeling generous."

"Just one," Travis answered. "My children, when they are born..."

"Children? I did not know."

"Yes, the midwife tells us there are twins. Tell my children that I was good. I did my best. Tell them I would have loved them very much."

"I'm going to tell your children you were great, Travis. Because you are."

Laura Lee regretted not saying goodbye, though she knew she would have regretted seeing Travis one more time even more. It was easier this way. He had killed their love; why pretend it survived in any form? She'd already dealt with the specter of false hope countless times—wondering if he could be restored to her, be the man he was supposed to be, the father of their children, her partner. Was there any way?

There wasn't. He'd betrayed her. Her father. Those poor creatures below.

She was angry at him. She'd held him at arm's length *for years*. She'd loved him for a long time, yet she'd always sensed his loyalty to Shai. She sensed her within him and knew that it would eventually bring them heartache. She'd worked so hard to resist him, but he'd worn her down, eroded her prudence—and now they'd both been hollowed out by what she always feared was coming. He was constantly kind. He was patient and gentle. He was everything he needed to be to convince her that she'd been worried about nothing and should give in to what they both wanted. And then, he reverted to being Shai—and shattered both of their hearts.

She left him waiting outside all night, and then stayed locked in the tower as he and his conspirators left Mountaintop.

She did watch his departure from her perch atop Brathius Tower. She stared as the group grew smaller in the distance, wondering if this had always been their destiny. It felt unavoidable. Why did the universe insist on drawing people together who were so uniquely equipped to devastate one another?

She didn't know whether he'd survive away from Mountaintop, though she sensed he would find a way. That was one of his skills—regardless of consequence, he always did what he needed to survive.

In any case, she thought bitterly, it didn't matter. She'd never know whether he survived out there or not—and either way, for her the result was the same.

The love of her life, Travis Nilsing, had died.

64

ICELYN

I enter the chamber and am struck anew by how beautiful it is—the falling water, the light diffused through colored gemstones, the mosaics, the music. I glide silently between the beds, touching the soft blankets. Horrid acts were dressed up here, as if they should be honored instead of condemned. Ugliness masquerading as beauty. I am angry at how soothing this place is, because I know what terror it has held.

I scoop two heaping handfuls of the red powder from the bowl and drop it into a waterfall. The color spreads, and the channels running throughout the chamber turn a rich crimson. Chimes sound from afar. I wait, but no one appears. I'm not sure why, but I pick up the bowl, dump the rest of the powder into the water, and then drop it on the ground. I want it to shatter, but instead it just clangs loudly. It's an ugly sound, and that pleases me. Finally, something that feels true to the nature of this place.

Finally a door opens, and I hear footsteps. A group of women stride into the chamber, their steps full of purpose, as if they've been choreographed and practiced. They stand before me in a line. I can tell they are confused, but they don't speak.

"Does anyone else live down here?" I ask.

Instead of answering, they spread out and head toward the beds.

"Please, no," I insist. "Are there any more women among you?"

They stare at me, disturbed by my breach of protocol. It's not anger—they know I can do whatever I wish. It's fear. In going off script, I've made their expected response a mystery, and they don't want to make a mistake.

"You have my permission to speak. I promise that you will not be punished for anything you say."

A tall woman who (unlike most of the women here) appears to be older than me steps forward.

"There are no women here, Sir," she explains. "Only Vessels. There are another four resting below. Along with the fruit of the highest tiers, whom we are honored to care for."

"The fruit? What is..." I trail off as I remember the sound I heard floating up from below. Now I can identify it: crying. "You have babies down there? Children?"

"Fruits of the highest tiers," the woman answers confidently. "The nourishment of these young masters is one of our greatest honors. We also care for future Vessels, of course, and train them to take their place here when they are old enough."

I address the woman who is speaking to me. "What is your name?"

"Vessels have no names," she declares with pride. "We live a life of service, not selfishness. Glorifying, never glorified."

"None of you have names?"

"You can call me whatever you'd like. That is your right."

I don't want to give this woman a name.

I look at all six of them, lined up. "None of you have names?" I see a younger girl, her eyes tender and shy, holding eye contact with me. I know she only does this because she's been trained to do so; she looks away desperately whenever she gets the chance.

"Nothing you call each other, terms of endearment, jokes between friends, anything?"

They remain silent. I step toward the younger one. "Please, tell me what you are called? Or what you would like to be called."

She's quiet, but I can tell she wants to say something.

"You have my permission to speak," I say, though I hate that I have to.

"Are we going to begin the Exchange of Gifts?"

"There will be none of that tonight," I declare. I see a wave of relief pass over them. "Or ever again. You are leaving this place. You are no longer Vessels. You are people who can live the life of your choosing."

They stare at me, like my words have no meaning. I remove weapons from the bundle and try to hand them to the women. The quiet one—who, from the bruises on her neck, I recognize as the woman who attempted to commit suicide—takes one from my hands, seemingly because she doesn't know what else to do.

"I've always thought the word *Delipho* was pretty," she offers. "I'd like to be called that."

"Vessels have no name," the older woman corrects her sharply.

"We sometimes call her Mama," Delipho confides in me, and she smiles.

I try to hand Mama a spear, but she refuses it.

"We will return to our quarters if there is no process tonight," she declares.

"We're leaving this place. I'm taking you away."

"We don't want to leave this place. We are Vessels. We are honored. Respected. Cared for. Protected."

"You are not Vessels. You are women."

Mama's eyes flare, but she knows better than to argue with me.

She calms herself and speaks with gentleness. "I'd ask you to stop calling us that. Women were weak. Women were hurt by their own foolishness. Women on their own were at risk. Vessels are protected, honored, revered—given everything one could want."

"*Given* these things. *Reliant on others* for this respect, this honor, this protection."

"As is proper and right, according to Travis, according to the ways and wisdom passed down to him, which have ensured our survival when all others have perished."

While we have been talking, four more women have entered the chamber, no doubt drawn by the odd conversation we've been having. They each hold a child. This distracts me—it's been so long since I've seen a baby.

I walk toward them. "Don't you want your child to choose her future? Don't you want to be free of this prison? Don't you want to know what it feels like to be equal? Because *you are equal.*"

None of them take a weapon from me. Only Delipho holds a sword. And she extends it, under the watchful eye of Mama, trying to get me to take it back.

"The One Who Walks in Shadow and Air has decreed that we are to be Vessels," Delipho recites, her disappointed eyes on Mama.

"No. Look at me. Look carefully at me, every one of you." I stand before them with a fierceness in my voice that surprises everyone, including me. "If you have not already realized, you will now. I am Shai, the One Who Walks in Shadow and Air. Your hearts confirm this, yes?"

Their eyes fix on me.

"Listen, as I am going to tell you a truth about myself that has long been obscured. Again, you already know this is true within your hearts." I work slowly remove my tunic, revealing my form to them. I let my hair fall.

"The One Who Walks in Shadow and Air is a woman—a mother, yes, but a woman first, and no mere Vessel. I am here to invite you to join me in my strength and leave this life behind. I've seen with my eyes the pain this life brings you and what some of you would do to escape it. Now take your weapon and fight for what you know you deserve."

Delipho pulls her sword back to her side.

"Learn what a woman can be. More accurately, insist on what you know a woman is. Let us shape this world into what it should be—and knock this accursed tower to the ground."

As a walk past the line of women, each of them takes a weapon.

Except Mama.

"Is this the choice you want to make?" I ask, realizing sadly that it is a lost cause.

"I am a Vessel. Women ceased to exist for a reason. This is not the proper order of things."

"I will not force you," I answer.

Dronmer and I can barely keep up with the women as they rush ahead of us. They scramble up the stairs two at a time, leaving us and our small army of men behind.

"Wait for us," I implore, worried that they'll be injured without us by their side. At the very least, the babies should be protected. But it's as if breathing air outside of the Underneath Forge has granted them extra strength and speed. They cannot be slowed.

They have been let loose upon the world.

I had imagined that we would talk strategy, how we'd escape this tower, how they'd have their revenge. But I realize now that they have sprung into an action where words would make no difference. A lifetime of misery animates them, infuses them with purpose. They are a cleansing force, the reckoning I have yearned to see since I first visited this accursed place.

I hear their screams up ahead as they reach a new tier. I scramble to catch up with them and when I do, I see that the higher tiers have gathered, no doubt having been alerted to the outbreak. They're accompanied by armed men from lower tiers, violent guards who frighten me.

"Vessels!" Dronmer's father shouts, and his voice echoes against the stone tower walls. "We yearn to show you mercy, but you must stop this abomination now. Drop your weapons and return to your rightful place."

I watch in pride and awe as the women take a unified step toward the higher tiers.

"You are our beloved," Dronmer's brother urges, his voice taking on a sickly sweet cadence. "And you bear our fruit. There is no one we cherish more—"

He catches sight of me in my true feminine form, while also dressed as Shai, and he begins to stammer. He loses his thoughts as I stare back at him defiantly. His face flashes shock and then anger before he recovers.

"Please, for the sake of the love we share, turn back. This is not you."

Delipho lowers her sword and steps toward Dronmer's brother. She bows her head in submission.

Dronmer's brother seems heartened by this, and he reaches his hand out toward her. "Yes. You remember who you are, who we are to you. We give you meaning, and you give us life. It is this mystical, beautiful tradeoff that has made us all who we are."

Delipho places her sword on the ground, then kneels before him.

"You may speak, my beautiful Vessel. You may tell me what's in your heart," Dronmer's brother says.

Delipho lifts her head and looks into his eyes. "We have remembered who we are. And we will never forget who you have been to us."

The highest tiers look alarmed by her tone, which is no longer lilting or warm. It's steady and cold. Vessels have never spoken this way. Even more unsettling, her face remains fixed in a steely expression. I watch as their eyes shift uneasily over all of the women, noting that all of their accommodating smiles have disappeared.

"You have done great wrong to all of us, each of you. You have cloaked the evil you've done in beautiful words, but that does not make what you've done any less horrible. And now, *you* will bear the fruit of your actions."

Delipho grabs her sword from the ground. With one swift movement, she plunges the blade into Dronmer's brother's belly. The higher tiers shrink back in shock.

The women take it as a rallying cry and charge forward.

I grab my own weapon, ready to fight by their sides, but something tells me to hold back.

It soon becomes clear—so clear, in fact, that I wonder why it wasn't obvious to me earlier.

These women do not need our help.

The highest tiers and their goons have no chance against the fury they have finally unleashed.

65

THEN

Travis and his followers suffered under the punishing sun. It hung huge above them, so hot that it felt as though it couldn't be more than a mile or so away. They might as well be hiking straight through the middle of it.

Travis had been astounded by the lack of Croathus down below. Compared to their earlier expeditions, when they'd see groups of the monsters throughout the day, now they'd go a week without seeing one. Alive, that is. They saw many dead. Travis was tempted to hang one from a phone pole, on display, the way they'd done to his mother and the other humans. But they had to keep moving.

He knew that multitudes had died in the explosions. He guessed that many others had scattered as far as possible from this dangerous place at the foot of the mountain.

His plan had worked! Why was he being punished for making everyone safer? None of those creatures would dare attack Mountaintop now, with the risk of explosions, great floods, earthquakes, and death hanging over their heads.

He'd done the right thing. Why couldn't Laura Lee see that? As much as he loved her—and he always would—he knew now that she was flawed. Hopelessly so. She had let her emotions override logic and the instinct to survive. Travis had wanted to raise a family with her, but now he could see that he'd been lucky. Now, when he had a child—another child, not the ones he'd left behind in Mountaintop with her—he could raise the next generation of Nilsings free from her defects.

He led his hearty pioneers through the rocky pass. They'd been in the desert for months now, and their water supply was running low. He consulted maps to figure out where they might find a spring.

Despite the scorched ground, Travis liked the desert. He could imagine they'd traveled to another planet, one Sean Brathius hadn't torched with his twisted genius. He was going to build another humanity out here, untouched by the weakness he'd just escaped.

They arrived at the crimson red stone pillar by sunset, and it was as if God himself was welcoming them to their new home. This was the spot. There was water below the ground, miles of flat land where nothing could hide, and stone stretching up to the skies like a prayer.

Travis dropped his heavy pack. They'd been traveling for a very long time. They'd lost ten people—two to the monsters, three to sickness, three to injury, and two to suicide. They'd earned this home.

"We're here," Travis declared. "Welcome to Apex."

ICELYN

It feels as if we're walking through fire, even though there are no flames. I don't think I've ever felt heat like this before, or even imagined it. Even the insides of my nostrils burn when I breathe in. The air around us scalds our skin like boiling water.

Yet, as unpleasant as it is, I like it. Fire purifies, and the tower of Apex has left me feeling soiled inside and out. Hopefully this hellish trek will burn away some of the sins that have draped themselves around me.

Apex.

I realize that Dronmer has stopped moving with me again. It's not due to exhaustion-–I wager he's as strong as Adorane. And it's not because of the heat, either. He mentioned that it was the perfect temperature at one point and wasn't even joking. No—he's looking back at the smoldering ruins of Apex. I study his face, trying to read what he's feeling without projecting onto him what I'd be feeling.

Regret, escape, guilt, relief?

That tower has stood for hundreds of years, a refuge against the sun, the wind, the Croathus who roamed below. But it harbored a rotten secret in its core. And instead of ridding itself of that darkness, the men of Apex merely decided to call the darkness good. We humans are awfully good at tricking ourselves into believing things that aren't true, even for hundreds of years. But nothing can stand forever when its foundation is decayed.

"What are you feeling, Dronmer?" I ask. It's a direct question, and not one I want to ask. But if there's a chance that the death of his father and brother and the destruction of his home might introduce some shadows into his own core, I'd rather shine a light on it as early as possible.

"Nothing, Icelyn. Less than nothing."

I know that feeling. It's nothing because it's everything at once. It's like hearing every animal on the planet roar or bark or screech at the exact some time—you'd hear nothing, because everything was so loud.

The few lower tiers who Dronmer said could be trusted are unsure what to make of the women they hadn't even known existed up until today. They keep a healthy distance between themselves and Delipho and the others. The women seem to relish the moments of rest, sharing their water with their children. Dronmer watches, his eyes moving between them and the plumes of dust and smoke rising from where Apex once stood.

"Are you angry with them for razing Apex?" I ask. If he is—and this would be understandable—I think it would be better for us to know.

"They didn't do it. Apex destroyed itself long ago. This was inevitable." We watch as one of the children giggles, paying no mind to the scorching sun, and playfully spits water into his caregiver's face. "It's a mercy any life at all escaped the desolation it had stored up over the ages."

He chokes on the words. I know that even though they are true, they are sharp and painful for him to say.

"Have you escaped the desolation?" I ask him.

He holds my hand in his and stares at it like he's trying to remember something he's afraid he's forgotten.

"Not yet. I haven't. But there's still a chance."

The sun has disappeared behind the jagged mountains but neglected to take the smothering heat with it. We make camp in a narrow, soaring slot canyon.

"Tell me about where you came from," Delipho urges. I smile, because the first time she asked this question I gave an answer that amazed them all without intending it. Now, whenever there's a lull in action or conversation, she asks again, and I respond in turn. Each time it's like I'm performing a deeply impressive trick, and we all laugh.

"The highest point in the entire world, where my father was the leader," I answer for what's probably the tenth time now.

"Higher even than Apex?" they chorus, laughing.

"Oh, as high as two Apexes at least."

They *ooh* and *aah* as if they didn't think this was possible. Dronmer gathers kindling and stokes a fire. The air is already so hot that I wondered at the wisdom building it in the first place, but now I can see that the soft light, the crackle of burning wood, and the homey, smoky scent combine to lift our collective spirits, his most of all.

"And you have slayed a Threatbelow?" they ask, though they already know the answer.

"I have—though I am not proud of that, and if I had the choice, I wouldn't have done it. Because I loved them. We are kin to each other." The impossibility of this answer mixed with my insistence that it's true—and their tender faith in what I'm saying—combine to form an irresistible potion.

"You will see them," I promise, "and you will become kin to them too." I'm unsure of how exactly I can make this claim. Sure, Eveshone and Adorane have formed their own odd unlikely bond, but outside of them, the Anaghwin have loved only me. And the Croathus still hate all of humanity, me included. Yet when I say it, there's a surety to my words, as if I'm talking about something that has already happened many times, not something that is yet to be.

The women cuddle alongside their sleeping children in a cozy bunch, tender and warm. Truly, I would love to join. Yet I am not one of them, and it would be an intrusion to enter. Dronmer senses it too. He and the lower tiers set up their beds at least twenty paces away.

I think of everything these women have been through and doubt that I could ever completely be one with them.

"The Anaghwin will love you all," I whisper as the women and children drift off to sleep.

One of the younger women sighs. "How do you know?"

I don't even have to think about the answer. "Because they love what I love. And I love you all so much already."

THEN

"As it is written true and clear, so shall it be," the gathered council stated in muted unison. Laura Lee nodded and finished signing the document.

"The Code has been updated, and we are better for it," she declared.

She passed the thick booklet around the room, and each leader signed it. Oliver Hailgard took an extra moment when it was his turn. But he could feel Laura Lee's eyes watching him, hungry for his approval. She'd been through so much: First being banished and forced to live alone; then losing Travis; and now Sean's transformation into a hermit, condemning himself to imprisonment in his tower.

Oliver added his signature. The stroke lifted Laura Lee's mood. He wasn't feeling as buoyant.

The Code had grown more restrictive as Laura Lee meditated more on what Travis had done to her. She was only trying to protect others from falling into the same traps she had. Now that she was married to another man—a calmer, more restrained person who didn't ignite her passions, but who would also never secretly sabotage her father's attempt to unify all of creation—she could see Travis more clearly for who he was.

Travis had made Laura Lee feel dizzy when they kissed. His touch made her forget all of her promises to herself.

Everybody would be better off if they saved kissing and touching until after they'd already made the most important decisions in life and settled comfortably into the well-worn grooves that would define their adult life. That much was obvious. No need to confuse matters by dabbling with that dark magic when you're young. This was now clear in the code: No physical contact between adolescents and young adults prior to marriage.

Sean had always had reservations about Travis as a match for Laura Lee. He'd wanted her to marry Holden Carroway. Holden was about as exciting as a piece of toast, but Laura Lee could see now that her life would have been simpler if she'd listened. Holden talked too much about rock formations and wore the same shirt nearly every day, but at least his children had a father in their life. This had been fixed in the code: Parents, using scientific principles derived from the study of relational success, would now choose their children's marriage partners.

Travis had scrambled Laura Lee's good sense with his voice and his guitar. He'd used his talents to deflect and distort. If she had concerns about marrying the son of Shai, he'd respond with a beautiful song. And how could anybody who crooned like an angel hold anything dark in his heart? His repertoire kept his true self hidden. This had been fixed in the code: Musical instruments and singing were prohibited in Mountaintop. Future generations would not have to contend with their bewitchment.

Laura Lee was still charming, warm, and friendly, so nobody protested her additions to the Code. Oliver wanted to, probably more than anybody else—but after all, she was only adding these restrictions because she'd learned firsthand the consequences of them not being in place. And if there was one thing they could all agree on, it's that nobody wanted to be at risk of marrying someone as dreadful as Travis Nilsing.

66

ICELYN

Perhaps it is the radiating heat, which comes from the ground itself now instead of the sky above, that deprives me of woefully needed sleep. But I suspect it's more. Even Dronmer, cloaked in grief, has managed to doze off. I've been so concerned for him all day; it's only now that he's sleeping that I realize that I carry my own angst, apart from his.

Eveshone.

She has always held an elevated, unique position in my heart. My love for her, and her love for me, never had to be questioned, analyzed, measured, rationed, or calibrated. It just *was*, and in far greater supply than I would ever need. I could trust that her every thought of me was good. I didn't have to wonder about her.

But now she's left me. I've scratched and clawed to pull myself from beneath that mound of misery, to the point where I can again love her as she needs to be loved. I'm determined to do that. But this effort was not without a cost. The love we have shared has been warped—and no amount of sculpting on my part can restore it to what it was.

I realize, with a terrible shock, that Eveshone is now in a category that includes my father, my mother, Adorane, and Torrain. I love them all dearly, but with caution. I cannot place my heart in their hands anymore. Inevitably they will drop it, or worse.

I scale the side of the slot canyon until I find a lonely perch. From here, I can see my caravan below and miles beyond them on the horizon. The mountain ridge obscures the exact locations, but I know generally where Torrain and Adorane are, and I can sense where the Priestess and Eveshone are too. And then even beyond that, I can sense Mountaintop, where Father and Mother are, and the Drowned City, where I left

Omathis behind.

I can feel the connection between myself and each of them—wispy and weak, but emanating from me toward them and back again, like a constellation of stars blinking in the sky overhead.

I love them all, I realize. I do. At times it's been a question. At times I've declared the opposite about each of them. From here, I can see the bonds between us more clearly. I understand that even as I've passed from early, easy love to a harder, more stressful kind, I love them each more now than ever. Early love is simple—like playing a game as a child where your parents let you win. But only after you've experienced loss, only after you've been damaged at their hands—only then can you graduate to the kind of love that you know is going to last. And I have that now with each of them.

But even so, I think, as tears flood my eyes, Eveshone was special. A dull ache pulsates in the space between my stomach and my heart.

I'm excited to see her again. But as I get closer to that time, I have to face the truth: My feelings for her have shifted. This makes me sad. More accurately, I think I'm sad because my new feelings for her make me sad. Our love used to be so pure. We got along easily; there were no complications, and I had no doubts. But now, though I still have a tremendously strong affection for her, it's crowded by pain. We will never go back to what we were. As much as I will continue to love her, I'll be haunted by what we once had but have now lost forever.

As I focus on Eveshone, the world around me shifts. I can no longer see the women and their children sleeping below, the horizon and the stars above. All I see is her. Far away, she sits on a balcony that juts out from the peak of a tower of stone. This stone has been polished to the point of gleaming and shimmering, even in the moonlight.

She's been drained of vitality. She looks very ill—even past the point where sickness normally transitions into death. I don't even call to her, because I know she cannot hear me. I'm seized by the fear that it's too late, that she's now lost.

Emerging from the shadows behind Eveshone, I see a fiercer, darker version of her—statuesque and beautiful, graceful and terrifying. This creature stands over my beloved Eveshone in a way that makes me want to die.

This must be her mother. Unlike Eveshone, this elegant creature can see me, and I stare back at her. *Come and let us decide who owns this poor, frail child.*

No one owns her. Anyone who loves her should know that, I respond.

How enlightened of you. Then you will face me, lest she be mine? she asks.

I am filled with dread, but I nod and agree.

I lose my vision of Eveshone, of her mother, of everything. I am left with only a terrible feeling inside, a persistent fear that if I don't go to Eveshone soon she'll cease to exist—and that maybe she already has.

I am released from my vision of Eveshone because Delipho has climbed up the rocky wall to find me. She gently squeezes my shoulder. I'm grateful to escape the horror of my vision and have my sight filled with her face. She is sitting next to me, observing me closely.

"You are having a nightmare?" she asks. I'm comforted by her presence.

"I was. Only it was real," I respond.

"Yes, I know what that is like." She stands and holds her hand out to me. "I invite you to join us below. The others have asked that you sleep among us if you wish. They like you."

I perk up, shaking off the experience I just emerged from. "They do?" I ask.

"Almost as much as I do."

She has no idea how much I need to hear this. Or maybe she does.

"I can't. I have to make a plan. I don't think I can sleep," I decline, despite wanting to do what she's asking.

"Join us. You need rest to make a plan. And you need us, if you're going to be able to do whatever it is that plan is going to ask of you."

I don't argue. If I've learned anything recently, it's that I'm wrong as much as I'm right, and that sometimes it's better to trust someone else's instincts now and then. I climb down after her and lay in the midst of the women. A few of them jostle from their sleep enough to smile and put a tired arm around me.

I have never felt whatever I am feeling right now, and I like it. Delipho was right. In the morning I will go to Eveshone. But tonight, this is what I need.

I awake before the sun has risen; I haven't slept for long, but I feel completely refreshed. Being in the center of so much kindness and acceptance has strengthened me, and I feel like I can do what I must. I inhale deeply and smell the slumbering humanity piled around me. It's earthy, slightly sweet, and warm. People can be so awful to each other, but sometimes I catch a glimpse of just how wonderful humans can be. It reminds me of the feeling I had when Torrain, Adorane, and I used to sit beside each other and watch the sunset and talk and laugh until it was dark. Humanity can be a force of nature as great as any flood or storm, earthquake or volcano—for good or bad. That's our curse, but also why we exist—and why we should continue to exist—in the first place. I feel the rhythmic rise and fall as they all breathe in and out, and enjoy the compression and release as their bodies pulsate against mine. It's all fragile and beautiful, and I never want to leave it.

But I must. I do my best to squiggle out from among them without awakening anyone, and I succeed. As the first rays of sunshine begin to appear over the ridge above, I climb to reach higher ground so I can figure out where I'm going.

I'll leave the maps for Dronmer, Delipho, and the others so they can meet up with Torrain and Adorane in the lab.

But I'm going elsewhere—to steal Eveshone back from the one who stole her from me.

NOW

Adorane and Torrain had set out early again this morning, just as they'd done every day since Icelyn left. They'd wasted several days on Adorane's insistence that he could track Icelyn, painstakingly following tracks and broken branches for hours only to find a rabbit or a desert rat. Then they'd spent just as many chasing Torrain's recollection of the map to Apex. He promised that he'd committed every tiny jot and line to memory, yet every time he insisted that a certain landmark should be just ahead, he'd been wrong.

Now they were left with nothing—no tracking expertise, no cartographic knowledge. Only a frantic desire to find her.

It didn't help that there were still stray Croathus skulking through the desert, especially after dark. Icelyn had taken the only weapon they could use to defend themselves against the creatures, too, so they could only search for her when the sun was at its most punishing. Still, at this point they were so desperate to find her, neither had any room for anger at her for leaving them.

They'd already spent the morning running between the brush and cactus for a few hours when they saw a wispy trail of smoke rising into the blue sky. Neither of them grew overly excited. They'd once thought they'd seen a footprint, but it led nowhere. One time they had found a sun-bleached and frayed piece of fabric, but it hadn't helped them find Icelyn. (To their shame, neither could remember what color clothing Icelyn had been wearing when they'd last seen her—and this created more arguments between them than it should have.)

They picked up their already quick pace. Since they'd grown accustomed to the desert sun and were powered by their steadfast need to find Icelyn, they often moved through the harsh landscape faster than should have been possible. Now they were moving as fast as the bighorn sheep up on the rocks, those sure-footed beasts that had adapted to this place over millions of years.

Their effort was rewarded as they reached the narrow mouth of a tall, deep slot canyon.

"Do you hear that?" Torrain asked, but he didn't need to. It was obvious. Adorane turned to him, stunned.

Voices.

67

NOW

Adorane and Torrain came upon a mass of people they did not recognize. They wiped the sweat out of their eyes and drank deeply from their water supply. Both stood staring in shocked silence; this had never happened before in either of their lives. They thought they knew every single person in the world by name and face. Yet here were more than twenty people they'd never seen before.

Adorane shoved aside his excitement at meeting all these new people and scanned the faces for Icelyn. Torrain pushed through his instinctual bashfulness to do the same.

"Icelyn," they cried. "Icelyn!"

Their hearts sank. She was not among them.

Somewhere in Torrain's head it registered that there were woman in this group, and even children—so their fertility problem was solved. But this didn't matter to him if Icelyn was still missing.

A man stepped forward from the crowd, no older than Adorane or Torrain himself. The strangers pointed their weapons at Adorane and Torrain.

"We are looking for a woman," Adorane said.

"As are we," the man answered. "You said her name. Where have you seen her?"

Adorane realized that these people suspected that he and Torrain had done something to Icelyn. Torrain noted Adorane's pose, like he was ready to pounce and fight at any moment. He lifted his arms in submission before Adorane got them both killed.

"We're looking for her too! For ages now. We love Icelyn. We're Adorane and Torrain. We are her friends."

The man stepped forward and looked at Torrain and Adorane with shrewdly critical eyes. "I was prepared to be more impressed. She mentioned you both. Briefly."

It seemed like he was trying to hurt them, but they were just relieved to hear she was alive. Or had been recently, at least.

"You've seen her?" Torrain exclaimed breathlessly. "Where? Where is she?"

The man hesitated, deep in thought, and Adorane grabbed and shook him impatiently.

"Tell us where she's been. What has she been doing? Tell us what you know."

The man shoved Adorane backward. Torrain noted that he seemed every bit as strong, which he'd never seen before. As jealous as Torrain had always been of his long-time rival, he didn't like this interloper shifting the balance.

"I am Dronmer of Apex. Icelyn visited our tower. She is a remarkable person—the embodiment of the goddess we call The One Who Walks in Shadow and Air."

"Are you telling me that she claimed to be a goddess among your people, too?" Adorane laughed, reluctantly impressed.

"How many gods can one girl be?" Torrain asked with a smile.

Dronmer didn't laugh. "She is Shai. For she uprooted the evil in Apex, as these women can tell you. And then these women destroyed Apex in their rage."

The women nodded, their eyes steely. This was a story Adorane wanted to hear, but they didn't have time now.

"But where is she?"

One of the women stepped forward. "I was with her last night. She was troubled by something she had seen. Someone was in danger. And she was eager to make a plan."

Adorane and Torrain could both guess what this meant and where she had gone. They hoped they were wrong.

THEN

The pain of labor washed away when Laura Lee heard the first plaintive cries of her beloved children.

"Give them to me," she whispered. "Let me hold them."

The midwife placed both warm, wiggling children on Laura Lee's chest, and she nuzzled their impossibly small faces with her own. They cried, more in an effort to inflate their newly working lungs than to communicate distress.

"This one's a boy, right?" Laura Lee asked. She'd always known—one boy and one girl—but now she was sure.

"Yes. A little boy. A new Brathius."

Laura Lee shook her head. She was aware of her unique position in Mountaintop—one where she was setting the cultural template for a new society. Her wedding to Travis had been imitated so often that their vows and ceremony had become the new traditions. Now she was going to demonstrate new practices when it came to naming a newborn child.

"He's not a Brathius. He's precious. He's adorable. He's mine, and I will love him always. But he is not a Brathius. No, this child is a Nilsing. He's everything I loved about Travis."

She turned her attention to the other child, a girl who stretched out her hand and grasped Laura Lee's finger.

"This is my Brathius. It's as obvious as the sunrise. Can you see?"

One Nilsing and one Brathius.

Laura Lee had encouraged Oliver and Tamar to start this tradition with their child, but they hadn't. Laura Lee did, and from that day on, parents in Mountaintop bestowed upon their children the surname that they decided best fit their child. In later years the bestowing of the last name would wait until the child was five. It could be the mother's, the father's, that of an ancestor from generations ago, or even a wholly new one, if the parents felt the child warranted it. Laura Lee felt this better reflected the individual nature of each child. It also dispelled the illusion that humanity was nothing more than multiple lines of notable men.

ICELYN

I'm moving as quickly as I can through the loose gravel and sand. Every step forward defies of the part of me that wants to turn back and forget this mission.

Not long ago, I heard something that made my legs give out completely—Adorane and Torrain, yelling my name.

I ached to go back to them, to embrace them, to tell them I was all right, and to introduce them to Dronmer and the women and children. Well, the women and children, at least. I hadn't thought of this before, but there is a very good chance that neither Adorane nor Torrain will like Dronmer at all. Oh, my, the two of them were complicated enough in their competitions and rivalries already. Imagine adding a third?

But I knew I could not answer. I know what they would ask of me. *With these women, our quest is completed! You do not need to do anything. We can all go back to Mountaintop now.*

But I cannot leave Eveshone.

Adorane would not understand. Or worse, perhaps he'd insist on rescuing Eveshone from the Priestess himself. But he would die before he could even reach Eveshone. This is my battle.

I push myself as fast as I can to outrun my desire to turn back and give in to Adorane, Torrain, and the life they want for me. The desire is almost too strong to bear, and not only because I miss them greatly—something else has been nagging me ever since I saw the Priestess in my nightmare. A voice in the corner of my mind that I've been trying to ignore.

This is a battle you may not win, it says.

But it's a battle I need to fight, I reply.

But you may lose Eveshone and yourself also. What a waste.

If I lose Eveshone, I lose myself anyway. So if that's the case, I am lost either way. I keep moving forward.

The voice grows more insistent as I get closer to where I know I must go.

It's not just that you may not win. You cannot win, it insists.

I fear the voice is correct.

This is a trap, it hisses. *Eveshone draws you there only because the Priestess asks her to.*

But I already know this. As sad as it makes me, I've accepted it. Even if it's a trap, it's one I must fall into.

I am her mother.

All I can do is keep running. This is a battle I need to fight—whether I can win it or not.

As the sun sets, I pass through a portal formed by a giant fallen boulder and approach the ancient, gleaming tower I saw first in my vision. Seeing it takes my breath away.

I don't belong here. Every grain of sand, every stone, every stalk of sage screams a warning to me. *Go away! Turn back!* But still I move forward, one foot in front of the next.

The massive wooden door on the tower swings open, and Eveshone stands in the opening.

"I am here. I see you! Let me hold you, dear Eveshone," I shout to her. She gazes at me sadly, then turns and enters the tower again. I push after her and slip in just before the door slams shut.

The inside of the tower is lit by torches. I enter a wide circular room whose ceiling arches dizzyingly high above me. On the second level, I see a series of openings that have been given great honor. They are adorned with gems and shining metals; mosaics, paintings, and beautiful carvings decorate the displays. But they are empty.

Eveshone stands in the center of the room.

"The Mothers are not here," she says to me in a flat voice. She sounds like she's had her spirit pressed out of her. "If that's who you are looking for."

I would hope she knows I'm not looking for the Mothers, whoever they are.

I put a hand on her shoulder. She won't look at me, and when I move my head in an attempt to make eye contact, she turns away in shame.

"I'm looking for *you,* Eveshone."

"You shouldn't have come here." Tears fill her eyes. "I'm not worth it. Not after what I've done."

"No," I protest, placing my cheek against her chest. I reach my arms around her and press my hands into the small of her back. I can hear the turmoil inside her body, swirling and raging. I want to share a Vibram with her. I want our roots to connect, but there is nothing to connect to. "That's not true. None of what you're saying is true."

"I left you for her," she says mournfully, and then her body shudders with regret. "You need to leave," she whispers.

"I'm here for you. But I'm also here for more than you."

She doesn't understand. Neither do I, but I keep speaking. "You're the doorway, Eveshone, into something even bigger. My love for you is..." My eyes fill with tears as I surprise myself with my own words. "My love for you is the most real thing in my life, and it's the only thing that can unlock who I'm meant to be."

"But I broke us. I pulled us apart. What I did—"

I cut her off.

"You didn't do this to me. This is something that happened to both of us, Eveshone. It's never been you doing something awful to me. It's you and I facing something terrifying together, because this is what we're meant to do."

I feel a hint of our roots brushing against each other, and it's enough to know that she's still there, and so am I. She looks at me for the first time since I've entered the tower. Some color has returned to her face, and a subtle purr rises deep inside her.

"But the whole reason I called you here was for her, Icelyn. I didn't want to. I fought it, but you're here for her," Eveshone confesses, but she doesn't look away. I press my face hard against hers until neither of us can tell where one of us ends and the other begins.

"I know you did," I whisper. "And I love you anyway."

I feel the Priestess' strong, cold hands clasp my shoulders and lift me off the ground. Eveshone tries to leap to my defense, but another creature who I am surprised to recognize as Amperous easily pins her down.

As I'm carried away from her, I feel no fear for myself, and only sadness for her.

This is a battle I must fight.

68

ICELYN

I awaken in darkness, with no light to help me puzzle out where I am. I don't remember falling asleep. I don't recall anything about how I came to be here. But I can sense that I am not alone.

"Priestess?" I call out. "Are you here with me?" My voice echoes in the silence. I stand and move slowly, exploring the space. Stone, cold to the touch, lies beneath my feet. Wooden bars stretch from the floor to above my head on every side of me. I am caged.

"Who is here?" I ask. "Where is Eveshone?" No response.

I try to be as still as possible. What can I learn in this moment? I actively seek information, because I can feel that if I lose focus, I'll be overcome with fear. I breathe in and detect no scent. But I can't shake the feeling that I'm not alone. I hum in an attempt to bounce sound off the walls of this echoey space. I know that bats can locate themselves by shooting sound waves off their surroundings. Why shouldn't I try?

I slowly rotate as I hum, and the melody I've chosen brings some comfort to me. Finally, I reach a spot where the echo isn't the same. I continue to rotate as a test, and the observation holds. Something is there in the dark.

"Are you going to say anything?" I ask. I reach through the bars toward the entity that absorbs my sound waves instead of bouncing them back like the stone walls.

Still silence. But now I hear the breathing and feel the pulse of a creature who has been doing its best to sync those operations to my own so I wouldn't detect it. Now that I've sensed it, it's obvious to me. Eveshone would sometimes practice this syncing when we were in a particular state of harmony, but this isn't Eveshone. This creature is larger, older, rougher.

"Amperous," I state. It's not a question. I know Amperous well from stepping into Omathis' memories. I've felt what it was like to be his brother, to be raised by his side. "If you're going to imprison me, at least have the decency to greet me properly."

His breathing quickens. I know I've caught him off guard, first by recognizing that I'm not alone and mostly by identifying him. But he remains silent, perhaps hoping I'll doubt myself and allow him to remain hidden.

"Fine. You don't want us to commune, for whatever reason." Suddenly I realize the true reason he's shielded himself from me. "Oh. It's because you are afraid your natural instincts will flow and you will love me, aren't you? And then you won't be able to do what she's asking you to do."

The creature sitting outside the cage moves. Despite its massive size, it glides with barely a whisper. The sound of a door opening echoes loudly. Light pours into the room, illuminating the silhouette of Amperous attempting to leave.

My eyes take in my surroundings. I'm in a windowless room, barren save the sturdy cage I'm trapped in, with polished thick wooden bars that extend from ground to ceiling.

Amperous hesitates in the doorway. He doesn't want to leave, even though he knows he should.

"Oh," I observe. "It's too late for that, Amperous. Do you love me already? Something like love, yes?"

He turns, and for the first time since the attack on Mountaintop I see his beautiful golden face. My heart flips. *I forgot how much I love him.* "Remember the soothing I gave you in Mountaintop? We can have that every day, Amperous. You can be reunited with your brother. It can all be as it was meant to be."

He turns away from me and leaves the room. He pushes the door closed, and I am in darkness once again.

NOW

Dronmer and Delipho hadn't figured out how to relate to each other in the absence of Icelyn, and adding Adorane and Torrain to the already volatile mix had resulted in chaos. None of them were accustomed to dealing with strangers. Indeed, the word *stranger* had had no meaning to them prior to this day; as far they were concerned, they had known every human who'd ever existed.

"You think she went to the gathering place of the monsters?" Dronmer asked skeptically.

"She has a connection to them," Torrain explained.

"To one in particular—Eveshone," Adorane added.

"Yes, she mentioned that name while in her vision," Delipho said.

"Then we will go there too," Dronmer concluded. Torrain noticed that Dronmer seemed to view the world in a simple way. For him, in any situation there was only one correct choice, not countless courses of action with their own gradations of good or bad consequences.

"Then we would die," Adorane responded. "A horde is gathering, and their rage against us grows. Torrain and I stumbled across one of their gatherings once while searching for Icelyn." Adorane felt a chill pass through him at the memory. The Croathus had grown organized and devoted in the presence of the Priestess. He and Torrain knew that if she'd ordered them, the monsters would have easily ripped them apart. "Fortunately, we were at a distance, and they were focused on her. Or we would have been stripped to bones and left to bleach in the sun."

Torrain raised his eyebrows at Adorane. *Stripped to bones and left to bleach in the sun.* Adorane seldom spoke like this. Was he trying to impress the strangers?

"We have weapons," Dronmer replied. "So we will go and get her."

"With children. With babies? With women?" Adorane asked.

Delipho looked offended. "Ask Dronmer what these women did to his father, his brother, and all the others who kept us locked in the Underneath Forge. We didn't need his help—or any man's help."

"What did they do to your father and brother, Dronmer?" Torrain asked.

"They slaughtered them. I thought maybe we could just capture or banish them. But no, they cut them into pieces."

Adorane watched the women, talking to each other, tending to their children. He tried to reconcile the gentle scene with what he was being told.

"...Okay, I apologize. I didn't know."

"We come from a place where women don't often, maybe even ever... kill," Torrain offered as an explanation.

"And where people aren't normally so... forgiving when their father and brother are murdered," Adorane added.

Dronmer shrugged. "It needed to be done. It wasn't murder; it was justice. They were terrible people."

Once again, Torrain marveled at Dronmer's straightforward manner. Apex must have been a very curious place.

"So it is decided," Dronmer declared. "We will go and save her."

"It's not that simple," Torrain answered. "Come, we need to go to the lab first. I'll show you what I mean."

ICELYN

My head pulses with dizzying pain, and my body is covered with sweat. My lungs refuse to take in enough air. When I try to breathe in deeply, it feels like the air is made of knives. I cough and spit up a warm liquid that I fear is blood, but I can't tell in the ever-present darkness.

I have made a terrible mistake in coming here. I know that now. My life has been a series of mistakes, one after another, and nothing anyone can do, myself most of all, can ever make up for them. Everyone I have met is worse off from having me in their life.

Everything is swirling. I fall backward and my head bounces off the floor. I welcome the novel pain that radiates through my body. At least it's not the same pulsing, dizzying despair I've been imprisoned by for days, years—who knows how long.

I hear a welcome sound. Any sound would be welcome in this hell devoid of senses, but this one is especially so; it's the door scraping against the stone floor. Amperous enters, along with rays of light, and for a moment I relish the reprieve from my misery.

Amperous returns often to the room where I am caged. He won't talk to me, but he listens as I speak. Most of his visits are unnecessary, at least for the Priestess' purposes. The last time he visited he even brought me a bone with some dried-out meat left on it, along with water. He seemed embarrassed as he passed them through the bars to me, but he didn't look away when I smiled and thanked him.

This growing connection to Amperous has been the lone bright spot for me while in this cage. But the rest is complete darkness, eating me from the inside out. It feels like an eternity has passed, though I have no way of marking the days.

He stares at me now, shocked and then concerned. I study myself in the torchlight and am grateful to see that I haven't coughed up blood—only vomit. Small mercies.

"Speak to me, Amperous. I am desperate to hear another voice," I beg.

He considers my request, truly considers it, for which I am grateful. But instead of saying anything, he exits back into the corridor, leaving the door open. He returns soon, carrying with him a thick column of wax, and places it in the corner of the room. He lights a wick on the candle with a torch, and a small warm glow spreads from that corner. I've never seen anything so beautiful.

"Thank you, Amperous."

"Don't tell the Priestess," he instructs, and then he leaves.

69

ICELYN

The candle gives me life. The flame is always changing, its form never fixed. I see in the flickering of the fire the shapes of my own memories played back to me. It's a frog, it's a mountain, it's an ocean wave. It's Adorane, it's Father, it's Dronmer, it's Delipho and the women who allowed me to slumber among them, it's Omathis. It's a river, it's a baby, it's an infant, it's a waterfall. It's Torrain, it's Eveshone, it's Istoch. Precious times, lovely people, moments I'd somehow forgotten until now. As I stare at it, it clears away the darkness in the room, while also overcoming the darkness that had overwhelmed me on the inside. This candle is saving me. Its light is a warm golden hue, just like Amperous' glorious fur.

After staring at the flame and finding my salvation in it, I am now at a place where I feel like I've escaped from this cage, from my own cage. I see the true nature of things. I am in Eveshone's heart. I am with Omathis. I am beside all of my beloved Anaghwin, and I am forever bound with Adorane and Torrain. I hear a dripping and realize it is tears falling from my face to form a puddle on the floor below me. I place my hands in the puddle and wash my face, my neck, my arms, my torso. I am cleansed, I am baptized, I am prepared.

"I am ready," I say, my words confident and clear. They echo off the walls.

And who are you? The voice is familiar by now, though I still have no idea who it belongs to. It began back when I decided to speak to Adorane's god—so I suppose it could be that. But perhaps some other god commandeered the conversation; who am I to know? The way Adorane and the other Veritas would talk about their god sounded so limited, but this voice feels boundless and expansive. Maybe the voice is just me—a deeper, wiser version of me who's not consumed by fear or reputation and is instead focused on being the strongest, bravest, and kindest person I can be. Maybe it's all of these things, or maybe it's something else altogether.

Who are you? it repeats.

"I am Icelyn Brathius."

But who is that?

I consider this a moment. "Many things. I am Lovely Brathius, I am Sean Brathius, I am god to the Anaghwin."

Yes. What else?

"I am the One Who Walks in Shadow and Air, the one who is not afraid to give power to those imprisoned so they can free themselves."

I continue to scrub my body with my tears, rubbing them into my skin.

Yes. What else?

Something falls out of me, and my confidence is gone. What else? I'm not sure there is anything more. Isn't that enough?

"…I'm just a girl. Afraid of all this. Afraid of what comes next. I'm wrong more than I'm right. I fail more than I succeed."

I am embarrassed to admit this—and yet, the voice sounds more pleased by this muddled, hapless response than any of my previous declarations.

Yes, you are all of these things. You are everything you need to be for now.

"But what if I can't do what I need to do? What if I am not enough?"

You will be everything you need to be when the time comes.

Suddenly my skin feels cleaner than it ever has. My heart is so buoyant that I feel as though I could pass through the bars and float out through the walls of this stone tower if I desired.

Amperous sits just outside the cage, watching me.

"You love me, Amperous," I say.

He nods.

"I would like to step into your memories," I request.

He studies me.

"I need to know," I press.

"I don't think the Priestess would approve," he answers.

"You're stronger than that, Amperous. You don't need her permission."

"I'm afraid that I'm not—and that I do."

"Well, where is she? I will ask her permission."

"She's preparing for the ceremony."

NOW

Barielta surveyed the basin below. The stone bowl formed by hundred-foot stone walls made an ideal gathering place. Scores of Croathus had arrived from afar. Some wore the skins of creatures found only in the frigid lands to the north, others of exotic animals that Barielta didn't recognize, though she assumed they were from the humid jungles to the south—the lands where her people had thrived in hiding long ago. Croathus who had settled far away to the east had found a land dominated by buildings and roads and cities, where the trees had been cleared and many of the larger animals wiped away; even after all these years, some of those places had still not recovered from the damage humans had done. You could tell which Croathus had come from these lands because their robes were stitched together from the skins, furs, and feathers of many smaller creatures. The patchwork coverings were jarring at first, but she'd grown to appreciate the custom—Croathus from across the land, making use of what they had.

The energy in the natural amphitheater had reached a fever pitch, though it was still only halfway filled. So much excitement, she marveled —yet only she knew what they were all there for.

The Priestess ducked into a cave and moved through a narrow stone corridor until she reached a spacious cavern.

The Mothers were arranged like living pieces on a game board: a mountain lion, a grizzly bear, an eagle, a cheetah, a wolf. As she walked between them, she reached toward each, and each responded to her touch. She sang a haunting melody, and they joined in the song.

She leaned against a clear cylinder filled with dirt, and ants gathered where she touched it. She moved on to another, watching the porous brown blobs pulse underneath where her hand met the glass. She moved on to the third, where pale luminous creatures, each like the moon in the sky, swirled in a whirlwind of activity to greet her. She bent to run her hands through the mountain lion's golden fur, and it purred with satisfaction.

Then she heard something that put a damper on her mood, and resented it. She left the mountain lion and strode toward a distant corner of the cavern.

"I had hoped being in the presence of all this greatness would cure you of your malaise," Barielta lectured.

Eveshone, her hands, feet, and neck bound by leather and metal, continued to cry softly.

"I have hope for you, Eveshone. My blood flows through your veins. I believe in it."

The words were technically encouraging, but the way she said them sounded threatening. The Priestess inhaled sharply, consciously improving her mood, and then turned away from her daughter.

"You'll enjoy the ceremony," the Priestess promised. Then she added ominously, "It will change you. It will change us all."

Barielta emerged from the cave and examined the platform her Croathus were laboring to build. They'd carved two shelves into the basin wall, one higher and narrower, where a wooden stake with shackles had been raised. Below the stake, a stone funnel had been carved, attached to chutes leading down to the second level. On that second level, eight majestic platforms were carved into the stone. The Croathus worked feverishly to decorate the platforms, redoubling their efforts when they noticed the Priestess was watching.

Below that level, a pair of giant bronze cauldrons had been set up on the ground. And below that, a forest's worth of dried wood had been stacked, ready to explode into flames.

Satisfied, she returned to the cavern.

"We are almost ready for your coronation, Mothers," the Priestess sang joyfully. "The basins will be filled with life, and the fires will burn so hot that we will breathe that very lifeblood into our nostrils."

She walked to the other side of the space, among and between more clear tubes, these housing the unformed faceless Croathus that so disturbed the others.

She looked at them with great love in her eyes.

"And then we will all be reborn. I promise you this."

Dronmer, Delipho, the lower tiers, and the women and their children marveled at the lab's machinery—the brightly flashing colored lights, the screens, the magical evidence of electricity and computing. They looked both exhilarated and frightened as they fanned out across the room, hesitant to touch anything.

"And so you see—by analyzing Eveshone's DNA, and comparing it to both Icelyn's profile and the lab results I found in the computers here, I can tell that there are unrealized features of the Croathus. They simply need to be unlocked, using the correct keying sequence."

Torrain was not gifted as a teacher, so no one would have understood him even if they were paying attention. But they were too busy being distracted by the parade of flashing lights and numbers to hear even one word.

"Dronmer! Delipho! Are you listening?" Torrain asked.

"Do you *think* they're listening?" Adorane asked wryly, as Dronmer repeatedly pushed a button that made a *bloop* noise.

In his frustration, Torrain flipped a series of switches that caused most of the lab to power down. Sighs of disappointment rose from the others.

"Why'd you do that?"

"I need you to pay attention," Torrain commanded loudly.

"I have been paying attention," Adorane whispered, "and I still have no idea what you're getting at. Make it easier to understand."

"The key to unlocking the Croathus' new features is Brathius blood," Torrain stated.

"The Threatbelows need Icelyn's blood?" Dronmer asked, starting to understand.

"Yes. In order to unlock their potential. That's the way they were designed. It's actually an elegant security feature, if you think about it, guaranteeing that only Sean would be able to—"

Adorane cut Torrain's tangent off before he lost everyone's interest again. "So we need to rescue Icelyn before they spill her blood."

Torrain pressed a series of keys and brought up another screen full of indecipherable diagrams and numbers. "But that's the thing… I'm not sure she wanted to prevent it. I think that's why she's gone."

70

THEN

She'd only closed her eyes for a few seconds—just to rest, *not to sleep*.

Laura Lee had been haunted by dreams for years, but lately they disturbed any chance she had of a full night's rest. And she was raising two young children alone, so sleep was already hard to come by.

Laura Lee knew the dream well by now: the vials. The needles. Her father. The pain. The anger. The hopelessness.

She'd never mentioned her nightmares to Sean Brathius before. Why was that? she had wondered recently.

Yet she knew the answer.

What if it wasn't just a dream?

She didn't want to find out.

She'd only closed her eyes for a few seconds, just to rest. She would never fall asleep and leave two eight-month-old children unsupervised in the tower. But she awoke to screams of pain and realized she must have fallen into a deep slumber due to exhaustion. She shook herself from her stupor to find little Revilo Nilsing crumpled in a pile at the bottom of the steps, clutching his left arm and howling in pain. She scooped him up, grabbed his sister Ciryl, and ran them both to the healing arts pavilion.

They set Revilo's arm and assured her he'd be healed in weeks. "Young bones mend themselves quickly," they promised.

This was all her fault. What if he'd landed on his head instead? Her son could be dead. What if Ciryl had also fallen? All this had happened because she couldn't sleep when she needed to.

She held Revilo closely that night. All three slept together in a makeshift bed on the floor at the bottom of Brathius Tower. He'd been too afraid of the stairs even if she carried him, and Laura Lee didn't want to add any more distress to an already terrible day.

"No, no, no," Revilo repeated while pointing at his injured arm. "No."

"I know, baby. That's not the way it's supposed to be. You're right. But it's going to stop hurting soon."

"Mama. Mama? Mama." He didn't know a whole lot of words, but was able to express a lot through the few he did. Laura Lee could hear his fear, his disappointment, his pain. Every time he said *Mama* it was with fresh sadness, as if he'd just learned that she wouldn't always be there to protect him. That he thought he was safe with her around, but had just realized he wasn't.

"Mama?"

She held him tightly, hoping her embrace could be the apology that words couldn't convey.

"I'm going to figure this out, baby."

ICELYN

Amperous stops in more often now.

"Are you lonely, Amperous?" I ask during one of his visits.

"I haven't thought of it. If I had to answer, I'd say no. I have the love of the Priestess now, and I haven't had love for a very long time."

Yet even as he says it, I can tell he's questioning the statement. Is it love that he has? Or something else?

Our thoughts are syncing more often, and I'm starting to feel the outside contours of his roots connecting with mine. I don't point this out, lest I scare him away. This closeness developing between us is better left unexamined and undiscussed. I fear if I shine a light on it, it will scatter.

But his visits grow longer and longer. Today, he lingers near the bars of the cage after sliding through my now-customary meal of bread and water. When I reach for the tray, our hands touch. It seems accidental, but nothing truly is. After all, when he first began his visits, he'd keep such great distance that an accidental touch could never happen.

When our hands touch, I feel a jolt pass through my fingers. I notice that he jumps back a little, and I am flooded with terror that he will leave the room and leave me alone once again. But he does not leave.

"I was wondering about stepping into your memories, Amperous. I know I mentioned it before, but… I wanted to ask again. It seems that maybe a shift has occurred, and it would be welcome now."

Amperous doesn't respond. Instead, he sits with his back against the wooden bars. He seems to be waiting. I sit with my back to the bars too, so that our backs press against each other in the spaces between the wood. I know that this is his way of saying yes.

"Don't tell the Priestess," he whispers.

"I know," I answer.

Many of the memories play out just as Omathis' did. At first, it feels as though I'm watching the same events again.

I'm back where I was before, lonely and cold, unable to speak, so hungry. Tiny, unable to walk. Screaming out, wanting something in my belly, wanting someone to calm me down. Then I see him—the man with the icy blue eyes. He holds me, and I start to feel the comfort he always brings. So warm, so giving. I want to lose myself in his eyes and never escape them.

"Forget Omathis' memories, please," Amperous urges me. "See through my eyes." He's right. Once I lose myself more in him, I'm awakened to another dynamic—not just what is happening, but how I feel about it.

I continue to cry. I am not comforted. I am held by this man, but it's not enough. More precisely, the comfort I feel only upsets me more. I still remember the hunger I felt before I was given something to eat, and I fear the cold will return. I know that he will put me down soon, and I will feel worse than I did before he entered the room.

"Stop your crying, little one," the man urges, and I can feel the tension coiled up in his body. I have upset him. We are making one another feel terrible. "Look at your brother, Ampy. See how he sleeps? How about you do that?" But I can't sleep, even though I want to. And I cannot stop crying. Finally, he puts me down and leaves, even though I am still screaming.

He feeds me the same food as he feeds the other. He holds me as long as he holds the other. But while the other is made whole by these things, I am not. I am still hungry. I can only think of how afraid I will be when he puts me down. The man puts the other down with great sadness, then picks me up, even though he doesn't want to. I can tell.

I awaken, fearful and alone. I cry out. This time, the man doesn't come. This time, I am met by another—one who doesn't want to be here. She smells bad, and her eyes are cruel. She lifts me roughly and commands that I be quiet. I do, even though on the inside I am louder. She holds me tight, and I can barely breathe. She shakes me, and it makes my head hurt. I fear my arms and legs might just fall off. But I know she will be angry and might try to hurt me if I complain, so I am quiet. From then on, I am quiet at night—because I know that if I am not, the scary, cold, cruel one will come.

I am shaken from Amperous' memory with a terrible confirmation. This is the Shai from Omathis' memories, and now from Amperous' too. I no longer have any doubt. The statue of The One Who Walks in Shadow and Air. Shadow Air is Shai. If I am Sean and Lovely Brathius, who raised Omathis since he was a pup with love and kindness, am I also this cruel, cold woman who damaged Amperous? How can that be? But I am, I know it is true.

"Amperous…" I begin. "I am so sorry."

"There is more to see," he reminds me.

I see now that even when you're raised in the same cage from birth with someone else, your life can be completely different. It starts as one being slightly more difficult than the other, but soon it grows to a point where every action is interpreted through a negative lens by those around you.

Omathis and I both snuck an extra apple out of the food bin. "You must be hungry!" Mister Sean laughs at Omathis, declaring him a naughty little boy, and gives him a third apple.

Then he smacks me on the back of the neck, hard! "You must not steal, Amperous." I am forced to go to sleep hungry.

Omathis often tells me how good Mister Sean is, and I can't blame him. Mister Sean is *good—to Omathis.*

Then the Sleeps begin. I remember suffering through that torture through Omathis' eyes, and thought it couldn't be worse. But compared to how Amperous experienced the Sleeps, Omathis' pain was only an inconvenience. I realize that what I'm missing as I'm living through Amperous' suffering are the years of trust and care Omathis had built up for Mister Sean. When I experienced this torture through Omathis, it all hurt, but at least I believed it was for the best.

For Amperous, it is pointless cruelty.

The Sleeps are torture. They fill my insides with hatred. I dream of the day when I can sink my talons deep into Shai. Her disgusting smell fills my nostrils. I pretend that I know I should not feel this way, but in truth I don't bother trying to feel anything else. Mister Sean I would spare because Omathis loves him, and I do love Omathis—but someday, I will kill Shai. I would kill her twice if I could, and still I'd be hungry to kill her again.

Mister Sean has taken Omathis out for a special training session. He does this often, because "he doesn't have time for my misbehavior." Hearing this makes me less obedient.

While he is a away, Shai visits and speaks to me from the other side of the clear wall. "He thinks you love him," she says, "but I know the truth about you. Omathis might love Mister Sean, but you don't. You look at us with murder in your eyes. Even though love for him has been built into your body, you manage to harbor hatred."

I don't respond. I don't agree, but I'm not willing to argue.

She holds up a file that she's retrieved from Mister Sean's desk. "Here's a secret that I'm going to tell only you, because Omathis would never believe it. You aren't his children. You are his weapons."

I look through the pages and find pictures of Omathis and me at different ages. Test results. Numbers and words, charts and diagrams. But what Shai points to is the title: CROssbred Anthropomorphic Tactical Hybridization for Ulterior Soldiers. *"This is what you are," she says. "Not his breath and his blood, not his children. Only his soldiers. He tells you he cares only because he knows it will make you train harder. You're killing machines, nothing more."*

I can see that she enjoys telling me these things. It brings her joy to watch me understand that we are not his children, but his soldiers. I can never tell Omathis, because this would break him. It's already broken me.

Later, I feel great love for another, for my mate, for my children. I am happy, finally, away from the stench of humanity. But then our green paradise collapses, and I am forced to spill blood again.

And then, when I am foolish enough to trust Omathis' vision of Sean Brathius just for an instant, I lose them all in the Great Death.

I emerge from his memories twisted and weak. "I'm so sorry, Amperous. Shai lied to you."

"No, she didn't. We were born to spill blood, and that is all we'll ever do."

I'm exhausted. I saw and felt Amperous' true love for his wife and children, only to watch them die. I felt him embrace his revenge. Omathis' descent had been painful, but Amperous' was worse, because it was justified. It was inevitable. It was righteous.

"I'm sorry, Amperous, for all the pain we've brought you."

"Why should you care? Every Brathius knows we were created for pain. To bring it and to bear it. Now prepare yourself. It is time for the ceremony of Mothers."

He blows out the candle and leaves me in the darkness.

71

ICELYN

When Amperous comes for me, I do not fight him. He gives me a bag of woven desert grass and asks me to place it over my head. I comply.

He binds my hands and feet with rope, and I don't struggle. I wonder why he bothers with these things. I can't fight him, and I can't run from him either.

While he wraps the rope around my wrists he accidentally touches my skin with his. I again feel the charge pass between us.

"No Soothing, please," he commands, but I sense a desperation in his voice.

Once the bag is over my head, he tightens the opening around my neck, and I am plunged into darkness.

"I am letting you do this without a struggle as a way to show you how sorry I am for what's been done to you," I say.

"You have no choice," he responds.

"We both know I do."

Amperous is much larger than me, and he straps me onto his back. I sense us exiting the tower, moving from the shade into the blistering sunshine. He bounds across the desert before climbing over rocky ridges and down into valleys.

I am thirsty. Before I can ask, he reaches back to unhook me, removes the bag from my head, and tenderly puts a jug of water to my lips. While I drink, he speaks to me.

"When you stepped into my memories, I was forced to dwell on them too. As you can imagine, I don't do that often. I had been tempted to grow closer to you until I was reminded, again, what your kind has done to me. Shai, Sean, you with your Soothing in Mountaintop, and the poisonous air."

"Oh, Amperous," I start, but he interrupts me with a growl.

"No. I had forgotten because of the pain you were in, but I know now. This is what you all do. You pretend to be kind, you make us care, you draw us in close—and then you attack."

"That is what we've done. And I am sorry. But I'm trying to end that forever between your kind and mine. That's what I'm going to do tonight."

"You're going to die tonight. Nothing more."

"Is that what you want? For me to die?"

"That's what the Priestess wants."

"Is it what *you* want?"

He pulls the bag over my head and straps me to his back.

I feel myself lifted until the rope around my wrists are hung from a hook high above my head. Then I am released, and my body sways until my feet are bound to a thick wooden stake behind me.

"If this is what you want, Amperous, then I accept it. You are owed the chance to determine my fate. I saw what we did to you. You are justified in choosing revenge."

He removes the bag from my head. The pole behind me, the one I am bound to and hanging from, is decorated with flowers and ribbons and the words *Hominum Brathius.* In front of me, a massive embroidered tapestry billows in the desert wind. Behind that beautiful curtain I hear what sounds like every creature in the world waiting to see me.

"Stop pretending this is my decision," Amperous whispers to me.

"Nothing you do is beyond your control. Don't ever give your choices away. They are your most precious possession."

I gaze down at him and then past him, at the beasts lined up on a stone ledge below me. I've seen some of these creatures before, like a mountain lion and a bear, but there are others I do not recognize. They each stand on their own platform, though none are bound to stakes like I am.

"Regardless of what happens here, Amperous, I want you to know that you are a noble creature, more than a killer. You are destined to do more than bring and suffer pain. I am honored to have gotten to know you."

I see that there are metal chutes lined up below me, like the aqueducts in Waterpump back in Mountaintop, each extending to a creature below. Though the desert air is already hot, a plume of a different kind of heat rises from below. I catch a glimpse of a large empty cauldron, surrounded by smoke and flame.

"I am not noble. I am a Croathus. I am a killer. That is what you made me to be. Only after we kill you and the rest of your kind can I be anything else."

"I think you're wrong, but there's no use arguing. After this is over, we'll all know for sure, one way or another. What do you think it's like… to die?" My voice cracks with fear.

"I think it's like falling asleep, only it never ends. Nothing worse. It's worse for those of us who are still awake. But those who slumber do not suffer."

"Well, if it's any different, I'm going to come back and haunt you. I'll haunt all of you. That I promise."

He only rolls his eyes and snorts quietly.

NOW

The basin was already filled to capacity, but more Croathus continued to pour in. Barielta studied the mass gathered below her with pride. Finally, they would become who they were meant to be. Untethered from their past, they could become more than any Brathius ever intended.

All the platforms were now complete. A great series of curtains woven from silk and studded with gemstones hung before them, shielding them from the view of the Croathus below. The Priestess heard many of the pups—and even some of the curious adults—wondering out loud what was hidden behind them.

The Priestess indulged herself in a way she hadn't for years. She thought back to her own humble beginnings and her desperation to birth something new in this world. She remembered Omathis' decrees making that impossible. She recalled—with a small smile—Eveshone's father, and how his rebellious streak and love for her made him disobey the rules and break from Omathis and the community. But even when she had her child, Eveshone, and had the family she thought she wanted, she'd still wanted more. She'd felt guilty about it at the time, but it was the truth.

Now that she saw this amphitheater packed with hundreds of thousands of her kind—looking to her, waiting on her, worshiping her—she understood what it was she'd needed all along.

She needed to be what her kind needed her to be—to be great, but not for herself. For them.

Eveshone's father had never understood this. Fortunately, Amperous did.

As soon as Omathis saw the desert, he was seized by panic. This had become an accursed place; the very land seemed to have dark intentions. He had a difficult time breathing. Every instinct screamed at him to return to the refuge he'd enjoyed.

He lost his connection to Soneyane as soon as he crossed into the hot sands. Yet he knew she'd want him to continue. And he wanted to continue too. Icelyn needed him.

He just hoped he wasn't already too late.

Torrain was finally able to explain what he had learned about Icelyn in the lab with enough clarity that Adorane and Delipho mostly understood. Even Dronmer partially did, in his way.

"You believe that she didn't go only to save Eveshone, but to…let the Croathus win?"

"I don't know what Icelyn knows. I'd be surprised if she knew all this. But maybe she knows it instinctively on some level, and that's what's driving her," Torrain answered.

"So not only was Brathius blood used to make the Anaghwin and the Croathus," Delipho puzzled, "but you're telling us that Anaghwin and Croathus blood was injected back into the Brathius?"

Adorane nodded his head, annoyed. "She always sensed that she was special—different. If she finds out how right she was, we'll never hear the end of it."

Dronmer grew impatient with the conversation. "None of this changes anything. We need to go and save her before it's too late. Can we agree on that?"

Adorane and Torrain still weren't sure how they felt about Dronmer, but in this they could find common cause. "Of course. What Icelyn might want and what she needs are two very different things. But where are the Croathus planning on doing what they want to do? The desert is vast—how are we to find them?"

Delipho looked out the window of the lab to the desert below. The day was clear, so she could see for miles. In the distance, a wall of dust and sand rose from the floor high into the sky.

"I'm going to guess it's wherever all those beasts are going."

THEN

"Are you doing something to me at night, father?" Laura Lee asked as she entered Sean Brathius' chamber at the top of Brathius Tower.

The tall narrow cylindrical room was darkened, even though it was the middle of the afternoon. Sean sat at his massive oak desk, pushing through stacks of papers and scrawling notes here and there. He acted as if he hadn't heard her, but she saw a flash of shock cross his face.

She took another step toward him. "Father. I asked you a question."

Without stopping his reading and writing, Sean replied monotonously, "Oh, Laura Lee. How delightful. You must bring your daughter sometime so I can meet her."

"You have a granddaughter *and* a grandson," she replied. Not that it mattered to him.

She'd brought Revilo and Cyril to visit with Sean countless times, and her father would hardly look at them—Revilo especially. The older Revilo grew, the more he resembled Travis. Laura Lee understood why this was difficult for Sean—it was not easy on her either—yet she grew more and more frustrated at his inability to look past it. Revilo was his own person who deserved to be judged on his own merits.

"Of course you do. Both a girl and a boy. How I would love to spend time with them. Bring them here, please."

"I have, father. You don't acknowledge them." It hurt Laura Lee to speak the truth about the person her father had become. She wanted to cherish him, look up to him, adore him. One of the worst things a parent can do is make it hard on their children to admire them.

"Whenever it's convenient for them and you, I'd like to meet her. That's all."

Was it madness, willful delusion, or overwhelming grief that caused him to ignore reality, shut himself up in his chambers, and act like this? What difference did it make?

"Father, what are you doing to me at night? I need to know." She held her hand out until her fingers touched his chin. She realized this was probably the first time anyone had touched him in over a year. She lifted his head and turned it until he was forced to look at her.

His eyes lost their murkiness as they focused on her.

"Nothing I'm not doing to myself, too, Laura Lee. I promise. I only want goodness for us."

Fury rose in her chest, followed by a deep, unfathomable sadness.

"What *goodness* are you doing to me?" she asked, her voice tight and controlled.

"It's better if you don't know."

"But I *do* know, Father. It clouds my nights and darkens my days. Revilo has a broken arm because of it."

"Revilo?" Sean asked, confused.

"My son."

"Oh yes, I'm…I'm sorry about him. And about how I've acted," he confessed in a rare moment of clarity. "I don't know why I can't be who I should be. I should visit with your children more than I do."

Something about the way he said this disturbed Laura Lee. "You stay away from them," she commanded. "Don't do anything to them."

"I don't need to. What I've done to you—it's passed down. I've given a gift to you and your children—and their children, too. I can't be sure when it will bear fruit, but one day there will be a harvest."

"What have you done to me? What will I pass down? Have you done this to anyone else?"

"Just myself, and…" he trailed off. "The less you know the better. But this is a gift, I promise. I wouldn't have given it to you if it weren't. But don't worry, I'm finished. It will not harm you anymore."

She'd always worked hard to understand the reasoning behind the decisions her father made. She'd contorted herself to paint him as a misunderstood hero. But now, for the first time, she gave herself over to the thought that maybe he was injecting evil into the world. Maybe that was all he'd ever done.

"Make sure this is the final gift you bestow upon this world, Father. We cannot bear any more."

72

NOW

As the moon rose over the stone basin and the first stars appeared in the sky, Croathus from the north, south, east, and west pounded on drums in haunting synchronicity. They rumbled with approval as the Priestess, holding a torch, rose from the front of the crowd and climbed the stairs below the tantalizing silken tapestries.

Once halfway between the crowd below and the ledges above, she planted her torch into the cliff wall and faced the crowd. Deafening roars washed over her.

"Tonight we witness the birth of a new dawn," she declared. With a flourish of her hands, the tapestries fall from the lower ledge above her head and revealed the Mothers.

The Croathus were stunned silent by the sight of them. Some had tears in their eyes. Other fell to their knees at the sacred feeling that had descended over the basin.

"Children! Allow me to introduce you to your Mothers. They course through your blood. They hold the promise of who we can and should be. Each of them loves you and will fight for you." With each rhythmic syllable, the crowd below her moved together, forward and back, left and right, in tight synchronicity with each other.

"And not only the Mothers—but the shape of what's to come!" A few Croathus walked forward on cue, carrying the glass cylinders containing the formless, faceless ones, and placed them between the Mothers, below each pedestal. Each creature pressed itself against the glass, revealing their disturbing unfinished shape to the crowd. While before those gathered had been quiet due to reverence, now it felt like the silence was born of terror.

Barielta didn't mind. Everything was happening as she had hoped. They would soon understand.

"But first, there must be a sacrifice," she declared. "One must die, so that all can be reborn."

ICELYN

When the silken curtain falls in front of me, I am ready. I am in an expansive bowl, and it is filled shoulder to shoulder with Croathus as far as I can see. I was expecting hatred and jeers. But instead they look to me in silence, waiting on the Priestess to know how to feel.

I scan the crowd until I find who I'm looking for.

Eveshone.

She stands at the front of the gathered crowd, just below me. In contrast to how vibrant and alive she'd been most of the time I've known her, she looks crushed and bruised. Not outwardly, not physically—but in her soul.

As I planned, I let my overflowing of care for her extend out to the others gathered. I will not die before I try to Soothe every one of them, starting with Eveshone.

"We were born with enmity in our hearts for their kind, but the truth is that they are part of us too…" I hear the Priestess, who is standing on an elevated platform just below me, projecting over the crowd with her hypnotic speech patterns, but I tune her out.

For the first time in ages, Eveshone can feel my roots. Color returns to her face as I Soothe her. She looks as though she's been shaken from a stupor—as if she's only now truly realized what is happening. She reaches toward me and cries out.

I am strengthened by my connection with her, and I move to Amperous. He does not fight it. I am already bound to him. I can feel his roots, and he can feel mine. He reaches up from beside the wooden stake and gently touches my foot. It only amplifies our connection.

I was afraid that trying to Soothe such a large amount of Croathus would be difficult, and it is—but my connections with Eveshone and Amperous are making me stronger. I extend the sphere of my Soothing out from both of them, and can feel my roots starting to entangle with those of more and more Croathus.

"…And so I declare that today, we are set free from you, and we are no longer indebted to the Brathius!" the Priestess declares, lifting her arms. "Amperous, sacrifice the Brathius."

Amperous, who I now notice is holding an angry, twisted metal knife, only flinches. He continues to touch my foot and bathe in our communion.

"Amperous," she shouts, her voice shaking with angry disbelief. "Do what you must."

He doesn't answer, and he doesn't obey. I continue to spread my Soothing, and the Priestess can tell she's losing her hold over the assembled Croathus.

"Icelyn Brathius, stop it. I command you." She speaks directly to me.

I find that while in the past Soothing has taken my strength, now my connection with all of those here has made me stronger, so I'm able to answer her with confidence. "I will not. You are one voice against thousands."

"You think they will love you? They will never love you," the Priestess bellows with a harsh laugh. Her voice echoes off the natural stone walls.

"Amperous, do you think she loves you?" the Priestess taunts.

Amperous remains silent, but his connection with me doesn't waver.

"Has she beguiled you? Speak."

But before he can answer, I feel a stab of pain explode in my side. And then another in my back. I look at Amperous, who still holds his knife harmlessly, away from me. No one has struck me. What is happening?

Cries echo from the back of the gathered.

I strain to see what is going on. And then I realize.

Oh no.

NOW

Adorane, Torrain, Dronmer, and Delipho, after debate and no clear leadership structure, finally decided that the best course of action would be to arm themselves and the women from the Underneath Forge, along with the lower tier men, with the ultraspears and ultraswords. They would storm the gathering and threaten to kill as many Croathus as they could unless Icelyn was set free. It was not an elegant solution, but they didn't have any better ideas.

Upon reaching the basin, they found the creatures transfixed and docile. They crept into the midst of the crowd and were able to sneak through the huddled beasts. But then they saw what the creatures were focusing on.

Icelyn, captive, hanging from a stake—with a beast holding a knife by her side.

Dronmer's protective instinct set in, and he angrily lashed out at a Croathus. Then another. He rushed toward Icelyn, intent on killing every single creature between her and him if he had to. The lower tiers followed, and soon they were striking down the creatures left and right.

ICELYN

"Dronmer, stop!" I shout, as soon as I realize what they have done. My voice is so powerful that he and the others freeze and drop their weapons to the stone floor. I concentrate on Soothing the creatures immediately around them so they are not eviscerated by Croathus while unarmed.

"You see, Amperous? She does it again," The Priestess accuses. "She draws her human servants in to slay us while making you think she loves us." I can tell her words are working; my connection to him is splintering.

"You cannot stand beside her and me at the same time, my love," the Priestess shouts. "Choose now. For I carry your child—and I want my child to be the first Croathus born into a world without humanity."

Amperous peers up at me, indecision filling his tearful eyes. I'm not sure why, but I hear myself say, "Do what you must, Amperous. I won't hold it against you."

He pushes the knife into my side, then pulls down diagonally, opening my abdomen. I feel as though I have burst into flames. I hear the screams from below—from Eveshone first, then Adorane, Torrain, and the others. But my head is light, and I can barely hold onto consciousness. Blood pours from me like a waterfall into the chutes, down toward the animals below—the ones Barielta called "the Mothers." I watch as the red river cascades down from me onto them, baptizing them in my life. Between the Mothers, there are a series of clear cylinders holding clear liquid—beings that look like unfinished Croathus. I watch, transfixed, as my blood mixes into the cylinders and turns the clear liquid red.

I struggle to breathe, because I know it's not time to die. I must continue to struggle, continue to Soothe, continue to connect. Now more than ever.

I strain to see as the current of my blood falls down into the cauldrons far below. The bronze hisses as the blood makes contact with it, and immediately the scent of my blood fills my nostrils. I can see a haze settling over the crowd. I can see the scent of my blood enter their nostrils too, though I am dimly aware that this is impossible.

I feel the relief of rest coming. I don't have to do this for too much longer. I can see it in the Croathus' faces—my Soothing and my connection will be made permanent soon. We are in unity now. We will share breath and blood.

But I must hold on longer. As I do, I watch Adorane and Torrain and the others rush through the crowd toward me. I hope they reach me before I go, so I can tell them one last time what they mean to me.

The Mothers below me have left their platforms, and they move through the crowd. It's strange, but they appear to know which Croathus to approach, and they reach out to touch them. I fear that my blood has transformed them, and I worry about what this may mean once I'm gone.

The cylinders filled with red liquid shatter. I hope my eyes are lying to me—because what emerges, dripping and clumsy like newborn deer, makes what little blood is left in my body run cold. They are Croathus, but some with wings, others transparent like the creatures we encountered on the beach. Still others shimmer and pulse, like they are being taken apart and rebuilt, over and over, faster than my eyes can track. But while the previous versions of these creations were weak and unfinished, these seem mighty and ready to dominate. They move out to the crowd, following the Priestess as she beckons them toward to her.

Amperous' face fills my vision. He releases my hands and feet from their ropes. He gently lowers me to the ground. I must be light, because I think I've been drained of almost all my blood. My mind flashes back to school, somehow, to a long-forgotten biology lesson. I must be eight and a half pounds lighter, I realize in my delirium.

"What have I done, Icelyn?" Amperous asks, panicked.

I struggle to look past the blood-soaked Mothers and the newly created Croathus creatures, past the Priestess. I see that the gathered Croathus are locked in with me, and I feel every one of their heartbeats in my own weakening pulse. We are connected.

"They have been changed, Amperous. You have been changed too. There was no other way," I say, and I mean it. "Today has erased all doubts, for you have all breathed my blood: You are all Anaghwin." I am at peace.

Amperous presses against my abdomen, trying to stem the bleeding, but it is far too late for that. Tears flow from his eyes.

Eveshone reaches me. I try to lift my hand to hold hers, but I can't. She falls to the ground and presses her face against mine.

My vision is blacking out. The darkness is closing in, and I am tired. I cannot hear anything. I can no longer feel anything. The only regret I have is that I am fading before seeing Adorane and Torrain one last time.

Other than that, I am flooded with a satisfaction stronger than anything I have ever known. Finally, I know that I have done what I was meant to do.

73

NOW

Adorane and Torrain climbed the cliff walls, but they could tell they were too late. Eveshone's scream echoed down to them, and her pure anguish told them what they didn't want to hear.

"This can't be," Adorane repeated over and over. Torrain grew pale and silent. Both tried to quicken their climb, but they were weakened with grief.

Above, Amperous and other Anaghwin gathered around the lifeless body of Icelyn Brathius, laying their hands on her, humming together, desperate to draw her back to life. Others in the basin locked in, and soon all those who had not left with the Mothers, the New Born, and the Priestess were calling to Icelyn.

Adorane and Torrain reached the ledge where Icelyn lay and pushed past Anaghwin to sit beside her.

"She's gone," Adorane said, and his eyes filled with tears. He grabbed Torrain's shoulders in frustration. "You said that parts of them had been injected into her, and you said they couldn't die, not easily, and if they did, they could be revived. You said stuff about jellyfish and…sponges… you said she could come back. Bring her back."

Torrain gently touched Icelyn's forehead with the back of his hand and was startled by how she felt. Cold as a stone. For once, he spoke simply. "It's not a guarantee that they come back. It's just that some do."

Adorane fell on top of Icelyn's body and cried. "This isn't real. No. Icelyn. No. You're the only one I ever cared about. This can't be. You can't go."

Eveshone felt a jolt. "Adorane! What have you done?"

Lost in his grief, he did not hear her. "Come back, Icelyn. Please," he begged, sobbing.

Eveshone grabbed Torrain. "We need more people who love her. Get them up here!" Torrain ran to the ledge. He shouted for Dronmer and Delipho and the women to climb up and join them.

Torrain laid down beside Adorane, and tears rushed out of him. All sense of embarrassment was gone as he mourned for Icelyn. He remembered their kiss, the time she'd basically pounced on him without warning. It had been his first kiss—and still, to be honest, his only kiss. He had always been afraid that none other would ever compare.

Dronmer, Delipho, and the women pressed in to touch Icelyn. Eveshone and Amperous joined, and they were touched by the Anaghwin who had climbed to the ledge and those who remained in the basin below. They begged, they howled, they promised. The Anaghwin were in sync, as one, while the humans were a chaotic explosion of raw pain and uninhibited sadness.

Eveshone was the first to notice Icelyn's eye twinge when Adorane had collapsed upon her. Now, she was the first to recognize that she wasn't so far gone anymore.

"I feel her, in my roots. I can feel her!" Eveshone exclaimed. Amperous was next. A ripple of excitement passed through the gathered Anaghwin as they felt her approaching in their roots too.

Blue and green lights started to glow from beneath her skin, jumping from her to the Anaghwin and back.

Where Amperous and Eveshone were holding Icelyn's wound, the skin slowly but steadily began stitching itself together—smoothing and grafting over, layer by layer. Color began to return to Icelyn's face. Torrain noticed that her skin didn't feel like rock anymore; it was growing warmer. Tears fell from Adorane's face onto hers as he sensed a pulse in her neck.

ICELYN

I open my eyes, and I've never been so crushed before. But it's a good pressure, a perfect weight. All those I love the most are here, laying on me, crying, begging for me to come back and be with them. I'll have to remind them of this next time we quarrel.

I'm disoriented. I can't remember what happened—only that it was terrible but also good. I feel at peace—I'm sure the memory will fill in over time, like how a dream comes back to you throughout the day.

"I've missed you all so much," I say, because it's true, and any other thing I can think to say seems weird.

Adorane smashes himself against me. "Don't ever leave us again, Icelyn Brathius."

But I cannot respond. My voice is silenced, and I feel the curious sensation of retreating back into myself. I am tired, and far away, and cold. Soon I am seeing all those around me not like I would if I were among them, but more like a memory—cherished and vividly remembered, but distant.

I want to tell them each so many things, but I am no longer in the body they hold. Actually, that's not quite right. I'm both not in my body and so deeply buried within my body that I cannot escape. I'm as far away as I can possibly be, and yet frozen within, too.

I focus on a few final fading sensations. The scent of Adorane's skin, Eveshone's gentle cradling of my head in her arms, the softness of Amperous' furry robe, the melodious tone of Torrain's voice, the wetness of Delipho's tears, Dronmer's sweat on my neck. I don't think it's possible, but I swear I see Omathis beside me, too, his tears hot against my forehead. I try to reach and hold his hand, but I cannot. The children of Apex run their chubby fingers through my hair. The Anaghwin sing their haunting songs, trying their best to revive me.

But I cannot be revived, because I am not here. Not anymore.

I am elsewhere.

It is time for me to rest. Perhaps to journey—but first to rest.

74

NOW

Adorane awoke and had to fight off the urge to return to sleep, as he did every morning since the event in the Basin. Once he was out and about, he could return to a semblance of life. But in this time when he emerged from slumber into waking, he was sorely tempted to give up. Life without her was more terrible than he could have imagined. He'd gone years without her, she lived in the Drowned City and he in Mountaintop —and though he suffered then, at least he knew where she was. She was apart from him, but alive and thriving.

Now he knew what truly missing her was.

He threw his blankets aside and pulled on his pants and tunic and coat. So much depended on him. They were building a new society, the Anaghwin and human. He couldn't sleep through it.

He walked through the formerly ruined city that was restored more every day, past Anaghwin and humans working together. This was all Icelyn had ever wanted.

He met Torrain where they did every morning, just outside a newly rebuilt building that soared tall and majestic overhead. They entered without a word.

The Apriori had originally built this place to honor their god, and it still held a heavy sacredness. They walked toward the front of the cavernous main chamber and stood before a small wooden door.

"You go first," Adorane whispered. They'd learned long ago that it was awkward for them to enter together.

Torrain opened the door, passed through, and closed it behind him. He sat on the ground, tears in his eyes, and looked up.

Icelyn Brathius, sitting peacefully in a chair, her eyes closed. Statue still.

"Omathis and Amperous have returned from their trip to the cavern in the south. Their Green Paradise. Their team has recovered many meaningful artifacts from the site. You should have seen them—they were both so happy."

Icelyn didn't reply. She never did.

"And your parents moved into the city just this week. More and more come from Mountaintop every day. The look on your father's face when he saw how beautiful it is Down Below—you would have laughed. And your mother stands in the ocean every day. Just up to her ankles, but she does."

Torrain waited, as he always did, but he knew Icelyn wouldn't say anything.

She had no pulse, no breath in her nostrils. Yet her skin was warm to the touch, and her body showed no sign of the decay normal in death. She was incorruptible, pristine, frozen in perfection. She was a mystery to all, human and Anaghwin alike—with them still, but nowhere. Not alive, but not fully dead either.

"Anyway," Torrain started, shyly, like he was embarrassed by what he was going to say next. "I miss you so much. But I wanted you to know that you're in everything we're doing here." He took a step toward her. He and Adorane had decided that until they understood what was going on, it would be best to lay out a few rules when it came to Icelyn. Only a few—Adorane, himself, Eveshone, Omathis, and Amperous—would have regular access to her presence. Certain others could enter on rare occasions, but only if one of the trusted few accompanied them. And though it was not a formal rule, none of them touched her. Whatever was going on here felt too holy, maybe even dangerous. It was beyond them—beyond even Icelyn.

So Torrain's approaching her was unusual. But he missed her so much, he didn't know what else to do. He grew nervous, weakened as he got closer to her. Because he was Torrain, who at his core was clumsy even as he'd grown stronger and more accomplished, he tripped over his own feet.

His head crashed into Icelyn's knee with an impact hard enough to make him see stars. His vision blacked out and then, just as quickly, restored.

He was puzzled to find that as much as his head hurt from the accident, more pain radiated from his knee. That knee hadn't even touched the ground when he fell.

He sat beside her. "I'm starting to think you aren't coming back. It's been years."

When Torrain emerged from the chamber, Adorane was rubbing at his left knee. A bruise was forming.

"What happened in there?" Adorane asked.

"Your turn," Torrain mumbled, eager to evade the question.

"Torrain, what happened?"

"I fell. It's not a big deal."

"What's wrong with your leg?" Adorane asked, because Torrain was limping, despite his best efforts not to.

"Nothing. My knee just hurts."

"Your left knee? So does mine. It just started while you were in there."

After Adorane had finished his visitation with Icelyn, they walked through the city of Anaghum. They noticed that many, both human and Anaghwin, had a slight limp. Torrain's eyes widened in shock as he saw the bruises forming on their left knees.

Istoch and Tranton hadn't spoken to each other in weeks. Persopile was their reluctant emissary. She hadn't chosen the role, but it reduced their arguments dramatically. Less conflict was exactly what she needed, being stuck on a boat with the two of them.

She let them sleep while she took a turn fishing. Istoch was good at it, but often felt bad for the fish and threw it back. "It's not bad to be a little hungry," he'd declare. "Better us a little hungry than that fish completely dead."

This had been a regular cause of Tranton and Istoch's arguments.

This late into the night, Persopile's vision would often grow blurry. So the first time she saw the light, she didn't pay much attention. But then she saw it again, blinking at the same steady pace, over and over.

She dug into Tranton's bag for one of his ocean maps. It was difficult to tell where they were, and she didn't want to ask. While Tranton pretended to be an expert, it was clear he had no better idea than anyone else. Another regular cause of arguments.

You couldn't have predicted it by looking at the map, but it seemed that they were finally approaching land. After months of seeing nothing but endless waves, Persopile was afraid to believe it.

But by the time the sun was rising, there was no doubt. Cliffs, beaches, and forest spread north and south as far as her eyes could see. This didn't appear to be an island, either—they'd found the land across the ocean, just as they had set out to do.

She shook Istoch awake first, so they could celebrate alone. They embraced, whispering jokes about leaving the boat and swimming ashore without Tranton. But they finally jostled him out of his sleep too.

He acted as though he wasn't the least bit surprised. He'd foretold it according to the maps, he insisted; he just hadn't mentioned it. Istoch and Persopile were in such giddy moods that they didn't even mind.

As they pulled their vessel through the crashing waves and onto the sand, all three fell to the ground and hugged it. The coast was littered with stones round and smooth, large and small. Istoch gazed back at the vast ocean, amazed that they'd somehow crossed it.

Persopile grabbed Istoch's hand. "Quiet. Do you hear that?" she asked.

Tranton tutted. "Just the waves," he declared. "I calculate that just north of here, we should be able to find some fresh drinking water." As if he knew where they were.

But Istoch heard it too. Something harsh, loud, and too staccato in nature to be the surf. "Quiet, Tranton. Listen. She's right. That's not the waves."

Now Tranton heard it too. It had grown so loud that he couldn't pretend otherwise.

"It sounds like marching," Persopile observed quietly.

They squinted into the distance. On the horizon, they saw dark figures approaching. Their movement was unnaturally regimented.

"What is that?" Istoch asked.

"I don't know," Persopile whispered. "But I think we should hide."